CO

Colin Forbes, born in Hampstead, London, writes a novel every year. For the past twenty years he has earned his living solely as a full-time writer.

An international bestseller, each book has been published world-wide, including the United States. He is translated into thirty languages.

He is an enthusiastic traveller and visits all locations appearing in his novels. 'It is essential for an author to see everything for himself to achieve vivid atmosphere and authenticity.'

He has explored most of Western Europe, the East and West coasts of America, and has made excursions to Africa and Asia.

Surveys have shown that his readership is divided almost equally between men and women.

Colin Forbes

SHOCKWAVE

THE
GREEK KEY

PAN BOOKS

Shockwave First published 1990 in hardback by Pan Books
and first published in paperback 1990 by Pan Books
The Greek Key First published 1989 by William Collins Sons & Co. Ltd
and first published by Pan Books 1989
in association with William Collins Sons & Co. Ltd

This combined edition published 1995 by Pan Books
an imprint of Macmillan General Books
25 Eccleston Place, London SW1W 9NF

Associated companies throughout the world

ISBN 0 330 34587 7

1 3 5 7 9 10 8 6 4 2

A CIP catalogue record for this book is available from
the British Library

Printed and bound in Great Britain

SHOCKWAVE

AUTHOR'S NOTE

At the [illegible] author would [illegible] to [illegible]
[illegible] would like to [illegible] to [illegible]
[illegible] recognition, World Success & [illegible]
[illegible] to [illegible]

AUTHOR'S NOTE

All the characters portrayed are creatures of the author's imagination and bear no relationship to any living person. Also, the organization, World Security & Communications, again has no equivalent in real life anywhere in the world.

FOR JANE

CONTENTS

CONTENTS

Prologue

At 4 a.m. it was purely by chance that Bob Newman first heard that Tweed had murdered and then raped a girl.

Returning from a London party, he was driving down Radnor Walk when he saw the unmarked vans parked by the kerb in front of Tweed's terrace house. Men in civilian clothes moved up and down the steps leading into the narrow three-storey building.

They walked quickly, as though in a hurry to complete some urgent assignment. A uniformed policeman stood under a lamp, his hands clasped behind his back. Otherwise the street was deserted.

Newman slowed his Mercedes 280E, parked it a dozen yards from the rear van. He cupped his hand to mask the lighting of a cigarette while he watched. One dark-haired man in a business suit he recognized as he hurried back inside the house. Harris, Harvey – some such name. Special Branch . . .

Two men in boiler suits emerged from inside the rear van. They carried a long plastic body-bag into the building. It looked very much as though the Clean-Up Squad was at work.

Newman climbed out of the car, locked it, strolled up to the entrance to the house. The uniformed policeman stopped him.

'You can't go in there, sir. Best get back to your car and go home . . .'

'I know the man who lives here. What's going on?'

The policeman looked uncertain how to reply. He

glanced up the steps and the dark-haired man peered out. Harvey. That was his name, Newman remembered. Chief Inspector Ronald Harvey. A thick-headed bureaucrat. He hustled down the steps to confront the new arrival.

'Newman, what are you doing here at this hour? Did Tweed phone you?'

'Why would he do that at this time of night?' Newman countered.

That was when Howard, Director of the Secret Service, appeared framed in the doorway. But not the immaculate Howard that Newman was accustomed to seeing. Tall, in his fifties, his plump reddish face was disfigured with a stubble of unshaven hair. His tie was badly knotted, his shirt had a crumpled look – everything about him suggested a man hastily summoned out of bed. His expression was grim and Newman could have sworn he was still feeling dazed.

'Better come in, Bob,' he mumbled. 'This is a terrible business. And the Minister is here . . .'

He was talking as he led the way along a narrow hall, mounting the staircase to the first floor. Harvey followed close on Newman's heels, protesting.

'This is no time to let a foreign correspondent into here.'

'I'll take full responsibility.' Howard addressed him over his shoulder, still ascending the steps. 'And you know perfectly well Newman is fully vetted, has often worked with us.'

'Which Minister are you talking about?' Newman asked.

'Minister for External Security. Buckmaster in person, which I could do without. Brace yourself, Bob. It's in here . . .'

*   *   *

Howard stiffened himself, walked very erect into Tweed's bedroom. The place seemed full of people. Curtains closed over the window, Newman noted. But his gaze focused on where 'it' lay. On Tweed's bed.

The girl would have been in her late twenties, early thirties, Newman estimated. A mass of beautiful blonde hair spread like a wave over the pillow. She lay with the sheet pulled down, exposing her naked body, her long legs, knees pressed together. A brutal sight. Her tongue protruded, flopped to her left side from between well-shaped lips. In life she had been glamorous. Her greenish eyes were wide open, staring sightless at the ceiling. Her neck was horribly bruised. She looked bloody awful, Newman was thinking.

A man in a dark suit, also unshaven, straightened up, reached down to lift a black bag off the floor. The doctor. Removing a pair of surgical gloves, he dropped them inside the open bag he'd perched on a chair, closed the bag.

Harvey plunged in. 'Well, Doctor, what are your findings?'

The doctor, short, plump with thinning white hair, raised his eyebrows. 'For heaven's sake, you'll have to wait for the autopsy. I'm not given to making guesses.'

'Perhaps not,' a fresh voice drawled, 'but you can tell me a few preliminary conclusions. Time, my dear chap, is of the essence, considering the murderer's identity.'

Newman swung round. A tall slim man stood in the doorway to the bathroom. His thick brown hair fell down the sides of his face. In his mid forties, he stood six feet and his aura of authority dominated the room. Unlike the others, he was freshly shaven and his swift-moving brown eyes were alert. He wore an expensive check sports jacket, a spotless white shirt, blue tie with a regimental tie clip sporting the symbol of the airborne forces. Lance Buckmaster. The Minister for External Security. Noted

13

for his attention to presenting a faultless appearance. The tone was clipped, public school.

'You know the Minister, Bob,' Howard said to Newman.

'We have met.'

'And I'm still waiting, Doctor, for a reply,' Buckmaster said with a snap.

The doctor sighed, pursed his lips. 'The girl was strangled and then savagely raped. More I can't say before—'

'The autopsy,' Buckmaster interjected impatiently. 'We know the form. But how do you interpret the sequence – strangulation first, then rape. Why not the other way round?'

'Despite the victim's slimness she looks agile and strong. If she'd fought the rape there'd have been skin from her attacker under the fingernails. There may be a trace under her index finger, but nothing more. And that's subject to the autopsy,' the doctor repeated firmly. 'I'd like to go now.' He looked at the group of waiting men. 'The preliminary examination is finished as far as I am concerned . . .'

Nodding to Howard, he walked out without a glance at Buckmaster. Harvey checked with the photographer, the forensic expert, who both said they didn't need the body any more. Two waiting men in boiler suits carefully wrapped the corpse inside a canvas swathe, lifted it on to a stretcher, removed it from the room on their way downstairs. Buckmaster, hands clasped behind his erect back, paced the room restlessly, pushed a shock of hair over his head.

'Why assume it was Tweed?' asked Newman, staring at Howard.

'Because he lived here.' It was Harvey who answered. Wearing plastic gloves, he was picking up a pipe from a glass bowl to slip it inside a transparent bag. 'He even smoked his pipe before he did the job.'

'May I look at that pipe?' Newman persisted. 'It's full of tobacco and barely been smoked.'

'So he had a few puffs before he grabbed her round the neck and got on with the job . . .'

Newman walked over to a small wall cupboard. 'Can I look inside here?'

'You cannot,' Harvey informed him. He sealed the bag holding the pipe. 'What's inside it that interests you?'

'Maybe a tin of tobacco.'

'Then we'll have a look at it, shall we?' Harvey stretched out a gloved hand, opened the door. A tin of tobacco rested on the shelf. He prised off the lid. Newman leant forward, sniffed at the half-empty tin. A stale musty odour.

'Satisfied?' Harvey replaced the lid, put the tin back on the shelf. 'And Tweed has disappeared—'

'Looks like he's run for it,' Buckmaster interjected. 'Our best hope is he'll do away with himself. All this has to be kept under wraps, Newman. You've signed the Official Secrets Act.'

'And the neighbours?' Newman enquired.

'A rumour will be spread Tweed has gone off on another insurance investigation. He had nothing to do with his neighbours. All they know about Tweed is he's supposed to be Chief Claims Investigator for an insurance company with a lot of business abroad. Howard told me that.'

'And you want this kept under wraps,' Newman reminded him. 'So what are you doing here – you're highly recognizable with your picture in the papers at every opportunity . . .'

'Don't quite like how you phrased that.' Buckmaster's tone was aggressive. 'You are talking to a Minister of the Crown, in case you've forgotten. As to my presence, Howard phoned me. And I've left my Daimler and driver round two corners from here. And it's time I left.' He

15

looked at Howard. 'I will be in touch with you by nine this morning. See you're available in your office.'

He pulled out a folded check golfing cap from his pocket and rammed it low over his forehead. He sneered at Newman. 'You think anyone will recognize me now on my way back to my car?'

He walked out of the room. Howard shrugged his shoulders as they were left alone. 'He's got a point. He normally never wears anything on his head—' He broke off as Buckmaster reappeared in the doorway.

'Funny business this. I'd never have associated a man like Tweed with such an atrocity.'

Then he was gone again. Howard waved his hands with the air of a man lost. 'And I'd never have thought Buckmaster capable of such a human remark. People are a funny mixture . . .'

'How did you first hear about this business?' Newman asked in a low voice.

'Anonymous phone call. Woke me up. "Tweed is in desperate trouble at his apartment in Radnor Walk. Better get over there before the police do." I think those were his exact words . . .'

'So it was a man who made the call? Recognize the voice? I want you to think – think hard.'

'No, I don't think I've heard that voice before. I dressed quickly. I was on my own. Cynthia is away, fortunately. I arrived about 1.30 a.m. The door wasn't locked. I found that out when I'd pressed the bell and no one came. I walked inside, came upstairs . . . and found her lying on the bed. No sign of anyone else. I phoned Buckmaster. Only thing I could do. When he arrived he alerted the Clean-Up Squad. We can't have a scandal like this made public. It would destroy the Service . . .'

'Who is – was – the girl?' Newman asked crisply.

Howard, still in a state of shock, stared at Newman. The foreign correspondent was in his early forties, well-

16

built, of medium height and with light brown hair verging on sandy-coloured. Even at that hour he had an alert look, as aura of controlled energy. The normally droll smile was absent.

'We've no idea of her identity,' Howard replied. 'They've torn the place to pieces and couldn't even find a handbag. Of course now they're recalling the fact that Tweed's wife left him several years ago for a Greek shipping magnate, that he hasn't had a lot to do with women since . . .'

'He likes girls,' Newman interjected sharply. 'He's been on the edge of having an affair more than once. But he blotted out his wife by dedicating himself to his job. You know that.'

'I thought I did . . .'

'Not you, too? That's great. That's really great.' Newman slapped a hand against his thigh, heard a noise, turned to find Harvey had come back.

'One thing strikes me as odd, Mr Newman,' he began, his manner officious. 'How you happened to turn up here at this hour?'

'I'd been to a party at Cipriani's in The Strand which went on all hours. To sober up I walked back to my flat in Beresforde Road. I wasn't sleepy, so I decided to drive round London a bit to tire myself.'

'That's a jolly long walk, if you don't mind my saying so,' Harvey remarked and smiled in a twisted way. Newman could have hit him.

'So what the hell are you getting at?' he asked quietly.

'Nothing. At the moment. But we can check your story later – find witnesses who saw you leave Cipriani's. Get someone to do the same walk at the same time, see how long it takes . . .'

'Why not do the walk yourself?' Newman rapped back. 'Might help to take an inch or two off your waistline.'

17

'No need to get personal. The main thing is, where is Tweed at this moment?'

Kneeling in front of the safe in his first-floor office at Park Crescent, headquarters of the Secret Service, Tweed turned the dial to the last numbers of the combination lock, hauled open the door.

The curtains were drawn over the windows looking towards Regent's Park and he hadn't turned on the light. He used a flash to see what he was doing. Pulling open a drawer, he took out several stacks of banknotes in German marks and Swiss francs. He arranged them neatly in the executive case open by his side, then concealed the bank-notes with several layers of insurance magazines and four paperbacks. He locked the case, closed the safe door, spun the combination dial, stood up.

In his mid forties, Tweed had a compact build, dark hair and wore horn-rim glasses. In repose his face was that of a kindly man with exceptional intelligence. The eyes behind the lenses were watchful and wary. He wore a business suit which lacked the elegance of his chief, Howard. The Deputy Director of the SIS was a man you could pass in the street without noticing, an effect he'd been careful to cultivate.

Still using the flashlight, he perched the case on his desk, took out his key ring, used the two keys which unlocked the specially reinforced bottom right-hand drawer. Reaching down, he delved beneath three code books, hauled out the six passports with his photograph – minus glasses – and all in different names. He chose the passport with the name William Sanders, thrust it in his breast pocket. The other five he spread out flat at the bottom of the executive case. He re-locked the drawer, stood up, and that was when someone switched on the main light.

* * *

Paula Grey, his attractive assistant, closed the door, leaned against it. In her early thirties, her raven black hair gleamed in the overhead light. She had excellent bone structure, a well-shaped determined chin, a good figure and long legs. She was wearing a dark blue gaberdine suit, a white blouse with a pussy bow, her check coat folded over one arm. The February early morning was chilly, with a hint of snow to come in the air.

Tweed, enduring high tension, concealed his shock well. His mind went cold as ice. His voice was completely normal when he asked the question.

'What on earth are you doing here at this hour?'

'I might ask you the same thing.' She nodded towards his suitcase standing next to the desk. 'Going somewhere? You never told me. And something's wrong. I can tell.'

His right hand went automatically towards his pocket for his pipe. Then he remembered he'd given up smoking the damned thing. His mind was moving at extraordinary speed.

'Something cropped up unexpectedly. I'm going abroad for a short time . . .'

She walked towards him, her movements swift and graceful. She put both her hands on his shoulders.

'This is Paula. Remember me? I came in to do some work – I couldn't sleep. Now, what's wrong?'

'Brace yourself. I'm going to be accused of murder and rape. A beautiful young girl I've never seen before. She's lying in my bed at Radnor Walk. Now you'd better ask the question – did I do it?'

It was the only hint of emotion he showed. She clenched her teeth, shook him. Tried to. He stood immovable. 'What the devil are you talking about? How dare you ask me that.' Her voice quavered with emotion, then she regained control. 'Are you mad? Fleeing like a common criminal. You're the Deputy

19

Director – in case you've forgotten. You must stay and fight it. Find out what really happened.'

'Can't. I have a secret project I was controlling. Only one other person over here knows about it. I have to remain free to carry that project through. A lot is at stake – maybe even the security of the whole western world. Which sounds melodramatic. I'm leaving, Paula. Catching the earliest plane to Brussels.'

'Why Brussels? And I still don't see why you're so certain you'll be accused of this dreadful thing,' she protested.

'Because someone very clever and ruthless has planned this frame-up. So they may have planted some more damning "evidence" somewhere in my flat. I had no time to search thoroughly. And why Brussels? That's only the first stage. I have to find a bolt-hole – somewhere I can operate from. They'll lock me up when they find that poor girl. Everything points to me as the murderer, the rapist. Who do you think I could trust with that hanging over me? No one for certain—'

'You bloody fool,' she snapped. 'You can trust me. I'm coming with you. My case packed for an emergency is in that cupboard over there. And a couple is less conspicuous than a man on his own . . .'

'Out of the question.'

Tweed forcibly removed her hands, walked across to the stand near the door, donned his old Burberry. He picked up the executive case, his suitcase. He paused by the door, looked back at her.

'Your job could be at stake. You live for your job. Stay here and keep the home fires burning.'

He left the room, closing the door behind him. That was when Tweed began running and running and running. The nightmare had started.

PART ONE

The Fugitive – Tweed

1

At 7 a.m. the same morning Lance Buckmaster arrived at
the headquarters of the company he had founded in
Threadneedle Street, World Security & Communications
Ltd. To avoid any risk of being noticed he drove his wife's
Volvo station wagon.

The twenty-storey building was empty at that hour.
Buckmaster parked the Volvo in the underground garage,
used the special key to open the executive elevator door,
ascended to the eighteenth floor. Gareth Morgan, his
deputy and confidante, waited for him in the large office
with windows overlooking the City. A white mist
obscured the view, gave the high-rise buildings a ghostly
look. It was going to be a bleak February.

'It worked.' Buckmaster threw his check cap on a
couch, strode across the room and lolled in his executive
chair. 'Special Branch bought it, swallowed it – hook, line
and sinker.'

'And Tweed?' his deputy enquired.

Gareth Morgan was forty-two years old and looked
more like fifty-two. Five feet six, he was overweight for
his height and his body resembled a large turnip in shape.
He had small neat feet and moved with agility. Dark-
haired, he had shrewd beady eyes, was clean-shaven and
showed the beginnings of a jowl. A slow deliberate
talker, he fixed his small eyes on the subject he was
conversing with, as though exerting a hypnotic effect. He
was a man of great energy, ability and ruthlessness. Buckmaster's wife, Leonora, had once told a woman friend,

'Lance and Morgan go well together. Two of the world's greatest con men . . .'

'Tweed has vanished off the face of the earth,' Buckmaster informed his subordinate in his lofty voice. 'Which is just what we hoped for – that he'd run for it.'

'Don't underestimate that man,' Morgan warned as he lit a cigar. 'He'll have headed for Europe . . .'

'So it makes your job easier. We have WS & C offices with trained staffs all over the Continent. I'm putting you in charge of the operation. Locate Tweed and eliminate him. Essential you make it look like an accident . . .'

Morgan pursed his thick lips, his expression grim. 'You mean go over there myself? I have to mind the shop here. When you became a Minister you appointed me Managing Director. Remember?'

'You like moving about.' Buckmaster's tone was brusque. 'The assignment should be right up your street. You fly to Europe, put the boot in to our top people, get them looking, then fly back here. Like a Kissinger shuttle, Gareth.' He checked his watch. 'And I'm not supposed to be here. I'm leaving shortly for the Ministry.'

Morgan ran a thick thumb across his jowl, puffed at his cigar. Buckmaster was right: he shouldn't be in the building. When he'd been appointed a Minister he'd handed over his parcel of shares to his wife, Leonora. And the idea did appeal to Morgan: a Kissinger-like shuttle. Appealed to his ego. He'd use the company executive jet.

'I'll have to return here frequently,' he said eventually. 'I find Leonora is becoming a bit active – curious about things – as chairman. And she's become chummy with that accountant, Ted Doyle . . .'

'Curious about what?' Buckmaster demanded.

'Company figures. The balance sheet. So far I've kept her away from the secret files. When is that fifty-million pound loan coming in? I can't bluff the City for ever.'

24

'Soon. And you've left off a zero. It will be five hundred million.'

'As much as that?' Morgan concealed his shock. 'That should put us back in business nicely. But where the hell can you raise that money?'

Buckmaster stood up, donned his check cap. 'Leave that to me. You deal with Tweed. And quickly . . .'

'It may take time,' Morgan warned. 'I told you not to underestimate him.'

'Not too much time. The deadline is running out. Fly to the Continent today. I'm off . . .'

Morgan sat in the leather chair facing Buckmaster's desk for some time after his chief had left, his bulk squeezed between the arms. He had come a long way since his early days as a security guard with a small outfit, had climbed with Buckmaster.

He recalled as almost yesterday the advertisement in *The Times* for an experienced administrator to join a new security organization. He'd called the number in the ad. from Cardiff and Buckmaster had answered the phone. Buckmaster had been off-hand in his reaction.

'I don't know you have the experience I need . . .'

'But I do have a first-class ticket from Cardiff to London in my fist. And I'm calling from the station. The express leaves in five minutes – I can see it from where I'm speaking. Give me fifteen minutes of your time and you'll hire me. If you decide not to I'll walk straight out of your office and you'll never see me again. Only four minutes now before that express begins to move . . .'

The audacious ploy had worked. Buckmaster had warned him there would be no question of paying his fare. Morgan had replied he paid his own way. He boarded the express with two minutes to spare.

It was Morgan's handling of the attempted bank raid a few days earlier in Cardiff which turned the trick. It had made the national press. Instead of travelling with the security truck carrying the money, Morgan had checked out the area round the bank the previous day. On the morning of the delivery he hid in an alley armed with a baseball bat concealed under his raincoat. Two armed men had jumped from a car as the money was being carried towards the bank. Morgan had appeared behind them, had first smashed the skull of the man carrying a machine-pistol and then crushed the kneecap of the second robber armed with an automatic.

At the interview Buckmaster had explained he was founding a new security firm specializing in protecting high-risk and valuable cargoes. His first reaction was to reject Morgan until he remembered the abortive Cardiff robbery.

'Routine. That's where established firms make their mistake,' Morgan had told him, speaking rapidly and with an air of total authority. 'And they use one of three alternative routes in recognizable trucks. The vehicles must be varied in appearance, the destination told to the driver in code as he leaves the depot – by you or me. We must have dummy runs to confuse the intelligence systems of the professional robbers. And I hire every member of the staff – I can smell a wrong 'un a hundred yards away . . . We infiltrate informants into the underworld to organize our own counter-espionage apparatus . . . In certain countries on the Continent we use tougher methods . . .'

'On the Continent?'

Buckmaster, who normally dominated a conversation, had found himself taken aback by the scale Morgan foresaw they would operate on.

'Of course.' Morgan had waved the unlit cigar he'd held clenched between his teeth. 'It is an international organization we are thinking of. Europe first, then the States . . .'

'And when could you start?' Buckmaster had eventually asked.

26

'As your right-hand man, now. I brought my packed case. It's waiting in the lobby . . .'

Buckmaster had hired him on the spot. A decision he had never regretted. Morgan had suggested the name, World Security & Communications. And that was twenty years ago. Long before Buckmaster's eyes had turned to politics and he'd become the youngest MP in the Commons, leaving Morgan to run the largest security organization in the world. It had expanded by leaps and bounds.

And that, Morgan thought as he stirred in the chair, was when I advised caution. That we consolidate what we had built up; but Buckmaster had the bit between his teeth. More offices had been opened up in many countries. Too many too quickly.

'And one day I'll own the whole outfit,' he said to himself. 'Providing it doesn't go bust first.' Through nominees he'd bought up a major holding in the company. Morgan thought of only one person in the world. Gareth Morgan.

Stretching, he yawned. He'd been up all night. First things first. The tracking down of Tweed.

2

Tweed moved fast. He caught the first Sabena flight to Brussels, using the William Sanders passport at London Airport. Arriving in the Belgian capital, he took a cab to the Hilton on the Boulevard de Waterloo.

He booked in at the special executive reception on the eighteenth floor, reserving an executive suite on the twentieth floor. Dumping his case inside the suite, he left the hotel.

. He hired a BMW from Hertz, showing a driving licence in the name of William Sanders. He parked the car in an underground garage near the hotel. He could have parked it in the Hilton garage, but if he needed to leave suddenly that might be dangerous.

'Do you really think we can disappear into the blue?' Paula asked as they walked back to the hotel.

'If we keep moving . . .'

The presence of Paula Grey was one thing he hadn't counted on. She had followed him in a second taxi to London Airport, taking her case with her. His first realization that he was not alone came when he booked a return Business-Class ticket at the Sabena counter. He turned and Paula was standing behind him.

'A Business-Class return to Brussels,' she informed the airline clerk.

Collecting her ticket, she came up behind him again as he checked in for the flight. Tweed was unable to argue with her -- it was too public and the last thing he wanted was to draw attention to himself. They were sitting alongside each other in the half-empty aircraft before he could protest.

'What on earth do you think you're doing?'

'Coming with you. I told you. Back at the office.'

'I can't risk having you with me. There are things you don't know. You could be in terrible danger.'

'I've been there before. Remember Rotterdam? For starters?'

'I want you to catch the first flight back from Brussels. I'm a common fugitive – wanted for murder and rape. It's a queer feeling I can tell you . . .'

'So you need every bit of support you can get. Back at the office you said something about a secret project. Is that why you have to go underground?'

28

'Yes. And don't ask me about it.'

'I'm not leaving you,' she warned him. 'Tell me later what really happened to you last night. First we must decide what to do, where to go, who we can trust.'

Tweed, reacting automatically to the danger, still felt stunned. Paula, he recognized, was thinking with her usual clarity. She had summed up his immediate task in a nutshell. For the first time he wavered in his determination to get rid of her. She sensed his uncertainty.

'Well, for starters, who can we trust?'

'No one,' he'd said bleakly. 'Absolutely no one – they'll react as soon as they guess I've left the country. The first move will be to alert all my known contacts, to request that I be held incommunicado if I approach any of them . . .'

'And you really think someone like Chief Inspector Kuhlmann of the German Federal Police is going to swallow this absurd idea that you're a murderer and a rapist?'

'He won't have any option . . .'

They had argued like this until the plane touched down in Belgium: Tweed uncharacteristically negative; Paula positive and working out escape routes. Tweed's mood changed as soon as they reached Brussels, reserving the suite at the Hilton, hiring the car.

Returning to the Hilton, they went straight up to the suite. It was Paula who had insisted they share the suite against all Tweed's objections.

'If we book a separate one for me,' she pointed out, 'I may have to show my passport. Being registered as Paula Grey will lead the baying hounds straight to you – once they grasp that I've disappeared too. I can sleep on a couch if they haven't twin beds . . .'

'They had twin beds the last time I was here,' Tweed recalled.

'Stop being so Victorian,' she'd snapped. 'If you register I can pass as your wife . . .'

It was Paula who, on the way back to the hotel, had dived into a shop, emerging with a folder full of Michelin road maps of different areas of Europe. 'Need these to plan our route,' she'd said briskly.

Now Tweed was staring from the suite window at the panoramic–view over the city. Close by reared the immense domed bulk of the Palais de Justice, a complex so large it covered a greater area than St Peter's in Rome. He found it ironic.

'If they catch up with me now,' he mused, 'I suppose that's where they'll take me . . .'

'Oh do shut up and look at these maps with me. Where are we heading for when we leave here?'

'Switzerland might be best.' Tweed shook off his mood of resignation, leaned over her shoulder to study the maps. Again her driving force was animating him, pushing back an insidious sensation of inertia. 'I'll have to risk contacting Arthur Beck, Chief of the Federal Police in Berne. Switzerland being neutral, it might be our best bet.' -

She carefully concealed her satisfaction at this first use of the word 'our'. Tweed's finger traced a route through Liège to the east and then down through the Ardennes, a remote hilly district.

'Not much traffic if we can make it into the forest,' he said. 'Definitely our best chance of not being spotted.'

'But where do we go from there? How can we safely cross into West Germany – assuming the alert has gone out by then?'

'Our best chance is to drive along the secondary roads in the Ardennes into Luxembourg. There's no check on crossing that border. Then, if we get lucky we drive over the Luxembourg frontier into Germany, head south down the Rhine for the Black Forest. There's a small place where I think we could slip over the German border into Switzerland. It's one hell of a long shot.'

'So we follow that route,' Paula said firmly.

'The big question is – will we ever reach the Swiss border?'

Paula asked the question which had preyed on her mind while they were drinking coffee from room service in Tweed's suite. She took a deep breath, nerved herself, dived in.

'Isn't it about time you told me what really happened back at your flat in Radnor Walk?'

'Like an idiot, I walked straight into a carefully prepared trap. If one of my staff had done the same thing I do believe I'd have fired him. I was so incredibly stupid I still don't know what got into me.'

Paula crossed her legs on the couch, facing Tweed who sat bolt upright in an executive chair. 'Well, what did you do?' she coaxed.

'I was working late at the office as you know. You'd gone home and only Monica was left in the building with me. She took the call and said it was for me. The caller would only tell her his name was Klaus. I guessed it was one of my circle of private informants on the Continent – the people even you don't know about. I've promised them all total confidentiality.' He paused, sipped at his coffee.

'I know you have these people. Go on,' Paula encouraged him.

'I took the call. It sounded like Klaus Richter, although there was a lot of background noise. People chatting, laughing. He said he'd flown over urgently to see me and asked me to come to the Cheshire Cheese, that pub in Fleet Street, at ten o'clock that night. He sounded edgy. I agreed. Where I made my mistake was in not checking back with his number in Freiburg at the edge of the Black Forest. Although they'd probably

31

covered that.' He spoke the last words grimly.

'Who is "they"?' Paula asked.

'I've no idea who's behind the conspiracy – because that's what it has to be. And a very dangerous conspiracy since I suspect it's connected with the secret project I was controlling alone. Don't ask me about that. I arrived at the Cheshire Cheese early deliberately – to spy out the land . . .'

'Your usual ploy in such cases. You did have all your marbles,' she encouraged him again.

'It was 9.45 when I entered the pub. Place was crowded. I ordered a glass of wine and sat in the corner where I could survey the whole place. No sign of Richter. I waited and waited. It was just before closing time when a girl dropped an envelope in my lap. Unsealed. The message inside was brief. *Came early. Had to leave. Being followed. Meet you at Radnor Walk. K.* I'd just time to read it when the girl returned. She whispered that Klaus told her she must take the message from me after I'd read it. A clever touch that. Klaus was a very careful man. I let her take it . . .'

'Seen that girl before?'

'Never. Head wrapped in a scarf and tied over her chin. It *was* a cold night. About thirty at a guess. About five foot ten, well dressed, pale white complexion, blue eyes. Then she was gone . . .'

Tweed stared into the distance, recalling the incident. Paula prodded again.

'So what was your next move?'

'As I said, it was late, near closing time. I walked back all the way from Fleet Street to Radnor Walk, which took a while . . .'

'To check that *you* weren't being followed?'

'Exactly, I wasn't. At least not on foot. There was an Audi which passed me soon after I'd left the pub. I believe now the driver – I didn't see who it was – was checking that I had left the pub. Eventually, after midnight, I arrived at Radnor Walk. The front door was slightly ajar. No trace of any forcing of the two security locks. I crept inside, picked up that heavy walking stick with the weighted tip I keep in the umbrella stand, explored the ground floor. Nothing. I had the strong feeling the place was empty. Then I went upstairs . . .'

He drank more black coffee slowly, the faraway look in his eyes again. This time Paula waited in silence. He put down the cup, stared straight at her.

'I entered the bedroom and the bedside light was on. I saw her at once, lying face up in my bed. The sheet rumpled. Brutally strangled. Big bruises round the neck.' Tweed was now speaking in a normal detached tone. 'The sheets had been pulled down over her long legs. She was naked, had a good figure. I soon realized she'd been raped – no need to go into the details. I also realized it was the perfect frame – that I'd be accused.'

Why?' Paula was leaning forward, watching Tweed carefully. 'You knew the girl?'

'Never seen her in my life. The murderer had added some subtle touches. My pipe, filled with tobacco, partially smoked, lay in a glass bowl.'

'You gave up that pipe several weeks ago. You said you were a wet smoker and didn't enjoy it.'

'Which is one thing about me the murderer doesn't know. But it doesn't mean a damned thing. I could have tried the pipe again before I set about her. A glass I'd left in the kitchen in the morning was on the bedside table – with a drop of wine in it. Chablis. From a bottle on another table which was almost empty. The glass would still have my fingerprints on it, I'm sure.'

'Could they still feel so sure you were guilty? People like Howard, for God's sake.'

'No option.' Tweed was cleaning his glasses with his handkerchief, a mannerism which Paula welcomed seeing. Relating what had happened was calming him. 'And no alibi,' he went on. 'I was walking back for over an hour through deserted streets. I doubt if anyone at the Cheshire Cheese would remember me – I was deliberately making myself inconspicuous . . .

'The girl who gave you the message from Richter. She knows you were there.'

'And is obviously part of the plot, hired to hand me the note, and take it off me afterwards. No evidence . . .'

'This Klaus Richter in Freiburg,' she suggested. 'Could he help?' She frowned. 'You used the past tense when referring to him. Why?'

'Because I think he's probably dead,' Tweed replied. 'The people who organized this are professionals – and ruthless as hell. What they did to that girl proves that. They've left no loose ends, I'm sure.'

'What on earth did you do after you'd found this unknown girl in your house?'

'Thought fast. I could see a noose had been thrown round my neck I'd maybe never get free from. The only answer was to run – in the hope that I can escape being apprehended while I find out what's happening to the project I was working on. As I said earlier, I'm a fugutive. We can't trust anyone . . .'

'There's Newman – and Marler.'

'A horrific crime like the one at Radnor Walk makes a man an outcast, a pariah without friends. We're on our own. Someone is counting on that.'

'But we're not just going to sit here until they come for us?'

'No. Instead we'll do the unexpected.'

3

'I've found out Tweed caught an early flight to Brussels. I'm having the staff of our office there check every hotel. I flew over copies of that photograph of Tweed you gave me,' Morgan reported as he drove the Daimler beyond Exeter towards Dartmoor.

His bulk was squeezed inside the chauffeur's uniform, which did not fit his turnip-like shape too well. A chauffeur's peaked cap was pulled down over his high forehead. Buckmaster sat beside him, staring at the bleak snowbound slopes of the moor.

Morgan had adopted his disguise because, as a Minister, Buckmaster was not supposed to have any further connection with the world-wide security organization they had built up. Buckmaster ran a hand over his lean face.

'It's essential at least to keep Tweed harassed and fearful – on the move until you can locate him and do the job.'

'There is one complication.' Morgan leered. 'Paula Grey has also disappeared you said earlier. Looks as though he's taken his bedmate with him to keep himself warm.'

'There's no record that their relationship is anything but professional,' Buckmaster snapped in a puritanical tone. 'That means they may be more alert. Bear that in mind. And if this Grey woman is with him when you pinpoint their whereabouts – she'll have to go too.'

'That can be attended to. I've contacted Armand Horowitz and he's meeting me in Brussels.'

'So, you've gone to the top,' Buckmaster commented as they turned on to the Okehampton road. It was getting dark.

'You need a real professional on a job like this,' Morgan responded. 'Horowitz has never failed to take out a target.'

'Don't want to hear about it. No details, no pack drill.'

Morgan subsided into silence. Buckmaster's habit of distancing himself from the seamier side of the company worried him. He had little doubt that if anything went wrong Buckmaster would let him drop over the cliff. Which, he reflected, is why he pays me one hundred thousand pounds a year. But, he also reflected, it means I'll have to watch my back. Treachery was the name of the game in politics. In business too. Because he had grasped this fact was why Morgan had risen so high.

'What are you going to do next about Tweed?' Buckmaster asked as Morgan turned off the Okehampton road and drove through the snow towards Moretonhampstead.

'Tell you in a minute. I'd better get out of these togs – I also suggest you sit in the rear of the car before we arrive at Tavey Grange.'

He stopped the car on the grass verge of the deserted road. Getting out, he tossed the cap on the seat, wrestled off the uniform, exposing the lightweight dark suit he wore under it. While Buckmaster sat impatiently in the rear and drummed his fingers on his knee, Morgan put on an expensive black overcoat, the collar trimmed with astrakhan, buttoned it up, got back behind the wheel and resumed driving.

Passing between the granite houses lining the main street of Moretonhampstead, he drove on, his headlights picking out the bends in the serpentine road. Tavey Grange lay half a mile beyond the Manor House Hotel. He answered Buckmaster's question as he turned off the road between lodge gates and proceeded down the long drive across open parkland. A half-moon was rising and the snow-covered slopes of Dartmoor glowed weirdly.

'I'm taking the chopper from your helipad here back to London. Tomorrow I'll take Stieber with me to Brussels, pick up the trail there.'

'You'd better know – unofficially – that an alert for Tweed has now gone out secretly to our counter-espionage friends and certain police chiefs in Europe. Locate and hold is the order.'

'That might handicap me.' Morgan grunted. 'Wish you hadn't done that.'

'Had to. It was the obvious reaction I had to make as Minister. If I'd held my hand it would have looked suspicious. The PM agreed. It will serve the purpose of isolating Mr Tweed from his old buddies, keep him running like a scared fox.'

'If you say so.'

Morgan felt more comfortable as he approached the Grange, still hidden by a copse of trees. It was only in London they had to keep up the pretence that Buckmaster had nothing to do with his company. The servants at the house were mostly foreigners who didn't know their arse from their elbow, as Morgan put it to himself.

They passed the copse and the lights of a large Elizabethan house came into view. Tall stately chimneys, the lights shining from behind mullion-paned windows. Morgan reduced speed and checked his appearance in the rear-view mirror, driving with one hand. Wanted to look his elegant best for the bitch, his nominal company chief, Leonora Buckmaster. He combed his hair. In the rear Buckmaster made a gentle hissing noise between his teeth. The sooner Morgan boarded the chopper and pushed off the better.

Leonora Buckmaster came to the front doorway as the Daimler pulled up. Morgan jumped out, opened the rear door. Buckmaster alighted. His wife called out in her well-modulated voice.

'Drinks are ready in the library. Then straight into dinner. I'm famished. Good evening, Gareth.'

'Good evening, ma'am.' Morgan dipped in a little bow and gave her his best smile.

Leonora Buckmaster was ten years younger than her husband. A slim blonde creature, she wore a Valentino black and white dress. Her husband gave her a hug and hurried inside, saying he was going to take a quick bath, then he'd be down for drinks.

'A drink in the library for you, Gareth?' she enquired.

He pecked her on the cheek. She managed to conceal the physical revulsion she always felt from close contact with this man. She might be chairman of the company with Lance's block of shares in her name, but Gareth Morgan was managing director and ran the organization.

'That would be nice, Leonora,' he agreed after closing and locking the car. The garage man would put the Daimler to bed. He followed her into the library, produced his cigar case, then hesitated.

'Not in here. Out on the terrace,' she informed him. 'I've got a drink. Do pour your own. Leave some in the bottle . . . .'

It was not a friendly joke: Morgan was aware she thought he drank too heavily. To hell with her, he thought and kept his coat on in the warm book-lined room. He poured half a glass of neat Scotch, raised it to Leonora who had seated herself in an arm chair, erect and elegant.

'Chin-chin,' said Morgan and drank a heavy slug.

He opened the door to the terrace spanning the full width of the rear of the mansion, closed it behind him. The ice-cold air hit him. He lit his Havana, took a deep satisfying puff. Leonora was getting to be a pain, probing into the affairs of the company. At least he'd kept the vital figures away from her.

He strolled along the terrace below which the grassy slopes fell away steeply towards an ornamental lake. A cottonwool mist was floating down towards the lake from the ridge in the moonlight.

On the terrace he took his decision. He'd board the chopper when he'd finished his drink, tell the pilot to take him to London Airport. His suitcase was in the boot of the Daimler. He could get a couple of hamburgers and a glass of beer at the airport, then catch the evening flight to Brussels. Get after Tweed.

At SIS headquarters in Park Crescent, London, Howard sat behind Tweed's desk, facing Bob Newman. Monica, Tweed's close associate for many years, sat at her desk, her head bent over some files while the two men talked.

'Do you really think Tweed is guilty?' Newman demanded point-blank.

'It's inconceivable, I agree,' responded Howard, waving a well-manicured hand, his plump face pink with embarrassment at the directness of Newman. 'But he made a great mistake fleeing the country. And taking Paula with him. Doesn't look good for his case . . .'

'His case!' Newman exploded. 'You talk like a bloody prosecuting counsel. He obviously had his reasons. What was he working on? And how do you know he's fled the country?'

'Can't talk about what he was working on,' Howard said stiffly. He paused. 'Didn't even know myself until I talked with the PM this afternoon. And you won't like this, but since you're fully vetted and have worked with Tweed in the past . . .' Another wave of the hand. 'A general alert has been sent out to certain security personnel in other countries to locate and hold him when found. All very hush-hush. The press mustn't get on to it – and you *are* the press. I'm invoking the Official Secrets Act form you signed on that one. Have to. Sorry and all that . . .'

'I said,' Newman repeated slowly, 'how do you know he's fled the country?'

'Well, Buckmaster gave the order. Check with airports, seaports. Show his photograph. Only to top security personnel, of course.'

'Of course!' Newman interjected ironically. 'Do get to the point of what I asked.'

'Jim Corcoran at London Airport made discreet enquiries. Found a girl with a good memory who remembered him checking in early this morning for a flight to Brussels. Appeared to have a girl with him. From the description Corcoran obtained I'm afraid it could be Paula Grey . . .'

'Makes sense,' Newman commented.

'Makes sense!' Howard's pompous manner changed, his voice went up several decibels. 'If it was Paula that means I have two of my staff as fugitives from justice . . .'

'Balls!' Newman lit a cigarette. 'Buckmaster's doing this all on his own?'

'Well . . .' Howard showed more indecision. 'Actually I wasn't privy to the decision to send the alert.'

Wasn't privy to . . . Newman controlled himself with an effort. Howard really was the most bombastic prig. 'Then who was?' he demanded.

'Buckmaster – after due consultation with the PM I was told at Downing Street to issue a discreet alert.' He leaned forward. 'I might tell you I persuaded her to cut down the list Buckmaster had drawn up of people to be informed. Only those I feel we can trust to keep it under wraps have been contacted.'

'Who are they?'

Howard hesitated again 'Why do you want to know?'

'For Christ's sake – because I believe Tweed is innocent, that he's been framed up to the hilt. And I'm going to do something about it, not just sit here on my tod wringing my hands.

'I can't do anything else, Bob,' Howard said quietly, 'except sit here on my tod, as you put it. I needed to know that you're also convinced it's a conspiracy. It's not a view I can admit to officially. I'm very relieved you're going into action – and you might like to know I reworded the signal Buckmaster was sending, made it, shall we say less positive.'

'Buckmaster seems to be running this outfit these days,' Newman snapped. 'I don't like that either . . .'

It was a recent experiment on the part of the PM – to create a new ministry to oversee the security services. The Ministry for External Security. The first man to be appointed as Minister, Lance Buckmaster, had seemed logical. He was youngish, energetic and a good orator.

It had seemed even more logical to choose this MP since he'd built up a vast international organization devoted to security. World Security & Communications specialized in the safe movement of high-risk cargoes – gold bullion, old-master paintings, large consignments of banknotes.

But WS & C as it was now known world wide had carried the development of security to the ultimate. It handled secret data for the research departments of major companies. It had gone into the communications field, using its own satellites to provide a watertight method for directors talking about vital topics over the phone from, say, Frankfurt to Washington, supplying the coded systems.

- With all this experience behind him, Buckmaster had proved a natural choice to control the new Ministry. The snag was it had deliberately not been made clear how much power he wielded over the Secret Service. Howard was still able to report direct to the PM. She had insisted on retaining ultimate control. Howard waved his hand a third time before speaking his mind.

'Just between you and me it's a running dogfight between myself and Buckmaster. I won't let him come here often. There are certain files I refuse to let him see. It may cost me my job, but so far the PM has backed me.'

'And what about Turnip Top, as the press has labelled Gareth Morgan? I met him at a party. His conversation is a lie a minute. His policy is to ingratiate himself with anyone who might be useful to him, a nauseating spectacle. But I detect something sinister behind the showbiz front, the big cigar.'

'I wouldn't have said sinister. Why use that epithet?'

'Rumours from contacts I have. Hidden inside WS & C is a well-organized industrial espionage section – run by an unpleasant character with a dubious background. Helmut Stieber. Not his real name, by the way. His father came from Czechoslovakia. Married an English girl. Both are dead. Stieber is Morgan's deputy. Spends most of his time on the Continent. Also rumoured they used strong-arm tactics during one of Buckmaster's many takeover bids to build up his conglomerate. Even to sabotaging competitors' plants.'

'I didn't know that.' Howard sat up straight. 'I can tell you one thing – Morgan isn't allowed anywhere near this place. But some of Buckmaster's requests for data I suspect emanate from Morgan . . .'

He broke off as Marler strolled in after tapping lightly on the door. In his early thirties, he was supposed to be the coming man at SIS. Among his talents was that he was the most deadly marksman in Western Europe.

Slim in build, wearing an expensively cut sports jacket and slacks, he was clean-shaven, had a strong face and spoke in a high-pitched drawl.

'Evenin', Bob. Haven't seen a story from you for ages. Living off the proceeds of that bestseller you wrote, *Kruger: The Computer That Failed*?'

Marler, five feet seven, perched his backside on Paula's desk and swung his legs. Newman looked at him with no particular liking. He'd noted that Howard had clammed up as the new arrival appeared. Why?

'You know perfectly well, Marler, that these days I only go after a story I think is really worthwhile. That's the advantage of being financially independent.'

'So you won't be doing a piece on the somewhat grisly events at Radnor Walk?'

'There's a "D" notice on that,' Howard snapped. 'We've led the press to believe some foreign diplomat was involved in a wild party. Drugs and all that. Put them off the scent.'

'Jolly good idea.' Marler lit a king-size cigarette. 'Can't have the world thinking Tweed broke loose at long last, had his way with an attractive girl and then throttled the poor dear . . .'

'You have such a nice way of putting things,' Newman commented. 'Life and soul of any party, you'd be.'

'Keep your hair on, old chum. I know it's a bit of a shaker.' He addressed Howard. 'Since Tweed appears to have scooted, are you sending out a general alert, setting the hounds after him?'

'All options are still under consideration,' Howard told him stiffly.

'Fair enough. Just came in to say I've been summoned to the presence. Thought you ought to know . . .'

'You mean the PM?' Howard's sense of outrage was clear in his tone.

'Lordy, no. Lance Buckmaster, our esteemed Minister for External Security has asked me to attend him down at the ancestral home, Tavey Grange on Dartmoor.'

'Why?'

43

'I'll know when I get there, won't I? I'd better get moving. It's a quite a drive – even at night. Our posh new Minister never sleeps.' He glanced at Newman as he stood up. 'The Radnor Walk episode would give you something to get your teeth into. Assuming you're still on Tweed's side . . .'

'Are you?' Newman rapped out.

'I always keep an open mind . . .'

'Because there's not much going on inside it?' Newman suggested.

Marler gave a mock salute, left the office without replying.

'You don't trust him,' Newman said with a slight sense of shock.

'You asked me earlier who had been informed in Europe. If you ever quote me I'll deny I ever said it.' Howard was now looking uncharacteristically grim. He spoke in a monotone. 'Chief Inspector Benoit of the Brussels Criminal Police. Arthur Beck, chief of Swiss Federal Police in Berne. Pierre Loriot at Interpol in Paris. Gunnar Hornberg of SAPO in Stockholm. René Lasalle of French Counter-Intelligence in Paris. And Chief Inspector Otto Kuhlmann, head of Federal Criminal Police in Wiesbaden. That completes the list.'

'Thank you.' Newman paused as Howard stood up to leave. 'It will be a miracle if the news doesn't leak out. And you really have closed him in.'

'The list was much longer as drawn up by Buckmaster,' Howard replied as he reached the door.

'And the signals included details of the crime committed at Radnor Walk?'

'Those men are his friends of quite a few years . . .'

'But will they still be his friends after receiving the signal you sent?'

'I edited the Ministry version,' Howard told him. 'My signal used the phrase "alleged offence". I must go now.

Good luck, Bob. I can't do another damned thing.'

He left the room and Newman swung round to face Monica who had remained like a piece of the furniture during the whole time since he'd arrived. Now she held one finger to her lips, picked up a portable radio from the kneehole beneath her desk and switched it on. Carrying it over, she placed it on Tweed's desk, switched it on, found a music programme, kept it on low volume and sat down close to Newman.

'Why that?' he asked.

'In case the Ministry has bugged the office. Some odd people with papers bearing Buckmaster's signature have been here.'

'Surely Howard realizes the danger? Yet he let me talk . . .'

'He can't believe a Minister would do that. I can – I've met the Right Honourable Lance Buckmaster. Honourable? You have to be joking. He's one of the biggest con men in politics, and that's saying something. Of course I may be prejudiced – he called me Old Faithful.'

'Patronizing swine . . .'

'Oh, he did it on purpose – to try and needle me. Part of his stock-in-trade when he wants to take over an organization. He sows dissension. Howard thinks Marler is in the running for his job.'

'Marler wouldn't play. I don't like him, but he's a cynical bastard and won't be taken in by the likes of Buckmaster.'

'Are you sure? It's a big carrot he's dangling in front of Marler's nose. That has unsettled Howard – all part of the well-known Buckmaster technique.' She leaned closer. 'Am I right in thinking you really believe Tweed had nothing to do with that beastly murder?'

'Yes.'

'Then you might like to know Tweed took a large sum of money with him. A small fortune in Swiss francs and

German marks. It's missing from the safe and only two people had the combination. Tweed and myself.'

'So he's OK for funds. That worried me . . .'

'And, Bob, he's also taken six dummy passports in different names, all carrying his photo . . .'

'Anyone know about that?'

'Only me. He kept them in his bottom right-hand drawer. I'm the only one besides Tweed with keys. I checked while I was on my own. Plus international driving licences in the same names. He's up to something.'

'He needs back-up. I have to find him.'

'He does have Paula with him as far as we know,' Monica reminded him.

'He needs more than that. I'm leaving for Brussels today. I always carry a large sum in one thousand Swiss franc notes.' Newman frowned as he worked it out. 'I won't even go back to my flat just in case someone is watching it. I can buy what I need in Brussels – clothes, shaving kit. Luckily it won't seem odd at the airport, travelling without a suitcase. Businessmen are travelling there and back in a day.'

'If only we knew who was behind all this,' Monica mused.

'I'll have to find out, won't I? Remember, I'm used to doing just that – as a foreign correspondent.'

4

Morgan had missed the last flight to Brussels the previous evening. Fog had delayed the landing of his chopper at London Airport. He stayed overnight at the nearby Penta Hotel.

In the morning he ate a large breakfast – double portion of ham and fried eggs, plenty of cream in his coffee. After he'd booked his Brussels flight he used a public phone to call Stieber, his Chief of Security, in Threadneedle Street. He gave Stieber the number he was calling from, told him to call him back from outside. Stieber was back on the line in five minutes. His cold voice, with a hint of the Czech accent he'd never eliminated, sounded a shade excited.

'The bug in you-know-who's office worked. It came over a treat on the radio transmitter when I played it back . . .'

'Give me the guts, then pick up your case from the office and get your backside out here. London Airport, Terminal One. At Sabena's reservation counter. Buy yourself a Business-Class ticket. From Brussels you'll fly on by yourself to Frankfurt, then maybe Freiburg. I'll instruct you on the plane. You have one and a half hours to get here. Give me your news. Fast . . .'

'Marler was on his way to see the chief on Dartmoor. What is really interesting is Bob Newman is getting into the act in some way.'

'The foreign correspondent?' Morgan's tone was sharp. 'So what is he up to?'

'I don't know. I think after Howard left the room there was maybe a further conversation between Newman and someone else . . .'

'You *think*?'

'Wait for me to finish, please. A radio was turned on and it played music, which I found odd. So there could have been conversation I didn't pick up – scrambled by the radio.'

'You're guessing. Unless Newman is a smart cookie. Forget Newman. He's a has-been. Get your arse over here.'

* * *

The evening before Morgan phoned Stieber, Marler had driven his second-hand red Porsche to Dartmoor. After dark he stopped at a Little Chef, had a quick meal of scrambled eggs and coffee, then continued his journey.

It was ten o'clock when he turned in between the lodge gates and guided the Porsche down the winding drive to Tavey Grange. Leonora appeared behind the Spanish butler, Fernandez, who opened the nail-studded front door.

'Mr Marler?' She gave him her best smile, liking what she saw under the porch lantern. 'Please come in. José will take your case up to your room. Have you had dinner? I've kept something for you. Lance is making long-distance calls from his study – he's looking forward to seeing you in the morning. A drink for you?'

Marler extended his hand, smiled back. Leonora had small, well-shaped hands and clasped his warmly. Marler, normally cold and distant, could exert considerable charm with attractive women.

'Very kind of you, Mrs Buckmaster. But I grabbed something to stay the pangs of hunger on the way down. If your husband isn't going to be available until mornin' I think I'd just as soon get some kip. Long drive and all that . . .'

Leonora escorted him up the massive oak staircase to his room at the back, wished him a good night's sleep and walked slowly back along the landing. She had excellent legs. Marler, still holding the executive case he'd refused to hand to José, noted the curtains were drawn the full length of the large room. He began his check.

There was no key to the door. Opening the executive case, he extracted a rubber wedge, jammed it under the door. He next pulled back a section of curtain, opened one of the mullion-paned windows. Icy air flooded into the heated room.

With a flashlight – also taken from the executive case –

he examined the exterior, leaning out. The beam illuminated the deserted terrace one floor down. He swivelled it to check the outside wall. No fire-escape, no convenient drainpipe anyone could shin up. But to the right of the window he'd opened he found an old ivy creeper clawed to the brickwork. A ready-made ladder for an intruder who wanted to search his possessions during the night.

He closed the window, drew the curtain back across it, glanced round the room. A small heavy porcelain vase on a side table caught his eye. He placed it carefully on the window ledge behind the curtain. That would make enough noise to waken him.

Satisfied with his precautions, he had a wash in the luxurious bathroom, cleaned his teeth, undressed and got into bed. What would the morning bring? He was still uncertain of Buckmaster's motive for wanting to see him.

The following morning, while Morgan was waiting for Stieber at London Airport, Buckmaster joined Marler in the dining-room.

'Good of you to come,' he announced breezily. 'Hope you don't mind, this will be a working breakfast.'

'You talk, I'll listen,' Marler replied and continued piling marmalade on his buttered toast.

'I'm not too happy with the way things are run at Park Crescent – under the present regime, I mean.' Buckmaster poured coffee for himself, Marler said nothing.

'What I'm getting at is our friend, Howard. Nice chap, right sort of background, but is niceness enough?'

'He's proved satisfactory to the PM so far.'

'So far. That's the operative phrase. But what about Tweed and the new emergency? If the Radnor Walk horror becomes public it would be the greatest scandal in the history of the Service. Can we afford that? Some of my advisers think the simplest solution would be if Tweed never came back.' Buckmaster paused to digest some crinkly bacon. 'I understand you are one of the best marksmen in Europe,' he remarked as though apropos of nothing in particular.

'What exactly are you proposing, Minister?' Marler demanded.

'Oh, no definite proposal, my dear chap. Just thinking aloud. Looking at the problem from all angles. And from what I hear you are the person most likely to smoke Tweed out of his hideaway, wherever that may be.'

'I wouldn't count on that,' Marler parried.

'We know he took a flight to Brussels with that girl, Paula Grey.' Buckmaster pushed a cardboard-backed envelope across the table with his fork. 'Inside are two photos, one of Tweed, the other of the Grey woman. I suggest you start with flying to Brussels today. We've notified Benoit that Tweed is wanted. Also Kuhlmann, Loriot, Lasalle and Arthur Beck.'

'You mean I could use them to help in the search?' Marler probed.

Buckmaster paused in the act of forking a strip of bacon into his mouth. 'Well, it would be entirely up to you to decide whether that really is the best way to go about solving this problem. If you see what I mean.'

'I'm not sure I do.'

'I glanced through your personnel file last night. An abbreviated version, I suspect. Howard is still a little jealous of his authority, hasn't yet quite grasped the new set-up since my Ministry was established. I got the impression you're something of a lone wolf. I like that.'

'And you're authorizing me to leave for Brussels, to handle the problem in any way I see fit? Have I understood you?'

'Broadly speaking, yes. In the interests of the Service. Draw any amount of expenses you need. There's my authority for you to do that inside the envelope. Mission unspecified, of course. For your protection.' Buckmaster gave his public smile now so well-known from his pictures in the press.

'Supposing I did solve the problem for you . . .'

'Not for me,' Buckmaster corrected him quickly. 'For the reputation of the Service. I'm only a cog in the machinery.'

'I was going to say,' Marler persisted, 'where would that leave me?'

'A good question.' Buckmaster dabbed at his thin lips with his napkin. 'We all have to think of ourselves from time to time, don't we?' Again, the public smile, showing two rows of perfect teeth. 'You have to remember that with Tweed gone the post of Deputy Director becomes vacant.' Buckmaster leant back in his chair, brushed a hand through his hair. 'And when it's all over who knows? Howard might decide the time had arrived for him to think of retirement.'

'No sign of that at the moment,' Marler pressed him.

'I wouldn't be too sure. Tweed was Howard's appointment. He might think it the honourable thing to do. With a little gentle persuasion . . .'

Buckmaster jumped up suddenly, left his chair standing away from the table. 'Let me show you something before you leave for Brussels. Upstairs in my study . . .'

He took the treads up the great staircase two at a time, a demonstration of his boyish energy. Marler followed at a slower pace. Inside the panelled room Buckmaster picked up a malacca cane, pointed to the wall over the fireplace.

The badge of the Airborne Division had been enlarged in colour and framed as a centrepiece. Below it was Buckmaster's beret, worn during his Army service. Four photographs of the wearer showed him in the act of jumping from an aircraft.

'We were taught to go for the jugular,' Buckmaster remarked.

'That was in the Army.'

'Oh, come, man. This is a war we're fighting now. A war to preserve the SIS against all enemies, against all who put its reputation in peril. Agreed?'

'I'm listening . . .'

Buckmaster folded his arms, leaned against his desk, still gripping the malacca. Almost as though he was posing for a fresh picture to be taken.

'You really are a close-mouthed character. I like that. Makes for good security. Now, you've had time to sleep on the problem. What's your first move against Tweed?'

'Search, locate, destroy. I'd better get moving now. I want to be in Brussels today . . .'

'This conversation never took place.' Buckmaster stood upright, towering over his guest. 'I have some phone calls to make. I'd give you a lift to London in the chopper which arrived back last night, but I'm inspecting a certain defence establishment *en route*.'

'And I have my car . . .'

Buckmaster watched the slim marksman leave. Everything was working out well: security and police chiefs on the Continent had been alerted; the whole apparatus of WS & C was looking for Tweed under Morgan's iron hand; and now he had Marler in the manhunt.

Buckmaster was banking most on Marler. He had one great advantage over all the others. He was working from the *inside*.

Marler collected his suitcase and executive case from his room and ran down the staircase in search of Leonora Buckmaster to pay his respects. To his surprise she was waiting in the large hall, wearing a mink-lined raincoat open at the front. Underneath it she was clad in a close-fitting N. Peal black sweater which showed off her figure to full advantage. A Liberty scarf was wrapped round her head and she picked up a travelling case.

'Could you possibly give me a lift to town if that's where you're going next?'

'My pleasure. Car's outside, rarin' to go.'

Marler concealed his surprise and opened the passenger door of the Porsche. She swung her shapely legs inside and began talking as he switched on the ignition.

'The chauffeur has a touch of the flu. Hence the Daimler isn't available . . .'

As the car moved away from the Elizabethan pile Marler glanced in his wing mirror. Behind him was the stable area, now used as garages. He saw a uniformed chauffeur polishing the bonnet of the Daimler just before he turned under a stone archway on to the drive.

'In any case . . .' Leonora laid a hand on his arm. '. . . I wanted to talk to you about this and that.'

They were well on their way, bypassing Exeter, before she spoke again in her throaty voice. The mist had lifted in the night and Marler was making good time.

'You're with General & Cumbria Assurance, my husband told me. One of the top executives. You're concerned with ensuring – and insuring – VIPs' security against kidnapping?'

'That's right.'

Marler decided Buckmaster was good at security if he didn't let his wife know that General & Cumbria was a cover organization masking the SIS.

'So you must be a real expert on all forms of security,' Leonora continued.

'I would hope so.'

'I'm sure you know that when Lance became a Minister he had to transfer his block of shares in WS to me – in my name. I'm the chairman and I can do what I like.'

'Really?' Marlet was concentrating on his driving.

'I don't too much like the man, Gareth Morgan, Lance appointed as managing director. He runs the whole organization as though I didn't exist.'

'You sound a trifle irked.'

'More than a trifle. The fact is I'm looking for someone who one day could take over from Morgan. A horrid man. And I've got another problem.'

'Unfortunately life is full of them . . .'.

'Don't be so coy.' She nudged him playfully in the ribs with her elbow. 'I feel you are a man I can talk to – knowing that whatever I say won't go any further.'

'Up to you to decide that, Mrs Buckmaster.'

'Please, Leonora.' She slid out of the sleeves of her coat, lit a cigarette, took a deep drag. 'The fact is my husband is playing around with women. One mistress I could ignore – but he's now on his sixth. I find that a bit much.'

'Are you sure? Rather dangerous – his being a Minister and all that.'

'Of course I'm sure. I could give you names. But he's very discreet. His training in security helps the bastard. Doubt if I could prove anything. Not sure I want to – it would ruin his career. Then he'd want his shares back. It could end up as a public dogfight. Not in my interest.' She spoke coolly. 'And it might lead to an investigation of my own background.'

'So, mum's the word. And why tell me all this?'

'I have to talk to someone. You don't imagine I could confide in my best friends, do you? They're the ones who'd love to dish the dirt. You're neutral. Besides, I wanted to put you in the picture. In case I can lever out that toad, Morgan.'

The rest of the journey she went silent, smoking and staring into the distance until Marler pulled up in front of the HQ of World Security in Threadneedle Street. He refused her invitation to join her for 'a cup of coffee, or something stronger.'

'Frightfully kind of you,' he said to her as they stood by the kerb. 'Trouble is I've an urgent appointment with one of those VIPs you mentioned. A millionaire. Business calls . . .'

He drove back to London Airport and stopped in the long-term garage. He sat there for a few minutes. Something of a record – to be 'head-hunted' by the husband and then the wife on the same day. A bright future spread out before him. Then he grabbed both cases and made for the airline counter to buy a ticket. To Brussels.

5

Tweed muddied the trail leading to him. After spending one night at the Hilton he reserved the suite for a week and paid in advance. He explained to the blonde girl receptionist who controlled the executive suites that he had to go to Bruges on business.

'We may have to stay there overnight but I need to have accommodation available for when we get back . . .'

After an early morning breakfast with Paula, he walked with her to the garage where the BMW was parked. They put their cases in the boot and within ten minutes he was leaving the outskirts of Brussels, heading east for Liège – the opposite direction to Bruges.

'Do you think the trick will work if they trace us to the Hilton?' Paula asked.

'It will confuse them. That is what we have to do from now on. Throw out smokescreens.'

Before midday they were across the border into Luxembourg, surrounded by cliffs looming over the narrow serpentine road. No other traffic in either direction. Paula's head was bent over the map, acting as navigator for the route to the point where they would attempt the crossing into Germany.

'Do we assume German security has been informed?' she wondered.

'Yes. We always assume the worst. If we can only slip inside Germany we can make for the autobahn and then for the Black Forest area.'

'You have a plan?'

'Ultimate objective Switzerland. Arthur Beck may or may not be cooperative. We can't assume he will be. After all, a murderer and a rapist isn't the type of person anyone wants to get mixed up with . . .'

'And you're assuming they'll believe that about you? Friends and allies for years?'

'That goes out of the window when you become an outlaw. I'm working on the premise we have no friends anywhere. We're on our own this time.'

'There's Newman and Marler. They'll never swallow the frame-up.'

'No friends anywhere,' Tweed repeated, twisting the wheel as he followed the lonely road through the limestone gulch. 'We will know something in less than two hours. That's when we'll hit the German border.'

Chief Inspector Kuhlmann of the Federal Police in Wiesbaden was chewing on his cigar as he read the *Most Secret* signal from London. His assistant, Kurt Meyer, watched his chief.

Kuhlmann was a small wide-shouldered man with dark hair and a mouth which was also wide. In his forties, he had thick dark eyebrows and an aggressive thrust to his jaw. His movements suggested great energy and he threw the signal on to his desk.

'You've read it, Kurt. What's your reaction?'

'This Tweed sounds a monster . . .'

'That's because you've never met him. He's totally incapable of committing any type of crime, let alone murder and rape – that signal is oddly worded, coming from Howard.'

He strolled over to the window, lit his cigar, stared down as plain-clothes policemen hurried across the courtyard one storey below. He grunted as Meyer took the two photos from the envelope delivered by secret courier. One of Tweed, the other of a dark-haired girl with an attractive face and intelligent eyes.

'What do we do?' Meyer asked. 'The Minister in Bonn suggested we circulate all frontier posts, after phoning them . . .'

'The Minister is a cretin. Another politician. Always pass the buck. Well,' Kuhlmann removed his cigar to gesture with it. 'He's passed the buck to me so let's get creative.'

'Creative?'

'The Minister said we ought to circulate Tweed's photo as well. It occurs to me we're just about to circulate the picture of that man, Stein, suspected of wholesale fraud - so maybe we get them mixed up, Kurt.'

'Mixed up?'

'That's it. The instructions are to have Stein followed without his realizing it. Not sufficient evidence for an arrest. So we send out Stein's photo as Tweed, and Tweed's as Stein.'

'Why are we protecting this Tweed?' Meyer enquired.

'Partly because I've known him for years. He's incapable of throttling a cat, let alone a woman. And the wording of the signal from Howard is intriguing. *Whereabouts required because of alleged complicity in the murder and rape of an unknown woman. Please report direct to me. Repeat direct to me. Howard.* He's sending me a message.'

'I still don't understand . . .'

'But then you're not supposed to – nor is anyone else except me. Howard doesn't believe a word of this crap. Something very funny is going on back in London. Better get on with it. Don't forget to switch those photos. A whole pile of messages are going out. Be surprising if we didn't slip up on one of them.'

Paula was tense as they approached the German frontier post beyond Echternach in Luxembourg. Tweed, who had refused to let her take over the wheel, appeared outwardly to be perfectly relaxed as he stopped and presented the passport in the name of William Sanders.

'What is the purpose of your journey to the Federal Republic?' asked the Passport Control official in German.

Some instinct made Tweed reply in German. 'We're taking a late holiday now the package-deal tourists have gone home.'

The official stared hard at Tweed and slowly turned the pages of the passport. Tweed put an affectionate hand on Paula's neck and she managed a wan smile. The official seemed to take for ever examining the passport before he handed it back and waved them on.

'Oh, my God,' said Paula as they drove out of sight of the frontier post, 'my palms are wet inside my gloves.'

'So what a good job you were wearing them. They look for little giveaway signs like that. Now we're inside Germany and we can keep moving.'

'What route?' asked Paula. 'And it's beginning to snow.'

'A devious one. I'm doubling back to Trier, still inside Germany, then on to Mainz and Frankfurt.'

'That's a funny way to Switzerland. And surely we'll be passing close to Wiesbaden, the HQ of the Kriminalpolizei?'

'Which is the last area Kuhlmann will expect to find us in if the hounds have been loosed. The route from there? South on the autobahn. Later we'll move on to the E35 – the autobahn to Basle in Switzerland. The idea is to move faster than London will ever dream we could. Later, you can take over the wheel.'

'I'd like that. It will take my mind off things – with no limit on the autobahn. I'm really beginning to think we might make it.'

Arriving at the Mayfair, the most expensive hotel in Brussels, on the Avenue Louise, Morgan immediately called the World Security office on Avenue Franklin Roosevelt. Horowitz sat in an armchair in Morgan's room, listening.

'I'm at the Mayfair, George,' Morgan began. 'Have you any info on the subject I told you was top priority?'

'Yes, we have. He's in Brussels. Very close to where you're speaking from. Maybe it would be best if you came over here.'

'Expect me in ten minutes.'

Armand Horowitz had been staring into space, mentally checking the measures he must take to trace Tweed. Six feet tall, he was in his forties, had a long bony face tapering to a pointed jaw. Clean-shaven, he wore steel-rimmed glasses and moved with calculated deliberation. He had already killed fifteen men – top industrialists and other VIPs.

His secret opinion of Morgan was not high. The Welshman was too fond of high living. His manner was too flamboyant for Horowitz's taste. But he paid the huge fee Horowitz demanded for accepting an 'assignment'.

Inside the luxurious villa on Avenue Franklin Roosevelt George Evans, chief of European Operations for World Security, greeted the two men in his office overlooking a trim lawn with a light covering of snow. Also in his forties – Morgan disliked older men in positions of power – Evans was a large heavily built man, simian arms hanging by his sides, with a moon-like face and dark hair. He reminded Horowitz of an ape.

'Get to it,' snapped Morgan as he whipped off his overcoat, refused any refreshments and eased his bulk into an armchair.

'Tweed, I suspect, is both tricky and cunning . . .'

'I didn't come here for a pen portrait. Where is he? Close to the Mayfair you said on the phone.'

'Since then I've had another report from one of my top security agents.' Evans played with a pencil as he leaned over his desk, staring at Morgan, who stared back with a bleak expression. All these people needed a boot up the backside at regular intervals to keep them up to scratch. 'My agent', Evans continued smoothly, 'phoned while you were on your way over here. We doubt whether Tweed and his mistress, Paula Grey, will ever return to the Hilton where he was staying . . .'

'Chapter and verse,' Morgan snapped.

'I was just coming to that. My agent took a dummy package to the Hilton, addressed to Tweed, marked "Personal and Confidential". Reception at the Hilton said no one of that name was staying there. My agent said Tweed was attached to the European Commission and often travelled incognito – under a different name. He had a forged authority signed by one of the Commissioners who is away on holiday. He also showed the photo of Tweed you sent over with the courier who travelled here by night ferry. The girl receptionist was reluctant to give any information. My agent chatted her up and she let slip Tweed and the Grey woman left early this morning after booking their suite – and paying for it – for another week.'

'He's slipped the net,' Morgan muttered half to himself.

'You said Paula Grey was his mistress,' Horowitz intervened in his slow way of speaking. Evans stirred in his chair: there was something sinister about Horowitz which made him feel uneasy. 'What positive proof have you about their relationship?' Horowitz enquired.

'Well.' Evans spread his large hands. 'From her photograph she's attractive and younger, so one makes the natural assumption . . .'

'Which could be quite wrong . . .'

'Does it matter?' Evans, conscious of his position, resented contradiction from the hired help. Then he became aware of the eyes behind the steel-rimmed lenses gazing at him and felt uncomfortable.

'It might matter a lot to me in my job,' Horowitz informed him. 'Knowing the true relationship between two people who are in flight can be most helpful.'

'Well, we haven't actually photographic evidence of copulation,' Evans responded brusquely.

Morgan watched the exchange with secret satisfaction. No harm in taking Evans down a peg. Horowitz nodded thoughtfully.

'Thank you for the data, Mr Evans,' he said politely.

'How did you get on to this Hilton business?' demanded Morgan.

'I've had my whole staff touring the best hotels in town. The extract from the file on Tweed you sent with the courier made the point he often stays at top places because he thinks he's less likely to be noticed.'

'And that's all you have?'

'No. I didn't stop there. Another group of my agents have toured the car hire firms, using the same tactics. Tweed has hired a BMW under the name William

61

Sanders. The doorman at the Hilton saw them driving east early. Here is the registration number.'

He passed a slip of folded paper to Morgan who handed it to Horowitz without looking at it. Standing up, he slipped on his overcoat, his expression still bleak.

'You lost him,' he told Evans. 'What are you going to do next?'

'Tweed was seen driving *east* out of the city. A logical move if I was in his shoes – Belgium is too close to Britain. He has to be heading for Holland, Germany or France . . .'

'Then alert our organizations in those countries. Pick up his trail . . .'

'If I may make a suggestion,' Horowitz, also standing, addressed Evans. 'You said you'd read an extract from Tweed's file, detailing some of his techniques . . .'

'Only an extract. Someone in London must be blocking complete access . . .'

'I was about to say,' Horowitz continued, 'that Tweed must have assumed something like this would happen.' He's a pro. So it's likely he'll change his normal habits. He could still be here, staying at some small hotel. Why not switch your agents to checking those places?'

'Do it,' said Morgan. 'I'll be back in a minute for a private word.' He marched to the door, followed by Horowitz who put his soft trilby back on his head, pulling the brim down. Outside in the corridor Morgan stood near the mahogany door he'd closed.

'What do you think? Holland, Germany, France?'

'Oh, definitely Germany,' Horowitz said promptly. 'Holland is a cul-de-sac, leading him nowhere. And with all the terrorist problems the French face their borders are watched closely. I would make for the Federal Republic.'

'Wait here.' Morgan went back into Evans' office, closed the door, marched back to the desk behind which

Evans was sitting, phone in his hand and about to use it. 'Put that thing down.' Morgan leaned across the desk, his face close to Evans's.

'That was a real cock-up, wasn't it? You had him in the palm of your hand and let him escape. Now, just for once try and earn that over-inflated salary we pay you. Use the satellite phone for top security. Call Frankfurt, tell them I'm coming. And while I'm on my way all our operatives in Germany hit the streets – with copies of Tweed's photo, and Grey's. All the hotels. But they're to concentrate also on car hire firms. Tweed may decide to switch that BMW for something else. I want a fix on that man. And fast.'

'Understood. I'll then fly to Frankfurt myself to oversee the operation. I may see you on the same plane.'

'I hope not.' Morgan straightened up. For the first time he smiled as he took a cigar from his case, laid it on the desk. 'Havana. May give you inspiration. I'm relying on you . . .'

He left the office. Horowitz stood in the corridor, hands in his trench-coat pocket, staring up at a framed portrait of the founder, Lance Buckmaster.

'No inspiration there for you,' Morgan commented as they walked to the elevator. 'We'll catch the first flight to Frankfurt after we've picked up our bags from the Mayfair. That way we should be ahead of Tweed.'

'Don't bank on it. I'm beginning to build up a vague picture of this man. A formidable opponent, I suspect. I shall want a met forecast for the weather over the whole of Western Europe. And while you go straight back to the hotel I want to buy some road maps.'

As Morgan walked back to the Mayfair alone he felt satisfied. He'd shaken up Evans, first bawling him out then ending up with a show of confidence in him with the Havana. The only way you kept the top brass in line, reminded them who was the boss.

6

Chief Inspector Kuhlmann put down the phone and looked at Kurt Meyer as though he'd never seen him before. It was a technique he employed when grilling a suspect he knew well. Meyer felt confused as he sat behind his desk and started examining a file.

'We've pinpointed him,' Kuhlmann said eventually. 'Stein crossed the border near Echternach in Luxembourg a few hours ago. He's on our patch.'

'Stein?'

'Tweed, you dumb bastard. Travelling in a BMW with a girl. Sounds like Paula Grey. The frontier post spotted him from the photos we rushed to the western frontier. I have the registration number too.'

'Shouldn't we record it?' Meyer, young and lean-faced, had his pen poised over a pad.

'It's in my head.' Kuhlmann walked over to a large-scale wall-map of the Federal Republic. 'I wonder where he's making for? Could be anywhere except near Wiesbaden, near me.'

'Shouldn't we inform the Minister?'

'Not yet, we haven't caught Tweed yet. That phone call never happened. Your job hangs by a thread,' he informed his subordinate cheerfully.

Hands thrust inside his jacket pockets, Kuhlmann went over to the window and stared down into the courtyard again. He had omitted to tell Meyer Tweed's BMW was being followed by an unmarked police car, a vehicle which would be replaced by another later to allay suspicion. Kuhlmann was notorious for playing a lone hand. The web was being spun, he thought. The big question was who was the spider?

Newman boarded the aircraft for Brussels at London Airport, fastened his seat belt. Into the empty seat beside him a passenger joined him. Newman turned his head slowly. His fellow passenger was Marler.

'Didn't know I was on your tail, old chum, did you?'

Newman clasped his hands. He said nothing until the machine was ready for take-off, moving forward to the main runway. When he responded it was in a monotone, as though reciting a catechism.

'You phoned Julia, who practically runs the house where I've an apartment in South Ken. Presumably from the airport. She told you I'd left with a bag. You waited at the entrance to Terminal One, saw me arrive in a taxi. You then followed me to the ticket reservation counter, chatted up the girl afterwards, found I'd booked a Business-Class seat to Brussels, did the same yourself and waited outside the final departure lounge until you saw me boarding.'

'Ten out of ten. And I kidded myself up you hadn't seen me.'

The plane lifted off the ground, climbed steeply through a dense cloud-bank, emerged into brilliant sunlight. Below was a sea of unbroken cloud like endless mountain ranges.

'Now you can tell me what you're up to,' Newman demanded.

'We're both on the same side. Trying to find Tweed and Paula, to protect them.'

'Well, that's reassuring, isn't it?' Newman suggested ironically.

'Cryptic remark.'

65

'Not really. Here comes the $64,000 question. Do you think he did it?' Newman lowered his voice. 'Strangled and then raped that girl?'

'You have to be joking.'

'I have a funny sense of humour. Maybe not on your waveband. You haven't answered the question. And who sent you?'

'I thought you knew.' Marler's tone was flippant. 'When Tweed is out of action, Howard is in control.'

Newman remained silent for the rest of the flight. He was thinking furiously. He had never liked Marler, although he recognized his great ability. Now he didn't trust him. Why? Some sixth sense he'd learned not to ignore.

He had two options, he thought, as the plane began the descent to Brussels. One, he could ditch Marler. It wouldn't be too easy, but he knew he could manage it. Two, he could go along with Marler, pretend to accept him at face value, and this way he could keep an eye on him. He decided on the second option as the wheels touched down.

Remembering where Tweed had stayed once during a desperate operation in the past. Newman told the cab driver to take them to the Brussels Hilton. He went up to his room while Marler went to his, dumped his bag on the bed, ran back to the elevator and walked out of the hotel.

It took him a few minutes to find a public phone booth. He took out his small notebook, found the number for Kriminalpolizei in Wiesbaden, dialled Kuhlmann's personal number.

To his relief the Chief Inspector answered the phone himself. His voice sounded as gravelly as ever, charged with energy. He told Newman to hold on and the Englishman heard him call out in German.

'Kurt, take that file down to the Registry and lock it away yourself. The combination hasn't been changed . . .' A pause. 'OK, Newman, what can I do for you?'

'Have you received a message from London to apprehend Tweed?'

'Where are you speaking from . . .'

'A public call box, of course . . .'

'OK. Keep your hair on. I had to check. The answer to your question is yes. Partially. Newman, what was the weather like when me met in Lübeck?'

'A bloody heatwave. Why . . . Oh, I see. Yes, it is me. You said partially. What does that mean?'

'Sounded like you,' Kuhlmann said calmly. 'I had to be sure. You think he did it?'

'For God's sake!' Newman was unusually vehement. 'Have you lost your marbles. He's innocent. It has to be some kind of conspiracy. Who's behind it I don't know. But Tweed badly needs help, back-up. I'm in Brussels. He came here but I'm sure he didn't linger. Not with the wolves after him. And he has Paula with him. I just don't know where to start looking.'

'Frankfurt might be a good place to start. Don't come here. Call me and I'll meet you somewhere. I've decided where. At the Frankfurt Hof. We'll fix a time over the phone. Speak to me only.' The tone of voice changed. 'I'll see to it – and thanks for calling, Lothar. Bye . . .'

Newman guessed Kurt had returned to the office. Kurt Who? And Kuhlmann was obviously trusting no one except himself. It was getting worse. The stench of treachery in the air.

As he re-entered the vast lobby of the Hilton Newman stopped, then moved to the right into the sitting area. Marler was standing at the reception counter, talking to one of the girls. He had an envelope in his hand. Newman watched him stuffing banknotes into the envelope, sealing it, writing on the front. Then he disappeared and the girl also vanished. Newman guessed they had gone to the security vault behind the counter. He was waiting when Marler reappeared.

'Unpacked your bag?' Marler enquired and lit a king-sized cigarette.

'Not yet. I had some coffee. I saw you at the counter.'

'Let's stroll a bit down the Boulevard de Waterloo,' Marler suggested. He waited until they were outside before speaking again.

'While you were quenching your thirst I was busy making a few enquiries. By devious means, of course. Tweed has been here. He reserved an executive suite for another week – but Tweed has gone. And won't be coming back is my guess.'

'How did you find that out? Hotels don't give information about guests easily.'

'Oh, I simply told the girl I'd agreed to leave a large sum of money I owed to a friend. Showed her Tweed's photo. Asked for a safety deposit box after she'd seen me cramming Belgian banknotes in an envelope. Two large denomination bills on top, the rest a small sum. Gave her the key, got a receipt, told her my friend was travelling incognito. She wrote *William Sanders* on the envelope she'd put the key inside. I *can* read upside down. Now all we have to decide is where to look next for him.'

'Frankfurt,' Newman said, and left it at that.

George Evans just managed to catch the same flight as Morgan and Horowitz, but the last seat available was Economy Class. When the plane landed at Frankfurt he left the airport first, bypassing the wait at the carousel which held up his colleagues.

World Security HQ was in Kaiserstrasse, a new building with armoured plate glass windows and a system of scanners covering the entrance and all corridors. Arriving an hour later, Morgan stepped out of the cab and looked around while Horowitz paid.

Morgan didn't like Frankfurt. He liked Hamburg and Münich, but he called Frankfurt the Machine City. Too much traffic clogging the streets, too many high-rise buildings, too little greenery. A concrete fortress of a place.

His first act on entering was to test the security. He walked straight towards the bank of elevators. Two uni-formed guards intercepted him, one reached for his suitcase.

'I'm Morgan. I run this show,' he snapped and waved his pass in their faces. 'And I'm short of time . . .'

'I'm sorry, sir,' one of the guards replied in English, 'but we have to check your case with the X-ray machine.'

Horowitz, more stoical, was already at the counter while his case passed through the type of machine used at airports. Morgan waited while his own case was pro-cessed, biting his lips.

'George Evans is expecting me. He may not have got here yet.'

'He's in his office now. Just stand in front of this screen while I call him . . .'

'What the hell for?'

'So he can see you on the screen in his office. All identities of callers have to be confirmed . . .'

The guard was talking to Evans as Morgan glared at the screen, then took out a cigar and clamped his teeth on it.

'If you're seeing me, get these people off my back, George – we're supposed to be running an operation . . .'

'You can go up now, Mr Morgan,' said the guard, replacing the phone. 'Room 401, fourth floor.'

'I run this outfit. I know where the hired help lives . . .'

Inside the elevator Horowitz made his comment. 'They were doing their job. And the security is reasonably good.'

'You have to keep people on their toes.' Morgan chuckled, a wheezing sound. 'Management must manage.'

Evans got his blow in first as he stood at the door, ushered them into a large office overlooking the Kaiserstrasse. Venetian blinds were half-closed over the windows to avoid any risk of observation from the buildings opposite.

'We've traced Tweed. I'm expecting another call from our informant. The connection was broken as you came up . . .' He broke off as his phone rang. 'Hello. That you, Kurt again? Make it snappy – I have important visitors.'

He listened, said yes, he'd grasped it. 'Keep me up-to-date on their progress. What we need to know is where they're heading for – so we can be ready for them. The money will be waiting in the usual safety deposit. Bye, Kurt.'

He offered drinks and Morgan said he'd have a double Scotch. Horowitz shook his head, nursed his small case on his lap and glanced at Morgan. On the plane his employer had downed several drinks: Morgan was a man who drank heavily. Maybe the pressure of the job was getting to him. No excuse.

'Tweed', Evans began as he handed a cut-glass tumbler to Morgan, 'has arrived in Germany. With Paula Grey, so far as we know. With a woman, anyway. He actually came into Frankfurt in his hired BMW, then changed it for a Mercedes. Here is the registration.'

Another folded slip changed hands, was again passed on to Horowitz. Evans looked pleased with himself as he settled behind his large antique desk. In his armchair Morgan drank half the Scotch, smacked his lips, scowled.

'A Mercedes. That doesn't help. This country is lousy with them. Look at the taxis – all Mercedes.'

'Which is maybe why Tweed chose that make,' Horowitz suggested in his quiet voice. 'Have you a toilet here?' he asked his host.

Evans gestured towards a door and Morgan waited until he was alone with Evans before he asked the question.

'How are we getting this info so fast? Who is Kurt?'

'I don't like to advertise my contacts.' Evans glanced at the closed toilet door, leaned forward, lowered his voice. 'Kurt Meyer. Chief Inspector Kuhlmann's assistant – an inside track right into the centre of the Kriminalpolizei at Wiesbaden. I can tell you that isn't easy to arrange.'

'But it's your job to do things like that. You've got something on this Kurt Meyer?'

'Pornographic pictures taken in a high-class bordello. And he's married. We pay him to put icing on the cake, and tie him to us. I have receipts signed by Meyer in the safe – he didn't want to provide them but a little arm-twisting works wonders.

'And that's all we know?' Morgan demanded. 'That Tweed and his girl friend are driving somewhere in a Mercedes?'

'No, that isn't all we know.' Evans made no attempt to conceal his satisfaction. 'Unmarked police cars are following him. They're using the leapfrog technique, one vehicle taking over from another at regular intervals. They radio in reports of their locations to Wiesbaden. When he can, Kurt then passes them on to me – from an outside phone, of course. *We* now have operatives following Tweed.'

Morgan twirled his cigar between his thick stubby fingers as he thought about it. Evans's news was better than he'd ever hoped for.

'Where was the latest sighting?' he asked.

'On the autobahn, heading south towards Karlsruhe. He could turn off east or west, of course . . .'

71

'Not west. He won't risk France. But he might head east.' Morgan put the cigar in his mouth, lit it as Evans pushed a heavy Rosenthal bowl towards him. 'He could just be heading for Russia via the Czech border . . .'

'From the little I've grasped about him I'd say that was unlikely, to say the least.'

'But it would be a good rumour to spread, step up the pressure all round. Feed it into the grapevine, use your press contacts.' He blew smoke into the air. 'But on no account let anyone know we're interested.'

'You know we have a department devoted to doing just that. Feeding rumours on behalf of a client about to make a take-over bid – rumours about the bid victim . . .'

'But no names,' Morgan warned. 'Just rumours about a highly placed British official defecting to the East.' He looked up as Horowitz reappeared. 'We have a tail already locked on to Tweed. Driving south on the autobahn. You'll have to be careful. The German police are tracking him – unmarked cars.'

Horowitz, tall and thin in the trench coat he still wore, and carrying the case he never let out of his sight, stared at both men. There was something remote, detached in his ice-blue eyes. Again Evans felt disturbed: it was almost like a hangman measuring his latest customer for the drop.

'I find that curious,' Horowitz remarked. 'I understood from you, Morgan, some kind of alert had been sent out. If so, why hasn't Tweed been arrested?'

'No idea.' Morgan disliked people who brought up insoluble problems. 'What do you propose to do?'

'I'd like an executive jet placed at my disposal at Frankfurt Airport. The company jet. To fly me to the small airport outside Freiburg near the Black Forest.'

'Consider it done,' Morgan replied before Evans could speak.

'It may be an hour or two before I arrive to board the

jet,' Horowitz continued. 'I have to pick up a helper. I'm on my way now.'

Evans watched him leave, noted how silently he closed the door behind him. He let out his breath. 'I'm not sorry to see him go – it's like having death in the room.'

'Maybe that's his trade.'

Armand Horowitz walked a hundred yards along Kaiserstrasse, disassociating himself from World Security before he hailed a cab. Looking back, he could see the complex of radio masts and satellite dishes on the roof of the building he'd left. WS operated a highly sophisticated communications system. But Horowitz, who had been born in Hungary, was no slouch himself at communications.

He had spent a while in the toilet, most of the time with his ear to the stethoscope-like instrument he'd pressed against the closed door. He'd heard quite clearly Evans's reference to his inside track with the Kriminalpolizei at Wiesbaden, to Kurt Meyer's treachery. Secret knowledge, Horowitz always felt, was power.

As the cab drove out of Frankfurt to the address on the way to the airport, Horowitz, sitting erect, case in his lap, reflected he was the only real professional in this game. He'd developed a contempt for men like Morgan and Evans. They carefully distanced themselves from the dirty work, but didn't hesitate to employ his services. Evans had been distinctly uncomfortable about Horowitz's presence in his office.

The cab stopped at the street intersection he'd been given, his passenger paid him, took time drawing on his gloves until the cab was gone. Horowitz then walked the last hundred yards to the decrepit villa standing back from the airport highway, pushed open the left-hand iron grille gate. He walked up the moss-infested path, mounted the

73

steps and pressed the bell-push two times, paused, then gave one long press. He'd seen no reason to reveal to Morgan and Evans that his helper was a woman.

7

Newman arrived at Frankfurt an hour later than Morgan. With Marler he took a cab to the Hessischer Hof, one of the two best hotels in the city. They registered and avoided using a porter. As the elevator ascended Newman made his flat statement.

'Wait in your room – or in the hotel. I have to go and check with someone.'

'I don't actually recall anyone putting you in charge . . .'

'Then get off my back and I'll work on my own.'

'No need to get shirty,' Marler responded mildly as they walked along a quiet, carpeted corridor. 'If that's the way you want to play it, fair enough. I'll mooch about the hotel . . .'

Newman dumped his bag, took out two spare suits, hung them on a hanger, left the case lid open and left the Hessischer Hof. He walked across the small park on the far side of the street towards the vast exhibition centre, glancing back frequently: he'd chosen this route because it was impossible for Marler to follow him without being seen.

From a public phone booth he called Otto Kuhlmann who answered immediately.

'I'm in Frankfurt. The heatwave man in Lübeck . . .'

'Meeting point changed. Can you be near the ticket

office at the *Hauptbahnhof* one hour from now?'

'I'll be waiting for you there . . .'

It was only a short walk to the main rail station. Newman went straight there. He spent half an hour in the restaurant, drinking coffee. When he emerged on to the vast concourse he saw Kuhlmann standing at the entrance to one of the platforms opposite the ticket office. The German saw him at once, walked over, shook hands, greeted him in his own language.

'Let's just stroll up and down, Bob. That way we can talk without being overheard.'

'You don't believe this incredible accusation against Tweed?' Newman asked him point-blank.

'No. Neither does Howard. But what about you? Any doubts?' Kuhlmann challenged.

'None whatsoever. Why the devil do you think I came haring over here? To try and find Tweed, give him some back-up, find out what the hell is going on.'

The tannoy was calling out a message about an express leaving for Basle in Switzerland. Passengers were hurrying to barriers. A locomotive was gliding in, hauling a trainload of coaches. Kuhlmann, inches shorter than Newman, wearing his normal dark suit, which emphasized the great width of his shoulders, took his time replying.

'There's the stench of treachery and conspiracy high up in London,' he commented eventually. 'Tweed – with Paula Grey, I assume – at this moment is driving south along the autobahn from Frankfurt. He crossed the Luxembourg border in a hired BMW with Belgian number plates. Since then – in Frankfurt – he changed cars. Now he's in a black Mercedes. My men picked him up as he came over the Luxembourg border. They're following him in unmarked cars. I thought only I knew this. I haven't told my Minister.'

'You said Howard doesn't think him guilty. That surprises me. How do you know?'

'Because the signal he sent spoke of *alleged complicity* in murder and rape, and only asked for his whereabouts. It also was emphatic that I reported back to him alone. I haven't even done that yet.'

'Why not?'

'Because my men tracking Tweed have reported a complication. Someone else is playing the same game – following him with a series of cars. I found out who they are just before I left to see you. Gave me cause to think, pause.'

'Who is it then?'

'Prepare yourself for a shock. The registration numbers of two of the cars were radioed back to me. I called Vehicle Registration. The cars belong to World Security & Communications GmbH. Lance Buckmaster's international colossus before he became your Minister for External Security. The damned fools omitted to *hire* cars.'

Newman was stunned. They walked in silence while he absorbed this new twist. He stopped to let a woman with a pram rush past him. Kuhlmann lit a cigar. They began walking again.

'You have to be quite sure about this?' Newman queried.

'I thought you knew me well enough by now to know I'm careful – very careful – about what I say,' Kuhlmann growled. 'Maybe you can also work out why I'm in no hurry to communicate with anyone in London. Who can we trust?'

'Maybe someone high up in WS is playing his own game. Buckmaster no longer has any control over his company.'

'Not like you to be naïve. We've had trouble with that outfit before now. They were suspected of trying to smuggle restricted high-tech equipment into East Germany. Aboard one of their own security trucks. I grilled a man called George Evans, the managing director of their operations here on the Continent. A crook if I ever saw one. I just hadn't enough evidence to bring the case to court.'

'What are you saying?' Newman asked, wanting the German to confirm his own growing suspicion.

'I'm saying that officially the WS organization is now run by Buckmaster's wife, Leonora. She has his block of shares. I did a little research at the time of the East German business. But do you think even a man like Evans, managing director for Europe, would risk his position by going into business on his own? I cross-examined him. He's not the type. He'd only carry out orders – coming from Lance Buckmaster.'

'And you think he's still doing that?'

'Yes!' Kuhlmann was emphatic. 'What it's all about is what I can't fathom. But now you can see why I'm in no hurry to contact London. First, Tweed is a man I like, admire. Someone is trying to put the fix on him – whoever they are they're not getting help from me. Second, I have a score to settle with World Security. They were guilty as hell over the East German business and made me look a fool. I even got a reprimand from my creep of a Minister. So now I watch and wait.'

'You're really relying on me.' Newman faced Kuhlmann, confronted him.

'Yes, I am. You have freedom of movement. I haven't.'

'I don't even know where Tweed is,' Newman pressed.

'So, you call me at regular intervals. Let's give you a code name. Felix. Speak only to me. I've worked out Tweed can't drive for ever – even if Paula Grey gives a hand with the wheel. Somewhere he's got to stop. I'll know when he does – and where. I'll have a police chopper waiting at Frankfurt Airport to fly you to the nearest airfield.' Kuhlmann took an envelope from his breast pocket, gave it to Newman. 'The pilot's name is Egon Wrede. That letter identifies you, authorizes you to be flown anywhere you tell Wrede. Best I can do . . .'

'Wait! There's something odd you haven't told me. Why did you think up this secret system of approaching only you? Code name Felix, etc. Sounds as though you don't trust anyone except yourself.'

'I don't. There's a lot of power behind this thing. Best I can do,' he repeated and walked away.

Tweed checked the small notebook he rested on his knee. Paula was behind the wheel of the Mercedes moving at between 140 and 160 k.p.h. – about ninety miles an hour. Ahead the autobahn E 35 stretched away into the distance. They were well south of Karlsruhe and approaching Offenbach with Freiburg beyond.

Paula had at last persuaded Tweed to hand over the driving to her for awhile. No great burden – she loved speed. Out of the corner of her eye she saw Tweed glance again in the wing mirror.

'They're still with us?' she asked.

'Indeed they are,' he said calmly as though working on a crossword puzzle. 'Seven cars spread out behind us and that silver Merc a quarter of a mile ahead. That makes eight cars – I've double-checked the registration numbers,' he remarked, glancing down at his notebook.

'It's a bloody convoy.'

'It's exactly that. Which is what I don't understand. Eight cars tracking us all this distance. At first I thought they were police cars.'

'Why shouldn't they be? They're probably looking for us now.'

'Because it's too many – even for using the leapfrog system. If Kuhlmann was waiting to pounce – waiting to see where we're making for – he'd use four cars at the most. Eight suggests two different groups.'

'Who could they be?'

'Your guess is as good as mine. It's OK for me to talk?'

'I want you to . . .'

She loved the speed but was only too aware of the danger of slipping into a hypnotic daze. The four-lane highway curved and straightened and curved. The scenery which might have relieved the monotony, kept her alert, was non-existent. It was like driving along an endless concrete canal. But she kept up her high speed. Tweed was desperately anxious to get to Freiburg and it was late afternoon already.

'What do we do when we reach Freiburg?' she enquired.

'*Before* we get to Freiburg,' he corrected her. 'I take over the wheel and we lose them, the whole shooting match.'

'Don't see how . . .'

'You will. Just keep moving.'

Horowitz gazed out of the window of the descending Sikorsky. Freiburg airfield came up to meet him. Alongside sat a girl in her early thirties with titian hair, good bone-structure and an excellent figure concealed beneath the windcheater she wore. Tight denims clung to her legs and she wore knee-length leather boots.

Horowitz had picked up Eva Hendrix from the villa on the way to Frankfurt Airport. It wasn't her real name and – like Horowitz – she'd been born in Hungary. Normally he mistrusted the use of women but he foresaw the opportunity of infiltrating her into Tweed's company in the future.

'Where are we going first?' she asked as the machine touched down with a bump.

'World Security HQ in Freiburg.'

'Funny place to have an office – I thought they had a main HQ in Basle, thirty minutes down the autobahn from Freiburg.'

'They have. Freiburg is more discreet. On the edge of the Black Forest.'

'Good place to bury the bodies,' she joked with black humour.

Horowitz froze for a few seconds. She had come nearer to the truth than she ever dreamed. Too busy lighting a cigarette, she didn't notice his expression. She glanced out of the window into the dark as the pilot entered the cabin.

'Oh my God, it's started to snow.'

'So for once the met forecast people got it right. Which is helpful.'

He didn't explain why it was going to be helpful and the pilot told him the car he'd specified was waiting for them. Horowitz nodded as he followed Hendrix out of the cabin, carrying the case he'd picked up from the Frankfurt villa in one hand, his executive case in the other.

Horowitz, who preferred travelling light, had suitcases with clothes packed deposited at various locations all over Europe. The car was a Ford, as he'd requested. Nothing flashy. He had perfected the technique of not being noticed to a fine art. Eva Hendrix started to chatter in her persuasive voice while the uniformed chauffeur drove them into the ancient town of Freiburg. The snowflakes were larger now, the windscreen wipers flicked back and forth.

'Is it a seduction job again?' she whispered.

'Not exactly. More an infiltration – if the chance arises.'

He feeds out information as though each word costs him money, she thought. Well, he was paying so let him get on with it in his peculiar way. She glanced at his strong profile, staring ahead at the snowbound road. He wasn't queer, she felt sure, so did he have a woman every now and again she wondered? If he did it would be a clinical performance, precise and calculated, like everything he did. Not for me, she decided.

'I'm not interested in you sexually,' he remarked, spacing out the words in his deliberate way. 'Just in the work you can do for me.'

Christ! she thought. A man who can read a woman's mind. It was supposed to work the other way round. When they arrived at the HQ of World Security in Freiburg the closed gates were opened for them immediately. At least someone with the car's description and registration number had been told they were coming.

Inside the lobby Horowitz handed the uniformed guard the letter of introduction Gareth Morgan had supplied.

'We've no photograph of you, Mr Schmidt,' the guard complained.

'Read the note at the bottom. You're not very good at checking documents, are you? Mr Morgan wouldn't like that.'

So far as he knew, no photograph had ever been taken of Horowitz. He'd been very careful about that. The photos in his collection of passports were blurred images of the real man – and without the steel-rimmed glasses he habitually wore.

'Sorry, sir,' the guard apologized. 'The chief's office is available for you. I'll take you up there – unless you'd like some refreshment first?'

'Nothing for me . . .'

'I'm starving,' Hendrix complained. 'I'd like a good steak, cooked rare, and a drink. A double vodka-martini.'

'See to her wants. Feed her. She can stay down here in that sitting area. Now, take me to the office,' Horowitz ordered the guard.

The office was a large room on the first floor equipped

with a desk on which perched three phones in different colours. Horowitz told the guard he wanted to call the Frankfurt office. Privately.

'I'll leave you alone, then. The blue phone is the one to use.'

Horowitz waited until the guard had gone, then placed his bags on a couch and studied the room. High up in one corner was a camera aimed at the desk. They do trust each other, Horowitz thought. Dragging a chair over, he stood on it, took off his scarf and wrapped it round the observation lens.

Before using the phone he checked the room minutely. He found the tape recorder attached to a small alcove carved out from underneath the desk. His keen hearing had caught the whirring of the tape. They'd probably switched it on by remote control while he was on his way up. This was one call they wouldn't be recording.

Crouching down, he examined the machine. He used the manual switch to turn it off. Then he extracted the cassette, hauling out the length of tape which had been recording and stuffed both items in his jacket pocket. He was seated at the desk, about to dial Frankfurt, when the door was thrown open and a uniformed guard entered the room. He pointed at the camera.

'That has to be left alone . . .'

Horowitz replaced the phone, stood up slowly without a word, walked slowly up to the guard. His right hand took hold of the guard's tie and collar and he threw him backwards through the doorway. The guard hit the far wall and slid to the floor.

'I have already said I wish to make a call privately. Stay out of this room. If there is another intruder I will break both his arms.'

The guard, still slumped on the floor, gazed at the slate-grey eyes behind the glasses. He had never felt so frightened. Horowitz had spoken quietly, the words spaced out. He closed the door and went back to the desk, sat down, dialled the number from memory. He was still wearing kid gloves.

'I wish to speak immediately to Gareth Morgan. No need for my name. He is expecting the call.'

'Morgan here,' a familiar voice rasped within thirty seconds. 'Is that . . .'

'No names are necessary. I'm speaking from your Freiburg office. Can you tell me where the subject is now?'

'Yes. A car radioed in only a few minutes ago. Coming straight towards you. On autobahn E 35. About midway between Offenbach and Freiburg . . .'

'Then I'd better go. You arranged for that vehicle I requested when I called from Frankfurt Airport? With a *reliable* driver?'

'I dealt with it personally. Driver's name is Oscar. He should be waiting for you in the transport yard at the back.'

'And the subject is still in the same vehicle?'

'He is . . .'

'Goodbye, then.'

Horowitz picked up his cases, retrieved his scarf from the camera, keeping clear of the lens, took the elevator downstairs. Eva Hendrix, an empty glass on the plate glass table, was sitting waiting for her food. Horowitz dumped his suitcase beside her.

'Look after that. I'll be back in a few minutes.'

He went out of the front entrance, made his way round to the back of the building as snow fell on him. He was hardly aware of the chill in the night air, his mind totally concentrated on his job. He found the enormous twelve-wheeler refrigerated truck parked inside a large shed with the doors open. A man sat in the cab attached to the trailer vehicle, smoking a cigarette, reading a newspaper. He folded the paper, opened the door, jumped out and threw his cigarette out into the snow as soon as he saw Horowitz.

'I'm Schmidt,' Horowitz said, examining the driver. 'Who are you?'

'Oscar. I need identification for this job.'

Horowitz handed him the authorization signed by Evans. Oscar read it carefully by the sidelights of his huge vehicle. The engine was purring like a tiger. Oscar reminded Horowitz of the Michelin tyre man – short and tubby, his belly bulging behind his belt, round-headed. But there was nothing amusing about Oscar. His rubbery face, unsmiling, was the prototype of the 'heavy' seen in 'B' films.' He handed the sheet back and Horowitz showed him the piece of paper with the registration number of Tweed's Mercedes. Oscar glanced at the paper and handed that back.

'You can remember the number?' Horowitz asked.

'It's my job to remember things like that. What make of car? What colour? Where?'

'A Mercedes. Colour black. Now driving down the E 35 from Offenburg. One man, one girl inside. What is that contraption mounted over the cab?'

'Show you, then I'm off.'

Oscar climbed nimbly back inside the cab, slammed the door shut and pressed a switch. On top of the cab was a very big circular disc with a grille over it like miniature venetian blinds. When Oscar pressed the switch half way a lamp like a huge searchlight came on, so strong Horowitz had to dip his head. The driver pressed the switch fully down and the beam became of blinding intensity. Peering up, Horowitz saw the narrow 'blinds' had swivelled to become mere rims. He guessed its purpose. It must have a range of three hundred yards.

He stood aside and the great vehicle moved ponderously out of the garage. Oscar sounded his deafening horn three times and the gates to the yard swung open.

Horowitz watched it turn on to the road and vanish. It should, he reflected, be more than large enough to finish the job.

Returning to the front entrance, he found Hendrix still waiting for her food, smoking yet another cigarette. He bent over to speak so only she could hear him.

'We're leaving now. On foot. So put your coat on and then we can get out of here . . .'

'I'm waiting for those sluggards to bring my steak.'

'No, you're not. I booked two rooms at the Hotel Colombi from Frankfurt Airport. You can have an eight-course dinner there, if you can cope with it. And I may not need your services now, so you could be on a train back to Frankfurt tomorrow.'

'The snow is getting worse. I'll get soaked . . .'

'Put this scarf round your head. Then get moving, woman. No more yacking. You know I don't like attention drawn to myself.'

As they plodded through the snow, which was falling even more heavily, Horowitz had a mental picture of Tweed in his Mercedes driving towards Freiburg, while Oscar in his refrigerated truck drove towards Tweed.

8

Night. Tweed had taken over the wheel from Paula. Visibility was bad. The falling snow was approaching blizzard conditions. He had the heaters full on. He was driving at 100 k.p.h. His undimmed headlights showed the curve of the autobahn ahead far enough to keep up that speed.

'It's getting worse,' said Paula. 'I calculate we're within twenty miles of the turn-off to Freiburg. Do we go on?'

'Yes. The vehicles are still behind us. We have to shake all of them off.'

The headlights behind him were blurred, the gap between pursued and pursuers had widened, but they were there. And the silver Mercedes was still somewhere ahead of them. He shifted his position: he was beginning to feel stiff and achy.

The view beyond the windscreen was weird. A belt of heavy snow along the highway south, the neon lights cast a weird light over the snow, reflecting back a ghostly glow. There were few headlights coming in the opposite direction beyond the barrier, and few travelling in his direction. He yawned.

'Isn't it getting too hot?' Paula suggested, looking up from her map. 'I'm happy to turn down the heating.'

He reached a hand out and switched off both heaters. There was a danger he'd lose his concentration if too much warmth built up. The belt of snow rolled on and on and on. Tweed straightened up, pushed his back hard against the seat, anything to keep alert.

'Will the snow make your manoeuvre to lose them more difficult?' Paula asked.

'Could make it easier. We can't be seen so easily. Please keep an eye on the signs. I need to know we're approaching the Freiburg turn-off well in advance.'

'Will do. We're coming up to one soon, but it's not the one for Freiburg.'

Oscar sat inside his parked truck at the top of the slip road leading down on to the E 35 for traffic heading along the autobahn to Freiburg and Basle. His engine was running and his windscreen wipers whipped back and forth to keep the glass clear of snow.

He held a high-powered pair of night-glasses pressed close to his eyes. From his vantage point he could see vehicles approaching from the north a good way off. The snow was falling more lightly, thank God, which increased his range of vision.

The manoeuvre he had planned was highly dangerous and quite illegal. He was banking on the size of the truck to make it easy, not all that dangerous and successful. He wore gloves, as he had since he'd first entered the vehicle – stolen from a food depot a hundred miles to the north. And he had added a subtle touch for afterwards when the police investigated the catastrophe. On the seat beside him was a half-empty bottle of bourbon – also handled with gloves.

An ex-amateur racing driver, Oscar was confident that after the 'accident' he could execute the necessary U-turn to head south again. If some other car became embroiled, bad luck. Only an army tank crashing into his truck could put it out of action. And that was what he had once driven when he had done his military service – driven a Leopard tank.

When the police eventually found the abandoned truck they'd assume the driver who'd stolen it had been drunk. The bottle of bourbon would convince them of that. Oscar felt sure he'd foreseen every contingency. But that was what Schmidt was paying him nine thousand marks for. Attention to detail.

He stiffened. A Mercedes was approaching. The snow had almost stopped falling and he had a clear view. A lone woman driving. In any case, it was the wrong registration number. The car seemed to float towards him. And she must be doing 140 k.p.h. Stupid cow – in these conditions. No wonder there were pile-ups on the autobahn. Probably racing on to meet her lover, he thought. The car seemed to take ages to reach the point where the slip road entered the autobahn. Then she was gone.

The incident reassured Oscar. He'd have plenty of time

to drive down when the target vehicle came into sight. He lit a cigarette, then frowned. The weather was changing. The snow had stopped coming down. The temperature had dropped suddenly. In the distance over the autobahn it was becoming hazy. Creeping in from both sides was a freezing fog. He lifted the pair of binoculars to his eyes again. At the moment he'd still have time to drive down on to the autobahn – providing the freezing fog came no closer.

'We're approaching another turn-off,' Paula warned. 'Still not the one to Freiburg, but we're getting closer.'

'I congratulate you on spotting that sign,' Tweed replied and gripped the wheel more firmly.

A sinister white vapour was floating over the autobahn. Snake-like curls of mist drifted downwards. His windscreen was icing up. The wipers kept knocking slivers of the ice off the windscreen. He turned up the heater. Raw cold was penetrating the interior of the Mercedes. The silver car ahead had disappeared. Could it have driven up the turn-off? He doubted it.

'It's stopped snowing,' Paula remarked, 'but this fog is going to make it difficult for you.'

'So we're lucky there's nothing just ahead of us.'

'The trouble is I can't see any more how close our friends behind us are. Let's hope they keep well back. We don't want one of them slamming up our rear.'

It was a thought which had occurred to Tweed. He wriggled and sat up straighter. For no particular reason he felt more alert and in control. Second wind. The adrenalin was flowing again. Probably the arrival of the fresh hazard had triggered it off. He would have liked to reduce speed but he was worried about what might be coming up behind him.

The ice made a crackling sound now as it froze harder and the wipers shifted it. In his headlights the endless lane ahead gleamed like glass. The surface was becoming very treacherous. Paula yelled an urgent warning.

'Oh, my God! Look what's coming. He must be mad . . .'

In the distance a huge truck was advancing towards them on collision course, its headlights blazing. Then mounted on top of the cab another light came on, a powerful beam like a great eye glaring at them. Paula froze with terror. The searchlight beam became much stronger, blinding her as the monster rumbled on towards them. Even above the sound of their own engine she could hear the drumming beat of Oscar's souped-up motor.

Tweed's mouth tightened. His eyes flickered for a second to the rear view mirror. No sign of any traffic behind his Mercedes. He kept his speed, resisted the temptation to lessen the pressure on the accelerator. The two vehicles rushed towards each other. The gap was closing to collision point in seconds.

'He's crazy as a fox,' Paula gasped.

'Brace yourself!' Tweed ordered.

He could see now it was an immense refrigerated truck weighing God knew how many tons. It would crush his car like an eggshell with its size and the combined speeds. He knew instantly the driver was intent on killing them. Still he kept up his speed, stayed in the same lane as the oncoming juggernaut.

Oscar was crouched over his wheel, his dead cigarette hung from the corner of his thin mouth. This was the target – everything was right. Number and sex of the people inside. Registration number. He pushed his foot down and the truck shook with the power of its movement. Oscar leant back in his seat, away from the wheel, ready for the shock . . .

Paula closed her eyes. She knew she was dead. The thought flashed through her mind that at least she would die with Tweed . . .

Behind the wheel Tweed sat immobile as a waxwork figure. His mind was as cold as the ice forming on the windscreen. The driver of the truck must now have assumed he was petrified with fright, unable to think, maybe even asleep as sometimes happened.

Tweed calculated the combined speeds of the two vehicles as best he could, his mind moving like lightning. When he judged the moment was right – that he could turn the Mercedes faster than the truck driver could alter the onward rush of his mammoth – he swung the wheel to the left, switching to the outer lane. The juggernaut loomed over him. He was skidding. Tweed drove into the skid, the car responded, he was free of the skid. The wall of the truck slid past on his right, inches away.

Oscar swore foully, then blinked. Headlights were racing towards him. Instinctively he swung the wheel and the truck hit the car. There was a grinding crunch of metal as the front of the car telescoped, a second crashing sound as the car behind it rammed into the wreckage – followed by a third. The truck was skidding all over the autobahn, skating over the ice-rink surface. Oscar fought desperately for control, saw the outer metal barrier rear up before him, swivelled his foot – too late – for the brake. The truck smashed into the barrier, broke through it, lurched down an embankment.

The cab separated from the trailer which turned over on its side, sliding down the slope. Freed of its burden, the cab sped on, rammed into a low concrete wall. Oscar was hurled through the windscreen like a fighter pilot jerking forward at G-speed. When the police found him later his head was almost severed from his neck, lolled through the fractured opening in a macabre way, the dead cigarette still tucked in the corner of the dead man's mouth.

* * *

'I don't know how you managed it . . .'

Paula used a handkerchief to wipe sweat off her brow, to dry her hands. She was breathing deeply, her breasts heaving, fighting to get a grip on herself. Tweed said the first thing that came into his head.

'Neither do I, but I did. At a cost. You realize there was a major pile-up? Lord knows how many vehicles – all of them following us, I suspect. How close to the Freiburg turn-off?'

He asked to switch her mind to something else, and because it was essential to leave the autobahn after what had just happened. He reduced speed and carefully wiped each of his own damp hands on his coat. Paula was already studying the map, looking up to check a sign.

'It's the next turn-off. We're stopping in Freiburg?'

'Yes, I know the place. Spent six months at the University once to learn German. We'll stay there the night. You'll find it relaxes you. Freiburg has a first-rate hotel.'

'What's it called?'

'The Colombi.'

9

On their way to the Hotel Colombi, their shoulders stooped to ward off the falling snow, Horowitz paused when he saw a car hire firm which was still open. Eva grumbled as she stood in the cold, carrying her case.

'I want something to eat,' she protested, clasping her coat collar round her slim neck.

Horowitz's patience was exhausted. Smiling, he put down his luggage, placed both hands on her shoulders. A good four inches taller than his companion, he bent down to speak to her.

'If I have any more moaning from you they'll find your body in a ditch. How would you like to end up that way?'

She trembled as he stared straight at her, and not with the cold. 'I'm sorry. What are we doing?' Her teeth chattered, and again not with the cold.

'I am going to hire a car. We'll then drive the last few metres to the Colombi. Are we feeling better now?'

'I'm OK. Anything you say, Armand . . .'

Horowitz used a driving licence in the name of Vogel to hire an Audi. The formalities completed, he drove away along the cobbled streets of the old town. It was important to have transport, mobility. He reserved two rooms at the luxurious hotel which had a large reception hall and modern curving staircases leading to the first floor. Hendrix mellowed in the warmth and the palatial surroundings, said she'd go up to her room to get ready for dinner. Horowitz handed his suitcase to a porter with his room key.

'I'll see you in the bar,' he told Hendrix.

It was with a sense of relief that he made his way alone into the bar and ordered a glass of champagne. At that time of year there were few people about and he sat at a table by himself. An infrequent drinker, he sipped his champagne. A radio playing somewhere was interrupted by a news flash. Horowitz froze, his glass half-way to his lips.

'A major pile-up on the E 35 near Freiburg . . . reported eight cars involved . . . heavy casualties . . . also reported a large refrigerated truck driving north along the southbound lane caused the latest holocaust . . . the truck driver believed to have died in the pile-up . . . more details in our next news bulletin . . .'

Horowitz put down his glass still half full. He ordered a second glass, checked his watch. When Eva Hendrix arrived he pointed at his own glass.

'You can finish that up before you start on the one I ordered for you. I have to go out – something I forgot to attend to. Start dinner without me – I may be a while.'

'And I got myself all dressed up for you . . .' She saw his expression and stopped. She was wearing a green off-the-shoulder dress which hugged her figure. 'Don't worry,' she went on quickly, 'I'll start dinner and see you when you get back . . .'

And maybe, she thought, if I'm lucky he'll be away a long time and I'll meet an interesting man. Horowitz was not even looking at her: opening his executive case, he lifted the base, sorted through several documents, found what he was looking for and shut the case. Still holding on to it, he nodded and went out to where the Audi was parked.

It took him half an hour's fast driving up the autobahn to reach the disaster point. Police cars with blue lights flashing, revolving. Uniformed police everywhere. Beyond, a glimpse of carnage – the pile-up on the southbound lane resembled a scrap metal yard. Police were directing the traffic, waving traffic on. He pulled up on the hard shoulder, switched off and got out.

He was careful to approach one of the older policemen: the younger ones gave out no information, delighted in exerting their brief authority by telling you to move on. The policeman he spoke to stood with his hands on his hips, had grey hair showing beneath his peaked cap. Horowitz began the speech he had rehearsed.

'I'm a state official, a commissioner of taxes.' He showed the forged document. 'I heard about this awful accident on the radio and I'm worried sick . . .'

'You think someone you know might be involved?' the policeman asked sympathetically.

'Yes. My wife. She was driving from Frankfurt and phoned me to say she was leaving late. But she could have arrived here about the time of the accident . . .'

'Registration number? We have managed to find all of those at least.' The policeman immediately regretted his choice of the last two words. 'What make of car?'

'A Mercedes.' Horowitz hesitated. 'You have a list of the numbers? You have? Would you mind if I looked down the list? I'd sooner see it listed for myself. I'm in a state of shock.'

The policeman nodded again, took a folded sheet of paper from his tunic pocket, unfolded it, handed it to Horowitz and held a flashlight while the tax commissioner checked the numbers, moving his index finger slowly down the list. Horowitz let out a deep sigh.

'She's not included. Thank God. Do you mind if I do a U-turn through that smashed barrier and get back to Freiburg? I may have missed her coming out here.'

'I'll guide you out, sir. This is your lucky night. No one survived that. Freezing fog and still they drive at high speed. Madness.'

'There's a lot of it about in the world. And thank you for being so helpful, officer . . .'

Horowitz drove back to Freiburg in a philosophical mood -- the registration number of Tweed's Mercedes had not been on the list. He was still loose, roaming about somewhere. The question was where? He tried to think himself into Tweed's position: what would he do?

By the time he had arrived back at the Hotel Colombi he had decided. He was going to have a busy day tomorrow.

Tweed got lost driving into Freiburg. They had altered the street route system since last he'd been in the place. He found himself in front of the main station.

'I think the bookstall is still open in the ticket hall,' Paula said. 'I'll nip out and try to get a street guide.'

She returned a few minutes later with an air of triumph, waving a folded map. Sitting beside Tweed, she stopped before opening the map and looked at him.

'If you want to go on further I'm game. Is it safe to stop so close to that accident? That truck driver tried to kill us – and he knew where to locate us exactly. Lord knows how but maybe we should get out of here.'

'You're dog-tired and hungry . . .'

'I told you, I'm game.'

'I'm dog-tired and hungry too,' he told her. 'and that's when I'm likely to make a major mistake. I know Freiburg. Let's see if we can find the Colombi Hotel.'

'It's on the Rotteck Ring. I saw an advertisement for it in the booking hall. Give me a moment.' Tweed waited and looked round. Modern buildings in front of the station he didn't recall – obviously erected since his stay years ago in Freiburg.

'Got it! And it's so easy. See that street over there – Eisenbahnstrasse? We simply go down there and turn left into the Rotteck Ring. The hotel is on the far side of the Ring.'

'Let's get moving, then. I could do with a bath and I expect you could. Then a decent dinner. The food is fabulous.'

It was only a short distance and Paula spotted the Colombi as they turned a corner. Quite suddenly Tweed pulled in at the kerb before they reached the hotel. Leaving the engine running he drummed his fingers on the wheel.

'What's the matter?' asked Paula. 'You're suffering a delayed reaction from that appalling business on the autobahn aren't you?'

'No. But a few minutes ago I said I was dog-tired and hungry. I also said that was when I was likely to make a major mistake. I think I was just on the verge of making one.'

'I don't understand. We can talk about it when we're settled inside the Colombi in the warmth . . .'

'Which is the mistake I was about to make.' He leaned back in his seat. 'Think, Paula. I'm wanted for murder and rape. So in London they're bound to have looked at my file – which gives some of my personal techniques while abroad. One is that I often stay at a first-class hotel to merge into the background. The Colombi is among the "Thirty Best Hotels in Germany" list – and we were followed close to Freiburg . . .'

'But,' Paula hesitated, then went on, 'it must have been a massacre when you evaded that truck. I heard it – a terrible sound of vehicles crashing into each other. They may all be dead.'

'More than possible. But someone sent those cars after us and whoever he is, he'll soon know we weren't involved. They'll check the car registration numbers.'

'You think then some high-powered organization is behind that pursuit. Probably the police . . .'

'And maybe someone else. I told you, eight cars following us was too many for one outfit. So we go to the Colombi, someone knows that habit of mine, we're walking into a trap.'

'Yes, you could be right,' she agreed. 'So what do we do?'

'Stay at a much smaller hotel, the one I stayed at when I was here to learn German. The Oberkirch on Schuster-strasse. It has the advantage of being tucked away behind the Munster – and there used to be a large car park there. Don't bother with the map. I know where I am now. I turn into the Kaiser-Josephstrasse, then turn off that down a side street and we're in the Munsterplatz . . .'

Tweed turned down the Kaiser-Josephstrasse, a long cobbled street bisecting the town from east to west. It was almost deserted at that hour, in the wintry weather. A yellow tram ran along the centre and the street was lined on both sides with closed shops.

Turning into the Munsterplatz, Tweed saw cars parked,

covered with a coating of snow. He drove round slowly, the wheels bumping over the icy cobbles, found an empty slot behind two rows of cars under the lee of the Munster, drove into it.

'We're nicely tucked away here in case someone comes looking for us,' he remarked as he switched off the engine. 'It's only a short walk to the hotel. Mind your footing.'

'The main thing is we're within sight of sanctuary for the night,' Paula said cheerfully. 'I don't really care how far it is. I'm stiff as a board and want to stretch my legs.'

Carrying their cases, they moved across the square, lonely and silent at night. The only sound was the crunch of their feet on the crusted snow. The great spire of the Munster loomed above them like an arrow pointing to heaven. Tweed turned into the Schusterstrasse, which was also deserted. Icicles were suspended from the roof gutters like daggers, gleaming in the light from ancient lanterns attached to the walls.

'It's a lovely place,' Paula remarked.

The street was narrow, cobbled, full of old buildings which were joined together and went back to medieval times. Tweed nodded towards a small four-storey building on the left-hand side of the street. It had cream-washed walls, brown shutters and beyond its rooftop he could see the tip of the Munster spire.

'The Hotel Oberkirch,' he said. 'Refuge at last.'

'Even from the outside it looks cosy,' Paula observed, keeping up a cheerful note. 'I think I'll skip the bath, settle for a nice hot dinner.'

'I'll join you, ' said Tweed as he held open the door for her.

A wave of pure warmth met them. Outside it was below freezing point. Inside the temperature must be forty degrees higher, at least, Tweed reckoned. He reserved two rooms in the name James Gage and arranged to meet Paula in the dining-room.

They stood in front of a blazing log-fire before they parted. Paula crouched down, held out her frozen hands towards the fire. They began to tingle almost unbearably. She gritted her teeth, held her hands in the same position. The tingle began to fade, she stood up.

'What are we going to do tomorrow?' she whispered. 'Keep on the move?'

'I haven't decided yet. I think better on a full stomach – but I know one thing I'm doing immediately after breakfast.'

'Which is?'

'Find the local car hire outfit. Exchange the Mercedes for a BMW . . .'

'We had one of those when we drove from Brussels to Frankfurt,' she objected.

'So it will confuse the trackers mightily – especially since I think they picked us up at the Luxembourg border crossing, then followed us in our Mercedes down the autobahn.'

It was late in the evening when Newman left the Hessischer Hof in Frankfurt and walked across the little wooded park. He had left Marler in the bar, saying he was going upstairs for a shower.

For the third time that day he called Kuhlmann from the public box. He wasn't sure the police chief would still be in his office but the gravelly voice answered immediately.

'Felix here,' Newman said. 'No more developments, I suppose?'

'You suppose wrong. There was a newsflash I caught of a big pile-up on the E 35 autobahn outside Freiburg . . .'

'God! Not Tweed?' Newman let the name slip in his anxiety.

'No,' Kuhlmann assured him promptly. 'I know definitely – I've phoned Freiburg police HQ – they've a list of the registration numbers of the eight cars involved from a radio car on the spot. Your associate is not on the list. But I think he was somewhere near the disaster. Eight of my men were killed in the pile-up.'

'That's appalling. You must be feeling sick . . .'

'Not sick – grim. Look, Newman, supposing we meet where we met before? Say in three-quarters of an hour from now?'

'I'll be there . . .'

Newman, puzzled, replaced the receiver. He had slipped up in using Tweed's name because it had sounded as though he'd been one of the casualties. But Kuhlmann had also slipped up – using 'Newman' at the end of the conversation. And Kuhlmann *never* slipped up. Unless intentionally.

Kuhlmann looked at his assistant, Kurt Meyer, as he replaced his own phone. Meyer had his head buried in files he was comparing, apparently oblivious to everything going on round him.

'I'm leaving for the night,' he informed Meyer. 'You expect to be here much longer?'

'Maybe another two hours, Chief. I'm still trying to make head or tail of this Gruninger case.'

'Get lucky . . .'

Kuhlmann left his office after slipping on his dark topcoat and scarf. He walked down to the next floor where two men sat working at desks facing each other. He leaned on the door he had closed, pursed his lips before speaking.

'This is just between the three of us. Friedl, I think it is possible Kurt Meyer may leave the building shortly. I want you to follow him without being spotted. See where he goes, who he contacts. Bork, you go with Friedl. Take that camera with you – the miniature job Zeiss developed for us where you get a picture within a minute of taking the shot.

The night version. No flash-bulbs. If Meyer meets some-one I want his picture taken in the utmost secrecy. Think you can handle it?'

'No trouble at all,' Friedl replied. 'It so happens with the weather changing I bought a new windcheater and also a beret this morning. Meyer has never seen them. And I'll wear phoney glasses. He won't spot me.'

'If you can,' Kuhlmann ordered, 'meet me in the bar of the Canadian Pacific Hotel to report any findings. I'll wait there till midnight. See you . . .'

Kurt Meyer left the Kriminalpolizei HQ at Wiesbaden ten minutes after Kuhlmann had gone. He drove towards Frankfurt, stopping on the way to make a call from a public booth. George Evans answered the phone himself, working late in his office in the Kaiserstrasse.

'Kurt here. I have urgent information. There have been serious developments. Can we meet? You'd want to know at once.'

'Where are you calling from?' Evans asked.

'A public call-box, of course. On the way to Frankfurt from Wiesbaden . . .'

'So you have transport?'

'Yes. My own Passat.'

'I'll meet you in the lobby of the Frankfurter Hof half an hour from now. It had better be important.'

He slammed down the phone before Meyer could reply, stared across his desk at Gareth Morgan, perched like a large evil gnome on the edge of his chair, cuddling a glass of Scotch.

'That was my Wiesbaden contact, Kurt Meyer. I'm meeting him, as you must have heard, at the Frankfurter Hof.'

Morgan swallowed the rest of his drink, wiped his mouth with the back of his hand. He sat frowning, staring back at Evans, then decided.

'May be to do with that newsflash we heard about the pile-up near Freiburg. You said one of your men was reporting to you when he cut out.'

'He cut out all right. Or was cut out, more likely. He was just saying: *Tweed is somewhere ahead of us but in this fog*— Then he let out the most chilling yell – *Ahhhhhhh* – and the link went blank.'

Imitating the scream of agony he'd lifted his voice. Morgan pursed his lips with distaste. Any dramatics were his department. He stood up, placed the empty glass on Evans's desk where the damp base left a ring on the highly polished surface. Evans affected not to notice the sloppy touch.

'I think I'll come with you, hear what this Meyer has to say for myself. You can introduce me as your bodyguard . . .'

'Is that wise? Putting yourself on view? And Meyer is running scared.'

'I'd like to hear for myself,' Morgan repeated. 'Got it?'

He saw no reason to explain that Buckmaster had emphasized he wanted Morgan to supervise the whole Tweed operation personally. And Evans might not handle this creep so he obtained every scrap of information available.

'By the way,' he continued as Evans fetched the coats from a cupboard, helped Morgan on with his black overcoat, 'your running expenses here are astronomic. I was going through the figures. Do you really need thirty operatives in Frankfurt? We have to watch expenses if we're to make a profit.'

'I was told by London that expense was no object. It was the image which counted – if we're to hold our position as the largest security organization on the Continent.

'But you do have a budget?' Morgan persisted.

He was well aware that the reference to 'London' meant Lance Buckmaster.

101

'What's a budget?' Evans asked airily.

Morgan grunted. 'Let's get off to see this chap at the Frankfurter Hof.'

'I still think your coming is risky . . .'

'We're in the risk business – in case you hadn't realized it.'

'I'm damned sure it was an attempt to kill Tweed,' Kuhlmann told Newman as they again strolled up and down the concourse of the main station.

It was much quieter at this hour. The whole tempo of the *Hauptbahnhof* had changed. It was almost empty of passengers and the few there sat huddled on seats. The tannoy seemed to have gone to sleep.

'What makes you think that?' asked Newman.

'I had unmarked cars following him. They reported that four other cars were also doing the same thing. We know who they were now – security guards from the World Security apparatus. Why am I sure? A stolen refrigerated truck drives the wrong way up the autobahn – that was seen by a driver coming up the northbound lane – and Tweed's Mercedes was somewhere not far ahead. Two sets of skid marks were found afterwards – one by the wheels of a car, the other by the truck before the driver went through the barrier and was killed. Oh, yes, that was an assassination attempt.'

'And where do you think Tweed is now?'

'Somewhere in Freiburg would be my best bet. They'd driven all the way from Brussels. The last section was through near blizzard conditions. The incident must have shocked them, so logically they'd rest up for the night.'

'Is that police chopper at Frankfurt Airport still standing by? Egon Wrede was the name of the pilot?'

'Yes to both questions. And Wrede will still be fresh. He's an expert at catnapping while he waits. And he'll have collected food from the airport.'

'Then I'm using it to fly straight to Freiburg.'

'I hoped you'd say that.' Newman had stopped walking for a few moments, his mind racing. Kuhlmann brushed past his right side, strolled round behind him, came up on his left side and his wide mouth broke into a grin. 'Better check your pockets. Careful. Nothing on view.'

Newman felt inside his right-hand pocket. He froze. He could recognize the feel of a gun. He checked his left-hand pocket and again his fingers touched metal.

'A Walther .38 automatic,' Kuhlmann told him. 'It's OK – the safety's on. Spare mags in the other pocket. Better take this bit of paper . . .'

Newman read the typed sheet quickly. An authorization to carry the weapon. On official headed paper. Signed by Kuhlmann himself.

'How did you manage that trick?' he asked.

'I used to know a pickpocket when I was on the beat a million years ago. A real pro. He taught me all he knew. Then I put him away for two years. Are you wondering why I've kitted you up?'

'Yes.'

They were strolling again to keep warm. 'Three of the World Security guards dragged out of the carnage down near Freiburg were armed. Which was naughty. No authorization. You may need protection. Tweed certainly does. Best I can do . . .'

Kuhlmann walked away. Newman also left the station, found a cab and was back at the Hessischer Hof inside ten minutes. During that time he took his decision about Marler: to continue keeping an eye on him. He brought him out of the bar.

'We're leaving now. Give you the details in the cab. Get your bag. Don't ask questions – you'll get no answers.'

'Supposing I won't leave unless you tell me what's going on?' Marler challenged him as they walked across the lobby.

'Then I'll dump you . . .'
'Meet you down here in five minutes.'

10

'We'll go to the bar,' Morgan said after they'd met Kurt Meyer.

'That's rather public,' Meyer protested.

'Not if we sit in that dark corner,' Morgan snapped, taking charge of the situation. He ordered a large cognac for himself and left Evans to deal with the other drinks. Then he leaned forward, tapped Meyer on the knee.

'You've never seen me after this meeting. Get any funny ideas and certain interesting photographs will be shown to your wife. She'll enjoy them, I'm sure.'

'I swear . . .'

'Don't. I can't abide bad language.' Morgan sat back, satisfied he was dominating the proceedings, waited until the drinks had been served, paid for by Evans. He leaned forward again, his voice a hissing whisper.

'Tell all. Make it quick.'

'Someone called Newman rang Kuhlmann. . .' He paused to watch the effect of his statement. Morgan remained very still, his eyes fixed on Meyer's like inert beads. 'I remembered Kuhlmann making a reference to Robert Newman, the foreign correspondent. Maybe that's who it was . . .'

'I'm waiting for the guts,' Morgan hissed again.

'Well, this Newman was told by my chief that Tweed wasn't involved in the big car pile-up on the autobahn near Freiburg. But he said he thought Tweed was somewhere near the pile-up when it happened. Then Kuhlmann made an arrangement to meet this Newman . . .'

'Where?' prompted Morgan.

'At the place they'd met before. He gave no indication where that was. They were to meet in three-quarters of an hour. And that was about it. You have heard the news-flash . . .'

'We heard. Everybody has heard,' Morgan told him. 'Time you walked. Not yet. Evans has something for you while I get a drink.'

Morgan padded over to the low curved bar, ordered another cognac. While he was at the bar Evans slipped an envelope containing banknotes under the table to Meyer.

'I don't like that man,' Meyer complained. 'In future I only deal with you.'

'You deal with who we say you will. Say thank you for your present, then push off before he returns.'

'Thank you.'

Meyer stuffed the envelope into his breast pocket, took a quick glance round the dimly lit bar and hurried out of the hotel. Morgan downed his cognac, licked his lips, came back, slipped into his overcoat and without a word made for the exit. Evans followed.

They climbed into the rear of the waiting stretched black Mercedes limousine, the chauffeur closed the door and sat behind the wheel, waiting for instructions. Morgan leaned forward, spoke through the opening in the glass screen dividing rear from front.

'Put on the radio. Music.' He waited until the chauffeur found a programme. 'Now take us back to Kaiserstrasse.' He closed the glass panel.

'He won't be able to hear a word we say now,' he commented.

'Hans is completely trustworthy,' Evans protested as the car moved away from the hotel's steps.

'No one is completely trustworthy. If Meyer got it right –

and I think the little creep did – Horowitz has made a balls-up of eliminating Tweed. Like I said, you can't trust anyone. Is the Lear jet which flew him down there back here?'

'Yes. With a fresh crew waiting at the airport in case of need . . .'

'Which is more expense. I wonder what that's costing? It would be cheaper to let them stay at home on a stand-by retainer.'

'I had orders from London.'

'I know. To keep the jet ready on a round-the-clock basis. Well, they'll earn their money – the crew. I'm flying to Freiburg tonight to take personal control.'

'Horowitz won't like that. He likes to operate on his own. And his track record is excellent.'

'His track record just got smeared. When we reach HQ leave me alone in your office. Use another phone to call Horowitz – you can contact him, I suppose?'

'In an emergency. He phoned me from Freiburg. He's staying at the Colombi . . .'

'Some dump of a boarding house?'

'Actually . . .' Evans sounded smug. 'It's the best hotel they have in Freiburg, and listed among the thirty best in the Federal Republic.'

'More expense. No wonder his fees come so high. I've changed my mind. Don't call Horowitz. Under no circumstances let him know I'm flying there tonight. Instead call the airport, make sure that jet crew is ready – and write out an authorization placing the Lear at my complete disposal. No time limit.'

Lance Buckmaster was in his study, the door locked, at Tavey Grange, when the call from Morgan came through. It was being transmitted by satellite via the radio-receiver dish nestling among the Tudor chimneys.

'Hold on a minute,' Buckmaster ordered.

He held his hand over the phone. 'Sonia, go to your room at once. I'll join you later.'

Sonia Dreyfus, twenty-seven, with long dark hair, daughter of a wealthy industrialist, sat naked to the waist on a long leather couch. She had a good figure. Whipping on a sweater she gathered up her clothes and left the study. She'd learned that when Lance said move, you moved. And what luck that his silly bitch of a wife, Leonora, was up in London at the Belgravia apartment.

'Carry on. What is it?' Buckmaster's upper crust voice floated up into the stratosphere and back down to Frankfurt.

Morgan was wily in his wording. 'The first attempt was made on the subject for treatment. We now know his location. The attempt smoked him out . . .'

'But was not successful? Is that what you're telling me in your roundabout manner?'

'Your assumption is correct.'

'I want the problem dealt with quickly. Report to me here – if I am here – when it's out of the way. I have to go now, urgent matters to attend to. Good-night.'

In Frankfurt, Morgan put down the phone, used a silk handkerchief to wipe sweat off his forehead. That had gone easier than he'd expected. *Urgent matters to attend to*? At this hour? Buckmaster was probably screwing his latest mistress, Sonia Dreyfus. By Morgan's count – and he believed in keeping track of such juicy info – this would be number six. One of these days Leonora was going to react.

He pressed the intercom switch, told the Welshman to come and see him. When Evans entered Morgan was leaning back in his chair, trimming the tip from a cigar.

'This Newman business is a complication I don't need,' he began.

'You think it is *the* Robert Newman, the foreign correspondent, as Meyer suggested?'

'I don't think, I know.' He made a ritual of lighting the cigar, revolving the match round the tip. 'Newman and Tweed have collaborated in the past. I was told Newman has full vetting. Now we hear he's cooperating with Kuhlmann. It has all the hallmarks of a conspiracy. This tells me.' He tweaked his pointed nose with his index finger.

'Maybe Newman has heard the rumours – that Tweed is fleeing to the East, senses a good story. These reporters will go to any lengths to make money, get a sensational scoop. No morals at all.'

Morgan raised an eyebrow, said nothing while he got his cigar going. That was pretty good, coming from Evans, considering some of the things he'd done without a qualm.

'It's not for money,' Morgan corrected him. 'You've forgotten – not so long ago Newman got lucky, wrote an international bestseller, *Kruger: The Computer that Failed*. Made him financially independent for life.' He puffed at his cigar, blew a perfect smoke circle which drifted towards the overhead fluorescent strip. 'We may have to remove him from this vale of sorrows in due course.'

'The potential body count is rising,' Evans objected. 'Tweed, the Grey woman, now Newman.'

'So you'd better get ready to shell out a large fee to friend Horowitz – after I've put my foot up his backside. I'm leaving now. You may not see me for a while. Look after the shop in my absence. . .'

Five minutes later Morgan was sitting in the rear of the limo on his way to the airport. He'd seen no reason to tell Evans that after Freiburg he'd fly back to London. It was necessary to keep an eye on what Leonora was up to. After all, she might be chairman, but he was managing director.

Newman and Marler arrived at Frankfurt Airport at 1 a.m. The chief of security, a thick-set man called Kuhn, examined the letter from Kuhlmann and then escorted them into the icy air of the airport to where the police Sikorsky was waiting.

Wrede also examined the document, then welcomed them aboard. They climbed the step-ladder and Wrede, an amiable man, showed them to their seats.

'You're taking us to Freiburg, please, near the Black Forest,' Newman told him.

'I know. I was told over the phone. Coffee in this thermos, sandwiches here.' He handed them two large greaseproof packets.

Wrede, a small roly-poly man – Newman almost expected to see jam on the sleeves of his woollen pullover – was about to retract the ladder prior to closing the door, joining his co-pilot, when Kuhn came running across the tarmac.

Wrede listened, came back to Newman. 'Sorry, there's an urgent phone call for you. You can take it in the security chief's office.'

'Come with you,' Marler suggested.

'You'll stay where you are . . .'

He joined Kuhn at the foot of the ladder and they hurried back to the main airport building. On the way Newman noticed a Lear jet parked under lights, close to a hanger. Some millionaire's plaything. For something to say he asked the question.

'Whose jet is that?'

'Belongs to World Security. A crew stands by twenty-four hours a day, seven days a week. Costs them a fortune – many times more than I'll earn in a lifetime.'

Newman stared at the jet again. His memory automatically registered the serial number painted on the fuselage. Inside the office he picked up the receiver lying off its cradle. Kuhn tactfully left the office.

'Who is it?' Newman asked cautiously. 'This is Felix . . .'

'Kuhlmann here. Hoped I'd catch you before you flew off. I have heard rumours our friend who escaped the

pile-up is fleeing to the East. Absurd, I know. Trouble is
the Minister also heard them. He's ordered all frontier
posts to keep on the alert. Especially those leading to East
Germany and Czechoslovakia. Switzerland as well,' he
added. 'The heat is really on.'

'Thanks for letting me know. I'm taking off in the next
few minutes.'

It was a very worried Newman who walked back to the
Sikorsky. The sooner he reached Freiburg the better.

11

When the Lear jet carrying Morgan landed at Freiburg
airfield he ordered the crew to find accommodation in the
town, to call him at the Colombi so he could contact them,
to have the jet ready for immediate departure. He omitted
to thank them for a smooth flight: no point in coddling the
paid help.

The car he'd told Evans to have ready for him transported him through the night to the Colombi. The room he'd
ordered Evans to reserve by phone was ready. It was 2.30
a.m. when he knocked on the door of Horowitz's room.

'He may be asleep,' the night porter had pointed out.

'Then he'll just have to wake up.'

There was a light under the door but it was several
minutes before the door opened a few inches on the chain.
Horowitz, flat against the wall on the opening side,
wearing a dressing gown, clasped the Browning .32 automatic inside his right-hand pocket.

'Who is it?' he called out in German.

'Speak bloody English for Christ's sake . . .'

'I said,' Horowitz repeated in English, 'who is it?'

'Me. Morgan. Surely you can recognize my voice. Hurry it up. It's half-past two in the morning.'

'Put both your hands through the gap and then show your face,' Horowitz ordered.

Fuming, Morgan did as he'd been told. Glaring through the gap, he saw Horowitz come into view, the Browning pointed at his ample stomach. Horowitz closed the door, released the chain, opened it. As soon as Morgan was inside he relocked the door quietly, put back the chain, slipped the Browning back into his pocket.

'Where did you get the weapon?' Morgan demanded as he sank into an armchair.

'From a friend near Freiburg who keeps things for me. What are you doing here?' he asked in the same quiet tone. 'Everything is under control.'

Morgan's eyes swept round the room. The bedclothes were rumpled, a lamp on the bedside table was on, a paperback novel lay face down on the bed, splayed open. A bottle of mineral water and a glass stood on a table.

'Sure,' Morgan said sarcastically, 'everything is under control. Tweed is still wandering around God knows where, but still living.'

'God may not know where, but I have an idea,' Horowitz replied as he poured himself a glass of water and drank some slowly, his eyes on Morgan. 'And you haven't answered my question – what are you doing here?'

'Finding out what the devil isn't going on.' Morgan leaned forward and glared at Horowitz who had hauled a chair forward and was sitting close to him.' 'You were paid a small fortune to do this job. *Avec vitesse* . . .'

'Don't ever try to pass for a Frenchman,' Horowitz remarked mildly. 'You'd be spotted as soon as you opened your mouth. I told you, everything is under control.'

'Well tell me how. What do you propose to do next?

111

And what was that remark about God not knowing but you do – where Tweed is? Where is he?'

'Oh, he has to be holed up somewhere in Freiburg. You want a few details? Incidentally, only half the agreed fee has been paid . . .'

'You get the balance when Tweed's lying on a slab.'

'Which was part of our agreement, and still is. I suppose the Lear jet flew you here from Frankfurt? You know, you're rushing about too much. And you're overweight. You should watch it, my friend. You could easily have flown down in the morning.'

Morgan gritted his teeth. 'I got to my present position by moving faster than the opposition. Also, my boss – who is ultimately your boss – is getting impatient. He wants results and he wants them fast. Lying in bed reading a paperback is not what we paid you for . . .'

'Actually, that is exactly what you paid me for.' There was an edge to Horowitz's tone. 'Instead of dashing all over the place in the middle of the night I prefer to *think* – really you should try it sometime. On the basis of the little I've learned about my target from the extracts from the file you gave me I can do that.'

'I'm listening,' snapped Morgan and took out his cigar case.

'While you are, I'd sooner you didn't smoke in here. I have to sleep in this atmosphere . . .'

'Jesus!' Morgan put away the cigar case, took out a hip flask and swallowed a generous slug of cognac. 'That's better. I'm still listening.'

'Tweed had been driving for at least twelve hours I calculate by the time of the pile-up on the autobahn. Incidentally, no danger of Oscar, the truck driver, talking . . .'

'I was going to ask you about that. The newsflash was vague. At least the one we heard in Frankfurt.'

'Since then we've had a very detailed news bulletin.

112

You'll grasp what I mean when I tell you it was amusingly titled – The Headless Maniac. Severed heads don't talk, so far as I know. He muffed the job – but the weather conditions were exceptional. As I was saying, Tweed had driven for many hours to reach Freiburg from Brussels in a day. Even allowing for his lady companion taking over the wheel, they'd both be very tired. Freiburg was their nearest refuge. Tweed would want a good meal and a good night's rest. He's here somewhere, I assure you.'

'Then how do you find him?'

'First by getting up early in the morning. My alarm is set for six. I can get by on three hours' sleep quite happily. I shall tour the town – which I know well – on foot before it wakes up . . .'

'On foot? Looking for what?'

'His parked Mercedes, of course. I have the registration number . . .'

'You could drive round faster.'

'Yes, and miss his car. It's not too large – Freiburg – and I walk fast. My long legs. Also I have from the photos you showed me the images of Tweed and Paula Grey imprinted on my mind. I might even see one of them. On foot.'

'OK.' Morgan was mellowing under the influence of the large slug of cognac he'd swallowed. 'But there's a complication. It's called Robert Newman. He was in Frankfurt – and secretly meeting Otto Kuhlmann.'

'I see.' Horowitz's long lean face became serious. 'Could he possibly be coming here?'

'Work it out for yourself. Police cars were tracking Tweed as well as our own. One of our drivers recognized a plain-clothes driver from Wiesbaden. All dead now. But Kuhlmann told Newman about the pile-up, so . . .'

'I'm ahead of you. The foreign correspondent could arrive in Freiburg, and the file said they'd worked closely together in the past. As the French say, Newman is *formidable*. I shall have to take extra precautions. Are you staying here?' A wisp of a dry smile crossed Horowitz's features. 'Or flying back to Frankfurt when you leave me?'

'Good God! What do you think I am? Superman? I need a good night's kip after what I've been through today.'

Horowitz stood up. 'Then I suggest you go to your room and get your beauty sleep. Don't join me if you see me in the breakfast room. Just give me your room number.'

'Sixteen.' Morgan stood up, suddenly weary and flaked out. He stifled a yawn. Must keep up an image of command and energy in front of this cool snake. He lowered his voice. 'Try and make it a quick kill.'

'I move at my own pace. One planned "accident" has gone wrong due to the weather. You'll get your money's worth. As you have in the past. Good-night.'

The Sikorsky descended vertically through the darkness to Freiburg airfield. Newman gazed down at the snowbound landscape, felt the wheels bump, the rotors slowing and turned to Marler seated alongside him.

'We've arrived. There's a police car parked close to the tarmac. Leave me to do the talking if we're approached.'

'Since I don't have a clue what this is about I'm hardly likely to have much to say.'

As they descended the ladder after Newman had thanked the pilot, a uniformed policeman, his peaked cap rimmed with snow, greeted them when they stepped on *terra firma*. A tall giant, he extended his identity folder with his left hand and shook Newman's hand with his right.

'Mr Newman, I believe,' he said in English. 'Chief Inspector Kuhlmann asked us to meet you. Sergeant Andris at your service. Where do you wish us to drive you to?'

'Before we leave, Sergeant Andris, I see there's a Lear jet parked over there. Could you tell me when it arrived, who it belongs to, and who, if anyone, flew in here?'

114

Newman already knew the answer to its ownership. The registration number on the fuselage was the same as that painted on the machine he'd observed waiting at Frankfurt. A jet would cover the distance far more quickly than a chopper.

'I watched it land about an hour ago. It nearly ran out of runway. It belongs to World Security. One man alighted, a short heavily-built man wearing a dark overcoat, the lapels trimmed with astrakhan fur. Clean-shaven, in his forties at a guess, he moved quickly and had the small feet you often see with very well-built men. A Mercedes was waiting for him. I have acute hearing and just caught his instruction to the driver. The Hotel Colombi.'

'Thank you. Excellent powers of observation you have. And we also would like to be driven to the Colombi.' Newman paused. 'We'd like to arrive quietly. Could you stop your car nearby, out of sight of the entrance to the Colombi?'

Andris glanced at Marler as he held open the door. Settled in the rear seat next to Newman, Marler spoke in a low voice.

'He'll know me again. He photographs people with his eyes.'

'So behave yourself while you're in the Black Forest area,' Newman responded, glanced back at the Lear, closed his eyes and dozed.

He woke up as the car slowed and stopped by the kerb. Andris had carried out his instructions to the letter. The car was parked a dozen yards away from the light flooding out from the entrance to the Colombi.

At Newman's suggestion, Marler joined him in his room after depositing his bag in his own accommodation. Marler never seemed to tire and looked fresh as paint. He'd run an electric razor over his growth of stubble before arriving.

'And who do you think was the mysterious passenger who flew in before us?' he enquired.

115

'Gareth Morgan,' Newman said promptly. 'Description fitted him perfectly. I've met the louse. Have you?'

'No.' Marler omitted to mention his trip to Tavey Grange, his interview with Buckmaster. 'If this Morgan knows you is it a good idea to stay here? You could run into him.'

'I intend to. And his presence suggests we're very close to Tweed. Morgan likes to supervise operations himself.'

'Operations?'

'Yes.' Newman sagged into a chair, gestured for Marler to sit down. 'There was a horrific pile-up on the south-bound autobahn just outside Freiburg late yesterday evening – and the cars following Tweed were World Security jobs. So it's beginning to add up. Tweed escaped the pile-up . . .'

Newman watched Marler's reaction closely.

'Thank God for that,' Marler replied blandly and lit a king-size cigarette, a sign of inner tension. 'What', he continued, 'is beginning to add up?'

'The identity of the people who want Tweed out of the way. Permanently. World Security. At least they're mixed up in this business somewhere – otherwise why should they be so anxious to follow him?'

'But you haven't asked the main question,' Marler objected. '*Why* should anyone want him eliminated. Just supposing you're right. And there's a hell of a lot of supposition in your thinking. Or is there something you're not telling me?'

'What on earth gave you that idea?'

Newman yawned. He wanted sleep, to be fresh for the many tasks he had to undertake in a few hours. The main point now was to get Marler back in his room, to feel sure he'd stay there for the rest of the night.

'I'll tell you what gave me that idea,' Marler rapped back. 'You keep disappearing, making mysterious phone calls I suspect. For some reason you knew it was a good

116

idea for us to fly to Freiburg, that Tweed is in this area. You're not clairvoyant.'

'Why not push off and get some shut-eye?'

Marler stood up slowly. 'I'm beginning to get the feeling that for some crazy reason you don't trust me . . .'

'And that's crazy reasoning. You'll feel more relaxed in the morning.' He mimicked Marler's voice. 'Be a good chap, get back to your room. Maybe we can talk some more after a good breakfast.'

Marler left the room without a word. Newman waited for a few seconds, then tiptoed to the door, opened it quietly in time to see Marler's back disappearing into his own bedroom further down the corridor. Newman checked his watch and waited fifteen minutes. Satisfied Marler was not reappearing, he closed the door, leant against it, forced himself to think.

He must set his alarm clock early, get out of the hotel, explore the town for some sign of Tweed and Paula. Try the smaller places. Tweed could have switched his habits. Then a confrontation with Gareth Morgan, preferably in the dining-room. If he could throw the top man at World Security off balance, Morgan might just let something slip.

12

Armand Horowitz walked out of the front entrance of the Colombi the following morning shortly after streaks of grey light had appeared over the Black Forest.

He wore rubber overshoes – the snow had become hard as a rock overnight, its surface solid ice in many places.

He walked into the old part of the town – most of Freiburg – in the direction of the Munster.

Despite the sub-zero temperature he was clad only in a lightweight raincoat and a silk scarf, his head bare. Horowitz could stand any amount of cold, found it invigorating. Walking at a steady pace, he checked the registration number of every Mercedes parked by the kerb.

Inside the briefcase he carried in his right hand was a Pentax camera. At least the outer casing appeared to be a camera. Horowitz, an explosives expert, had sat up half the night in his room preparing the bomb which contained Semtex explosive. Attached to its back were four magnetic feet.

When he found Tweed's car it would be a simple matter to bend down, adjust the trembler mechanism by moving the shutter speed dial, then clamp the device to the underside of the car with the magnetic legs. The trembler would trigger the bomb when the car began to climb the slightest incline.

When the Mercedes had exploded Horowitz, on hearing the news over the radio, planned to call the local newspaper anonymously. He'd say he represented a splinter group of Baader–Meinhof, that they had 'executed' the industrialist, Martin Schuler. It would be assumed they'd mistaken the target. Another 'accident'.

Horowitz had collected the bomb from the same contact outside Freiburg who had supplied him with the Browning automatic and certain other equipment. He walked along the Kaiser-Josephstrasse where some shops were already open. Cleaning women with spades were levering ice off the sidewalk, pushing the slabs into the gutter.

He had changed his mind about checking the Munsterplatz car-park next. Tweed, he decided, would hide on the perimeter of the town, ready for a swift departure in an emergency. He turned along Schusterstrasse. In the distance was the Hotel Oberkirch.

Horowitz kept moving at his even pace, watching his footing. Just before reaching the Oberkirch he turned right again along a shopping arcade which led him out into Oberlinden, another street of ancient buildings. Every variety of paving had been used: cobbles, pavé and pebble mosaic. He reached one of the medieval gates, Schwabentor, the road passing under a tall decorated tower. He changed direction again, checking more parked Mercedes.

Now he was moving down Konvikstrasse, a narrow curving street. The old houses had dormer windows projecting from the roofs, leafless creepers stretching down the walls from window boxes high up. The water from a fountain surrounded by a circular stone basin was a frozen jet suspended in mid-air. The water in the basin was a solid sheet of blue-grey ice.

Tweed was also up early. He washed, shaved, dressed quickly and made a brief phone call. The car-hire firm he'd found in the directory was open for business. He left the hotel, hurried to the Munsterplatz. He was sitting behind the wheel, about to turn on the ignition, when he got out again.

He had to wrench the hood open and ice cracked. He checked the engine. No sign of tampering. He closed the hood and crouched down to check the underside of the vehicle. Again, all seemed well. He was driving slowly out of the square when he saw the tall man with steel-rimmed glasses in his wing mirror. Carrying a briefcase, he had paused and was examining a parked Mercedes. Tweed drove off, disappeared round a corner.

He exchanged the Mercedes for a BMW, using an international driving-licence with a fresh pseudonym, James

Gage. Before breakfast was served at the Oberkirch he had parked the BMW in the same slot beneath the Munster. The moment he arrived back he knew something had happened. Paula was waiting for him in the hall, an odd expression on her face.

Paula unlocked the door of her bedroom, stood aside, ushered Tweed into the room. He took four paces beyond the doorway, paused for a fraction of a second, then turned to speak to Paula who was relocking the door.

'You might have told me,' he chided her.

'I thought it would be a wonderful surprise.'

'It is.' Tweed turned back to grasp the hand of Newman who had stood up from the chair he'd sat in. 'And how did you find me?' was his first question.

Newman grinned. Nothing wrong with Tweed's mind: his first thought had been that if Newman could find him someone else could.

'It's all right,' he assured him. 'I used a long-shot trick in case I was coming to Freiburg. And I know this town. It was here that I picked up the trail of Kruger – remember, I explained how in my book.'

He took a folded telegram from his pocket, handed it to Tweed. It read: *Gerald seriously ill in St Thomas's, London. Please contact his brother urgently*. The telegram was addressed to Robert Newman, care of Hotel Colombi, Freiburg. Tweed handed the telegram back.

'I don't understand.'

'I sent it from the post office at the main station in Frankfurt, knowing the hotel would hang on to it for a week or two. They gave it to me when I arrived at the Colombi last night. This morning I toured all the smaller hotels, showed them the telegram, then your photograph. No one even questioned what your name was. That telegram acted as a kind of *Open Sesame*, as I thought it would.

120

When I arrived here they told me you booked in last night and called Paula's room. It's a gambit I used several times when I was an active foreign correspondent, tracking someone.'

'Clever.' Tweed sank into a chair, relieved. He reflected that the only two people in the world he could fully trust were now with him.

'Want to hear what I've found out?' Newman asked. 'Kuhlmann, by the way, is on your side. Doesn't believe for a moment you were involved in that murder and rape of a girl . . .'

'Have they identified her yet? I'd never seen her before in my life . . .'

'Paula has told me all you explained to her about that night. Now listen to me. I have to get back to the Colombi to have a crack at Gareth Morgan. Going back to that night in Radnor Walk, I was strolling back from a late party . . .'

While Paula perched on the edge of her bed, Tweed listened with great concentration to every word Newman said. Afterwards he could have written down the whole of the foreign correspondent's account. The warmth of the room steamed up his glasses. As he cleaned them on his handkerchief he recalled he had seen someone else perform the same action. A tall thin man with steel-rimmed glasses who had paused by a parked Mercedes at the edge of the Munsterplatz. Why had that incident come back to him?

'. . . and then we were driven from Freiburg airfield in the police car to the Colombi,' Newman concluded.

'We?'

'Marler flew with me from Frankfurt. Sorry, left that bit out. He's back at the Colombi. I've been keeping him in the dark about what I've been doing . . .'

'Why?' Tweed asked, his eyes alert.

'You'll say it's because I don't like him. Frankly I'm not sure we can trust him on this one.'

'Very wise,' interjected Paula.

'Why don't you trust him?' Tweed prodded.

'The way things are, a lot of people might assume your job will be vacant soon. I've a feeling Marler would very much like to be Deputy Director in your place.'

'It's possible.' Tweed considered for a moment. 'He's ambitious. Nothing wrong with that. I don't think that you're right, but you're sensible to take precautions. I'm a fugitive from justice. Best keep it between the three of us for the moment. Bob, could you go over that scene you witnessed at my apartment that night. Buckmaster was there, you said?'

'Yes. Howard phoned him after he came to the apartment himself.'

'And you said he was the only one who was clean-shaven – that is, looked freshly shaved. At that hour.'

'Yes. What are you driving at?'

'Only that if a man has an assignation with a girl he often takes care to shave himself before they meet.'

'My God!' Newman stood up abruptly. 'You don't mean that it could have been Buckmaster who . . .'

'I don't draw any theoretical conclusions.' Tweed blinked, looked at both his companions. 'I think it's about time you both knew what this is all about. The secret project I mentioned to Paula – without telling her all the details. It affects the whole security of the West.'

Tweed began talking after Newman and Paula had pulled chairs close to him, speaking in a low voice, against the sound of music from the bedside radio he'd switched on. The precaution seemed unnecessary to Newman: Tweed and Paula had arrived only the previous night and without any advance booking. As Tweed went on talking, he understood the reason for Tweed's ultra caution.

'With the aid of two British computer scientists, Arthur

Wilson and Liam Fennan, the Americans have cracked the Strategic Defence Initiative problem. They've found a fairly cheap way of ensuring a defence system can be hoisted into the atmosphere which will guarantee no Soviet rockets launched against the West will get through the screen . . .'

'You mean this system is watertight, absolutely fool-proof?' Newman sounded incredulous.

'They've done exactly that. And Washington accepts it could never have been achieved without the work put in by Wilson and Fennan. To simplify a complex problem, a giant computer called Able One – or *Shockwave* as we call it – has been built. It's really two huge computers linked together, their systems merged like twins. Since we contributed so much Washington is supplying us with the second of the only two *Shockwaves* in existence.'

'How and when?' asked Newman.

'Our *Shockwave* is on the way from the United States. We're going to install it at Fylingdales in Yorkshire. It has one drawback – a limited range. But once the system is functioning we can protect ourselves and the whole of Western Europe. *Shockwave* can detect up to five hundred rockets in flight – and destroy every one within seconds of being launched. The rockets and their payload would detonate over the Soviet Union. It's an amazing – and totally unexpected – breakthrough. The Russians are years behind us.'

'How is it being transported?' Newman pressed.

'That's what worries me. I wanted it brought in by one of the giant transport planes the US have. But someone persuaded the PM that it would be safer with such a huge cargo to bring it across the Atlantic by freighter, the *Lampedusa*.'

'So this is the secret project you referred to,' Paula remarked. 'How many people know about this clandestine voyage?'

'Only three in Britain and three in the US – the President himself, the Chairman of the Joint Chiefs of Staff, Admiral Tremayne, and Cord Dillon, Deputy Director CIA.'

'Where is the *Lampedusa* now?' asked Newman.

'On the high seas. I calculate it's about midway across the Atlantic, and due to berth at Plymouth in the early hours of the morning it arrives. Arrangements have been made to offload *Shockwave* at night, to transfer it to a huge trailer. The police will escort it to Yorkshire. Roads will be closed to give it free passage.'

'You did say that using this freighter worries you. Who are the three people in Britain who know about it? Who persuaded the PM to bring it by sea?'

'Lots of questions.' Tweed gave a wry smile. 'And the three people are the PM, myself and Lance Buckmaster. It was the Minister, Buckmaster, who opted for sea transport.'

No one spoke for a short while. Newman and Paula were absorbing the magnitude of what Tweed had revealed. Tweed checked his watch: they'd be serving early breakfast in the dining-room. But there was more to tell. His tone was calm.

'You had better know everything – in case anything happens to me. Someone else would then have to carry on the task . . .'

'What task?' Paula interjected.

'Patience. We have to communicate with the wireless operator aboard the *Lampedusa* as soon as we can – to check that all is well. The crew has been hand-picked by Cord Dillon, Deputy Director of the CIA. He personally vetted every man. Dillon, as you know, is an old colleague of mine. In London I had a secret system of communication by radio with their wireless op.'

124

He opened his battered briefcase, took out a thick code book.

'We have a system of code signals to be exchanged at specific intervals. I am Monitor. Buckmaster also personally has the code system – he uses the Admiralty's communication network. I used our high-tech communications system in our other building further along Park Crescent. At nine in the evening I called the *Lampedusa* – the evening of the murder at Radnor Walk – and all was well.' He looked at both of them. 'I'm now telling you something no one else in the world must know. Unknown to anyone except Dillon and the wireless op aboard, I invented a simple check system. I insert into the communication the signal "Tray" – not Troy. The wireless op should then respond with "Helen is OK". The second trick signal is "White". The response from the *Lampedusa*, if all is well, should be a reference to "Cowes" – the yachting port on the Isle of Wight. Buckmaster has no knowledge of this secret check system. Now, you both know something about codes. See if this makes sense.'

He handed the code book first to Newman and sat back while the foreign correspondent studied it. Newman nodded, handed it on to Paula.

'You've kept it simple. One question. The wireless op aboard that vessel presumably has a duplicate of this code book?'

'He has . . .'

'But does *his* code book contain the two trick signals with the required responses?'

'No, it doesn't,' Tweed replied. 'He carries that data only in his memory. Cord Dillon agreed that would be safer.'

'Seems quite clear to me,' Paula said, handing back the code book. 'But it seems useless to me now – you can't contact the *Lampedusa* because you've no equipment to transmit a signal.'

'You're right. At the moment.' Tweed paused. 'But if I can get Arthur Beck's cooperation I can use his high-powered transceivers from either Zürich or Berne . . .'

'That's assuming Beck is as helpful as Kuhlmann,' she pointed out. 'Which is a highly dangerous assumption. Arthur Beck is, after all, head of the Swiss Federal Police.'

'And I've further bad news,' Newman told him. 'Kuhlmann warned in Frankfurt that an alert has been sent to all frontier posts on the East German, Czech and Swiss borders.'

'East German and Czech?' Tweed sounded stunned. 'Why those borders?'

'Because someone has spread the rumour you're fleeing to the East.'

'That someone has been very busy.' Tweed looked unusually grim. 'But there is a roundabout way I might be able to slip across the frontier into Switzerland, then contact Beck. The hounds have been loosed on me, so it won't be easy.' He looked at Paula. 'I think we ought to split up. You stay with Newman and I'll go on alone . . .'

'Forget it!' she snapped. 'I've come with you this far. If you think you can just drop me overboard you've lost your marbles . . .'

'And,' Newman broke in, 'it took me one hell of a job tracing you. Face it, you need help. Think of *Shockwave*, of what is at stake. We worked as a team on other dangerous operations in London – but nothing as vitally important as this.'

'You're right, of course.' Tweed spread his hands in a gesture of surrender. 'We'll work together again. Now I have to decide our next move – and fast. Freiburg could turn into a trap.'

'And it could be a great mistake to leave here now,' Paula persisted. 'From what Bob has told us I'm convinced Buckmaster and World Security is behind this. They may well be watching all the exits from Freiburg.'

'She's right,' Newman agreed. 'Some of those cars involved in the big pile-up contained World Security men who were following you. And they have an office in Freiburg. Quite close to the Colombi, I noticed.'

'Breakfast first,' Tweed decided. 'I'll think better after a good meal. And Paula hasn't eaten for hours either. What are you going to do, Bob? Join us?'

'No. Just promise me you'll stay here. Good. I'm going back to the Colombi. I'm looking forward to a cosy little chat with Mr Gareth Morgan . . .'

On the first floor of the World Security building near the Colombi, Morgan sat in the local commander's office with Horowitz. It was a conceit of Buckmaster's originating from his days with the Airborne Division that he conferred pseudo-military titles on top personnel. In Freiburg the top man was 'Commander' Ken Crombie, a stern-faced thirty-year-old who had served in the same airborne division as Buckmaster. Morgan loathed him, was waiting for the first excuse to remove him, but concealed his dislike. Sitting offside to Crombie's desk he gave an oily smile.

'I'm very pleased with the way you're running this apparatus. The fact that you speak German makes you the perfect man for the job. And I gather you have stationed cars at all exits from Freiburg to watch out for Tweed's Mercedes?'

Horowitz grunted. 'Fat lot of good that will do. Tweed is nobody's fool. He's changed the Mercedes for a BMW again.' He reached for a pad in front of Crombie, used his pen to write neatly on it, pushed it back across the desk.

'That's the registration number they should be looking for. You'd better get on the blower, Crombie. Your cars do have radio contact, I presume?'

'You're sure about this information . . .' Crombie's general air of pompous self-confidence faded as his eyes met

Horowitz's. He jumped up. 'Excuse me', he said to Morgan, 'while I dash to the communications centre . . .'

'How did you come up with that?' demanded Morgan.

'I spent over two hours early this morning checking every Mercedes parked in Freiburg. No sign of Tweed's vehicle. Then I toured the car-hire people, showed them an insurance certificate in the name Weber. Told them a Mercedes with Tweed's registration number had ground up against my car when he overtook. Naturally the agency he'd handed it back to immediately checked the car for damage. While the receptionist was absent I checked his record book. There it was in black and white. The Merc changed for a BMW. In the name of James Gage. So now we know who we're looking for. I'll be touring all over Freiburg looking for that BMW when I leave here. Which I think should be now . . .'

Morgan sat thinking for several minutes before Crombie returned. Horowitz was like a machine, relentless until he'd completed his assignment. Even Morgan found it frightening.

'You've contacted them all?' he asked when Crombie came back. 'Good. We might have thought of checking the car-hire people ourselves. I'm off for some breakfast.'

And in my report, he thought as he climbed the steps of the Colombi, I'll put that *Crombie* might have thought of that but he didn't.

'Mind if I join you? Shortage of places.'

Morgan was piling fried eggs and bacon into his mouth when he looked up. He chewed the food for longer than was necessary. He immediately recognized the man sitting opposite as Robert Newman, foreign correspondent. His picture had appeared in the newspapers often enough. He concealed his sense of shock by taking his time plastering a piece of toast with butter. Then he smiled and buttered up his companion instead of the toast.

'Don't I know you? Yes, it's coming back to me. You're the famous correspondent who broke the Kruger scandal and wrote that blockbuster of a book afterwards. Made you rich. Good for you. I was a green security guard at the time.'

'But you've come a long way since, Morgan, weaselling your way up to the top. MD of World Security. Buckmaster's trusted servant.'

Newman ordered one fried egg and bacon from the waiter who had appeared, said he'd have coffee. Morgan had stopped eating, was wiping his thick lips with his napkin when Newman looked at him again, smiling affably.

'I don't like your language, Newman. Weaselling and servant were the words you used, I believe.' His expression and tone were ugly. He recovered quickly. He had to find out what Newman was doing, where he was staying. 'First thing in the morning,' he went on, 'I never am at my best until I've had breakfast.' He smiled again. 'Your reputation for getting a story is international. What might you be working on now? Another Kruger to chase?'

'You might say that. A different form of Kruger. But in the field of fraud again, yes.'

It had been a shot in the dark, the first thing which came into Newman's head. The reaction surprised him. Morgan's eyes stared at him as though he could hardly believe he'd heard correctly. For a moment he was at a loss for something to say. Then the crocodile smile appeared again.

'You're staying here – or just in for the excellent breakfast they serve?'

'Oh, yes, I'm staying here, as you are. Department of coincidence. How is the security business? Tell me, do you often cooperate with the police?'

'Depends.' Morgan gave himself time to think. That also

was near the mark – bearing in mind Kuhlmann's troops had also been following Tweed. This was a dangerous opponent – Morgan decided to deal with him aggressively, to frighten him, but Newman struck first.

'I've heard rumours that a British agent is on his way to the East, identity unknown.' Newman leaned across the table his voice low, grim. 'What intrigues me is where those rumours came from, who started them? You mentioned Kruger – well, I hunted him down and I'm going to hunt down whoever initiated these rumours. And more important, why?'

'Sounds like a dangerous mission . . .' Morgan began.

'Very dangerous. For the guilty men. I smell a conspiracy. I hear the police are investigating World Security . . .'

'That's a lie . . .'

'Well, you should certainly recognize one.' Newman switched moods, became amiable. 'And this isn't the first time that the police have been interested in you. There was that case of high-tech equipment being smuggled into East Germany – at least your organization attempted it and then failed.'

'You just listen to me for a moment.' Morgan had regained his self-control. He spoke in measured tones. 'You have a reputation for working on your own. A lone wolf is what you have been called. One day you'll come up against something you can't handle. It will blow up in your face.'

'You mean a car bomb?' Newman enquired casually.

'I never said anything of the sort. I didn't ask you to sit at my table. If you must stay there, shut up.'

'Just thought I'd warn you,' Newman continued in the same affable manner. He drank some coffee. 'After all, your job is on the block. Buckmaster drops people who become an embarrassment to him. Doesn't give them a second thought, however long they've served him. And you've just dropped butter on your suit.'

Morgan glanced down, used his napkin to wipe the butter from his sleeve. He forced himself to eat more toast and marmalade. He felt badly shaken. He never knew the details of how Horowitz carried out his assignments, but there had been a case of a car blowing up a hostile director of a company Buckmaster had taken over. And Newman's use of the word 'conspiracy' had rattled him.

He looked round the restaurant where most of the tables were occupied. A short slim man in his thirties sat by himself. Morgan's eyes passed over him. The presence of Marler meant nothing to him.

Within minutes of returning to his room, Newman heard a gentle tapping on his door. It was Marler, wearing a bulky raincoat. Newman told him to sit down, asked if he was going somewhere.

'Yes. Here. From my room.' He slipped off the raincoat, felt inside one of the pockets. 'This was the best way to conceal this.' He produced the special compact camera developed by the boffins in the Engine Room in the Park Crescent basement.

'Handy little gadget,' Marler went on. 'Easy to hide and when you take photographs it develops and prints them within a minute.' He extracted two prints from his breast pocket, perched them on Newman's lap.

'Where did you get these?'

'You weren't the only one up early this morning. I tapped on your door, no answer, so I guessed you'd gone out. I went out myself. I positioned myself where I couldn't be seen but I'd a perfect view of the entrance to the World Security offices down the street. Those are pictures of three men who left or entered the building separately.'

'I see.' Newman masked his puzzlement by studying the three prints. Was Marler cleverly trying to build up confidence? He felt uncertain, but still not sure enough to reveal to the agent Tweed's whereabouts.

Marler, reading his mind, watched him with amusement. Sooner or later he'd gain Newman's trust. He'd no doubt about his ability to do that.

'This one is Gareth Morgan, the man I set out to shake to the core at breakfast,' Newman eventually remarked. 'The other two I don't know. I don't like the look of the tall man with steel-rimmed glasses.'

'Your sixth sense is getting quite good. Keep working at it. You're looking at Armand Horowitz, a Mittel-European, and one of the world's most successful assassins. A real pro, Armand. No suspicion has ever attached itself to him and yet my contacts tell me he's killed at least fifteen men. All for a big fee. And in every case the murder was passed off as an accident.'

'How do you know all this – if he's kept under cover so well?'

'Never believe a word anyone says, do you?'

'Not without positive corroboration. I was an active foreign correspondent once – and noted for reliability.'

Marler sighed. 'All right. Once Tweed sent me underground. I posed as the finest marksman in Europe, for sale only for a monumentally high price. We even built up a "background" for me – I was supposed to have knocked off several top political and industrial figures. I got lucky – I was hired for a job which put me on the inside of a gang of monsters Tweed was after. The man who hired me told me if I'd refused he'd have hired Armand Horowitz.'

'And you think Morgan has hired him to take out a fresh target?'

'Obvious, I'd have thought. His target is Tweed.'

more cheese. It took precedence that moment when he retreated to the alcove. Tweed's handkerchief was soaked. . . .
Bottin, watching the sound of footsteps from the railway
track echoes no in the tunnel, gradual he re-
emit his hand through his smeared. . . .

13

Later that day, just before twilight, a carload of four
armed World Security men saw Tweed's BMW leaving
Freiburg, heading south on the E 35 autobahn towards
Switzerland. As the Mercedes began its pursuit, Savage,
the driver, a man in his thirties, gave the order to his
companion in the front passenger seat.

'Warn HQ immediately . . .'

His companion picked up the microphone. They had a
direct radio link on a high-frequency waveband. He gave
the day's call signal.

'Champagne here. Eiger now proceeding south on
E 35. We are escorting. Over and out.'

Listening to the amplified message in the communications complex in the basement of World Security HQ near
the Colombi, Horowitz pursed his thin lips. He had
caught the note of triumph in the operator's voice. Beside
him sat Eva Hendrix.

The large basement room had a clinical appearance,
the walls painted white, the steel tables supporting every
type of sophisticated apparatus. Including the satellite
system for receiving messages from the dish perched on
the building's roof.

'I wonder,' commented Horowitz and stood up.

'What's the matter?' asked Hendrix. 'We've got him.
And you were right – you said you thought Eiger would
head for Switzerland.'

Eiger was the code name Horowitz had given for
Tweed. Hendrix also stood up and slipped on her fur-

lined jacket. She wore underneath it a thick polo-necked sweater, a loose skirt and knee-length boots with flat heels. She guessed Horowitz was ready to leave. They had an Audi waiting for them outside.

'We're joining Savage?' she asked.

'Yes. It's the only thing to do at this stage. I can catch them up on the autobahn.'

Savage pressed his foot down as the Tweed BMW increased speed suddenly. There was a one-hundred-yard gap between the two vehicles and they had the autobahn to themselves. The speedometer on the dashboard of the Mercedes crept up from 140 k.p.h. to above 150 k.p.h. – approximately one hundred miles per hour.

'What's he up to?' asked the passenger in the front seat as he extracted a Luger .45 from his briefcase.

'Trying to shake us. He won't. Get ready. At this speed he'll go clear off the autobahn.'

Savage calculated they were approaching a long wide curve, the ideal spot for the killing ground. And still there was no other traffic on the autobahn. It was the time of day.

The previous day Savage had been behind the wheel of his silver Mercedes driving *ahead* of Tweed minutes before the catastrophic pile-up. Which is why he'd escaped undamaged, even alive. The bones of his lean face were taut with concentration. A tough Geordie from Newcastle, he had his eye on Evans's job. Too soft for this type of work. If he could eliminate Tweed he'd score a lot of Brownie points with Morgan.

'I'm going to close the gap, so be ready,' he warned his companion.

'He's crossing into the next lane? Why?'

'I'm going to close the gap. Get ready, I said . . .'

The man with the Luger pressed the button which

lowered his window. Air hammered inside the car like the slipstream of an aircraft taking off. The forearm of the hand holding the Luger rested firmly on the window edge. He took careful aim as the Mercedes rushed forward, the gap closed.

Behind the wheel of the BMW, Newman kept glancing in his rear view mirror. He nodded to Marler by his side.

'They're falling for it. Up to you.'

Marler used the seat retracting lever, pushed himself back to the fullest extent. They were alone in the car. Marler pressed down the arm-rest, began wriggling and squeezing himself through the gap between the two seats. Only a man as small and slim as Marler could have conducted the manoeuvre.

As Marler slithered into the rear of the car Newman increased his speed further, drawing away from the pursuing Mercedes for several seconds. Which distracted the man with the Luger who was about to press the trigger. The range had altered, become too great. He glanced at Savage, but the driver was already stepping up his own speed.

In the rear of the BMW Marler hauled the sniperscope rifle he'd obtained from his friend outside Freiburg from under the travelling rugs. He released the safety catch, lowered the window on the right side. The two cars remained in their different lanes but the gap was again closing.

It was closing because Newman had seen in his mirror that Marler was in position. He had gently lost speed. Even the small reduction in tempo was closing the gap in seconds. Inside the Mercedes Savage smiled thinly. Jerry would wait with his Luger until suddenly they were within yards of the BMW. The gun held eight rounds. Jerry would empty the weapon. At least two shots were bound

135

to find their target. In his mirror he saw another vehicle coming up behind him in the distance, its headlights like two small eyes. To hell with it. They'd be away, long gone before it arrived . . .

Approaching the Mercedes from the rear Horowitz sat in the passenger seat, a pair of night-glasses pressed against his eyes, his steel-rimmed spectacles pushed up over his forehead. Behind the wheel Hendrix was demonstrating that when a woman driver is good she's very good.

Horowitz lowered his binoculars, sat relaxed with them in his lap. Hendrix glanced at him.

'What's going to happen?'

'Exactly what I am wondering.'

She didn't say any more. Horowitz was not a man you questioned. She always had the impression of iron self-control. And he could spend hours travelling with some-one without saying one word. She could read nothing from his expression. Suddenly he leaned forward. She had a sensation of intense concentration. He spoke tersely.

'Drive a little faster. But keep a good distance behind that Mercedes.'

Inside the BMW Marler had kept the barrel out of sight below the level of the window. He looped the strap round the handle of the door to give maximum stability. The Mercedes was rushing towards them like a torpedo. The Luger was fired twice. There was no chance to fire it a third time.

Marler raised the muzzle, the front right tyre of the Mercedes leapt into his sight, he fired four times. Two of the high explosive bullets he'd fed into the rifle hit their mark. The target wheel unsheathed lengths of rubber, scattered them over the snowbound highway. Savage felt the car going out of control, slithering into a lethal skid, compounded by the speed at which he was travelling. The

136

Mercedes skated across the autobahn, swivelling in a half-circle. The rear struck the crash barrier with immense force, smashed through it and then the vehicle turned over and over on its sides, rolling across a field. It was slowing down when it burst into flames, became a fireball, lighting up the night like a small bomb detonating.

Black oily smoke rose from the funeral pyre as Newman continued to drive on. Marler reloaded the rifle after closing the window. He lit one of his king-size cigarettes.

'Good shooting,' Newman observed.

'Fair to middling. I suspect only two out of four hit the mark. It should have been at least three . . .'

'Well, you saved us. I'm taking the next turn-off, returning to Freiburg.'

'Jolly good idea. I'm getting a bit peckish.'

'That was horrible,' Eva Hendrix gasped as she slowed down, worried about skid-marks as they passed the fireball.

'It was worse. It was amateurish,' Horowitz commented. 'I find it pathetic. They *will* send boys to do men's work. And keep your speed as it is – I'm watching the northbound lane.'

She glanced at him again and he sat with his back pressed hard against his seat. He was holding the night glasses close to his eyes again, scanning the empty northbound lanes of the autobahn.

'Expecting something?' she asked, then wished she hadn't spoken.

'Yes,' Horowitz replied simply.

Several cars skimmed past on the northbound lanes. Horowitz scanned the registration numbers of each car which was a BMW. About ten minutes later he grunted as a pair of headlights appeared and sped towards them. The registration number came up clearly. Two men in the car. One driving, one smoking in the back. Neither of them Tweed. Of course. The car raced past, was gone.

'Take the next turn-off. Then drive us back to Freiburg. You can press your dainty foot down,' Horowitz suggested.

'What's happening? Where's Tweed?'

'If I were Tweed I'd have gone only one way. East out of Freiburg into the Black Forest. And Evans will have called off the watchdogs at the Freiburg exits. Another amateur . . .'

It gave Horowitz no pleasure to find he was right when they'd arrived back at World Security HQ on Rotteck Ring. Evans explained as he poured drinks in his office for Hendrix and himself.

'Once I had the report the BMW had been spotted I called in the operatives from the other exit points. The cost of running a total lookout like that is considerable. All those involved are on overtime. And we've been ordered to cut costs.'

'By whom, if I may enquire? No, nothing for me,' Horowitz remarked when offered a drink.

'By Morgan. Nothing else you require, I imagine? I gather Savage is continuing to track Eiger? We've had no radio report from him for a while.'

Horowitz gave Hendrix a warning glance. Keep your mouth shut. Let Evans find out another of his teams was *kaput* in due course. Maybe he'd have to talk fast to the police. That was what he was paid for.

'Where is Morgan now?' he enquired.

'Pushed off back to London, didn't he? Flew there in the Lear jet from Freiburg. Went as though the hounds of hell were after him.'

'Maybe he felt they were.'

It was a relief to Horowitz to hear Morgan was hundreds of miles away. Now perhaps he could do the job he'd been paid for without interruption. He stared at Evans who was consuming a large Scotch. These people drank too much.

'You asked if there was anything else I required,' he reminded him. 'Yes, there is. I need five of your German shepherd tracker dogs. With German handlers. The fiercer the better. I want them now. Plus an unmarked wired van to transport them.'

'That would leave me without guard dogs,' Evans protested. 'I have only five left in reserve. The rest are hired out . . .'

'I said I needed five. So that's fine.' Horowitz was still gazing at Evans whose eyes dropped. 'I understood that Morgan had told you to supply me with anything I wanted.'

'That's correct, but I didn't expect to be left without any dogs. We've quoted for a contract which includes those animals . . .'

'Then you'd better inform your potential customer he'll have to do without guard dogs.'

'And I have no unmarked van with a wired compartment left,' Evans informed him with scarcely concealed satisfaction.

'Go and buy one. A station wagon. Preferably a Volvo. And get your technical department to build a wire cage in the rear compartment for the dogs. I'll need the vehicle ready five hours from now.' He saw Evans open his mouth to protest. His tone became cold. 'Do I have to tell you how to fulfil a simple request like that quickly? You're supposed to hold down your job because you're effective.'

Evans's ruddy face became redder still. He sat behind his desk, picked up the phone and gave the instructions in German. He told the man he was speaking to he needed the vehicle ready in four hours, slammed down the phone.

'That's better,' Horowitz commented softly. 'Now I want you to take Hendrix and myself to that side office overlooking the operations room. The office with a one-way mirror so we can watch.'

'And what precisely would you like to watch?' Evans snapped.

Horowitz continued as though he hadn't heard the interruption.

'Assemble in the operations room all the men who were watching the other exits from Freiburg – all except those checking the one Eiger left by. You had a large-scale map to control the operation? Good. Put that on a wall where I can see it from the one-way mirror window. What time did Savage report in on his radio that he'd spotted Tweed's BMW leaving, that he was starting to follow the vehicle?'

'At exactly 4.15 p.m.'

'Thank you. When you have assembled all the watchers, find out the times they left their exits. In which sequence. There'd be a few minutes' delay between one radio message being transmitted and the next.'

'I'll have to call some of them back. They'll have gone off duty . . .'

'Then call them back.'

'I don't see what you're getting at,' Hendrix ventured as she sat down inside the office next to the operations room with another glass of vodka.

Horowitz stood, hands in his coat pocket, staring through the 'window' which had a mirror on the other side, making it impossible for the men gathering in the operations room to see him. On the table where Hendrix sat was perched a two-way microphone which would enable Horowitz to communicate with Evans when the conference started.

'The whole thing was a cock-up,' he said, standing with his back to Hendrix. 'Cobbled together without proper research and planning. It was Tweed who did the planning. Neither of the two men in that BMW we saw speeding back up the north lane to Freiburg was Tweed. The key time is 4.15 p.m.'

'I still don't get it : . .'

'And neither does Evans, I'm sure,' Horowitz said sardonically. 'I'm certain now that there was synchronization of watches between Tweed and the two men in the BMW. Timed to the minute – so when the BMW was spotted leaving Freiburg by Savage – and reported to this operations room – Tweed drove out of Freiburg ten minutes later at the outside.'

'But which way?'

'That is what I am attempting to discover. The vital time span is approximately 4.15 p.m. to 4.25 p.m. – say 4.30 p.m. at the latest. We have to hope one of those watchers was observant even after he'd heard the bird had flown. And I must remind Evans of something else . . .'

He walked back to the table with his deliberate tread, picked up the microphone, pressed the switch and spoke to Evans who stood looking at the enlarged wall map of Freiburg while operatives entered and sat in the rows of chairs facing the wall.

'Evans,' Horowitz said into the mike, 'you haven't forgotten the screen for projecting the target's picture?'

'It's being brought in at this moment,' Evans responded in a terse edgy tone.

'Show it first when everyone is seated, please . . .'

The lights in the operations room went out as Horowitz began speaking. The twenty operatives, all men, stirred restlessly. The amplifier added a curiously sinister, eerie tone to Horowitz's voice. The projectionist flashed

Tweed's picture on the screen. A head-and-shoulders three-quarter view, his face in repose. Horowitz spoke again, still standing, holding the mike close to his lips which distorted his speech to a sibilant hiss.

'All of you were waiting at your designated exits from Freiburg. You were on the lookout for this man, Eiger, travelling in a BMW with a specific registration number.' Horowitz paused.

From where he stood he saw rows of the backs of heads tilted upwards, staring fixedly at the screen. The projectionist was holding the image of Tweed steady. Horowitz waited, hoping the image imprinted on their minds would trigger off a memory. He continued speaking.

'I want you to wipe out of your minds any thought of that BMW. The vital time is between 4.15 p.m. and 4.30 p.m. – the period when you were being released from duty, no longer on the lookout. But even as you waited, maybe smoked a cigarette before returning to base, you subconsciously saw another car.'

He paused again, allowing them to soak up each statement before adding further data to their minds. He spoke again. His voice had an almost hypnotic effect on his audience as they sat motionless.

'Another car, but a different make. Not a BMW. Probably not a Mercedes. And inside that car was Eiger, the man who you see now on the screen. Think back, gentlemen. Please concentrate.'

'I just drove straight back to HQ,' a voice reported.

'At what time?' Horowitz demanded.

'At exactly 4.20 p.m. when I received the order over the radio to abandon surveillance.'

'One of you may well have seen this man,' Horowitz persisted. 'He could have been dressed in any garb. Maybe he wore some kind of headgear to change his appearance . . .'

'An astrakhan fur hat,' another voice called out

excitedly. 'That's what he wore. I thought the features were familiar.'

'Where did you see him? What vehicle was he driving?'

'A blue Audi. I was stationed at the Schwabentor, at the edge of the Altstadt. He came from the direction of the Konvikstrasse and turned away from the city along the Schwarzwaldstrasse. I'm sorry, but at the time the fur hats fooled me. In any case, we'd been called off duty, so I guessed someone else had picked him up.'

'No need to apologize. Have you any idea of the time when you made that sighting?'

'I can tell you exactly. It was 4.30 p.m. – I monitored it for the record. The radio signal had just come through to return to base.'

'You used the word "hats" – in the plural. Why?' Horowitz prodded gently.

'Because the girl sitting beside him also wore a fur hat.'

'Thank you for your help, gentlemen. That is all for now.'

Horowitz switched off the microphone and turned to Hendrix who had just finished her vodka.

'If you need another drink, make it coffee. We want clear heads for tonight.'

'Tonight?' she asked. 'That sounds like no sleep.'

'I don't need sleep.' Horowitz sat down opposite her and made a clenched fist gesture. 'It all fits. As I suspected, Tweed did the planning. He foresaw all the exits would be watched. He handed over his BMW to two other men and it acted as the decoy vehicle. At 4.15 p.m. It leaves Freiburg and drives south down the E 35 autobahn. Savage reports he has tabbed it. Evans falls for the trick, calls off all other watchers one by one. Fifteen minutes later Tweed is driving the new vehicle he has hired – an Audi – out of the city. Everything was carefully synchronized by Tweed. He calculated radio cars would be used, that within fifteen minutes other exits would be left unguarded. Even the route he took is significant.'

'Why?' Hendrix asked.

'Because he is heading for where I would head for if I were in his position. Along the Schwarzwaldstrasse – and then deep into the heart of the snowbound Black Forest. We must get on his trail quickly . . .'

Horowitz was walking to the door when Hendrix asked her question.

'But how do we go about it? The Black Forest is enormous – and the snow won't help.'

'The snow *will* help,' Horowitz rasped, showing the first signs of impatience with a mind slower than his own. 'We have one helicopter here. We will bring in more from Frankfurt, from Basle. We will scour the Black Forest from the air. And the snow may well locate Tweed because it will reveal tracks – the tracks of an Audi turning up a side road into the trees, the foot tracks of Tweed and his friend when they leave the Audi to seek shelter. According to the met forecast – which you heard yourself before we came down into the basement – all the roads south from the forest to Switzerland are impassable. I would appreciate it if you would move fast . . .'

'But what are we going to do?' she persisted as she followed him with quick footsteps.

He turned at the bottom of the stairs.

'We are going to ensure Evans provides tracker dogs which are killers. We shall travel in the Volvo with radio contact to all the choppers searching through the night. Must I spell it out in words of two syllables? We are organizing a vast dragnet, a manhunt.'

14

Gareth Morgan's Lear jet landed at London Airport early in the evening. He was amiable with Customs and Passport Control and they passed him through quickly. His mood changed as he settled himself in the rear of the waiting limousine and told the chauffeur, Hanson, to make all speed to HQ in Threadneedle Street.

'Those officials get on my wick. They know me but still I have to go through their bureaucratic formalities. Put a man in a uniform and he thinks he's God.'

'Yes, sir,' responded the uniformed chauffeur. Typical of Morgan to overlook the implied insult. But it was Morgan who paid him a fat bonus every Christmas in cash out of subsidiary research. Which meant the money was never accounted for – and that Hanson didn't declare the two thousand pounds for tax.

'What's been going on in my absence?' Morgan demanded of his private spy.

He stared out into the night. It was dry, cold and the sky was studded with huge diamonds. Oncoming headlights had an unusual clarity and power. Morgan lit a Havana while he absorbed the chauffeur's confidential report.

'Mrs Buckmaster has been spending a lot of time in her office checking various files . . .'

'What files?'

Morgan was instantly alert. He leaned forward over his now noticeable paunch. The doctor had said he ate too much and drank to excess. Stuff him!

'Well, sir, I used the duplicate key you had made for me to Mrs Buckmaster's office when she was out to lunch recently. Her desk was covered with files from our companies all over the world. Australia, America, South Africa, various countries in Western Europe. They were full of columns of figures. I took the liberty to use the camera you gave me to photograph some of the pages at random.' The chauffeur handed over his shoulder a plastic box. 'You could see for yourself on the scanner . . .'

Morgan prised off the lid with one hand, clenched the cigar between his teeth, took out the first cut film and inserted it inside the scanner attached to the roof of the rear compartment. He switched on the light, adjusted the focus, turning a small wheel. The figures on the page came up clearly.

He inserted a dozen pages, aware that Hanson was watching his expression in the rear-view mirror. He let nothing of his sense of shock show, but when the last page came up he swore to himself.

'Something wrong, sir?' enquired the chauffeur who had acute hearing.

Hanson was in his late forties. A good-looking man, his voice well-educated, he'd taken on this job after a chance meeting with Morgan in a bar. An excellent driver, he lacked application and had failed to pursue his studies to become an accountant. But he still had the ability to read a balance sheet.

'You looked at these?' Morgan asked in a mild voice.

'Had to, sir – to make sure they'd come out well. Not all of them, but they make interesting reading, I thought. Oh, if you could see your way to increasing my bonus this year. What with inflation, and the mortgage interest payments . . .'

'Consider it done.'

'That's very generous of you, sir.'

Hanson smirked in the mirror and Morgan had an

146

almost uncontrollable desire to hit him hard. It wasn't the fact that Hanson was driving – although at that moment they were stopped in a traffic jam – which forced Morgan to smile back. He recognized immediately that Hanson had grasped the significance of what he had photographed.

'Not at all.' Morgan smiled again, an oily smile.'You are a great asset to the company. Merit should be rewarded.'

Today's friends are tomorrow's enemies, he reminded himself. One of his favourite maxims. Only trust people for as long as it is in your interests to trust them. Soon he would have to dispose of Hanson. But in a way which rendered him neutered as a potential hostile force. Well, he'd managed that more times than he could add up. He smiled and nodded to Hanson as the car moved again.

'There is one other thing, sir,' Hanson continued, satisfied that he'd made his point about the bonus. 'Mrs Buckmaster has been closeted for hours with Ted Doyle. I don't mean anything naughty,' he added with exaggerated respect.

'Any idea what they've been doing?'

Morgan made his tone casual. He stared out of the window to avoid meeting Hanson's eyes in the mirror, showing too eager an interest. And Hanson was now definitely for the chop – he'd held back this juicy bit until he was sure Morgan would play along on the bonus issue. Which amounted to a devious form of blackmail, the kind of tactic Morgan used on others. He was furious a mere chauffeur should hold him up.

'I've had to take in sandwiches and coffee several times,' Hanson continued. 'Doyle was sitting alongside Mrs Buckmaster at her desk. They had a lot of leather-bound ledgers in different colours in front of them.'

147

'Doesn't tell me much, Morgan commented. 'Get to HQ fast as you can . . .'

The information told him a great deal and he was even more furious. Leonora had obtained the top secret ledgers showing the financial position of major World Security offices all over the world. And Doyle, who should have kept them hidden, was cooperating with her. Doubtless angling for a seat on the board.

It never occurred to Morgan that Doyle might be honestly worried about the position of Lance Buckmaster's empire. Honesty was a motive foreign to Morgan's way of thinking.

It was nearly 8 p.m. when Hanson drove down Threadneedle Street. No traffic about. Morgan craned his neck to look up at the eighteenth floor. It was a blaze of lights. He frowned. Could Leonora still be in her chairman's office at this hour?

Alighting from the limousine in the underground garage, he told Hanson to wait. Using his special key, he inserted it into the slot beside the elevator. Within seconds the high-speed elevator arrived. He stopped inside, pressed the button, got out at the eighteenth floor and paused as the doors closed behind him. He'd left his case in the car and stood there in his dark overcoat, listening. The silence of an almost empty building at night hit him. He headed for Leonora's office.

He had almost reached the suite when the door opened, Ted Doyle walked out, carrying a red leatherbound ledger, closed it and looked up in a surprise as Morgan waited for him a dozen feet from the sound-proof door.

'Mr Morgan! I had no idea you were due back . . .'

'I guessed that.' Morgan took hold of the red ledger, pulled it from Doyle's grasp, tucked it under his arm. 'What are you doing with this in my absence?'

Doyle was a tall, lanky man in his thirties with a lean, clever face and pebble glasses. A top flight accountant and the man Morgan had on his agenda for dismissal under a cloud when the right opportunity occurred. Something to do with money missing and fiddling the figures was needed. Doyle had to be discredited to the outside world when he left. The fact that this would ruin him never crossed Morgan's mind. The world was a jungle; survival of the fittest, the most ruthless, the only law.

'Simply casting an eye over some figures,' Doyle replied.

'Nice to know someone is holding the fort.' Morgan smiled, patted the accountant on the shoulder with his free hand. 'I'll hang on to this for the moment.'

He was walking away when he turned back.

'Oh, Doyle, I may want to chat with you later this evening. So maybe you could wait for me in your office? Get some food sent in to stay the pangs of hunger.'

He smiled again and unlocked the door of his own office. Once inside his expression became grim. Something drastic had to be done about Ted Doyle. And soon. He locked the ledger in his desk after studying at it.

Taking off his coat, he went into his private washroom, cleaned himself up, brushed his thick dark hair, buttoned up his jacket and left his office. He walked slowly towards Leonora's suite. Outside the closed entrance door the red light glowed. *No admittance. In conference.* That had been while she was talking to Doyle. He tapped on the door. The light turned green. He walked inside.

Leonora Buckmaster sat behind her large desk facing him. She sat very erect. The only illumination, a desk light, caught the golden glints in her blonde hair. Her expression was cold and frozen. She gave no sign of being glad to see her managing director. Open in front of her was a green ledger.

'What are you doing here at this hour?' she asked.

Morgan gave her his best smile. 'Just back from touring some of the European offices. Came straight here from the airport.'

'Did you by any chance examine the books at these European offices?'

'I didn't go there for that. I was checking on the latest contracts.'

Including, he thought, the contract with Horowitz to kill Tweed.

'You do know we're pretty near bankrupt?'

It was Morgan's turn to freeze. Inwardly he cursed Doyle for cooperating in his absence. Her statement – the fact that she now knew – was a body blow. He managed to look surprised and pulled a chair up to face her.

'No, I don't know anything of the sort, Leonora. Has that crazy accountant been misinterpreting the figures again?'

'The figures speak for themselves. My father did teach me to read balance sheets – even doctored ones.'

'So, Doyle has been fooling around with the figures . . .'

'Doyle has been showing me the position here, in Australia, the States, in South Africa – and Western Europe.'

'But then he doesn't know about the loan for five hundred mil I'm negotiating. Kind of changes the picture, wouldn't you agree? May I smoke a cigar?'

She was so stunned she didn't object. He clipped off the end, took his time about lighting the cigar with a match, running it round the tip. A display of supreme confidence.

'And may I ask where this gigantic loan is coming from? The banks won't lend us one more red cent. That I *do* know. So what is the source of this loan?'

'You will learn in due course. Part of the deal is complete confidentiality . . .'

'It was my money which started this company . . .' Leonora took a deep breath. She had been going to add that she now thought that was why Lance had married her. But she detested Morgan and had no intention of exposing her private life to him. She had successfully concealed her intense dislike of Morgan and forced herself to relax.

Morgan puffed at his cigar. He sensed he had her over a barrel. Once again he'd played his cards right. The ironic factor in the situation was that Morgan had no idea where the loan was coming from. That was something Buckmaster had not revealed during their conversation at Tavey Grange. Morgan's innate cunning caused him to phrase the next phase of their conversation carefully.

'Fortunately we have a brilliant accountant in Ted Doyle. I'm sure he realizes the present problem and will be discreet.'

'I'm sure of it too.' Leonora played with her gold pen. 'Ted is a loyal member of the company. I trust him completely.'

Morgan nodded to conceal the shock he felt. She had just confirmed that Doyle knew World Security was heading for the rocks. Very drastic action would have to be taken. There was now the risk that Doyle would confide in one of his City friends. If he did, that was the end of World Security.

'If there's nothing else to discuss, I think I'll go back to my office, just glance over what came in while I was away. Then I'm off home for some sleep – something I didn't get much of while I was abroad.'

'Those trips are tiring,' Leonora agreed and smiled. 'You push yourself too hard, Gareth. Try to pace yourself a bit.'

'You're probably right.' Morgan held his cigar in his

hand as he stood up, walked round the desk and kissed her on the cheek. She endured his closeness without flinching. 'And maybe you should go home,' he suggested as he walked towards the door.

'I think you're right. It's getting late.'

As Morgan closed the door her pleasant expression changed. I must find a way to dump him overboard, she thought. She was the chairman, after all, she considered as she opened her compact and dabbed on powder furiously where Morgan had kissed her. She slipped on her sable while she continued turning over the problem in her mind.

The trouble was Lance had appointed Morgan as managing director, and Morgan – the son of a coal-miner – had helped to build up World Security from nothing. He knew the organization inside out, including the Industrial Research Division, which he directed personally. She had heard disturbing rumours about that Division which had a secret section inside every HQ across the face of the earth.

I'll talk some more with Ted Doyle, she decided as she checked the contents of her Ferragamo handbag. And we'll look at the red master ledger again. She went to the door, switched off the lights and headed for the private elevator to which only three people had a key – herself, Lance and Morgan.

It always gave her the shivers, leaving the eerily silent and deserted building late in the evening. Her footfalls echoed along the marble-tiled floor. She stood in front of the private elevator, pausing before inserting the key.

She had the uncanny feeling she was being watched. But there was no light under the door leading to Morgan's suite of offices behind her. Staring at the closed elevator door she wondered again whether this wasn't a loophole in security. The elevator could bypass all floors, ending up in the underground garage. She would pass no security guard before getting into her car. When she had pointed this out to Morgan he had dismissed her fears as groundless, reminding her only three top people had a key. She inserted hers, stepped inside when the doors had opened, pressed the button for the garage.

Morgan's right eye was pressed against the spyhole in his door. He squinted like a voyeur at Leonora's legs below her hip-length sable jacket. He'd been waiting for her to leave for ten minutes. She seemed to take for ever before she operated the key and disappeared inside the elevator. He sighed with relief, wiped sweat off his forehead with his handkerchief, switched on his office lights.

He sat for ten minutes behind his desk, quenching his thirst with slugs of cognac from his hip flask while he skimmed through the red master ledger. He couldn't imagine how Doyle could have got hold of it. In his absence the ledger was stored in a special compartment in the vault and he alone had the combination to open it in his head.

Well, there was one person who could enlighten him. And that was the only other person in the building above the ground floor where the security guards watched the main and rear entrances. Ted Doyle.

Hugging the ledger across his broad chest, he walked out of his office and down the long corridor to the room at the far end. He opened the door without knocking. Doyle, seated behind his desk, studying a file, looked up. There was a carton of sandwiches on the desk, another containing coffee. Both were untouched.

'I have been talking about you with Leonora,' Morgan began as he sat in the leather chair facing the accountant. 'I don't think it's too long before you'll be invited to take a seat on the main board.' He smiled, still hugging the ledger.

'That's very gratifying, Mr Morgan.' Doyle peered at

him through the pebble glasses. 'I take it you've been talking things over with Mrs Buckmaster.'

'Exactly.' Morgan's small eyes gleamed with satisfaction. Doyle had gained the wrong impression as planned – that Morgan had been discussing the contents of the master ledger with the chairman. 'One point I omitted to ask her. How did you get access to this ledger when I was the only one who knew the combination?'

'Oh, I see what you mean.' Doyle relaxed, leaning back in his chair. 'She raised the point that there must be a master ledger. I told her where it was kept but only you knew the combination. She very much wanted to see it. So I got her to sign an authorization and we brought in an expert at opening safes. Had to tell him a fib, that we'd lost the bit of paper with the combination on it. With her signature he had no hesitation in opening it for us . . .'

A wave of fury swept through Morgan. He managed to smile and conceal his rage. Doyle had been too clever by half. He had become a more dangerous and immediate menace than Morgan had suspected. Very drastic measures were called for. He checked his watch.

'We actually discussed your joining us on the board in depth. There are one or two questions I'd like to ask. Then, you know me – once I've decided I like to get on with it right away. But would you wait until I get back? I have a call expected in five minutes from New York. You don't mind waiting?'

He smiled again, stood up and padded towards the door. That should hold Doyle in his office for hours if necessary. Back in his own lair he took a deep breath, then picked up the telephone.

Leonora lay in her bed alone in the Belgravia apartment fast asleep when a sound woke her. She sat up, switched on the bedside light. 2 a.m. Oh, Christ!

Sleeping by herself was her way of putting pressure on Lance. She had moved into her own bedroom when detectives had reported Lance was seeing his sixth girl friend, a tart of a German girl from Frankfurt. It was the only method she could think of bringing him to heel. His reaction had been disappointing when she informed him of her intention.

'I've decided I want to sleep in the guest room. It will help me to sort things out in my mind.'

'Fair enough.' He'd grinned, waved a dismissive hand. 'You need your beauty sleep and I'm often late dealing with those infernal boxes. Good idea. Then I won't have the added worry of waking you up.'

'Oh, you have other worries?' she'd asked sarcastically.

'Loads of them, darling. Organizing a new Ministry is hardly child's play.'

'I thought you'd done that by now . . .'

'Only just beginning,' he had replied and walked off to the main bedroom.

She heard a creak of wood in the corridor outside. Gathering up her dressing-gown, she threw it on, picked up a heavy silver candlestick and tiptoed to the door. She opened it quietly and stared at Lance creeping towards the main bedroom. He wore his military-style raincoat and there was a hint of moisture on the cloth. He turned as he heard her opening the door.

'Did she keep you up late?' she enquired.

His reaction startled her. He strode towards her, his face distorted with fury. She stepped back a pace and he stood in front of her.

'Don't worry – I'm not coming in there. I thought the idea was you could get some sleep on your own.' His voice rose. 'Do you have to pry into every minute of my bloody life? Have you still no idea of what it means to be a Minister, for God's sake? The hours I have to work? And when you decided to move in here my life became my own.' He paused, his facial muscles working. His tone become cold, arrogant. 'Also don't forget how you savour the reflected glory of being the wife of a Cabinet Minister . . .'

He reached forward, grabbed the handle of the door, slammed it shut with his wife still inside the room. She was trembling. Lance was very fit, very strong. He could have felled her with one blow. She locked the door, went back to bed and lay awake until just before dawn.

At precisely 4 a.m. a patrolling policeman found the body of Ted Doyle sprawled on the sidewalk below his office window eighteen storeys above the corpse.

15

At 6 a.m. Chief Inspector Roy Buchanan of the Homicide Squad stood bent over the slumped figure of Ted Doyle. The skull had been crushed from the immense impact of the fall. Buchanan, a slim man in his forties with a quiet, cynical manner, forced himself to concentrate, to observe by the beams of the flashlights held by detectives. The pathologist, Dr Kersey, stooped alongside the chief inspector, his bag resting on the sidewalk.

'Did he fall or was he pushed or did he jump?' Buchanan commented as he straightened and stared up at the light streaming from the open window on the eighteenth floor. 'That's what it comes to, wouldn't you agree?'

'Gives you plenty of options,' Kersey observed. 'Maybe the clue is up there.'

He gestured upwards and Buchanan crossed the street to get a clearer view of the high window. Not that the different angle helped him at all. He was trying to calculate the angle of a body falling from that height. So far as he could tell it would naturally have hit the outer edge of the wide sidewalk. Exactly as it had done, in fact.

The night guard on duty near the ground floor entrance opened up the building for the Scotland Yard team. Following Buchanan they all crowded into the elevator – Forensic, the fingerprint men, photographers – all the apparatus of trained personnel who spent part of their lives attending the death of men and women they'd never heard of before. It made for a certain outward appearance of callousness, which was really no more than professionalism.

The guard showed Buchanan and his younger assistant, Sergeant Warden, into Doyle's office. Buchanan restrained the guard from entering with a gentle hand on his arm.

'You can leave it to us now. No one else in the building. Only two guards? Tell them to wait until I've interviewed them. Yourself, too, please. Pop off downstairs now.'

'Window wide open,' Buchanan commented as they entered the office. 'Light still on. Everything normal, what I'd have expected. So far.'

'There's a note in that typewriter,' Warden observed.

Both men wore rubber gloves. Buchanan walked slowly across to the machine, his eyes scanning the carpeted floor. He stood looking down at the typed sheet.

No way I can pay my gambling debts. Pressure has become unbearable. Only one way out. Ted Doyle.

'Seems we have everything,' Warden remarked. 'You make a habit of visiting a gambling club. You get in too deep, can't pay your debts. They send along the heavies to persuade you it's serious. You're trapped and decide to end it all.'

'Except we don't know yet that he did gamble,' Buchanan replied. 'And there's something odd about that note. Name typed, not signed in Doyle's hand.'

'We've seen that before,' the phlegmatic Warden recalled.

'But it's all just a little too perfect. Call it sixth sense.'

Buchanan wandered over to the window, examined the ledge which was wide and damp with the drizzle which had fallen since midnight. He'd noticed Doyle's grey suit had been damp. The ledge was clean, no sign of foot-marks, but again he'd observed Doyle had been wearing rubber-soled shoes without a trace of dirt. So he wouldn't expect to find footmark traces.

Supporting himself with one hand, he stared down into the abyss. Plain-clothes men with torches were moving round the corpse. Several flashbulbs exploded, pinpoints of light from that height. Buchanan gritted his teeth: he suffered from vertigo. He turned back into the office to speak to Warden.

'Make sure the fingerprint boys check the keys of that typewriter. And I'd like them to pay particular attention to the edges of the window frame. All against Doyle's fingerprints, of course.'

'Of course . . .'

'And have you found out who is in charge of this organization – as I asked you on the way here?'

'Yes, sir. It came through on the radio while you were on your way into the building before I caught you up. Gareth Morgan is managing director, has a house in Wandsworth. The chairman is something else again – Leonora Buckmaster, wife of Lance Buckmaster, Minister for External Security. She lives in Belgravia. The press could make something big of this.'

158

'Oh, I don't know. They're obsessed with that earth-quake which just hit the Soviet Union. I think I'd like to see this Gareth Morgan first. See if you can contact him. Just say a tragedy has occurred at the World Security building and we'd appreciate his presence.'

'Consider it done.'

Warden was walking out to find a phone in another office when Buchanan called after him. 'And the pack can come in here and start their ministrations. I'll wait for Morgan.' Buchanan beckoned to Dr Kersey who had appeared in the doorway, holding his bag.

'The body is on the way to the mortuary,' Kersey informed him. 'You'll want my PM report in due course . . .'

'Yesterday would do nicely.'

'I'll be on my way then . . .'

'Just before you go, Tom. You've seen the corpse. Just for once I'd like you to give me an idea when Doyle died. Off the top of your head.'

'You know I never guess.' Kersey, a portly red-faced man in his fifties, shook his head. 'After the PM I'll know . . .'

'It would help me enormously at this stage of the investigation if I had *some* idea.' Buchanan clasped his gloved hands lightly together. 'No one's asking you to commit yourself.'

'At a wild guess, between midnight and 2 a.m. from the state of Doyle. And that *is* subject to my PM. Yesterday, I think you said. I'd better be going, hadn't I?'

At 7.30 a.m. Gareth Morgan stepped out of the limousine driven by Hanson, showed his identity folder to the uniformed policeman on duty, and walked across the wide -marble floor to the private elevator, key in hand.

Sitting beside the security guard, Buchanan observed

him with care. He always attached importance to his first sight of a witness. Jumping up, he joined Morgan as the managing director inserted the key.

'Chief Inspector Buchanan. In charge of this investigation,' he introduced himself.

Morgan let go of the key and stared up at the tall man beside him. His small eyes gazed straight at Buchanan's grey ones which had a remote look.

'Then perhaps you can tell me why I've been summoned here at this hour? All I got out of Sergeant Warden on the phone was a tragedy had occurred. What tragedy? And would it be possible to replace that uniformed policeman with a plain-clothes detective on duty at the front? It's bad publicity for the top security organization in the world to have the police on view. I'd appreciate the consideration.'

Morgan was unsmiling but his expression relaxed as he made his plea. Buchanan nodded, asked him to wait a moment, went and gave instructions for a more anonymous replacement, came back to the elevator.

'This is an executives-only elevator?' he enquired.

'Yes. Only two people have keys. Myself and the chairman.' He turned the key, the door opened and they stepped inside. 'You haven't answered my question,' Morgan persisted as the elevator shot up to the eighteenth floor.

'I see this elevator goes to the basement,' Buchanan replied.

'To the underground garage. We're often in a hurry to get away, to catch a plane. This is an international organization.'

'I'm aware of that, Mr Morgan. I also noticed there were no lights above the doors, indicating the position of this elevator. Presumably the security guard on duty behind his desk at ground floor level has no knowledge of anyone arriving by or leaving by this special elevator?'

'His bank of TV monitors doesn't include the garage,' Morgan replied shortly. 'Now will you please tell me who is involved in this so-called tragedy.'

'Oh, it was a tragedy all right for the person involved. Maybe we could go to your office where we can talk in private.'

They had stepped out on the eighteenth floor as Buchanan made his suggestion. He nodded to Warden, standing outside Doyle's office, to join them.

'That is where I'm taking you,' Morgan snapped, opening the door to his office suite. He paused as he saw Warden, wooden-faced, stop alongside Buchanan. 'I thought you said you wanted a private talk.'

'This is my assistant, Sergeant Warden, who will also be present at the interview . . .'

They stood while Morgan took off his black overcoat, checked his appearance in a wall mirror and went behind his desk. He gestured and Buchanan noticed the short thick hand with nails trimmed short. A man possessed of considerable physical power.

'Sit down, gentlemen. Tell me what's happened,' Morgan began.

'I regret I have to tell you that early this morning your chief accountant, Ted Doyle, was found dead on the sidewalk below his open office window.'

Buchanan sat in a relaxed position in his chair, his long legs crossed. His deceptively sleepy eyes watched Morgan for his reaction. The managing director spread his hands.

'This is terrible news. Doyle has worked for us for ten years. What do you mean he was found dead on the sidewalk? A heart attack?'

'Hardly. Perhaps I didn't explain myself too well. His body had fallen eighteen storeys – apparently from his office window.'

'You mean he slipped out of the window?'

'Again, that's hardly likely. You must know his office.

161

Even if he was drunk he would have had to climb up to reach the outside ledge, which is very wide. Did he drink?'

Warden kept his face expressionless with an effort. The cat-and-mouse interrogation was typical of Buchanan. He extracted information likè a skilled Queen's Counsel. Morgan opened a box on the table, selected a cigar, clipped off the end and lit it.

'To the best of my knowledge he did not *drink*,' he replied eventually. 'I find all this very upsetting.'

'You look upset.' Buchanan paused and Morgan glanced at him quickly. He had detected the note of irony in the remark. Warden was becoming intrigued: he began to think Buchanan was facing a worthwhile antagonist. 'And', his chief continued, 'I noticed the emphasis you laid on the word "drink". Had Mr Doyle other vices then?'

'We all have something. I expect you have.' Morgan waved his cigar. 'I smoke. You're beginning to make me think poor Doyle committed suicide.'

Buchanan thrust his hands inside his trouser pockets. 'May I ask what gave you that idea?'

'Logic. You pooh-poohed the idea that it was an accident. So naturally – much as I dislike the idea – suicide is the natural alternative.'

'Had Doyle other vices?' Buchanan repeated.

'Well . . .' Morgan hesitated, took several puffs at his cigar, 'I hate to say it, but I had reason to suspect he was a gambler. Very keen on the ponies. Horse-racing.'

'May I ask how you found that out? Not a very desirable pastime for a chief accountant, I'd have thought.'

'I first got the idea into my head about two months ago. I was working here on a Saturday and called him at home to ask about some figures. He seemed irritated and impatient. In the background I could hear the TV going – with a racing commentary.'

'Not a lot to go on to jump to the conclusion you did. How many other people like racing, watch it on TV, and never lay a bet in their lives.'

'Exactly the same thing happened on two other Saturdays. I admit the third time I made up a reason for calling him just to see whether it was every Saturday. He always refused to work on Saturdays when we were under pressure. Sundays, yes. Saturdays, no.'

'Still not conclusive, Mr Morgan . . .'

'But what happened last night made me feel pretty certain I was right. And you remarked that it wasn't a very desirable pastime for a chief accountant. You must understand that Doyle had no access to large sums of money. All major cheques here have to be signed either by myself or Mrs Buckmaster, the chairman. Also, the title of chief accountant was really a reward for faithful service. We have a finance director, Axel Moser, who handles the main financial problems. He's in Australia at the moment.'

'What did happen last night?'

Morgan hesitated again, pursed his lips as though reluctant to blacken the name of a dead colleague. 'He asked me for a loan of two thousand pounds in cash. Said it was for the interest on his mortgage. I refused his request point-blank. I guessed its real purpose was to bet on the gee-gees.'

'How did he take your refusal?'

'Rather badly. Said the sum meant nothing to a company our size . . .'

'You had a row then?' Buchanan interjected. His hands were now clasped on his knee and he leaned forward, staring hard at the managing director.

'No. Nothing like that. He just seemed – well, disappointed. As though he'd banked on my agreeing.'

'What time did this conversation take place? And where?'

163

'In Doyle's office. I left the building at 10 p.m. So it must have been about 9.30 when we had this conversation.'

Buchanan relaxed again, changed the angle of the questions without warning. 'How do you know it was precisely 10 p.m. when you left this building? Anyone who can confirm your statement? Just routine.'

Morgan tapped ash from his cigar into a crystal-glass bowl. Giving himself time to think, Warden noted. Morgan was reflecting that this tall lean chief inspector was a formidable opponent. He sat back in his chair, determined to dictate the tempo.

'It's a simple question I asked,' Buchanan said gently.

'I thought it was two questions . . .'

'My apologies. It *was* two questions. By now you should have the answers . . .

'My time is valuable,' Morgan said aggressively. 'I'm being paid a lot of money to use it positively. So I keep an eye on the time. Look . . .' He reached forward and turned round a wide black box so it faced Buchanan. It held various clock faces. The time in London, New York, San Francisco, Frankfurt, Sydney.

'Useful little gadget . . .' Buchanan began but Morgan went on talking.

'I know it was 10 p.m. because I checked that clock just before I went down to the underground garage. My driver, Hanson, was waiting for me. He drove me home to Wandsworth.'

'And you arrived at your home when? I'm sure you know – you live by the clock, you said . . .'

'At 10.25 p.m. I'll anticipate your next question for you. My wife can confirm I didn't leave the house until this morning. In response to your request to see me. Now, if that's all I have an international organization to run.'

'Not quite all, Mr Morgan. You were in this building until ten o'clock. Doyle was presumably in his office after

164

you left. Was anyone else here during last evening?'

'Yes, Mrs Buckmaster. I'd just come back from abroad. So we had a lot to talk about. I'd made a tour of some of the European offices. She wanted to know how I'd got on. That's it.'

'And Mrs Buckmaster was still here when you left?'

Beads of moisture were appearing on Morgan's forehead, Warden noticed. He'd seen this happen so often before. Buchanan going on and on, changing moods, lines of questioning, matching his stamina against that of the witness, but always keeping his temper.

'No,' Morgan replied. 'She left about 9 p.m. I was opening my door to walk around the place, stretch my legs, when I saw her leaving by the private elevator.'

Buchanan stood up and Warden joined him. Morgan also stood up to escort them to the door. Always leave an impression of amiability. Buchanan waited until Morgan had opened the door before he sprang his last surprise.

'Perhaps you'd like to accompany us to Doyle's office? After all, he was your employee for ten years. The place will be a bit cluttered with my men – but that can't be helped . . .'

Buchanan walked down the corridor, Warden stood aside, and Morgan felt obliged to follow. Inwardly he was seething: it was Buchanan's imperturbable manner that had got to him. He stubbed out his cigar in an ash-stand and paused by Buchanan who stood at the entrance to Doyle's office. Suddenly he turned round and asked another question.

'When you came down here to see Doyle did you notice an untouched carton of take-away food and a cardboard container of coffee on his desk?'

'Yes, I did. I simply assumed he was working late and had popped out to the deli round the corner for fodder.'

'You're quite sure about that? That the food and the coffee were untouched?'

'I've said so, haven't I? A security man trains himself to notice details.'

'Thank you. I really think this is a bad time for us to go in there. Too much activity . . .'

'Then, if you don't mind, I'll get back to my desk. This Doyle tragedy is very upsetting but it has to be business as usual for the company.'

'Just before you go, I'll need an office as my temporary HQ here while the investigation proceeds . . .'

'Moser's snuggery. I told you he was in Australia.' Morgan took a key-ring from his pocket, extracted one key from the ring, opened a door, handed the key to Buchanan. 'That's the only key,' he lied, 'so you can have all the privacy in the world.'

'Thank you for your cooperation,' Buchanan said politely. He added, as though an afterthought, as Morgan turned away. 'Oh, there will be more questions I'll have to ask you. But they can wait until I've assembled more data.'

They entered a large office with picture windows overlooking other high-rises. Between two of them a solid curtain of freezing fog was drifting in from the direction of the river Thames. Buchanan stood gazing at the blurred view.

'What was your impression of Morgan?' he asked Warden.

'A strange man. Self-made. Came up from nothing. Glories in his present position.'

'That's all right as far as it goes.' Buchanan rattled loose change in his pocket. 'But his reaction to the news of Doyle's death wasn't quite right. A terrible tragedy and so on – but not a sign of shocked *disbelief* when he was first told.'

'Maybe he thinks only of himself. What do you think happened, sir? Suicide?'

'I might have gone along with that except for the empty

food-carton, the empty cardboard coffee cup in his waste-paper basket.'

'Not quite with you . . .'

'Oh, come on. You're in such a state you're thinking of jumping from an eighteenth-storey window. Morgan replied to my question off guard, I suspect. He said the cartons were untouched when he saw Doyle, refused him the alleged loan. Can you see Doyle – in that frame of mind – waiting until Morgan had gone and then sitting down to eat a substantial amount of ham sandwiches, downed with a cup of coffee? Forensic found traces of ham and crusty bread in that large crushed carton. Plus coffee traces in the smaller carton. Well?'

He swung round and faced his subordinate.

'No, I can't visualize that happening,' Warden said slowly.

'So, if I'm right,' Buchanan continued in the same even tone, 'it wasn't an accident, it wasn't suicide. That means we're investigating a murder case.'

Morgan unlocked the security drawer in his desk, took out the typed list of employees. Each had a number alongside the name. Doyle was 35.

Delving inside his metal box full of keys, Morgan extracted one with a tab carrying the number 35. As a precaution against a possible 'mole' inside the organization, Morgan had ordered the Research and Development Division to make duplicates of all the keys to employees' homes.

If suspicion fell on a man – or a woman – someone could be sent along to wait until the house or apartment was empty. He would then use the key to enter the suspected employee's home to make a careful search. Quite illegal, but this emphasis on total security, regardless of ethics, was one factor which had made World

167

Security the largest and most successful organization of its type in the world.

With the key in his pocket Morgan opened his office door, peered out into the empty corridor and hurried to the private elevator. He found Hanson behind the wheel of the limousine in the underground garage, reading a paperback and munching an apple. He handed him the key.

'You know Doyle's address in Pimlico. You've delivered papers there. He's a bachelor so the place will be empty.'

'I make a search?'

'The reverse. You go to the races. You bet on the Tote?'

'That's right . . .'

'So no one can trace ownership of a Tote ticket. They're anonymous. You usually have some losing tickets . . .'

'Some in here now.' Hanson opened the glove compartment. 'I have another lot in my wallet. Don't know why I keep them – I have a clear-out periodically. Due for one now . . .'

'Which is exactly what you're going to do. Use gloves, wipe those tickets clean, then crumple them up. Drop them inside a drawer in Doyle's apartment. Anywhere will do – don't make them look hidden. And Hanson . . .' Morgan gripped his arm. 'Before you enter that apartment make sure there are no police about. They'll be going there soon. And use the Ford Cortina, not this limo. Too conspicuous. Now, move, man, move . . .'

16

At 10 a.m. Leonora Buckmaster parked her Volvo station wagon at the main entrance to the World Security building as snowflakes drifted down into Threadneedle Street from a leaden sky. The whole of Western Europe was being smothered by the blanket of snow drifting in from the East.

She opened the door, swung her legs out, locked the door and glanced up at the office block looming above her. Her expression was grim as she walked through the door opened by a uniformed security guard. In one hand she held her pass, in the other her elevator key and the car keys. A man in civilian clothes stepped forward to look at her pass which carried her photograph.

'Police, Mrs Buckmaster . . .'

'Then I want to see Chief Inspector Buchanan immediately – that is his name, isn't it?' She handed her car keys to the security guard. 'Keith, could you please park my car inside the garage. Thank you.' She turned to the plain-clothes detective. 'What exactly is going on here? I'm the chairman.'

'The chief inspector is waiting to see you on the eighteenth floor.'

'Is he? How very kind of him . . .'

She crossed the marble floor to the private elevator with long elegant strides. Behind her back the plain-clothes man nodded to his colleague at the reception desk who had taken control of the switchboard. The second man picked up a phone.

When the doors opened at the eighteenth floor Leonora found a tall slim man standing a few feet away. His grey eyes surveyed her, assessing his first impression. A handsome woman in her mid thirties, he estimated. She wore a hip-length sable jacket and relics of snowflakes clung to golden curls in her long mane. It reminded him of the Christmas fairy, a trivial thought he dismissed immediately.

He noted the good bone-structure, the alert blue eyes, the firm but full mouth which suggested a hint of sensuality. A woman who would make an instant impact on most men. She made no such impact on Buchanan. To him she was simply a witness to an as yet unexplained death.

'Mrs Buckmaster? I'm Chief Inspector Buchanan. Could we possibly have a private chat in your office?'

'What the devil is going on? Your men appear to have taken over the security apparatus in this building. Your Sergeant Warden phones me, asks me to come here as soon as I can, says there has been a tragedy, then refuses to elaborate . . .'

As she spoke she was striding along the empty corridor to her office suite. With his long legs Buchanan easily kept pace with her. His manner was neutral, almost everyday.

'I'd prefer to discuss this in the privacy of your office. And Sergeant Warden was acting under my explicit orders.'

She paused before inserting her key, glancing back along the corridor. Men with cameras were emerging from Doyle's office. She frowned, which did nothing to spoil her physical attraction.

'More of your men? What are they doing in Doyle's office?'

Buchanan gestured towards the door. A moment later Warden appeared from the doorway leading to the executive toilets.

'This is Sergeant Warden. If you don't mind, I'd like him to be present at the interview.'

She glanced at Warden, made no reply, unlocked her door and led the way inside. While she took off her sable, shook it, hung it inside a wardrobe with sliding doors, she asked them to sit down.

'Would you like some coffee?' she enquired as she sat behind her desk on which rested only three phones, one red, one blue and one white.

'Thank you, but not for the moment,' Buchanan replied. 'I'm afraid I have some distressing news. Ted Doyle's body was found eighteen storeys below his window during the night.'

'Oh, no. I don't believe it.' Her shapely right hand flew to her throat and held her polo-necked green sweater closer. 'It's not possible. I was talking to him in this office only yesterday evening. He was in perfect shape. I just can't believe it, take it in. Has there been a break-in? Did he disturb an intruder? How is he? From the way you worded it . . .'

All in a rush of words. Her voice was low and husky, throaty. She stared from one man to the other, her left hand clenched into a fist on the desk top. Buchanan spoke quietly.

'Yes, it is the worst news. He's dead. You can't fall from this height and survive. Can you imagine the impact when he hit the sidewalk?'

It was brutally phrased and Warden winced inwardly. At times he felt his chief went over the top. Buchanan's eyes were cold as he studied her. He folded his arms and waited. Either she was an excellent actress or her reaction was genuine. Impossible to say which at this stage.

She fetched a carafe of water from a side table, poured herself a glass, swallowed a generous quantity. Then she sat upright.

'Please tell me what this is all about.'

'You said you were talking with Doyle yesterday evening. What time would that be?'

'Roughly between seven and eight o'clock. I can vouch for the second time. Gareth Morgan, my managing director, arrived back from London Airport. I was surprised to see him. I remember checking my watch when I heard his voice. It was 8 p.m.'

'You heard his voice?' Buchanan leaned forward, holding her gaze. 'Talking to who?'

'He bumped into Ted – Doyle, that is – as Ted was leaving my office.'

'And you heard what Morgan said?'

'I'm afraid I didn't. He was speaking in a quiet way. But of course I recognized who it was.'

'And Doyle came back into this office with Morgan?'

'No.' She swallowed. 'I never saw him again.'

'So normally where would Doyle have gone?'

'Back to his own office . . .'

'And had you completed your business with him for the day?'

'Yes . . .'

'So what would keep him from going home?'

Warden listened with increasing interest. Buchanan had built up the tempo, was firing a fresh question as soon as she'd replied to the previous one. She reached for the glass of water.

'Please. It hasn't even sunk in that Doyle is no longer with us. You're going too fast.'

'Perfectly straightforward questions, Mrs Buckmaster. Surely nothing I've asked so far requires thought before you answer. I ask you again – what would keep Doyle from going home? Because', he continued ruthlessly, 'we know he certainly didn't go home.'

'He might stay to work late when there were no phone calls to interrupt him.'

'I see.' Buchanan gazed round the large office as though he'd not seen it until that moment. A smaller desk was angled at a distance to Leonora's. Presumably her secretary's. He looked back at her, spoke suddenly.

'According to what you said earlier you were conferring with Doyle for about one hour. Seven to eight. That's a long time. What were you talking about?'

'Is that relevant?'

Her long lashes blinked briefly. For the first time Buchanan sensed a wariness in her. Why? He pressed home his interrogation.

'It could be very relevant. It was the last but one conversation he apparently had before he died. The last one being with Gareth Morgan – after he'd seen you leave at 9 p.m.'

'How could he know that?'

The question slipped out before she realized it. She sat very still and stared hard at Buchanan. He replied offhandedly.

'He said he was opening the door of his office and saw you in the elevator just before it descended. Now, what were you and Doyle talking about for about one hour?'

'We were going over the figures for various European offices. We do have an organization in every West European country. It is one of our major markets. Both in the Common Market and in those countries still outside it. Including Switzerland. So there were a lot of figures to study. It was a matter of comparing the results of one office with another. One point was to see if we could improve our service in any particular area.'

'I see,' Buchanan commented again and paused.

That had been her longest answer yet. Full of unasked-for detail. Almost as though she was covering up what they had really talked about. He attacked from another angle.

'How important is – was – Ted Doyle? He had the title of Chief Accountant. But you have a finance director, Axel Moser. So where does the division in responsibilities come?'

'Ted handled all the day-to-day problems. He had quite a lot of power . . .'

'Including access to all the books?'

Again she blinked. Again she reached for the glass of water, took her time sipping the liquid. Placing it

173

carefully on a mat, she dabbed at her lips with a lace handkerchief.

'Naturally. How else could he do his job? I'm beginning to wilt under this continuous barrage.'

'I apologize. But I'm sure you are as anxious as I am to get to the bottom of why Doyle died. And I'm nearly finished. Was Doyle married? And if you could give me his address it would help our enquiries. My last two questions, Mrs Buckmaster. For the moment.'

She replied as she wrote out the address from memory on a blank card. She handed it across the desk and Buchanan gave it to Warden.

'He was a bachelor. Not from choice, I sometimes thought. But he was very shy where women were concerned.'

Buchanan stood up. He cast a slow glance round the office before he joined her as she escorted them to the door. He asked the question as she grasped the handle.

'How many keys are there to your private elevator? Someone has a spare, I presume? In case of loss.'

'No one has a spare. Bad security. And there are only three keys in existence. I have one, Gareth Morgan has another.'

'And the third key, Mrs Buckmaster?'

She looked him straight in the eye. 'Lance had one, naturally. He was going to hand it in when he was appointed Minister, but found he'd lost it. He never comes here since his appointment, of course. Against the rules.'

'Of course. And thank you for your cooperation, Mrs Buckmaster. I'll keep you informed of progress into our murder investigation . . .'

Buchanan left her staring after him as he walked away with Warden down the corridor.

174

17

The Black Forest was like a vast icebox. Tweed's hands were freezing as he gripped the wheel. Beside him Newman clapped his hands together to get the circulation moving. In the rear seat Paula pulled the fur-lined coat she had bought in Freiburg closer to her neck.

The hired blue Audi, with chains on its wheels, glided over the icebound surface of the hilly country road. On either side the dense stands of the fir forest walled them in, made for a claustrophobic atmosphere. It was night, the undimmed headlights reflected weirdly off the ramparts of snow lining the road. During the day a snow-plough had obviously fought to keep the route open.

Paula glanced back through the rear window. The lights of the second Audi, a neutral grey colour, driven by Marler, showed as a blur beyond the iced-up window. The temperature outside was way below zero. Above the sound of the engine she heard a crackling noise as their wheels broke the crusted snow ridges.

'Are you sure you know where we're going?' she asked. 'It was a long time ago since you were in Freiburg learning German.'

'I thought you'd grasped I have a photographic memory for routes,' he told her as he drove into a slow skid, then the car came back under his control. 'I drove all over the Black Forest in my spare time. We're heading for a small spa town called Badenweiler. From there we can drive down to the German border with Switzerland. The trick is to cross that border unseen. I think we can do it at a small place called Laufenburg on the edge of the Rhine. Part is in Germany, part in Switzerland. It straddles the river. We have to cross a bridge between the two frontiers. But that's for later.'

'And what's for now?' she persisted.

'We find a refuge for the night when we can. Freiburg was a deathtrap.'

'Maybe then we can talk about what happened back in London,' she suggested.

'Not while Marler is around,' Newman objected. 'And not one word about that *Shockwave* computer on the high seas.'

'You wouldn't be letting your personal dislike cloud your judgement? Tweed asked.

'No, I wouldn't . . .'

After conducting the decoy manoeuvre planned by Tweed – when Newman had taken over the BMW and driven it on to the autobahn – he had driven back to Freiburg. By then Tweed had slipped the net thrown round the city and was driving to the agreed rendezvous with Newman in the Black Forest.

As they parked near the Colombi Hotel Newman had been in an uncertain frame of mind regarding Marler. Certainly he had cooperated to the full on the autobahn – shooting the tyres on the pursuing Mercedes which had ended up as a fireball. But still Newman had reservations. How far would Marler go to prove a fake loyalty? A long way in Newman's opinion.

Without telling Marler where he had been going, Newman had returned earlier on foot to the Oberkirch. It was there that Tweed had explained his plan to evade the watchers he felt sure would be watching all exits.

'And what about Marler?' Newman had demanded. 'I don't trust him one inch . . .'

'Then this will give you a chance to test him,' Tweed had insisted. 'Take him with you – you may need him. You said he'd collected a rifle from some friend – and he's the best marksman in Europe. If there's an emergency and he backs you up, bring him to the rendezvous – but tell him to hire another Audi. A different colour from the one I'll be driving. Leave the BMW at the car hire agency in Freiburg and you drive Marler to meet us in the Black Forest here . . .'

Tweed had indicated a small village high up in the Black Forest on a large-scale map spread out on the bed. Paula, perched alongside the map, was also worried.

'Marler has always struck me as an unknown quantity,' she commented. 'If he's joining us I agree we should not risk telling him where we're headed for – Switzerland.'

'Then neither of you tell him anything. Leave me to handle Marler . . .'

When Newman and Tweed had eventually arrived at the crossroads just outside the village, Tweed had suggested Newman should transfer to his Audi.

'Marler,' he went on, 'we may need to use the decoy method again. That photograph of Horowitz you took outside the World Security HQ in Freiburg shows me someone will stop at nothing to make sure I don't reach a transmitter alive. So you take over driving the grey Audi on your own from now on. Following me into the forest.' He had smiled drily. 'I just hope you're as good a driver as you think you are. We're driving up into a white hell . . .'

Paula stared out of the window. It was like driving between two giant black tidal waves about to overwhelm them. When Tweed swung the car round a bend the headlights shone over the dense palisade of firs and there was no sign of life anywhere.

'We're close to where we turn off up a wide timber track if it's still there,' Tweed remarked.

They completed the nerve-racking swing round another curve and ahead the country road straightened, marched up a steep hill for about half a mile so far as Paula could tell – it was difficult to estimate distance even by the light of a rising moon. The weird glow reflected off the dangerous sheen of ice on the road, glittered on ice crystals in the ramparts of banked snow. Tweed suddenly reduced speed and then stopped. Lowering his window, he listened. There it was again, the distant chug-chug of a helicopter's rotors.

The sound was approaching fast. At the same moment coming in the opposite direction a car's headlights breasted the crest of a hill, drove down towards them. Behind he heard Marler tooting his horn.

'Marler has switched off all his lights,' he said.

'He's driving close to us,' Paula called out, 'using your lights to guide him. I think he wants us to stop . . .'

It all happened at breathless speed. Tweed slowed, stopped. Seconds later Marler was beside the window he'd lowered. He spoke tersely.

'Chopper with a searchlight approaching from the south-east. I think it's a trap. I'm turning round, driving back with lights full on. I'll act as a decoy . . .'

'Thanks,' said Tweed rapidly. 'When you get clear fly back to London. Organize surveillance on two targets – Ministry for External Security . . . and the World Security outfit . . . I'll leave a number on your answerphone at your apartment . . .'

'After the country code add digits four and five as second and fourth numbers . . .'

' 'After I've reversed the whole number . . .'

'I'm off. Good luck . . .'

Then Marler was gone. Tweed released the brake, pressed his foot down. The oncoming car was coming much closer. He saw in his wing mirror Marler had already executed a three-point turn, was driving away, headlights blazing. The chug-chug was much louder.

'Watch that vehicle coming towards us,' warned Newman.

Tweed was leaning forward, glancing constantly to his left. 'We've got lucky. Hold on ...' He swung the wheel, turned across the road on to a wide timber track driven through the forest like a great avenue. The wheels began bumping over deep ice-hard ruts. He fought with the steering, felt the wheels slip into wide grooves carved out over the years by timber wagons. He drove on sensitively, feeling his wheels locked in by the iron-hard sides of the grooves. The disadvantage was he was moving along runnels of solid ice. Newman released his safety belt, hauled out the Walther from his hip holster, glanced back through the rear window. No sign yet of blurred headlights, but the oncoming car must have seen them turn off. Of course, it could be an innocent driver. Newman doubted it. Always assume the worst. They hadn't met a vehicle for miles, then one turned up at the same moment the chopper appeared. He looked ahead.

'We're heading for a dead end up here,' he remarked.

'Not necessarily.' Tweed called over his shoulder to Paula who sat tense, frequently looking back. 'When I stop bring the bags out of the car. We may have to run for it.'

'Run where?' snapped Newman.

'There used to be an old hunting lodge hidden in the forest. A winding footpath leads uphill to it. The lodge was for the timber workers who stayed out here. There was an electric cable leading to it which powered the freezer. There may be food and drink still there ...'

'Fat chance ...'

'But we have to hide the car before that chopper finds

179

us. Yes, look! I was right. See that big boulder at the side of the track . . .'

'What about it?'

'That's where the path starts. Fasten your seat belt. I'm increasing speed.'

'God help us . . .'

Tweed pressed his foot down. The Audi slithered and glided over the ice channels but kept moving. Tweed had his window open an inch and cold bitter air was making the interior like a refrigerator. He was listening to the growing sound of the helicopter coming closer. He swung to the left. The wheels rasped and hacked at the walls of the ruts, then broke through. They shot off the track through a narrow opening with the firs pressing closely on either side. They were in the middle of an open space of virgin snow when Tweed doused all the lights, turned off the engine. The bonnet was buried beneath snow-covered undergrowth.

When he leapt out of the car, shoving the ignition key in his pocket, Paula was handing out three small cases to Newman. He plodded back quickly and peered down the track. He wore climbing boots purchased in Freiburg, a dark overcoat and a fur hat on his head. Tweed took his own case as Paula and Newman reached him.

'They saw us turn in,' he commented, his voice calm. His mind was as ice-cold as the night. His instincts for danger asserted themselves. He had mentally gone back years to the days when he operated as an agent in the field.

A few yards from where the track ended at the distant road two small eyes, the headlights of a car, moved slowly towards them.

'We cross the track to the path,' he ordered. 'They're too far away to see us yet . . .'

'You cross with Paula.' Newman's tone was grim. They heard a click as he checked the magazine in his automatic.

'I'll come after you. These people have to be stopped . . .'

Tweed didn't argue. He grabbed Paula by her free arm. 'Get moving, they're coming closer . . .'

Crouching down, they stepped carefully over the pitfalls of the timber track. The lights of the car were still too far off to illuminate them. They made their way up the path into the forest.

Inside the Volvo station wagon Horowitz sat beside the driver as the vehicle climbed the road into the Black Forest. Horowitz stared ahead through his steel-rimmed spectacles, his lean face showing no particular expression. His right hand gripped the microphone of the high-powered transceiver installed in the boot. The automatic aerial was extended to its fullest extent. Then the message from the helicopter came to him.

'Elbe Two calling Bismarck. Elbe Two calling . . .'

'Bismarck listening,' Horowitz replied tersely. 'Have you news?'

'Eiger may have been located. A blue Audi proceeding along route . . . Also escorted by a grey Audi following closer behind . . .'

'Continue surveillance. Await fresh instructions.'

Horowitz used a pencil torch to examine the road map spread across his lap. Beside him, the driver, Stieber, a small squat individual built like a barrel, glanced sideways. 'Keep your eye on the road,' Horowitz said softly without looking up.

'Have we found them?' Eva Hendrix called out from the rear of the car. She was cold and frightened. Behind her was the wire cage hastily constructed at the Freiburg HQ. Inside the cage, far too close for her comfort, five German shepherd dogs were standing up, prowling restlessly. Every now and again one of the killer dogs gave a low snarl and she edged a little further away from the beasts, holding on to the back of Horowitz's seat as the vehicle skidded round a steep corner.

'I guessed well,' Horowitz commented almost to himself. 'You turn left at the next intersection, step on the gas.'

'These bloody roads are like a skating rink,' Stieber growled.

'And', Horowitz continued, ignoring the comment, 'Gustav is driving his Mercedes towards them from the opposite direction.'

'Is Gustav armed?' enquired Hendrix breathlessly.

'Yes, now shut up.' Horowitz called the chopper which had located the target. He now had four helicopters patrolling above the Black Forest. 'Are you there, Elbe Two? Good. Don't lose Eiger or you're out of a job. Next, radio Gustav that the target vehicle is approaching him. Make regular reports of the situation to me. Over and out . . .'

'How long before we reach them?' Stieber asked while he took the left turn at the intersection as instructed. They were climbing a steep hill, driving conditions were becoming worse as they plunged deeper into the Black Forest.

'If you keep this thing moving, less than ten minutes. Then you can do your job – unless Gustav has done it for you.'

Stieber nodded with satisfaction. He was the dog handler and was only really in his element when he was loosing his dogs after a fleeing target. Man or woman, it was all the same to Stieber. He loved his dogs. Human beings he found expendable.

Despite his wool-lined gloves Newman was frozen stiff as he stayed crouched behind a patch of undergrowth. The screen would have been useless except for the thick snow cloaking its branches and twigs. His right hand held the Walther and he'd decided that to fire it he'd have to use his bare hand when the time came.

The time was coming. The beams of the undimmed headlights were already showing on the section of track beyond the small glade. The car's engine was labouring. The vehicle was approaching slowly. Clearly the driver did not possess Tweed's skill in moving up the obstacle course of a track.

Frequently there was a sound of metal grinding against the unyielding ground. The driver wasn't keeping to the runnels: he kept losing them and the chassis was hitting the murderous ridges. Newman wriggled his toes which felt like ice. He hoped he wasn't getting frost-bite.

The lamps of the headlights appeared suddenly. Newman dipped his head to avoid the glare, slipped off the glove from his right hand, gripped the Walther, decided he needed both hands in the dark, slipped off the other glove, gripped the weapon in both hands.

The Mercedes had stopped. They had seen the place where Tweed had turned the Audi across virgin snow inside the glade. How many men? Four at the most, he guessed. And the most dangerous would be those alighting from the far side of the car. The Mercedes moved a short distance more and stopped again close to where the Audi was concealed.

The headlights were now angled away from the undergrowth and Newman had a better view of the whole car. The rear was empty and in front there was only the driver, a heavily built man wearing a peaked cap. He opened the door and stared round. Newman saw he was holding a gun in his right hand: he thought it was a Luger. If he could take him alive he might extract valuable information . . .

The man stepped out, stood close to the car, head cocked to one side as he listened.

'Drop the gun!' Newman shouted.

The man swung up his Luger, fired, but in the heavy silence of the forest Newman's voice had echoed. The bullet went wide. Newman fired three times in rapid succession. The man sagged against the car. His fingers lost their grip, the Luger fell into the snow. Its owner slumped slowly to the ground and lay very still.

The silence was broken by another sound. The distant chug-chug of a chopper coming closer. Newman ran forward, felt the neck pulse. Nothing. The gunman was dead. Reaching inside his breast pocket, Newman slid out an identity folder which held the owner's photograph behind a transparent shield. *Gustav Braun. World Security. Industrial Research Division.* All in German.

He slipped the folder inside his raincoat pocket, peered down the timber track where the chopper's rotors sounded much louder. It was flying just above tree level and had a searchlight switched on in the nose. The beam was proceeding up the track.

Newman dashed back for his case, grabbed hold of it, ran across the track before the searchlight reached him. He paused under the trees to insert a fresh mag into the Walther. As the rotors became a roar he vanished along the path in the direction Tweed and Paula had taken.

The moon was a blurred glow from behind a screen of clouds as Marler drove the grey Audi downhill. He was sure that the chopper had seen him but it had passed him and seemed to be concentrating on Tweed's Audi.

Marler drove without lights. The route followed by the road was clear enough in the meagre moonlight. Ahead he saw a bridge crossing the road. Moments later he saw the headlights of an invisible vehicle coming uphill towards him – invisible because immediately beyond the bridge the road, he recalled, turned in a sharp curve.

Apart from the lone car coming downhill towards Tweed's Audi he hadn't seen any form of transport for over an hour. He took his decision on sixth sense.

He had almost reached the bridge when he swung across the road on to the snow-covered verge on his left. He pulled up alongside the bridge – the last few yards he was carried to his hiding place by a skid. Lowering the window facing the road, he switched off his engine, reached for the rifle under a travelling rug alongside, aimed the muzzle through the open window. He sat very still, finger on the trigger.

The Volvo station wagon navigated the turn under the bridge at speed – too much speed for the road surface. The driver was lucky. The vehicle continued up the hill. As it had passed Marler had a glimpse of two men in the front, a girl in the back, and behind her a cage with four or five dogs. No one looked in his direction.

'Oh, Christ!' Marler muttered. 'Tracker dogs . . .'

He decided not to go back. Tweed had given his orders and Newman would have to cope. After all, he'd had training in the SAS for that article he'd written about the elite attack force.

'Elbe Two to Bismarck . . .'

'Bismarck here. Please report present situation . . .'

Inside the Volvo Horowitz held the mike lightly, his body relaxed. Had Gustav Braun rammed the Audi with his Mercedes? Anything to delay Tweed until they caught up.

'Elbe Two reporting. Blue Audi with Eiger has turned off the road you are proceeding along. Look out for wide timber track on your left. Am now flying zero height along track. Braun's car has turned down same track.'

'Continue surveillance. We will be there shortly. Over and out . . .'

Horowitz replaced the mike on its hook. The climax was very close. Tweed had tried to lose himself in the forest. The chopper had frightened him off the road. He was trapped. He glanced at Stieber who was hunched over the wheel, bare hands now gripping it tightly despite the cold.

'Don't miss the turn-off along that timber track.'

'Can't miss it. The chopper's searchlight shows where that track is. Hope we can use the dogs . . .'

Horowitz pursed his lips at the look of eager anticipation on Stieber's face, lips drawn back over his teeth. The man was a sadist. His greatest pleasure was watching his dogs rip another human being to pieces. If he wasn't such a good tracker Horowitz would have dispensed with his services. A job required a professional – a clinical – approach.

Stieber swung the Volvo off the road and bulled his way down the track, moving too fast, relying on the weight of the car to carry him along. It was a recipe for disaster. Horowitz was about to tell him to slow down, when the Volvo slewed out of control, skidded diagonally off the track and stopped. In the headlight glare they saw the Mercedes with one front door open, stopped under the trees.

'We made it,' exulted Stieber.

'Put the dogs on the slip-leashes before I get out,' ordered Horowitz.

There was something disturbing about the parked Mercedes – and now the Volvo's engine had stopped Horowitz realized the Mercedes' engine was still ticking over. The helicopter had flown much further up the timber track, searchlight probing, the rotors a faint chug-chug. 'You stay in the car,' he ordered Hendrix and she was thankful to remain inside.

Stieber was already opening the rear of the cage, leashing the restless animals, telling them to keep quiet. The helicopter was returning down the timber track and it hovered now above the parked vehicles. Horowitz, a Browning .32 automatic held by his side, stepped out of the Volvo. He waved a hand in a downward chopping motion and the pilot switched off the blinding glare of the searchlight.

Horowitz approached the Mercedes cautiously, crouching by the side furthest away from the open door. He peered round the back. It was then he saw the slumped body of Gustav.

Still crouching, he made a quick examination. Two bullets through the skull, a third in the chest. He switched off his pencil torch and thought. No signs of powder burns so Gustav's killer was a first-rate shot. Something to bear in mind for later. Stieber, the five dogs straining on a multiple slip leash, was on the far side of the track.

'Tweed went this way,' he called out. 'They've picked up Tweed's scent.'

'There's more than Tweed to track,' Horowitz warned.

He was recalling the extract from the Tweed dossier he had read. There had been a clear indication Tweed never used firearms. So who was the killer?

'They can't be far away,' Stieber called out impatiently. 'That Audi that's disappeared turned up this track only a short while back . . .'

'Wait!'

Horowitz walked back to the Volvo, settled himself in the passenger seat and called Elbe Two. The radio op responded at once.

'Bismarck here. You know the position of the cars where you hovered. Fly east of that point over the forest. Use your searchlight. I want Eiger – he's now on foot – harassed, kept on the move. Understood? Then get to it . . .'

He walked over to where the five dogs were heaving at the leash, switched on his pencil flash. A clear footpath

187

into the forest showed up. He bent down, found a freshly snapped twig, straightened up.

'Get after them,' he told Stieber. 'Hurry – before those savages lose the scent. I'm not sure how many you're chasing. Two at least. I want them all. I'll follow with Hendrix at a distance.'

'Don't worry.' Stieber grinned, licked his lips. 'They're dead meat.'

18

Tweed led the file up the steep twisting path through the trees. The route was marked by snow-covered boulders of limestone and a small frozen stream ran to their left. Behind Tweed Paula plodded in her knee-length flat-heeled boots. A dozen yards behind her Newman brought up the rear.

Each of them carried their small case and Tweed climbed upwards confidently as though he'd passed this way yesterday. Just enough moonlight percolated through the dense ceiling of forest above them for him to see ahead. And his night vision was now excellent.

The heavy silence, broken only by the soft tread of their feet sinking into the snow, oppressed Paula. They came to a level stretch and she looked round and up. The palisade of endless vertical trunks sheered up like a stockade. The giant firs spread their branches like huge outstretched hands, hands weighed down with frozen snow. She jumped as there was a sound like a rifle shot. Tweed paused, looked over his shoulder.

'That was only an ice-encased branch snapping under

the weight – sounds like a gun going off.'

'It's horribly cold. How much further?'

'Less than a mile,' he lied. He estimated it was much further to the hunting lodge. 'Just keep moving. Don't watch your feet. Keep your head up . . .'

'Then I'll slip,' she protested.

'Plant your feet down flat. Watch the way I walk . . .'

She was amazed by his stamina, by the way he kept up an even pace going uphill. But then for over a year now he had taken to walking between three and four miles every day to and from Park Crescent to his Radnor Walk flat. The thought of that flat – and what had happened inside it – came back to her with a reaction of horror. She must ask him about it when they reached the hunting lodge. That was then Tweed heard the distant chug-chug of an approaching helicopter and a second moon appeared faintly above the tangled mass of branches. Newman came up behind them rapidly, joined them as the machine came closer and closer.

It was after midnight when Chief Inspector Otto Kuhlmann walked into police headquarters at Freiburg. Inspector Wagishauser, the top officer, and a small dapper man with a neat moustache, stared open-mouthed as he automatically stood up from behind his desk and came forward to greet the new arrival.

Kuhlmann, although small in height, reminded him of old movies he'd seen of Edward G. Robinson. Wide-shouldered with a large head and a wide mouth, he radiated a physical aura which made people look as soon as he entered a crowded room. He wore a grey overcoat, which he stripped off, and a cigar was clenched between his teeth.

'Chief Inspector Kuhlmann!' The surprise showed in Wagishauser's tone. 'Wiesbaden asked me to wait, said someone was flying down to see me – but I had no idea it would be you.'

'You should know by now I rarely announce where I'm going,' Kuhlmann growled. As he spoke he padded over to a large-scale wall map of the *Lande* – the state – of Baden Wurttemburg covering south-west Germany to the Rhine and the Swiss border. Various flags on pins had been inserted into the map.

'What's going on?' Kuhlmann demanded.

'There was a terrible pile-up on the autobahn . . .'

'I heard about that. Sorted out the corpses yet? Who was involved?'

'It was all very odd. I'm afraid several of my men died – following that Mercedes as you ordered. Some maniac drove a huge refrigerated truck the wrong way – up the southbound lane. Four of the cars involved belonged to the World Security organization. Nine of their operatives were killed. No survivors . . .'

'What happened to the Mercedes is my main concern.'

'It disappeared. We thought it must have continued on to Switzerland. But I set up a road-block and it never appeared. I called our frontier control at Basle and they hadn't seen a car with the registration number you—'

'Sounds like my man. You'd expected him to drive on to the Swiss border. He never does the expected. My bet is he took the next turn-off, drove back up the north-bound lane. Any other developments?'

'Only that patrol cars have reported unusual aerial activity over the Black Forest – still going on . . .'

Kuhlmann swung round, removed his cigar. 'What unusual activity? Spit out the details, man.'

'Several choppers are criss-crossing the Forest. We think they belong to World Security. The airport tower reported two had flown in from Frankfurt, one from Basle. They refuelled and took off immediately . . .'

'And they're still flying over the Black Forest on a night like this?'

'So it would seem . . .'

'You have a police Sikorsky at the airfield, I noticed when I came in. It's still there?'

'Yes, Chief Inspector . . .'

'I wanted it equipped with a swivel-mounted machine-gun inside thirty minutes.' Kuhlmann was slipping on his overcoat. 'And the machine must be fully fuelled. By the time I get there. Thirty minutes from now . . .'

The helicopter was hovering just above them as Newman stood with Paula and Tweed. They were sheltering under an enormous overhang of snow perched on the lower branches of a huge fir. The invisible machine was slowly rotating its searchlight over the forest below.

'He'll spot our tracks in the snow,' Paula whispered and then wondered why she was whispering. The beat of the rotors would have drowned a shout.

She pointed to the path alongside the frozen stream they had walked up. In the snow their footsteps were clear imprints and there were gaps in the tree cover. Tweed put his arm round her shoulders and gave her a reassuring squeeze. She smiled gratefully. The raw dry cold was penetrating her coat and her feet felt like blocks of ice.

'Keep still,' Newman warned in his casual voice.

He had taken off his gloves, tucked them under his arms. He held the Walther ready for use. There didn't seem to be anywhere the chopper could land but he wasn't taking any chances. The probing searchlight passed slowly across the platform of snow hiding them. Seconds later Paula nearly shrieked, clapped a hand to her mouth with fear.

It was probably the proximity of the vibrating rotors which caused the near catastrophe. Without warning the platform of snow collapsed, covering them with snow, exposing them to view. Newman repeated his warning and stood like a statue, staring upwards. He could see the faint outline of the chopper now.

It appeared to be poised just above the treetops, a long luminous shape as the moon reflected off its fuselage. He could even see the dizzying blur of the whirling rotors. Paula had clenched her teeth tight. Tweed was gripping her more firmly to keep her still. Their cases, which they had placed on the ground, were mounds of snow. The stream, about two feet wide, was frozen solid where it had once tumbled downhill over and between rocks. In places the moon gleamed on pure ice which made her feel even colder. Oh, God, she thought, how much more of this nightmare can I stand?

The helicopter began to ascend and then flew slowly away. As its chug-chug faded they heard another sound as they were on the point of continuing their trudge uphill. Tweed heard it first and placed a restraining hand on Paula's arm as she stopped to dig in the snow to locate the handle of her case. She straightened up, her gloved hand gripping the handle. It felt heavier – the snow was freezing solid on the suitcase.

'What is it?' she whispered again.

Then she noticed Newman had turned his head in the direction they had come, listening intently. He lifted his ear flaps from his fur hat, cocked his head sideways. Tweed stood like a waxwork figure, his expression grim, staring down the path. Then Paula heard it.

'Oh, God, no!'

'Tracker dogs,' Newman said tersely.

'And coming this way,' Tweed commented.

Newman glanced all round, stared at the frozen stream, then looked up. He delved into the snow, found Tweed's case, handed it to him. As he burrowed for his own case Tweed knocked the snow from the surface of his case and Paula automatically cleaned off her own.

The eerie howl of the pursuing dogs echoed weirdly in

the white wilderness. They seemed terribly close to Paula, a whole tribe of the ghastly hounds. Newman stood up, holding his case and looked at Tweed, speaking quickly.

'You head for the hunting lodge with Paula. I'm staying here. We can't out-run those beasts. No argument. Just one thing. How can I be sure to find the hunting lodge on my own?'

'Follow the stream, Tweed told him quickly. 'Higher up it flows past the side of the lodge . . .'

'I want you both to leave this path,' Newman snapped. 'The only way to kill your scent is to make your way up that icy stream. Can you manage that?'

'We'll have to. You have a plan?'

'Yes, but for Christ's sake get moving . . .'

Both Tweed and Paula wore footwear with crêpe soles, but Tweed's boots were corrugated. He took a long stride, gripping Paula by the arm, placed one foot on the stream, felt the snow holding him steady and started moving uphill fast. Several times Paula slipped, but always Tweed held her up, saved her balance. In half a minute they were out of sight. The banshee-like howling of the dogs was much closer. Newman bent down, opened his case.

Horowitz, his eyes calm and cold behind the steel-rimmed spectacles, trudged at a steady pace up the path as Hendrix struggled to keep up with him. He noted the muddle of footprints in the snow – the many small impressions of the paws of the dogs, the broad marks of Stieber's footprints and other footprints. What worried him was he could hear the dogs growling in blood-lust fury and the sound was close and stationary. He walked round a dense strand of trees and found Stieber holding the multiple leash, staring back at him.

'Why have you stopped?' he demanded. 'And quieten those savages.'

Stieber gave an order and the dogs fell quiet, circling each other in frustration. Hendrix caught him up, breathless, as the two men faced each other.

'You heard the dogs?' Stieber asked.

'I could hardly fail to hear them. Why were they suddenly making such a terrible row?'

'Because the meat is close,' Stieber gloated. 'Very close. They can sense it. I waited for you to get your agreement.'

'Agreement to what? Get to the point . . .'

'To release the dogs. Let them go on ahead by themselves – finish the job.'

'I don't want to see it,' muttered Hendrix.

Horowitz considered the request. 'How far away do you calculate the targets are?' he enquired.

'No more than half a mile.'

Not only the dogs were straining at the leash. Horowitz sensed Stieber couldn't wait to bring the hunt to its bloody and final end. He brushed snow off his sleeve, spoke quietly.

'Release the dogs . . .'

The snapping, snarling animals, freed from the leash, bounded forward, leapt up the path, vanished from sight. Slipping and slithering all over the ice, Stieber followed, far behind his creatures.

Newman sat about ten feet above the ground, his legs dangling over the branch of the giant fir they'd sheltered under. His case was perched in a crook of the tree. Lying in the snow directly below him was a soiled shirt he'd extracted from the case. In his right hand he held the fully loaded Walther.

The sound of the baying dogs had changed, was coming

nearer much faster. He guessed the handlers had released their charges. Almost frozen stiff, he flexed each arm, transferring the weapon from one hand to the other. He waggled his legs backwards and forwards to keep the circulating moving. Fortunately when the platform of snow had collapsed it had left the thick branch bare so he sat on wood but he could still feel the cold infiltrating his clothes. The joyous barking was much closer. He saw movement lower down the path. He gripped the Walther firmly in both hands, aimed it.

'Come and get it,' he said to himself.

The unknown factor was how many there were. He had eight shots in the gun and hoped he wouldn't have to reload. He could have perched higher up, but they would be moving targets. He wanted point-blank range. The first hound came into view, a massive beast, mouth open, sharp teeth showing. Newman remained quite still.

The dog was faster in its reactions than he'd expected. It sniffed briefly at his shirt, stared round, looked up, saw him. It gave a deep-throated growl as four more dogs joined it, then it crouched and sprang upwards. Newman whipped up the Walther, shot it through the head, slicing off the right side. A second dog made the leap, almost reached his feet. He shot it in the chest. It hung in mid-air for a fraction of a second, collapsed as a still heap in the snow. A third dog leapt for him. It rose so high its head was level with his feet, inches away. He fired twice. The dog fell like a stone, lay on its side. The remaining two beasts paused, circling the bodies. He fired twice more and they sagged, one lying twitching.

A heavy hush descended on the forest. Newman stared down the path as he reloaded, throwing the rejected magazine as far as he could. No sign of the handlers yet. The dogs would have outpaced any human being.

He took hold of his case, leaned down, dropped it on a pile of snow which cushioned its fall. Shinning down the tree, he approached the animal which was still twitching, aimed the muzzle, pulled the trigger. The dog jerked convulsively, lay still.

Newman walked away from the tree across the snow to the south, a different direction from that taken by Tweed and Paula who had climbed east. He came to a bare patch of moss-covered ground where the snow hadn't penetrated, walked a few more paces. Then he slowly walked backwards, placing his boots in the footprints he'd already made until he reached the tree.

Picking up his case, he took a long stride, placing one foot on the frozen stream. Then without a glance back, he plodded on upwards, out of sight.

Horowitz, followed by Hendrix, heard a howl compounded of fury and misery echoing through the forest. Not the sound of a dog. The sound of a human being. He climbed higher and walked slowly round a stand of trees, the Luger in his hand and concealed behind his heavy raincoat with a belt and epaulettes.

Stieber stood looking down at the carnage of his destroyed animals. He swung round as he heard Horowitz and his face was contorted in such rage he reminded Horowitz of one of his charges when alive. Shaking, he pointed.

'They killed my dogs, the bastards . . .'

'The dogs were trying to kill them,' Horowitz reminded him in a mild tone.

Stieber stared wildly at the Hungarian, his right hand slid inside the lapel of his own raincoat. Horowitz whipped up the Luger, aimed the muzzle at Stieber's chest.

'Take your hand out slowly. There had better be nothing in it. Now, that's more sensible. Feeling calmer now? Good. Oh, while I remember it, Stieber – if you ever threaten me again I shall shoot you. Understood?

Now let's fix our concentration on the job in hand . . .'

'There's a trail of footprints heading to the south. I'm going to check them . . .'

Horowitz stood quite still as Stieber trod through virgin snow, walking alongside the footmarks. Behind Horowitz Eva Hendrix shivered, tore her eyes away from the corpses.

'I don't see how they managed it,' she gasped. 'Five dogs attacking at the same time.'

'Oh, it wasn't Eiger. He never carries a gun. But some-one with him does.' He looked up. 'And that someone is clever and dangerous. You see that bare branch? He cleared off the snow, then waited – out of reach of the dogs but in an ideal position to pick them off. Hence the shots we heard.' He used one foot to poke at a crumpled shirt on the ground. 'The gunman even left one of his used shirts – to make sure the dogs would pause beneath where he waited. Eiger has a formidable protector. Ah, here comes Stieber with nothing.'

Stieber looked depressed. 'The tracks disappear. They went on over bare ground.'

'I wonder.' Horowitz made an impatient gesture. 'We can't waste more time here. I have an ace to play. The helicopters. We must return to the Volvo so I can re-establish contact.'

19

Aboard the police Sikorsky Kuhlmann stared down at the endless sea of the Black Forest as the machine headed towards the small spa town of Badenweiler. They were flying five hundred feet above tree level. From that height the forest was a criss-cross of black and white. Black where snow had fallen from the firs, white where it clung frozen to the treetops. The moonglow cast a ghostly light on the empty world below. Kuhlmann glanced up, stiffened.

Maybe half a mile away on the port side flew another chopper. It appeared to be skimming the treetops and from its nose a searchlight was angled downwards, turning slowly as it scanned the forest.

'See that chopper over to port?' he growled into the mike attached to his headset, addressing the pilot in the control cabin for'ard. 'Reduce height, fly towards it, when you're within forty yards of it fly on a parallel course.'

'Forty yards?' the pilot almost yelped. 'That's too close.'

'Which is what that other pilot will think . . .'

'Chief, my co-pilot has been watching it through night glasses. It's a World Security machine.'

'Pull alongside it. That's an order.' He addressed the gunner who was seated in front of him next to the door. A swivel-mounted machine-gun had been secured in front of him. 'When we're in position,' Kuhlmann continued, 'they may need to be persuaded to obey my orders. When I tell you, open fire, give them a burst a dozen yards ahead of their control cabin. That should prove an effective persuader . . .'

'It's illegal,' the gunner protested.

'If I say so, it's legal.'

The machine had altered course, was losing altitude, as Kuhlmann wrenched off his headset, stood in the narrow passage-way and held on to the backs of seats, making his way towards the pilot's cabin. Entering it, he held himself upright with one hand; with the other he reached towards the co-pilot and grasped the night glasses. The co-pilot was also acting as the radio op. He glanced up nervously while Kuhlmann splayed his feet, angled his back against

198

the side of the entrance, focused the glasses. The co-pilot glanced at the pilot, raised his eyes to heaven. Kuhlmann's reputation for taking chances had preceded him.

Within minutes the police chopper was flying alongside the World Security machine, which still had its searchlight on. Through his glasses Kuhlmann was now scanning the forest beyond the second chopper. He suddenly switched them back. Yes, he'd been right. In the middle of a clearing on top of a peaked hill stood a snow-covered mountain lodge. No sign of life. No smoke from the chimney. He didn't think the other chopper had seen it yet. He handed back the glasses, reached for the microphone in front of the co-pilot.

'Calling World Security chopper 4902. This is the police. I am ordering you to return to base immediately. Return to Freiburg airfield immediately. Kuhlmann of Kriminalpolizei speaking . . .'

The co-pilot was gesturing, pointing north. Kuhlmann gazed in that direction and saw three more machines with searchlights spread out over the forest. The co-pilot, who had been staring through his night glasses, handed Kuhlmann a spare headset.

'They're all World Security machines. What's going on?'

'That's what we're here to find out.'

They were still flying parallel to the other chopper, which continued on course. Kuhlmann gestured for the mike, gripped it tightly.

'Calling World Security chopper 4902. Chief Inspector Kuhlmann here again. I repeat – just once more. Return to base immediately. Return to Freiburg airfield . . .'

There was a lot of atmospheric crackle and then a reply this time. The voice of the radio op aboard the other machine was disjointed.

'4902 calling. Kuhlmann, I can't hear what you said . . .'

199

Kuhlmann handed back the mike, spoke into his head-set mike, his tone grim. 'Hans, I said give them a burst. I'm still waiting. That's an order.'

Nothing happened. 'God Almighty,' Kuhlmann muttered to himself. The co-pilot caught his expression, looked away. Kuhlmann swung round, re-entered the passenger cabin. Hans sat frozen, holding the machine-gun. He looked up, shook his head with a gesture of hopelessness. Kuhlmann reached down, grabbed his arm, tugged. Hans tore off his headset, scrambled out of his seat, the chopper wobbled, Hans fell into the seat opposite.

Kuhlmann was already easing his bulk into the gunner's seat. He fastened his belt. He used both hands. One pressed down a lever, slid open the door. Ice-cold air rushed inside the cabin. Hans shuddered with shock. The drop in temperature didn't seem to affect Kuhlmann. He swivelled the barrel of the gun, peered through the sight, fixed the crosshairs on a point about thirty feet in front of the other chopper's nose, pressed the trigger. One short burst, one much longer . . .

The World Security climbed vertically, turned through one hundred and eighty degrees, headed back towards Freiburg airfield. Kuhlmann leaned forward, grasped the door handle and hauled it shut. He felt like a block of ice. He rammed the headset in position again, addressed the pilot.

'Escort him back to Freiburg. Now patch me through to police HQ, same place. Ask for Inspector Wagis-hauser . . .'

He waited, rubbing his large, stubby-fingered hands together. Jesus, it was a cold night. A few minutes later Wagishauser came through. Kuhlmann began speaking rapidly.

'Arrange for a reception committee at Freiburg airfield. And three more World Security choppers are flying over the forest. Order them to return yesterday to Freiburg. I'm escorting a fourth machine back. I had to fire a burst of machine-gun fire across his nose to persuade him to obey my recall order.'

'You did what?' Wagishauser sounded appalled.

'You heard. Now contact those other three choppers. They have to be grounded. And that's an order. Any difficulty, get off your butt, drive round to World Security HQ, locate their communications room, pressure them to recall the other three choppers. OK?'

'But what is this all about? What are the charges?'

'Suspected involvement in drug-trafficking, of course . . .'

Sitting in front of the stationary Volvo, Horowitz couldn't contact the chopper, Elbe Two. No reply. He had a moment of inspiration, sensing trouble, and switched to the police radio band. He was just in time to hear the latter part of Kuhlmann's transmission:

'Arrange for a reception committee . . . I'm escorting a fourth machine . . . I had to fire a burst of machine-gun . . .'

He shushed Hendrix, again sitting in the back, while listening to the rest of the transmission. Beside him, Stieber, still fretting over the massacre of his precious dogs, showed alarm. As Kuhlmann signed off, Horowitz turned off the radio and gazed ahead in silence.

'Shit!' Hendrix called out. 'That's torn the whole ball game wide open . . .'

'We'd better get out of here,' Stieber snapped. 'Once I was interrogated by that bastard, Kuhlmann. He's no feelings at all.'

Horowitz was secretly amused at Stieber concerning himself with other people's feelings. He looked over his shoulder – Hendrix was shredding a lace handkerchief between her teeth.

'You two are easily disturbed,' he remarked. 'A couple of setbacks is nothing in my business. Eiger is still a target. I'm convinced he will run for the Swiss border when the roads south are open. The latest met report forecasts milder weather. We have to be patient. Meanwhile I'll organize a fresh team of World Security operatives . . .'

'At least eight have already been killed,' Stieber interjected, 'in that autobahn pile-up.'

'Please listen. They were all British. This time Evans must supply German operatives – men who really know the area.'

'Which area, for God's sake?' Hendrix asked.

'The Swiss border-crossings, of course. Basle, Konstanz, etc. When Eiger tries to slip over the frontier we'll be waiting for him.'

Landing at Freiburg airfield, Kuhlmann climbed into the car he'd radioed to be waiting for him. He was driven straight to police headquarters. Behind him followed a convoy of two police vans bringing in the crews of the four WS choppers.

Inspector Wagishauser greeted him with the news that the Minister had called him three times from Bonn.

'He sounded agitated. News of the aerial activity over the Black Forest has reached him. He sounded very upset . . .'

'His permanent state of mind. Can I use your desk and phone?'

The two men were alone as Kuhlmann put in the call to Bonn. As he expected, the Minister was still up, answered the phone himself on his private line.

'What is going on down there, Kuhlmann? I've had a

complaint from a man called Evans, managing director . . .'

'I've met the crook. Interrogated him over that business of a truck with high-tech equipment trying to slip over into East Germany . . .'

'Case not proven . . .'

'If you'd listen to me, Minister, I might save you a whole heap of political embarrassment. This thing could go up to the Chancellor. He might be asking *you* some pretty loaded questions.'

A long pause. 'Go on,' the Minister said, and Kuhlmann knew he'd got him.

'First, the original request was for us to locate Tweed. But they didn't tell us they were hiring a British outfit – World Security – to hunt him down and liquidate him on Federal territory. At least that's the way it's beginning to look. How well do you think that would go down with the Chancellor?' He didn't wait for a reaction. 'It's all wrapped up with four WS choppers patrolling the Black Forest in the middle of the night. They've already tried to kill Tweed once, hence that pile-up on the autobahn when eight plain-clothes men ended up on slabs. Maybe you'd prefer to let me go on handling things?'

'What does it all mean?' bleated the Minister.

'If Tweed is caught and taken back to Britain, imagine the public scandal. A quiet death over here would solve the problem nicely, thank you,' Kuhlmann continued smoothly.

'I'm more than happy to leave the case in your hands.'

I thought you would be, Kuhlmann reflected to himself and grinned at Wagishauser who stood listening with fascination.

'One more problem I'm not sure of handling – it might affect how you deal with the problem.' The Minister paused again. I really have you on the run, Kuhlmann thought. 'Lance Buckmaster, their Minister for External

Security, has been on the line to me. He wants to know how we're progressing in the search.'

'Tell him the hunt is continuing. But Tweed is a fox – he'll appreciate that phrase – and difficult to locate. We are now narrowing the search area. No specifics. And ask him if he's questioning our ability to cope.'

'That's a good ploy. Leave it all to you. *Carte blanche* to solve the problem . . .'

Kuhlmann grinned again as he put down the phone. The best detective in the whole of Germany, Kuhlmann was also past-master of the art of handling the politicians he despised. Wagishauser sat down in the chair facing his visitor.

'I'd never have dared talk to him like that, Otto.'

'Which is why you're here and I'm sitting behind my desk in Wiesbaden.'

Kuhlmann lit a cigar and reflected for a moment on the present situation. He was convinced Tweed was the last man to be involved in a murder and a rape, for Christ's sake. And he'd had enough experience weighing up criminals. There had to be a conspiracy. He couldn't actively help Tweed, but he would put roadblocks in the way of his discovery. Give his old colleague time. That, he guessed, was what Tweed needed: time. He looked at Wagishauser.

'The next move is to put the squeeze on Evans and his hirelings. Call Evans, get him out of bed, I want him here in thirty minutes. Counting from now.'

20

The hunting lodge was perched high up on top of a small peak with a clear view from the upper-storey windows over the Black Forest which lapped the sides of the peak like a sea. Standing shivering by a window she had opened, Paula gazed down, searching for any sign of a helicopter. The moonlit sky was empty. She closed the window and made her way down the wooden staircase of the timber-built structure.

'It's all right,' she informed Tweed, 'I can't see any sign of life on the ground or in the sky.'

'Then we'll light this up and get some warmth before we perish.'

He was crouched in front of a huge brick fireplace piled up with logs. While she was upstairs he'd found some old newspapers inside an airtight chest and tucked sheets among the logs. He used his lighter to ignite the paper and within minutes the logs were flaming.

They had reached the lodge to find it closed and shuttered. Tweed had picked up a short straight branch on their way up the mountain: he had seen it as a crude makeshift weapon and had used it as a walking stick up the final steep ascent. After walking all round the large lodge, he had utilized the stick as a crowbar to prise open one of the shutters. Hitting the exposed glass window beyond with his gloved hand, he had reached in through the hole and turned the handle to gain access.

The interior was ice-cold and had a musty odour. Paula had caught whiffs of pine cones scattered over the log fire.

The power had been turned off, the freezer and the fridge were empty. Tweed had grimaced at her discovery.

'So, we go hungry.'

'Hardly. Isn't it a good job that I did some shopping while I was out in Freiburg on my own.'

'What shopping?'

'At a supermarket.' She perched her case on a heavy wooden table, fumbled it open with her gloved hands, started taking out supplies. Two cans of baked beans, two of canned meat, two camping gas canisters with metal frames and grids, two cans of coffee, one of powdered milk, two loaves of bread and a wrapped pack of butter. 'We should survive on that – but not for long,' she warned.

'I should have thought of all that myself.'

'Men!' she chided him with friendly contempt. 'They assume food appears out of thin air.'

'I'm afraid I assumed the power would be switched on for lost travellers – with frozen food in the freezer.'

'But did you ever come up here in winter?'

'No,' he admitted, 'It was in autumn. Now, I'd better get that fire going before we freeze to death.'

'The smoke will show for miles coming out of the chimney,' she warned.

'So you explore upstairs where you get a panoramic view – check if there are any signs of life. Meantime I'll prepare to get the fire going – when you've made your check . . .'

When she ran down the wooden staircase and reported to him she repeated her warning. 'We're perched in the open on top of the highest point for miles. The smoke could locate us.'

'We'll have to risk it – otherwise we freeze to death,' he'd repeated before he set light to the paper.

Paula explored the ground floor, found a modern kitchen with a Calor gas stove – but no Calor gas. The

206

lodge was furnished with rough-hewn wooden chairs and tables and cupboards. In one cupboard in the main living-room she found a stack of sleeping bags. Tweed, still crouched over the fire, using an ancient pair of bellows to fan the flames gently, looked up.

'So, we have something we can sleep in.'

'Just dive inside one of them, you mean?' she suggested.

'Why not? We need sleep . . .'

'Men!' she said again as she sniffed at a sleeping bag and held it to her face. 'They're damp, need drying out.'

She hauled chairs in front of the fire, opened one sleeping bag and looped it over a chair. That was when Tweed stood up suddenly, put a finger to his mouth with one hand, grabbed her with the other, gestured towards the kitchen.

'What is it?' she whispered.

'Someone coming. I heard a faint crunch of feet on crusted snow. No noise. Get into the kitchen . . .'

Moving silently, he picked up the heavy stick which would serve as an effective club, then took up a position on the opposite side of the front door he had unlatched earlier. He was pressed against the roughened wall away from the hinged side. Paula had disappeared. He took a firm grip on the club, waited.

The door moved a millimetre. Tweed would never have noticed had he not been watching it. Seconds later the heavy door was thrown inwards as though struck by a hurricane, slammed back against the wall. Newman dived inside, crouched low, Walther gripped in both hands, swinging the weapon in a wide arc.

'Relax, Bob,' Tweed said in a quiet voice, staying pressed against the wall.

'You might have put out the welcome mat.' Newman slid the gun inside its holster. Tweed closed the door quickly to shut out the cold as Newman went on talking. 'I arrived and saw footprints leading up to this place. No guarantee they were yours.'

Paula appeared from the kitchen. 'Bob! What happened to those horrible dogs we heard coming?'

'Meat for carrion-eaters. Five of them. I shot the lot, then hoofed it up here over that frozen stream. Where does it end? We seem to be on top of a small mountain.'

'I'll show you,' said Tweed. 'It's remarkable.' He paused. 'Any chance you were followed?'

'Oh, come off it. I left the hounds at the foot of that big fir we sheltered under, then trudged up the stream for a short distance. Next move, I climbed another tall tree from where I could just see the corpses. I watched the area with these.' He took a small pair of binoculars from his pocket. 'Two men and a girl arrived. They spent about five minutes there – one of them followed a false trail I'd laid and then came back. Brief discussion. They all went back downhill the way they'd come. I continued on up the stream. What did you want to show me?'

Tweed led the way through the front door on to a wide verandah, walked down the steps and, with Newman and Paula following, took them round the side of the lodge where the frozen stream ran. He pointed to a snow-covered mound.

'That's the origin of the stream, frozen solid now. A very powerful spring gushes up there normally. After winter the stream becomes a rushing torrent when the snow melts.'

'Could you melt it now?' Paula asked. 'That would give us fresh water for our coffee. I have a plastic bottle of water but fresh would taste much better.'

'It would be a cold job,' Newman commented, crouching down, moving layers of snow until he exposed a thick jet of ice.

'So', Paula told him, 'get on with it while I prepare us all a meal under conditions I regard as somewhat primitive. And, Tweed, you keep an eye on that fire . . .'

She left them. Newman glanced at Tweed. 'Ever occur to you that women can be pretty bossy?'

They ate their meal off cardboard plates on the table, which had been hauled near the blazing fire. The pine logs oozed resin, sputtered and crackled, but Paula welcomed the sound. It helped to counter the brooding silence which pressed down on the isolated lodge.

She had served them meat and baked beans cooked on the camping gas, crusty bread and butter. They used plastic cutlery and at one stage Newman made the mistake of cracking a joke.

'This is just like a meal served by an airline – even down to the plastic knives and forks.'

'Really?' Paula folded her arms. 'Maybe you'd have preferred metal cutlery? But then I'd have had to carry it. The weight of my case was quite something coming up through the forest.'

'I assumed it just contained a few clothes. Sorry, I was just trying to lighten the proceedings.'

Tweed intervened. 'Difficult to do that. Under the circumstances. We're all – including Paula – feeling the strain.'

'Then if it's all right by you,' Newman said soberly, 'I'd like to hear what happened when all this started – back at Radnor Walk. I walked in on it and no one has told me much so far.'

'Hardly been time, Bob. But you're right,' Tweed agreed. 'And this is as good a time as any. So this is what happened . . .'

Newman listened in silence as Tweed recalled the late phone call allegedly from Klaus Richter asking Tweed to meet him urgently at the Cheshire Cheese pub in Fleet Street on the fatal night. Tweed gave a concise account, omitting no relevant detail. Paula watched him anxiously, wondering how re-telling the grim story might affect him in his state of near-exhaustion. Newman nodded as he completed his story.

'It all fits with what I observed while I was in your flat. Down to that damning detail of your half-smoked pipe in the ash-bowl. But what about this Klaus Richter? You said he lived at the edge of Freiburg.'

'In an apartment in a new development at the very end of Schusterstrasse . . .'

'But that's where we stayed the night,' Paula burst out in surprise. 'The Hotel Oberkirch was in Schusterstrasse – so why didn't we visit Klaus Richter to find out what was going on?'

'Because I'm sure it would be a death-trap,' Tweed assured her. 'Work it out for yourself. Richter was the bait to lure me away from going home to Radnor Walk until very late. To give someone time to strangle and rape that poor unknown girl. So, either Richter phoned me under pressure – maybe with a gun pressed to his skull. Or if someone else did a good job of imitating him they would still put a close watch on Richter's apartment in Freiburg – especially when they realized I was heading in this direction. Which they obviously did – hence the assassination attempt on the autobahn. No, Richter's apartment was the last place I was going to call on. He's probably dead, anyway.'

'I still think it should have been checked,' Newman commented.

'Oh, it is going to be checked. One of the special instructions I gave Marler when I was alone with him at the Oberkirch was to visit Richter's place. He'll be very careful.'

'Marler?' Newman queried. 'You still trust him?'

'I have to, I'm short of personnel. I need you, Bob, to protect me. I'm the only one who knows about the secret project *Shockwave* I was working on.'

'Care to enlighten me?'

'Now is as good a time as any . . .'

Tweed repeated what he'd told Paula in Brussels about the new computer which was the key to a viable Strategic Defence Initiative. The computer travelling aboard the freighter *Lampedusa* and bound for Plymouth by a devious route.

'Devious?' repeated Newman.

'Yes. It is following a course which avoids all the major shipping lanes.'

'And you have the code book for contacting the *Lampedusa* – with two trick questions to check all is well. Apart from the ship's radio op, does anyone else have the code book?'

'Only the Minister – Lance Buckmaster. He'll carry on making contact with the ship in my absence. From a room with radio equipment at the Admiralty. But he doesn't know about the trick questions. Like the radio op, I have them in my head. Not in the book.'

'What I want to know,' Paula said in a low tense voice, 'is who killed that girl at Radnor Walk?'

'Which is another mission I gave Marler, who is returning to England after checking Richter in Freiburg. You have to grasp the fact that all this was carefully planned by the opposition well in advance. Every contingency was foreseen. And Marler is rather good at unravelling other people's plans.'

'But who is the opposition?' Paula protested vehemently. 'We are working in the dark, on the run, getting nowhere.'

'I think I can answer your question about the identity of the opposition,' Newman replied. 'Someone tried to shoot me from the Mercedes down on that timber track. I shot him instead. I searched him and came up with this.'

He produced a folder from his pocket, threw it on the table. Paula picked it up, examined it, then stared at her two companions.

'Gustav Braun. An employee of World Security & Communications.'

'That's the opposition,' said Newman. 'I've heard rumours of WS using some pretty ruthless tactics in business – but this is the first time I realized they operated murder teams.'

'It could be for a very special operation,' Tweed mused.

'It is. For hunting down and killing you. The big question is who is running the operation? Gareth Morgan, Lance Buckmaster – or Leonora Buckmaster, now chairman. It has to be one of those three. Only power at the top would dare risk going so far.'

'What was your impression of Gareth Morgan when you confronted him over breakfast at the Colombi?' asked Tweed.

'Tough as granite, wily as a cobra, the biggest liar since Baron Munchausen. Very ambitious.'

'So the motive might be complicated – if Morgan plans to take over the whole organization. His first move would be to discredit Lance Buckmaster.'

'How would he do that?' Paula asked.

'By compromising him – maybe to the extent of having him convicted of murder. And if that's the case Morgan is using me as his cat's paw. Marler may uncover a nest of vipers.'

'He'll have his work cut out – considering what you've sent him back to do,' Newman commented.

'Oh, he has a lot to do,' Tweed agreed. 'One line of enquiry he will pursue is to try and obtain the findings of the Special Branch pathologist who conducted an autopsy on the body of that girl. There were traces of blood on the girl's wrists and on the sheet. I think she was tied up before she was foully assaulted – strangled and raped. So identification of the blood groups becomes important. The pathologist's report will record them.'

'You should have left Marler to protect you,' Newman told him. 'Sent me to London instead to dig up all this stuff . . .'

'Except that Marler is a member of the Service and can walk into places you'd never be admitted to. I know you're fully vetted, Bob – but it was always on my say-so that they let you travel to top secret establishments. Now I'm disgraced, to say the least. You'd also be suspect.'

Tweed has really foreseen all the problems, Paula reflected. She asked the question which had been bothering her for days.

'But why did someone go to all that trouble to set you up – have you suspected of this awful crime, go all the way by committing the crime. Why?'

'When we know the answer to that we'll know who murdered the girl in Radnor Walk,' Tweed replied. 'I think we're all at the end of our tethers. We need sleep. We'd better arrange a roster of guard duties – someone must be awake upstairs to watch the approaches to this lodge. I'll take it in turn with Newman. Two hours on, two hours off.'

'Not on your life,' Paula said firmly. 'I thought I was a member of the team. I'll take my turn. But what do we do next – in the morning? It would be dangerous to stay here too long.'

'Which is why we won't stay beyond the morning,' Tweed decided. 'We'll have to try and make it to Switzerland in one day. Move faster than anyone will expect.'

'With no transport?' Paula pointed out.

'There's the blue Audi still hidden inside that copse near the timber track,' Newman reminded her. 'And Tweed drove it deep into the undergrowth, which should give some insulation for the engine. I predict it will take me a while to get it going, but get it going I will.'

'Agreed,' said Tweed.

PART TWO

The Assassin – Horowitz

21

During the night after the abortive hunt for Tweed in the Black Forest, Horowitz had slept soundly for several hours in his bedroom at the Colombi. At precisely 5 a.m. the automatic alarm clock inside his head woke him. He got out of bed, immediately alert, washed, shaved and dressed swiftly.

Wrapped against the cold in a thick scarf and an overcoat, he told the night porter he hadn't been able to sleep and was going for a walk. The porter shook his head.

'It's bitterly cold out there, sir. And watch your footing. The sidewalks and streets are like a glacier . . .'

Horowitz thanked him for the warning and made for the Altstadt. The street lamps threw an eerie glow over the snow and no one else was about as he headed up Schusterstrasse, continued along Munzgasse to a T-junction where Konvikstrasse crossed it.

His breath created small puffs in the sub-zero air and from the roof gutters on either side hung rows of icicles. He had reached the edge of the town and ahead a flight of concrete steps led upwards. To their left was a colony of new houses, their architecture carefully designed to merge with the medieval dwellings facing them.

They had steep-tiled roofs and large dormer-windows projecting from the roofs. Beyond them in the near distance rose a wall of dense forest. Several of the houses – all of them divided up into spacious apartments – had pleasant gardens in summer with trees and shrubs and plants. Horowitz looked round one last time, then gently prised up the latch of the grille gate leading into a courtyard. Despite his care the ice splintered under the pressure of his gloved hand and the sound was like a pistol shot.

He closed the gate behind him, walked up to the house, peered inside an uncurtained window. Klaus Richter sat upright in an armchair facing the TV set. Horowitz went back to the front door, rapped on it with a certain irregular tattoo, turned the handle and walked slowly inside. A wave of warmth met him.

'Keep your hands where they are or I'll disembowel you,' ordered a throaty voice.

Horowitz froze, turned his head slowly. Stieber sat in a chair against the wall, a sawn-off twin-barrelled shotgun aimed at Horowitz's stomach.

'Oh, it's you.'

He sounded disappointed. Horowitz remained perfectly still as he spoke in his soft voice.

'First, point that thing away from me – at the far wall.' When Stieber had obeyed he spoke again. 'Now put the safety catch on and place the gun on the floor, muzzle aimed at the wall.'

Stieber grinned unpleasantly as he obeyed the order. 'Nervous, aren't we?'

'Just cautious. You have been here all night? Good. At least I find you alert. Has anyone been near the place? Eiger might have come back to contact Richter – or he might have sent the girl.'

'You see no bodies,' Stieber answered truculently. 'No, no one has been here so far,' he replied quickly as he saw Horowitz's expression. A night spent in the dark had done wonders for his night vision.

'You'll be relieved soon after daybreak. Meantime, stay here.' He glanced at Richter and now an unpleasant stench assailed his nostrils. He wondered how Stieber had stood it through the long hours, then remembered his other profession was that of pig farmer. Richter had been killed by the

218

simple process of injecting air into his veins. Morgan had said something about his first making a phone call to London. Horowitz calculated Stieber had killed him well over twenty-four hours before. He was about to leave when Stieber made the remark.

'I wonder whether anyone has been blown to pieces by the bomb you placed under that blue Audi we found hidden near the timber track?'

'We can always hope.'

'Gives me quite a kick thinking about that bomb. Helped to pass the time while I was sitting here with Zombie over there. The idea of Eiger coming back for his transport, turning on the ignition time and again to get the frigging motor going. That should have set off the bomb – the vibrations. Or maybe he'd got it going and was backing on to the track when – *Boom!* I'd like to have been there to see that – from a distance, if you see what I mean. It would have given me a real kick . . .'

'I'm going now,' Horowitz said. 'Tell the man who relieves you to stay inside here on duty until nightfall, then leave. No one will come after that.'

Horowitz was glad to leave the house. The reactions of the toad he'd left behind filled him with distaste. And he doubted if anyone would come near the apartment to check on Richter.

Marler, who had driven back to Freiburg the previous night in the grey Audi as soon as the chopper disappeared, also slept at the Colombi. The alarm clock on his bedside table woke him at 5.30 a.m.

'You're the second guest to brave the elements this morning,' the night porter remarked.

Marler paused at the front entrance. 'Really? Perhaps that was my friend who also likes fresh air before breakfast. What did he look like?'

'Tall, thin chap. Older than yourself. Maybe forty. Hard to tell. And he wears steel-rimmed glasses. Got a very deliberate walk. He'll need that this morning. So will you. Bloody ice all over the place. Was he your friend?'

'No. The description doesn't fit. I'll heed your warning.'

And that, Marler thought, as he walked through the eerily silent town, was more of a warning than the night porter could ever have guessed. The description fitted perfectly the photograph he'd taken the previous day of one of the men entering WS headquarters. A perfect word description of Armand Horowitz.

Why would Horowitz be prowling Freiburg so early? Marler noticed the single file of footprints leading from the Colombi imprinted in the snow. It was a long shot chance but he followed the footmarks to see where they led.

His suspicions strengthened as he followed them along the street called Schuster, continued along Munzgasse. They were leading him to the address of Klaus Richter, 498 Konvikstrasse, given to him by Tweed. Was it possible that Horowitz was waiting at Richter's address, foreseeing someone would sooner or later arrive to question Klaus? He decided it was not only possible – it was probable. Horowitz never missed a trick.

As he approached the long flight of concrete steps leading to the colony of new houses, eventually to the footbridge which crossed the ring road, he put his hands inside his trench-coat pockets, checked their contents. A .32 Browning automatic, a knuckleduster – and an aerosol filled with Mace gas. The last weapon was quite illegal.

He paused outside the shuttered café called *Wolfshohle* – the Wolf's Lair. Appropriate enough if Horowitz was in the vicinity. To his right was a fountain which would normally project water into the stone basin surrounding it. The jets were frozen solid, the water in the basin a sheet of ice. And still he had seen no one.

He strolled slowly up the steps, noted that Konvikstrasse

498 stood to his right, the way into the courtyard barred by a small grille gate. He also noted the footmarks leading inside, the fractured ice on the latch. He continued higher up to look the place over from the back.

There was a small rear garden enclosed by walls. Bareheaded, his hair gleaming under a lamp, Marler could stand up to any amount of cold weather. He thought for a moment.

At the main entrance lower down the flight there had been a second trail of footmarks, leading *away* from the apartment, continuing along Konvikstrasse towards the Munster. Marler was puzzled. Was the place empty now? A dangerous assumption.

He climbed over the wall, dropped into a heap of snow which broke his fall, made no sound. He approached the rear door. No lights inside the place. Extracting a leather pouch from his jacket pocket, he studied the lock, chose a pick-lock, inserted the instrument inside the lock, fiddled gently. He felt the lock turn. He slipped the pouch back inside his pocket, took out the Mace gas aerosol, slowly turned the handle of the door, pushed it inwards with great care. Well-oiled hinges. No sound. Warmth rushed out to meet him. He stiffened.

The central heating was turned on. Why – if no one was inside the apartment? He half-closed his eyes, blinking in the gloom. He was in the kitchen. He sniffed. A faint aroma of coffee recently made. He closed the rear door with equal care. His eyes were becoming accustomed to the dark.

The inner door was open and beyond was a straight passage which presumably led to the living-room at the front. He'd been puzzled on his arrival by the fact that no net curtains were drawn across the front windows downstairs, no curtains at all – unlike all the other apartments.

The passage was tiled, which was fortunate. Less risk of giveaway creaks. He walked slowly down the passage, holding the Mace aerosol at chest height like a gun. The door to what he felt sure was the living-room was wide open. He listened. A quiet creak, like someone changing position in a wooden chair. His nerves went like steel, as they always did at the moment of crisis.

He reached the doorway, peered through the gap between the door and the wall. One man, facing him, sat rigidly still in an armchair. Too still. Against the inner wall by the passage a second man sat, short, squat, with a rounded head. Across his lap rested a sawn-off shotgun. Charming.

Marler retraced his steps silently to the kitchen. A can of coffee stood on a wooden working surface. There had been a peculiar smell drifting from the living-room. To Marler it had been the smell of death, decomposition. He lifted the can of coffee, made sure the lid was pressed on tightly, then knocked over the can. It rolled, rested against the rear wall.

Marler was now squeezed against the wall alongside the door and opposite the hinged side. From the living-room came the sound of the same creak, but louder. Like a man slowly getting up. The man moved so quietly Marler's first intimation that he had reached the kitchen was when he saw the barrel of the shotgun poked through the opening. The squat man took two more paces. Marler took a deep breath, held it, squirted a limited jet of Mace into the jowly face.

Everything after that happened very quickly.

Stieber gasped, staggered into the kitchen. His left hand flew to his eyes, blinded temporarily by the gas, groaning with the pain. His right hand still gripped the shotgun. Marler moved behind him, his crooked right arm looped round Stieber's neck, jerked it backwards, just short of the point where it snapped.

'Just a little more pressure,' he hissed in German, 'and your neck snaps like a stick of celery. Put the safety catch on that gun. Now!'

In agony, Stieber grasped the message from the chilling voice of his unknown assailant. He fumbled with the shotgun. More by luck than judgement he found the safety catch, put it on.

'That's better,' Marler told him. 'Now we're going to walk back into the living-room. Shuffle with your feet. I'm not relaxing my hold. But I might take it that extra inch tighter . . .'

Stieber was disorientated, in a state of shock. Awake all night, he was in no condition to resist, even to think clearly. One emotion dominated his mind. Fear. He turned round, shuffled slowly along the passage in Marler's grip, clawing at his eyes with his left hand. The smarting sensation was growing worse.

Marler guided him through the doorway into the living-room, told him to place the gun on a table. *Very carefully.* He then guided him to the carver chair where Stieber had been sitting – probably to keep himself awake – and sat him in the carver. Stieber sagged, used both his hands to rub his eyes while Marler patted him all over for other weapons. Nothing.

The dead body of Richter had been propped up inside a chair to give him a lifelike appearance from the window. Marler stopped several feet away from the corpse, wrinkled his nose. He turned his attention again to Stieber.

'I'm going to ask you questions. I know most of the answers. Lie to me once, I'll know, I'll break your neck. Play along with me and you'll live to see another day. Understood?'

Stieber nodded. His right hand massaged the back of his neck which was aching horribly. But his vision was coming back. To protect himself, Marler had used only a small quantity of Mace. Stieber could now see him as a blurred silhouette. He was careful not to stare at the silhouette. His eyes fell on the outline of the shotgun, a few feet from where he sat.

223

'Understood,' he replied in German, the language this bastard had addressed him in from when he first spoke.

'Klaus Richter made a telephone call to London. You forced him to make that call. How?'

'I held a knife across his throat . . .'

'The call was made from here? From that telephone over there?'

'Yes . . .'

'I warned you.' Marler's voice was cold, detached. 'The man who took the call in London heard a lot of noise in the background . . .'

'Tape recorder . . .' Stieber's throat hurt and he was croaking. He pointed. Marler noticed the finger pointed straight at the recorder perched on a sideboard. Stieber's vision was clearing.

Marler, watching Stieber, crossed to the recorder, switched it on. The sound of voices with music in the background filled the room. That was how they had made it sound convincing to Tweed: noises like a pub. He switched off the recorder.

'Name of the man Richter called? Don't hesitate . . .'

'Tweed, whoever he may be—'

'When Richter ended the call someone killed him.' He aimed his Browning. 'I don't give a damn who. Just tell me—'

'I did. Injected air into a vein with a hypodermic—'

'Who ordered you to do this?'

A long pause. Stieber stirred restlessly. Marler holstered the Browning, flexed his hands, approached Stieber.

'Horowitz,' Stieber croaked quickly. 'Armand Horowitz. And don't ever let him know I told you, for God's sake.'

'Or for yours. I won't. Where is Horowitz now?'

'No idea.' Another pause. 'He came here about half an hour before you showed – to make sure I was waiting in case Eiger came here to check on Richter like you've done.

224

Then he left. I don't know where for. I don't think he'll come back. Hope to God he doesn't – my neck must be bruised and he'd notice that.'

'Show me the hypodermic you used on Richter. I need proof of that part of your story.'

Stieber stumbled to his feet, staggered to a sideboard, opened a drawer. 'In here—'

'Show it to me,' Marler ordered.

Stieber picked up the hypodermic out of the drawer. Marler nodded. That ensured the instrument carried his fingerprints.

'Put it back in the drawer. What is your name?'

'Helmut Stieber.'

'Who do you work for?'

'World Security in town here. As a guard. Richter was a freelance job I did on the side . . .'

I'll bet, Marler thought. Stieber was swaying about, having trouble keeping his balance. He staggered back towards where he'd sat, then lunged suddenly for the shotgun. Which was the move Marler had been expecting. Before Stieber reached the weapon his crooked arm closed round his neck for the second time. Stieber yelped with frustration and terror, sagged like a sack of potatoes.

'Stand up straight or this is it,' snapped Marler.

Stieber forced himself upright. Marler tightened the death grip, then released a little of the pressure. Stieber croaked out the words, his voice trembling.

'I've told you the truth.'

'I'm sure you have. But it was naughty trying to reach that shotgun. A good try, I'll give you that. Now, I'll tell you what I'm going to do. I need to get away from here . . .'

'I won't say a word. I'll stay here as long as you—'

'Yes, you will do just that. Why? Because we're going up that staircase to one of the bedrooms. Then I'm going to use adhesive tape to tie your wrists behind you, and I'm going to tape your ankles. You'll be left on one of the beds.

When I'm a long way from here I'll phone any friend you name to come and release you. Got any friends, Helmut?'

He was guiding Stieber into the hall as he spoke. He looked round the room and everything was perfect. Stieber's fingerprints on the shotgun; more important – Stieber's prints also on the hypodermic. The police should be able to work out something. At the foot of the stairs he used his left hand to take out the Browning. He thrust it against the German's back, then released his grip. 'This is a Browning. Walk slowly upstairs.'

Stieber climbed the treads one by one. Marler had released his grip, but the muzzle of the Browning was pressed hard into Stieber's back.

Marler ordered his captive to lie face down on a bed in a room at the back. Taking a small reel of adhesive tape from his pocket, he bound Stieber's wrists together behind his back, then performed the same action with his ankles.

'I have a friend—' Stieber began, turning his round head on the pillow.

'So have I,' Marler informed him.

Closing the door, he slipped on a pair of surgical gloves, ran downstairs and picked up the phone in the living-room. The lifeless Richter stared at him as he dialled police HQ.

'I'm reporting a murder in Freiburg. I have to speak with Chief Inspector Kuhlmann. No, no one else will do. And I'm going off the line if he doesn't come to the phone in thirty seconds. If he's sleeping somewhere else I want the number now . . .'

'He's here. Hold on—'

'For thirty seconds.'

Kuhlmann, freshly shaven, had been up all night and was in the canteen, drinking a cup of black coffee. He had got nowhere interviewing Evans. The Welshman insisted he had just returned from a conference at their Basle headquarters in Switzerland. He knew nothing of recent operations and was only prepared to talk with his lawyer present.

'Kuhlmann followed the uniformed policeman who had told him he was needed on the phone. No, the man at the other end had given no identification. Another crank call, Kuhlmann thought.

'Kuhlmann here. Who am I talking to?' he asked in German.

'A friendly informant,' the voice replied in the same language. 'Konvikstrasse 498. A case of murder. The murderer is still on the premises. So is the victim. That's it.'

Marler put down the phone quietly. His acute hearing caught the sound of footsteps approaching the front, crunching the snow. The sound of the grille gate being opened.

He walked rapidly back down the hall into the kitchen, shut the door, opened the back door, shut that door. Ice-cold air hit his exposed face. He ran to the wall, climbed it, hanging on to the metal rails at the top for support. He had changed his surgical gloves for his leather pair. He hauled himself over the rail, peered down the deserted staircase.

A fresh trail of footsteps were planted in the snow, footprints which stopped at the entrance to the house. He crept down until he could see the front of the house. A familiar figure stood with his back to him outside the front door, a tall thin man. Armand Horowitz had returned for some reason.

Marler waited until Horowitz had disappeared inside, then he ran down the remaining flight, turned left and walked along the Konvikstrasse towards the city gate, the Schwabentor. It was going to be a race against time. Kuhlmann might arrive soon enough to trap both men. Horowitz might move swiftly enough to free Stieber and both men might escape. That was Kuhlmann's problem. Marler's problems lay much further away. In England.

22

It was 7 a.m. in London. Buckmaster sat behind Morgan's desk at World Security HQ in Threadneedle Street. He had driven early from the Belgravia apartment in Leonora's Volvo – one advantage of her insistence on sleeping in her own bedroom. He could come and go without her knowledge. The Volvo was parked in the underground garage.

Morgan, wearing another dark suit buttoned tight over his ample stomach, sat in a chair facing his chief. He felt sleepy from the flight during the night in the Lear jet from Freiburg but his eyes were alert, like two blackcurrants.

'So, Tweed is still on the loose.' Buckmaster ran a hand through his unruly hair, leaned back in the swivel chair and placed one foot, shod in a handmade shoe, on the desk top. 'I thought you'd have cleaned up that little problem by now,' he said sarcastically, and clasped his hands behind his neck.

'Not so little.' Morgan toyed with a long cigar without lighting it. 'We have made great progress. We know he's somewhere in the Black Forest area—'

'*Was,*' Buckmaster snapped. 'What guarantee have you he's there now?'

'One attempt was made on him along the autobahn—'

'No details, please. When are you going to complete the job?'

He spoke in his bored voice, the one so often used

addressing an idiot questioner in the House. He had the satisfaction of seeing a flash of resentment in Morgan's eyes. Keep them on their toes. Especially the top people.

'The snow will help,' Morgan said emphatically. 'There has been a heavy fall in that area. Which means a car can be spotted more easily. He has to move out of the area soon – and we know the car he'll use.'

'I want him kept on the run.' Buckmaster leaned forward and slapped the flat of his hand on the desk. 'I want him harassed to death. Literally. I want him so confused he can't think. I want him driven out of his mind with terror. Maybe the best route to get at him is through Paula Grey.' He smiled sadistically. 'You do get my meaning?'

Morgan had always prided himself he could stand up to any pressure. But during his ranting Buckmaster had raised his voice until he was almost shouting. His expression was vindictive, his complexion red with fury. There were times when Morgan had wondered whether he was close to the edge – of insanity.

'I get your meaning,' Morgan said slowly. 'We've been faced with problems like this before. We have the apparatus to solve them—'

'*You* have the apparatus!' Buckmaster's voice rose to a manic shriek. He leaned across the desk, hair awry. 'I want this man destroyed. You can't do it sitting on your fat backside here in London. You said Freiburg, the Black Forest. So that's where you should be. Leading the manhunt.'

'I'll fly back today. Leave it all to me. You've never known me to fail . . .'

'There's always a first time . . .' Buckmaster's tone dropped to a sibilant hiss. 'This had better not be it.'

He used both hands to straighten his tie, tucking the end back inside his trouser top. Then he gave a broad smile, steepled his hands in a praying-mantis gesture, elbows rested on the desk.

'I do have every confidence in you, Gareth. Without you I'd never have built up this organization. You're the one person in the world I really trust.'

Morgan nodded while he thought. He'd just witnessed a typical Buckmaster performance. First, the use of threats and a mood of almost uncontrollable rage. Then, a swift change of mood to sweet reasonableness. He was familiar enough with the technique. But always before it had been practised on minions. He didn't appreciate being the recipient. He changed the subject.

'The killing and rape at Radnor Walk. Has anyone identified the victim yet? I might be able to use it in my pursuit of Tweed. The Special Branch net closing in – that kind of tactic.'

'Not a clue yet.' Buckmaster was relaxed again, hands behind his neck, legs stretched out under his desk. 'The Chief Inspector in charge of the investigation thinks she was probably a foreign girl. Tweed travelled abroad a lot.'

'Why foreign?' Morgan couldn't conceal the anxiety in his voice.

'Because all the makers' labels had been removed from her clothes. Her underclothes were newly bought – probably the first time she'd worn them. Same with her handbag, shoes and her tights. Inside her handbag was a bill listing the purchase of some of those items from Harrods the day of the murder. No credit cards. Only fresh banknotes in her purse.'

'All of which must have made her appear to be very English,' Morgan ventured.

'Too English for the Inspector's liking. More like a foreign girl who had been equipped with everything English.' Buckmaster yawned. 'You seem very interested in her identification.'

'I just told you why.'

'I must go.' Buckmaster stood up, straightened his jacket, reached for his overcoat. 'Before Leonora arrives.

She gets in early sometimes. How are you coping with her?'

'I can handle her. She's a woman. They're all subject to becoming emotional, even hysterical. That's why they make lousy top executives.'

'God! Look at that weather.' Buckmaster had wandered over to the window. The panoramic view was blotted out by a curtain of thick snowflakes drifting steadily down. Buckmaster spun on his heel. 'I'm off. I was never here.'

'Of course.'

Half an hour later, as Morgan checked through recent contracts, the summons came over his intercom.

'Gareth? Could you pop along to my office? For a short chat?'

He was startled to hear Leonora's voice. His first thought was Buckmaster had left just in time. His second thought was to wonder what she was up to. Her voice sounded very husky, very appealing. The tone she adopted when she wanted to throw someone off balance.

She was sitting behind her desk, dressed in a Chanel suit. Her blonde hair gleamed in the desk lamp she'd switched on: outside it was like night. As he settled himself in a chair on the opposite side of her desk she stood up, hauled a stiff-backed chair round the end, sat beside him, crossed her shapely legs.

'Lance has been here to see you, hasn't he? This morning.'

'No,' Morgan lied smoothly. 'As a Minister he can't . . .'

'I know. He's not supposed to have anything to do with the running of the company.' She had been tapping her perfect white teeth with a pencil. Now she used it to tap the knuckles of his stubby-fingered hand resting on his knee. 'But I can keep a secret. Come on, Gareth, give.'

And I can keep a secret, Morgan thought. 'I was here at

231

7 a.m.,' he told her. 'I've been working in my office on my own.'

'So why did he take my Volvo early this morning? I had to be driven here in the Daimler by Hanson.' Her blue eyes gazed into the distance. 'Still, if he wasn't here he must have been visiting a friend. Feminine sex. The stamina of the man. At this hour of the day. I ask you!'

'He's Minister for External Security,' Morgan persisted. 'He could have gone anywhere in that capacity – maybe somewhere it wasn't good policy to be seen. Hence his taking your Volvo.'

'Gareth, if he's fooling around, I want to know who with. I'm putting a first-class detective agency on his track. Sooner or later I'll know who she is.' Her tone became coaxing. 'You know, I haven't many people I can trust. I'm not such a fool as to confide in women friends. I need someone I can talk to. You fit the bill.' She tapped his knuckles again with the pencil. 'You do know, I hope, that Lance has plans to ease you out of the company?'

Morgan stirred uncomfortably in his chair. This was a dangerous situation. Which was the best way to play it to his future advantage? Leonora had dumped a time bomb in his lap.

'No, I didn't know that,' he said eventually.

'It doesn't mean he'll succeed,' she continued. 'Provided you have me on your side.'

'I'm grateful for your support,' he said quietly, wondering how he could bring the conversation to an end.

'We'll talk some more later, Gareth.'

She gave him her winning smile, stood up, walked back behind her desk and waved a slim hand at her in-tray. He stood up, said he also had a whole load of work to get through and left her office.

He locked the door of his own office, went to his desk, pressed the button which lit up the red *Do not disturb* light outside and sank into his chair. He mopped his damp forehead and hands with a handkerchief, took out his hip flask and swallowed a large slug.

He was badly shaken. Was it possible that Buckmaster was planning to get rid of him? Or was Leonora playing some devious game of her own. His second worry was her idea of hiring some detective agency to follow Buckmaster. Sooner or later the detectives were bound to come up with evidence of dalliance with some attractive female.

Should he warn Buckmaster? He decided he'd better leave the whole thing alone until he saw how it developed. Either way lay a trap. If he didn't warn Buckmaster and he found out about what Leonora had said, then he was out. And these fools of women had a habit of losing control in an argument and telling their husbands about things they shouldn't. But if he did warn Buckmaster, and Leonora won in a battle for control of the company, her first executive decision would be sack Morgan.

Inside her own office Leonora studied her appearance in a wall mirror, searching for traces of the dreaded wrinkles. She was satisfied she had planted doubts in Gareth's mind. He might even play along with her. She smiled at her image. Morgan had no suspicion that if she gained control her first pleasant task would be to throw him into the street.

Walking briskly to her desk, she took her notebook from her handbag, checked the phone number Marler had given her during their ride back to London from Dartmoor. Her slim fingers dialled the number and she soon grasped she was in touch with one of those beastly answerphones. Marler's voice came over the line.

'This is . . .' He gave only the number. No name. '. . . I am not available at the moment. Leave a message when you hear the tone . . .'

She thought quickly, worded her response carefully: she never trusted recorded phone calls.

'This is the lady you gave a lift to from Dartmoor. Please

call me at the office as soon as possible. At the office,' she repeated and broke the connection. A call to their Belgravia apartment could be dangerous; Lance was so often there.

What a wicked web I'm weaving, she mused. The thought gave a lot of satisfaction.

Marler took a cab from London Airport to the address of a man who ran a picture library of well-known people. He obtained the picture he wanted – a better photograph than he'd hoped for – and paid the large fee. He next took a cab to his flat in Chelsea, dumped his bag, checked the answerphone.

Leonora had made her voice sound very sexy in the few words she had spoken. Marler listened twice to the message before he put down the phone. I wonder what you're up to my devious lovely, he was thinking. He made himself a cup of black coffee, using the percolator in the tiny galley kitchen, and drank the whole cup in two swallows. Before leaving the flat he rammed a peaked check cap over his fair hair, took a cheroot from a packet, tucked it in his breast pocket. Clutching the cardboard-backed envelope containing the photograph, he left his flat.

The next cab took him to Wardour Street in Soho. He paid it off and walked the half-mile to his real destination, a first-floor office in Greek Street. The area was a mix of respectable restaurants, recording studios, and less respectable sex shops.

'Grubby' Grundy, as he was known in the trade, worked inside a small fortress. Running up the greasy staircase, Marler used the metal speakphone attached to the door above a plate which read J. GRUNDY, PHOTOGRAPHIC AGENCY.

'Grundy? This is Freddie Moore. Got a job for you . . .'

234

'I'm pretty busy now. Wait a minute,' a gravelly voice replied through the grille.

Marler lit a cheroot. He knew he had plenty of time. He could hear the grind of the steel inner door beyond the wooden one he faced, opening on its hinges. Then came the sound of bolts being drawn, three locks being unlocked. Marler pulled down the peak of his cap. He had the appearance of a racecourse tipster.

The wooden door opened on a heavy chain and a face like a wrinkled walnut peered through the gap. Impossible to guess Grundy's age. Wearing an old-fashioned waistcoat over a soiled shirt, his hooked nose supported a pair of *pince-nez*. The cuffs of his shirt were worn and hadn't seen a laundry for a long time.

'It is you,' Grundy commented and released the chain.

'You should be able to recognize my voice,' Marler commented.

He spoke again with the cheroot in his mouth, which altered his voice.

'Can't be too careful these days,' Grundy mumbled. 'Folks can mimic voices. Come in. Like I said, I'm pretty busy so you'll 'ave to wait for a few weeks, whatever it is you're wanting.'

Marler said nothing as Grundy went through the process of reconstructing his fortress. All this gab was an attempt to put up the price. Grundy shuffled over to a wooden work-table covered with photographs, a pot of glue, various photographic mounts in different sizes. All window dressing.

'What is it you be wanting?'

Grundy drank some liquid which looked like stale tea from a chipped mug. The large room overlooking Greek Street had the musty odour of an office which hadn't been polluted with fresh air for weeks. Marler opened the envelope, placed the photograph upside down after clearing a space on the table.

235

'I want one of your famous artistic fake-ups with some girl. Not a tart. Someone who looks classy, even if she isn't . . . No, don't touch!' he warned as Grundy reached for the photo. 'There's a little matter of the price to decide first. The girl will have to be reclining . . .'

Grundy snickered. 'Ah! A dirty picture. That comes very expensive . . .'

'How much? Just one copy. And I'll collect it this afternoon.'

'Don't know if I could manage that . . .'

'Then I'll go elsewhere . . .'

Marler was reaching for the print when Grundy's gnarled hand slapped down over it. He shook his head, his expression resigned.

'You always want everything yesterday on the few occasions we've done business. Five hundred nicker . . .'

'Five hundred pounds!' Marler took the cheroot from his mouth, flicked ash on the floor, replaced it between his lips. 'You are out of your crazy mind. One hundred is my price. For one photo.'

'You don't know what skill I 'ave. I 'ave to make two master prints – one of your pic, one of the girl. Then I 'as to merge the two, make another master print. I then 'as to take another master – after the retouchin' to hide the linkin' of two pics into one—'

'I do know,' Marler snapped. 'And since I'm in a generous mood I'll make it a hundred and fifty.'

'Two hundred,' Grundy snapped. 'And that's my final offer – the door is there.'

'Done. Two hundred. And that includes the negatives. You forgot to mention them.' Marler reached up with both hands, grasped Grundy by his waistcoat and shook him, his ice-blue eyes staring at the photographer. Feeling the slippery texture of the waistcoat he wished he'd been wearing gloves. 'I wouldn't like to have to call back for a missing negative, so be a good lad. Now, show me the girl.'

He released his grip and Grundy was trembling. Mumbling to himself, he took a key-ring from his trouser pocket, shifted a pile of framed blow-ups leaning against a wall and exposed a safe. Squatting on his haunches, he opened the safe, riffled through a pile of glossy prints, selected three, closed the safe and stood up.

'One of these should do you. They're all nudies . . .'

'Show me.'

Marler studied the three prints Grundy spread out over the table. They were mildly pornographic, showed three girls in the act of making love to a man. One was a blonde whose appearance surprised Marler – surprised him that she would permit such a photo to be taken. She was sprawled sideways.

'That one, I think. If you can marry it up.'

Grundy grinned lecherously. 'Oh, I bet I can marry them up all right . . .'

He reached for Marler's print, turned it over. Buckmaster fully clothed, had been photographed sprawled on his back along a couch, hands clasped behind his head. Grundy swore foully, glared at Marler.

'Moore, that's Lance Buckmaster. The bloody Minister. If I'd known you wouldn't 'ave got it for a penny less than the five hundred nicker I asked . . .'

Marler lifted a hand as Grundy crouched over the table and pressed his fingers hard on a certain muscle. Grundy yelped with pain. Marler's voice was quiet, sinister.

'One other thing I'm paying for. You've a bad memory. If I hear you've been talking about this I'll be back.' He looked round at the messy room, the shelves stuffed with a collection of brown folders. 'Some people might wreck this room, but it's a wreck already. You talk, I'll hear about it, and you'll be the wreck.' He let go of Grundy. 'You *can* marry them up?'

'They're both in a perfect position. The subject will be 'avin' the time of his life when I've finished my work.'

'I'm off. I'll be back at five this afternoon. And you've a job to do. Make it perfect. I have an artistic eye and I'm expecting a masterpiece. Go to it, Grundy.'

Marler stood on the pavement in the middle of Waterloo Bridge, the collar of his trench coat turned up against the bitter wind. Snowflakes were drifting down again.

He had given Leonora precise instructions when he called her from a public phone. She was to borrow a car from one of the directors, drive south of the river, head for Waterloo, then turn north along the bridge, *crawling*. She had told him she'd be inside a silver Mercedes after she'd asked him to hold on while she checked which car was available. Now he saw a silver Mercedes crawling towards him. A cab driver overtook her, shouted at her as he passed. She continued her crawl.

Marler stared hard at the vehicles behind her, checking for a car following her. There wasn't one. She pulled up alongside him. He opened the front passenger door, glanced back, dived inside, slammed the door, reached for the seat belt.

'Move! Now! And head down the Strand underpass and keep going north . . .'

'Anything you say. My, you can be masterful. I like masterful men . . .'

While she flattered him she did as he said, swinging across into the next lane skilfully and speeding up. Then they were disappearing down inside the underpass and, with a clear road ahead, she roared, pressing her foot down.

'Mind if I smoke?' he asked, glancing in the wing mirror.

'Of course not. You can light me one.'

He lit a king-size cigarette, passed it to her. She inserted it between her lips, took a long drag. Glancing at him, she smiled.

238

'That tastes especially good.'

'Keep your eye on the road. I want us well away from here in no time. We could have been followed. You could, that is.'

'Who would do that?'

'Morgan – or, rather, one of his minions. If he's in town.'

'He is. He came into the office early this morning. Just back from abroad some place. You know Europe well, Marler?'

'Funny question.'

'I don't see why. You told me you were with an insurance company which covers VIPs against kidnapping all over the world. Plenty of them in Europe. I need someone who's an expert investigator to find out what's going on inside the World Security offices on the Continent. I've heard some strange rumours about the Research and Development Division. That's under Morgan's direct control.'

'What sort of rumours? Keep straight on.'

For a change traffic was light. They were driving towards Euston Station.

'Rumours that we're mixed up in industrial espionage action. That's strictly between you and me. I don't want any nasty surprises. That division makes money – but as chairman the responsibility is mine.'

'You want to hire me?' Marler enquired.

'Yes. The fee would be thirty thousand pounds for starters, plus expenses. If you insist, we could draw up a secret contract.'

'No contract. No money. Not until I've sniffed around a bit. I'll see what I can do for you. And when I contact you at your office it will be Freddie Moore calling. Now, drop me off by Euston Station.'

'You don't take long to make up your mind. I like that. I like the idea of dealing with you. When you get back maybe we can have dinner to discuss what you've found out?'

'We can decide that later . . .'

Marler climbed out of the car when she'd stopped it in front of the station entrance. He gave her a little salute and she drove off. Marler bought a paper from a newspaper stand, pretended to read it while he watched the traffic. No one was following Leonora. He wondered what she'd think if she knew his next meeting was with Lance Buckmaster.

23

Seated behind his desk, Morgan braced himself. The guard at the main entrance had phoned to announce the arrival of Chief Inspector Buchanan. Morgan pressed the button which converted the light outside his door to green. He would have liked to say he was not available, that he was in conference, but felt it would be unwise not to show willing.

The door opened, his secretary, Melanie, ushered inside the tall policeman. Once again he was accompanied by his assistant, Sergeant Warden. Morgan remained seated, waved a pudgy hand.

'Please make yourselves comfortable. Coffee? Tea?'

'No, thank you, sir,' Buchanan replied as he took one of the two chairs facing Morgan. He hauled it back a couple of feet so he could cross his long legs.

Morgan shook his head at Melanie, who left, closing the door behind her. He clasped his hands on the desk and waited for Buchanan to speak. The Chief Inspector took his time.

'We are definitely treating the death of your accountant, Ted Doyle, as a murder enquiry.'

'May I ask why?' Morgan asked.

'Certainly. Suicide is out – lack of motive. The post-mortem showed no traces of alcohol in his system. That rules out an accidental fall – especially from that window. Which only leaves murder.'

'But I thought . . .'

'If you don't mind, I haven't quite finished, sir.' Buchanan's tone was firm, his grey eyes steely. 'I think you were about to say Doyle was a gambler. We have visited his flat. We did find some betting slips tucked under a coffee pot in the kitchen – tickets bought at the Tote . . .'

Buchanan, his right hand resting inside his trouser pocket, paused, but Morgan had learned his lesson. He remained silent, clasping his hands a little more tightly. Buchanan resumed what he had been saying.

'One odd thing about those tickets was they were completely clean of fingerprints. If Doyle had handled them I'd have expected to find some of his prints. You don't go round wiping useless tickets – or any kind of tickets, for that matter.'

Buchanan paused again. Morgan felt obliged to react. 'It does sound odd,' he agreed. 'What was the other odd thing?'

'I beg your pardon?'

'You did say *one* odd thing. That implied something else was odd.'

'Sorry, sir.' He glanced at Warden who sat quite still, staring at Morgan. Buchanan turned back to face his host. 'I was just coming to that. We have a witness.' For the third time he paused. Morgan's knuckles were white. 'The other odd thing was what this witness saw. She lives opposite the entrance to Doyle's ground floor flat. A reliable witness – we don't get too many of them . . .'

Morgan was beginning to feel the strain. This bastard was playing cat-and-mouse with him. He ignored the drops of moisture forming on his high-domed forehead.

Buchanan again continued after the pause.

'This woman saw a man entering Doyle's flat. Dark trousers – the type worn by a commissionaire ... or a chauffeur, and a hip-length suède jacket. Any idea who that might have been?'

'None at all,' Morgan lied. 'Was this before Doyle ... died?'

'No, afterwards. Later that day, in fact. He stayed inside for no more than a few minutes. When he left our witness had a good view of his face. It puzzles me considerably.'

'Perhaps he had a friend,' Morgan suggested.

'A friend with a key to Doyle's flat?'

'Sorry. I'm not following you.'

'I just explained. The woman saw this unknown man entering Doyle's flat. He used a key to unlock the door. According to the woman, who knew Doyle, he was a bachelor whose main interest was listening to classical music. Mainly Wagner. By himself. He had a fairly expensive hi-fi system in his living-room. Or perhaps you know that, sir? Ever visited him at his flat?'

'Never!' Morgan's reply was swift. 'Why should I?'

'I thought maybe because of his position you might sometimes have called on him after office hours to discuss some knotty accountancy problem.'

'I'd discuss that with our Finance Director. He's abroad at the moment ...'

'So you told me during our previous interview.' Buchanan uncrossed his legs, took his hand from his pocket and leaned forward. 'Would you know who might have had a spare key to Doyle's front door?'

'No one here, I'm sure,' Morgan lied again, then clamped his lips close together.

'You can see where all this is leading, sir?'

'I'm afraid I don't.'

'An unknown man enters Doyle's house with a key. In the living room, as I mentioned, is a hi-fi system worth

242

several thousands pounds. Just the kind of thing a burglar would whip. So this mysterious caller didn't go there to take anything. Maybe he went there to leave something. Betting slips with no fingerprints. Incidentally, he wore gloves. I told you the witness is unusually reliable.'

Morgan shrugged his heavy shoulders and made no comment as though it was all beyond him. Buchanan stood up and Warden jack-knifed erect at almost the same moment.

'I think that's all, sir. For the moment.' Buchanan gave one of his rare wintry smiles. 'I thought you'd like to be brought up to date with the present stage of our investigation.' He turned towards the door, then swung on his heel. 'Oh, you weren't thinking of leaving the country, were you, sir?'

'What the devil does that mean?' Morgan glared malevolently at the Chief Inspector. 'I'm managing director of an international corporation. I happen to be flying over to the Continent later today.'

'Anywhere we could contact you?'

'The Basle office should be able to locate me. In any case Mrs Buckmaster is here all the time if you need someone.'

'Of course. She would do very nicely. Excuse me, I'd overlooked her. Better not let her know – ladies don't like to be overlooked, do they? We'll be going now. Have a good trip . . .'

Buchanan said nothing as they left the building, a frown of concentration on his face until they were inside their car. Warden took the wheel, Buchanan sat beside him.

'What do you think, Sergeant?'

'He was very tense, sir. Very keyed up. His hands gave him away. He clenched them tighter when you mentioned the betting slips, tighter still when you told him about having a witness.'

'Yes, I noticed that. It doesn't necessarily mean anything. People get nervous when they're talking to the police. And I'd just told him it was a murder case.'

'And later he had beads of sweat on his forehead.'

'Again, could be natural tension. He's still in a neutral zone as far as I'm concerned at this stage of the enquiry. Let's get back to the Yard.'

Morgan was in a cold fury. Hanson had allowed himself to be seen while entering Doyle's flat to plant the betting slips. He'd even been wearing his dark chauffeur's trousers. At least he'd had the sense to wear a suède jacket.

Morgan decided to tear a strip off Hanson at the first opportunity. And to warn him never to go anywhere near that district again. Morgan was also worried about Buchanan. A sly piece of work; full of little verbal tricks. For the first time Morgan felt he had met his match when it came to low cunning. No time to dwell on that now.

Riffling through the dial-card index box, he extracted the card for Freiburg, slipped it into the phone slot. Then he pressed the button which lit up the red light outside. He didn't want to risk intrusion while he made this call. The phone began ringing.

'World Security, Freiburg? Put me straight through to Evans. Morgan here. Make it fast . . .'

'That you, Evans? Now listen carefully. I'm only going to say this once. I'm flying to Basle today. That will be my HQ for the next few days. Any news of the target?'

'No more than when you left,' Evans reported.

'He's making for the Swiss border. This is what you have to do. Send men to watch every frontier crossing from Germany into Switzerland. Along the Rhine from Basle to Konstanz.'

'I haven't the manpower,' Evans protested.

'Do I have to teach you how to tie on your bib? The best operatives you do have should be stationed at the major

244

crossing points. For the smaller ones hire outside help. Tell the people you hire to take cine-cameras. They're to station themselves where they can watch – from the Swiss side – and use the cameras to record everyone crossing.'

'And just supposing the target does put in an appearance?'

'They play it off the cuff. If they have a car or truck at their disposal they use it. Providing they can make it look like a genuine accident. Do I have to spell it out in two-syllable words?'

'Understood . . .'

'And once you've organized our watch on the Rhine you fly to Basle. I'll expect you to be waiting for me at our HQ when I arrive.

'Understood . . .'

A thought struck Morgan. 'This conversation isn't being recorded, I take it?'

'Well . . . as a matter of fact, it is. You've always insisted every conversation *should* be recorded.'

'Heaven save me from professional idiots. Evans, your first job when this call ends is to erase the tape. You heard me? *Erase the tape* . . .'

'Will do. Personally.'

'And now, set in motion the manhunt. The target must be found within the next twenty-four hours.'

24

A major weather change over the Black Forest. The morning sky was a dazzling blue. From the verandah of the lodge Tweed half-closed his eyes against the blinding glare.

The sun was reflecting off the snow, the ice crystals clinging to branches of immense firs. The temperature was still below freezing but the air was crisp, invigorating. Behind him Newman and Paula emerged with their own cases. Tweed had taken the decision as soon as they woke.

'We're moving south soon after daylight – heading for the Swiss border.' He had a map spread open on the table. 'We are close to Badenweiler – that's a spa inside the forest. There will be few people there at this time of the year – and a good road leads south through Kandern. Then we're out of the forest. From there we make for the A 98 autobahn which runs east close to the Rhine. Our objective is Laufenburg, a small town which I know. I told you earlier it straddles the Rhine – at that point the river is the frontier. We have one bridge to cross and we're in Switzerland.'

'Where are the checkpoints?' Paula had asked.

'On either side of the bridge.'

'Isn't it risky?'

'Of course it is.' Tweed had spoken with relish at the prospect of action. For the first time since they'd fled from England he seemed his normal resourceful self, calm, determined. 'It will be risky wherever we try to cross. But it's far more risky hanging about here. Horowitz knows we're in this area. Those tracker dogs Newman shot last night prove that.'

'That Horowitz frightens me.' Paula had shivered.

Before they had gone to sleep Newman had produced the two photographs Marler had taken outside the Freiburg HQ of World Security. The photos showing Gareth Morgan and Armand Horowitz entering the building. Tweed had recognized the Hungarian.

'Only one other photograph has ever been taken of that man. Pierre Loriot of Interpol showed me it. He's the most dangerous assassin in Western Europe. Morgan

246

certainly has some peculiar contacts for a so-called respectable businessman . . .'

That had been a few hours earlier. Now, as they prepared to leave, Paula asked another question.

'And what are we going to use for transport? We're marooned.'

'Not necessarily,' Tweed had replied as they ate the breakfast she had cooked. Tinned meat and toast. 'The Audi we travelled in from Freiburg may still be down that path we came up. Let's hope so. We did conceal it in the undergrowth – and when our pursuers arrived they'd be taken up with the abandoned Mercedes and the guard, Braun, Bob shot . . .'

'Could be tricky. I'll lead the way back, arrive first,' Newman had commented.

Before they left he helped Paula to clean up the lodge. He emptied the Elsan bucket they'd used as a toilet down a crevasse in the snow, then had sprayed it with a can of disinfectant Paula found in a cupboard. To lighten their load, the rest of the uneaten food went down the crevasse.

'No sign – or sound – of a chopper,' Newman remarked as he followed Tweed down the slippery steps from the verandah. 'And everyone had better watch their footing – a twisted ankle we don't need . . .'

Then he went on ahead, holding his case in his left hand, the fully-loaded Walther in his right. The going was very treacherous once they disappeared inside the trees, following the path of the frozen stream. Muffled up with a scarf over her head, Paula shivered as she followed Tweed. Not from the penetrating cold. The atmosphere of the dark and silent forest closed round them like a vast tomb. The only sounds were the crunch of their boots on crusted snow, the crackle of ice. Newman had disappeared below them, making greater speed.

'I wonder if they've identified that poor girl they found in your flat?' Paula mused.

I doubt it. I think someone – the murderer – brought her in from outside Britain. To cover his tracks.'

'Any ideas yet as to who the murderer could be?'

'I think I know now. Either Lance Buckmaster or Gareth Morgan.'

'My God. What makes you think that? Wouldn't they bring in a minion, maybe even a hired killer?'

'No. Too great a risk. Whoever killed and then raped her was going to be sure no one else could point the finger. The idea was to get me out of the way, which they have done.'

'Why do you also suspect Morgan?' she asked.

'Keep your voice down. Sound travels a long way in this silence. Why Morgan? Because of that folder Newman extracted from the pocket of the man who tried to shoot him by the Mercedes. The folder which identified him as Gustav Braun, member of World Security. Braun was small fry, would never dare use a firearm without backing from the top man. Gareth Morgan. I hope to God Arthur Beck is friendly – I need to have the use of a long-distance transmitter as soon as possible. To contact the *Lampedusa*.'

They reached the bottom of the path and Tweed peered out along the timber track they'd driven down the night before. No sign of anyone, not even of Newman. Paula gave a sigh of relief as she ran across the track. She could just make out the snow-covered silhouette of the blue Audi where they'd left it concealed in the undergrowth.

'Stop! Don't move one inch further. Don't touch that car.'

Newman's voice. Paula turned round and he emerged from behind the trunk of a massive fir. She heard a soft *plop!* She stared round to locate the source of the sound as Newman walked towards her. He waved her back across the track to where Tweed still stood.

She had recrossed the track when she saw a solid wedge

of snow slide from a fir's branch. It made the same *plop!* sound as it hit the ground. Newman gestured towards the fallen snow.

'The temperature has risen above zero. There's a snow melt. Both of you go back a dozen yards up that path while I check that Audi.'

'Check it?' Paula queried.

'Look round you. There are the ruts under a film of snow where they turned the Mercedes and drove off – with Gustav Braun's body in the boot would be my guess. I've been waiting to make sure they hadn't left behind a couple of men in ambush. Not a sound. But even in the dark they may have seen the Audi – and left us a birthday present. A final birthday present.'

'He means a bomb,' Tweed said quietly and, taking her by the arm, led her back up the path.

Newman walked all round the white mound which was the Audi. He walked slowly, placing each foot carefully. He doubted whether they had planted landmines but World Security was capable of any devilry – especially if Horowitz had been with the pursuers.

He studied the bonnet. Using his gloved hand he whisked some of the snow off it. The front of the bonnet was sealed with a coating of ice. Unlikely that the engine had been tampered with.

He continued his circuit. On the driver's side snow had drifted against the lower side of the chassis. Except in one place. There was a gap about eighteen inches wide – the width of a man's body. He stooped down, used his gloved hand to whisk away more snow.

Lowering himself to the ground, he eased his way slowly under the body of the car, feet first. He paused to extract a pencil flash from his trench coat pocket, then vanished underneath the Audi. Sprawled flat on the snow, he hauled the glove off his right hand, switched on the flash, moved the beam round slowly. *Bingo!*

*   *   *

The explosive device was a slim black metal box attached to the underside of the Audi by small protruding legs. Newman remembered his training with the SAS in Wales when he'd been writing a series of articles on the outfit. The man in a Balaclava helmet whose face he'd never seen. The man known as 'Sarge'. He could hear his voice now on the bomb disposal course.

'So, you've been smart, you've found the bomb. Take it easy, lad. Locating the bastard is only the first step. Check it for booby traps, you stupid bugger . . .'

Newman swivelled on his back, aiming the flash along the edges of the device. Looking for tell-tale wires. None. At one end a metal lever protruded a quarter of an inch, something he'd never have seen without the flash. He clenched the flash between his teeth, reached up with his bare hand, took hold of the box and pulled gently. It remained solid as a rock.

He was pretty sure the four small legs at each corner which clamped it to the car were magnetic. That the protruding lever controlled the magnetic system. Press the lever in and the box would be released. He suddenly realized he was sweating despite the cold. If he was wrong, if the lever was a trap, this would be the end of Bob Newman.

But they needed the car. He took a deep breath. His right hand reached up again, index finger extended close to the lever. You bloody idiot! He dropped his hand, took off the glove from his left hand and cupped that beneath the box to hold it when – *if* – it fell away from the chassis. Another deep breath. Get on with it. You're either right or wrong.

His right index finger tip touched the ice-cold metal of the lever. He paused. Again he examined it with the flash and was no more certain of its function. His index finger pressed the lever. The metal slid inside the slot, the box

250

dropped free into his extended left hand.

He let out his breath. Easing his way back into the open –
holding on to the box – was an endurance test of nerve. He
stood up slowly, walked back into the centre of the timber
track. He shouted up to Tweed and Paula hidden on the
path.

'Wait for one bloody great bang. I'll be OK. I'm going to
hurl a bomb.'

He turned to face along the timber track away from the
main road. Like a cricketer bowling, he threw the container overarm with all his strength, then dropped flat in
the snow. The device described an arc in mid-air, curved
down and landed at the base of a fir tree. The tremendous
boom of the explosion nearly cracked his ear-drums. A
cascade of snow plunged down from the nearby trees.

Newman watched grimly as he saw the tree the bomb
had landed nearest sway. There was a wrenching, cracking
sound. The big fir tilted, toppled, fell across the track,
tearing up its root system. Then an eerie silence descended. The tree lay across the track, barring the way. Newman thanked heaven he'd had the sense to throw the bomb
away from the main road.

'Oh, my Lord!'

Paula had run down the path, slipping and sliding. Now,
seeing Newman was safe as he climbed to his feet, she was
gazing at the stricken fir. As Newman slapped the front of
his coat to clear it of snow she used her gloved hands to
brush it off his back.

'So, they did leave us a goodbye present,' Tweed commented.

'The car is safe now, anyway,' Paula said. 'I'll be glad to
get inside it. I'm frozen stiff.'

'You'll have to freeze a bit longer,' Newman warned. 'I
want to check it further . . .'

It was half an hour before he had used his gloved hand to
de-ice the bonnet, to lift it cautiously and check the engine.

Then he had to use his gloved hand again to de-ice the lock before the key would turn. Still cautious, he made them stand well away while he tried the ignition. The engine fired at the twentieth attempt. Paula gave a muted cheer.

They dumped their cases inside the boot. For ten more minutes they sat inside the car while Newman turned on the heaters and waited for everything to warm up. Eventually he turned to Tweed who sat beside him.

'We're ready to go.'

'Then let's get moving. Head for Badenweiler and then south for the border.'

The Audi slithered all over the place as Newman drove back along the timber track, skidding over solid ice from one rut to another. He drove at a slow speed, expertly following the skids, then turning the vehicle back to the centre of the track. Paula said something to keep her mind off the ordeal: she was scared stiff the car would stop, that they'd be trapped in this awful white wilderness.

'That bomb you found, Bob. How did it operate?'

'My guess is it had a trembler mechanism. Anyone starting up the car, causing vibrations, would have detonated it.'

'Thank God you found it. We seem to be up against some grim people. Worse than the opposition from the Soviets in the old days . . .'

She relapsed into silence as Newman reached the end of the track, turned on to the main road away from the direction leading back to Freiburg. The road climbed steeply, began following a series of bends, and again the dense wall of fir trees hemmed them in on both sides. The road surface was virgin snow; no other traffic had passed this way since the previous fall of snow.

Whenever he arrived at a level stretch Newman braked, lowered his window. Icy air dispersed the warmth instantly. He leaned his head out and listened. The heavy silence was broken only by the occasional *plop!* of melting snow sagging to the ground.

'What are you listening for?' Paula asked.

'Something I can't hear, fortunately. The sound of a chopper. They don't seem to be out this morning. Odd.'

'Unless Kuhlmann has grounded them,' Tweed suggested. 'Last evening I heard the faint sound of a machine-gun when two choppers were in the air.'

'That would make sense,' Newman agreed. 'Kuhlmann is tough and independent-minded. But to cover himself he'll still warn the frontier posts to look out for you. When we get there I'll spy out the land first.'

'You won't be with us,' Tweed informed him.

'What's the plan?'

'You drive us to the German side of Laufenburg, drop us there, then drive back to Basle. I want you to check on the World Security HQ in that city. It's a big one. Time we began to hit back, to find out exactly what kind of outfit it is.'

'And how do I go about that? Just walk in and ask? I think not.'

Tweed was scribbling on the one-time pad he always carried. He tore off a sheet and handed it to Newman. 'Contact that man. Use my name as reference. He'll get you inside.'

Newman read what Tweed had written. Alois Turpil. An address in Berne. A phone number. He looked at Tweed.

'That World Security HQ in Basle is probably a fortress. How can this Turpil character help? Who is he anyway?'

'One of my underworld contacts. And the most professional safe-cracker in Europe. Also an expert on security systems. He'll get you inside – and out again – and no one will know . . .'

'You hope . . .'

'If you find interesting data, call Arthur Beck at Federal

253

Police headquarters in Berne. That's the second number I've added at the bottom of the sheet, the one without a name. You'd better call him in any case. As I said, let's hope he's as friendly as Kuhlmann. If you run into a road block, make for Zürich. We'll be staying at the Hotel Schweizerhof, facing the main station.

'If you ever reach Switzerland.'

'You have a point,' Tweed agreed. 'A few miles after we've driven through Badenweiler we descend to Kandern – and then the forest has ended. We'll be completely in the open.'

'And that sounds like running a gauntlet. Especially if this clear weather lasts, which I think it will.'

Horowitz stood next to Evans, looking out of the first-floor window of the Basle headquarters of World Security. Below the Rhine flowed swiftly westward, a river as wide as the Thames even at Basle, hundreds of miles before it flowed into the North Sea. A huge barge, its hold covered with canvas, coated with snow, surged past. Horowitz peered down to where a narrow stone promenade followed the river bank.

'Are all the watchers in position along the frontier?' he enquired, adjusting his steel-rimmed glasses higher up his nose.

'They should be,' Evans replied. 'It was a devil of a rush to get them in place. I phoned instructions from Freiburg before flying here.'

'What about the more obscure crossing points – like Konstanz where you can walk over the border. Or Laufenburg where you stroll over a bridge and you're in Switzerland?'

Evans looked surprised, glanced at the motionless thin man. 'You seem to know the area very well. Are you by any chance Swiss?'

'That is something I never discuss,' Horowitz responded in his slow deliberate way. '. . . my origins.'

He turned to gaze at his companion. Evans again felt uneasy as the eyes stared at him unblinking behind the lenses. An aura of deadly purpose, ice-cold control, emanated from this strange individual.

'And you haven't answered my question,' Horowitz reminded him.

'I called the Zürich office for reinforcements. They, too, were short of manpower. They've hired other operatives to cover the smaller places. Not that I'd expect Tweed to know about the obscure crossings.'

'If I were Tweed it is exactly one such place I would choose to slip across the border.'

'What do we need that girl for?' Evans asked to change the subject. He gestured with his head to Eva Hendrix who was sitting out of earshot at the far side of the large office, drinking a cup of black coffee.

Horowitz glanced round. Hendrix was reading a German fashion magazine. She raised both hands and ran them through her titian hair. The curls fell back into the same place: it was an unconscious mannerism she practised frequently.

'She may come in useful at some stage of the operation,' Horowitz told him and left it at that.

He saw no reason to inform Evans that he hoped to infiltrate her alongside Tweed. He had already drilled into her the story she should tell him, a story Horowitz felt certain would convince Tweed of her innocence. The phone rang and Evans picked it up off a nearby table. He spoke briefly in German, put it down, and looked smug as he reported what he'd heard to Horowitz.

'That was the two men who have arrived at Laufenburg. One called to tell me they are in position overlooking the bridge you mentioned.'

'Then now we must wait.' Horowitz turned away from

255

the window to join Hendrix. 'Waiting is the key to success in such a task as we are engaged on. Moving around a lot is a mistake. I only move when I have located the target and *he* has stopped moving.'

Due to the altitude, the air in the small spa town of Badenweiler was mountain fresh. It was deserted at that time of the year as Newman drove slowly along the curving roads. On either side trees and shrubs laden down with snow increased the atmosphere of a town from which the inhabitants had fled, as from some dreaded plague.

They drove past great hotels half-hidden by the foliage, all unoccupied with the shutters closed. Tweed peered out of the window as they glided past the sign for one hotel. The Romerbad. He had once had lunch in summer there in a restaurant at the back overlooking a distant view of hills towards the French Vosges beyond the Rhine.

'The whole town is like a great garden,' Paula whispered.

'And someone I talked to in the Oberkirch at Freiburg told me that during the season the police close certain roads from 1300 to 1500 hours,' Tweed remarked.

'Why?'

'So the rich who come here in summer to take the waters can have their afternoon nap undisturbed by vehicles.'

'They must have been joking,' she protested.

'No, it's that kind of town. A haven for the rich . . .'

Tweed took his decision on the spur of the moment as they approached a signpost. He leaned forward to read the directions, than spoke quickly.

'Don't take the Kandern turning, Bob. Drive straight on.'

'Anything you say. May I ask why?'

'It's a more devious route, takes us right up into the forest before we emerge into the open. If Morgan and

256

Horowitz have people watching for us they'll be more likely to assume we'll take the direct route for the border via Kandern . . .'

They left the small town behind quickly. They drove past a few splendid private villas – again shuttered – and suddenly civilization vanished. Newman was driving up a steep, winding and lonely road where again the surface ahead was virgin snow. The dense palisade of firs on both sides turned the road into a dark corridor, a tunnel of white. The road seemed to climb forever and Newman was constantly turning the wheel to negotiate a chilling series of dangerous zig-zag bends, praying he wouldn't meet a snow-plough coming from the opposite direction. To his left were the trees, but to his right the ground now fell away like a precipice. One skid and they would dive into eternity.

'You've been driving a lot,' Tweed remarked. 'Want me to take over the wheel?'

'I think I've got the feel of the ice. It's just below this coating of snow.'

'Can we just stop talking about it and just get on?' Paula said through her teeth.

It was the first display of nerves she'd shown so far. Newman looked briefly at her in the rear-view mirror and grinned. She managed a wan smile in return and eased herself across to the left side of the car. Away from that awful chasm. Couldn't bear to watch it any longer . . .

'We're close to the summit,' Tweed reassured her a little later. 'I remember this road in summer.'

'But now it's winter,' Paula replied. Then, 'Sorry, I'll keep my big mouth shut.'

The precipice had disappeared. They were driving uphill along a winding avenue lined with the forest on both sides. Paula wiped her damp hands with her handkerchief. Newman had increased speed, and then they reached the crest and the whole world changed.

Newman slowed, swung the car off the road on to a vast platform of land. He put on the brake, left the engine running, leaned back in his seat. Tweed opened the door and got out followed by Paula and Newman. Paula gasped.

'It's like being on top of the world.'

'We are,' Tweed agreed. 'At least in this part of the Black Forest. Look at that board.'

The sign read: *Waldparkplatz Kreuzweg 1079 m.* They were perched over three thousand feet up. In the distance an endless valley spread away to the south, a valley without trees. The descending plain was a blanket of snow and the intense glare of the sun off the whiteness was almost painful. Paula took in a deep breath of air and then spluttered. It was very like breathing in liquid ice.

Tweed had taken a pair of compact binoculars from the pocket of the sheepskin he'd bought in Freiburg. He stood on the eminence scanning the vast panorama. Newman, shielding his eyes against the glare, was also gazing all round.

'What are you looking for?' Paula asked, banging her gloved hands together.

'Movement,' Tweed replied. 'On the ground, in the air. It looks deserted.'

'Agreed,' Newman commented, 'so let's get back to the car and head for Laufenburg.'

'There's a ski-lift up that slope . . .'

Paula pointed to their left. A small closed-up cabin stood at the base. The cables shone like silver wires, encrusted with solid ice. They climbed back into the car and Paula relaxed: they were leaving behind the claustrophobic forest, the dreadful ascent alongside the precipice. Minutes later as Newman drove at controlled speed downhill her nerves were twanging again.

The steeply descending road between vast open fields was a crazy and dangerous route. Newman was guiding the Audi round endless spirals, ferocious hairpin bends. Paula braced herself as they swung and skidded round yet

258

another hairpin which turned through a hundred and eighty degrees to the level below.

'Aren't we going rather fast?' she ventured.

'We're in the open,' Newman said tersely. 'The sooner we're clear of this lonely area and hit the autobahn the better.'

If we ever reach it, she mumbled under her breath. They drove past isolated farmhouses and steep-tilted rooftops over barns with ramps leading up to them. They passed through a series of deserted villages. Kalbelesch. Schinau. Neuenweg. Burchau. Then they were down in the plain as they reached Tegernau and a crossroads.

'We drive straight on for the autobahn,' Tweed warned, the map open on his lap.

An hour later they reached Laufenburg, a small medieval town toppling down the side of a hill to the Rhine. Newman parked the car and turned to Tweed.

'I could drive you over to Switzerland, risk it,' he said.

'Too big a risk. We've been travelling in this blue Audi ever since we left Freiburg. Paula and I will walk from here. There used to be a guest-house perched at the end of the bridge over the Rhine. I hope it's still there. We'll use it to spy out the crossing. And, if you can, I'd advise you to turn in this car for another vehicle before you cross the frontier at Basle.'

Their parting was brief. Newman gave the thumbs-up sign, drove back westward. Tweed stood in the snow, holding his case, and smiled at Paula.

'It's not far down this hill. Watch your footing.'

'And you watch yours.'

She trudged after him, placing her booted feet carefully. No one about. The town seemed uninhabited. They turned a corner and Tweed walked faster, then stopped, waiting for Paula to catch up.

'There it is. The border crossing. And the guest-house is still there.'

259

She stood looking down the hill. At the bottom was a small single-storey building with parking lots in front of it. Outside stood a German guard in a blue overcoat and a peaked cap. The frontier post at the end of the bridge. Facing it was a colour-washed building with a legend in ancient German script inscribed on the wall. GASTHOF LAUFEN.

25

Basle. The German checkpoint was located north of the main part of the city and north of the Rhine. Uniformed guards were stopping cars, asking for identification, taking a good look at the passengers inside each vehicle.

Stieber, his round head leaning forward over the wheel, had parked his Mercedes close to the checkpoint and was watching each approaching car. Beside him sat another security guard from the main HQ at Basle.

'Don't forget, Klaus,' he rumbled in his throaty voice, 'we are looking for a blue Audi. Maybe with three people inside. We see it, we follow it into the city. At the first chance we take them.'

'You've told me all that before,' Klaus, a six-foot giant remarked. 'And let's hope no one checks us with the armoury you've brought.'

'The guards know me,' Stieber snapped, 'know I'm from World Security. They just wave me on without a second thought.'

The armoury Klaus referred to was a pair of knuckle-dusters Stieber carried in his jacket pocket, the 9-mm. Luger tucked inside a shoulder holster and the hand grenade hidden inside the glove compartment. They sat and waited. It was mid-morning and a glorious sunny day. The snow was melting to slush.

It was mid-morning as Newman drove towards the Basle checkpoint. Now that he was well clear of Laufenburg he began to worry about Tweed and Paula. Could they really slip over the frontier unseen? Was the border being watched?

He was driving through the suburbs of Basle and in the distance he could see the checkpoint. He carried no weapons. He'd dumped the Walther – minus the magazine – out of the window into a deserted field. Without the magazine in case some child picked it up. Later he'd thrown all the mags one by one into another field ten miles further along the highway. There was a queue of vehicles at the checkpoint.

Unusual. He slowed down, stopped behind a Volkswagen Passat. While he waited he studied the road beyond the checkpoint. A Mercedes was parked by the roadside, facing his direction. Two men inside, one round-headed character leaning forward over the wheel, taking a great interest in the queue.

'Amateurs,' Newman thought. 'Too close to the frontier. Too obvious. Definitely not Kuhlmann's men. Which only leaves the World Security thugs.'

He worried a little more about Tweed and Paula. Then decided he was being silly. Tweed was one of the most experienced field agents in the world. And spending several years behind a desk at Park Crescent hadn't dulled his tradecraft. In any case he'd broken with tradition on several occasions and gone back into the field in recent years.

The round-headed man was staring at Newman's vehicle now. He said something to his companion and lit a cigarette. Then he slumped behind the wheel. As the queue moved forward Newman felt relieved he'd seen a car-hire agency on his way in to the city. He'd told them he didn't like the Audi, had shown his international driving licence, had changed the Audi for a cream BMW which he was now driving. The queue moved faster. Newman, keeping his eyes off the parked Mercedes, looked at the frontier-control guard.

'Papers, please.'

Newman produced his driving licence, his passport.

The tall guard glanced at the licence, took a few seconds longer to look at his passport, handed everything back and waved him on. Newman drove on into the centre of the city. The Swiss control-point officers didn't even stop him.

Back at the German checkpoint, the guard waited a few minutes, examined the papers of several more vehicles, then spoke to his companion.

'Take over, Hans. I have to make a phone call.'

Inside the cabin he called Police HQ at Freiburg, asked for Chief Inspector Otto Kuhlmann. He had to wait a few minutes before a voice growled.

'Yes, what is it?'

'Frontier Control, Basle, sir. Sergeant Berger speaking. Robert Newman, the foreign correspondent, crossed into Switzerland a few minutes ago. Driving a BMW. Registration number—'

'Don't bother about that. Who was in the car with him?'

'No one, sir. He was alone.'

'Thank you for the information. No report necessary. I want no written record of this incident. That's all.'

Kuhlmann put down the phone, chewed on his cigar, walked over to a wall map of Southern Germany and Switzerland. 'You're being clever, Tweed,' he said to himself. 'But I'll bet my pension you'll be back. And then the people after you had better look out.'

* * *

Gareth Morgan landed at Basle Airport and a waiting limo drove him straight to World Security headquarters. He showed his pass to the guard and took the elevator to Evans's office. It was late afternoon and already night was falling and they had the lights on. Evans stood up from behind his desk and on a couch Horowitz sat with Hendrix while he worked at a crossword puzzle. Stieber was staring out at the Rhine and turned round, giving Morgan a little salute.

'Well?' demanded Morgan, dumping his case on the couch next to Hendrix. 'What's happened? Where are we? What is the latest situation report?'

Always let them know the boss had arrived. His manner was aggressive, his mouth a tight line. Horowitz finished writing a word on the crossword, laid the newspaper carefully aside, glanced up.

'Nothing has happened.' He smiled grimly. 'We are in Basle. The latest situation report from Stieber is that no one has passed through the Basle checkpoint. Not that I ever expected a man of Tweed's experience to come that way.'

Morgan glared at Stieber. 'What are you doing here? You've left the Basle border crossing unwatched – when Tweed might try to slip across after dark?'

Horowitz answered in the same deadpan tone. 'Other guards took over the watch when Stieber came off duty. You know, Morgan, you really must learn to wait . . .'

'I make things happen . . .'

'Then make Tweed cross the Rhine. We have men with cine-cameras observing the minor crossing points. Couriers are standing by to collect the films. By tomorrow afternoon I'll be sitting in your cinema in the basement, watching those films.' He picked up his crossword. 'Patience is the maxim for the moment.'

'I don't pay you to sit around doing crosswords . . .'

Horowitz's pencil was poised to write a fresh word. He

raised the pencil, pointed it like the barrel of a gun. 'You pay me to get results. In my own way. In my own time. Understood?'

Morgan's eyes flickered away from the eyes behind the steel-rimmed glasses. He twisted his lips and transferred his gaze to Evans. 'We'll go to the accountant's office. I want to check the books. Now.'

Horowitz had already resumed filling in his crossword. Beside him Hendrix let out her breath, unnerved by something in the tone of Horowitz's voice.

Tweed had reserved two rooms at the Gasthof Laufen. He had asked for his room to overlook the Rhine and from his window he gazed down on the bridge dividing the two countries. Beside him Paula stared through the heavy net curtains at the far end of the bridge, at Switzerland.

Swiss Laufenburg also clung to the side of a steep hill dropping to the river. To the left of the bridge ancient houses, rooftops weighed down with snow, fell sheer to the Rhine like a cliff. Tweed scanned the crossing through his binoculars, then let them hang from a strap round his neck.

'So near, yet so far. How long do we wait here?' Paula asked.

'The rest of today, all night, then tomorrow we attempt our move into Switzerland. From here I can see what the form is, whether people are stopped at either – or both – ends. It's an ideal observation post.'

Paula walked across to Tweed's bed, perched herself on it and crossed her legs. She picked up a German fashion magazine to pass the time.

Tweed had raised his binoculars again. The sun was shining brightly, had moved round a fraction. It was reflecting off something which glittered in one of the houses to the left of the bridge. A car from Germany arrived at the checkpoint below him. The German guard stopped it, examined the driver's papers, walked round to the back, opened the boot, glanced inside, slammed it closed and waved the car on to Swiss control. Arriving at the other side, the driver was waved on without examination.

The sun had moved another fraction. The glittering reflection in the window of the house perched high above the Rhine vanished. Tweed focused his glasses, gazed through them for several seconds, grunted.

'Something catch your attention?' Paula enquired.

'Yes, I've found what I was looking for. Someone in one of those houses across the bridge is operating a cine-camera, photographing everything that crosses.'

'Oh, my God!' She dropped her magazine and rushed to join him. 'Where? Who do you think it is? The Swiss police?'

'No. They could check people at their frontier post. These are clandestine watchers. Undoubtedly men sent from World Security – and waiting for us.'

'Had we better find some other place to cross?'

'No, this will do very nicely. It's all working out according to plan. We cross here tomorrow morning.'

And with this cryptic remark Tweed lapsed into silence and Paula couldn't get him to explain any more. She was left wondering why he was in such a good humour, even humming a little tune as he continued to survey the bridge.

Once inside Basle, Newman had driven to the best hotel in the city, probably one of the best in Switzerland. The Drei Könige, The Three Kings. It had the advantage of being situated overlooking the Rhine less than a mile east of World Security HQ.

He parked the BMW a short distance from the hotel, collected his bag from the boot, walked into the large reception hall he remembered from previous visits. The concierge greeted the foreign correspondent warmly.

'It's a little while since we've had the pleasure of your company . . .'

Newman asked for a double room overlooking the river, registered, left his bag on the bed with the lid open, left the hotel and took a tram to the main station. He called Alois Turpil in Berne from a phone booth in the station. The mention of Tweed's name acted like magic.

'What can I do for you, Mr Newman?' a guttural voice asked in German.

'I have a job requiring your professional services in Basle. I know your fee. Tonight, if you can make it. You can? Good. I can meet you off the express from Berne if you let me know when you're arriving. 1800 hours? Yes, that would be convenient. I can explain the details over dinner. Too complicated for the phone . . .'

'Of course,' the voice purred. 'We meet on the platform at the *Hauptbahnhof* when my train arrives?'

'Agreed. I'll be wearing a blue suit with a chalk stripe, a pale trench coat and carrying a copy of the *Financial Times*.'

'Mr Newman, I've seen your picture in the papers. It's part of my profession to recognize international VIPs. I'd know you if you were naked.' The voice snickered.

'It's a bit cold for that. See you at 1800 hours. And don't forget your equipment.'

'And don't you forget the fee for my consultation.'

Newman broke the connection and frowned. There had been a touch of flattery he hadn't liked. And the snicker had an unpleasant flavour. He picked up his executive case, which he had wedged against the rear of the phone booth. He recalled what Tweed had said while he sat in a huge restaurant inside the station and drank coffee.

'You may not take to Turpil. He's not my favourite person, but his skill is extraordinary. As to his fee, you'll have to negotiate. He'll be nervous about operating inside

266

Switzerland – against his normal rules. He'll make a big thing about his objection to drive up the price. He'll probably demand thirty thousand Swiss francs. Haggle. You'll get him down to twenty thousand. Especially when you show him the cash. He's greedy for money, is our Alois . . .'

Tweed had then opened his own executive case and handed Newman several stacks of high-denomination Swiss banknotes at the lodge high up in the Black Forest. Only then had Newman realized why Tweed had instructed him to buy his own executive case in Freiburg.

Newman decided he wouldn't let Turpil know where he was staying, that he would take him to dinner at the Merkur restaurant he'd noticed from the tram on his way to the station. He would, in fact, remain as anonymous as possible. He just hoped that when he did meet Turpil he liked him better than he had talking with him over the phone.

When he did meet Turpil he took an instant dislike to the safe-cracker. Worse still, he mistrusted the man.

When Marler phoned the Ministry for External Security, asked for Buckmaster, identified himself, he was transferred three times to different girls before he reached Miss Weston. She sounded as though she'd swallowed something unpleasant and her tone was falsetto.

'Mr Marler, you said?'

'That's right. For the third time. The Minister knows me – I'd like a word with him.'

'The Minister left a message in case you called. He's driven to his home in the country. I can't give you the address.'

'Thanks a lot,' Marler snapped and rang off.

He thought it unwise to tell her he knew that meant Tavey Grange on Dartmoor and he swore as he walked back to his mews flat in Chelsea. Inside five minutes he had backed his second-hand Porsche into the cobbled yard and was driving west.

The journey to Devon was uneventful but when he turned on to the moor for Moretonhampstead the snow was much deeper. The white ridges were stark against the clear blue sky like a series of tidal waves frozen in mid-air. Another red Porsche was parked in front of the main entrance in the cobbled courtyard.

The surface was icy. He nearly skidded as he pulled up. He almost sprawled on the ground as he walked to the arched porch. Why did the English love leg-breaking cobbles? José, the butler, opened the heavy door in response to his jerking the chain-pull bell.

'Ah, Mr Marler. Please come in, sir. The Minister is expecting you.'

'He is?'

'Indeed, yes, sir. Miss Weston phoned from London.'

Marler mentally revised his impression of Miss Weston and was glad he'd told her nothing. He stepped into the warmth of the centrally-heated hall and Lance Buckmaster ran down the massive staircase. Clad in hip-length, fur-lined driving jacket, the uniform for the upper-class driver in winter, Buckmaster was on top form, began talking before he'd reached the bottom tread.

'You made good time. It's a marvellous day for a spin over the moor. You can wait for refreshment until we get back, I'm sure.'

It would have been nice to have the option, Marler thought, but he followed the tall agile figure back through the doorway. Buckmaster halted suddenly when he saw Marler's car.

'So you run to a Porsche as well.' He sounded aggrieved. Behind them the door closed as José disappeared inside the mansion. 'We'll take mine. Give you a few tips on how to drive the beast.'

'Yours is new,' Marler pointed out as he climbed in beside the Minister. 'I couldn't run to this on my salary.'

'Let's get away from here before you give me your report,' Buckmaster snapped as though addressing the foreign housemaid.

He drove straight out on to the main road between the gates of the lodge, tooting his horn, not pausing to check whether anything was coming in either direction. Marler adjusted his seat belt and made no comment on the atrocious behaviour.

He was capable of racing along himself but as Buckmaster took his Porsche across the moor the experience was hair-raising. They drove past a field where a small frozen lake lay beyond it. Buckmaster gestured, driving with one hand.

'That's the Miniature Pony Centre. Fascinating to see them in summer. They're rather like big dogs. Very sweet.'

'Mm,' responded Marler.

It was beyond the steep hill leading down into Postbridge, a tiny hamlet, and the equally steep hill leading out of the place, that Buckmaster let rip. There were wheel ruts in the snow-covered road, just a few. Soon they were climbing higher into the vast openness, swerving round murderous bends at high speed. There were patches of ice gleaming on the road, Marler noted. Buckmaster had his window open and a blast of Arctic air filled the interior. Marler buttoned the collar of his topcoat. Buckmaster glanced at him and gave his braying laugh.

'Invigorating, isn't it? Blow the cobwebs out of your system.'

'We just passed a dangerous-curve sign.'

'I know this road like the back of my hand.'

'But we're not driving on the back of your hand.'

'Insubordinate bastard, aren't you, Marler? They said that in your file – or words to that effect. In the usual Civil Service jargon . . .'

He stopped talking. The Porsche was sliding into a skid. They were very high up, no other traffic, sweeping views and, on Marler's side, a sheer drop into a chasm as Buckmaster fought for control, just managed to ease the Porsche round the bend. Marler looked down into the abyss. A massive rock shaped like the snout of a shark loomed up below.

'That's Shark's Tor down there,' Buckmaster shouted breezily. 'Enjoying the spin? Not frightened, I trust?'

'Just cautious.'

They were on top of the moor and to the south in the sunlit distance the moor rose to a ridge topped by a huddle of rocks which Marler guessed would be huge seen close up. Buckmaster gestured again.

'Haytor there in the distance. Really makes you glad to be alive on a day like this.'

'Just so long as we stay that way.'

The braying laugh again. Buckmaster was getting a kick out of playing on his passenger's nerves. Just like a bloody great schoolboy, Marler was thinking. And naturally the choice for a Minister of the Crown.

'Give me your report,' Buckmaster said suddenly. He fished a cassette out of the glove compartment, rammed it inside the slot, turned a switch. Nothing happened. Not a sound. Buckmaster shrugged. 'Should be playing Stravinsky's *The Rite of Spring*. That's the third time the cassette player has gone on the blink. Pay a small fortune for this tin can they call a car and nothing works. That building on the right we are approaching is an inn – the only habitation for miles. Now, get on with it. Give me your report.'

The inn, half-submerged in snow which had drifted up to the height of the ground-floor window sills, had an abandoned look. Who the devil would visit a place like that for half the year, Marler wondered.

'Tweed is alive and well,' he began. 'I located him,

talked with him, in Freiburg on the edge of the Black Forest.'

'You did what! You actually had him under your gun and you tell me he's still alive and well. What the bloody hell do you think you're playing at, Marler? Didn't I make my meaning clear before you flew to Europe?'

Buckmaster's voice had risen to a shout closely verging on a shriek with the last sentence. His gloved hands slipped on the wheel. Now the road fell away sheer to their left into a rocky valley. Marler's hand moved, gripped the wheel and turned it towards him a fraction, then released it.

'Don't you ever dare touch the wheel again when I'm driving,' screamed Buckmaster, his face contorted with rage.

'You were within an inch of the edge – and there's ice under this snow.' Marler's voice was cold, terse. 'Concentrate on your driving and keep quiet until I've finished . . .'

Buckmaster struggled with his emotions, startled and sobered by something he had never heard before in Marler's tone. He reduced speed as his passenger continued.

'You don't try to assassinate a man when he's surrounded with armed bodyguards. There were three other men in the room at the Hotel Oberkirch on Schusterstrasse. And Tweed thinks I'm on his side. That's a big plus. At the moment he's somewhere inside the Black Forest. His objective is Switzerland. Probably it's that country's neutrality which appeals to him. I'm going back there shortly and I'll find him again. So not to worry . . .'

'I am worried. I *shall* worry.' Buckmaster's mood changed to one of near-petulance. 'Until the problem of Tweed is solved. Permanently. If there was a trial on a charge of rape and murder the scandal could bring the government down.'

'Murder and then rape . . .'

'Whatever.' Buckmaster was pressing his foot down again suddenly. Marler watched the speedometer climb.

Forty-five m.p.h. Fifty. Sixty. On a snaking road coated with snow and ice. The only thing which had saved them so far was the lack of any other traffic. Buckmaster glanced quickly at Marler. 'How do you know which came first at Radnor Walk? The murder or the rape?'

'Tweed talked about what he alleged he found when he arrived back at his flat. Few signs – if any – of a struggle by the unknown girl victim. Some blood on a sheet. Traces of skin under her right index finger. It looked like she had known the murderer, wasn't frightened of him. To start with.'

'Alleged is the word. So that's the story he's going to relay – if he ever reaches the witness box alive. That's your job, Marler. You suggested it was the solution when you came to see me at Tavey Grange last time.'

'I did?'

'We're coming in to Princetown. I'm turning back here. I have to be in the House this afternoon. Answering a lot of damnfool questions.'

'You're driving back to London?'

'Lordy no. The chopper is standing by. I never liked this town. The prison may be on the other side but the whole place reeks of it.'

Which was a graphic description, Marler thought. The houses where the warders lived with their wives were long bleak stone terrace blocks. They passed a building with a sign, *Prison Officers' Association*. Something like that. When they'd left Princetown behind and were back in the open Buckmaster opened up the engine. Marler braced himself for yet another endurance test.

The sunshine had now gone, the sky was a ceiling of leaden clouds full of snow to come. As they ascended back on to the moor Marler stared at the bleak aspect, the tors rising up like prehistoric sentinels. This was Doomsday country.

'I don't think Howard is up to the mark,' his companion

said suddenly. 'I may have to ask for his resignation – and that would leave the post of Director General vacant.'

Another sprat to catch a mackerel, Marler thought, and I am the mackerel. No commitment, just a devious hint. Buckmaster's unstable temperament bothered him. When he'd told the Minister Tweed was alive and well Buckmaster's reaction had been beyond all reason, a near-manic fury. His most public posture was of the commanding ex-Airborne Division officer. But Marler had seen a very different side to the man.

'That pathologist who conducted the autopsy on the murdered girl is coming to see me,' Buckmaster remarked, going off at another tangent. 'A boring chap, this Dr Rose.'

They were approaching the dangerous bend with the steep hill beyond it, the precipice now on Marler's right with Shark's Tor spearing up out of the snow. He spoke in the cold tone he'd adopted earlier.

'You slow down here. If you want to commit suicide wait until you're on your own.'

'Damn your impudence . . .'

But Buckmaster reduced speed as he negotiated the diabolical bend. He was descending the hill when Marler leaned forward, pressed the eject lever for the cassette, grabbed it with his left hand and hurled it out of the window he'd lowered a few minutes earlier. It sailed over the drop towards Shark's Tor.

'What the hell did you do that for?' Buckmaster demanded.

'You inserted a cassette with nothing on it – to record our conversation. *My* conversation mainly. I don't like tapes existing which can be held over my head.'

Buckmaster grinned wolfishly. 'You must admit it was a good try.'

26

At Park Crescent in London, Howard's first question to Marler showed him which way the wind was blowing.

'What have you been up to – or shouldn't I ask?'

Howard was sitting in Tweed's office, but, significantly, not in Tweed's chair behind his desk. He occupied the armchair, his legs crossed, wearing an expensive grey Chester Barrie suit from Harrods. For Howard it was the only shop in town. Marler thought Howard's plump pink and well-fed face showed signs of strain.

Tweed's faithful, long-time assistant, Monica, sat behind her own desk, watching Marler like a hawk. She fiddled with her bun of grey hair. Without Tweed, the familiar office had a ghostly feel of no one being there.

'May I smoke, sir?' Marler asked.

Howard waved an indifferent hand, then gestured towards the hard-backed chair close to him. 'Sit.'

Marler perched himself on the chair, lit one of his king-size cigarettes. He threw the question at Howard, studying his reaction.

'You're convinced that Tweed is guilty of that murder and rape at his Radnor Walk flat?'

'Are you?' Howard flashed back, one leg waggling up and down.

It was a stand-off, an *impasse*. It was Monica who broke it, her voice accusing.

'The whole idea is just damn ridiculous. What I'm trying to find out is who really did it -- and why.'

Howard turned to Monica. 'Do you believe in him?'

274

'Probably . . .'

'Thanks for the vote of confidence,' Marler snapped. 'But I have to believe the two of you. I do. Probably.'

Howard stirred. 'We're talking in Tweed's office because Harry Butler has just flashed this office for listening devices. It's clean now. He's checking my office at the moment.'

Marler was stunned. 'What's going on, for God's sake?'

'Harry found this phone was bugged. He's just called me before you breezed in to tell me my own phone was also bugged. Last night someone broke in here in the early hours, bashed our guard, George, over the head. He's at home, slightly concussed. A clumsy attempt had been made to break open one of the filing cabinets,' Howard continued. 'I wasn't satisfied that was the real purpose of the visitation. Hence my getting Harry to check the whole building, room by room. The intruder was bugging the place. Identity unknown.'

'Could you guess?'

'I never guess,' Howard replied stiffly.

'I do,' interjected Monica. 'Buckmaster wants to know what's going on here. His authority over these premises, the SIS, is limited – thanks to a directive from the Prime Minister. So who has the expertise? We've heard some funny rumours about an organization called World Security.'

'No proof, Monica,' Howard warned. He pouched his lower lip over his upper. Marler waited. Howard was on the verge of a decision. He reached for a green file on Tweed's desk.

'Might as well tell you. In complete confidence. I found out from Special Branch the name of the pathologist they used on the autopsy of the murdered girl. Identity also unknown as yet. Pathologist is a Dr Rose. He doesn't like Buckmaster – who has been badgering him for the report on the post-mortem. He also doesn't like the fact that the

Minister asked for only one copy of the report to be typed and brought to him. He sees his lordship this afternoon. But Dr Rose was here this morning at my request. Secretly.'

'What does his report reveal?'

'An interesting fact.' Howard opened the file, riffled the typed sheets. 'On this page he confirms the victim was first strangled, then raped afterwards. Underneath the right index finger of the girl's hand he found traces of skin and blood. Rose believes – although there were no other signs of struggle – that she managed to claw her murderer's naked back while he was throttling her.' Howard looked up. 'Are you sure you're convinced of Tweed's innocence?'

'Oh, for God's sake, what do you want from me? A sworn affidavit?'

'Fair enough. Now we come to the interesting fact. The blood type under the girl's fingernail corresponds to a patch of blood which stained the sheet. She was blood group O Positive.'

'Do keep me in suspense. No hurry at all . . .'

'The blood group of the stain and under her finger was a rare blood group. AB Negative. The murderer's blood group.'

He closed the file, replaced it on the desk, and paused. Howard was not averse to a little drama. His tone was grim when he continued.

'Tweed's blood group is A Positive. That lets him out. You see how vital the Rose report is? Lucky I have this photocopy.'

'Could I have a copy of that photocopy?'

'No,' said Howard.

'Oh, give it to him,' Monica interjected again. 'I can make a copy for him and no one will be any the wiser.' She glanced at Marler as Howard handed her the file. 'You must promise not to lose it.'

276

'Promise.'

Marler gave her a mock salute, waited until she had left the office. 'You said that lets Tweed off the hook. You're not suggesting it would be safe for him to surface, to come back?'

'No. Definitely not. Buckmaster is trying to push me out, to take over the SIS by remote control. I'm fighting him tooth and claw. He demands a file, I provide only a doctored extract – just one example of the battle that's raging. The PM is adopting a neutral stance. So far. How is Tweed? Does he want to get back here quickly? He had some secret project on the go. I didn't know a thing about it. Resented the fact to start with. Now, after what's happened . . .' he waved his manicured flipper in a dismissive gesture.

'Tweed's OK,' Marler replied after a long pause, 'I doubt if he's in a hurry to return. He's up to something. They tried to kill him on the autobahn near Freiburg . . .'

'Good God! I didn't realize it had come to that. Now tell me, who are "they"?'

'Difficult to be sure.' Marler blew a perfect smoke ring, watched it float up, disintegrate after forming an oval shape. 'World Security has a big office in Freiburg.'

'You mean that fat toad, Gareth Morgan, is going into business on his own account?'

Marler was surprised at Howard's swift reflex. He was equally surprised at the transformation in Howard's character. The SIS chief who had spent half his time at his club had become a tiger: there was the light of war in his blue eyes. Buckmaster had performed a miracle – had turned Howard into a gut fighter.

'Could be Morgan, I suppose,' Marler replied. 'He was present in Freiburg when a noose was thrown round the city to trap Tweed. He slipped through it, of course. Bob Newman is with him. Paula, too.'

'I was going to ask where she was. Does Tweed need

back-up? I could fly out Harry Butler and Pete Nield at an hour's notice.'

'Hold them in reserve – until you get a phone call saying we need a butler and an assistant for a banquet.'

'And you're going your own way, of course, as always?'

'Of course.'

By arrangement Marler met Leonora at the World Security HQ in Threadneedle Street at nine o'clock that night. She was waiting for him in her office. By the side of her desk stood a silver bucket filled with ice on a tripod. A bottle of Bollinger champagne protruded its head above the ice as though signalling, 'I'm chilled. Rescue me . . .'

'Anything to tell me?' Leonora asked as Marler extracted the cork, poured the liquid into two tulip-shaped glasses perched on her desk. She was wearing a form-fitting N. Peal polo-necked sweater, a mid-length pleated cream skirt slashed to her thighs. Marler speculated whether she was wearing anything else except her tights. She tucked a blonde curl into the corner of her red-lipped mouth and reached out the other hand for her glass.

'To us.'

'Down the hatch,' responded Marler.

It was very quiet in the building on the eighteenth floor. He had the impression the only other people in the tower were the guards at the main entrance. Ignoring the chair drawn close to hers, he sat facing her with the desk between them like a frontier pole.

'I have something to show you,' he began. 'But before I show you it might be better if you had a refill.'

'That's what it's for.'

She extended her glass and looked up at him as he leaned to pour more champagne. She nodded to a large couch beneath a window. Marler had noted all the curtains were drawn shut. He carefully avoided following her gaze.

'We might be more comfortable on the couch,' she suggested, and drank half her glassful.

'Might be safer sometime when I visit Tavey Grange when Lance is up in town,' he parried.

'No.' She shook her head and her blonde hair swept across her face. 'José, the butler, is a creep. Reports everything to the boss, Lance. We're far more likely to remain alone and intimate here.'

'I'd better show you what I've brought you,' he said quickly. Lifting the cardboard-backed envelope off his lap he took out the glossy print he'd collected from Grubby Grundy. Holding the print so it faced him, he made a performance of hesitating.

'Oh, come on, Marler. Show me, whatever it is. And why are you still wearing those kid gloves? It's warm enough to fry an egg in here.'

'Which is what I was doing – or trying to – when I badly burned my hands. One of those cheap pans which conduct heat up the handle. Bit unsightly. Here you are. Brace yourself.'

She took the print with one hand, her lips tightened, she drank the rest of her champagne, held out the glass as she went on staring at the photo: the picture Grundy had created of Buckmaster sprawled, fully clothed, on a couch with a nude girl lying on top of him.

'I don't know her,' she said eventually.

'Sorry. It's a bit pornographic.'

'He's found a new way of doing it. He's fully dressed – and she's starkers. Maybe he's found he enjoys them undressing him.'

'Maybe.'

'Who is this particular cow?'

'No idea,' Marler lied.

'And may I ask how this came into your possession?'

'You just did.' Marler sipped more champagne. 'A detective – private – I know who is a whizz with a zoom lens took it. You won't expect me to supply his – or her – name and address.'

She had put her glass on the desk, was handling the print and plastering it with her fingerprints. When she threw it down on the desk he whipped it up with his gloved hands, slipped it back inside the envelope, then leaned forward to pour more champagne in her glass.

'I'd like to keep that photograph, Marler,' she said.

'I'll get you three more prints. I need this copy for the photographer to select the right negative.'

'He takes so many? Of that kind of picture?'

'I told you, he is a detective.' He raised his glass to her, took a sip. 'Lord knows how many he takes in a year. And not necessarily of that sort. Often a picture of a man and a girl entering a flat is sufficient.'

'Then get me three prints.' She frowned. 'If Lance goes on the way he's doing he's going to end up with a nervous breakdown – what with his big job and his women on the side. Talking about women on the side, it really would be more comfortable on that couch.'

'Next time, if you don't mind.' Marler checked his watch and stood up. 'I have exactly ninety minutes to catch a plane.'

'Be like that. You can find your own way out?'

'I can . . .'

As he drove through the night to London Airport Marler reflected that by showing the photograph he'd laid the groundwork for a lot of aggravation for Lance Buckmaster.

The Minister made the call from a public phone-box inside the Post Office off Trafalgar Square. He got through to Freiburg and they told him Morgan was at the Basle HQ. He dialled the Swiss number and caught Morgan just before he left for the company flat.

'You know who this is,' Buckmaster said. 'No names, no pack drill.'

'What can I do for you, sir?'

'I have obtained the pathologist's report. Only one copy in existence.'

In Basle Gareth Morgan sighed with relief, but not audibly. He made no comment, waited for the next instruction.

'I'm worried about a Dr Arthur Rose,' Buckmaster continued. 'I think he's accident-prone. He has a consultancy at St Thomas's Hospital on the Embankment.'

'I know the place. You want me to send someone to attend to him?'

'Under the circumstances, don't you think it would be wiser?'

'Agreed. Consider it done . . .'

Buckmaster broke the connection and in his Basle office Morgan turned to Stieber, who spoke pretty good English. The German looked expectant as Morgan opened the wall safe, took out several bundles of bank-notes, tossed them on his desk.

'You're paying a visit to London. Catch the plane tomorrow morning. A Dr Arthur Rose, consultant at St Thomas's Hospital. Near Waterloo – on the Thames Embankment and facing Parliament. The good doctor is accident-prone. Be careful but make it a quick job. You know your way round London.'

'These for me?'

Morgan nodded and Stieber picked up the banknotes, stuffing them into his jacket pockets. He was leaving the room when Morgan called out to him.

'And the first thing you do when you reach London Airport is to change those Swiss notes into pounds sterling. The lot. Anything left over, change it at another bank back into Swiss notes before you fly back here.' His voice became menacing. 'Don't forget, change the lot into pounds sterling.'

'Will do.'

And that, Morgan thought as the door closed, will eliminate my fingerprints from any money he has on him if he botches the job. He mopped his moist forehead. This Tweed business was getting complicated. Morgan always worried if operations became complicated.

Arriving in London the following day, Stieber changed the banknotes, then took the Underground into the city. Cab drivers had good memories. He eventually emerged from the mole world at Regent's Park station. Ironically, when he stepped out of the elevator and walked east he crossed one end of Park Crescent, which meant nothing to him.

His destination was the street leading down into Fitzroy Square which is lined with used-car dealers and their dubious wares. Stieber's knowledge of London was mostly confined to the less salubrious areas.

He decided on a Ford Escort, which had seen better days, on the basis of the price, the vehicle's anonymity. He insisted on driving the car a long distance north with the dealer, a cunning lout with a soiled open-necked shirt.

'Petrol costs money, mate,' the dealer informed him as they turned back.

'So does this heap of scrap metal.'

Stieber was wearing an outsize pair of dark glasses and a cap he had brought with him, a piece of headgear purchased on a previous stay in the British capital. It gave him the look of a wide boy who might have had something to do with horse racing which the Jockey Club would not have approved of.

Parking it back at the kerb in the same street, Stieber

spent another half hour haggling over the price. It was expected. The deal concluded, he drove straight to St Thomas's, being very careful to obey the regulations. Especially to drive on the wrong – the left – side of the road. Stieber wanted to leave no official record of any kind of his lightning visit to Britain.

Morgan had trained him to operate in this manner abroad. If he ran into trouble he had in his memory the name and phone number of a lawyer who specialized in 'difficult' clients.

Driving to the hospital, he crossed Westminster Bridge from the north side and automatically registered there was a pedestrian crossing near the southern end. He drove slowly and found an empty parking slot nearby. Another car was about to occupy it. Stieber accelerated, drove across its bows, forcing the other driver to pull up with an emergency stop. As he slid inside the slot the competing driver jumped out of his vehicle and strode over. A City gent, wearing a bowler hat. Stieber didn't know there were any of them left.

'You've taken my slot,' Bowler Hat fumed. 'And you nearly caused an accident.'

'You are correct.' Stieber leaned out of his open window, extended his large paw. 'Shake.'

Bowler Hat was taken aback, uncertain how to react. Assuming that Stieber was giving way, he extended his own hand. Stieber grasped it, squeezed hard, almost crushing Bowler Hat's fingers. He yelped with pain as Stieber released him and spoke.

'Don't push your luck, matey.'

Stieber was reproducing the vernacular of the used-car salesman back near Fitzroy Square. The other man swore, retreated to his own vehicle, decided not to mix it with this brute and drove off.

Feeding the meter, Stieber collected the cardboard-backed envelope he'd bought at a stationer, an envelope crammed with sheets of blank A4 paper. Adjusting his tinted glasses, tilting his cap at a rakish angle, he walked to the entrance to St Thomas's.

He knew Dr Rose was on duty with his consultancy somewhere inside. He'd phoned from a call box on the way after buying the Ford Escort. He entered, spoke to the nurse on reception duty. This was the tricky part.

'I have some important papers for Dr Arthur Rose. Not urgent.'

'You can leave them with me . . .'

"Can't do that. I've been told to hand them to him personally. Like I said, it's not urgent, but he needs them by the end of the day.'

'He's in conference . . .'

'Then I'll come back. Any idea when he'll be leavin'?'

'About seven this evening.'

'I have a parking problem,' Stieber continued. He stared at the receptionist through his glasses. 'If I may say so, you look very smart in that uniform. Really suits you . . .'

The girl, very plain, coloured, then resumed her posture of the correct receptionist as Stieber continued.

'So if I could just get a glimpse of Dr Rose? Then I'll recognize him, hand him these important papers and dash back to my car before I'm nicked for a ticket.'

'I think I can arrange that.' She called out to a nurse hurrying across the lobby. 'Susan, could you take this gentleman to the third-floor conference room where Dr Rose is addressing the symposium? He just wants to be able to recognize him later.'

Stieber said nothing to the stern-faced nurse who accompanied him in the elevator. She led him down a corridor, then paused by a large window. A dozen or so men in white coats were seated, listening to a man in outdoor clothes standing on a dais.

'That is Dr Rose. On the platform.'

A well-built man of about forty, chubby-faced and wearing rimless glasses. Hair greying at the sides. Clean-shaven. The nurse stood on guard and wasn't going to leave him. Stieber didn't want to depart by the main entrance, to be observed more closely a second time by the receptionist.

'Thank you . . .' He suddenly put his hand to his mouth. 'Lord, my stomach. I'm going to throw up. I thought that hamburger tasted funny . . .'

'Toilet through this door,' the nurse said briskly. 'You know your way out? Good.' She held the door open. With all she had on her plate she could do without a mess on the floor to clear up.

Stieber disappeared inside, walked into a cubicle, locked the door, sat on the seat, clutching his envelope. He waited several minutes, flushed the toilet and peered out into the corridor. Empty. He walked quickly to the door marked *Fire Exit*. Beyond a flight of iron steps led to the ground.

No one was about as he left the hospital by a rear entrance and made his way back to the car. He drove off into Lambeth, found a pub with a free parking slot, walked inside and ordered a ham sandwich and a mild and bitter.

When in London pubs were his favourite haunt. Not for the beer, which tasted awful compared with its German counterpart, but for the conversation which he eavesdropped on. It was the perfect place to polish up his English, absorb the accents, note the colloquialisms which were the passport to acceptance.

'Are you a cabbie?' asked the barman as he brought the second half-pint. 'It's a hobby of mine – guessing my customer's profession.'

'No. I'm on the dole.'

'Bad luck. A lot of people are. Been out of a job long?'

'Only a month. Seems like a year . . .'

Fortunately another customer came up to the bar.

Stieber had removed his glasses and stuffed his cap into the pocket of his windcheater before entering the place. Like cab drivers, barmen had good memories.

He killed the rest of the day visiting two more pubs, where he drank orange juice – no point in being stopped by the police and being breathalized. Then he drove round south of the river, noting the layout of the streets. He had to circle the area close to St Thomas's several times before he found a parking slot.

It was dark now. Six o'clock. Three slots became vacant all at once. The British were going home early. Trains were late due to iced-up rails, frozen signals. Stieber had read about weather conditions in a newspaper he'd bought before entering another pub. The temperature had nose-dived, there was a sheen of ice on the streets. The lack of people and the ice would help. Stieber had a feeling this would be an easy one. Unlike the Tweed problem. But that was his experience – jobs were either a piece of cake or bloody difficult. A piece of cake. That was a phrase he'd picked up in one of the pubs: at first he'd thought they were talking about their favourite food, but the subsequent chat had given him the real meaning of the phrase.

He was parked where he had a good view of the main entrance to St Thomas's. He'd arrived an hour early to be on the safe side. He just hoped that Rose would leave the place by himself.

As he sat with his gloved hands on the wheel – he had worn gloves ever since leaving the plane that morning – with the engine ticking over, he thought about the British. They did not work like the Germans did. And they spent so much time in their awful pubs, chatting or just sitting alone, maybe reading one of their boring newspapers. Stieber's idea of relaxation was to visit a blue movie, watch a couple of girls frolicking.

At seven on the dot Dr Charles Rose, wearing an over-coat and carrying a briefcase, emerged by himself. As

Stieber backed out of his slot, Rose walked towards Westminster Bridge, placing his feet flat on the treacherous surface. Stieber couldn't believe his luck.

He checked ahead, behind him in the rear view mirror. Not a soul in sight. Not even a car. He drove slowly towards the bridge. Then he blinked. What incredible luck. A piece of cake. Rose had stopped by the pedestrian crossing, pressing the button and waiting.

The light turned red for traffic and Rose stepped off the kerb. Stieber gunned his engine, raced forward. He saw Rose turn at the sound, saw his horrified face, then the car slammed into him at speed. Stieber felt the soft thud of metal meeting flesh and bone. Rose's body was lifted off the ground, arms flailing, briefcase describing an arc in mid-air. The body fell back, sagged on the road. Stieber kept up his speed, felt the vehicle wobble as the tyres rolled over the corpse. Best to make sure, Stieber thought, and sniggered.

He drove through central London to Finchley where he'd had a bed-sit during the three months he'd once spent in England at Morgan's suggestion to polish his English. Moving slowly down a suburban side street he spotted a house in complete darkness. He drove on, parked round the corner.

Walking back, he studied the semi-detached house again, then pushed open the gate and made for the side entrance, creeping over a mossy path. There were no lights at the back. He pressed the bell, ready to run if he heard sounds inside. Nothing.

It took him five minutes to break a glass pane in the back door, reach in and turn the key, enter the kitchen, close the door behind him. A cloth was laid over the table. He whipped it off, tucked it under his arm and went down the hall into the front room. A pair of silver-plated candlesticks and a silver-plated bowl were perched on a table. He grabbed them, wrapped them in the table cloth, left the house by the way he had come in.

Snow had begun to fall again in the eerily silent street when he reached his car. He opened the boot, shoved the wrapped articles he'd stolen inside, closed it quietly. Half an hour later he abandoned the car five miles away and close to an Underground station.

One hour later Stieber was alighting from the Underground carriage which had transported him to London Airport. There were no flights until the following morning so he booked a room at the Penta Hotel and after dumping his case in the bedroom he went to the restaurant.

As he ate he checked over the details of his brief visit. He had used no car hire, no taxis. Of course the police would, sooner or later, possibly connect his abandoned car with the murder of Rose. The front of the car was bound to carry relics of its encounter with the doctor. But it would all look like the work of a petty thief, an accidental killing of a pedestrian. The 'loot' found in the boot would confirm the theory. The work of what they called a 'lager lout' these days. No fence would look twice at silver plate.

Stieber enjoyed his meal, treated himself to a bottle of German Riesling. He'd earned it. Tomorrow he'd fly back to Basle, congratulating himself on a very neat job.

27

At the Gasthof Laufen Tweed was out of bed as soon as it was daylight. He washed, shaved, dressed and packed his night things inside his case in ten minutes – an exercise he'd learned years ago as an operative in the field. You always had to be ready for a swift departure in an emergency. Then he stood by the window, binoculars pressed to his eyes. He dropped them to hang suspended from the loop round his neck.

He was gazing down at the bridge, where the red-and-white striped frontier poles were raised on both sides, when Paula tapped on his door. He unlocked it, let her inside, relocked it and joined her by the window. He could sense the tension inside her.

'Shouldn't we wait a day or two longer?' she suggested.

'No, we cross mid-morning. We've been in the same place for one night. That's long enough. We have to keep on the move.'

'You sound horribly fresh, horribly confident. I wish I did. What's happening?'

'It's a good job I took this room to observe that bridge. I know their routine now.'

Paula compressed her lips, stared at the bridge and the river. At this point the Rhine curved in an S-bend. On the German side officers clad in green overcoats and peaked caps stood by the frontier control building. On the far side their Swiss counterparts wore blue overcoats and blue peaked caps. All their coats were buttoned to the neck against the cold.

'The routine is important?' Paula queried.

'Vital. They stop all cars on this side, check drivers, their papers and their vehicles. They even stopped girls going over on bicycles. But they don't stop people on foot. That's the point. So, we have to get rid of our suitcases. Even on foot I think we'd be checked.' Tweed's voice was terse, fresh. 'It means we have to transfer our few clothes to plastic bags — several people have walked over with them and no one bothers.'

'I remember there was a supermarket, a small one,

where Newman dropped us. I could go there, buy a few things, collect some plastic bags.'

'After breakfast . . .'

'But what do we do with the cases?'

'Shove them in here. I've been exploring.' Tweed led her to a small door under where the roof sloped. He opened it, shone his pencil flash inside while Paula peered in. She stood up.

'Won't the chambermaid find them?' she objected.

'Not immediately. I'll hide them under those two spare duvets on that shelf. Before I do that I'll break the locks. That will give a reason why they were left. But when they discover them we'll be long gone.'

'Will we?' She wandered over to the window again. 'Are those men with the cine-camera still watching from that house?'

'Of course.'

'They'll photograph us then . . .'

'I hope so . . .'

She spun on her heel. 'Another cryptic remark. What the hell does it mean?' she flared. 'And I hate these clothes. Do I pass inspection?'

Paula was clad in worn blue jeans and a padded wind-cheater. Her feet were shod in trainers. She had bought this clobber, as she called it, at Tweed's insistence in Freiburg.

'You look fine. You look like everyone else. It's a uniform these days. So you merge into the background. Now, breakfast. You'll feel better on a full stomach.' He smiled. 'So will I.'

'I'm sorry', she said, and hugged him impulsively, 'for that attack of nerves. I'll be all right when we're on the move – really I will.'

'I know. A good breakfast. Now . . .'

* * *

Tweed walked down the hill to the German frontier post first, followed by Paula, a dozen yards behind him. He'd insisted on this sequence, partly to steady her nerve, but he'd also issued a stern instruction.

'Nothing is going to happen to me – but if it does you keep walking and you go up to that Swiss police car parked near their border post.'

As he came close to the frontier post the blue-coated guards stopped a BMW. In each hand Tweed carried a plastic carrier-bag containing the contents of his suitcase. Paula also was similarly burdened. They looked like two people who had completed their shopping, two people who had nothing to do with each other.

Tweed paused at the edge of the kerb, looked back as though to check no car was coming, saw Paula stepping it out, her head high. He walked past the post at his normal pace. The sun was again shining brilliantly, reflecting a hard glare off the chrome of the BMW.

He was on the bridge now, moving along the left-hand sidewalk, his pace steady. He had passed the German cabin without anyone taking any notice of him as they checked out the driver of the BMW, opening his trunk. Tweed was half-way across, the Rhine flowing swiftly below him, when he paused and stared straight at the house concealing the cine-camera.

Paula was appalled. It took all her determination to keep moving. What the devil was Tweed up to? It was almost as though he'd deliberately challenged the invisible watchers behind the curtains. Then he was walking again, approaching the Swiss control.

'It's going to go wrong where we least expected,' Paula said to herself. 'The Swiss guards will have the description sent from London . . .'

She gritted her teeth as Tweed drew closer and one of the Swiss officers walked across the road. He was going to intercept Tweed. It was all over. After they'd gone through so much already . . .

The officer stood on the sidewalk, hands on his hips, facing Tweed, who continued walking towards him. The officer gazed over the parapet of the bridge as a police launch passed beneath it, shouted something down to the men aboard, waved his hand, crossed back to the post and began talking to his companion. Tweed walked past and began climbing the hill where the road turned off the bridge.

He would have given anything to look back to see how Paula was faring but he resisted the temptation. He went on climbing the road which curved round to the right past the ancient houses. The railway station was less than ten minutes' walk from where he was now.

He knew he was out of sight of the bridge when he heard the crunch of feet coming up fast behind him. Still he didn't turn his head. Paula drew alongside him, breathing heavily. It was so cold that, like Tweed, her breath was coming out as puffs of white vapour.

'Don't you think we might co-habit now?' she enquired.

'Depends what you mean – it's a bit public here.'

She dug him affectionately in the ribs with her elbow. 'You know what I mean! And look at that sign. We've made it.'

By the roadside a large sign pointed back the way they had come. DEUTSCHLAND. Tweed grinned at her as they continued trudging uphill over the icy slope.

'Want to go back for a second look?'

'Not bloody likely. Eliza Dolittle in Shaw's *Pygmalion*.'

'I have seen a few plays in my time, I'd have you know . . .'

They were joshing each other like a couple of school-children. It was for both of them the release of tension after their ordeal. They passed several expensive-looking villas with grey colour-washed walls, then they were on

292

the level. At an intersection was another road sign. *Altstadt*. The Old Town.

Tweed nodded his head to the right. 'It's a wonderful example of an old medieval town. Pity we haven't time to explore it. Ah, there's the station. We turn left here.'

Paula glanced to the right. A straight cobbled street led to an old tower. The arched entrance to the Old Town was cut out of the base of the tower. Below the sloping roof was a clock with roman figures painted in gold. It was so large she saw the minute hand jerk forward.

Normally she'd have loved to explore, but she was frozen and couldn't wait to get far away from the border. As they turned left she saw the *Bahnhof*. Laufenburg's rail station was a compact two-storey building with coral-washed walls and shuttered windows. More like a private residence than a station.

Tweed entered the booking hall, studied the timetable on the wall. He walked up to the ticket window, put down his plastic bags as Paula stood alongside him, then he stared at the clerk.

'I – want – two – top – tickets – to – Zürich. Single . . .'

To Paula's astonishment he spoke in English, spoke to the clerk as though addressing a mental idiot. The clerk looked at him, nodded, produced two tickets from the machine while Tweed was fiddling with Swiss banknotes. Then he examined the tickets and stared again at the clerk.

'These – are – first – class?' he mumbled.

'I beg your pardon,' the clerk said in perfect English.

Paula's patience snapped. 'Erste Klasse fahren,' she said.

'Ah, first class? I did not hear you friend clearly . . .'

The clerk changed the tickets, sorted out the banknotes Tweed pushed under the window, gave him half of them back, leaned forward, spoke slowly and clearly.

'For Zürich you change at Eglisau. The train is due in five minutes. The next train.'

'I eventually worked that out from your timetable,' Tweed grumbled. 'British timetables are much better than German.'

'Swiss,' the clerk corrected him. 'You are in Switzerland.'

'I know that. You think I am stupid?'

On the deserted platform Paula, still suffering from the reaction of crossing the bridge, exploded.

'Have you gone mad? Half-way across that bloody bridge you stopped and stared up at the house where they have a cine-camera. Now you make a scene with that ticket clerk, you talk in English when you could so easily have spoken in German. That clerk is going to remember us, if someone enquires after us.'

'I hope so.' Tweed's mood had changed. He was his normal alert self. 'I am springing a trap.'

'What does that mean? Sometimes I feel humiliated by the way we keep on running, running, running. It's not our style.'

'So,' Tweed repeated, 'I am springing a trap. Laying a powder train in our wake, if you like – a powder train which in due course will blow up in the face of our pursuers.'

28

Newman used the same phone at the main station in Basle to call Alois Turpil. The idiot hadn't kept his appointment the previous evening. Newman had met the train arriving at 1800 hours. Passengers had alighted as he stood with his copy of the *Financial Times*. Then the platform was deserted, the train moved out, and no one had approached him. He swore, went into the restaurant and ordered a large Scotch.

'Who is this?' the same voice as previously enquired in German at the other end of the line.

'You should bloody well be able to guess. You never came to Basle last night. What the hell are you playing at?' Newman responded in the same language.

'If you had told me where you are staying, given me a phone number, I would have called you,' Turpil purred. 'Something most urgent, most unexpected came up. I couldn't leave here. Where are you calling from now?'

'A public box at the *Hauptbahnhof*, of course . . .'

'I can meet you tonight. Most definitely. At the same time and the same place.' The tone had become deferential.

'Let me tell you something, Turpil. Stand me up again and I am going to report your behaviour to our mutual friend. You won't ever get another commission from him again. Or from me. No, don't interrupt. Just listen. 1800 hours this evening. On the platform where your train arrives. Look for the *Financial Times* under my arm. It's pink in colour . . .'

'I know that . . .'

'Glad to hear you know something. Last chance, Turpil . . .'

Newman slammed down the phone and walked away.

'Wake up. We're at Laufenburg.' Horowitz, dug his elbow into Morgan's overweight bulk settled in the seat beside him.

'Where are we?'

Morgan had eaten a large lunch with all the trimmings. An aperitif for openers. White wine, then red wine with the four-course meal. Followed by a large cognac with coffee. He blinked. They were seated in the dark in the

295

cinema in the basement of World Security HQ in Basle.

More pictures were being flashed on the screen, films projected from the cine-cameras which had photographed the more minor Rhine crossings the previous day. It was mid-afternoon. The films had been brought in fast by couriers on motor-cycles. They had watched eight films from eight different crossings before Morgan fell into a deep sleep.

'I just told you,' Horowitz said quietly. 'This is Laufenburg.'

'Another negative result,' grumbled Morgan, reaching for his cigar case. He extracted a cigar and twirled it between pudgy fingers. If he lit it that puritanical bastard, Horowitz, would object. He forced himself to concentrate. More people crossing the bridge. Another blank . . .

Horowitz leaned forward. Morgan sensed his companion was coiled like a steel spring. He blinked again, yawned, sat up more erect to keep himself awake.

'Freeze that frame!' Horowitz called out to the projectionist behind them. 'That's it. Now, zoom it up. That man crossing and carrying two plastic bags . . .'

Morgan frowned, stuck the cigar in his mouth, chewed on the tip as the frame froze, the picture became enlarged, showing the head and shoulders of the hatless man trudging across the Rhine. Horowitz's voice was a sibilant hiss.

'That is Tweed. When was this picture taken?' he called out.

'Yesterday morning.'

The projectionist's voice was a weird disembodied echo. There were only two other people watching. Horowitz and Morgan. The Welshman stared hard at the frozen face which was looking straight at the camera with a grim expression. The image was blurred but, now Horowitz had pointed it out to him, Morgan felt sure it was Tweed. Horowitz was calling out to the projectionist again.

'There may be a girl with him. Continue running the film now.'

The blurred image vanished, the screen went white for a few moments, then the focus was back to normal, taking in most of the bridge. Morgan settled back, but Horowitz still leaned forward, motionless. His deliberate voice broke the silence again.

'That girl – also carrying plastic bags – in denims and the windcheater. 'Freeze *that* frame. Zoom it up. Quickly!'

Morgan sucked at his wet cigar end. Another head-and-shoulders image filled the screen. Again the image was blurred but her features were clear. Horowitz sank back in his seat and turned to Morgan.

'I studied the photos closely enough to be sure. That girl is Paula Grey. The two of them have crossed over into Switzerland.'

'Well, he'd want his girl friend with him,' Morgan commented. 'All home comforts on tap . . .'

'According to the file Grey is his trusted assistant. There was nothing said about an intimate relationship.'

Horowitz sounded severe, as though he found Morgan's attitude to life repellent. Yes, a ruddy puritan, Morgan reflected, and a cold-blooded assassin into the bargain. Who is he to come out with moral lectures? Instead he said:

'Well, there's your target. What's your next move?'

'Where is Stieber?'

'He won't be back till tomorrow,' Morgan replied quickly. 'I sent him to check something for me in Germany.'

'Then I need a car immediately. To drive me to Laufenburg. It will only take a short time and I wish to question the men who filmed those shots. Also I may make further enquiries in Laufenburg. I wish to leave at once. With a print of both those frames.'

'I'll come with you.' Morgan heaved his bulk out of the chair. 'I'll tell the projectionist to provide the prints within five minutes. And there's a Merc waiting in the car park. Which should get us there fast.'

'You can stop wasting any more film,' Morgan told the operator of the cine-camera as they entered the room of the old house perched above the Rhine. 'You filmed the target, Stutz. And is there an ash-tray in this dump, Jost?' he asked the other man, waving his lighted cigar.

'Mr Stutz,' Horowitz began more politely as the operator pressed a switch, stood up from behind his camera and stretched his arms. 'Mr Stutz, this is a frame of a man you've filmed crossing the bridge. Yesterday, I understand. Do you by any chance remember this man? You are concealed behind net curtains – hence the blurred image – but the strange thing is he appears to be looking straight at you.'

Stutz, a small lean-faced man, studied the print, scratched his head. He handed back the print and slipped a peppermint in his mouth.

'Oddly enough, I do remember him. And I had the weird sensation that he *was* looking at me. Which is impossible.'

'Not necessarily. He is a very clever man. And this print of a girl – you remember her?'

Stutz reacted more quickly, glancing at the print before he returned it. 'No. I don't recall her . . .'

'She was walking not a dozen metres behind the man,' Horowitz insisted.

'Then that explains it. I was so startled by the man staring straight up at me I don't think I took a lot of notice of what I was filming for the next few minutes.'

'Thank you, Mr Stutz. Incidentally, what time of the day was it when the man crossed?'

'Mid-morning. Maybe a bit earlier. Hard to be exact.'

'Thank you again, Mr Stutz. One final question. In Laufenburg is there a car-hire firm, even a small outfit?'

It was the other member of the team, Jost, small and stocky, who answered. 'No, there isn't. Quite definitely not.'

'You sound very certain, Mr Jost.'

'I spent a holiday here last year. Which was one reason I was chosen for this assignment. I knew where we could site the camera for a fee. No car-hire people in Laufen-burg . . .'

Morgan waited until he was alone with Horowitz back in the icy street, standing by the parked Merc, before he asked his question.

'You think they hired a car to make their getaway after they'd slipped over the border?'

'I don't now.' Horowitz gave Morgan a glance verging on the contemptuous. 'Not when there's no place to hire a car. So, we have two people on foot, carrying heavy carriers in each hand. The bags sagged, I noticed. And in this weather. They need to leave here quickly. They have overcome a nerve-racking hurdle – crossing the frontier. They would wish to leave this town quickly. How? The railway station is our next visit . . .'

Once again Horowitz slipped quickly behind the wheel. He had noted Morgan's reaction to too large a meal. Sluggishness. Driving needed swift reflexes, especially in these conditions. His judgement was confirmed when he started the engine and the wheels spun futilely on ice. He released the brake, let the car slide back a few feet, braked on packed snow. The car moved forward up the curving hill.

In the front passenger seat Morgan glanced to his right as they reached the level area at the top of the hill. He gestured with his cigar.

'There's a Hotel Bahnhof over there. They could be sitting inside that place while we drive past.'

'No.' Horowitz crawled forward, saw the station to his left, turned the wheel. 'I am beginning to think myself inside the mind of this Tweed. He is a clever and resourceful opponent. He knows when to wait. He must have spent one night inside the Black Forest at least, maybe two – before he drove here. And he must also have detected the bomb I attached to the Audi we found in the undergrowth off the timber track. You have your World Security pass for Switzerland with you?'

'Yes. Why?'

'I am going to question the station staff. All you have to do is to flash your pass, say "Police", and then leave me to do the talking. That pass looks very like a Swiss detective's identity pass. Which, I suppose, is why you had it designed like that. One day the police will complain.'

'We do a lot of business in Switzerland. They don't bother us.'

'That won't influence the police in this country. Ah, here is the station . . .'

Morgan did as instructed. Standing beside Horowitz in front of the ticket window, he flashed his pass. '*Polizei*.'

'We think you may be able to help us,' Horowitz began in his soothing voice. 'We are looking for a dangerous criminal. A German who can pass for an Englishman. He may have been accompanied by an attractive girl. Here is his picture. It is a little fuzzy, but still a good likeness. Have you ever seen this man?'

'Yes,' the ticket clerk said promptly. 'I'm hardly likely to forget him . . .'

'Oh! Why is that?'

'He was very aggressive, talked to me like a schoolboy and was rather stupid in the way he asked for the two tickets to Zürich. I don't think he knew Switzerland at all well – he spoke in English word by word, and of course I know the language well.'

'Of course,' Horowitz agreed amiably.

'He was so muddled,' the clerk continued, 'that I gave him two ordinary tickets and he wanted first class. The girl

300

with him had to say "first class" to me in German. Then I got it sorted out for him.'

'Two return first-class tickets to Zürich?' Horowitz enquired.

'No. One-way. He did know he had to change at Eglisau.'

'And can you recall about what time of day this was?'

'In the morning.' The clerk reflected. 'Sometime about mid-morning. Has he done something awful?'

'Possibly a question of taking money which doesn't belong to him.' Horowitz smiled. 'You have been most helpful. I thank you.'

Morgan stamped his feet to clear his shoes of snow before he climbed back into the Mercedes beside Horowitz. Then he clasped his gloved hands together to get the circulation going.

'So now we know. It's Zürich.'

'I find the behaviour of Tweed very curious,' Horowitz commented. 'It bothers me more than a little.'

'What behaviour? Seemed pretty clear to me.'

'I said earlier I was beginning to know Tweed, how his agile mind works. First, while crossing the bridge, he gazes straight at the camera. A coincidence? I think not. I believe that somehow he knew that camera was there. Then when he reaches the station he makes a great fuss, goes out of his way to draw attention to himself so he will be remembered. Why? We will drive back to Basle now. Later I will go to Zürich, perhaps with Stieber. But Zürich worries me. I shall tread very carefully, I promise you.'

29

Newman had spent some time parked in a slot opposite to the entrance to the eight-storey modern building over-looking the Rhine which was World Security HQ. He had then parked his car in another slot out of sight and had explored on foot.

Six steps led up to the large plate-glass entrance doors. Beyond them uniformed guards with dogs patrolled. He walked down the side street next to the building and came to the river. A flight of steps led down to the Rhine near one of the bridges spanning the wide river.

At the bottom was a pedestrian walk alongside the Rhine. He looked up as he strolled along with a bitter wind blowing in his face. More snow on the way. There were plenty of footprints in the snow covering the promenade and under them the snow was packed hard. Above him on each floor windows gave a view across to the opposite bank. Attached to the river wall was an iron-rung ladder leading down to a mooring point for boats.

The rest of the day he was careful not to go near the building. It began to snow heavily in mid-afternoon. Would that help or hinder their entry into the building? That was assuming Turpil turned up this time.

At 1800 hours, having eaten an early dinner at the Hilton, he was standing on the same platform as the train glided into the *Hauptbahnhof*. Passengers again alighted, girls clutching scarves close to their throats as they left the warmth of the coaches and the icy air hit them.

Newman stood well back, the *Financial Times* tucked

under his arm. All the passengers disappeared down the exit steps, the train moved out, leaving a deserted platform except for Newman. He swore.

'All right, Turpil,' he said to himself, 'that's it. And thank God I didn't tell you where I was staying . . .'

'Mr Newman? Mr Robert Newman?'

The guttural voice was familiar. Newman swung round. A man had emerged from the top of the nearby steps, had moved with the silent tread of a cat. A small man, inches shorter than Newman, slimly built, but with a remarkable face. Very strong bone structure, his nose hooked, a wide thin-lipped mouth and a pointed chin. His eyes, a pale luminous blue, stared hard at Newman.

Alois Turpil wore denims, the bottoms nipped tight to his ankles with bicycle clips, a close-fitting dark wind-cheater buttoned to the neck. Perched on his head above a high forehead was a woollen pixie cap. He reminded Newman of a pixie, a formidable pixie.

'You came this time,' Newman remarked in German.

'I explained that on the phone, Mr Newman,' Turpil replied in English. 'Shall we go into the restaurant out of the cold so we may talk?'

'Where did you spring from?' Newman asked as they walked towards the restaurant. 'You didn't alight from that train.'

'Always do the unexpected. That is the only way to survive. I drove here by car, parked it. I have been watching you from the opposite platform – from behind that trolley of luggage. I wished to make sure you were alone . . .'

They chose a table in a corner. Probably it was the weather, the time of the year, the time of day – the place was three parts empty. A waiter wearing a white apron arrived.

'You'd like something to drink?' Newman suggested.

'Nothing alcoholic. Coffee would do nicely.' Turpil, still

303

wearing his woolly cap, waited until they were alone. 'I never drink alcohol when I'm working. It muddles the brain. Now, Mr Newman, what is it you wanted me to do for you?'

Newman shifted his executive case more firmly between his legs under the table, offered his cigarette pack, took one when Turpil shook his head. The direct approach, he decided.

'We have to break into World Security HQ down by the Rhine. I want to photograph their most secret records. I'd guess in the so-called Research & Development Division section – wherever that may be. I have a camera. You get us inside, open up filing cabinets, any safes you can locate. I photograph certain documents, you replace them exactly where you found them. When we leave I don't want them to know we've paid them a call. Especially I don't want them to know that we've copied some of their records.'

He paused as the waiter brought coffee. They drank it in silence while Newman waited for Turpil to react. He guessed his age as about fifty, maybe a little older. Hard to tell, he was so slim. The silence went on. Turpil frequently gazed at Newman with his strange luminous eyes. The Englishman was not happy about the eyes – they had a remoteness which hinted at a man who cared not a fig for his fellow human beings.

'This place is too public,' Turpil said after finishing his coffee. 'Surely there is somewhere else where we can discuss this problem more privately?'

Newman sighed, paid his bill, led the way out of the station to where he had parked the BMW. He saw Turpil glance at the front number plates and congratulated himself on his precaution. Before leaving the car he had scooped up handfuls of snow in his gloved hands and plastered it over the registration. Both front and rear plates.

Turpil settled himself in the front passenger seat. Newman climbed in behind the wheel, turned on the engine and both heaters. The interior was like the inside of a refrigerator. Ice had formed on the windscreen.

'What you propose is a dangerous operation, very dangerous,' Turpil began. 'World Security is an unpleasant crowd. If we were caught we'd be liable to end up floating in the Rhine, unconscious.'

'So, you know the building,' Newman said with a flash of insight.

'I didn't say that. You've told me the problem. Now I need to know the fee for my services.'

'Fifteen thousand Swiss francs . . .'

'Ridiculous. I've wasted my time coming here. Your friend, Tweed, would know better.'

'I'm talking about cash, Turpil.'

Newman rested the executive case on his lap, unlocked it and raised the lid. Turpil glanced at the neat stacks of banknotes inside and for a second Newman saw a flash in the pale eyes. He closed the lid.

'And I only deal in cash,' Turpil replied. 'We're wasting time. What time were you thinking we'd make the break-in?'

'Around midnight . . .'

'No. Three o'clock in the early morning. The morale of the guards, their alertness, will be at the lowest ebb.'

'You do know the building,' Newman persisted. 'I'll raise the fee. Twenty thousand francs. My last offer. In fact it's all I've got in this case, all I can afford.'

He omitted to tell Turpil that for his own travelling expenses he had deposited ten thousand of the francs Tweed had provided in the safety deposit at the Drei-Könige. He snapped the catches shut on the case, lit a cigarette and stared out at the bleak deserted street.

'I make a rule of never operating inside Switzerland,' Turpil informed him in his quiet purring voice.

Newman didn't reply. He glanced at his watch. 6.30 p.m.

'You drive a hard bargain,' Turpil commented, and Newman knew the fish had taken the bait. It had been the sight of all that cash. Turpil's next remark confirmed he'd assessed the man's character correctly.

'Do you mind if I look inside that case for myself?'

'Be my guest . . .'

After checking the contents and handing back the case Turpil sat silent for several minutes. Newman was catching on to his tricks, mannerisms. He also said nothing. Then Turpil tapped the closed case resting on Newman's lap.

'I normally receive an advance before I do the job. Fifty per cent of the agreed fee.'

Newman shook his head. It wasn't only letting go of so much money: Turpil would have thought him a soft touch if he'd let him get away with it. They were conducting a ritual dance and Newman's patience was wearing thin.

'What is the next move – between now and target time?'

'You amuse yourself on your own until 2.30 a.m. Then I pick you up from your hotel . . .'

'The Hilton,' Newman said promptly. He turned to face his passenger. 'Let me ask you a couple of questions before you disappear into the wild blue yonder. Where is your equipment? And what are *you* going to be doing?'

'My equipment is in my car, parked not a dozen yards from where we're sitting. It's an Audi with a souped-up engine. I shall be checking the World Security building again thoroughly.'

'Again?'

Turpil smiled for the first time. 'My earlier profession was security expert. I installed the security system inside that building. I know my way around it better than I do the inside of my own apartment.'

So, all that talk about how tough the job was going to be was pure sales pitch, Newman thought. But he was relieved that Turpil would be working on familiar territory so he said nothing as Turpil opened the door. He leaned inside before he closed it.

'The main entrance to the Hilton just down the road. 2.30 a.m. prompt. Timing is everything.'

He slammed the door shut before Newman could reply.

Tweed had phoned his old friend Arthur Beck, Chief of the Federal Police in Berne, from a call box in the main station as soon as they reached Zürich. Paula stood a few feet away, guarding the plastic bags. It was a tense moment for both of them. How would Beck react?

'Arthur Beck here,' the familiar breezy voice came over the line. 'Who is this?'

'Tweed speaking . . .'

'Give me the name of that lovely girl assistant of yours – it sounds like you, but . . .'

'Paula Grey. And last time we were here you held a plane *en route* to Athens while we talked at Kloten Airport.'

'That's enough. Excuse the precaution. Where are you calling from?'

'A public call-box . . .'

'I have been waiting for this call ever since you crossed the frontier over the bridge at Laufenburg, my friend.'

'And how the devil do you know about that?'

'Oh, I had Howard's report about your unconventional behaviour in London, plus photographs of yourself and Paula flown to me. I circulated copies to the frontier posts. Surely you noticed the Swiss official who stood staring at you on the bridge and then went back to a police car? He recognized you from your picture, reported back to me over his radio. Now, where are you?'

'Zürich. I need to get to a high-powered transmitter

very quickly, to use it in secrecy. I may tell you why if – when – we meet.'

'Oh, we must meet. I'd arrange for a car to bring you here from Zürich police HQ but I think you should keep under cover. Do you mind taking an express to Berne? No? Good. Get a cab from the station. I suggest you enter the Taubenhalde by the rear entrance. Remember where it is? Then when may I expect you? Give me time to get out the welcome mat.'

'It will be a few hours yet. We have to eat and then take an express to Berne.'

'Good. Arrange it so you arrive after dark. When we meet you can tell me who has gone stark raving bonkers in London. Not Howard, from what I read between the lines. Take care.'

Tweed smiled as he replaced the receiver, partly with relief, partly at the English colloquialism – Beck prided himself on his use of the English language.

'He seems friendly,' he told Paula. 'Now, first we must buy two suitcases to pack our things. Then lunch.'

'I know just the place in the Bahnhofstrasse to get suitcases. There's a café over there where you can get coffee. Wait for me. I'll be as quick as I can . . .'

Horowitz sat alone with Morgan in the latter's office in Basle. He had sent Hendrix back to her apartment in Frankfurt after paying the girl a large fee. He now saw no opportunity to infiltrate her into Tweed's company.

'The time has come for me to fly to Zürich,' he announced. 'I wish to take Stieber with me. When is he due back – from Germany you said?'

'Any minute now.'

'You must alert as many operatives in Zürich as possible about Tweed and the girl. They have photographs, I assume?'

'Yes. I'll phone, tell them to run off more copies.'

'Those operatives are reliable, I hope? They can throw a dragnet through as complex a city as Zürich?'

'Of course.' Morgan was indignant. 'I have an old woman on a cycle who can cover an incredible distance. We have motor-cyclists, men on foot who look like young louts. We have men selling toys and balloons at strategic points no one would suspect. We can scour Zürich . . .'

'Send two top operatives, a man and a girl, to the main station. Tweed and the girl probably arrived there. Check all the hotels. Give them a cover story for when they show their photographs of Tweed. I suggest they say he has to fly urgently to New York. His wife is seriously ill. They can pretend to represent some big insurance company and Tweed is one of their top executives. The Prudential. Have you the facilities to print fake Prudential visiting cards?'

'Yes. On the premises in Zürich.' Morgan suppressed his resentment at this stream of instructions. 'You're flying to Zürich today?'

Horowitz stood up. 'No, tomorrow. That gives you time to get your people in Zürich moving . . .'

'Manpower will be stretched to the limit,' Morgan protested.

'Send men from here. The focus has switched to Zürich. I'll see you later.'

Horowitz left the office without another word and walked back to the Drei Könige where he was staying. Morgan sat fuming, puffing his cigar, when the phone rang. It was Buckmaster. The pressure never eased up.

'Just a brief word,' the lofty voice told him. 'I'm sorry to have to tell you Dr Rose met with a fatal accident. A hit-and-run driver according to the papers. Sorry to be the bearer of ill tidings. Must go.'

Morgan sank back in his chair and sighed with sheer

relief. At least that call counter-balanced his conversation with Armand Horowitz.

Newman drove back to the Drei Könige for dinner when he had watched Turpil leave his parking lot inside his Audi. From what Turpil had told him he seemed to be making careful preparations for the break-in at World Security. He parked the BMW near the Drei Könige, walked into the lobby, acknowledged the concierge's greeting, went up to his room and had a quick shower.

The drive through the night from the station had been short but a gruelling experience. It had stopped snowing but the temperature had nose-dived. The tram-lines were bars of ice, there had been shot ice as he turned the bends and twice he had skidded.

After the refreshing shower, which warmed him up, he changed into a heavier suit for the night's work and went down to the dining-room. The promenade deck overhanging the Rhine where tables were laid in the open in summer was closed and ankle-deep in snow.

There were very few people in the dining-room. The head waiter was leading him towards a table when Newman spoke quickly.

'I think I'd like that table for two by the wall, please.'

'But certainly, sir . . .'

Newman sat down with his back to the wall. Pretending to examine the menu, he watched the tall thin man with steel-rimmed glasses seated four tables away, providing Newman with a three-quarter view of him. Newman had had a bad shock.

He recalled the photographs Marler had taken of the men entering the World Security Building in Freiburg. The turnip-figured man Marler had identified as Gareth Morgan. His tall companion, Marler had explained at greater length, was one of the top assassins in Europe. And now, apparently like Newman, Armand Horowitz also considered the best hotel in town was good enough.

30

Latitude 30. 10. N. Longitude 41. 0. W. The mid-Atlantic south-west of the Azores. Captain William North, American skipper of the *Lampedusa*, a 20,000-ton freighter with a single smoke-stack, gave the order to heave to. Hundreds of miles away from the well-used sea-lanes, he was worried about the stricken vessel half a mile to starboard. His First Officer had just reported to him on the bridge.

'Radio op reports a Mayday signal from that ship, sir. I gather they have a sick woman aboard. Fell down a companionway and broke her left leg. Compound fracture. They've no doctor. They also have engine trouble. Permission to take the lady aboard?'

North stood, feet splayed, binoculars pressed into his eyes while he scanned the vessel. It was motionless, swaying on the gentle swell. He then swept the horizon and, as he had expected, there was no other vessel in sight. It was broad daylight and the sun rippled off the wave crests.

'We do have a doctor,' his officer persisted. 'If she is left there and they can't repair the engine trouble she could be in real trouble.'

'Let me think.'

North lowered the binoculars. He had a lot to think about. The stricken vessel was the *Helvetia* and flew the French flag. About twenty thousand tons, he estimated. It could have drifted a long way south if the engines had broken down a while ago.

Yes, he had a lot to think about. In the hold of the *Lampedusa* rested the giant computer, *Shockwave*. So enormous it almost filled the large hold. North had a crew of twenty American seamen, all of them armed. Underneath the canvas-covered erection on the foredeck was concealed a high-powered machine-gun. Seen through his glasses the *Helvetia* had a frail look as she rolled helplessly.

'Supposing we just sail on,' North suggested, thinking out aloud. 'Get the hell out of it and continue *en route* for Plymouth. Then we can hand over that lump of hi-tech to the Brits, go ashore, try out the Limey beer.'

'Then I wouldn't sleep too well for the rest of the voyage,' his officer replied.

'Don't suppose I would either,' North agreed. He took his decision. 'Tell the radio op to signal them to send the lady over to us in one boat. Repeat one boat. Warn Dr Schellberger he has a patient coming aboard. Wait! Also tell the radio op to report what we're doing to Langley on the agreed waveband. I presume you've checked with the sonar team that there are no subs in the area?'

'I did that before I came to the bridge. Normal procedure in an emergency.'

'Well, OK. Get it moving. We can't hang about here for the rest of the year. And, just to make assurance doubly sure, tell the gun team to stand by their weapon. But don't take off the canvas. We don't want to give that skipper of the *Helvetia* a heart attack. That would make for another patient for Schellberger . . .'

North stood, hands on his hips, staring at the other vessel, then called back his officer who was running off the bridge.

'Another precaution, Jeff, warn the guard crew to be on the alert. Assemble them close to the foredeck. Get to it.'

North, a six-footer, wrinkled his forehead. Why was he

312

taking all these precautions? Because something about this goddamn situation bothered him. Couldn't put his finger on it. Everything looked peaceful enough. He checked his watch. Should take them about a half-hour to get the lady aboard the *Lampedusa*. The *Helvetia* crew was white, European. Something he'd checked when he'd scanned the deck of the vessel.

He glanced over his shoulder as a short heavily built man heaved himself up the ladder. White-haired, Dr Schellberger was very spry for his age, his weight.

'Hear I've got work to do, sir,' he remarked. 'A hip fracture and a broken leg. That will make for a deal of pain.'

North nodded. Then another possible solution occurred to him. He suggested the doctor could go aboard the *Helvetia* to tend to the patient. Schellberger shook his head.

'With a compound fracture you never know. I'd prefer to have her aboard here to keep an eye on her.'

North nodded agreement. The First Officer reappeared, reported. 'The radio op is sending your signal to the *Helvetia*. He was delayed responding to a signal from London. Then he'll be contacting Langley.'

'Thank you. I guess we'll be under way in the next half-hour.'

Several thousand miles away to the north-west Lance Buckmaster left the special room at the Admiralty which had been put at his disposal at the specific request of the PM. Inside the room, for which he had the only key, was a high-powered transmitter which he had no trouble operating by himself. They had similar advanced transceivers at all the main headquarters of World Security & Communications.

He returned through the dark to his office at the Ministry

for External Security. Alone, he sat down before a type-writer and tapped out a brief memo to the PM. He read it once, initialled it with a flourishing 'B', put it inside an envelope, sealed it, addressed it *Highly Confidential. Personal attention of Prime Minister*, called a messenger, gave him the envelope and told him to hand it direct into the hands of the PM.

Alone again, he clasped his hands behind his neck, stretched and yawned. Now all that remained to be done was to work his way through his red despatch boxes. As suited the PM, the memo had been brief.

1810 hours. Contacted North. Cargo proceeding according to schedule.

On the bridge of the *Lampedusa*, Captain North watched the activity aboard the *Helvetia* through his glasses. A staircase had been lowered, the platform resting just above the lapping waves. A large boat had also been lowered from its davits and was being brought alongside the platform. Two crew members ran down, tied up the boat securely fore and aft to the platform.

More crew appeared at the top of the staircase, men moving slowly as they handled a stretcher, manoeuvring their burden down the platform at an angle. Inside the stretcher North had a glimpse of a girl with long dark hair splayed, a girl who lay very still and appeared to have a piece of wood strapped to the side of her left leg.

North lowered his glasses, checked the situation on his fore-deck. As ordered, several seamen stood round the canvas-covered machine-gun. Others, their hand-guns concealed, lounged at the port side, gazing at the *Helvetia*. Because his vessel was riding the sea with the bow pointed towards the stricken ship, North felt he had made his dispositions. No need to waste manpower at the stern.

*   *   *

Aboard the *Helvetia* ex-Sergeant Greg Singer, late of the SAS, stood at the head of the staircase, checking the operation. A six-foot-tall man, he was heavily built, his large head was like a sculpture carved out of teak. His dark hair was cropped close to the skull and he wore a pea jacket and denim trousers.

Thirty-three years old, he had been drummed out of the Special Air Service for brutality in his treatment of young recruits. His CO had been sorry to lose him.

'Singer is as tough as a rock,' he'd remarked. 'Pity that he went too far on that training course ... He has brains ...'

Too far had been British understatement for the incident when Singer broke the jaws of two trainees climbing the Brecons in Wales. They hadn't been trying hard enough, according to Singer. Now he glanced at the stop-watch held in the palm of his large hand. Timing was everything in this operation. Seconds counted. And his fee of £100,000 was at stake. For that kind of money he was prepared to go the limit. And that was exactly what he was going to do. He slid his right hand inside the jacket, felt the butt of the Luger shoved down his leather belt. The skipper, Captain Hartmann, born in Austria, appeared alongside Singer.

'Radio op reports they've given permission for us to move the wounded passenger aboard.

'Time to start the jamming,' Singer snapped, his expression a graven image.

'We've already started that. No further signals from the *Lampedusa* will go anywhere. What about the frogmen?'

'They went over the port side five minutes ago. They'll reach the stern about the time our boat arrives ...'

Singer ran down the steps, leapt into the boat. The stretcher had already been carefully laid inside near the bow. Five men were aboard, including Singer, when they cast off. Rolls of canvas were littered untidily inside the large boat as Singer gave the order and the engine fired.

315

The mooring rope was unhitched, thrown on the platform, and the boat headed across the gentle swell for the *Lampedusa*.

The attention of all the men on deck aboard the vessel was concentrated on the approaching boat, a factor Singer had banked on. Nothing like insatiable curiosity to bugger up security. He checked his stop-watch again. 'Slow her down a bit,' he ordered.

It was all a question of synchronization. The five frogmen under the waves had to reach the *Lampedusa*'s stern about one minute before Singer's boat hove to under the staircase North had now lowered over the side of his vessel. Three minutes was the maximum period Singer had planned for completion of the operation.

It was a peaceful scene, North thought, arms folded as he waited on the bridge. The clearest of blue skies, the sun gleaming off wavelets, the approaching boat now close enough to see down inside it. The injured woman would be in her twenties he estimated. Her suède jacket was open, exposing her tight sweater, the two mounds of her breasts thrusting against the wool. Her denims seemed pasted to her long shapely legs. Several members of the *Lampedusa*'s crew gave wolf whistles. The girl smiled briefly, waved her right hand. North stirred restlessly. The wolf whistles irked him.

'Cut that out!' he shouted. 'Prepare to bring the casualty aboard . . .'

At the stern of the *Lampedusa* something like a nightmare was appearing. Hands grasped the gunwale, bodies heaved themselves over and on deck. They were clad in frogmen's suits, which masked their faces, and as they came aboard they carried waterproof bags which they dumped on the deck.

They moved silently and with great speed. Unzipping the bags, they wrenched off their flippers from their feet, their masks from their faces. From inside the bags they hauled out gas-masks and breathing apparatus. Fitting them over their heads, they hauled gas pistols from the bags and ran along either side of the deck. A crew member of the *Lampedusa* appeared suddenly at the top of a companionway. He stared in amazement at the hideous figures running towards him, reached for his gun inside his holster. One of the masked intruders aimed, fired his gas pistol. The seaman clutched at his throat, gave a horrible gurgling sound, collapsed backwards down the companionway. He was dead before he reached the bottom.

The invaders fanned out, one group diving down the companionway, a second couple ran up towards the bridge, another man dived up the port side. They paused at the top behind the bridge. One man crept forwards and peered round the corner.

The boat from the *Helvetia* was now moored to the platform of the *Lampedusa*. Crew members had run down the platform and were lifting the stretcher, easing it carefully on to the platform. Singer grabbed something from under a roll of canvas, fitted the gas mask on swiftly, bent down again and hauled out a Uzi machine pistol. He ran up the staircase and was on deck before North realized anything strange was happening.

'Man the gun!' He shouted. 'Open fire on the terrorists . . .'

He broke off in mid-sentence as a short burst from the Uzi cut his body in half. Singer swung the barrel towards the crew manning the machine-gun. They had ripped off the canvas, were swivelling the muzzle under the instructions of the First Officer. Singer fired several more short bursts. Four men slumped to the deck. Blood began to seep from the corpses, staining the woodwork. Singer pressed a lever, put his weapon on single shot, fitted in a fresh magazine.

He ran from his bridge, down a companionway below decks, still wearing his gas-mask. The cyanide gas was lethal at one sniff. Two of his masked men were moving further along the corridor. He jumped over two bodies, heading for the wireless room. Automatically he made a body count. Seven so far. Including North, the captain, there was a crew of twenty to be accounted for. He burst into the radio cabin.

The operator, an American called Hoch, held a clutch of code-books in one hand. With the other he was fumbling to open the porthole. Singer raised his mask clear of the lower part of his face, pressed the muzzle of his Uzi against Hoch's skull.

'Put those bloody books down on that table. There's a good boy. Now, I'll ask you once only. You contacted Langley?'

Hoch, a tall, very thin man, opened his mouth and nothing came out. Then he swallowed, tried again.

'I tried to do that. No dice. A lot of interference – you know, atmospherics. No contact . . .'

Singer experienced a wave of relief. The jammer aboard the *Helvetia* had worked. He stepped back a few paces, gestured at the floor.

'You're the one who may survive. We need you, *Kamerad*. Lie flat on the floor. No, on your belly.'

Singer fished a pair of handcuffs from his pocket, jammed the Uzi muzzle into Hoch's neck to scare him a bit more. He laid the Uzi on the floor, stooped over the prone figure who was shaking with fear. Wrenching both hands behind his back, Singer attached the handcuffs. Hauling the American to his feet, he clenched his huge right hand, hit his victim on the jaw. Hoch fell down unconscious. Yes, they'd need Sparks, Singer was thinking. For radio transmissions. At the other end they'd be familiar with Hoch's 'fist' – his touch when he tapped out a signal.

Singer picked up his Uzi, adjusted his mask, opened the door, jumped into the corridor, swinging his weapon in both directions. One of his men, gas-mask in place, kicked open one of the cabin doors. From inside there was a crackle of gunfire. As his man was hurled back against the other side of the corridor he performed a reflex action, pressing the trigger of his pistol. A gas shell hurtled into the cabin. Silence.

Singer approached slowly, waited by the open door, peered inside, a quick jerk of the head forward and back. Then he stood in the doorway. Six crew members of the *Lampedusa* lay piled on top of each other, still clutching guns in their lifeless hands. One man's face was already turning a bluish colour. Cyanosis.

Singer heard a muffled groan, swung round. His man lying in the corridor was shot but still alive. No time to waste on looking after casualties. Singer glanced up and down the deserted corridor, slipped inside the cabin, pulled a Smith & Wesson .38 from a dead hand, went back into the corridor and bent over the badly injured man. He placed the gun muzzle against his skull, pulled the trigger. The fallen man gave a convulsive jerk, lay still. Singer replaced the gun in the hand of the dead American.

No point in letting his team know what he had done. Bad for morale. His memory made another body count. Twenty aboard the *Lampedusa* – including Hoch. That left nineteen. So far he made the body count thirteen. Another six to be accounted for.

Emerging up the companionway on to the aft deck, he found one at the foot of the companionway, two more on deck. That left three. The engine-room. Had the bloody fools checked there? He doubted it. He went down more steps, stopped in front of a steel door, turned the handle, opened it and stepped on to the metal grille beyond. A ladder led down into the works of the tub.

Three engine-room men stared up, paralysed by the sight of the apparition. He picked them off one by one.

319

Nineteen. A clear field. He ran back up on to the bridge. There was a lot to do.

Singer, minus gas-mask, stood on the bridge and sucked in good fresh sea air. The Swedish girl, Ingrid, who had acted as decoy, had been freed from the stretcher, had removed the dummy splint from her leg, and was leaning over the rail.

'Naylor,' he called out to a seaman from Liverpool. 'Put on your mask. You know the layout of this tub. You damn well should, you studied the layout along with the rest of us back in Antwerp. Go right through her, open up every port-hole. I want the ship clean in one hour. Get rid of all traces of cyanide gas. We're going to have to sleep and eat aboard this vessel.'

'On my way, Sergeant.'

'Lapointe,' he called out to the Frenchman. 'You put on your mask, too. But first assemble a working party. I want all the bodies transferred to the *Helvetia* within an hour. Dump them in the engine-room. And don't forget – every body must be handcuffed to a metal support. You'll find one of our own – Johnson – in a corridor. They shot him. Take him with the rest. We can't afford incriminating evidence. You all want to be hanged in Turkey? No, I thought not.' He smiled grimly. Nothing like a little joke to release the tension.

'On my way,' reported Lapointe, and hurried down the companionway off the bridge.

'Next the second funnel . . .'

Singer joined Ingrid by the rail. The launch which had transported them from the *Helvetia* had returned to berth alongside the freighter. An immense cylindrical object was being loaded on the motor-boat, roped securely. It was so large it projected over the bow and the stern. As he watched he saw through the binoculars he'd hauled from round Captain North's corpse, that they had completed the job. Lapointe and a helper had now moved the body close to the step-ladder still slung over the side.

'Everything went well, then, Sergeant?' Ingrid enquired, as though referring to a banquet.

'So far, so good.'

Singer glanced at her, then looked away. He had found her running a small brothel in Rotterdam. She was expendable – before they reached their destination she'd have to be dropped overboard one night with heavy weights tied to her ankles. Women were a nuisance aboard a ship crewed by so many men. And women couldn't resist opening their big mouths.

Singer had recruited his team by travelling round all the ports of Western Europe – from Oslo to Marseilles. He was very choosy. No prison record and the potential candidate must know his job.

Captain Hartmann was a case in point. A first-rate skipper, he had almost lost his ticket when drugs had been found on board his ship. The charge had been dismissed for lack of positive evidence, but afterwards Hartmann had trouble finding employment.

'What are you thinking about?' Ingrid asked and pressed her arm against his. He shifted further along the rail. Singer was a clever organizer and was constantly checking in his mind the next steps in the programme.

'Pearson,' he called out half an hour later, 'stand by to erect the funnel. Got your tools ready? I want a reliable but quick job.'

Pearson, a ship's carpenter, bent down to his tool bag and came up with a power drill. He brandished it and grinned.

The boat had arrived and men were slowly hauling up the considerable weight of the dummy smokestack. It was Pearson's job to fix it to the deck behind the existing funnel. Other men were already slung over the ship's side in a cat's cradle, painting out the name *Lampedusa*, substituting *Helvetia*, the name of the vessel still floating half a mile away.

'Everybody give Pearson a hand,' Singer ordered. 'That metal funnel is bloody heavy.'

He made his second trip to the hold which he'd visited after checking the body count. All the corpses had been transferred to the *Helvetia* by fast motor-boat making several trips. Descent by ladder into the huge hold was a tricky operation. There was so little space between the ladder and the cargo.

Singer, smoking a cigarette, once again gazed up at the computer, *Shockwave*. He felt dwarfed by a small building. A monster of a computer, so he'd been told by the voice on the phone which gave him all his instructions while on the European mainland.

Looking up, he thought the description good. There was something frightening about its sheer size, by the thought of the vast number of circuits packed inside its metal coat. I am earning my money, Singer thought, and then hurried back up the ladder. More jobs to do: he had to check everything himself.

On deck he climbed over the side, ran down the staircase to the motor-boat moored to the platform. Naylor, who had reported all portholes opened, that the gas was clearing, was sitting by the engine which he started up when Singer gave him the nod.

A few minutes later Singer was climbing aboard the almost deserted *Helvetia*. The abandoned ship had an eerie feel. Alone, Singer made his way to the engine-room. Only one live man awaited his arrival. Marc, the Belgian explosives expert. Short and stocky, he was his usual passive self.

'Where is the bomb?' Singer asked.

'Behind you, against the bulkhead. That large black box.'

322

Singer turned round. 'And that will send it to the bottom? You are certain?'

'No, sir,' Marc replied in his polite way. 'It will blow it sky-high. That is the expression?'

'It is . . .'

Singer was touring the nineteen corpses which had been put aboard, each handcuffed to a steel upright, each with a rope attached to its ankles, a rope also attached to a huge metal ring. Even so far from the shipping lanes Singer wanted no risk of a body floating to the surface. Satisfied, he asked one more question before leaving the ship with the Belgian.

'You said you could detonate with that radio gadget. Can you be certain it will work from the *Lampedusa* – that is, from the *Helvetia* as we must now always call it.'

'It will blow sky-high,' Marc repeated, showing no resentment at this checking of his skill.

'OK. Let's move it . . .'

Singer paused on the deck before running down the steps to the motor-boat. He was gazing at the other ship where they had now erected the dummy funnel. It was extraordinary how convincing the addition looked. They had done their research well – checking the precise measurements of the real funnel from Lloyd's shipping records. The height, the diameter, the colour.

'That's it . . .'

Five minutes later Singer was on the bridge of the other vessel with *Shockwave* in its hold. Still he hadn't finished checking as he talked to the skipper, Captain Hartmann.

'You did bring with you all the papers? The manifests showing we're transporting bauxite from Jamaica to Turkey?'

'In my cabin, Sergeant.'

Everyone had been trained to call him by his rank. It made for good discipline. Singer scratched his stubble, thought of one more point.

323

'You know we're heading for the eastern Med to make the rendezvous. But you must pass through the Straits of Gibraltar during the night.'

'I have timed it for that. Our course is planned.'

Singer turned to Marc who stood holding a small gadget like a camera. 'Blow her!' Marc turned to face the original *Helvetia*, paused, then pressed a button. Like the eruption of a volcano, the *Helvetia* exploded into an inferno of flames and smoke. The bow section soared into the air, turned in an arc, plunged bow first down into the ocean like a gigantic torpedo, vanished. Amidships the vessel lifted clear of the water, shattering into a thousand fragments which showered back into the water. The stern split in two, rode the waves for a short time, then dived deep down towards the ocean bed.

The destruction of the *Helvetia*, an awesome spectacle which caused Singer's crew to freeze, gazing motionless, was accompanied by an ear-splitting *boom*! Then a small tidal-like wave swept towards the *Lampedusa*. Men gripped the rail and waited for it to reach them, still hypnotized by the power of the explosion, by the sight of a large freighter disappearing completely. The wave rolled majestically forward. Singer splayed his feet, took a firm grip on the rail. The wave reached them and the freighter rolled at an angle close to forty-five degrees. Next to Singer, Ingrid was petrified, sure their vessel was going to capsize. The vessel righted itself, the wave rolled on beyond the starboard side. The relics of the *Helvetia* sank and the sea resumed its normal appearance. Singer turned away from the rail, looked at Captain Hartmann.

'That's it,' he said laconically. The thought that nineteen men had been cremated never crossed his mind. With Singer it was always the next step to take.

'OK, Skipper,' he called out. 'Make your own waves. Head for Gibraltar. How long before we get there?'

'Several days. Depends on the weather conditions.'
Hartmann gave the order to start up the engines.

31

During the few hours they spent in Zürich Tweed and
Paula were very active. Paula bought two suitcases in the
Bahnhofstrasse, returned to the main station with them.
Tweed took one case and they visited the public lavatories.
Inside a cubicle Tweed perched his case on the toilet seat,
quickly transferred his belongings from the two plastic
carriers inside the case, locked it. He stuffed one bag inside
the other, flushed the toilet and met Paula by the refreshment counter.

She was also carrying her case and had screwed up the
plastic carriers. They dumped the carriers in a litter bin.
Paula looked at Tweed.

'What's next on the agenda?'

'We book two rooms at the Hotel Schweizerhof across
the *platz*. Remember, I told Bob he could communicate
with me there.'

'Of course. I'm not quite myself yet. Can I show you
something really interesting in a shop before we go to the
hotel? It's only a short distance down the Bahnhofstrasse,
just round the corner from the hotel.'

'Why not?'

Tweed thought it best to humour her. She had been
under pressure ever since they arrived in Brussels, which
seemed a year ago. Paula led the way down an escalator
into Shopville, the shopping precinct beneath the *platz*.
They crossed the large complex, past shops selling fruit and

chocolates and mounted a second escalator, emerging at the beginning of the Bahnhofstrasse.

It was only a brief walk down the great banking and shopping street before Paula stopped in front of a shop window. Tweed gazed at the display. The shop sold Walkmans. Slung across the inside of the window was a hammock and inside it sprawled a large toy monkey. On its head was attached a Walkman and the toy had an expression of pure bliss.

'Isn't it sweet?' said Paula.

'Very comic,' Tweed agreed. 'But those things are the instruments of the devil. Half our young people are going to end up deaf . . .'

Inside the Schweizerhof Tweed reserved two rooms for a week. He insisted on paying for the rooms in advance after registering.

'We'll go up to our rooms,' he explained, 'but then we have to visit a business associate in Interlaken. So we'll leave a few of our things in the rooms, then take our cases with us. We may be kept in Interlaken overnight. But we'll know our rooms are waiting for us when we do get back.'

'That's perfectly satisfactory, sir,' the girl receptionist assured him in English.

'Now, a word with the concierge . . .'

Tweed explained the situation briefly again. 'The point is I am expecting a message from one of my staff. Could you please hold any messages until we get back?'

He handed the concierge a banknote. 'Certainly, sir. Thank you. All messages will be carefully recorded . . .'

Inside his corner room overlooking the main station and the Bahnhofstrasse, Tweed took out a few clothes, stored them in drawers. In the bathroom he left a spare toothbrush and tube of toothpaste, then rejoined Paula who had just arrived back in the lobby.

'We could have lunch here,' she suggested. 'Remember?

The restaurant on the first floor is elegant, the food excellent, the service very good.'

'No, not here,' Tweed whispered, clutching his case. 'They have us recorded on the register. We'll eat at the first-class restaurant in the station. More anonymous. Safer.'

'I'd really better get a grip on myself,' she commented.

They had a late and leisurely lunch at the station, lingering over their coffee. It was well after dark when they caught the 1710 express for Berne. The journey through the night took a little less than an hour and a half. They stepped down the steep drop to the platform in the large cavern of Berne *Bahnhof* at precisely 1829.

Outside the station Tweed fiddled with his suitcase until two other passengers had taken the first two taxis, then he told the driver of the next cab to take them to the Bellevue Palace Hotel. It had started snowing again as he paid off the cab, waited for it to drive away and then picked up his suitcase.

'A bit of a walk, I'm afraid,' he warned. 'We go up this side street to reach the back entrance to the Taubenhalde, Federal Police HQ.'

'I'll have to wear a heavier coat,' she said, buttoning her hip-length suède jacket at the neck.

'And mind your footing,' he warned as they started walking up the hilly side street alongside the Bellevue Palace.

'Where does this lead to?'

'The famous *Terrasse* above the river Aare. In good weather you get a marvellous view of the Bernese Oberland range . . .'

'This is hardly good weather . . .'

'The *Terrasse* runs past the Parliament building. There's a small funicular, the Marzilibahn, which we can take down to the lower level.'

A bitter wind raked their faces as they plodded through

327

the snow. Tweed glanced up and swore briefly. 'Looks as though the funicular is iced up. *Kaput.* That means a dicey walk down a steep path.'

'Great!' she commented and left it at that.

Workmen with lamps and wearing orange boiler suits worked on the iced-up rails and the funicular cabin, perched at the top, was in darkness. Slithering down an icy path they reached the bottom and Tweed headed for the entrance to a modern building. At reception inside he presented his passport to the uniformed police guard.

'I have an appointment with Arthur Beck. He is expecting us.'

Paula revelled in the warmth inside the building while Tweed waited, the guard used the phone, spoke briefly in Switzer-Deutsch, which she didn't understand, then handed back the passport to Tweed.

'You know the way, Mr Tweed? To the Taubenhalde – it is rather complex.'

'I've been here before. Ready, Paula?'

Paula was fascinated as she followed Tweed through a long subterranean passage and then ascended an 80-metre-long travelator to the main entrance inside the Tauben-halde. Another uniformed guard escorted them inside an elevator to Floor Ten. The door remained closed until the guard inserted a special key inside a slot. Arthur Beck was waiting for them when they stepped out.

'You arrived safely. Good.'

Beck hugged Paula, kissed her on both cheeks, said she was very welcome, then turned to shake hands with Tweed.

'I suppose you're welcome, too. Come to my office.'

Beck, in his forties, was plump-cheeked; his most arresting feature was his alert grey eyes under dark brows. Of medium height, he moved his hands and feet quickly, his complexion was ruddy and he wore a smart grey suit, a blue-striped shirt and a blue tie which carried a kingfisher emblem woven into the fabric. Inside his large office overlooking the front street he took their coats, hung them on hangers, and offered them coffee.

'Or something stronger after your long and arduous journey?'

They both asked for coffee when he had stored their cases in a corner. Beck used the intercom on his desk, ordered coffee for three, ushered them to armchairs and joined them. Typically, his first question was direct.

'How urgent is it, Tweed, that you have the use of a transceiver? The communications complex is in the basement.'

'Very urgent. And I have to request that I be permitted to use it on my own.'

'Within ten minutes he'll have taken over the Taubenhalde – he'll be sitting behind my desk,' Beck joked to Paula, who smiled. She liked Beck, the man Tweed had once called the cleverest policeman in Europe.

Beck's manner changed as he gazed at Tweed. 'Before I let you inside our sophisticated communications apparatus I have to know who you are calling – and why.'

Tweed nodded and paused. He had expected this and now he had reached his Rubicon. He either had to reveal top secret information, known only to Buckmaster, the Americans, the PM, Newman, Paula and himself – or sacrifice the opportunity to call the *Lampedusa*. He waited until a uniformed girl brought in the coffee on a tray laid with a cloth, supporting a silver pot and Meissen china, placed the tray on a table Beck had hauled forward, then left the room. As they drank the steaming liquid, he told Beck about *Shockwave*.

'I know Swiss colonels who would give an arm and a leg to have this information,' Beck observed.

'I warned you it was in complete confidence.'

'Agreed. But you explained this *Shockwave* computer has made the Strategic Defence Initiative a reality, that it would defend not only England against all Soviet-launched rockets, but also Western Europe. That means Switzerland also would be protected by this extraordinary scientific umbrella.'

'That is so.'

'Then I suggest I entertain the delightful Paula while you work away in the basement. I will have to accompany you to the complex.' He turned to Paula. 'I will be back in three minutes. While I am away please be thinking of what you would like to eat. A nice steak, well done? Some river trout? It is an important decision. Ponder it . . .'

Beck left Tweed alone in a room in the basement after asking him if he could operate the model of the transceiver resting on a steel slab projecting from the wall. Tweed said that he was familiar with the machine, omitting to say it was exactly the same model they used in the communications complex in the second building they occupied at Park Crescent.

Adjusting the headphones, he turned to the correct waveband. It took him ten minutes to make contact with the vessel he was calling. The codename for the *Lampedusa* was *Valiant*.

'Monitor calling,' he began, using his code-name for this operation. 'Are you proceeding on schedule?'

'We are on schedule. We are on schedule,' the answer came back.

'Is the cargo is good condition?' he asked, making it sound as though the vessel was carrying perishables. No one expected eavesdroppers on this waveband but it was a precaution.

'The cargo is in excellent condition,' the reply came back.

'Are the weather conditions clement and is Tray in good health?'

330

Tweed tensed after he'd made the reference to Tray. The first trick question known only to himself and the radio op aboard the *Lampedusa*.

'Weather conditions clement so far. Atmospherics garbled the rest of your signal.'

Tweed froze. His mind went as cold as ice. He sent a fresh signal, including the second trick reference.

'Is the crew in good health? Give my regards to White.'

'Crew all well. Transmission not perfect. Again the rest of your signal was garbled.'

'Signing off, I will call you again as arranged. My regards to North . . .'

Tweed sat for several minutes in front of the transceiver like a waxwork. He had received a nasty shock. The second trick question had also not been responded to correctly. The reference to White should have been answered by a reference to Cowes in the Isle of Wight. Some such statement as, 'White was taken sick before we sailed, was sent home to Cowes.'

Now he had to decide whether to tell Beck the real situation. He weighed up the pros and cons quickly. He was on the run, a fugitive. Only Beck could help him now. And he already knew about *Shockwave*.

He stood up, altered the waveband he'd transmitted on, then he pressed the bell by the door Beck had locked. The Swiss came down in the elevator quickly to release him, locked the door. Tweed was silent as the elevator ascended. When he re-entered Beck's office he saw Paula was sitting up to a table covered with a spotless cloth. She was devouring the last of an omelette.

'You also would like some sustenance?' Beck suggested.

'I think I'd like a drink. A stiff cognac.'

Two pairs of eyes stared. Tweed rarely drank. On the few occasions when he imbibed it was always wine, never spirits, except to fight a cold. Beck nodded, went to a cabinet, poured a tot into a balloon glass, handed it to Tweed without a word.

Paula swallowed the last of her omelette, drank coffee quickly, dabbed her lips with a napkin, and swung round in her chair, crossing her shapely legs as she studied Tweed. Beck sipped at a glass of beer, leaning back in his chair, eyes half-closed while he waited.

'Someone has hi-jacked *Shockwave*. It's a disaster area,' Tweed announced.

32

'We've pin-pointed Tweed already in Zürich.' Morgan stabbed at his blotter with a paper knife as though spearing Tweed to its surface.

He was leaning back in the chair behind his desk in his office at World Security HQ in Basle. On the other side of the desk, summoned from the Drei Könige, sat Armand Horowitz and by his side in a hard-backed chair was Stieber. Morgan puffed his cigar with satisfaction and then continued.

'He's staying at the Hotel Schweizerhof. We've got him.'

'That hotel is opposite the main station,' Horowitz observed with a frown. 'He draws attention to himself in Laufenburg, buying tickets for Zürich. Now you tell me he walks out of the station at Zürich and books in at the nearest large hotel.'

'That's about the size of it. He's not so smart as you make out. Maybe he's exhausted. How would I know? You want me to hand him to you on a plate? Well, I've done just that.'

'I'll take him before sunset tomorrow,' Stieber interjected. 'Just leave it to me.'

'Like we did in Freiburg?' enquired Horowitz. 'I go back to Richter's house on Konvikstrasse and find you trussed up like a chicken. Lucky I had a hunch about that place.'

'That was a nasty experience,' complained Stieber. 'That English bastard who ambushed me in the kitchen was as cold as ice. A pro to his fingertips. He scared the guts out of me – and I don't mind admitting it.'

'What's your beef?' Morgan demanded, staring at Horowitz.

'It's all too easy. The trail from Laufenburg was too easy to follow. Now he chooses the obvious hotel. How did you find out so quickly?'

'Because my apparatus is organized. I told you I was sending people round to check the hotels with Tweed's photo and a phoney story. They started with the major hotels first. Bingo! One team calls at the Schweizerhof and hits pay dirt. And that's not all.'

'What else?'

Horowitz sounded weary. He also sounded troubled and unconvinced by Morgan's flamboyant confidence.

'I told you I was well-organized. I'm using the Walkman technique of observation and communication. You know what I am talking about?'

'No, I don't.'

Morgan leaned over his desk and pointed with his cigar, a mannerism Horowitz found irritating. 'You know those Walkmans all the kids walk about with, listening to pop music from one of those gadgets clamped to their heads and ears. They even ride bikes wearing them, which is damn dangerous . . .'

'Yes, I understand now. Please explain further.'

'So, I've trained a large team of youngsters – in their early twenties. Don't worry, they've no idea they're employed by World Security. They think they're working for a debt collection agency. We train them in a building we hired for the purpose in a Zürich back street.'

'Maybe we could hear what they do?' Horowitz suggested.

'They have these gadgets – headsets – strapped to their skulls with a wire leading to a jacket pocket. Looks just like one of the musical Walkmans. Actually they're disguised walkie-talkies – high-powered and good for operating over a radius of two miles. They can take instructions from the communications vans located carefully to cover the city. And they can communicate back by talking into a concealed mike. Get the idea?'

'Go on, please.'

'They have been shown a blow-up picture on a cinema screen of Tweed, another of the Grey woman. They'll be patrolling the streets until they spot one or both. They report back to the nearest communications van the moment they spot one of them. The stage is set for the final denouement.'

Morgan waved his cigar in a grand gesture and settled more comfortably in his chair.

'It's all too straightforward,' Horowitz commented. 'Tweed is one of the wiliest and most dangerous opponents I have ever been up against. He avoided the bomb I attached to the Audi in the Black Forest.'

'It probably failed to detonate . . .'

'When I place a bomb it detonates,' Horowitz told him. 'I am going to earn my fee with this one, I can sense that already.'

'I don't know why you've got an attack of nerves,' Morgan responded, and studied the tip of his cigar.

'My nerves are in perfect condition,' Horowitz said in such a cold voice that Morgan blinked. 'I am flying to Zürich and I will take Stieber with me. I want to study the situation on the spot, see for myself what is really happening. Phone Zürich, tell your managing director there that he will take all his orders from me.'

'If you insist . . .'

'I do insist.'

'Then you'll be dealing with Evans. He's already aboard a flight for Zürich.'

Horowitz nodded, picked up his suitcase, left the office without another word, followed by Stieber. Morgan sat frowning behind his desk. Why did Horowitz always leave him with this worried feeling, verging on fright? He checked his watch. It was 6 p.m. Time for a snifter. He reached for his hip flask.

Inside his office at the Taubenhalde Beck had listened with great attention, his eyes never leaving Tweed's, while the latter gave him a summary of what had happened from the moment he'd discovered the unknown girl's body in his flat in Radnor Walk.

Paula was puzzled by how much Tweed omitted from his account. No reference to the attempt on his life on the Freiburg autobahn, nor to the bomb attached to the Audi in the Black Forest. But he had talked about Bob Newman and Marler. Newman knew Beck, had once sat in this very office.

'That's about it,' Tweed concluded as he finished the story of their flight across the Rhine at Laufenburg, their arrival in Zürich, their reservation of rooms at the Schweizerhof.

'I see,' Beck said eventually. 'That murder in your apartment is most mysterious. Who has a motive for such a brutal killing?'

'I'm not sure yet.'

'Come, you must have some suspicions. And it's a very odd factor that the girl has still not been identified.'

'You know that? How?'

'Simple. I phoned Howard in London to ask him how the case was progressing.'

335

'And didn't he express an opinion?'

'No, he didn't. He seemed completely mystified. And rather worried about you, to use British understatement.'

'What do you know about an organization called World Security?' Tweed asked him suddenly.

'One of the West's great conglomerates. While he was running it Buckmaster made takeover bid after takeover bid, bringing many smaller security outfits into his fold. Sometimes using very aggressive methods. But that seems to be the way of big business now.'

'Is that all you know about them?' Tweed persisted.

Beck drank some more coffee. Tweed waited, glanced at Paula. She sat with a wary expression. Beck put down his cup.

'The man to put that question to is Colonel Romer, Director of the Zurcher Kredit Bank. You remember Romer?' Beck took a pen and began writing on a pad of headed notepaper as he continued. 'At one time you suspected Romer of being mixed up in criminal activities. Wrongly, as it turned out. He has now moved to their headquarters in Zürich. In Talstrasse. Give him this letter from me.'

Signing what he had written, he folded the sheet, wrote the address on an envelope, slipped the sheet inside, tucked in the envelope flap without sealing it, handed it to Tweed.

'Thank you. Now, I said I needed a hideout, some remote refuge where I can ponder my next move in comparative safety.'

'I've been thinking about that. Brunni is the answer. A nowhere place up in the mountains of Schwyz canton. Beyond the town of Einsiedeln. There is a chalet a friend of mine has for the summer, at the very foot of the Mythen, a dramatic mountain. You should be safe there.'

'And a means of radio communication with the outside world?'

336

Beck looked at Paula and smiled. 'He doesn't want much, does he?'

'*Shockwave* is at stake, the salvation of the West, including Switzerland,' she told him.

'But you said this great god of a computer has been hi-jacked, Tweed. What do you think is its ultimate destination now?'

'Russia,' Tweed said promptly.

'Does such an act fit in with *glasnost*, *perestroika*?' Beck asked cynically.

'Gorbachev is in deep trouble,' Tweed replied. 'We know he is up against both the Left and the Right in his country. Both factions have formed an unholy alliance. They think they are the guardians of Leninism. So, news reaches Moscow that they can lay their hands on *Shockwave* – which will protect Russia from any missile attack by the West. The Red Army generals are already restive because Gorbachev is clipping their wings. How can he reject the chance of acquiring this marvellous machine? If he did so it could cause his instant downfall. God knows there are enough hardliners praying for just that to happen.'

'You are guessing,' Beck suggested.

'Yes, I'm guessing,' Tweed admitted. 'Theorizing might be a better word.'

'We have talked enough. Paula looks tired.' Beck stood up. 'You both need a good night's sleep. I have reserved two rooms for the night in false names – at the Bellevue Palace.'

'False names?' Tweed was puzzled. 'The Swiss registration system at hotels is very strict.'

'But I am accompanying you there. I will deal with the paper work. Give me your passports. I will flourish them. I have a car waiting.'

'It's only a short distance. We could walk,' Tweed suggested.

'But then you might be recognized. Tomorrow, have breakfast brought up to your rooms. I will call for you both at ten, if that is all right. Another car will drive you to Zürich. An unmarked car.' He paused by the door as Tweed and Paula collected their cases after slipping on their coats. 'And a plain-clothes guard will be placed outside both your rooms. I trust you do not object?'

'Have we an option?' Tweed enquired with a wry smile.

'No, you haven't . . .'

Paula tapped on the interconnecting door between their bedrooms. Tweed, unpacking his case, walked over, drew the bolt on his side. Paula stormed into the room with an expression like thunder.

'We're prisoners,' she protested. 'Guards on our doors. An escort from a building five minutes' walk away from this hotel. And another escort tomorrow morning in a car to Zürich. Beck doesn't believe you.'

'Calm down. He's cautious. I had rather a dramatic story to tell him. He's had this report from London about murder and rape in my flat. He's just taking no chances. Can't say I blame him.'

'And', she fumed, 'you left out the terrible incidents which might have convinced him. No mention of the attempt to kill you on the autobahn. No reference to the bomb Bob found beneath the Audi . . .'

'Deliberate omissions,' he told her. 'They would have made my account of events even more dramatic. I foresaw all this from the moment we arrived at the Hilton in Brussels. So I worked out a plan to convince him in due course. Remember, this is a neutral country.'

'What plan?' she demanded.

'You'll see what I mean as events develop. The opposition is going to help us.'

33

Basle. 2.45 a.m. It was snowing again as Turpil drove the
Audi through the deserted streets of the centre of the city.
By his side Newman peered out at the medieval buildings.
He caught a glimpse of the Munster rearing up and then it
was gone as they headed down towards the Rhine. The
rear seats were empty, he had noted.

'Where is your equipment?' he asked.

'In the boot of the car, of course. If we're stopped by a
patrol car I have in my pocket a typed phone message from
a doctor saying my sister is ill. You're a close friend of the
family.'

'What's your sister's name?'

'Klara. She's had a bad fall down a staircase. Lives on St
Johannsplatz. That's not far from the World Security
HQ.'

'This Klara, I take it, doesn't exist?'

'Of course not.' Turpil waved a small hand. 'But it's the
best excuse for being up at this hour.'

Newman settled down to watch the snow falling. Turpil
had planned the operation better than he'd expected. They
turned down a side street and Turpil stopped the car. He
lowered his window, listened, then raised it.

'I can hear a footfall half a mile away, let alone another
car. Here, take this. Put it in your ear when I tell you after
we get inside. It's an ear-piece.'

'For what purpose?'

Newman examined the small pink-coloured cylinder
which was like a small sweet with a tiny grille at one end.

'To increase your hearing powers. Be sure to insert it in your ear so the grille projects outwards. That's the microphone.'

'I've never seen anything like this before . . .'

'I should hope not. I invented it myself. I used to be a watchmaker – precision work. Don't lose it. Now, we'll collect the toolkit.' Turpil produced another of the tiny gadgets, grinned as he inserted it in his own right ear. 'I'll hear anyone coming with my ear-drummer.'

Opening the boot, he hauled out a slim rectangular canvas holder, handed it to Newman. 'You start working for your loot.' Taking another smaller leather hold-all out, he closed the boot. The snow was falling less heavily now as Turpil extracted a pair of rubber overshoes from the holdall, slipped them over his shoes. 'Gives a firmer grip.' He looked down at Newman's footwear. 'I hope those don't slip on ice.'

'Rubber-soled, corrugated with a grip surface.'

'Then let's march.'

They emerged on to a wide street and to his right Newman saw the entrance to the World Security HQ. He could hardly avoid it – overhead searchlights illuminated the plate-glass doors. No sign of life inside, but he was viewing the interior from an oblique angle.

'Guards walking about inside,' Turpil whispered.

'I can't see them.'

'No, but I can hear them – their footfalls on the marble floor. With my ear-drummer. Now, down to the river . . .'

Newman recognized the side street he had walked down when he had checked the geography of the area. They were close to the Rhine and Turpil went ahead, running nimbly down the six ice-covered steps. Newman paused, inserted the ear-piece, turned sideways. The sudden deafening sound almost made him lose his balance. It was like the surge of a great ocean. It took him a moment to realize he was listening to the flow of the Rhine, enormously magnified. He snatched out the ear-piece, put it in his trenchcoat pocket as Turpil peered round the corner at the bottom, then gestured for him to follow.

Newman trod carefully down the steps to the promenade, holding the canvas carrier by the handle. A raw breeze raked his face as he turned the corner. There were no footprints on the promenade beyond where Turpil had walked. How was he going to enter the building from the back, Newman wondered. The first row of windows were a good twelve feet above them. Turpil was gazing up, waited for Newman to join him.

'No danger of early morning lovers in weather like this,' he commented, his left ear bent towards Newman.

'They come along here?'

'In summer you step over them. The Swiss youth has developed uninhibited habits. Give me your satchel.'

Turpil unfastened the straps, hauled out what looked like an aluminium grid with large rubber suckers along one rung. He extended it, section by section, and Newman realized it was a ladder at least fifteen feet high. Perching it against the wall, Turpil adjusted the height, swung it sideways and rubbed handfuls of snow against the suckers, then melted it with the warmth of his gloved hands.

'Now it will be firmly attached to the wall,' he explained, and hoisted it again, positioning the top carefully just below a window sill before he pressed hard against the whole ladder.

'This is World Security,' Newman reminded him, bending to speak into his left ear. 'Those windows probably have the best alarm systems in the business.'

'They do,' Turpil assured him. 'But for summer ventilation they can be lifted sixteen centimetres before they contact the alarm bolts. Inside on the right is a switch. You lift it once, then down, then up, and the alarm is cut off. In

341

hot weather they can then lift the window up wide open. It's just a precaution. They considered it impossible for anyone to get inside this way.'

'And how can you be certain they haven't added refinements?'

'Didn't I tell you?' Turpil grinned slyly. 'They called me in a couple of months ago to repair a defect. I checked the whole system and they haven't changed a thing since I installed the original system.'

'That was a couple of months ago. Let's get on with it.'

Newman, always careful, wasn't completely reassured. Morgan's organization might well have its own security specialists who had added a few booby traps. Alarm systems of which Turpil had no knowledge existed.

'Use your ear-drummer,' Turpil told Newman. He pointed along the promenade. 'Then you can check no one is coming along by the river while I go up the ladder. I'll wave when I'm inside the building. Then you follow me up the ladder. Ready? I'm on my way . . .'

He was climbing the ladder, holding on with one hand, the other clutching his hold-all, while Newman adjusted his ear-piece. The roaring surge filled his head until he grasped his gadget was beamed towards the Rhine. He faced the wall, aiming it along the promenade. The deafening surge was replaced by a curious swishing sound. Startled, he looked quickly along the promenade, moving his head only slightly.

The breeze was blowing swirls of light snow along the surface of the frozen promenade, a sound he'd been unable to hear before. It made him realize how sensitive the instrument was. He looked up.

The snow had almost stopped falling. Perched at the top of the ladder, Turpil was brushing his clothes clean of snow with one hand. He raised the window a few inches, reached inside with one hand, held it there a few seconds, then lifted the window wide open. Climbing in over the sill, holding his satchel, he peered out and waved.

Newman listened for a short time, heard only the swish of the swirling snow. He extracted the ear-drummer, slipped it into his pocket and shook the ladder. The base remained firm, the rubber-covered legs now held fast by the frozen snow. He began the ascent.

Heavier than Turpil, he felt the ladder whipping under him as he pressed his feet carefully into each icy rung. The higher he went the stronger the breeze became, flapping his trench coat. The intense cold began to penetrate his gloves, freezing his hands.

He resisted the temptation to hurry, to look down, staring at the wall as he continued his ascent. One foot slipped off a rung. He gripped the ladder more tightly, ignoring the bitter cold. Recovering his balance, he climbed higher. He reached the level of the open window unexpectedly. Turpil reached out a hand, placed it on Newman's shoulder and pulled, indicating he should climb inside quickly.

Newman needed no encouragement. Swinging one leg over the sill, he dipped his head under the open window, heaved himself inside. Despite the open window warmth met him and his fingers began to tingle.

'Now we must haul up the ladder,' Turpil told him.

'Why? We need that to escape . . .'

'No! No! We use another method. We may be here some time. Someone may see the ladder. Don't argue. Help me haul it up.'

They both took hold of the top rung and heaved with all their strength. The feet embedded in the frozen snow came loose suddenly and the ladder was free. As they hauled it up Turpil telescoped it until it was converted to the grid Newman had carried in the canvas container. Turpil slid it back inside the container he had carried up with his tool-kit.

'I'd just like to know how the hell we *do* get out of this place,' Newman snapped.

'Everything is prepared – for an emergency . . .'

Turpil produced a pencil flash after drawing a curtain over the open window. He handed another flash to Newman, who was beginning to be impressed. Turpil seemed equipped for the job.

'But how do we get out of this place?' he repeated.

Turpil lowered the beam of his flash. Coiled on the floor was a mountaineer's rope, knotted an intervals. One end had a large rubber-sheathed ring. The ring was attached to the steel leg of a large table. Newman stooped to examine it more closely.

There was a join where the ring was looped round the table leg, rather like two claws meeting. And a wire was wrapped round the full length of the rope, a wire which had a small handle at the other end of the rope.

'That table is screwed to the floor,' Turpil explained. 'It is used for computers and other machines, so they need good stability.'

'I still don't see how this rope works. We throw it out of the window in an emergency, I assume, and then abseil like a mountaineer down the wall. Why can't we use the ladder?'

'You said we shouldn't leave any traces of the break-in. It would take too long to remove the ladder. When we've both gone down the rope I operate that handle. The two claws round the table leg open and we can haul it out of the window. Another of my inventions. Now, we're wasting time – so what is it you want here? We're in the main Research & Development room, as they like to call it. The dirty tricks set-up. Plus confidential records . . .'

'Dirty tricks? What do you mean?'

'In a few words, blackmail and sabotage. They're bidding to take over another company. Right? So they sabotage their security trucks, tip off the underworld, and

344

the contents of the truck are grabbed. The target company's reputation is ruined. I'll tell you about the blackmail later. What do you want?'

'Evidence of illegal – criminal – activity . . .'

'Now you're talking. First, I de-activate the whole alarm system. Then I'll open the wall-safe I installed. Of course, sometimes they play clever, hide something important in an unlocked drawer under a pile of notepads. So if you want to ferret around wear these.' He handed Newman a pair of surgical gloves, then slipped another pair over his own hands.

He opened the control box attached to a side wall, holding his pencil flash gripped between his teeth. Inside was a complicated arrangement of coloured wires and plugs inserted into sockets. Turpil went on talking as he began moving plugs from one socket to another.

'Don't smoke in here. Smoke lingers. Later I'll want you to open the door into the passage – after you've inserted your ear-drummer. Beam it down the passage to the right where the elevators and the staircase are at the far end. You'll hear anyone coming a mile off. And when you open that door don't put a foot in the passage. There's a pressure pad outside. Not one of your crude mats – it's part of the woodblock floor.'

Wearing the surgical gloves, holding the pencil flash in his left hand, Newman began opening drawers quietly in a large desk. He'd found nothing when he came to the last drawer at the bottom on the left. A pile of printed memo pads, A4 size.

'Alarm neutralized,' Turpil whispered. 'If I've made a cock-up the alarm will sound in their Zürich HQ. The systems are linked. Added precaution. The Zürich guards find nothing, phone this place.'

Turpil removed a large grid chart hanging from the wall which was headed *Gross Turnover*. The line on the chart climbed to new heights of business activity. Behind it a large safe was embedded in the wall. Turpil inserted his ear-piece. Newman glanced up, expecting the little man to produce a stethoscope.

'No stethoscope,' he called out quietly.

'You've been watching too many films. My ear-piece picks up the fall of the tumblers.' Turned sideways, his ear close to the safe, his gloved hand turned the combination slowly. Newman went back to checking the drawer. Carefully lifting up another pad he found a desk diary for the current year. Why conceal that?

Underneath at the very bottom of the drawer was another desk diary. For the previous year. He flicked through the pages from the beginning. Full of appointments. What attracted his attention was certain days which had an initial letter prominently written in with a felt-tip pen – unlike all the other entries inscribed with an ordinary pen. The initial letter was 'M'.

Alongside each initial there was a time. Always late in the evening, 9.30 p.m., 9 p.m., 10 p.m., 9 p.m., 10.30 p.m. All the dates were between January and April. He double-checked. No date later than April 25.

Newman flicked over the pages of the current year. January and part of February. More appointments at intervals but no more 'M' entries. He was intrigued, partly by the fact that no name was given alongside the times for these entries, unlike every other appointment noted which *did* have a name.

Newman looked up, saw that Turpil was opening the large wall safe. He walked over and Turpil dived a hand inside his hold-all, brought out two wash-leathers which he gave to Newman.

'Now, all the snow has melted off our shoes. Could you clean up the floor? No traces that we've been here, you said . . .'

Newman swore inwardly. But Turpil was right: Newman had noticed the pools of liquid from the melted snow on the woodblock floor and had been going to mention them. He crouched down, used the wash-leathers vigorously. One to mop up most of the water, the other to polish the surface. Finishing the job he gave the leathers back to Turpil who put them inside a plastic bag, then shoved the bag into the hold-all. Turpil gestured towards the open safe after checking his watch.

'Up to you now. Remember exactly how everything was stored.'

The wall-safe was shoulder high. Newman used his flash to check the contents. To the left several wads of bank-notes tied together with elastic bands. He ignored them. In the middle were piles of large envelopes. He lifted the top one out carefully, took it over to the desk, extracted the sheets inside.

Records of income and expenditure for the company the previous year. Certain items were underlined in red ink; all for the sum of 6,000 Swiss francs. Alongside each was the same phrase. *One-time cost.* Bribes? Newman glanced down all the sheets, then went through them a second time, again to double-check.

He frowned. Certain sheets carried a flourishing initial at the bottom and all were dated. The initial was a 'B'. He examined other sheets with references to 'Sab.' and names of companies taken over by WS & C. The German for 'sabotage' was the same as the English word. Newman looked round. Turpil had opened the door to the corridor. He closed it, came across to Newman.

'Not a sound. We have to be careful now. The time element.'

'Turpil, take these sheets and photograph them. You said you had brought a camera.' The little man felt in his pocket, produced a compact horizontal-shaped camera with a flash-bulb attached.

'Won't there be a danger the flash will be seen?' Newman asked.

'Curtain is drawn. There's no window on to the passage. I'll lay them out on the desk . . .'

'And while you're at it, there's a last year's desk diary I've left out. Photograph five pages. January 15, January 28, February 16, March 4 and April 25. And just inside the front cover you'll find the owner's name. Morgan. Photograph that, too.'

Newman turned back to the safe. He found nothing that interested him until he came to the sixth large envelope. Inside were four glossy prints of different girls. All attractive, all a head-and-shoulders picture, all in colour, all the girls in their late twenties or mid thirties.

A titian-haired beauty, a blonde and two brunettes. All had a provocative smile and half-closed eyes behind long lashes. Again Newman frowned as he studied the blonde-haired girl. Memorizing the sequence, he took them over to Turpil, glad that he he'd checked about the camera. The room had been lit up time and again with flash-bulbs going off. Turpil worked at great speed. Newman placed the photos on the desk top.

'I'd like good copies of these,' he said. 'They'll have to be black-and-white, I suppose?'

'I'm using a colour film . . .' Another flash. 'Only way to record the red underlines. I'll leave you to put the desk diaries back – you know how they were stored.'

Turpil glanced at the four photos Newman had spread over the desk. He paused as he saw the picture of the blonde-haired girl, then looked at the other two and nodded, continuing to photograph the last two cost sheets. He glanced at his watch as he turned to the photographs.

'You've got three more minutes to look for anything else. Then it gets dangerous.'

Newman walked back to the open safe, carefully piled the other envelopes in the sequence he'd found them ready to go back into the safe. Reaching inside, he drew out a thick red master-ledger. Full of figures, it meant little to him.

On an impulse he turned to the last page where the balance was drawn up. He carried the ledger over to the desk, open at the last page.

'Last item. A copy of this page. Then maybe we'd better call it a day . . .'

'A night.'

Newman collected the five cost-sheets, arranged them in the original sequence with the rest, slid them inside the envelope and carried them back to the safe. He dealt with the photos when Turpil handed them to him. Finally he slid the ledger back into its place at the bottom. When he turned round Turpil was by his shoulder.

'I have to close the safe, turn the combination to its original setting, then reactivate the alarm system. Go to the door, use your ear-drummer, listen to the right down the passage. We have to be careful but quick. Don't forget to slip those diaries away first . . .'

Newman dealt with the diaries, placed the notepads on top and crept to the closed door. Inserting the ear-drummer, he opened it and thrust his head only outside. No sound of movement.

When it happened Newman nearly jumped out of his skin. He was almost deafened with the sound of ferocious dogs snarling, followed by several pairs of footsteps, then more dog sounds. Had he not been staring down the endless passage he would have sworn they were almost outside the door.

He turned to warn Turpil. The little man had closed the safe, was replacing the alarm system plugs. Some instinct made Turpil glance over his shoulder. Newman crept across to him.

'Big trouble. I can hear guard dogs and men's feet. They sound to be very close, coming this way . . .'

'Keep calm. They're a long way off and they'll be

checking each office. Close the door quietly.'

Turpil had even produced a large waterproof for Newman to slip on over his dried-out trench coat. Despite the open window the air-conditioning inside the building was almost tropical. Turpil had earlier pulled aside the curtain for a few seconds. It was snowing heavily.

Newman was tense as Turpil coolly handed him the canvas carrier containing the telescoped ladder, advising him to fix the handle firmly to his belt. Then Turpil pulled back the curtain, picked up the coiled rope, leaned out of the window to check the promenade and dropped it.

'I'll go first. You watch how I go. You can abseil down a cliff, I assume?'

'Just get on with it . . .'

Newman couldn't get out of his mind how close the guard dogs had sounded. Turpil reminded him to pull the window down, to turn the alarm switch on from outside.

'Press it down once, then up, then down. The alarm is then active. The reverse of what I did before I entered . . .'

'Got it! Now, move! They could be here any minute.'

Turpil had attached the handle of his hold-all to a belt he'd taken from inside it and wrapped round his waist. He tugged at the rope, climbed over the sill, disappeared. Newman peered out.

Turpil had rammed his woolly hat over his head before leaving and from above he looked like a gnome as he descended, using his feet to kick himself away from the wall. Newman was surprised at the speed of his descent. Reaching the promenade, Turpil gestured for him to follow.

Newman had already tucked the surgical gloves inside his coat pocket with the ear-drummer and was wearing his leather ones. Grasping the rope, he heaved himself over the edge, remembered just in time the window and cursed. Holding on with one hand above a knot, he reached up, hauled down the window to within a few inches of the sill,

350

reached inside, fumbled around for the bloody switch which seemed to have moved, found it, operated it and closed the window to within inches of the sill.

By now, supported only by his right hand and arm, his whole body was feeling the strain. Thankfully he gripped the rope with his left hand and began his descent. The knots were a godsend: they prevented rope burn from a prolonged slide. The snow was not a godsend – getting in his eyes and penetrating down behind his collar as he abseiled down the wall, kicking his feet against it, arching his back outwards, hoping the damned thing would support his heavier weight. It seemed to take an eternity before his feet slammed into the promenade.

'We must be quick,' Turpil hissed.

'Now he agrees on the need for speed,' Newman thought bitterly, but he kept his mouth shut.

Turpil told him to move well up the promenade, then stooped to grasp the handle at the end of the wire. Looking up, he turned the handle, rammed it upwards, hauled on the rope. Newman realized the claw apparatus at the other end had got trapped behind the sill. He stamped his feet as the cold seeped into him. Turpil, still staring up, hauled with all his strength. The claw shot out of the window and Turpil ran towards Newman, dropping the rope end. The claw ring hammered into the snow. Turpil ran back, coiled the rope swiftly as Newman joined him.

'Back to the Audi?' he asked. Turpil shook his head, slung the rope over his shoulder and went to the edge of the river.

Newman waited for him to slip over the edge. Turpil gestured for him to follow, knelt down and then disappeared. Newman glanced up at the building, walked to the gap in the railing and looked down. Attached to the river wall was an iron ladder leading to a small landing stage. A boat was moored to a bollard and Turpil was stepping aboard.

Newman took a deep breath, clenched his fingers, and with his back to the Rhine descended the ice-coated rungs. Turpil beckoned to him to hurry. The motor boat had a canvas awning protecting the wheel and the controls. Newman stepped aboard, Turpil reached out, untied the mooring rope, hauled it on to the deck and the swift flow of the Rhine swept them out towards mid-stream. Seated under the awning, Turpil made no attempt to start up the engine as Newman sat beside him and released the canvas container from his belt.

'What's the idea?' he said.

'If there's an alarm in that building they have a drill. A number of the guards immediately rush outside, men carrying secret guns, and surround the whole building. Look, there are lights.'

Newman stared back at the building receding in the distance. The curtain had been pulled back from the window they had left by. Powerful torches shone down on the promenade and searched from left to right. The motor boat was already too far away for them to have any chance of seeing it and soon the flashlights were blotted out by the snow. Above them, the awning sagged under the weight of snow it had already collected.

'Too early to start up the engine?' Newman enquired and shivered.

It was incredibly cold as they drifted fast into mid-river. A cutting wind penetrated Newman's waterproof and his trench coat under it. The boat was moving much faster as the main current caught it up in its westward flow.

'Too soon,' Turpil agreed. 'They might just hear it from the building. In any case, we don't want anyone to hear us at this hour. Don't worry. We are heading for where the Audi is now parked.'

'Impossible,' Newman protested, 'we're drifting miles away from the *platz* where we left it.'

'But it is not there,' Turpil explained, as though to a

child. 'Shortly after we walked to the building Klara, who has a key, drove the Audi across the Rhine and parked it on the opposite bank. We are close now, so I will start up the engine.'

'Just a second. Who is Klara? Not your imaginary sister?'

'My real sister from Berne. Earlier she parked her own car at the same spot, took her bicycle from the boot, cycled to that *platz*, and as I have just said, drove the Audi to the same secluded spot.'

He was starting the engine when Newman stood up to stretch his aching legs and wandered out towards the stern as the boat rocked. Turpil shouted to him before starting the engine.

'Better give me back that ear-drummer while we re- member it.'

'Got it in my pocket.' Newman pulled out the surgical gloves, transferred them to his other pocket, brought out the ear-drummer, appeared to lose his balance and grab- bed the edge of the gunwale.

'Sorry, Turpil, I've dropped it overboard.'

He palmed the ear-drummer and slipped it inside his trouser pocket. A useful little gadget, which you couldn't buy in the shops.

'I'll have to charge you for that,' Turpil shouted and fired the engine.

Newman hurried back under the awning, sat down. 'How long before we reach the parked Audi?' he called out.

'A matter of minutes.' Turpil glanced over his shoulder as he held the wheel and began to steer the boat towards the eastern bank. 'It's awhile since I've seen Tweed. Maybe I could meet him soon? Say "Hello", and all that . . .'

Newman was frozen, the back of his neck was damp with melted snow, he was aching in every limb, but his mind was

353

still alert. There was something a shade too casual in Turpil's reference to Tweed. He made a vague gesture with his hands while he thought.

They were close to the high river embankment on the east, heading for a mooring landing with a flight of steps leading up to the promenade, when a searchlight came on, began probing the chopping surface of the Rhine. Turpil reacted instantly.

Turning the wheel, he headed back for mid-stream, out of the range of the searchlight, then he cut the engine and let the boat drift again. Once again the boat was caught up in the powerful current of the Rhine. Newman stood up as Turpil beckoned and joined him by the wheel.

'We cannot use the Audi,' Turpil told him, his teeth chattering. 'The police have found it. We have to change our plans.'

'I thought that searchlight was mounted on a patrol car,' Newman commented. 'Start the engine up and make for the nearest landing stage on the west bank. We must get ashore as fast as we can.'

'If you say, so but why?' Turpil fired the engine.

'Because,' Newman explained patiently, 'the men in the patrol car will radio for a police launch to come and find us. The nearest landing stage. Then we push the boat out, let it go downriver, drift with the current.'

The sudden crisis had made Newman forget the cold, his aches, and he automatically took charge. Within a few minutes they found a landing stage, Turpil moored the boat, they climbed out. The only sounds were the surge of the river, the thump of the boat against the landing stage. It had stopped snowing.

'What do we do next?' Turpil asked.

'Walk. Back to where I've parked my car. You can wait inside it while I pay my hotel bill. Is there anything inside that boat which could identify you?'

'No. I stole it earlier this evening . . .'

'Then set it loose. Quickly.'

Turpil unlooped the rope from the bollard, threw it on to the deck and the boat slid away, moving out towards the centre of the Rhine. Newman was still carrying the canvas carrier containing the ladder. Turpil's toolbag lay on the wooden platform.

'It's not safe to walk through Basle in the middle of the night carrying incriminating break-in kit,' Newman warned.

'I suppose you're right . . .'

Turpil picked up the hold-all and hurled it out over the river. It hit the water with a splash, sank immediately. Newman threw the container with the ladder after it as Turpil produced the camera from his pocket. Newman grabbed it off him, tucked it inside his trench-coat pocket.

'That is more dangerous evidence,' Turpil protested.

'So why should you worry? I'm carrying it. And we worked damned hard to get it. I can see a launch coming downriver with a searchlight. Let's get back up the steps. And', he added as an apparent afterthought, 'we'll drive to Zürich and you can meet Tweed.'

As they mounted the steps and disappeared into a side street Newman was convinced he had fed the bait well – with the promise to Turpil to meet Tweed. That remark aboard the boat had definitely been more than a shade too casual. Newman was determined not to let Alois Turpil out of his sight.

34

All roads led to Zürich.

The following morning Tweed and Paula had breakfast

early in their rooms. When they left they found new plain-clothes guards had taken up duty in the corridor outside. One of them came forward, showed Tweed his police identity card.

'We have to escort you to the car. Your bills have been paid. The Mercedes is waiting at the front entrance.'

'Nice to be treated like royalty,' Paula joked.

'Or like prisoners,' Tweed whispered.

Beck was waiting for them in the rear of the car, perched on a flap seat. He gestured for them to enter quickly and they climbed inside clutching their suitcases. The door was shut, the driver, also in plain-clothes, operated the central locking system. Tweed looked at Beck as the car moved off.

'Worried we're going to dive out at a traffic-light stop?'

'It's security,' Paula said quickly.

'Paula is right,' Beck agreed.

Tweed stared out of the window as they were stopped by traffic lights. The glass was amber-tinted, which neutralized the sun glare. As they'd walked down the hotel steps the sunlight reflecting off the snow-covered street had been blinding. And, Tweed reflected, it made it more difficult for anyone to see who was inside the car.

To his right a long bridge spanned the Aare. A tram trundled across it, passed in front of them. Why didn't the British go back to using trams? The car moved, turned left past the Casino. As they drove on through the ancient city the Mercedes bumped over the exposed cobbles where the snow had melted.

'We want to go to the Schweizerhof Hotel in Zürich,' Tweed remarked. 'We left some of our things in the rooms I reserved.'

'The driver can collect them . . .'

'No, Beck, we'll collect them ourselves. Get the driver to park near the hotel when we arrive, not outside.'

'As you wish . . .'

'And Bob Newman may want to contact me. He'll probably call you to find out where we are. It's essential that I see him.'

'As you wish . . .'

'I do wish.'

Tweed settled back in his seat and said not one more word until they reached Zürich.

Newman made no attempt to break any records as he drove the BMW through the night towards Zürich. Alongside him Turpil clasped and unclasped his hands in his lap. Well away from Basle they stopped at an all-night café for truckers.

'We'll get some coffee and something to eat,' Newman said.

'I am hungry after what we've been through,' Turpil grouched.

It had been a long walk back to the Hotel Drei Könige. Newman had taken Turpil to his car, told him to sit in the rear seat and had given him a notebook taken from the glove compartment. 'If a patrol car spots you, tell them you're waiting for Newman, the foreign correspondent. You've been into France? Good. To do a few jobs, I expect. So scribble a few notes in that book about Albert Leroux – tell them I am writing a story about him. There's been enough in the papers about Leroux and his suspected embezzlement for you to make something up . . .' Newman had then lowered a rear window a few inches and locked Turpil inside the car.

Driving the BMW into the car park at the back of the eating place, Newman alighted with Turpil and went inside. Several huge ten- and twelve-wheeler juggernauts were parked near the BMW. At the plastic-topped tables rugged-looking men wearing leather windcheaters sat talking, eating ham rolls, drinking coffee.

'Tweed is in Zürich?' Turpil asked as he devoured a ham roll.

'Say that again. Can't hear you with a mouthful of food . . .'

It gave Newman a few seconds to think up an answer. Intriguing that once again Turpil was showing interest in Tweed's whereabouts. Turpil repeated the question, then drank more coffee greedily.

'I didn't say that,' Newman replied. 'But when we get there I'll know how to contact him, find out where he is, go to see him.'

'On his own, is he?'

'No idea.' Newman grinned. 'You know Tweed, a regular will-o'-the-wisp.'

'I'd like a bath when we get there. Where will we be staying? And I'm short of clothes.'

The hook-nosed little man began destroying a third ham roll. As he asked the questions his ferret-like eyes watched Newman.

'We'll put up at a hotel I know. You can get your bath there. And you can buy some new clothes anywhere. I have a question for you.'

Turpil hooded his eyes, looked guarded. 'What is it?'

'In the camera I've got in my pocket there are pictures of four attractive girls. I've got an idea about them – how they make their living. It's the blonde-haired beauty I'm really interested in.'

Newman drank coffee from his mug and waited. A knowing gleam came into Turpil's eyes. He smirked, waited until he'd finished his roll before he spoke.

'Fancy the lady, do you? Well, why not? Mind you, she's expensive. But you can afford her. That huge fortune you made out of that big bestselling book you wrote. Sold all over the world. What was it called?

'*Kruger: The Computer That Failed*,' Newman said shortly. 'Get back to what we were talking about. This highly expensive girl. 'What exactly does she do for a living? What's her name? Where does she hang out?'

'Information costs money.'

Turpil made a gesture, rubbing his thumb over the tips of his fingers. Newman, about to explode, thought again. If he paid, Turpil was less likely to get restive in Zürich – hoping for more loot.

'How much money?'

'A thousand francs will give you the answers – and the girl.'

'You don't come cheap, do you?'

'She doesn't come cheap.' Turpil leered. 'Very classy . . .'

'I'm talking about *you*,' Newman snapped. It would be a mistake to agree too easily. 'A thousand francs is too much.'

'Then let us talk about something else.'

'No, let's talk about this girl, about . . .'

What he was going to say was muffled by the sudden boom of twin exhausts outside. One of the big diesel trucks was leaving. The atmosphere inside the canteen was over-heated, polluted with the stench of cheap cigars mingling with the smell of cooking. Newman shrugged his shoulders, drank more coffee. Turpil leaned forward.

'You were going to say something?'

'I've lost interest. I don't think you know anything about the girl.'

'But I do! I have used her.' He saw the expression on Newman's face. 'No, you misunderstand. Not in that way. She has provided me with information. For a fee. She is English. She came to Switzerland to work as a secretary in Geneva. It was not long before she saw how she could make much more money, a great deal of money. There are wealthy Swiss who feel taking a mistress, setting her up in a flat in a different city from where they live, is a constant expense. Bankers and businessmen. So they hire her services for a night, pay her the fee in cash, and there is no more expense. She also services wealthy Frenchmen and Germans across the borders.'

'A high-class call-girl.' Newman sounded as if he had lost interest. 'You said you used her. How?'

Turpil hesitated, then couldn't resist showing Newman how clever he was.

'I have an arrangement with her. She is going to visit some German in Stuttgart. His wife is away but he does not risk using his apartment – in case the neighbours see his friend. A banker, let us say. He meets her at a hotel in Ulm. She tells me this and I know I can enter his apartment safely. It is amazing how much money some of these Germans keep in cash.' He winked. 'The tax inspector never knows.'

'I've grasped your system,' Newman commented. 'How long is it since you last used her?'

'Oh, several months. The opportunities only crop up occasionally.'

'And her name? And where does she live?'

Turpil went quiet. He made the same gesture with thumb and forefingers, then took hold of his last ham roll.

'Stop eating,' Newman snapped, and handed him a folded banknote. One thousand francs.

'Her name is Sylvia Harman. She lives in the Altstadt in Zürich. An expensive apartment. Her address is Rennweg 1420.'

'And what does she charge for the pleasure of her company for a night?'

'Six thousand francs.'

Horowitz caught the 1055 flight from Basle Airport for Zürich. Alongside him sat Morgan and several rows behind them Stieber sat alone. The aircraft was three-quarters empty so they could talk freely.

'I've been up half the night,' Morgan grumbled. 'I was called out of bed by an alarm at HQ. Funny business. The alarm went off at the Zürich HQ. When they found no signs of trouble they phoned Basle. The alarm systems sometimes cross.'

'What did you find?' Horowitz asked to be polite, his mind on something quite different.

'Panic stations. And no sign of forcible entry. I can't put my finger on it, but the incident bothers me.'

'Better tell the police,' Horowitz suggested ironically, wishing his companion would keep quiet.

'You have to be joking. Now, what are your plans when we get to Zürich?'

'Oh, I'll prowl around certain districts, ask a few people I know certain questions . . .'

'Time is running out. I had a call from London while I was in my office. London wants results.' Morgan paused. 'If you move fast, get the job over with, there could be a bonus for you.'

'London can wait.' Horowitz's tone was chilling. He turned to face Morgan who had the corridor seat. 'Now you listen to me, Morgan. The fee for my services, plus expenses, has been negotiated. I do not work on bonus systems. I regard the word – bonus – as an insult. You're not hiring a hoodlum to put sand in the gear boxes of a competitor's vehicles . . .'

'It was just a suggestion,' Morgan said hastily. 'Well-meant but . . .'

'I loathe the little people of this world who mean well.'

There was a long silence while Horowitz stared out of the window. Morgan fiddled with his cigar, twirling it between his fingers. A stewardess bent over him.

'I'm sorry, sir, but smoking is not allowed in this section. And, as the captain announced earlier, pipes and cigars are frowned on even in the smoking section.'

Morgan glared up at her. 'Something wrong with your

eyesight, little lady? This cigar is not lit. May I suggest that your first call when you leave the aircraft is to an optician to get your eyes tested.'

'I'm very sorry, sir. I mistakenly thought you were about to light it. Could I fetch you something more to drink?'

'A large cognac to get over the lousy service . . .'

Morgan sat fuming as the stewardess hurried away to fulfil his order. It was Horowitz who had insisted they sat in the non-smoking section. Morgan struggled to control conflicting emotions. He was furious with his companion but aware that Horowitz was not a man to get on the wrong side of.

The stewardess brought his drink. Morgan tôok it from her without a word of thanks. He swallowed half the contents at a gulp. Horowitz spoke, still staring out of the window as the machine began its descent.

'I really can't think of any better way in which you could have ensured her attention was drawn to us, that she would remember us after we've left the flight.'

'OK. You're right. You always are. It's the lack of sleep which made me blow my top. No excuse. When we get to Zürich I'll take you straight to our HQ – if that suits you. A car will be waiting for us. Then after we've arrived you can hear all the details of the dragnet we've thrown out. Anything you don't like, change it. I won't say a word. You're the boss.'

'That is the way to handle it,' Horowitz responded and lapsed again into silence as the captain announced they were landing and the *No Smoking* and *Fasten Seat Belts* signs were illuminated.

35

On the outskirts of Zürich Beck had argued with Tweed, but had eventually given in. Reluctantly. He was still very unhappy with the risk element involved.

'I want you to drop us both immediately outside the *Hauptbahnhof*.' Tweed had insisted. 'Paula and I will then go across to the Schweizerhof and pick up our things.'

'And then do what?' Beck had demanded.

'Why, come back to join you,' Tweed had responded as though surprised at the question.

The Mercedes was now parked outside the main station by the cab rank. Beck had left the rear of the car and sat next to the driver as he picked up the radio microphone and used the agreed call sign.

'Commander speaking to all cars. Which of you is closest to the main station?'

'Car Nine responding. We are just crossing the *Bahnhof* bridge in the direction of the main station . . .'

'Pull up by the cab rank. I'll come and see you.'

Beck returned the mike to its cradle and spoke to the driver.

'Keep your eye on the entrance to the Schweizerhof. You know what our two passengers look like. If the man comes out you follow him. I can contact you from the other radio car.'

'What about the raving beauty of a girl?'

'Watch it, Ernst. Remember, you're a married man,' Beck replied with mock severity. 'If she's with him, so much the better. If she comes out on her own, ignore her.

It's the man we have to keep under surveillance. Back in a minute.'

As Beck walked past the huge station he wondered again what he should do. Tweed had spun a plausible story, had told him about his escape route from England via Brussels and the Black Forest. But Beck was convinced Tweed had left out a great deal from his narrative. It seemed impossible that he could have murdered and then raped a girl in his flat in London. The trouble was Beck had experienced many shocks in his career as a policeman. There was no certainty about Tweed's innocence. The only answer was to watch him closely.

To reach the Schweizerhof after leaving the car Tweed and Paula had descended one of the escalators into Shopville, the shopping precinct beneath the Bahnhofplatz. There were many exits and Beck recalled his anxiety when they had seemed to take too long to appear at the entrance to the hotel. Then, to his relief, they *had* appeared.

Car Nine was parked at the end of the cab rank. An unmarked car. He was glad to see the two plain-clothes men in the front seats were Tanner and Graf, two very reliable detectives. He stopped to speak to Tanner in the passenger seat.

'A man and a girl have gone into the Schweizerhof. Leave the car here and tag them. The man is medium height, medium weight, mid forties, wearing a pale grey suit and he has horn-rim glasses . . .'

As he gave the description it crossed his mind how easily Tweed could pass unnoticed in the street. Normally one of his virtues, but damned inconvenient now.

'And the girl?' Tanner enquired.

'About thirty, a mane of raven black hair, good bone structure, also of medium height but slim – a good figure. Dressed in denims and a windcheater. Pale grey.'

'We're on our way, Chief . . .'

Beck returned to the Mercedes to resume his own watch. Now nothing could go wrong.

Walking across the lobby with Paula by his side, each carrying a case, Tweed approached the concierge, who handed him their room keys.

'I have a message for you. And something else to tell you.' As he spoke the last sentence the concierge leaned over the counter and lowered his voice. He passed a folded sheet of paper to Tweed. The message, dated and timed earlier that morning, was simple.

Am at the St Gotthard with a friend. Bob.

'Thank you,' Tweed responded, 'and the other thing?'

'Two men called earlier this morning asking if you were staying here. They even had a photograph of you. One of them flashed an identity card inside a plastic folder and he said, "*Polizei*". Something about their manner, about the card, made me suspicious. I told them you were staying with us but you had gone to Interlaken. I also said it was not certain when you would be back, maybe a few days. You will excuse me for changing your message about your return, and I should have examined the card more carefully . . .'

'That's all right,' Tweed said easily, 'they sound like business rivals.'

He handed the concierge another banknote, refused the aid of a porter and they went up in the elevator to their rooms. Tweed waited while Paula unlocked her door, told her to dump her case and come along to his room. She waited until he'd closed and locked the door.

'Someone knows we're here.'

'They do,' Tweed said grimly.

He handed her Newman's message.

'Bob has been clever. He knows I normally stay here

when I'm in Zürich, so he avoided this hotel. The St Gotthard is just behind us on the Bahnhofstrasse . . .'

'And this reference to a friend?'

'My guess is it's Alois Turpil, although why he brought him here I've no idea. We must move fast. Go back to your room, change into quite different clothes . . .'

'Thank God for that. I hate these denims . . .'

'Make yourself look as different as possible, but hurry it up. I'm also changing and I'll come along to you when I'm ready . . .'

'I can always change quicker than you,' she said with an impish smile and left the room.

When Newman drove into Zürich the city was just going to work. Streets and trams thronged with people. He parked near the St Gotthard, locked Turpil inside the car after taking his passport off him, went into the hotel. He reserved two rooms, took his suitcase to his room, left it there and called the Schweizerhof to leave a message in case Tweed turned up.

The first part of the morning was taken up with furious activity. Returning to the car, he threw the question at Turpil.

'The films in this camera. I want them developed, printed, and fast. Also discreetly. An ordinary shop won't do.'

'I do have a contact.' Turpil paused. 'It will cost money.'

'You should have that phrase printed on a card. How much – and how far away is this friend?'

'He is very close. Also very discreet. To develop and print those films? Two thousand francs . . .'

'Not on your life! Don't waste my time . . .'

'Well, as a special favour I might persuade him to do the job for a thousand francs . . .'

'Which includes your commission?' Newman said cynically. 'So let's get moving. Where to?'

'Lindengasse 851. I'll guide you there. It's near the Sihl and difficult to find . . .'

Following Turpil's instructions, Newman drove down the Bahnhofstrasse. The city was ankle-deep in a mush of well-trodden snow and overhead leaden clouds drifted so low Newman felt he could reach up to touch them. More snow on the way, a lot of it.

He turned right into the Pelikanplatz and then Turpil was constantly instructing him as he drove through a maze of backstreets. The snow was deeper here with fewer footprints. He parked outside a villa near the end of Lindengasse. Newman realized they were close to the Sihl, the second river of Zürich which joined the main river, the Limmat, near the *Hauptbahnhof*.

To his surprise Turpil's 'friend' was a stooped old crone who was introduced to Newman as Gisela. A forbidding woman, her first question showed the sort of business she was involved in.

'These are dirty pictures?'

'No, they are not,' snapped Newman and glanced round at framed photographs on the walls of nude girls in provocative poses.

'A thousand francs is the fee,' Turpil said hastily.

'Only because you give me other business,' Gisela replied and took the films Newman handed her.

'And that includes the negatives,' Newman told her. 'Also I will be present when you do the work.'

'You don't want much, do you . . .'

But inside the dark-room she was skilled at her work. Newman watched the prints of the four girls emerge as clear images. He had asked for two copies of everything. She took time with the girls' prints and then dealt rapidly with the documents. When they were dry she inserted them inside two cardboard-backed envelopes with no printed indication of their source.

Newman returned to the St Gothard with Turpil.

* * *

Inside the World Security HQ in Zürich on Belle-rivestrasse Morgan glowed with triumph. He sat in a large black leather executive chair facing Horowitz and Stieber, seated on a couch.

'We have located Tweed, gentlemen. Here, in this city. I know the hotel he is staying at. Opposite the main station where, undoubtedly, he alighted from the train he travelled on from Laufenburg.'

He puffed at his cigar and glanced out of the window. The modern building looked across towards a park, and beyond, the Zürich See – Lake Zürich – was like a plate of molten lead. His office was on the fourth floor. He switched his gaze to the other two men.

'The Hotel Schweizerhof,' he told them.

'Are you sure of that?' Horowitz asked.

'Of course I'm sure,' Morgan rapped back. 'You're always asking me that question. Two of my men report he is registered there.'

'But has anyone actually seen him?' Horowitz per-sisted.

Morgan controlled his temper with an effort. The hired assassin wasn't a man at all: he had a mind like a Swiss watch with his obsession with precision.

'Not yet,' Morgan replied. 'Are you never satisfied?'

'I find it most peculiar. The location,' Horowitz con-tinued. 'As you say, the main station is probably where he got off on his way from Laufenburg. But look how easy it has been to follow him. The way he stared up at the man supposedly filming him in secret as he crossed the bridge. That absurd fuss over buying the tickets at Laufenburg station. Now, in Zürich, he stays at the nearest large hotel to the *Hauptbahnhof*. I told you before, I am beginning to know my opponent. His behaviour does not equate with his record of cleverness.'

'So he's scared witless. Loses his judgement. Goes to earth like a rabbit in the nearest burrow. And I have my lads with Walkmans on patrol. It is only a matter of time before they report a sighting.'

'It is not Tweed's normal pattern,' Horowitz insisted. He stood up. 'I think I will take a tram to the Schweizerhof to see for myself what is going on.'

'Suit yourself. Why a tram? I can give you a limo . . .'

'Because a tram is one of the most anonymous forms of transport.'

Inside his corner room at the Schweizerhof Tweed was very active. First he changed from his plain grey suit into a navy blue business-suit with a grey chalk stripe. He left the grey suit on a hanger in the wardrobe.

Next he sat at a desk, took a sheet of headed hotel paper and wrote a note to Beck. He slipped it inside an envelope and wrote on the outside. *A. Beck.* It was a common enough name.

It was exactly midday by the station clock when he dialled the St Gotthard and asked to speak to Mr Robert Newman. In less than half a minute the familiar voice answered.

'You know who this is, Bob,' Tweed began. 'I'm at the Schweizerhof with Paula . . .'

'Your timing is perfect. I've just returned with my friend.'

'Good. We must meet urgently. On our own, if you get my meaning. Without my protector, or maybe my escort would be a better word.'

'Understood.' Newman lowered his voice. 'Can I bring my friend with me – I don't want to leave him on his own. If you get my meaning . . .'

'By all means bring him. You know the Hotel Baur en Ville? Good. They have a small and very good restaurant – a café – which you enter from the side. You do know it? Splendid. It is a split-level layout – on three levels. I will be at a table on the top level. Say in fifteen minutes from now.'

'I'll have certain things to show you. Bye,' said Newman and rang off.

Tweed was changing his tie when someone tapped on the door to the small lobby. He unlocked the door on the chain, saw it was Paula, let her in. She wore a light raincoat over a sweater and had tied her hair into a pony-tail, which completely altered her appearance.

'Told you I'd be ready first,' she joshed him. 'Men take for ever . . .'

'We're going to lunch to meet Newman. I've just called him and we meet at the Baur en Ville. He has someone with him. It could be Turpil. If it is, occupy the little man's attention so Bob and I can talk in private. Now to slip out of here without Beck knowing.'

'Which I'd have said was well nigh impossible . . .'

Tweed had also substituted a blue topcoat for the rain-coat he'd worn earlier. He paused in the hotel lobby, had a further word with the concierge, handing him the sealed envelope.

'I want you to send that envelope by a porter over to the silver Mercedes parked outside the station. But please wait five minutes until after we have left. Here is the tip for the porter, and this is for your help.'

'Please wait just a moment, sir.'

The concierge strolled towards the entrance, looked at his watch as though waiting for a taxi he had ordered, then came back to Tweed.

'I've seen the car. Please leave it to me . . .'

Paula, puzzled, followed Tweed as he crossed the lobby towards the bar, glancing across the *platz*. Then he changed direction, walked towards the entrance and turned left as the automatic doors opened leading to the small café attached to the hotel. Paula followed him, saw a stationary bus was blocking Beck's view, and went down the steps inside the café. At the front it was open to the public and several smartly-dressed Swiss women were eating omelettes. The bus was still stationary as Tweed slipped out of the front door and turned left, away from the Bahnhofstrasse.

The *platz* was choked with a traffic jam and every vehicle was stationary as Paula followed Tweed down a side street alongside the hotel. She caught him up.

'Keep at least a dozen yards behind me,' he ordered. 'And when we reach the Bahnhofstrasse walk on the opposite side to me. They'll be looking for two people.'

Reluctantly she dropped back, wishing to God she had her Browning automatic in her handbag. Tweed was in danger: she sensed it. That was why he was distancing himself from her.

Walking three-quarters of the way round the block, Tweed entered the great banking and shopping street of the Bahnhofstrasse and turned right along the wide sidewalk, away from the Schweizerhof and the station. His rubber over-shoes sloshed through the snow mush as he walked slowly, glancing round as though it was the first time he'd seen this street. Paula waited for a tram to pass and crossed to the other sidewalk.

A youth clad in the usual uniform of jeans and windcheater, a Walkman attached to his head, pushed in front of Tweed, glanced at him, apologized in German. Tweed, shoulders hunched, gloved hands inside his coat pockets, trudged on. A girl on a bicycle, moving in the same direction, stopped and gestured with her head for a couple to cross. She also wore a Walkman headset. Over-polite, Tweed thought: she'd had plenty of time to cycle past without inconveniencing the couple.

He looked across the street where Paula was stepping it out. Another youth equipped with a Walkman turned his head away, stopped to stare in a window. The display was of ladies' underclothes. Not his scene, Tweed thought, unless he was kinky. An attractive girl, braving the elements in a

371

short skirt, walked towards the lad who had resumed his stroll. The girl had excellent legs. The lad turned to watch her as she passed. Definitely not kinky. Tweed suddenly recalled the window Paula had shown him – the shop display with the monkey sprawled in a hammock, a look of bliss on its face, the Walkman clamped to its head.

Tweed came to a tram stop. Feeling in his pocket for a one-franc coin, he inserted it into the machine, took his ticket and waited. The youth who had walked in front of Tweed was trudging behind him. He went to the machine and collected a ticket for himself.

Tweed stared at him. The youth looked away, shuffled his trainers in the snow, building a ridge of snow, then looked around vaguely. In every direction except where Tweed stood.

There was a whining noise as a tram approached. Passengers moved forward, ready to board. Tweed glanced at the destination plate, took two paces back. The youth leaned against the machine. The tram, a heavy blue juggernaut with three coaches linked, stopped.

The automatic doors opened, the passengers on the pavement waited as people got off, then climbed aboard. Everything was automatic – the doors, the platform step which dropped and then was raised as the tram moved off. The tram was still stationary. The doors began to close. Tweed leapt forward, just escaped being caught by the closing doors.

As it moved off he sat down and looked out of the window. The youth had jumped forward too late. His expression was one of fury and frustration. The tram glided on. The girl on the bicycle with the headset pulled alongside, pedalling vigorously. She glanced up. At the wrong moment. She failed to see the patch of ice in the road. The cycle toppled, dropped her into a pile of snow swept up earlier by road cleaners.

Tweed stayed aboard until the tram reached the stop

before the lake, then alighted. He crossed the street, bought a fresh ticket, boarded another tram coming in the opposite direction.

36

'Blast it!' said Beck.

Sitting in the passenger seat of the Mercedes he read again the note which had just been handed to him.

My dear Beck: I am so sorry to absent myself for a few hours. Urgent business which must be attended to. I will contact you at police HQ in Zürich. Please excuse my playing truant!
Tweed.

He dived out of the car, threaded his way through the stationary traffic. Wandering inside the lobby, the concierge saw him leave the car, recognized him as the man Tweed had asked to have the envelope delivered to. He was behind his counter when Beck strode in, his manner brusque.

'You have a Mr Tweed and a Miss Paula Grey staying here. I have an appointment with Mr Tweed.'

Could this be the husband of the girl who called herself Paula Grey? – wondered the concierge. He liked Tweed, and not only for his custom and the generous tips.

'Maybe he is in his room,' he suggested. 'I will call him.'

'No reply,' he said a little later, 'and now I see his key is missing. He may be in the restaurant . . .'

'I'll check for myself,' Beck snapped and ran upstairs. The next place he checked was the bar, and finally the small café. He walked out in search of Tanner, who stood a few yards to the right of the exit, pretending to read a newspaper. Beck was told he had not seen Tweed, but the pavement had been crowded. Beck checked with Graf who had taken up a position round the corner in the Bahnhofstrasse. No luck there. Beck said, 'Blast it!' again and went back to his car.

'Hell's teeth!' said Morgan and slammed down the phone. The report had just come in from the communications van parked near the Quai-brücke, the bridge where the Limmat ran out of the lake. He glared at Stieber, as though it were his fault.

'They had him – Tweed – in the palm of their hands.'

'What happened?' enquired Stieber cautiously.

'They picked him up walking down the Banhhofstrasse. Would you think anyone could give them the slip once they'd seen him?'

'But he did?'

'Oh, yes, he did. He tricked them. Oldest ploy in the world. Pretended not to be boarding a tram, then he dives on to it at the last moment. Vanishes into thin air. Why do I employ such idiots?'

Stieber was careful not to reply as the phone rang. Morgan snatched it up.

'Yes? Who is it?' he rasped.

'You know who it is. You sound agitated. Something gone wrong?'

There was no mistaking Horowitz's quiet sibilant voice. Morgan gripped the receiver more tightly. He'd better own up.

'We have located our target,' he announced.

'You have? Where is he?'

374

'Well, he was spotted in the Bahnhofstrasse, walking towards the lake. Then he disappeared. We have to start again, which we are doing, of course.'

'Of course.' The tone was mocking. 'Precisely where and how did he *disappear*, as you put it? Vanish in a cloud of blue smoke, did he?'

Morgan explained, Horowitz listened, then put down the phone. Horowitz had been calling from the main station. Patience. He would travel round this area on trams until he saw Tweed.

Tweed walked into the Baur en Ville café-restaurant and found Paula waiting for him inside. He took her by the arm.

'We'll go up to the top level – you can see everyone coming into this place from there . . .'

He asked the head waiter to reserve an extra table across the aisle, explaining that two more people were arriving to join them. The café had dark wooden walls and when they sat down with their backs to the wall they had a good view of the entrance from their elevated position at the third level.

'Are you all right?' were Paula's first words. 'I saw you dive aboard that tram at the last moment. Is there trouble?'

'There was.' Tweed picked up the menu. 'I'll tell you about it later. Here comes Newman with friend Turpil. What I want you to do is to entertain Turpil at that other table. He was once a watchmaker . . .'

He broke off as the two men arrived. Tweed noticed that Newman was shepherding Turpil in front of him. The little man greeted Tweed like a long-lost friend.

'How wonderful to see you again. It has been too long since last we met. You remember Geneva?'

'Of course.' Tweed shook his limp hand. 'Now, I have some business to discuss with Mr Newman. This is Paula.

375

She will keep you company. You'll enjoy being with her more than you would with us.'

'Yes, indeed . . .'

Paula had hung her coat up and Turpil stared at her figure with interest. She shook hands with him and guided him to the other table. Turpil offered her the inside seat against the wall but she demurred.

'Please. I'd much sooner sit on the outside. More leg-room.'

Tweed smiled to himself. She had manoeuvred the seating so that Turpil was penned in. Also he was too far away to catch any of the conversation between Tweed and Newman. They both ordered veal paillard and mineral water.

'What happened when you crossed the frontier at Basle?' Tweed enquired.

'Someone was waiting for you. Two men parked in a car close to the frontier post. Not police. The driver was a round-headed thug – like a football.'

'He spotted the Audi?'

'It wasn't there to spot. I'd changed it for a BMW on the outskirts of Basle. Since then I've been busy with Turpil – breaking into World Security in Basle at dead of night. I've things to show you, but how have you got on? You made it here, thank God.'

'Zürich is a trap,' Tweed replied, coming straight to the point. 'On my way here I noticed a lot of youths with Walkmans. The only trouble is they're not genuine Walkmans – they're mobile radio communication gear. I saw one talking into what looked like a microphone after he'd spotted me.'

'That's a diabolically clever idea . . .'

'The idea is. The operators aren't, fortunately. Amateurs. When we leave here you know what to look for.' He paused as the food came, then switched the subject. 'I keep telling myself the key to this business is who killed that girl in my London flat. And the identity of the girl. You've something to show me?'

Without saying a word, Newman glanced at the table across the aisle. Paula had Turpil engaged in conversation, had asked him about his days as a watchmaker. The little man clearly loved having an attractive girl as an attentive listener. Newman extracted one set of photographs of the four women, spread them out in front of Tweed.

'Copies of photos we found in a safe at the Basle HQ,' he said and started his lunch.

Tweed's eyes swept across the display, then stopped. He was staring at the blonde-haired beauty. He tapped it with his finger, looked at Newman with a frozen expression.

'This is the girl who was murdered in my flat. Who is she?'

'A Sylvia Harman, according to Turpil. English. Lived here in Zürich. Address, Rennweg 1420 . . .'

'A stone's throw from where we're sitting,' Tweed commented.

'She was a high-class call-girl . . .'

Newman described the information Turpil had given about her. Tweed listened, watching Newman, eating automatically. He put down his knife and fork as Newman said this wasn't all, extracted from the cardboard-backed envelope the copies of the cost sheets and the pages from the desk diary, and handed them across the table.

'Items of income and expenditure and pages from last year's desk diary. Also from the World Security HQ in Basle. I had to search to find the diary.'

Tweed scanned the copies quickly, then at Newman. 'You said she charged six thousand francs a night for her company.'

'That's right. Over two thousand pounds. Expensive, wasn't she? You see the point?'

'Yes. The item, *One-time cost*. Always for six thousand Swiss francs – Sylvia Harman's nightly charge. Also the five dates from January to April in the diary with an appointment marked with the initial "M". They are the same dates as the *One-time cost* items. It forms a pattern of liaisons between someone inside World Security at Basle and Sylvia Harman.'

"And "M" suggests Morgan . . .'

'That could be a cover for Buckmaster. The dates for last year are January to April. He vaulted from the back benches to be appointed Minister for External Security in June last year.'

'I find that too subtle.'

'Whatever you find it, I congratulate you. You see what all this means – at one blow you've achieved something I thought we'd never manage. You've identified the dead girl in my flat. And these sheets give us a direct link between her and World Security. After all, you found her photo in the company's safe.' Tweed gave a sigh of sheer relief. 'I congratulate you, Bob,' he repeated. 'The next move seems obvious.'

'It does?'

'Yes. We break in to Sylvia Harman's flat on Rennweg.' He glanced across to where Turpil was still chattering away non-stop to Paula, who kept nodding her head, bobbing her pony-tail up and down. 'And we have the means to do that at the next table. Friend Turpil . . .'

The argument which raged for some time was vehement. Tweed and Newman had joined Turpil and Paula, sitting opposite them while they all drank coffee.

Tweed proposed the break-in to Turpil. There was the normal haggle over the fee until Tweed, who sat facing Turpil, agreed a generous amount. Newman had just volunteered to accompany Turpil when Paula spoke.

'It's no good your searching that apartment. You've no idea where a girl would hide something. Only another

378

woman knows where to look. I'll go with Turpil . . .'

'Out of the question,' snapped Tweed.

'Oh, stop being so macho,' Paula burst out. 'I've been trained to be careful,' she said, phrasing it carefully in front of Turpil. 'I repeat, only another woman knows where to look.' She flared up with a pretended burst of temper. 'Or is this your way of saying I haven't got the bloody nerve? If so, I would greatly appreciate it if you'd come straight out with it . . .'

They talked about it for several more minutes and Paula refused to give way. It was Newman who cooled the argument as he turned to Tweed.

'She is right, you know. And I can go with them and act as lookout. So if something goes wrong and a little muscle is called for I think I can provide it. Unless you're going to argue about that?'

Tweed threw up his hands. 'Outnumbered, out-voted, talked down. You're a couple of rogues and rebels . . .'

'But at long last you agree?' Paula said and smiled. She turned to Turpil. 'You said you knew the flat, that you'd been there, so you know how to get in, presumably?'

'Easy as jumping a low hurdle,' the little man agreed.

'So', Paula continued, 'wouldn't it, on balance, be safer if we did the job in daylight? You said she lived alone? You're sure about that?'

'Positive. She had the money. She didn't need to share the expenses with another girl. She didn't like the idea of sharing. She lives alone. All I have to do is to make sure she isn't in. She usually exercises about this time of day. A great one for keeping fit. Can't guarantee she will be out, of course.'

'Yes, we can.' Newman had been puzzling over how he could reassure Turpil without letting him know the girl was dead. 'I'll tell you now, while you were using the bathroom in my room at the St Gotthard I called a friend in need of some feminine company, gave him Sylvia's phone number

379

out of the directory. He called back and said she'd agreed to go with him back to his hotel this afternoon.'

'Then what are we waiting for?' Turpil asked. 'I carry a portable kit which will get us inside that place in just a few minutes.'

Tweed noticed Turpil had been eyeing him furtively at intervals during the long argument. He leaned forward.

'We may have another job for you later. But you'll have to come with us to a place in the mountains where I'll be resting up for a few days. In the canton of Schwyz. Near the town of Einsiedeln.'

Newman stared across the table at Paula in blank amazement at this extraordinary breach of security. Paula had trouble not showing her alarm and incredulity. Tweed said he would meet them at Sprüngli, the chocolate shop with a tea-restaurant on the first floor further down the Bahnhofstrasse. He nodded towards Turpil.

'Don't forget to bring our friend back with you.' He stood up, then bent down to whisper in Newman's ear. 'I'm trusting you to take very good care of Paula.'

It was still light when they made the break-in at Rennweg 1420. Renneweg was a street of small shops which branched off Bahnhofstrasse at an angle and led to the section of the Altstadt on the west bank of the river Limmat.

Newman was glad to see there were plenty of shoppers moving up and down the street. The entrance to Sylvia Harman's apartment was a straight staircase open to the street. The door was latched back and Newman assumed it was locked after nightfall.

Turpil disappeared off the street and Paula followed him up the steps. He paused in front of a heavy door on the first landing, then pressed the bell and waited. He looked at his watch to time three minutes. Then he took a bunch of keys from his overcoat pocket and began trying one after another.

It was very quiet inside the building and Paula found herself glancing at the upper flights in case someone was descending. On the pavement below Newman was leaning against the side of the entrance, smoking a cigarette.

'It's open,' Turpil whispered.

Paula stood looking down a narrow hallway, listening for the sound of a shower gushing, a bath emptying of water. Then she strode inside and Turpil followed, closing the door behind him. Paula was very suspicious Turpil had the key to the heavy door and had performed a pantomime to conceal the fact.

She checked the layout of the flat. There was a living-cum-dining-room, one large bedroom, the kitchen and the bathroom. She had the impression of an expensively, tastefully furnished apartment. Opening a wardrobe door in the bedroom she surveyed a quantity of fashionable clothes that also suggested good taste. On the floor rows of good shoes were neatly arranged.

Neatness, tidiness, expense and taste were the words she used mentally to sum up the occupant. She heard the squeak of wood being moved, returned to the living-room to find Turpil starting to search through a sideboard.

'Don't you touch anything,' she snapped. 'You've no idea as to the best places to look.'

'I'm a pro—' he began indignantly, then broke off in mid-sentence.

He closed the drawer and Paula sent him back into the lobby to stand guard in case Newman came rushing up the stairs. It took her ten minutes to find the inconsistency she was looking for. In the bathroom stood a laundry bin. She lifted the lid and stared.

Inside used clothes were crammed higgledy-piggedly. A mess of clothes hastily shoved into the bin. She bent

381

forward, began to sort through the clothes. She found the diary for the previous year at the bottom.

'I want to phone my sister, Klara,' Turpil said.

They were walking down a side street leading to Bahnhofstrasse. Paula had slipped the diary into her shoulder bag after a swift examination. On their way to the break-in Newman had quietly told Paula the sort of thing she should look for. Lists of phone numbers with names; any kind of financial record; diaries, especially for the previous year.

'You should have phoned her from the St Gotthard,' Newman told Turpil. 'We're on our way to Sprüngli . . .'

'And when did I have the time?' Turpil demanded. 'I have to call her before we go to the cake shop.'

'Why the urgency?'

'I want to make sure she got back safely.' Turpil glanced at Paula as they emerged on to Bahnhofstrasse, a sneaky look. 'You understand, I'm sure. And Klara may have a business message for me.'

'Business messages can wait . . .' Newman began, then he swore under his breath.

Turpil had darted from his side, had run to a ticket machine. Newman was moving after him when Paula grabbed his arm, warned him to be careful. A police patrol-car, which Turpil had undoubtedly spotted, was parked nearby and the two uniformed men inside were looking their way.

Newman ran to the ticket machine as a tram approached the stop, moving towards the main station. He bought two tickets as the tram stopped and Turpil scrambled aboard a coach. Newman ran for the same central door with Paula by this side and passed her a ticket.

'Something funny going on,' Newman said quickly. 'He

gave two reasons for making a call. Keep an eye on him . . .'

She mounted the step to the interior of the coach, saw that Turpil was occupying a seat near the door, walked past him as the doors closed and sat down a few seats in front of the little man, choosing a divan seat with its back to the side of the tram. She could now keep him under observation.

Newman went in the opposite direction from the central doors, occupied an outer seat next to the aisle. They had him in a pincer movement. The tram stopped again, several passengers alighted, but a whole crowd boarded the coach, most of them standing. It was now difficult for Newman to see Turpil.

The next stop was close to Globus department store on the other side of the street; close also to the *Hauptbahnhof*. Newman stood up as a lot of people alighted. He caught a glimpse of Paula who was leaving the tram, beckoning to him furiously. Newman managed to leave the coach just before another horde came aboard. Rush hour was starting and now it was dark. He stood on the wide pavement, looking in all directions. Turpil had vanished.

Paula ran up to him, her coat flapping. She was out of breath and couldn't speak for a moment.

'I saw him,' she gasped out. 'Heading for the *Hauptbahnhof*. I think I saw him going down an escalator. Into Shopville. I'm not certain it was him . . .'

'You walk round the *platz*. Watch all the exits from Shopville. If you spot him grab him by the arm, tell him you'll accuse him of trying to interfere with you, call the police, unless he comes back with you to Sprüngli. I'm going down into Shopville . . .'

Paula was away, walking briskly as Newman reached an escalator, descended into the underground shopping precinct. He slowed down inside Shopville, looking everywhere. The bloody place was like a labyrinth. Plenty of people down here, men and girls hurrying back and forth.

Newman kept walking slowly, scanning the whole area. He saw Turpil's back suddenly. There was a row of telephones under perspex hoods. Turpil was using the phone at the end of the row. Newman started walking forward, then remembered the ear-drummer.

Taking it out of his trench-coat pocket he inserted it inside his right ear, which was turned towards one of the escalator exits. A deafening growling rumble followed by a high-pitched whine filled his ear. A tram was turning round off the *platz* down Bahnhofstrasse.

Newman swivelled his stance, standing opposite the phone compartment where Turpil was making his call. The sound of footsteps clacking like hammerblows on the floor; then, quite distinct, Turpil's voice.

'It's taken me long enough to get through to you. Morgan. You want to know where a man called Tweed is to be found soon? I know. Twenty thousand francs? Agreed. He's going to hole up in the mountains, in the canton of Schwyz, near Einsiedeln . . .'

The connection was broken as Newman's left hand wrenched the phone out of Turpil's hand, replaced it. His right hand gripped Turpil by the forearm, just above the elbow, on the nerve. Turpil yelped with pain as Newman hauled him out, turned him towards the escalator leading to Bahnhofstrasse.

As they walked side by side, with Newman holding on to the elbow, Turpil began to babble.

'I had to speak to Klara . . .'

Newman showed him the palm of his bare left hand, the ear-drummer resting inside it, then put it back in his coat pocket. Turpil swallowed several times before he spoke again.

'You dropped that in the river . . .'

'Pretended to. Is Morgan your pet name for Klara? Who is she?'

'My mistress. She looks after me. Cooks for me.

384

Manages the apartment in Berne . . .'

'But you were talking to Morgan of World Security. Selling Tweed for thirty pieces of silver. No, for twenty thousand francs. You're a lump of dirt. How did you know Morgan was interested in Tweed?'

'They've spread the news on the grapevine, the under-world. A reward of twenty thousand francs for news of his whereabouts. I'm getting old, Mr Newman. I'm getting near retirement. I need every franc I can lay my hands on . . .'

They were on the automatic escalator now, standing together as it carried them up towards the Bahnhofstrasse exit. No one behind them. No one in front. After the warmth of Shopville the icy temperature of night met them.

'And you were supposed to be a friend of Tweed's,' Newman commented. 'With friends like you who needs . . .'

They had stepped off the escalator. The temperature had dropped rapidly. Newman didn't see the patch of ice, slipped on it, loosened his grip. Turpil snatched his arm away and ran.

He ran across the street without looking. He tripped almost as soon as he'd left the kerb. He never saw the great hulk of the blue tram swinging round the corner into Bahnhofstrasse. He sprawled forward full length over the track. The tram driver jammed on his emergency brake. The rails were coated with ice. Too late. The tram slid forward a few more feet. There was a screech. Which could have been Turpil. Or the tram grinding to a halt. The wheels sliced through the prone body like a mincing machine. Spurts of liquid gushed from under the tram. Splotches of deep carmine splashed on the white snow. Blood. A woman began screaming. A crowd was gathering.

Newman walked further down the street. He saw Paula's

385

horrified face on the other side and crossed to join her.

'We must get to Tweed quickly. It's an emergency.'

37

At a corner table inside Sprüngli on the first floor Tweed listened while Newman tersely reported their experiences. Paula sat beside Tweed staring out at the leafless skeletal trees lining Bahnhofstrasse. A tram appeared. She looked away. Tweed squeezed her hand.

'Would you like a cake?'

'I couldn't face anything to eat. More black coffee please.'

Tweed gave a waitress the order and glanced again at two men sitting at separate tables a few yards away. One was a poker-faced man in his thirties, wearing a business suit. The other, who sat closer, was a youth eating a cake, a Walkman clamped to his head. Newman drank coffee: he had finished his story. He put down his cup, said quietly to Tweed:

'What I don't understand is why you let Turpil know you were heading up into the mountains, to this place in the canton of Schwyz, Einsiedeln.'

'The plan is working,' Tweed replied. 'Although I didn't foresee it would have such grisly consequences.'

'Turpil asked for it,' Newman told him. 'He set out to betray you for money. To some pretty grim people. Don't forget the bomb I found under the Audi back in the Black Forest.'

'True . . .'

Tweed was thinking that Newman had grown harder

386

since his ordeal travelling secretly in East Germany a few years earlier. Not less human, but tougher.

'What plan, for God's sake?' Paula burst out, still shaken.

'We need Beck's full cooperation. As I realized before we ever reached Switzerland, it would be difficult to convince him completely of my innocence, that we are being hunted by professional killers. We have to *demonstrate* the situation to him, bring the enemy out into the open.'

'In the . . . excitement . . . I forgot to give you this diary. I found it hidden in the linen bin in Sylvia Harman's apartment,' said Paula and handed the book to him.

'Last year's diary.' Tweed riffled through the pages, stopping briefly at certain dates, then he looked at Newman. 'A further link in the chain linking World Security with the girl I found dead in my flat. The same dates as those in the desk diary you found in Basle, Bob. January 15, 28. February 16. March 4. April 25. Alongside each date is the initial "M". Even the times are the same in both diaries. 9.30 p.m., 9 p.m., 10 p.m., 9 p.m., 10.30 p.m. I remember them distinctly.'

'But how would Sylvia Harman turn up in London?' Paula asked.

'Easy,' Newman replied. 'Whoever used to spend the night with her – Buckmaster or Morgan – could fly her in by the Lear jet. For six thousand francs she'd fly there without a second's hesitation . . . What's the matter?'

Tweed had slipped the diary into his pocket and was staring behind Newman as the poker-faced man approached their table. He drew up a chair at the end, next to Tweed, sat down. He showed Tweed a folder in the palm of his hand.

'Norbert Tanner, Federal Police. Working for Arthur Beck. I don't know whether you realize it, Mr Tweed, but you're being followed. That youth sitting by himself with

387

the Walkman. He tagged you here from near the Baur en Ville. Shall I take him in with us?'

'No. Leave him alone. Pretend you haven't noticed him.'

'If you say so. And now, if you don't mind, I'd like you all to accompany me to police headquarters. Orders of Mr Beck. There's a Merc waiting outside, the one with amber-tinted glass . . .'

'We've got Tweed this time,' said Morgan, standing by the window of his office on Bellerivestrasse, staring out into the night. 'He's headed for Einsiedeln, a nowhere place up in the mountains in the canton of Schwyz. All I have to do is to send my Walkman lads up there ahead of him in a bus.'

The only other occupant was Armand Horowitz who sat in a hard-backed chair. He'd refused the offer of an armchair: they relaxed you, made you less alert. And Morgan had the heating turned full up, compelling Horowitz to remove his raincoat. He wore a drab grey suit, but it was well cut and fitted his thin tall frame perfectly.

'Might I enquire how you know this?' he enquired.

'You might!' Morgan, his turnip-shaped bulk emphasized by the thin stature of his guest, was in flamboyant mood. He walked back to his desk, settled himself behind its vast size. They laid a lot of emphasis on status symbols, the size and quality of the desks, Horowitz was thinking.

'Then get on with it,' he said.

'A little turd called Alois Turpil – we've used him occasionally for break-in jobs – phoned me. Tweed himself must have told him . . .'

'Another out-of-character action,' Horowitz observed.

'Can it!' Morgan burst out. 'This is the real McCoy.'

'Describe this Turpil.'

Morgan was thrown off balance. 'A small man,

mid-fifties, a hooked nose, looks a bit like a gnome . . .'

'Looked,' Horowitz corrected him.

'What's that?'

'I spent the afternoon travelling on trams round the station area and the immediate vicinity. Sometimes the long arm of coincidence reaches out to help persistence. Was it a lengthy phone call?'

'No. As a matter of fact he broke off in mid-sentence. I don't know why. Maybe the connection was broken accidentally . . .'

'Or by someone else.' Horowitz had an amused look in the eyes watching Morgan. 'This time I believe you. I was on the tram which mowed Turpil down, turned him into goulash.'

Morgan paused in the act of placing his cigar between his lips, held it in mid-air like a conductor grasping a baton. 'What are you talking about?'

'Turpil – from your description – is very dead. He came up from Shopville on an escalator with a man who was holding him by the arm. Turpil broke free at the top. He ran into the street and my tram rolled over him.'

'I see . . .'

'No, you don't. I have a photographic memory and the man holding on to him was the foreign correspondent, Robert Newman. His picture has appeared in the papers often enough. More to the point, in Basle the arm of coincidence was stretched to breaking point. Newman was dining in the restaurant of the Drei Könige when I was staying there. And you said something about an alarm going off here in Zürich for no reason.'

'Oh God! Was there a break-in at Basle? I'll have to get them to double-check nothing is missing. Turpil was an expert break-in artist. For hire by anyone who had the money.'

'That's your problem. Mine is Einsiedeln. Cancel that fool idea of sending up those Walkman louts. They'll stand out like clowns in a small town.'

389

'Someone has to go there,' Morgan objected.
'Someone is going there. I am. With Stieber. At once.'

Police headquarters on Lindenhofstrasse is a four-storey old block of grey stone. One side overlooks the river Limmat which divides Zürich into two separate districts. Through the net curtains masking Beck's office window on the third floor Tweed could see the dim bulk of the university perched high up on the opposite bank.

'You've got a nerve – wandering round Zürich.' Beck said to Tweed. 'And in your present position I suspect you need it. *If* you are being followed.'

'Mr Tweed *is* being followed, sir,' interjected Tanner. 'No doubt about it. I picked him up near the Baur en Ville and he walked to Sprüngli. During that short distance I spotted three of them. Two youths on foot and a girl on a bicycle. All equipped with fake Walkmans.'

'Fake?' Beck queried. 'A bunch of kids has you worried?'

'It's the equipment, sir. It has to be very sophisticated. I saw two of them reporting to someone through concealed microphones. You called them a bunch of kids, but who-ever has organized them is pretty professional. With equipment like that. And another one on a motor-cycle followed us to here. A man. He could still be outside, waiting for Mr Tweed to leave the building.'

Beck looked bleak. 'I don't like that. Go down and see if he's still there.'

'And if he is, permission to bring him in for questioning downstairs? I think I can persuade him to talk.'

Newman and Paula, sitting on chairs close to Tweed, stared at Tanner. Yes, Newman thought to himself, you'll make him talk if you get your hands on him.

'Agreed, Tanner,' Beck decided. 'And I do want to know who his employer is.' He waited until Tanner had left the office. 'Tweed, while you've been running round Zür-ich I have been to see Colonel Romer of the Zurcher Kredit in Talstrasse. He has now been waiting all after-noon and part of this evening to see you.'

'Something I said caught his attention?' Tweed suggested.

'Yes, it did.' He looked at Newman before turning his attention back to Tweed. 'All of this is highly confidential – but I know you've been fully vetted. Now, Tweed, you can be awfully frank with Romer. He carries a lot of clout in military circles in this country.' Beck checked his watch. 'Romer has gone out to get something to eat. He'll be back in three-quarters of an hour. Meantime, who wants some refreshment?'

Tanner returned half an hour later. 'He talked – the motor-cyclist. There's a control communications van parked near the Quai-brücke.'

'Is there now? Tanner, send a patrol car to check it out. It will have an aerial – so our men can say it is interfering with the police radio band.'

Beck waited until Tanner had gone. 'Who do you think these people are, Tweed?'

'World Security.'

'I see.' Beck thought about it. 'Even if it is, it would be logical for Lance Buckmaster to pass the word through to his organization to keep a lookout for you, to back up the continent-wide alert Howard sent to police chiefs.'

'I see,' Tweed replied tersely.

'Now,' Beck continued. 'Colonel Romer will be back at Talstrasse. I'm sending you there in a car. Whatever you say to him, he is totally trustworthy and discreet. He will discuss the matter only with myself. He might just hold the key to this weird business.'

Colonel Romer was a tall, well-built man with a trim moustache who held himself erect and was in his early

391

fifties. He wore a dark grey business suit. His thick brows and hair were grey and there was a hint of humour in his blue eyes.

His office, overlooking a narrow side street, had stripped pine panelled walls, the furniture was English antiques. He had drawn up an armchair alongside Tweed's and had two glasses of Montrachet and the bottle on the low coffee table near them.

'I am a good listener, Mr Tweed,' he said and smiled. 'I recall our rather tense meeting in Basle a couple of years ago. Since then I've become chief executive of Zurcher Kredit – it simply means more work.'

'And you're a colonel in the Swiss Army,' Tweed commented.

'Correct. And as such much concerned with national security,' Romer responded in English. 'I am also a good listener . . .'

Tweed had already decided Romer was as discreet as Beck had indicated. He began. He started with the discovery of the dead girl in his flat. But he was careful not to refer directly to the Strategic Defence Initiative. Instead he used the phrase, 'The most advanced hi-tech system of defence for the West ever invented . . .'

'And you say that when you contacted this vessel, the *Lampedusa*, from Beck's communications complex in Berne, they did not know the replies to the two trick signals? So the ship *has* been hi-jacked?'

'I'm sure of it . . .'

'And only two people in England check its progress – yourself and the Minister for External Security, Lance Buckmaster?'

'That's right.'

Romer sipped his wine, looked grim as he put down the glass. 'What I am going to tell you is highly confidential. In my position I hear a lot on the international financial grapevine which never gets into the papers.' He paused. 'World Security is bankrupt. Buckmaster is a megalomaniac. He went on borrowing vast sums for expansion to further his ambition to build one of the ten top companies in the world. He has over-reached himself. He needs about five hundred million pounds to save his company from going under.'

'Where on earth is he going to lay his hands on a sum like that?'

'Not from any of the major banks. They have loaned him too much already.' Again Romer paused, sipped more wine. Tweed remained silent. 'There is one intriguing development, some people might call it sinister.'

'And that is?'

'Through the Narodny Bank, which is, of course, the Russian bank operating in the West, the Soviets have placed in reserve, ready for some huge business deal, the equivalent of five hundred million pounds in gold bullion. The transfer will take place in Switzerland – not through this bank. I just wonder what the Kremlin is buying for such an amount.' Again he paused. 'Unless, in view of what you have told me, you could guess?'

Tweed sat very still. Romer *had* given him the key to the whole bizarre sequence of events. He now knew positively who was behind the murder and rape of Sylvia Harman in his London flat – to get him out of the way. The only question was which of the two men had committed the crime. But for the first time he now knew the *motive*.

38

A world of snow and ice. Horowitz, wearing knee-high fine leather boots, a fur coat and a Russian-style fur hat, walked slowly through the small town of Einsiedeln. High up in the mountains, the old buildings crowded in on the narrow streets. On one side of him walked Stieber, on the other he had Morgan, who had insisted on accompanying them in the car.

'It's bloody cold,' grumbled Morgan and shivered.

The temperature was well below zero. From the roof gutters of the buildings long spear-like icicles were suspended. The snow underfoot was a foot deep, hard-packed by the tread of the locals. A bell began to toll, a sound laden with doom. It was four in the afternoon.

'What the devil's that?' asked Morgan.

'You'll see when we turn this corner,' Horowitz told him.

Women shoppers, well muffled, some with only the top halves of their faces showing above woollen scarves, shuffled along with plastic bags. Turning the corner, the street opened out into a large space with the ground rising behind it steeply. Perched on top was a vast and ancient façade with twin towers.

'The Benedictine monastery,' said Horowitz as the bell continued its mournful dirge.

Morgan suddenly had the premonition of something awful. Around this part of the town the dense forest closed in, branches bent under the weight of frozen snow. Away from the shopping street, it was very quiet, the grim solitude of an Arctic wilderness.

'That is one of the most famous monasteries in all Europe,' Horowitz continued. 'In summer, pilgrims come from everywhere to visit it. The area inside its wall is immense, like an enclosed town cut off from the world.'

A woman dressed in black, her head covered, had climbed the slippery path and pushed open one of the huge double doors. From inside came the sound of singing, again a dirge-like sound. Morgan shuddered again. He hated the atmosphere of this place which reminded him of some huge tomb.

'What is that yodelling?' he asked.

'Not yodelling,' Horowitz chided him. 'That is the monks' choir which sings at this hour each day.' He stooped down to pick up his case from the snow. 'Wait here, Morgan. We are going to reserve rooms in the Hotel St Johann. Unless you are going to stay with us?'

'No,' Morgan said hastily. 'I have to get back to Zürich. I have an international business to run. In case you'd forgotten . . .'

But he was speaking the last sentence into space. Horowitz and Stieber were plodding away with their cases through the snow. Swearing to himself, stamping his frozen feet, Morgan watched them disappear inside a small five-storey building with a grey slate roof. The St Johann.

It was ten minutes before they returned without their cases. In that time Morgan watched a monk emerge from the monastery, a figure clad in a black robe with a cowl pulled over his head to protect himself against the snow which had begun to drift down.

'I have phoned for a taxi to take you back,' Horowitz informed him. 'It should be here soon.'

'A taxi? I'm going back in the Mercedes we parked in the main street . . .'

'No.' Horowitz's tone was firm. 'We need transport when Tweed arrives – so we can follow him.'

'You're confident he will do that?' Morgan demanded while he brushed snow off his coat, his fingers frozen inside his gloves.

'You were, back in Zürich,' Horowitz reminded him. 'And I sense this is the kind of place he has been making for – a remote refuge.'

'Well, enjoy yourselves . . .'

Morgan took a step forward, slipped on a patch of ice which nearly upended him. Recovering his balance, he swore again as a Mercedes taxi stopped close to them. Horowitz handed him a brochure of the St Johann.

'I did a sleight of hand with my passport when registering. I'm staying under the name of Anton Thaler. If you want to call me the phone number is there. You were lucky with the cab – the company they phoned radioed to one just on its way back to Zürich. And you can see why I told you not to bring your Walkman louts up here – they'd stand out like clowns.'

'See you,' mumbled Morgan, 'and I'll collect the chauffeur from the parked car on the main street.'

He collapsed into the rear seat of the taxi, sighed with relief at the warmth, and thanked God he was returning to Zürich from this benighted wilderness.

Horowitz smiled as the taxi departed. 'I think our esteemed friend is glad to be on his way to civilization. What is it, Stieber?'

The German was staring at several monks leaving the monastery clad in their black robes and cowls.

'I just had an idea,' he said. 'Doesn't matter now. What do we do next?'

'Wait for Tweed.'

At police headquarters in Zürich, after listening to Romer's call to him, Beck put down the phone and looked at Tweed as he stood up.

396

'I'm going downstairs to make arrangements for transport to take you up to Einsiedeln – and then on to Brunni. That was Colonel Romer, and you convinced him at least.'

'But not you?' Tweed commented quizzically.

'I'll be back in a few minutes . . .'

'Could we use your phone? To call London?'

'Go ahead . . .'

'And,' Newman interjected, 'where is this place, Brunni?'

'At the end of the world,' Tweed told him.

'In that case,' Newman continued, gazing at Beck, 'I'd like a weapon to guard Tweed. There have already been two attempts to assassinate him. A juggernaut tried to drive him down on the autobahn near Freiburg. Then a bomb was placed under his car in the Black Forest.'

'And I can confirm both attempts,' Paula said. 'Because on both occasions I was there.'

Beck's expression froze. 'Why on earth didn't you tell this to me earlier?'

'Would you have believed it in Berne?' Tweed challenged him. 'I thought it would have sounded too dramatic, that I was bolstering my story.'

'What weapon had you in mind?' Beck asked Newman.

'Something like a Magnum .45. Preferably just that. With plenty of spare ammo.'

'And I'd like a Browning,' Paula chimed in. 'You know I've experience with the gun.'

'Plus temporary permits to carry the weapons,' Newman added.

'I'll have to think about it. I'll be back within ten minutes . . .'

Tweed drank more coffee. It will be coming out of my ears, he thought. He looked at Newman.

'It's time we had back-up. I sense a climax is coming. Up in the mountains. Can you call Howard? Ask him to fly out Harry Butler and Pete Nield to Zürich immediately? They

397

can take rooms at the Schweizerhof, wait there for further instructions. They may catch the last flight tonight.'

'I'm sure Howard will play. I talked about using them when I saw him in London. I'll call him now -- before Beck gets back.'

While he made the call Paula moved closer to Tweed.

'Surely with that evidence you told me about in Sprüngli that Bob found in Basle – plus the diary I took from the flat in Rennweg. And plus the fact that we've now identified the dead girl in your flat – and can link her with World Security. Surely with all that we could return to London and prove your innocence?'

'It's all circumstantial. And I have to solve the problem of *Shockwave*. That takes priority over everything. Beck has now agreed to provide a mobile transmitter. I have to contact the *Lampedusa* again, make sure she's been hijacked.'

'Can't that wait until we reach London?' she persisted.

'It cannot! I'm convinced that vessel with its vital cargo is on its way to Russia. We're racing against time to stop it.'

'And how are you going to do that?'

'I have no idea yet,' he admitted as Newman put down the receiver.

'Butler and Nield will be on the first flight here,' he reported. 'Officially they'll be helping to track you down. Howard is playing it clever with Buckmaster . . .'

He broke off as Beck entered the office, carrying a large hold-all. He dumped it on his desk, thrust his hand inside and it came out holding a Browning .32 automatic. He handed it to Paula who checked that the safety catch was on, released the magazine and checked that there wasn't one up the spout. She shoved the magazine back inside the butt, slipped the weapon inside her shoulder bag. Beck had watched her.

'If you hadn't done that I'd have taken it off you,' he said with a wintry smile. 'Here are spare mags.' He reached inside the hold-all again, brought out a Magnum .45, gave it to Newman.

'Here's your cannon. Plus spare ammo. And for each of you a temporary permit to carry firearms.' Beck leaned against his desk and looked severe. 'I may tell you I wouldn't have supplied weapons, but I made a quick call to Chief Inspector Otto Kuhlmann. He confirmed that there was a pile-up on the autobahn outside Freiburg. Tweed, what was the name of the informant you said lured you to the Cheshire Cheese pub in London?'

'Richter. Klaus Richter. Lives in Freiburg . . .'

'Kuhlmann also told me they found the body of a Klaus Richter – in his Freiburg apartment. A case of murder.'

'I see. And the mobile transceiver?' Tweed prodded.

'Already on its way to Einsiedeln. Concealed inside a plain van carrying on the outside the name of a Zürich builder, Ingold. The driver will park outside the monastery and wait for you. I thought it wiser if you travelled up there in a car without the van tagging on. The codeword for contact with my driver is simple – Limmat. He'll then go where you tell him to.'

'And where is this Brunni you mentioned earlier?' asked Newman.

'A tiny summer resort at the end of a remote valley. Brunni,' he repeated, 'not Brunnen, which is near the capital of the Schwyz canton. We have a chalet there where we have kept key witnesses in hiding. The driver of your car, Georg, will unlock the place for you.'

'What about food and tea and coffee – provisions to keep us alive?' asked Paula.

'I was coming to that. You won't get anything in Zürich now. In any case I don't want any of you wandering around the city again. There are good cooking facilities at the chalet which is regularly cleaned. And only a very few locals live there in winter.'

'The food,' Paula persisted.

'As you drive into Einsiedeln there's a small super-market to your left – it stays open late and you'll be able to get anything you need there.'

'Then what are we waiting for?' Tweed asked.

'Nothing more. The car is waiting for you outside. Tanner is downstairs and will escort you to it. There's a phone in the chalet. Keep in touch. This whole business worries me.'

'And what do you think it does to us?' Paula asked.

Horowitz stood by the window of the room he'd reserved at the St Johann. He'd asked for a room at the front and now he stood with Stieber alongside him, a pair of night binoculars pressed against his eyes. His steel-rimmed spectacles rested on top of a chest of drawers as he examined the van which had parked opposite the monastery.

'It's a builder's van,' he remarked. 'Some Zürich company called Ingold. Why he's parked there at this time in the evening I can't imagine.'

He lowered his binoculars, replaced them with his spectacles. The window gave an excellent view of the great hulk of the monastery with the open space in front of it. Horowitz bit his lip and went to the phone.

'We need reinforcements,' he decided.

He dialled the World Security number, asked to speak to Gareth Morgan. The operator wasn't sure whether he had left the building. A minute later Morgan's voice, irritable, came on the line.

'Who is it?'

'You can guess who is talking.' Horowitz paused. 'I have now surveyed the territory and need extra manpower. It must be your top men. Professionals. I emphasize that. And they must come up here on motor-cycles equipped with radios. And tooled up. I expect them to arrive within one hour . . .'

'That's impossible . . .'

'Then make it possible. I'm not prepared to argue the point. Call them at their homes. I know you have men who are skilled motor-cyclists. The leader reports to me, Anton Thaler, at the St Johann as soon as the team arrives.'

'Tooled up, you said.' Morgan made his final protest. 'This is Switzerland.'

'My knowledge of geography is pretty good, too. One hour from now . . .'

Horowitz broke the connection. Stieber, his round head damp with sweat from the high temperature of the heating, stared at Horowitz.

'You usually work alone. Why the motor-cyclists?'

'Because I am not sure we know Tweed's final destination. We need outriders to scour the whole area. Of course, when the final confrontation comes, I shall be alone.'

39

Latitude 32. 10. N. Longitude 21. 30. W. The *SS Helvetia* – formerly *SS Lampedusa* – was steaming through heavy seas well south-east of the Azores in the Atlantic. It was late afternoon, the cloud overcast was threatening, and Greg Singer, late of the SAS, was in the hold. Beside him stood Captain Hartmann.

'It's a huge brute,' Singer observed as he gazed up at the giant computer *Shockwave*. 'I suppose it won't shift in this swell?'

'They protected it against all weathers,' Hartmann replied.

Shockwave, its immense face exposed at the front, was packed on the other three sides, at its base and the top, inside a wall of six-inch timber. The base was reinforced with steel.

Singer, leaning against the outer hull to hold his balance, watched as the vessel swayed. *Shockwave* appeared to be totally stable. Singer's great fear was that it would break loose, smashing its incredible weight against the hull.

'How long now before we pass through the Straits of Gibraltar into the Med?' Singer asked.

'If this weather continues, it may be several days. If it improves, we may move through the Straits earlier. I cannot predict . . .'

Singer swore to himself as he followed Hartmann up the ladder out of the hold. All these bloody skippers were like that: they wouldn't commit themselves. In its approach to Gibraltar, the *Helvetia* was still following a devious course to keep clear of the commercial sea lanes.

'I'll go see Hoch,' Singer said as they stepped into the passageway, 'then join you on the bridge.'

It never occurred to Singer that Hoch, the radio op. was the sole survivor of the massacre of the *Lampedusa*'s original crew. That was a detail which belonged to the past. Singer reckoned he had Hoch under his control – psychologically as well as physically. He had warned the American that his wife and family on Cape Cod in the eastern United States were under constant surveillance.

'One code-word from me and on a dark night that nice frame house of yours will go up in flames – with no exit for those inside. They'll roast to death, Hoch. When they reach the bodies they'll find cinders . . .'

Hoch, a lean-faced man with a strong jaw, had regarded Singer with pure hatred. Now Singer nodded to the armed guard outside the radio room, opened the door and walked inside. A second guard, a pistol in his hand, sat facing Hoch who was perched at the edge of his bunk.

'Just to remind you once again, Hoch,' Singer told him, 'we have the code-books. When London contacts you again you'll behave yourself, won't you?'

Hoch merely nodded. They might have the code-books but he carried inside his head the two trick questions and answers. The odd thing was Monitor had only contacted him once so far, and it was Monitor who had posed the trick queries in his signal. Hoch, nerving himself, had not replied with the correct answers.

Hoch didn't really grasp what was going on in London. The other contact, Prefect, contacted him daily – but never once had he introduced the trick words. It was almost as though Monitor was the only man who knew them. He wished to God Monitor could contact him again.

Tweed, seated in the back of the Mercedes, gazed out as the car moved along the highway above the southern shore of Lake Zürich. It was a clear cold night. On the opposite shore lights of towns glittered like stars fallen to earth. By his side sat Paula, still seething over Beck's apparent lack of total trust. Beyond her Newman, the Magnum nestled inside the hip holster Beck had also supplied, was asleep. Georg, their driver, opened the glass screen dividing him from the rear compartment.

'This is where we turn off up into the mountains to Einsiedeln.'.

Despite the heavy snow-covering Georg swung the car skilfully off the main highway and they began to climb a steep and twisting road into lonely country.

'I thought Beck had more faith in us,' Paula burst out after Georg had closed the screen.

'He's in a difficult position,' Tweed squeezed her arm. 'I think if I were in his position I'd be equally cautious. He can't be one hundred per cent convinced of my innocence yet.'

'You should have showed him the photo of Sylvia Harman . . .'

'And admitted we had made two break-ins? Bob in Basle and the two of you in Harman's apartment in Zürich? The Swiss regard burglary of private property with the same severity as murder. I'd have put him in an impossible position.'

'I suppose you're right.' She sounded edgy. 'Don't forget to remind Georg to stop at that supermarket in Einsiedeln. We must have provisions. There'll be nothing at that chalet.'

'Don't worry. I told him before we left. Relax . . .'

As they continued climbing the tortuous road a team of motor-cyclists overtook them, moving over the icy surface at high speed. Tweed automatically counted six of them. Sinister figures clad in black leather with helmets and snow-goggles. He also noted each driver had an aerial for radio transmission spearing up from behind his saddle.

'Lunatics,' Paula commented. 'Riding at that speed on roads like this.'

'Youth will have its mad fling,' Tweed commented.

'They didn't look all that young to me,' remarked Newman, who had been woken by the zoom-zoom of the powerful machines.

As they entered Einsiedeln they passed the *Bahnhof* on their left, the end of the single-track railway from Zürich. Georg pulled up in the near-deserted main street in front of the supermarket. Tweed turned to Paula.

'It will take you a little while to do your shopping. Do you mind if we drop you here, then drive on to where the mobile transmitter van should be parked? And, Georg, could you go with her as bodyguard? Good. How long do we have, Paula?'

'Thirty minutes at least. It's not the shopping – finding where everything is in a strange supermarket takes the time. It's all right – I've got enough money. See you . . .'

Newman took over the wheel, they drove on and the snow was deeper; drifts were piled up on either side of the road. The car turned a corner and the monastery came into view.

'Park here,' said Tweed. 'That looks like the van.'

'I'm coming with you,' Newman said, struggling into his coat as Tweed slipped on his own topcoat. 'This could be hostile territory.'

Standing by his hotel window Horowitz stiffened, snatched up his binoculars, focused them on the Ingold van. Two men were facing him, talking to the driver. One familiar face came up so clearly he could see light reflecting from a lamp in the street off the lenses of the horn-rim spectacles. A face familiar from his study of photos, of the film of a man who had crossed the Rhine at Laufenburg. *Tweed*.

'What is it?' asked Stieber.

Behind him stood a figure clad in black leather, holding a motor-cyclist's helmet. Bruno Zeller, leader of the team.

'Shut up!' said Horowitz.

His blank expression concealed his excitement, the exhilaration of the chase when he was hunting a target. This was his first live sighting of Tweed. The brilliant Deputy Director of the British Secret Service. The wily man who had eluded the ambush on the Freiburg autobahn, the man who later had escaped the bomb he'd personally placed beneath the Audi. The man who seemed to have gone out of his way to advertise the trail of his flight to Switzerland. He looked so mild.

Horowitz swivelled the binoculars a fraction to the other man. Robert Newman. You're a long way from Basle, my friend, he thought. So now the clan gathers. Excellent. He lowered the binoculars, handed them to the motor-cyclist.

'Zeller, study the smaller man by that builder's van. Then the second man. You'll have to follow them – without them knowing.'

'Who is it?' asked Stieber impatiently.

'Tweed himself at long last. The taller man is Robert Newman, the foreign correspondent. A dangerous man who, according to the file I read, has worked closely with Tweed in the past.'

Stieber, unable to conceal his exultation, unlike Horowitz who had spoken in an offhand manner, slapped his ample thigh.

'We've got him! Why don't you take him now?'

Horowitz gave him a scornful glance. 'First the range is too great. Second we'd never escape in time. Or have you forgotten? We're up in the mountains. Only two ways out. Back to Zürich or along a precipice road to Brunnen.'

'What are we going to do then? Morgan will be furious—'

'Morgan can put his head in a bucket of cold water. We wait. This is not the end of their journey.'

Tweed, hands thrust into his coat pockets, was wandering slowly back and forth across the open space in front of the monastery. Newman caught him up, glancing all round. First he checked the few parked cars. Then he scanned the hotels and restaurants.

'What the devil are you doing?' he demanded. 'Strolling about in the open. A perfect target for a sniperscope rifle.'

'I don't think so.' Tweed was watching his footing on the treacherous slope. 'That photo Marler took in Freiburg near World Security's HQ. Armand Horowitz. Europe's top assassin. Reputed to have killed fifteen men. And not a jot of evidence against him. He's very careful. My guess is he's here now.'

'Then . . .'

'Wait, Bob. You heard Turpil reporting my presence to Morgan in Shopville before his macabre death. The fact that he also mentioned Einsieden. This information will be known by now to Horowitz. But if he attempted to kill me here how far would he get? One phone call from you and Beck would have road-blocks surrounding the whole area. And Horowitz could not escape across the mountains. In the snow? Impossible. He'll know all this. And if possible I want him to see me.'

'In God's name why?'

'So he'll walk into the trap I'm setting for him. That is why I wanted an isolated hideout in the mountains. A cul-de-sac. No way out.'

Tweed and Newman had disappeared from view as Horowitz paced his room. Zeller had left, to instruct his team. Horowitz was frowning, had an abstracted look. Stieber shifted restlessly in a chair.

'Something wrong?'

'Yes. Again with Tweed's behaviour. He puzzles me, and if I don't understand something it worries me. He spent five minutes wandering about in the open, almost as though he was deliberately showing himself. The same pattern as in Laufenburg – on the bridge, at the station. Even in Zürich he puts up at the obvious hotel. What game is he playing?'

'I just hope we don't lose him.'

'Zeller and his team won't lose him. And they can contact us by radio in the Mercedes. We'll go to the car now and wait for news. I don't think it will be long coming.'

'We haven't eaten for hours,' Stieber complained and rubbed a hand over his ample stomach.

'You have a genius for stating the obvious,' Horowitz told him.

Newman drove Tweed the short distance back to the supermarket. Paula, avoiding the sub-zero temperature, was waiting just inside the entrance with Georg and a collection of carrier bags. Tweed and Newman got out, helped Georg to carry the provisions to the car. Paula dived into the rear of the Mercedes and glowed in the warmth. While Georg slipped behind the wheel, Tweed pointed out to Newman a signpost to the left. *Apthal*.

'The road to Brunni . . .'

They soon left Einsiedeln behind and the narrow road ran straight through a wilderness of snow and forest. Paula was reminded of the Black Forest after they had passed through the hamlet of Apthal – in the headlights the black firs closed in on both sides. To the left below the unfenced road ran a small river. The headlight beams shone on it as they turned round a sharp curve. The river was frozen solid, a tumble of wavelets formed of ice and frozen waterfalls.

'This is a pretty lonely area,' Paula commented and pulled her coat collar closer.

'Where we're going,' said Tweed, 'under the Mythen, it's the end of the road. I was here once years ago for a few days.'

'The Mythen?'

'A mountain few foreigners ever see. A magic mountain.'

'Now you're being fanciful . . .'

'But I'm not being fanciful when I say we're being followed.'

It was Newman who had spoken as once again he glanced through the rear window. He still had his coat unbelted and open so he could reach the Magnum quickly. He glanced back once more.

'Do we want the actual chalet where we're staying located?' he asked Tweed.

'Preferably not. Who is following?'

'A motor-cyclist. Like one of those who passed us on the way up to Einsiedeln.'

'I don't think we can ask Georg to drive any faster.'

The Mercedes was speeding over the dangerous surface which shone like glass in the headlights. Newman tapped on the window and Georg opened the screen.

'Mind if I take over the driving now?'

'As you wish. Mr Beck said I was under your orders,' he replied in German.

'Then pull up for a moment and I'll take the wheel. You sit alongside me . . .'

The raw intense cold hit him like a hammer as he climbed out of the car and looked back. The pinpoint of light which was the motor-cyclist's front lamp was stationary. A giveaway. Now he was certain. He got behind the wheel, waited until Georg had fastened his seat belt, then left the engine running and lit a cigarette.

'What are you doing?' Tweed called out.

'A battle of wills. Will he wait there all night in these freezing temperatures – or will he decide to follow from in front . . .'

He had hardly finished the words when the motor-cyclist came speeding up behind them, overtook slowly, and then rode ahead. Newman began driving at speed. The motor-cycle swung round a steep curve, skidded, recovered its balance. Newman pressed his foot down. Paula tensed. Tweed leaned forward, intrigued by Newman's tactics. He drew alongside the motor-cyclist, swung the wheel, tipped the motor-cycle. The machine spun wildly off the road, the rider somersaulted as his machine hit the ice of the frozen river. The motor-cycle skidded for a few yards, met an obstacle, a small waterfall of ice, its momentum vaulted it into the air and then it fell back with a crumping crash. The rider, sprawled on his back, slithered a short distance over the ice, turned painfully on his side.

'You've got a bad memory,' Newman told Georg as he drove on.

'Why? Did something happen?' Georg asked.

40

The Mythen.

The mountain looked enormous by the light of a rising moon. Its slopes, shrouded in deep snow, towered over the scatter of chalets which was Brunni in the valley below. The Mercedes was moving slowly as Horowitz peered out, first at one side, then the other.

'I thought we'd spot where they'd made for by the wheels of their car in the snow,' he observed.

'But there are so many recent turn-offs,' Stieber replied as he drove the vehicle even more slowly.

'There can't have been so much traffic in this isolated spot at this time of the year, at this hour of the night,' said Horowitz.

There were wheel tracks leading off the road in all directions, leading to the chalets dotted about the lower slopes. Horowitz was perplexed. He had no way of knowing that Newman, approaching the end of the road, had deliberately driven off the road at many points, then carefully backed the car on to the road through the same ruts without altering the angle of the wheel.

'We spent too much time trying to get some sense out of the injured motor-cyclist who ended up in the river bed,' Horowitz decided.

'He did manage to tell us the Tweed car rammed him off into the river,' Stieber recalled.

'And bearing in mind where we found him – that it was beyond Apthal – Tweed and his friends must have driven as far as Brunni,' Horowitz insisted. 'They have to be hiding in one of these chalets.'

'A few of them have lights on behind drawn curtains. Why don't we call at each place and see who is inside?'

'Because Tweed is not so foolish as to permit anyone to turn on the lights. He has to be concealed inside one of the chalets without lights . . .'

'Then what are we going to do?'

'We drive back to Apthal and talk to Zeller. By now he must have called up a car to take that injured motor-cyclist to hospital. This is a cul-de-sac. The road ends by that cable station which takes skiers up the mountain. Tweed is trapped.'

From behind the dormer window in the unlighted room on the first floor of the chalet, Newman watched the Mercedes turn in the road and head back towards Einsiedeln. He went downstairs to where all the lights were turned on behind closed curtains, put his night glasses on a table.

'That car had Horowitz inside it. And I'm pretty sure the driver was the same round-headed thug I saw watching at the frontier crossing in Basle. They've driven away.'

'So you were right,' Paula said to Tweed. 'With our decision to put on the lights. I thought you were crazy.'

'There are enough other chalets with lights on. I imagined it would be Horowitz who would come to spy out the land for himself. He'd assume we were inside one of the many chalets without lights. There, that's burning nicely.'

He stood up from the log fire they had found laid, which he had lit and was now crackling and flaming. He rubbed his hands together.

'But don't forget it was a clever idea of Bob's to drive up to all those other chalets and make wheel tracks in the snow. That must have confused them more than somewhat.'

Paula still wearing her coat, sleeves folded up, shivered.

'It's like an ice-box in here. I'll be glad when that fire warms us up. And, by the way, a meal will be ready shortly. Thank heaven they have electric power even out here – and an electric cooker in the kitchen.'

'That's the Swiss for you. All home comforts laid on for us.'

'But what's the next move?' Newman asked. 'We must expect an attack at any time now Horowitz has appeared.'

'Use the phone, report to Arthur Beck that elements of World Security have appeared in Brunni. Meantime I'm going to the van parked in the barn at the back to call the *Lampedusa* on the mobile transceiver.'

Georg, the driver, opened his leather coat and exposed the gun he wore inside a hip holster. 'I'll come with you, if that's all right, Mr Tweed.'

'Be my guest . . .'

'And what about the meal?' Paula protested. 'I suppose you want me to slow it down?'

'You always could read my mind,' said Tweed and smiled as she marched off to the kitchen, head in the air.

Latitude 35. 20 N. Longitude 10. 0. W. Twilight fell over a sea the colour of deep purple. The offshore winds carried a faint musky aroma from the invisible coast of Africa to the east. The *SS Helvetia* was sailing at full speed across an ocean as smooth as a summertime pond.

In the radio room Hoch was receiving – and responding to – the signal from Prefect. By his side sat a seaman who had a reasonable grasp of Morse code. Behind him stood Greg Singer, holding a Luger pistol.

Hoch, tense inwardly, was calm outwardly as he attended to his job and wondered why Prefect never inserted the two trick questions. He completed the transmission, signed off, sagged back in his chair. The seaman by his side nodded approval to Singer, stood up and left the cramped cabin.

'That's a good boy. Now you can have your dinner,' said Singer and walked to the door.

He was opening the door when a fresh transmission started to come through. The American, Hoch, scribbled a note on his pad. Singer ran back, read it. *Signal now from Monitor*. Singer rushed to the doorway, peered down the deserted passageway. The seaman who understood some Morse had disappeared. Singer swore, closed the door, went back to the transmitter, stood over Hoch with his Luger as the radio op communicated.

Hoch responded to the innocent questions. Then came through what he had been waiting for.

'Are you still proceeding on schedule? And how is Tray?'

'We are proceeding on schedule,' Hoch replied. 'End of reply.'

'Is the cargo in good condition? And my regards to White.'

The reply to which should have been a reference to Cowes in the Isle of Wight. Hoch responded.

'The cargo is in excellent condition. Last part of your signal unclear.'

'Signing off. I will call you again as arranged. My regards also to North . . .'

Hoch removed his headset. He turned in his swivel chair and looked up at Singer. The ex-SAS man was watching him with a suspicious expression.

'Why would Monitor suddenly contact us again? We haven't had a signal from him for a while – and then only one. But Prefect signals us daily. What's going on?'

Hoch shrugged. 'I could guess.'

Singer placed the muzzle of the Luger against Hoch's skull and grinned. 'Then guess. And you'd better guess good.'

413

'Two possibilities. One, Monitor has been sick. Second, it's part of the intense security. First a signal from Prefect – then a signal from Monitor from the same transmitter. Just the kind of double-check they made earlier when I was aboard the *Lampedusa*.'

'You guessed good,' said Singer.

He nodded towards the bunk and when Hoch had lain down on it he fastened the handcuff to Hoch's wrist. The other cuff was attached to an iron leg screwed to the deck. Singer left the cabin and met a guard on his way to the bridge.

'Go to the radio op's room and keep an eye on Hoch,' he ordered.

It was very nearly dark when he reached the bridge. The *Helvetia* appeared to be gliding across the surface of the ocean. Captain Hartmann turned to watch Singer as he walked up to the skipper.

'When do we pass through the Straits of Gibraltar?' Singer demanded.

'In the middle of the night. When the lookouts are trying to stop falling asleep. By morning we shall be well inside the Mediterranean.'

'On the last lap. Turkey here we come.'

In London Lance Buckmaster returned from the special room at the Admiralty where he had just communicated with the ship at sea using his code-name, Prefect.

Arriving after dark at the Ministry building he ran up the staircase to his office. It took him only a few minutes to tap out the brief memo to the PM on his typewriter. He read it quickly, initialled it with his flamboyant 'B', put it inside an envelope, sealed the envelope, addressed it: *Highly Confidential. Personal attention of the Prime Minister*, called a messenger and told him to place it direct into the hands of the PM.

414

As with his previous memos on the subject, it was terse and to the point:

1930 hours. Contacted North. Cargo proceeding according to schedule.

Tweed was frozen stiff as he closed the padlocks on the outside of the barn door. Inside the building was the van containing the mobile transceiver he had used to contact the *Lampedusa*. Georg, who had provided the keys for the padlocks, stood beside him, glancing round.

The incredible silence of the night in Brunni was like a sinister pall pressing down on them. Tweed stamped his feet in the snow and paused on their way back to the chalet close by. In the moonlight the immense cone of the Grosse Mythen – the Big Mythen – loomed above them like a threat.

To the right of the 6,000-foot-high mountain rose the Little Mythen, a twin-peaked giant. Little? Its snow-covered slopes soared into the night. There were far higher mountains in Switzerland, Tweed reflected, but isolated above the dead end of the valley, the mountains seemed immense.

'They're dangerous,' Georg remarked in German.

'Why? How?'

'The exceptional weight of snow which has fallen. And with only a slight rise in temperature the danger would increase. The danger of a major avalanche.'

'Let's get inside, it's cold . . .'

The four of them were settled at the table, eating ravenously, when Paula asked Tweed how he had managed with the transceiver.

'You look pretty grim,' she added.

'I contacted the *Lampedusa* more easily than I expected – considering how hemmed in we are by mountains. The news is bad. The ship has definitely been hi-jacked. The radio op didn't respond to either of the trick questions.'

'You're worried, naturally.'

'I'm very worried about what may have happened to the original crew. This is a ruthless opposition we're fighting.'

'One thing I can't understand,' Paula continued. 'Something I've been going to ask you before. Why on earth did the PM agree to *Shockwave* being transported by sea? The Americans have giant cargo planes – one of them surely is big enough to have flown the computer across the Atlantic?'

'The answer is simple.' Tweed's tone became vague and his eyes were half-closed. 'Buckmaster insisted using a plane was unsafe. Planes crash. The PM accepted his argument. Simple as that.'

'Really?' interjected Newman. They were talking in English so Georg wouldn't understand what they were saying. 'Simple you said? Then, if the PM trusts Buckmaster so much, why did she arrange for you also to check the *Lampedusa*'s progress? And why did she agree that only you – not Buckmaster – would know the trick questions to put to the radio op?'

'Normal security precaution,' Tweed replied with the same vagueness. 'Now, let's finish our meal.'

'When we have,' Newman suggested, 'I'd like to phone Marler at his flat in London. If I can get hold of him I want to find out what he's up to back home.'

'Do it,' said Tweed, who spoke as though his mind were miles away.

'And I'd better check with the Schweizerhof in case Harry Butler and Pete Nield have arrived. We do need reinforcements.'

'Do it,' Tweed repeated. 'If they're there, tell them to contact Beck at police headquarters.'

'What on earth for?' asked Paula.

'Just do it,' Tweed repeated again.

'What's that noise?' Newman asked suddenly and jumped up from the table.

He dashed up the open staircase leading to the first floor in the dark. Without switching on any lights he fumbled his way to the bedroom at the front with the large dormer window. He opened the door, slipped inside. The chug-chug of an approaching helicopter was much louder, heading straight for Brunni.

Newman peered out of the uncurtained window and stared. A Sikorsky was hovering over Brunni no more than a hundred feet up. The moonlight shone off its fuselage. An unmarked machine. Like an evil great bird it maintained its hover, rotors whirling, motionless in mid-air.

Newman moved back to the side of the window. The occupants of the machine could be using night glasses. The machine began to move forward slowly, heading for the Mythen. With great skill the pilot turned away from the cliff-like walls which meant death to the machine, cruised slowly over the chalets, then flew off back down the valley towards Einsiedeln.

At a remote sector of Kloten Airport outside Zürich four Sikorsky helicopters were drawn up on the tarmac. Men in leather jackets and heavy trousers tucked inside knee-length boots, were boarding the machines.

Morgan sat inside a Mercedes with Horowitz alongside him. Behind the wheel sat Stieber, clad similarly to the men climbing inside the helicopters. The engine of the car was running and, at Morgan's insistence, the heaters were turned full up.

'What do you hope to achieve by this airborne attack force?' Horowitz enquired ironically.

'They are all trained skiers. Their equipment went aboard earlier. In case of casualties, they're all wearing German clothes and carry no identification. I have thought this out to the last detail.' Morgan was unable to conceal

417

the satisfaction in his voice. He tapped the phone by his side. 'I am now waiting for word from Zeller that he has located the chalet where Tweed and his colleagues are hiding out. We'll wait for days, if necessary.' He gave Horowitz a sideways glance. 'I'm just wondering what you are doing for the big fat fee we're paying you . . .'

Horowitz's left hand gripped Morgan's right wrist. It felt like a steel manacle, screwed tight. Morgan had trouble not wincing. Horowitz's voice was a soft whisper.

'I'm not accustomed to taking personal insults lying down.'

'Sorry. Maybe I didn't phrase that very diplomatically. I withdraw the remark.'

He flexed his fingers as Horowitz released the grip. The assassin continued in the whispering tone so Stieber couldn't hear him.

'I am waiting patiently for Tweed to make one slip. Sooner or later they always make a slip.'

'Tweed has walked into a trap,' Morgan asserted, trying to recover his position. 'Brunni is a cul-de-sac. No way out. Except one road back to Einsiedeln. No route over the top of the mountains at this time of the year . . .'

'I was there,' Horowitz reminded him. 'I was the one who described the geography to Zeller. And someone is walking into a trap.'

Newman came back from the kitchen where he had used the extension phone to avoid Georg overhearing him. He sat at the table and drank fresh coffee poured by Paula.

'Thanks. That's better.' He looked at Tweed. 'I managed to contact Harry Butler at the Schweizerhof. He'd just flown in with Pete Nield. They're going to see Beck first at police HQ. Then they're coming up here right away on motor-cycles – courtesy of Beck. Harry called him while I waited. They're going to wait by the ski-lift at the end of the road until I fetch them. I didn't trust an open phone to give them our exact location.'

'You've done well . . .'

'That's not all. I called Marler and caught him at his flat just before he left. Had a very intriguing conversation with him. Howard has given him a photocopy of the report by the pathologist who examined the dead girl in your flat. It showed traces of skin and blood under one of her fingernails. Same type which stained the sheet. She was group O Positive. You're blood group A, if I remember?' He continued as Tweed nodded, watching him intently. 'The blood group of the stain on the sheet – and under her fingernail – was a rare blood group, AB Negative. The murderer's blood group. All we're needing now is the girl's identity, Marler said.'

'You told him?' Tweed enquired. 'About Sylvia Harman. The call girl from Rennweg, Zürich?'

'No. Never said a word. I still have a funny feeling about Marler. He said you could come home now. Wanted to know where you are. I said somewhere in Europe.'

'Then in God's name why are we staying here any longer?' exclaimed Paula.

'Because we need Arthur Beck's full cooperation,' Tweed told her, 'and he's still not convinced of my innocence. But a full-scale attack on me here *will* convince him.'

'We could fly back,' she protested.

'I'd risk it myself. Alone. But we're dealing with ruthless professionals. Don't forget Armand Horowitz. If he did find out I was flying back he's quite capable of putting a bomb aboard the flight. I can't risk the lives of innocent passengers.'

'Then let's use trains,' she pressed.

'Bombs have been placed on trains. In Italy and other places.'

'Then how the devil do we get back when the time comes?'

'Only one way. And for that we need Beck.'

She turned to Newman. 'I think you're wrong about Marler.'

41

Marler left his London flat after the call from Newman. It was dark as he drove his Porsche to the Buckmaster flat in Belgravia. He was careful to park a good hundred yards from the entrance and in a side street. Leonora answered the speakphone and released the front door.

Half an hour later he smoked a cigarette in her bed as she disappeared into the bathroom wearing only a flimsy silk slip. She had attended to her blonde hair he had mussed up when she reappeared and slipped back under the sheets.

'Have you got a girl friend?' she asked after lighting her own cigarette.

He considered his reply. Unmarried, the love of his life was his Porsche and his independence. He did have girl friends in half a dozen countries in Europe. Variety was the spice of life.

'You're my girl friend,' he said eventually. 'Are you sure we won't be interrupted by an outraged husband?'

'Lance is down on Dartmoor. He flew there early this evening. He has his fun. Why shouldn't I have mine?'

'How did you know that?' he enquired as she slid her naked arm under his back.

'I employed detectives to follow him . . .'

'Dangerous. He's an expert on security.'

'We all spy on each other. People think spies are foreign agents after another country's secrets. But I spy on Lance, and he spies on me. I had the devil of a job to shake the man who was following me this evening, but I managed it. He thinks I'm still back in Threadneedle Street. I left on the lights in my office before I sneaked off to meet you. Have you not realized how many wives spy on their husbands? They check their suits for the wrong hairs, go through their pockets for theatre tickets. And husbands do the same thing with their wives. They notice when their woman spends a lot of extra time on her make-up before she goes out on her own. Suspicion rears its lovely head. And a woman gets to know her husband so well she can tell from his expression when he's been up to something. Because she watches him – *spies* on him.'

If a lot of marriages are like this thank God I'm single, Marler was thinking. She laid her head on his shoulder.

'Did you bring that compromising photograph you promised to give me? The one with Lance lying on a couch with the girl? You did promise.'

'Yes. It's in my jacket. I'll give it to you after I've been to the bathroom. And I suggest you get dressed.'

He closed the bathroom door and heaved a great sigh. Anything to get away from that coaxing, insinuating voice. He knew she might well now be going through his jacket. Let her. He'd checked carefully before he'd left his flat. In his wallet all she'd find would be the fake card showing he was a senior executive of the General & Cumbria Assurance Company, the cover for the SIS.

When he returned she had dressed. She was sitting in front of her dressing-table mirrors, brushing her golden hair. His jacket over the back of a chair was not in exactly the same position as he'd left it. He put on his clothes very quickly. Extracting the envelope from his jacket, he took out the photograph, using a handkerchief to avoid leaving fingertips. She was absorbed in repairing her make-up.

'The photo's on the bed. Are you going to use it?'

'What do you think? Time I scared the louse. I'll say

I've got several copies – and how would the tabloid press like to see it?'

'Up to you,' he warned. 'But if you do go ahead show him it in a public place, a restaurant full of people.'

'My!' She swung round on her stool with a radiant smile. 'You're feeling protective towards me. That really is most sweet of you, Marler.'

Stuff it, he thought, but she was going on again in the same syrupy tone.

'Surely you don't think Lance is capable of violence towards a woman?'

The remark hit him like a blow in the solar plexus. It was so obviously a serious question masked by a whimsical tone. His mind flashed back to what had happened in Tweed's flat. He kept his expression blank.

'I just think he has a hair-trigger temper and you'd be much wiser to have any confrontation in a public place – if you must have one.'

'Don't forget what I said about the managing directorship of World Security. It could become vacant soon. I'm getting really pissed off with that horrid Gareth Morgan. Kiss me again before you go. And think about my offer . . .'

Marler stood on the steps of the portico of the old building with a Georgian façade before he descended onto the pavement. It was because he paused that he saw the small man standing in the portico on the opposite side of the street, a man standing well back and holding something up to his eyes with both hands.

Marler glanced both ways as he hurried down the steps, saw no one as snow began to fall. At speed he continued straight over to the building on the far side. The swiftness of his movement caught the little man off guard. He backed, tried to enter the building, pushing open the door to the empty entrance hall.

Marler followed him, grabbed his right arm above and

below the elbow, pressing his fingers into the nerve centres. The little man, a camera dangling from a strap round his neck, yelped with pain as Marler manoeuvred him inside the hall.

'Make any more noise, try to get free, and I'll break your arm. For no extra charge I'll make it a compound fracture.'

It was the calm, chilling tone of Marler's voice as much as the pain which petrified the man. He stood very still while Marler whispered in his ear.

'Now tell me. Who are you? Who hired you to take my picture?'

Marler waited. He was confident he knew the answer to the second question. If the right answer didn't come up he'd have to exert more pressure; maybe break one arm to start with. The little man, illuminated by a dim wall sconce, had a pasty complexion, a shifty expression, and his suit was frayed at the lapels. He gasped out the words.

'Halbert. Of Halbert Investigations. A private detective.'

Holding him with one hand, Marler reached into his breast pocket. He hauled out a wallet, told the little man to extract the contents with his free arm. With trembling fingers the man found a grubby printed card, showed it to Marler.

Halbert Investigations. Willy Halbert. With an address in Clerkenwell. Not exactly the most high-class district in London. Marler tucked the card inside his own pocket.

'I asked who hired you? Do get it right first time, chum.'

'She didn't say there'd be any rough stuff,' Halbert bleated in an aggrieved tone. 'Mrs Buckmaster. She lives in the house you came out of. Told me to be here an hour ago, to photograph any man who left the building.'

'You did? There was no flash and it's dark.'

Halbert nodded his weak chin downwards to the

423

camera. 'It's an infra-red job. A security camera. Cost me a fortune. Worth more than my office and the sticks of furniture inside it.'

'I see.' Marler paused. 'Now I'll tell you what we're going to do. First, you'll extract the film from the camera and hand it to me. You can do that without spoiling the negative? Good. Next,' he lied, 'I'm an ex-SAS man. I could snap your neck like a celery stalk. So you tell Mrs Buckmaster the film didn't come out. Technical hitch. And you never mention our cosy little conversation. Is it a deal?'

'Anything you say.' Marler had released Halbert, who moved away from the sconce and extracted the film with difficulty. His right arm was hurting him. He handed the cartridge to Marler.

'That's going to cost me money,' he grumbled. 'She won't pay the rest of the fee.'

Carrot and stick. Marler took out his wallet. 'How much was the balance. Don't try and fleece me, my friend.'

'A hundred nicker,' Halbert said quickly.

He stared in surprise as Marler gave him two fifty-pound notes. He couldn't make out this pale-faced, well-spoken intruder whose manner spelt out killer to the petrified Halbert.

'I've had another idea,' Marler continued. 'You phone Mrs Buckmaster and tell her there's a technical hitch with the picture you took, that you've had to give it to a specialist in printing and developing. That it will take up to a week.'

'Then what do I do?' Halbert asked, massaging his arm. 'You have the film.'

'I'll call you. Only then can you tell her it didn't work. No picture.'

Now the stick. Marler's hands moved in a blur. They grasped the injured arm, squeezed it. Halbert yelped again.

'Don't have second thoughts,' Marler warned. 'Bad for your health – to start thinking. And I know where I can always find you down Clerkenwell way.' He released his grip and grinned. 'At least you're not out of pocket with this transaction. Put it down to experience.'

The following morning, as previously arranged, Marler flew from Battersea helipad by the Thames in the heart of London to Dartmoor. As he travelled in Buckmaster's private chopper he reflected on the events of the night before.

We all spy on each other. The seductive Leonora carried her idea to its ultimate conclusion: she even spied on her lover. Before travelling to Battersea, Marler had visited Grubby Grundy, the Soho photographer.

Grundy had developed the film in double quick time, providing Marler with two excellent prints. They showed him leaving the Belgravia building as he'd paused at the top of the steps. And there was no doubt where he was leaving – the number on the pillar had come out clearly.

It didn't take too much imagination to foresee how Leonora might use the picture if the devious need arose. She could tell Lance that Marler had arrived unannounced.

'He said you had sent him. He had a message for me. I never learnt what this bogus message was. He tried to rape me. I hit him with my hair brush and he collapsed. He's small and slim – so while he was unconscious I dragged him into the hall and left him there to recover. It was a frightening experience . . .'

Some such story. And the photograph, 'taken by a reporter who happened to be watching the building,' had been bought for a good sum by Leonora. Or, on some occasion, she might threaten Marler with the cooked-up story. Anything to give her a hold on him.

She also used stick and carrot. Stick was the photograph, backed up by her lying story. Carrot was her veiled offer of the managing directorship of World Security. Was she planning to ditch her husband while she had control of the huge conglomerate, World Security? And the photograph he had given her could be a counter in the elaborate game she was playing. A threat to have it published, to destroy his political career?

I'm walking a tightrope, Marler thought as the chopper lost altitude and the snow-covered ridges of Dartmoor appeared. Ten minutes later they landed on the helipad in the grounds of Tavey Grange. Lance Buckmaster was waiting in his study.

'On time as always. I like that, Marler.'

Buckmaster clad in an immaculate sports jacket and slacks, sat behind his desk, his right leg perched on the desk top. The hand-made brogue shoe gleamed like glass. Buckmaster raised both hands and ran them through the unruly locks of his thick brown hair.

'Help yourself to coffee,' he said in the exaggerated public school voice he used to such good effect in the House of Commons. 'You've located Tweed by now I hope? The problem of his disappearance – to avoid a scandal – has become urgent.'

Marler thought quickly, concentrating on holding the coffee pot. Newman, the bastard, had refused to reveal where Tweed was hiding. But when he had met them both last in Freiburg Tweed had been heading for Switzerland. He added milk. All this took only a few seconds.

'I now know which country he's taken refuge in. And it's not a very big one.' He looked up at Buckmaster who was watching him closely. Time to guess. 'Switzerland. And I know his haunts there.'

Buckmaster clasped his two powerful hands behind his

426

neck and nodded. It had been a test. Morgan had already informed him that Tweed was in some nowhere place up in the mountains called Brunni, south-east of Zürich.

He twisted his foot on the desk while he thought. Morgan was confident he could solve the problem. And for back-up he had Armand Horowitz. But they'd muffed the job twice. Once on the Frieburg autobahn, then with a bomb in the Black Forest. Marler, on the other hand, was the best marksman in Europe.

'Howard is really not up to the mark,' he said suddenly. 'I do think the time is coming when I'll have to appoint his successor.'

He studied his manicured fingernails and Marler was careful not to say anything. Another big carrot was being dangled under his nose.

'You're sure you can smoke out Tweed?' he asked eventually.

'He trusts me. That's the key. The answer to your question is yes.'

'I gather Tweed also has with him that foreign correspondent chap, Newman.'

'I know that,' Marler told him.

'He's SAS trained. I've met that bunch in my capacity as Minister. Suppose Newman gets in the way?'

'We're all expendable.'

Buckmaster adjusted the crease in his slacks. 'And Tweed also has Paula Grey with him.'

'We're all expendable,' Marler repeated in his cold voice.

Buckmaster whipped his leg off the desk, stood up, straightened his jacket. 'Then you'd better get after them. Finish the job, for God's sake. Sorry to drag you down here, but it's the only safe place for a chat.' He gave his wolfish grin. 'And don't forget what I said about Howard's job needing a replacement.'

'I'll fly to Switzerland today.' He paused before he left

427

the study. 'I read a bit in the paper about a Dr Rose being killed in a road accident. Wasn't he the pathologist who carried out the post-mortem on that dead girl found in Tweed's flat?'

Buckmaster froze for a second, then shrugged his wide shoulders; a powerfully built man, the Minister for External Security.

'How did you know about Dr Rose?'

'Howard mentioned he was still waiting for the pathologist's report. Named him as a Dr Rose from St Thomas's.

'I see. Yes, I read the same bit myself. Dreadful how many of these hit-and-run drivers there are these days.'

Marler stared out of the window as the chopper flew him back to London. But he saw nothing of the snow-streaked countryside. In a mental trance, he recalled recent events.

He was being offered the top job by Buckmaster. And within the past twenty-four hours Leonora had suggested he could be the next managing director of a vast conglomerate. The income for each post would be enormous.

He pictured himself buying the latest Maserati, even a Lamborghini. Racing along the autobahns in Germany, overtaking everything in sight. A red job. It would drive his girl friends into a frenzy, sitting by his side. A leap into the stratosphere of the Service. Or the world of business where you lived like a king. Dreams . . .

The nightmare would be finding Tweed inside Switzerland.

PART THREE

The Killing – Shockwave

42

Langley, Virginia, USA. Cord Dillon, Tweed's opposite number, Deputy Director of the CIA, picked up the phone with his own special number. Prepared for most things, the crag-faced officer received a shock.

'Is that Cord Dillon? Good. This is Monitor calling. I've grim news. The *Lampedusa* has been hi-jacked in mid-Atlantic.'

'Jesus! Where are you calling from, Tweed? There have been some funny rumours about you . . .'

Dillon was a tall, well-built man with a thatch of thick brown hair, clean-shaven, and above a strong nose his eyes were a startling blue and ice-cold. Sunken cheeks emphasized the cheekbones and the mouth was wide, thin-lipped, and expressed determination.

'Just for once, Dillon, listen. Don't worry about the rumours. I have enemies. You know that. I've contacted the *Lampedusa* three times now. On none of these transmissions did the radio op answer the trick questions.'

'Sounds like you're right . . .'

'I am right. You've distributed those silhouettes of the *Lampedusa* as we planned two months ago?'

'Sure I have. To every naval ship in the world. In sealed envelopes as you suggested. Only to be opened and the signal acted on when I send the word . . .'

'Send the word. I want you especially to alert the US Sixth Fleet in the Med based on Naples. They're to look for a freighter with that silhouette – bearing in mind the hi-jackers may have altered its appearance, and its name, but they can't change the basic silhouette. Once located, the vessel must be stopped, boarded.'

'Listen here, Tweed. What makes you so Goddamn certain it's heading for the Mediterranean?'

'Because from its original course it only had two alternative routes to reach Russia. One was to head north for the Barents Sea and the ice-free port of Murmansk. It wouldn't go that way – because of the NATO naval exercise, *Sea-Trap*, now in progress. The other route is via Gibraltar – sailing through the straits in darkness and linking up with a Soviet warship in the Eastern Mediterranean. That's the route I'd have chosen.'

'You sound Goddamn sure of yourself, Tweed . . .'

'I am. So, for Pete's sake, alert the Sixth Fleet. Now!'

The connection was broken and Tweed was gone. Dillon sat at his desk for a couple of minutes and thought. He wore his plain grey suit, which was neatly pressed, but clothes were something you simply had to throw on in the morning. Then he decided, reached for the red phone.

'Get me Admiral Tremayne at the Pentagon. Urgently. If he's in one of those endless conferences, drag him out. Tell him we have to send a *Leopard* signal. That will move him.'

One hour later a flotilla of vessels from the US Sixth Fleet got under way from Naples, each ship heading on a different course to sweep the Mediterranean. The commander of each vessel had opened his sealed *Leopard* order. He studied the terse signal, looked at the stack of photocopies of the silhouette of the *Lampedusa*, and distributed them to selected officers and other rank lookouts.

Among the flotilla despatched from Naples was the missile-armed Kidd-class destroyer DGG 997 *Spruance*. Its commander, Hank Tower, was a short, thick-set man, clean-shaven and with an easy smile. His course was due south for the Straits of Messina. Passing through them he would turn east, heading towards Crete and the Eastern Mediterranean. Speed: 30-plus knots.

The Soviet heavy missile cruiser *Sverdlov* had left its base at Novorossiisk and sailed across the Black Sea. It was now approaching the Turkish Bosphorus strait. It would pass down the strait in the night, proceeding across the Sea of Marmara and down the Dardanelles into the Eastern Mediterranean. A rendezvous east of Crete had already been established.

Prior to its departure, there had been a special meeting of the Politburo in Moscow. President Gorbachev had expressed doubts about the operation. But his military adviser had urged him to seize this unique opportunity to acquire for the defence of the Motherland the new Strategic Defence Initiative, *Shockwave*, perfected by the British and the Americans.

'There must be no major confrontation,' Gorbachev had warned.

'The *Sverdlov* will rendezvous with the *Helvetia* and escort it by night back into the Black Sea. After that, the *Helvetia* and its vital cargo will simply disappear. No one will ever know what happened to the original *Lampedusa*.'

'Just so long as there is no crisis,' Gorbachev had insisted.

He knew he had no choice but to agree. There were more than enough hostile elements massing against his *glasnost* policy. To alienate the military establishment could well end in his being removed from power.

Latitude 36. 54. N. Longitude 16. 30. E. The *Helvetia* was sailing south of the Straits of Messina on an easterly course. Its speed was fifteen knots and there was a heavy swell under an overcast sky. It pitched and tossed gently under the swell.

It was four o'clock in the afternoon and not the kind of day you expected in the Mediterranean, Singer thought as he clung to a rail on the bridge. Behind the wheel, Captain Hartmann reflected that the ex-SAS man was tireless. He seemed to get by on three hours' sleep a night. The rest of the time he was prowling the ship, checking, checking, checking . . .

'Will we make the rendezvous on time?' Singer called out.

'It all depends on if the weather eases. I guarantee nothing. The met forecast is not good.'

'Make this old tub move faster.'

'This old tub is a freighter. She is moving at top speed, Mr Singer.'

Hartmann was always polite. In his position many would have pointed out he was the skipper. And Hartmann was also a careful man. Singer carried a loaded Luger shoved down inside his belt and had already displayed his ruthlessness. Hartmann was secretly appalled by the massacre of the crew of the *Lampedusa*. No one had told him about that in advance.

Singer nodded and left the bridge for the aft deck. He had a problem. He was worried about what would happen when they made contact with the Russian vessel. Would the Soviets let him – or any of the crew aboard the vessel – go free?

He was beginning to doubt it. Clinging on to a rail as he descended a companionway, he thought of the fifty thousand pounds – half the agreed fee – he had deposited for this job in a Luxembourg bank. Was it worth risking disappearing for ever inside Russia for the other fifty thousand?

He stood at the bottom of the steps and stared at the surf-topped grey waves rolling towards the vessel. No sign

434

of land anywhere. The second problem was how to escape from the ship.

In its circuit two hundred miles above the earth the American satellite *Ultra* passed over the Black Sea. Its sophisticated cameras recorded everything happening below. A continuous flow of information was passed down to Langley, Virginia.

A specialist hurried into Cord Dillon's office. He laid two prints on the Deputy Director's desk.

'What the hell do these show?' Dillon demanded.

'That tiny black mark has been identified by our analysts. It is the Russian missile cruiser *Sverdlov* approaching the Bosphorus. On its way to the Mediterranean would be my guess.'

'Jesus!' Dillon grabbed his red phone. 'Get me the Pentagon. Admiral Tremayne. Tell him it's a *Leopard* emergency. To call me back. Fastest.' He slammed down the receiver, muttering to himself. 'God help us. Tweed was right . . .'

It was dark outside the chalet at Brunni. The moon had gone down, the temperature had dropped again. Newman piled logs on the fire as Tweed sat with Paula and drank more coffee.

It was the middle of the night. No one had felt like going to bed. Georg was upstairs, on watch by the dormer window. Newman had suggested a duty roster for a watch to be kept on the road back up the valley. Georg had dismissed the idea, saying he'd slept during the day. The night seemed endless as they waited cooped up inside the chalet.

'I managed to get through to America on the phone,' Tweed remarked. 'Last night. I reached Cord Dillon.'

435

'That rough diamond,' snapped Paula.

'That rough diamond is a very able man. In an emergency he can react with the speed of light. You might as well know he was going to contact the US Sixth Fleet to search for the *Lampedusa*.'

'Assuming it is headed for the Mediterranean?'

'Knowing the distances involved, the speed of the *Lampedusa*, I'm gambling that ship is now well inside the Med.'

'Even if you're right, it's like searching for a needle in a haystack,' Paula objected.

'Not quite. The Sixth Fleet has a lot of ships. I have done all I can. It's the original crew of the *Lampedusa* I'm worried about, that I have on my conscience.'

'Time to change the subject,' Newman said briskly, brushing his hands together as he stood up from the fire. 'In the general excitement of coming up here I forgot to tell you a couple of things.' He opened his briefcase and brought out a sheaf of photocopies. 'These are other documents I asked Turpil to photograph when we broke into World Security at Basle.'

'Don't mention Turpil,' Paula protested. 'I can't get out of my mind that horrible moment when he disappeared beneath that tram.'

'He was betraying Tweed,' Newman reminded her. 'He asked for what he got.'

'What are these?' Tweed asked quickly, picking up the photocopies.

'Evidence of how World Security operates. Their so-called Research & Development Division is the spearhead they use when they bid for another company. To build up their huge conglomerate Buckmaster and Morgan have used sabotage, blackmail and intimidation on a huge scale.'

'I see what you mean,' Tweed commented, skimming through the copies. 'And you're right.'

'That's really awful,' said Paula. 'Think of the misery

they must have caused to countless people. That's awful,' she repeated.

'That's big business,' Newman told her. 'A lot of conglomerates operate that way these days. Human beings don't exist. Only winners and losers.'

'And what was the other thing you were going to tell me?' Tweed enquired.

Newman glanced at Paula. 'When I was talking to Marler he also told me the pathologist who examined Sylvia Harman's body from your flat in Radnor Walk was killed in a so-called hit-and-run accident.

'So-called?' Tweed asked sharply.

'Marler said it was cold-blooded murder.'

'That does it.' Tweed jumped up from his chair and looked at Paula. 'I've been unhappy ever since you insisted on coming with me. We have to find a way of getting you away from this chalet and back to Zürich. Beck will find a safe way of transporting you back home.'

'We've had this argument before,' Paula reminded him. 'I would like to know what's changed.'

'Nothing. But the murder of this pathologist ...' He looked at Newman. 'Who was he? Do you know?'

'A Dr Rose from St Thomas's.'

'The murder of Dr Rose,' Tweed continued, 'highlights the fact that World Security will stop at nothing to eliminate me – and any witnesses. You're going back to Zürich.'

'Really?' Paula extracted the Browning automatic from her shoulder-bag, checked the safety catch, turned the weapon in her hand. 'Why do you think I'm carrying this? And why are we still waiting here?'

'I've already told you,' Tweed said in an exasperated tone. 'An attack will be launched on us here soon. I need that to happen to convince Beck. Damnit, I've already explained it to you.'

'And I've explained I'm sticking with you until this is all over.' She paused. 'One way or the other. The only way you'll get me out of here is to carry me. You're going to need all the support you can get. There are few of us with weapons anyway.' She checked her watch. 'My turn to relieve Georg on the night watch. And the two of you had better get some sleep. See you . . .'

Newman waited until she had disappeared up the stairs. 'She has a point, Tweed. She takes her job very seriously. You send her away now and she'll never forgive you.'

'But at least she'll be alive . . .'

'You think so? What do you think she might run into going back down the valley – even if we did give her the car?'

The attack Tweed had predicted came just before dawn broke.

43

Paula, stiff from sitting on a chair in front of the dormer window, a pair of night-glasses slung round her neck, was pacing round the bedroom when she heard the machines coming.

She ran to the window, stood to one side, and waited. The sound of the approaching engines was growing louder in the stillness of the night. She heard the creak of the door opening behind her, swung round, the Browning held in both hands and pointed at the shadowy figure.

'Don't shoot the cook, he's doing his best.' Newman said.

'In case you've forgotten, *I'm* the cook. And you shouldn't creep up on me like that. You're supposed to be sleeping.'

'I heard those motor-bikes coming. Maybe it's starting.'

'Of course! I couldn't identify the sound.'

With Newman alongside her, she turned back to the window, the gun still in her hand, the safety catch slipped on. The engine sounds were now a roar. A headlight shone on the snow below the chalet. Slowing down, the large motor-cycle came into view. The rider wore a black leather suit, helmet and goggles.

'Oh, God!' she exclaimed, 'it's one of those thugs who passed our Mercedes on the way up from Zürich.'

'But what's he doing? Give me the glasses.'

The motor-cyclist had stopped, the powerful engine purring, then it swung across the opposite side of the road and carefully followed one of the false trails Newman had made when they first arrived. The ruts had frozen solid. The cyclist stopped, raised both hands, took off his helmet and scanned the area.

'That's Harry Butler,' said Newman. 'And if I'm not mistaken here come Pete Nield.'

The second motor-cyclist appeared and performed a copycat manoeuvre of the tactic carried out by Butler. He nudged the spiked wheels of his machine inside another set of frozen ruts created by Newman. Paula grasped what they were doing immediately.

'Nobody following them will be able to detect where they've disappeared to . . .'

She was talking into air: Newman had dashed out of the room and downstairs. He grabbed up his coat, threw it on and ran out of the front door and down the icy steps. Both Butler and Nield had wheeled their machines out of sight behind the chalet on the far side of the road.

'We're in the chalet opposite,' he told Butler as he almost collided with him round a corner.

'I know. Beck told us, drew a map. And he gave us the key to this chalet which is another safe house.'

Nield appeared from the back of the chalet in time to overhear the remark. 'What's safe about this place?' he asked. 'It's a dead end – and I emphasize the word *dead*.'

'Come across and meet Tweed. He woke up when he heard you coming . . .'

The two men were a contrast in personality. Butler was well-built, in his thirties, clean-shaven, deliberate in his movements and speech and poker-faced. Nield was a few years younger, slimmer and he sported a neat black moustache. He was agile, quick-thinking and sometimes impulsive. They complemented each other and made a good team with Butler normally taking the decisions.

As they plodded over the iron-hard snow each man carried a canvas satchel looped over his shoulder, a heavy satchel which bulged. Tweed, fully dressed, met them at the head of the steps and ushered them inside. He came straight to the point.

'Welcome. I'm relieved to see you. We're expecting a full-scale onslaught from the opposition any time now. How did you get on with Beck?'

Newman was piling more logs on the fire; a freezing wave of air had penetrated the chalet during the short time the door had been left open. Butler and Nield stripped off their jackets, warmed their hands in front of the fire. Newman checked his watch.

'Time for Georg to take over watch duty from Paula. I'll go wake him up.'

Georg appeared at that moment, coming down the stairs from the second bedroom at the rear. He stared at Butler and Nield, nodded to Tweed and went into the kitchen to wash his face with cold water. No better way of getting the corpuscles racing after a short deep sleep. He went back upstairs and Paula joined them.

Nield greeted her with a grin and a kiss on the cheek as Butler dropped his satchel on the table and began to unpack.

'Beck,' Butler informed Tweed, 'was surprisingly helpful. I got the impression he's begun to worry about you. We tried to persuade him to provide us with hand-guns, but he refused. Instead he supplied these. They could be more effective – he told us he'd given you weapons.'

'That's right,' said Paula. 'But what on earth are those?'

Butler had produced a short-barrelled, wide-mouthed and ugly-looking object like a large squat pistol. He extracted a second object, a similar instrument but with an even wider mouth, followed by large shells.

'This one is a tear-gas pistol. And this one is a smoke gun. Acrid, choking smoke – and lots of it from one shell.'

'Me, too.' Nield grinned again at Paula and took the same objects from his own satchel. 'And back home Butler has given me lessons in how to ride a Honda on skid-pans. Most stimulating.'

'Sounds dangerous to me,' Paula commented.

'You should see Butler skidding at speed with a sharp turn. His machine is tilted at an angle of forty-five degrees and he keeps control. A real tearaway. That's what he's been teaching me . . .'

'I doubt if you could use those machines here,' Tweed said.

'The surface is ideal,' Butler commented. 'We tested it on the way here from Apthal. Went off the road up the slopes. The snow is frozen hard. Now, what's the pro-gramme?'

No word about what had happened in London, Paula noted. No reference to the dead girl in Tweed's flat. No doubt about whether Tweed was innocent or guilty. They'd just come to help out their chief, to do their job. She blessed them.

'We face an attack on us by a determined and profes-sional opposition,' Tweed told them. 'They want to kill me. So far they have tried twice. This third assault, I predict, will be quite something.'

441

'So we'll sort out the sods when they come,' Nield responded cheerfully.

'How about weapons?' Butler asked. 'Beck said you had some.'

Newman produced his Magnum .45. Paula fetched her Browning from her shoulder bag. Butler nodded at Newman.

'That's quite a cannon. But it's still only two handguns. Right?' He looked at Nield. 'We're going to have to spring a surprise on our expected visitors. Tactics rather than firepower.' He switched his gaze to Tweed and Newman. 'If you agree, Pete and I will take up quarters with our motor-bikes in that chalet across the way. If they come down the valley we have them in a crossfire. If they come down the slope behind here out of the forest Pete and I will go up after them. Surprise is worth a lot of firepower.'

For Butler it was a major speech. Tweed glanced at Newman who nodded. 'I like it. Harry has the right idea.'

'Then we do that,' Tweed decided.

'See you then.'

Butler and Nield repacked their satchels, looped them over their shoulders. Nield winked at Paula who gave him her warmest smile. Then they were gone, the front door slammed shut. The only sound for a short time was the crackle and spitting of the logs in the heavy silence.

'I'm so glad they've arrived,' Paula said. 'It gives us a fighting chance.'

A slim one, Newman thought, but he didn't say anything.

No one slept any more. Paula made more coffee. Georg came down briefly to report smoke rising from the chimney on the chalet opposite. Tweed told him not to worry and he went back to his post.

The chalet had the same musty odour of the lodge they

442

had occupied in the Black Forest, an odour which mingled with the scent of burning logs. Tweed paced around a lot, his brow furrowed.

'I wish now I had asked Beck for a gun,' he said at one stage.

'You'd only have shot yourself in the foot,' Newman joked.

'That's rubbish,' Paula snapped. 'He's a first-rate shot.'

'Lost your sense of humour?' Newman enquired and grinned.

She put her tongue out at him.

The monk appeared about one hour before dawn. He drove in from the direction of Apthal in an Audi and continued slowly past the chalets to the ski station at the end of the road. Paula ran up the stairs and then called down for Newman to come up.

Newman entered the front room where Georg and Paula stared out of the dormer. It took him a minute to adjust his vision to the night. The chalet opposite was in darkness.

'Look what he's doing,' Paula said. 'It doesn't make any sense.'

A door opened in the stationary Audi and a short figure clad in the robe and cowl of one of the Benedictine monks walked to the ski station building and stared up at the Mythen. Both hands were clasped in an attitude of prayer. It was one of the most bizarre sights Paula had ever witnessed.

'What on earth is going on?' she asked in German.

'Some of the monks have a mystic feeling about the mountain,' Georg told her. 'Personally I can never work out where one begins and the other ends – religion and mysticism.'

'In the freezing cold? At this hour?'

Newman's tone expressed sheer incredulity. Georg nodded and smiled.

'Suffering is their pleasure, their way of life . . .'

*   *   *

By the cable station Stieber stood motionless. He had grabbed a Benedictine monk on his way back to the monastery in a side street earlier the previous evening. In what was really a deserted alleyway, he had hauled the monk inside a doorway, one arm round his neck in a hammerlock. He had increased the pressure, intending to truss up the unconscious man and to hide him. He had felt his grip loosen and the neck had flopped sideways. Checking his pulse, he had found none. He had broken the monk's neck.

Couldn't be helped. Stripping off the monk's robe, footwear and cowl, he had thrust the body into a trough of frozen water. The weight of the corpse had broken the ice and Stieber had thrust it down deep. The ice had almost immediately formed afresh, sealing in the monk. The man's face stared up at him as he waited to make sure the ice was thickening. Then he had hurried away, stuffing the clothing into the boot of the Audi.

Now he bowed his head, concealed beneath the cowl. Turning slowly, he surveyed the chalets. As he began to swing round Newman jumped to one side of the window. Without asking why Paula moved quickly out of view of the other side.

'Get away from the window, Georg!' Newman hissed in German.

Georg moved, but his reaction was a little slow. Down at the ski station Stieber saw movement behind the uncurtained dormer window. He was careful not to stare at the chalet as, head bowed, he walked slowly back to his car. At this hour why should anyone be watching from a window in an unlit room? He counted chalets, marked mentally the position of the one where he had seen movement, climbed back behind the wheel of the Audi and drove back slowly the way he had come.

'Well, now I've seen everything,' exclaimed Paula. 'What do you think, Bob?' Tweed's voice.

Newman turned round. He'd forgotten how silently Tweed could move. Tweed stood to one side of the room where he had a view down through the dormer window towards the ski station.

'I think it's damned peculiar,' Newman said savagely. 'A monk driving here in the middle of a sub-zero night – just to stare up at the mountain. Convincing?'

'I think not,' Tweed agreed. 'A monk. It's a perfect disguise for a man to reconnoitre the area. I sense the hand of Horowitz.'

'So they could be arriving any time now,' Paula said grimly.

'Any time now,' Tweed repeated.

Stieber drove back less than a mile from Brunni and pulled in to the side of the road where a Mercedes stood parked, its engine ticking over. A short distance behind it stood a second Mercedes.

Sitting by Morgan, the driver in the first machine, Horowitz blinked through his spectacles as Stieber approached, opened the rear door and slipped inside, slamming the door shut.

'Well?' asked Morgan.

'I've located the chalet where they're holed up. Very near the ski station – the last but one chalet on the left from this direction.'

'You're sure?' demanded Horowitz sceptically.

'No more of that, please,' Morgan burst out. 'Stieber is reliable. I'm calling Kloten now. Let's get it over with.'

He reached for the microphone, gave the call sign, received an immediate response and gave the order.

'Operation Mountain Drop . . . Objective is . . . Repeat, commence Operation Mountain Drop. Confirm. Over . . .'

The confirmation came through from Zeller, brief, terse,

then Morgan hooked the mike back over the cradle. He checked his watch.

'They'll launch their attack just before dawn. Perfect. A man's morale is at its lowest ebb. So is his alertness. We may catch them all asleep.'

'And what about Zeller's motor-cycle corps?' Horowitz asked in his ironic tone.

'I sent them back to Kloten to join the assault team. What kind of reaction do you think we'd get from the locals with a fleet of motor-cyclists vrooming about at this hour? One of the chalet owners might even call the police.'

'And choppers don't make any noise? Is that what you're saying?'

'Of course they do. But in this weather you get the Rescue Service sending out choppers at any hour if they hear someone is in trouble on the mountains.'

'Theoretically you seem to have thought of everything.'

'*Theoretically?*' Morgan queried irritably.

'If Zeller withdrew his motor-cycle team who were those two motor-cyclists who drove past us towards Brunni like bats out of hell?'

'How do I know? Maybe Zeller decided to send a couple back to reinforce the assault. I give Zeller a pretty free hand.'

'I need this car solely for my own use,' Horowitz announced. 'You can use the one behind us.'

'Thank you very much. May I ask why?'

Stieber called out from the rear of the car. 'God, it's hot in here.' He had pulled back the cowl off his head but it was impossible to remove the robe. 'And about this use of transport. I need a car to take me back to the agreed look-out point beyond Apthal. So I need transport just as much as Horowitz seems to.'

'Use the Audi again,' snapped Morgan. He turned to Horowitz. 'I asked you why you want this car for your own use.'

'Because I always work alone. No passengers. That's final.'

'If you say so.'

Morgan was feeling jittery. He was convinced Horowitz had not given him the real reason for his insistence on using the Mercedes by himself. He sighed as he reached for the door handle and glared at his companion.

'It's all yours then. I suppose you're getting ready to run if the going gets tough.'

Horowitz ignored the sneer as he looked over his shoulder at Stieber who was clambering out of the car.

'What did you do with the original owner of those clothes? I told you to tie him up and leave him inside any empty shop so they'll find him in the morning.'

'Didn't work out like that.' Stieber sniggered. 'By chance his neck was broken. Had to hide the body somewhere. Shoved it in one of those water troughs. Had to use the body weight to break the ice. You should have seen him as the ice froze over him and his face stared up through it.'

Horowitz hid his disgust. Stieber was a man who enjoyed his work. A dangerous attitude. For Horowitz, killing a target was a clinical operation to be carried out efficiently without emotion. He was even more glad to have the car to himself. The discovery of a murdered monk would set the police on fire.

Nor was he too confident of Morgan's assault plan. From Horowitz's point of view it would at least serve one purpose – it would smoke Tweed out of his refuge. And I'll be waiting, he thought as Morgan stepped out of the car and shivered with the cold. Horowitz called out to him before he slammed the door.

'What is it now?' snapped Morgan.

'Just remember you're dealing with Tweed.'

'The guy's not superhuman.'

447

'He is the most dangerous and wily antagonist I've ever been up against.'

Silence. Like the grave. It was getting on Paula's nerves. The bloody silence of the mountains. The fire glowed but had stopped crackling, as though waiting. Tweed sat at the table, going through the photocopies of the documents in the safe at World Security in Basle, the documents recording sabotage, blackmail, intimidation. A damning indictment.

The front door opened and Newman came inside, locked and bolted it. He had been double-checking the heavy closed shutters protecting the windows on the ground floor. He started up the stairs.

'Where are you going?' asked Paula to break the silence.

'To check the rear bedroom now no one is sleeping there . . .'

On the landing he opened the door, switched on a pencil flash. The curtains were closed over this dormer. Walking across the room, he switched off the flash, drew back the curtains. He opened the first window, then the second one beyond which served as double glazing. The view was up a shallow slope of virgin snow. At the top great fir trees were staggered at intervals, row upon row, one behind the other. That was when he heard the faint chug-chug sound.

He listened as the noise came steadily closer. Nothing to see – the trees obscured the view. He shut both windows, went back to the door and ran downstairs. The swift clatter of his feet made both Paula and Tweed stare at him.

'I think they're coming at last,' Newman reported. 'More than one chopper from the sound of it. Approaching us from the back and behind the trees . . .'

'I'll go up and warn Georg in the front room,' said Paula, jumping up. 'Hadn't you better go across to Butler and Pete Nield?'

Georg appeared half-way down the stairs. Paula noticed he had unbuttoned his holster flap, exposing the butt of his Walther. Tweed had stood up from the table, was cleaning his glasses, his head cocked to one side.

'I heard them from the front,' said Georg. 'I'd better get back up. Agreed?'

'Agreed,' said Newman. He looked at Tweed. 'I'll watch the back. No need to warn Butler. He'll have heard them coming.'

'What about me?' Paula asked, the Browning in her hand.

'You stay down here . . .'

'For safety?' she flared.

'No.' Newman's voice was rough. 'To take care of the windows down here. They may try to smash in one of the shutters – so don't think you're not in the line of fire. You are . . .'

He ran back upstairs and into the rear bedroom. Opening both windows again, he listened. The steady chug-chug of several machines was close but still he couldn't see a sign of them. He leaned out of the window, peered round the edge of the dormer at the roof. A few places he could get a hand-hold. He sat on the edge of the window and thanked God he was wearing a long heavy windcheater. The cold was already penetrating through to his backside. He put one foot on the ice-filled gutter, tested its strength. Holding on to both sides of the window he put both feet on the gutter, eased his weight on it. The gutter held. He hauled himself back inside, closed the outer window. Now he could hear the chopper engines clearly through the closed window. They were landing. Out of sight.

In the living-room Tweed put on his glasses. He went to the fire and picked up the iron poker. It was a weapon of a sort. He glanced at Paula.

'At least the waiting is over,' he remarked.

'I'm glad. Now we'll know the worst.' She corrected that. 'Soon they'll know the worst, whoever they are.'

Upstairs in the front room Georg had left the door open – as had Newman in the rear room – so they were able to shout to each other. Newman held his Magnum .45 with spare mags laid out on the inner ledge. The sound of the helicopters flying in had stopped. They were on the ground. The loaded pause – while they prepared something nasty.

It went on, the pause. Nothing happening. No sound, no sight of any intruders. Newman's night vision was pretty good now. To the east streaks of pallid light appeared, the first of the dawn. Perfect timing on the part of the attackers. They'd be coming soon.

He saw them suddenly. Through half-closed eyes a twitch of movement appeared high up amid the trees. Dark figures moving at astonishing speed. Zigzagging in and out among the tree trunks. Of course! He shouted back to Georg and they heard him downstairs.

'It's a ski attack! Coming at us through the forest . . .'

Tweed appeared at the door as though by magic. Holding his poker, he joined Newman who was crouched over the window, holding the Magnum in two hands. The tiny figures were growing larger. They skied with great skill. Tweed lifted his glasses, saw each man carried an automatic weapon looped over his shoulders. A formidable force.

He heard a roaring sound from the other side of the chalet. Dashing across the room and the landing, he ran to the window where Georg stood, Walther in his hand. The front door of the chalet on the far side of the road was open. Butler was manoeuvring his powerful motor-cycle through the doorway, down the steps, swung on to the saddle and raced over the road and up the slope past Tweed's chalet. Nield followed on his own machine, but headed for the other side of the chalet.

Tweed reached Newman's window in time to see Butler riding his Honda up the slope to the left as Nield appeared to the right. They were executing a pincer movement on the flock of skiers who had emerged from the trees and were converging on the chalet. And Butler had been right: the surface of the snow slopes was perfect for the spiked wheels of the motor-cycles. Butler was roaring up the slope, out-flanking the advancing skiers. Way over to their right Nield was executing a similar manoeuvre.

'I'd better get downstairs with Paula,' Tweed said as Georg joined Newman.

He hurried agilely down the treads. Paula was crouched behind the table, holding her Browning. She glanced over her shoulder.

'What's happening at the front?'

Tweed told her. She smiled grimly and took a firmer grip on her weapon. It was again a question of waiting to see what happened.

Upstairs in the rear bedroom Georg threw open both of the other windows and crouched beside Newman. Zeller, clad in black leather like his men, leading the onslaught, saw the open window. He slowed down, stopped, whipped his rifle off his shoulder and aimed at the window. He was still out of range of a handgun. Nield rode his bike with one hand for a few seconds, raised the other, holding one of the pistols, fired. In the greyish light Newman clearly saw the shell arc through the air, land close to the leader. Black smoke poured into the air, became a cloud, enveloping Zeller. Newman heard the *crack!* of a shot which went wild.

Several skiers behind Zeller changed direction as the black cloud spread. Butler was now guiding his machine inside the trees, zigzagging as the skiers had done, taking the high ground. Over to the right Nield also disappeared inside the firs. The skiers appeared confused, leaderless.

Then Zeller skied out of the cloud, shaking his head,

451

coughing as he cleared his lungs of the acrid smoke. The whole group halted briefly. Newman glanced at Georg.

'They're going to change tactics . . .'

The words were hardly out of his mouth when the skiers were on the move again. Earlier they had moved down in a phalanx. Now they separated over a wide area. A more difficult, widespread target. Ski-ing down towards the chalet individually.

Several skied a long way to the left, heading down for the road. And the sound of the motor-cycles had vanished. It was briefly so quiet Newman could hear the swish of the on-coming skiers. He waited for them to come within range.

'Some of them will come at the side of the chalet,' Georg warned.

'I know. They'll cope downstairs . . .'

One of the skiers who had circled round the chalet carried a crowbar. His companion was armed with a grenade. The skier with the crowbar skied up to a side window, inserted the bar where the shutters met and heaved.

The first warning of lethal danger downstairs was when both Paula and Tweed heard the wrench of the crowbar. Tweed, grasping the poker tightly, ran to the side of the window. There was a terrifying splintering noise and both shutters flew outwards. A gloved hand grasped the window ledge to haul the owner inside. Tweed brought the poker down on the hand with all his strength. The unseen man screamed. The hand disappeared.

His companion, much taller, grenade in his hand, appeared at the window. He wore a ski-mask and goggles. Paula stared at the horrific apparition, saw the right hand move back to a throwing position. She fired twice in rapid succession. The skier, who had taken out the pin, fell out of sight. There was an explosive detonation. Miraculously the glass of the windows remained intact but its surface was smeared with a red stain. Tweed glanced out, saw below a goulash of dark red flesh and bone staining the snow. He reached out, hauled the shutters closed.

'What happened?' gasped Paula.

'Hand grenade. Finished them both off.'

No point in going into the gory details. He smiled his admiration for her. She nodded, shoved a fresh mag into the weapon so it was fully loaded. It went very quiet again for a short time.

At the rear window upstairs Newman calculated the first skiers would be within range any second. Then he heard the roar of the motor-cycles coming again, speeding out of the forest as they raced for the skiers at top speed. A clutch of skiers had formed opposite the rear of the chalet for a mass onslaught. Butler raised his pistol, fired a projectile. It landed in front of the enemy group. White vapour billowed in a cloud, creating a wall between attackers and chalet. The lead skiers reached it and suddenly there was chaos as the tear-gas hit them. Choking, blinded, they fell, skis projecting criss-cross upwards.

The second line of skiers curved to left and right to avoid their fallen comrades. One halted, raised his rifle. There was a *thuck!* close to Newman's head. A bullet had lodged in the woodwork. He swung his Magnum, took swift aim with both hands gripping the butt, pulled the trigger twice. The skier flung up his arms, dropped the rifle, collapsed backwards. Georg aimed at another skier standing, rifle thrust into his shoulder, fired three times. The skier sagged, fell face forward.

Butler and Nield were now racing their motor-cycles amid the mêlée. Nield rode past one skier and used the large muzzle of his pistol to hit the man. Barrel connected with skull. Nield almost lost his grip on the weapon but left the man behind sprawled in the snow. The heavy silence was no more. The roar of the cycles mingled with the rapid fire of shots. From the skiers, from the chalet. This was the decisive moment. It was also the moment when downstairs Tweed and Paula heard vehicles approaching at speed along the road from the direction of Apthal, vehicles with sirens blaring like banshee wails. And above the siren sounds they heard the heavy thump-thump of helicopters approaching.

Stieber, who had no difficulty in breaking the neck of a defenceless monk, had halted his Audi well back from Brunni. Too many bullets would be flying around for his liking. He had driven the car off the road behind a barn. He sat behind the wheel in his heavy suit: the monk's robe was buried under the snow a mile back.

He saw the four cars, marked *Polizei*, tearing past him towards Brunni. The lead car, driven by Beck, skidded round the bends, recovered control, raced on out of sight while the other three cars followed. Stieber reached for the ignition key, then withdrew his hand. He'd heard the sound of choppers coming. Opening the door, he grabbed his binoculars and waited. One helicopter flew almost at rooftop level, following the road. On the side of the fuselage the word *Polizei* stood out in the weird light of dawn which was like grey smoke. Stieber focused the binoculars. Despite the cold the door of the chopper was open. Projecting from it was the barrel of a swivel-mounted machine-gun.

Stieber waited until two more helicopters had flown past at a greater height, then tried to start the engine. It fired after three attempts and he drove round the barn and on to the road, turning away from Brunni, heading back towards Einsiedeln.

Beck stared up the slope as he skidded the car to a halt in Brunni. Skiers, lying in grotesque attitudes, dotted the slope behind the chalet. Two men on motor-cycles circled

454

the scene warily. The side wall of the chalet was stained with a dark crimson splash and below it was a huddle of two bodies.

'A massacre,' he muttered to himself.

He snatched the microphone from its cradle. The waveband was already tuned in to his three helicopters hovering overhead. A handful of skiers were making their way back up the slope into the forest.

'Beck here. Ground all choppers behind that forest. If they attempt to take off, use the machine-guns . . .'

He rammed the mike back on to its cradle and ran out of the car up to the entrance to the chalet. The rear door of his car had opened earlier and uniformed police with automatic weapons were heading up the slope, joined by more men from the other three cars. He ran up the steps, stood to one side of the door and hammered on it.

'Open up. Police here. This is Beck talking . . .'

Tweed opened the door after unlocking it and drawing back the bolts. Poker in hand, he stood to one side. In the middle of the room crouched Paula, her Browning aimed at the doorway. She straightened up, lowered the weapon. Beck stamped snow off his boots and walked inside. Tweed shut the door.

'Better late than never,' he observed.

44

At Einsiedeln, inside his room at the St Johann, Horowitz stood by the window. It was from here he had watched the four police cars arrive. From here he had watched through his night-glasses as Beck got out of the lead car and stared all round the deserted open space, then climbed back inside and drove off, leading his motorcade.

It was from here that Horowitz had seen the three choppers with *Polizei* on their fuselages overfly the town and head towards Brunni. None of this had surprised Horowitz – this was Switzerland. He had warned Morgan when the Welshman had called in briefly to see him on his way back to Zürich. Morgan had shrugged his wide shoulders, had said he had urgent business to attend to and had left.

Outside his room Horowitz heard the floorboards on the landing creak. The room was in darkness to let him see clearly what was happening outside. He picked up the Luger pistol with a silencer off the table, walked to the door, stood to one side.

'Yes? Who is it?'

'Stieber. Just back from you-know-where.'

'So what is happening?' Horowitz asked after unlocking the door and letting Stieber inside.

'All hell's let loose out at Brunni.' Stieber was sweating despite the cold outside. 'I saw four police cars and three of their bloody choppers racing towards the Mythen.'

'I know. I saw them. Now you've arrived you can make yourself useful. I paid for this room in advance for three days. You stay here and report by phone what happens.'

'And where are you going?'

'That doesn't concern you . . .'

'I don't like it. Suppose they find that monk I dumped in a trough? They might come looking for me.'

'And why should they suspect you? Were there any witnesses to the incident?'

Horowitz was closing his case. He had packed earlier ready for a swift departure.

'No, the alley was deserted. No one saw me.'

'And you've got rid of the monk's clothes?'

'I buried them in the snow outside Apthal.'

'Then you have absolutely nothing to worry about. Should a member of the police call to ask why you're here, tell them World Security is thinking of opening a bank account. You know the name of the bank in the High Street?'

'Yes . . .'

'Then I'm off. Just keep your eyes open. Don't go to sleep. Report by phone to Morgan any development.'

'You're clearing out, leaving the whole business behind?'

Horowitz stared at Stieber. 'You seem to have forgotten – I have a job I undertook to do. What has happened out at Brunni will help me to complete that job.'

Beck had made Tweed's chalet his temporary HQ. 'While we clear up this mess.' He sat at the table in the living-room with Tweed, Newman and Paula. Police came in, reported to Beck and went again. Ambulances had arrived to transport the injured and the dead from the blood-spattered slopes behind the chalet. Tweed faced Beck across the table.

'Do you believe me now?' he asked brusquely. 'Believe that there exists an opposition out to kill me?'

'Yes. I apologize for not believing you completely earlier. And we have identified the opposition.' He picked up a green identity folder a policeman had brought him. 'Most of those skiers had no means of identification on them. A deliberate ploy. But one man slipped up, had this folder inside his pocket.' He read from it. 'World Security, Zürich. Heinrich Locher. Then a number. That gives me what I've been waiting for ever since Otto Kuhlmann in Wiesbaden told me about the World Security truck they caught trying to smuggle classified high-tech equipment over the border into East Germany.'

'What have you been waiting for?' Paula asked.

457

'A legal excuse for turning over World Security HQs in Zürich, Basle and Geneva. Of course what happened out here was not all that legal.'

'We protected ourselves against armed attack – with weapons supplied and authorized by yourself,' Newman pointed out.

Beck smiled. 'Yes, you're right, of course.'

'And how did you happen to turn up here in the nick of time? We would have been overwhelmed by sheer numbers,' Tweed commented.

'Simple. I do know what's going on inside Switzerland. That is my job. It was reported to me from Kloten that World Security helicopters were assembling, that they were taking on board large numbers of men with ski equipment. The official reason was they were being sent on leave. I didn't swallow that one. I organized a strike force to stand by – choppers and cars. When that chopper fleet took off from Kloten it was tracked by radar – in this direction. I left Zürich to come up here at once. Now, Tweed, what are you going to do next? Have you any idea?'

'I'm returning to London. But I need your help, then Kuhlmann's. I can't fly back on a scheduled flight – they might put a bomb aboard the plane. I can't risk the lives of the other passengers.'

'Then why not use a chopper?'

'World Security will stop at nothing to make sure I never reach London. They could use Stinger missiles to destroy the machine. Lord knows what they have secreted away. I have decided the least risk to myself – to other people – is to cross Europe by car along the German autobahns, then to cross the Channel secretly by boat. For the first part of the journey I'll need your cooperation, Beck. Once I drive over the frontier at Basle I'm on my own.'

Beck looked dubious. Georg came in through the front door to report three more skiers had been transported into the waiting ambulances. Beck nodded and asked him to leave them alone, to take charge of the operation on the slopes. Only when they were alone again did he comment.

'Who do you think is behind all this?'

'Buckmaster or Morgan. Maybe both. I think one of them murdered that girl they found in my London flat. Not a job to hand over to a lackey – it would have provided a potential danger to the instigator of the crime if the murderer were caught. It's one of those two men – and I think I know who.'

'And the motive?'

'Colonel Romer of the Zurcher Kredit Bank could guess at that.'

'All right, you're evading the question. Now, your route to London. You do realize you will be the target of the entire World Security apparatus. They'll pull out all the stops to make sure you never reach London alive.'

'I'm counting on that.'

The reply was so curious they all stared at Tweed. Paula leaned forward, searching her chief's face. It was devoid of expression.

'What are you up to now?' she asked.

'Just trying to get home in one piece,' Tweed said amiably. He paused and looked at Beck. 'Isn't the Zurcher Kredit one of the banks which has provided Buckmaster with a huge loan?'

'I believe that may be the case,' Beck replied cautiously.

'The phone is in the kitchen. He's a friend of yours. Why don't you call him now – get him out of bed, if necessary. If my judgement of Romer is correct it will be a loan subject to swift recall. Maybe even at forty-eight hours' notice. Give Romer a message from me. I strongly advise him to call in that loan immediately. If Buckmaster tries to delay repayment Romer should hint he won't be able to keep the news from the press for long.'

'If you say so . . .'

'The phone is in the kitchen,' Tweed told him as the Swiss stood up. He waited until Beck had closed the door, then stared at Newman. There was something implacable in his manner which made Paula watch him with fascination.

'Bob,' Tweed began, 'when you were a foreign correspondent all the time, I gather you built up a network of contacts all over the world?'

'That's true.'

'You still keep in touch with these people?'

'Yes. In case some big story I like the sound of breaks. As you know, I still write the occasional piece.'

'Reporter friends in Tokyo, Sydney, San Francisco, New York and London?' Tweed persisted.

'In a lot of places – including all those you mentioned.'

'Then you could phone them at intervals and ask them as a favour to spread the question, *is World Security solvent?*'

A heavy silence descended on the room. Newman straightened in his chair and his eyes narrowed. Paula parted her lips and looked excited: like Newman she had grasped what Tweed was doing. It was Newman who broke the silence.

'Of course the major stock-markets of the world are in those cities you've mentioned. And World Security shares are quoted in those centres. Yes, I could phone friends who would regard that as an international scoop – and they'd begin to dig deep for follow-up stories. When Beck's come off the phone I could call Tokyo.' He checked his watch. 'The market is still open there.'

Tweed held up a hand. 'Not yet. I want to give Romer the chance to get his money back before the avalanche descends.'

'And just exactly what are you up to now?' Paula

asked. 'I detect a ruthless purpose behind what you're saying. That's not like you.'

Tweed had the same implacable manner but he spoke in an almost offhand way.

'It was Colonel Romer who gave me the missing link I was seeking behind this conspiracy. He told me the Russian Narodny Bank is holding five hundred million pounds in gold bullion ready for an urgent transaction. The potential recipient of that huge sum is a closely guarded secret. While I was in London I was working on a secret project known only to three people in Britain. The PM, Buckmaster and myself. It concerned the movement by sea of the key to the defence of the West. Further, only two people had the codes to contact the ship transporting the high-tech project, which I call *Shockwave* . . .'

'Something the Soviet military would give five hundred million pounds to lay their hands on?' interjected Paula.

'Exactly. I repeat, only Buckmaster and myself could contact the ship transporting *Shockwave*. Which is why I had to be got out of the way, sent running like a common fugitive. So, a murder is carefully planned – with Sylvia Harman's corpse found in my flat. I do start running – which leaves Buckmaster as the sole contact with the ship carrying *Shockwave*. At least, that is what he believes. That man, a minister, is handing over our defence against a rocket onslaught to the Russians to save his company. It's me against him – and I'm going to bring him down.'

'World Security is a huge international conglomerate,' Newman warned. 'And Buckmaster always wins in a business battle. If he's after a company to take over he always wins – by intimidation, by the power of his reputation, by using every trick in the book. You think you can defeat him?'

'I'm going to bring World Security crashing down across the face of the earth. The tricky part is to avoid involving a Minister of the Crown in a murder case because that could

461

destroy the government. That one I haven't worked out yet.'

'There are other people I could phone,' Newman mused. 'I've been thinking – people who spread rumours high up in the financial world behind closed doors.'

'When the time comes, do it,' said Tweed.

Beck opened the kitchen door and walked in to join them at the table.

'I phoned Romer. He was already up. He's an early riser.'

Tweed produced a sheaf of photocopies from his brief-case, a selection of the copies Newman had obtained from Basle. He handed them to Beck.

'It occurred to me after you'd gone that Romer might like to know something about the methods they've been using in the so-called Research & Development Division of World Security.'

Beck scanned the sheets. He frowned, still standing, checked back through several sheets, then looked at Tweed.

'This is damning evidence . . .'

'I suggest you might like to make a fresh call to Romer.'

'I think I will at that . . .'

Paula waited until the kitchen door had closed. Again she leaned towards Tweed.

'What game are you playing now? I don't think for a moment that occurred to you after Beck went to make his call.'

'A small question of psychology. Romer is up. He gets the first call from Beck with my message. He's a cautious Swiss banker. So at this moment he's weighing up whether to act or not. He gets a second call from Beck with evidence of the most appalling malpractice on the part of World Security. As I said, he's a Swiss banker. That second call reporting the evidence will decide him. He'll pull out.'

'You really are being devious,' Paula remarked. 'Is there any other titbit I've missed?'

'On my instructions, Marler is attacking Buckmaster inside his citadel. We're getting at him through his wife.'

'My! This really is a no-holds-barred battle.'

'Buckmaster is a cobra . . .'

Tweed stopped talking as Beck reappeared. 'Romer is calling in that loan. Now we have to take a few days trying to plan how you'll get back to London alive. If that's possible.'

45

At 8 a.m. London time, Lance Buckmaster received the call in his Belgravia flat from Zürich. Colonel Romer himself was on the line. Buckmaster greeted him affably and then stiffened in his chair as he detected the coldness in Romer's voice.

'Could you say that again slowly?' he asked curtly.

'At a meeting of the board this morning it was unanimously decided we must request you to repay the loan we made to World Security.'

'You're getting good interest on the money, Lord knows. I paid over the odds for that loan. You've received all the interest payments on time. And you shouldn't be talking to me. I'm a Minister now, in case you've forgotten.'

'Since the loan was agreed before you became a Minister – was negotiated with you personally – I thought it courteous to call you. You would prefer I get in touch with the chairman, Mrs Buckmaster?'

'Hold your horses, Romer. This comes out of the blue. I've had no hint of this before now, no warning.'

'The agreement does not mandate for any warning notice. We have taken our decision.' Romer's voice hardened. 'It is irrevocable.'

'How many months before you need the money back?' Buckmaster snapped.

'Not months. Not weeks. The time here is just after 9 a.m. We require payment of the entire loan by 11 a.m. your time, within forty-eight hours.'

'That's ridiculous with a company like World Security . . .'

'Read the agreement you signed. I'm sure you have a copy at hand. Or should I go through the strictly regular channels and call Mrs Buckmaster?'

'No. As you said, I negotiated the loan with you. May I ask why this sudden decision was taken?'

'Oh come, Mr Buckmaster. You know well it is the policy of my bank never to reveal reasons for decisions.'

'I'm asking you for thirty days to repay,' Buckmaster said.

'My regrets, Mr Buckmaster. I said the board's decision was irrevocable. The loan must be repaid in forty-eight hours. By 11 a.m. London time, two days hence. A courier will be flying to you with written confirmation.'

'Not necessary. No courier. Save your money.'

Buckmaster slammed down the phone in the living-room, swore slowly, with calculated venom. Running his hands through his hair, he stood up and walked round the room. Why? Why? *Why?*

His brain began to function. Zürich. Switzerland. Tweed was in Switzerland! That had to be it. *Tweed.* Assuming he was still alive. The phone rang again. He snatched it up.

'Who is it?' he demanded brutally.

'Morgan. Speaking from Basle. Is is OK to go ahead?'

464

'It is.'

In his Basle office overlooking the Rhine, the snow-encrusted rooftops on the opposite shore, Morgan pressed his prominent belly against the edge of his desk. It didn't sound too good a moment to report what had happened, but Buckmaster had to be told.

'We still have a problem . . .' Morgan talked fast – get it over with, exude confidence. 'The first major onslaught on the target was made and, as so often occurs, it did not succeed.' Morgan began to embroider the story. 'The target would have been removed but he had official help up in the mountains.'

'The police took him into custody?' Buckmaster said quickly.

'Something like that. You can guess the rest. But this is just the start of the take-over campaign.' Morgan phrased it carefully. He never entirely trusted a phone: he had bugged too many in his time. The police might be tapping the wire from outside. 'I am moving to Freiburg as soon as I have completed this call,' he went on. 'The campaign will continue from there. I have people here who will keep me in touch with developments . . .'

'Is Tweed still alive?' Buckmaster shouted down the phone.

'Yes,' Morgan admitted reluctantly. 'It was very odd. After the first phase of our campaign he appeared in the middle of Einsiedeln, got out of a car, walked around. Our accountant, Armand, found that odd.'

'And how does Armand view the situation?'

Morgan took a stronger grip on the phone. He was on firmer ground now. 'Armand is cool as a cucumber. Says the situation is developing as he expected. We have someone on the inside who reported the target is travelling back to England by road. God knows why, but Armand says that suits him fine.'

'Travelling back to England?' Buckmaster's voice rose

several decibels. 'When for God's sake?'

'Within a few days. We even know the route the consignment will take. Which is why I'm leaving for Freiburg to take overall command of the situation.'

'As you have up to now,' Buckmaster commented sarcastically. 'You say Armand has a plan?'

'Yes. I won't bore you with the details . . .' Morgan thought he'd got out of that trap skilfully. Buckmaster would assume he was being cautious over the phone. The fact was that Morgan had no idea what Horowitz's plan was. Buckmaster's tone was like ice when he spoke again.

'Hand over complete control to Armand. Offer him a large bonus to deal with the problem. Permanently. You're out of a job if you let me down this time. I already have your successor lined up . . .'

Morgan opened his mouth to protest and heard the click. The connection had been broken. Buckmaster had gone off the line. He replaced the receiver and mopped his damp forehead. The conversation had been an ordeal. Was Buckmaster serious in his threat to sack him? You never could tell. He always kept you off balance.

To take his mind off the phone call Morgan went over in his mind the events of the past few hours. The assault at Brunni had been a débâcle. Worse still, his paid contact inside Police HQ at Zürich had warned him to expect a raid on all three World Security HQs in Switzerland. Staff were busy burning incriminating documents. A detail he had felt it wise to omit mentioning to Buckmaster at this stage.

His police contact had also told him Tweed was leaving for London by road during the next few days – that he would be travelling on the autobahns in Germany from Basle. This seemed madness on the part of Tweed to Morgan. He had said as much to Horowitz on the phone when he had called from Zürich from a public call box.

'It is the first slip Tweed has made,' Horowitz agreed. 'I have been waiting for that slip . . .'

For a time Morgan had refused to believe Tweed was still alive. Then Stieber had reported the news from Einsiedeln – that he had seen Tweed step out of several cars in broad daylight and walk around in front of the monastery.

Strangely enough to Morgan, who had taken the call from Horowitz in a public box after a brief message from Zürich, giving him the location and number of the box, this episode had impressed Horowitz more than the massacre at Brunni.

'He's playing the same devious game,' he had commented to Morgan. 'He got out of that car in Einsiedeln and showed himself in a very public way. He's using the same strategy as when he crossed the bridge over the Rhine at Laufenburg, when he then made a fuss over the tickets at the station, when he booked rooms at the hotel nearest the *Hauptbahnhof* in Zürich.

'And what strategy is that?'

'Cat and mouse,' Horowitz had replied.

'And who is the cat?' Morgan had rasped.

'I shall be. In the end . . .'

That had been several hours ago. Morgan checked his watch. The car would be waiting to take him over the border into Germany. He had to clear out before the police raid hit the Basle HQ. He picked up his case and went down in the elevator.

The Mercedes was waiting for him at the kerb. Morgan had another bad shock. Wearing a chauffeur's uniform and a peaked cap, Armand Horowitz opened the front passenger door for him. In case someone was watching he said nothing and climbed inside. Horowitz, who had taken his case, deposited it in the boot, slammed it shut and got in behind the wheel.

'How the hell did you get here so fast?' asked Morgan.

'Encouraging to receive such a warm welcome.' Horowitz drove the Mercedes away from the kerb, headed for the bridge over the Rhine and the frontier control post

467

beyond. 'It's quite simple. I flew in one of your remaining choppers from Kloten to Basle airport. Fortunate that your chauffeur is my height and·build. I noticed that earlier. I borrowed his uniform.'

'He gave it to you? Just like that!'

'A little gentle persuasion was needed. He's lying unconscious in your communications room in the basement.'

'Why the disguise?'

'We are crossing the border into Germany . . .'

There was silence for the next few minutes. Morgan was uneasy about the checkpoint. Had Beck alerted the guards? Sent them his description? He couldn't get out of Switzerland quick enough. He'd heard what it was like inside Swiss prisons.

'Just relax,' Horowitz ordered as he slowed the car, joining the short queue waiting to pass the control point.

Morgan had his passport ready inside his coat pocket as a Swiss official approached the car. Would they get through?

The Swiss leaned down, stared hard at Morgan, who gazed back. The stare was transferred to Horowitz who sat erect, looking ahead. The Swiss, a short stocky man, waved them on. They were through. Horowitz drove on to German soil.

The short stocky man hurried inside the building to an empty office. Standing up, he pressed the numbers typed on a slip.

'Freiburg Police HQ? This is Swiss control at Basle. You have a Chief Inspector Kuhlmann who is expecting this call urgently.'

He had to wait a few minutes. Then a gravelly voice came on the line.

'Kuhlmann here. That's Swiss control at Basle?'

'Yes. I'm carrying out the instructions I received from Berne. A World Security Mercedes has just·left Switzerland for Germany. Inside were Morgan and a uniformed chauffeur.'

'How do you know it was World Security? How can you be sure it was Morgan?' Kuhlmann demanded.

'Berne supplied a complete list of registration numbers of all cars belonging to World Security. They also gave me a detailed description of Gareth Morgan. He's fat as a pig, grossly overweight, medium height, mid forties, clean-shaven, very black hair. Looked like a giant turnip . . .'

'Describe the chauffeur.'

'Just a chauffeur. Tall, thin, lean-faced, wore steel-rimmed glasses . . .'

'O.K. And thank you.'

Kuhlmann put down the phone and turned to his assistant. 'Get me Arthur Beck of the Swiss Federal Police. You'll contact him at Zürich police HQ . . .'

46

In the living-room of his Belgravia flat Buckmaster sat in a state of shock. An hour earlier he'd had the phone call from Colonel Romer. The withdrawal of the loan was a disaster. The withdrawal of any of his many bank loans at this point would be a disaster.

It was so nerve-racking. It was also going to be a race against time, maybe a matter of hours making all the difference. As soon as the Soviet military took possession of *Shockwave* half the enormous sum of five hundred million would be paid to him in gold bullion in Switzerland. From a portion of that sum he could pay off Colonel Romer and his bloody gnomes. The balance of the other two hundred and fifty million would be paid after their technical analysts had examined *Shockwave*.

Tweed. It had to be Tweed's hand behind this cata-strophic news from Zürich. Tweed was in Zürich. The coincidence was too great. It all depended on Armand Horowitz doing yet another smooth and perfect job. Tweed must never get back to England. The thought of the man filled Buckmaster with venom.

. He took a deep breath and remembered a long article which had featured him in *Forbes Magazine* in the States. The writer had traced Buckmaster's phenomenal rise to power and riches. He had used a phrase which leapt back into Buckmaster's mind. *This man is at his best with his back to the wall*. He stood up. He would beat down the opposition once again – emerge from this temporary difficulty stronger than ever. It was at that moment that Leonora, who had slept in after a late night at the office, appeared from her bedroom.

'I'm glad you're still here. I'd like a word with you, Lance.'

Something in her tone made him stiffen. She was holding a cardboard-backed envelope. From it she extracted a large photograph, holding the blank side towards him.

'I've decided I can't stand your playing around with so many girl friends any longer.'

'What the devil are you talking about?'

His voice was dangerously quiet, his expression frozen. She had chosen the wrong moment to make a scene. Half his mind was wrestling with the problem of the loans. The last thing he wanted was more trouble – and so close to him. He felt the fury bubbling up inside him and with a supreme effort he preserved an impassive manner.

'I'm talking about this. Photographic evidence of your fooling around with your hired tarts.'

She extended the photo towards him and he took it from her. He was careful not to snatch it out of her hand. Taller than Leonora, he towered over her as he examined the print. His eyes were cold as he raised them and looked at her.

'Where did you get this garbage?'

'Yes, that would be a good description of her,' she continued. 'Garbage. How much does she charge for a quick lay? Or do you buy her presents? A diamond choker? I wouldn't mind choking her myself.'

'This is a fake,' he told her in the same quiet tone.

'Of course!' she laughed in his face. 'A fake. That's a good one. Really, Lance, you're a Minister of the Crown. At the moment. I'd have thought you could do better than that.'

'I asked you where you got this from.' He advanced towards her. 'I want an answer.'

'Haven't you heard of private investigators? Lots of women employ them when they've learned to mistrust their sneaky husbands. And sometimes they get lucky – they get photographic evidence. Like I got.'

'You . . . stupid . . . cow.' He spaced out the words. 'I recognize this picture . . .'

'Really?' She put up a hand and touched a curl into place. 'You mean you get someone to photograph you while you're doing it? Kinky as well as randy as a goat. May I look at your photograph album sometime?'

'This photograph,' he repeated in the same over-controlled tone, 'is a fake. This picture of me on the sofa was taken by a press photographer. God! I've lost count of the number of pictures taken of me. But I do remember this one. You've been cheated. I've never seen this girl in my life—'

'You would say that—'

'Shut up!' he roared at her. He resumed his controlled tone. 'Someone has produced clever artwork – they have superimposed the girl – a picture of her – on top of me. Then they'd photograph the whole thing again to hide the joins.'

'You really expect me to believe that? I do believe you are losing your grip when it comes to telling convincing lies. Maybe you're losing control of everything.'

It was just something savage to say out of the blue. But it had a different meaning to Buckmaster. His mind raced. Could she have something to do with the withdrawal of the Swiss loan by Romer? Treachery behind his back? His fury boiled over.

He transferred the photograph to his left hand. He raised his right hand and slapped her across the side of the face with a backhander. Her head jerked back. She lost her balance and fell sprawling on to a nearby couch. For one moment the ex-captain of the Airborne Division thought he'd hit her too hard. He took a step forward and then she was lifting herself upright, leaning back on the couch, her eyes blazing.

'You bastard! That's the first and last time you'll hit me . . .'

'You're going to feel silly when I go through the publicity files and find the original photograph of myself this girl has been linked up with. Now, I need to know who gave you this piece of rubbish.'

'And the police need to know who had access to the Threadneedle Street executive elevator – everyone – on the night Ted Doyle was murdered . . .'

'Murdered? What fanciful nonsense are you talking about now? The press has reported Doyle fell out of the window.'

'Oh, yes,' she jeered, 'and you also were fooled by the report Chief Inspector Buchanan spread. He's not satisfied, I can tell you. Buchanan is investigating it as a case of cold-blooded murder. Only three people had keys to the executive elevator which comes straight up from the underground garage. Me, Morgan – and you.'

'You told this Buchanan I still have a key?' he asked quietly.

'Not yet.'

'You have some sense. Now, listen to me, Leonora. I can remove you as chairman and put Morgan in your place tomorrow.'

'I don't think so . . .'

'Then you'd better read the articles of association governing the conduct of the company. I can throw you out just like that.'

He snapped his fingers at her contemptuously. Leonora stood up and touched the side of her face with her fingertips. A blue weal marked her where Buckmaster had struck the blow. She could see it in the wall mirror behind him. She spoke through her clenched teeth, spoke with great emphasis.

'At the first sign that you're trying to remove me I'll go to Buchanan and tell him who still has the third key to that elevator.'

'You can't drag me into the Doyle business.'

'You want to bet?' she mocked him. 'Bet your whole career? How long do you think you'd last as Minister for External Security if the press splashed you across its pages as one of the murder suspects?'

'You . . .'

'And,' she continued with deadly calm, 'if you call me a cow a second time that's it. Come to think of it, I don't have to go and see Buchanan. He's made another appointment to visit me at my office. That third missing key intrigues him.'

'Let's leave things as they are,' he decided. 'We're having too many domestic tiffs . . .'

'Tiffs!' she snorted. 'When you say leave things as they are, you mean I'm staying on as chairman. Is that it?' she pressed.

'You caught me on the raw.' He was under icy control now. 'Yes, that's it. Of course. I need someone I can trust in that position. Morgan is insatiably ambitious. Keep your

473

eye on him.' He checked his watch. 'Hanson will be waiting to take me to the Ministry. Give me that envelope. I will hang on to this photo until I've found the original.'

'I do have other copies,' she warned him as she handed it to him.

'Fair enough. I really must go now . . .'

Outside the entrance he was his normal affable self with his chauffeur, Hanson, who opened the rear door of the Daimler. Once the car was on the move he sat tensely, thinking over recent events. His whole world was coming apart.

There was Romer and the withdrawal of the Swiss loan. He'd have to visit the room inside the Admiralty, check on the progress of the *Lampedusa*. The ship must be close to its rendezvous point. And now he had a fresh anxiety. He had read the papers and there had been no further mention of Doyle's death. Just a small report that the inquest had been adjourned at the request of Chief Inspector Buchanan. 'While we continue our enquiries . . .' What enquiries?

As Buckmaster was driven to Whitehall, Marler was not far away, driving his Porsche to Scotland Yard. He had delayed his departure for Switzerland after reading the papers. His attention had been caught by the item on the postponement of the inquest on Doyle, the chief accountant who had fallen out of a window at World Security.

Leonora had told him about the strange death of Doyle during pillow talk at her Belgravia apartment. By asking a few offhand questions Marler had built up a picture of what had happened during the fatal night. She had chattered on, relieved to have someone she could talk to about the weird episode.

Marler had made a brief phone call to the Yard. He had spoken to Buchanan briefly and they had arranged this appointment. He parked his car and walked inside the famous building. He was shown up to Buchanan's office immediately and had a shock when he entered to room.

There were two men inside the office. One of them Marler recognized. Chief Inspector Harvey of Special Branch, the weasel-like officer Tweed had always disliked. Marler concealed his sense of shock. What a contrast the two men were.

Buchanan, tall, elegant, cordial, got up from behind his desk, walked round it, extended his hand. His grip was firm. He wore a smart grey suit, a white shirt, a pale grey tie which matched the colour of his alert eyes.

'Thank you for coming to see me, Mr Marler. Do please sit down. I gather you know Chief Inspector Harvey of Special Branch?'

'We've met.'

Marler nodded to the other man. Black-haired, shorter and bulkier than Buchanan, he wore a blue business suit which didn't seem to fit him properly. A sneer lingered at the corners of his tight little mouth. His eyes darted all over the place.

'I don't quite understand,' Marler began when Buchanan had sat down again behind his desk. 'You're the Met – Metropolitan Police. Harvey is Special Branch. It's unusual to find the two separate forces working together.'

'What's that to do with you?' Harvey snapped.

'I do think we owe our visitor an explanation,' Buchanan intervened politely. 'You are, of course, quite right, Mr Marler. The two forces normally operate independently – and most of their activity is connected with your organization. Of which, I confess, I know very little . . .'

'Do you really think this is necessary?' Harvey snapped.

'I do. Mr Marler, I'm investigating the circumstances surrounding the death of Edward Doyle, chief accountant with World Security. Apparently he fell to his death from a window late one evening. There are aspects of the case which puzzle me. The investigation is continuing. Now, this is where Harvey comes in. There was – only a short time before Doyle's demise – the murder of an unknown woman in the Radnor Walk flat of a man called Tweed. I understand he is your immediate superior?'

'Correct.'

'Harvey is getting nowhere with his enquiry into this brutal murder . . .' He paused and Marler glanced at Harvey who was glowering. Not a welcome disclosure. '. . . and so far,' Buchanan continued, 'he hasn't had any luck identifying the victim. He found himself facing a dead end.' A grim smile appeared on Buchanan's face. 'Excuse me, that unfortunate pun was unintended. Am I explaining this clearly so far?'

'So far. I'm still waiting for the connection.'

'Which is what I'm coming to. Harvey has managed to keep the Radnor Walk murder out of the press – for obvious security reasons. Then he heard about the death of Doyle at the offices of World Security. That has appeared in the press. On the night of the murder in Radnor Walk three people turned up at that address. And this was in the early hours of the morning. One was Robert Newman, the foreign correspondent. Another was your ultimate chief, Mr Howard, alerted by an anonymous phone-call. Tweed subsequently disappeared. All clear so far?'

'I get the picture.'

Buchanan paused. Marler was beginning to grasp his mannerisms, his technique. He paused before saying something significant. 'A third man also turned up very promptly at the flat. Lance Buckmaster, Minister for External Security.'

'Really?'

'When are you going to talk, Marler?' Harvey burst out.

'I am talking.'

'Oh, yes.' The sneer was pronounced. 'In single sentences?'

'That's right.'

Marler answered Harvey's questions without looking at him. Buchanan was watching him closely with a hint of amusement. He turned to Harvey and smiled.

'Why don't you pop down and get yourself a cup of coffee at the canteen? I'll join you there in a few minutes.'

'I think I'd prefer to stay where I am.'

'Harvey, I started out by making it a request.'

'We're not getting anywhere with this iceberg.' Harvey pursed his lips and stood up. 'Maybe you'll find me in the canteen, maybe you won't.'

He closed the door quietly after leaving the room. Marler asked Buchanan if he could light a cigarette. The Chief Inspector told him that was quite all right. Marler lit his cigarette, blew a smoke ring, watched it circle above him, then spoke.

'What's the connection? I'd like you to spell it out.'

'The only possible – I repeat possible – connection is that Buckmaster arrived at Radnor Walk soon after the body was found. Then, shortly afterwards, we have another corpse at the headquarters of World Security – Buckmaster's company – in Threadneedle Street. I am beginning to wonder whether the two incidents are linked. I have no evidence, I stress. Why did you come to see me, Mr Marler?'

'I can't reveal my source. I work under the Official Secrets Act. But someone told me there is a private executive elevator from the underground garage at Threadneedle Street to the suites on the eighteenth floor. Is that so?'

'Yes, it is.'

Buchanan was no longer looking at Marler. The soul of relaxation, he played with a glass paperweight on his desk. He looked up as Marler asked his question.

'I take it this interview is between the two of us? That

477

you won't repeat this conversation to Harvey? I'm still talking about the Official Secrets Act.'

'You have my word. You may talk freely. In complete confidence.'

'Staying with that elevator. I understand there are only three keys which operate it. Mrs Buckmaster has one. Gareth Morgan has another. The third key is supposed to have gone missing.'

'That is the way I understand the situation.'

'Lance Buckmaster has the third key. It isn't lost. He kept the key when he became a Minister. So he has discreet access to the executive suites at Threadneedle Street.'

Buchanan stopped playing with the paperweight. He gazed into the distance, his manner still relaxed. This man could coax the truth out of most people, Marler thought.

'I'm greatly obliged to you, Mr Marler, for that interesting piece of information. I won't conceal from you it opens up a fresh line of enquiry. After all, Doyle was Chief Accountant. As the Americans say, he would know where the bodies are buried.'

'And we're talking about two bodies.'

'Indeed we are.' Buchanan paused. 'Would it be too much to ask why you didn't want to talk about this in front of Harvey? He is, after all, also covered by the Official Secrets Act – as you are.'

Marler checked his watch. He'd soon have to leave to catch his flight for Zürich. He gazed straight at Buchanan.

'I never flannel people. But I've been assessing you ever since I entered this office. I know Harvey. He'll make a balls-up of the whole business. I think you'll do rather better in bringing the investigation to a conclusion.'

'Thank you,' said Buchanan. 'I take that as a compliment.'

* * *

Driving to London Airport, Marler checked over in his mind what he had achieved. He remembered a friend whose security company had been taken over by Buckmaster with a hostile bid.

Every form of intimidation and pressure had been employed to demoralize him. Rumours had been spread that his family would be kidnapped and held to ransom. There had been a burglary at his home which seemed pointless – until too late he discovered his phone had been bugged.

A number of his security trucks had been sabotaged – involving very late delivery of consignments to old customers who had consequently withdrawn their business. His wife had suffered a nervous breakdown. To stop the pressure – none of which could be proved to the police – his friend had accepted a bid from World Security which hugely undervalued his firm.

Well, thought Marler, Buckmaster is going to enjoy a taste of psychological warfare himself. He felt confident that Leonora would show him the compromising photograph sooner or later. Probably sooner.

Now Buckmaster was going to face discreet but persistent cross-examination by Chief Inspector Buchanan into Doyle's death. The combined pressure was bound to have some effect on the Minister's morale. Most of all he'd worry about the press getting hold of one of the two stories. Well, chum, he said to himself – you're not the only one who can set about destabilizing the morale of an individual. With a sense of grim satisfaction he boarded the Zürich flight.

47

Marler made the call to Buchanan from a phone at Kloten Airport soon after landing. He had to wait awhile before the Chief Inspector's voice came on the line. Buchanan had just arranged an appointment to see Lance Buckmaster that evening at his apartment in Belgravia.

'Who is this?' Buchanan enquired.

'Marler speaking. Didn't they tell you? I gave them my name.'

'Just to check your identity, what were you wearing when I saw you last?'

'Check sports jacket, grey slacks, blue shirt, yellow tie.'

'And give me the name – just the surname – of the man who was with me when you arrived.'

'Harvey. You are a suspicious character . . .'

'Merely careful. Where are you calling from?'

'A long way from London. Don't ask me the location. I am careful, too.'

'I'm satisfied. What is it, Mr Marler?'

'Another possible lead I overlooked to mention when I saw you.' Marler paused: Buchanan should grasp the significance of that conversational ploy. 'The lead is a hit-and-run – so-called – death which took place in London recently. A man called Dr Rose of St Thomas's. Buckmaster might be able to help you on that one.'

'Who is this Dr Rose? As you kept saying, what is the connection?'

'Dr Rose was the pathologist who examined the body of the unknown girl murdered at a flat in Radnor Walk. Bye . . .'

Marler picked up the phone again and dialled police HQ in Zürich. He asked to speak to Arthur Beck, gave his name, and said he'd also like to speak to Paula. He waited and was put on to two different people. The second was a woman. He had to repeat what he'd said at the beginning. Another wait. He kicked snow off his shoes: they had brought a mobile staircase for disembarkation from the flight and the snow was thick on the ground.

'Arthur Beck speaking. Who exactly is this?'

'I thought they'd have told you by now. I'm speaking from Kloten. I just flew in from London. I'm trying to contact a man called Tweed. My name is Marler.'

'Who?'

'Tweed. Come on, Beck, you know him. You've worked together in the past. His assistant, Paula Grey, is probably with him. And Bob Newman, the foreign correspondent.'

'I think you'd better report to police headquarters. A taxi driver will bring you here.'

'You haven't answered my question about Tweed . . .'

'A taxi driver will bring you here. Goodbye, Marler.'

Now what is happening, Marler wondered? He picked up his case and headed for the taxi rank. Was Beck hostile towards Tweed? He'd have to box clever when he arrived at police HQ.

'That was a man called Marler,' Beck said to Tweed, Paula and Newman after he'd put down the phone. 'Just flew in from London, so he said. What do I do with him when he arrives here? You know him?'

'A key member of my team,' Tweed replied.

481

He looked up as a policewoman showed Butler and Nield into the large office overlooking the River Limmat. It was night and across the water lights glittered along the waterfront. Reflections from street lamps vibrated in the dark water. Butler and Nield had just returned from taking baths at the Hotel Schweizerhof. They sat down and watched Tweed.

It was two days since the massacre at Brunni. Since then Beck had installed Tweed in a guarded house in the Altstadt. He was brought to police HQ only after night had fallen. Beck flexed his hands.

'You haven't told me what I do with this Marler. Could he be someone else impersonating Marler? We can put him in the interrogation room and you can take a look at him unseen through a one-way window. World Security is like an octopus with its tentacles everywhere. I've only grasped that recently.'

'It might be a wise precaution,' Tweed agreed. 'Then if it is Marler he can join us . . .'

'I don't think so,' Newman intervened vehemently. 'How do we know we can trust him? He could be in Buckmaster's pocket by now.'

'I agree with Bob,' Paula chimed in. 'We can't risk it.'

Tweed looked at Butler and Nield. 'Your opinion of Marler?'

'He's always been a lone wolf,' Butler replied. 'But where Tweed is concerned I'd trust Marler with his life.'

'Which is exactly what you would be doing,' Paula exclaimed.

'Pete?' Tweed enquired, facing Nield.

'I go along with Butler. And on this cross-country run we are going to need all the help we can get.'

Beck stood up from behind his desk. 'One piece of information I omitted to pass on to you, Tweed. Chief Inspector Kuhlmann phoned me from Germany a couple of days ago. He reported that Morgan crossed the border into Germany at the Basle frontier post in the direction of Freiburg. Driven by a chauffeur – wearing steel-rimmed spectacles.'

'And that sounds like Armand Horowitz,' Newman said grimly.

'So,' Beck continued, 'do you still think, Tweed, it's a good idea to travel back to England by road? And along the German autobahns? I've had my doubts about that ever since the idea came up.'

'That's the route I'm taking,' Tweed told him. 'And we have made all the preparations for me to go by road.'

'You're stubborn.' Beck shrugged. 'Now you must excuse me while I go downstairs and make arrangements to receive this Marler.'

Tweed waited until they were alone. He then walked across the office and turned on a transistor radio. It was tuned to a police waveband. He noted its position, turned the station knob until he found music playing. Standing, he addressed his team.

'That's probably unnecessary – but it guards against the room being bugged. World Security have penetrated this building in another way. They have an informant inside the organization.'

'How on earth do you know that?' Paula asked.

'Because Morgan and – more important – Horowitz have crossed into Germany. And Beck said that they were pointed towards Freiburg – which is on the route I will be taking. Beck phoned here several times before we left for Brunni – and made advance preparations for my journey. The coincidence is too great.'

'Then we must change the route urgently,' Paula stated.

Tweed shook his head. 'No, we keep to the original arrangement. The same route.'

Paula glanced at Newman. He was sitting with the ghost of a cynical smile. She looked at Butler and Nield.

Butler showed no reaction. Nield winked at her. She turned back to Tweed.

'This is madness.' Her eyes narrowed. 'You look too innocent. What are you up to now?'

'I have already told you. I am going to smash World Security, I am going to destroy Buckmaster. The second part will be the more difficult – to accomplish it without a great national scandal. We'll have to play it off the cuff. Now I am going down to the transceiver inside the van Beck had driven down from Brunni and parked outside. I want to see if I can contact the *Lampedusa* again. It may be close to its rendezvous with the Soviet military establishment.'

'Then we're close to a major disaster,' said Paula.

Tweed turned the radio knob back to the police band, switched off the radio. Newman joined him as he left the room.

'I'm coming with you. It's dark outside . . .'

While they waited Paula poured everyone more coffee from a percolator on a hot-plate. They sat in silence. From outside the only sounds were the occasional wail of police sirens. Fifteen minutes later Tweed returned with Newman.

'I made contact. No reply to the two trick questions – as I expected. My main idea was to keep up the morale of Hoch, the radio op. I recognize his "fist" – we practised before the *Lampedusa* sailed. The position aboard must be very tense by now.'

Latitude 34.10.N Longitude 25.50.E. The *Helvetia* was sailing south of Crete on an easterly course. Although no land was in sight the freighter was about midway along the huge Greek island. Its scheduled progress had been considerably slowed down by worsening weather. Under a lowering sky twenty-foot-high grey waves like small mountains rolled towards it. The foredeck was awash as the massive waves broke over it. The glass was dropping, a storm was brewing.

Greg Singer fought his way up the companionway to the bridge as the vessel pitched and tossed violently. He had checked once more the vast bulk of the monster computer in the hold. By some miracle it had still not shifted its position. He staggered across the bridge to where Captain Hartmann stood alongside the helmsman behind the wheel.

'How much time have you to make up?' Singer shouted.

'Make up?' Hartmann stared at the rugged-faced Singer as though he were mad. 'We are six hours behind schedule – and the latest met forecast promises a Force Seven gale. We shall be lucky to stay only six hours late. There is just a chance the gale will pass to the south. But look at it now.'

He waved a hand beyond the foredeck. The view was hardly encouraging. Giant rollers swept towards them from all directions. In the distance clouds like a black hand had smothered the horizon. Singer tightened his lips: there seemed little point in bullying the skipper any more.

And the problem he'd had on his mind earlier now seemed to be more menacing. When they made the rendezvous would the Russians simply let him go? He was beginning to doubt it more and more. On shore it had seemed a straightforward deal. Now at sea with nothing in sight but the accursed surf-topped rollers Singer felt trapped. Somehow he had to escape.

The missile cruiser *Sverdlov*, one of the Soviet Navy's most modern and heavyweight ships, had emerged from the Dardanelles Straits and was sailing south at high speed through the Aegean Sea for the rendezvous close to Eastern Crete.

The weather was good, the sea was calm, the huge

warship was proceeding at top speed. The commander had no doubts: he would reach the rendezvous with the freighter on time. His only worry was the latest met report. A fierce gale was raging south of him. But he didn't expect it to slow his ship's speed by more than a few knots.

The unseen eyes of the spy satellite *Ultra* looked down on the earth. Its circuit took it over the Black Sea, the Aegean Sea and then across the Mediterranean to Libya, its main target. At Langley, Virginia, Cord Dillon studied the latest photographs *Ultra* had transmitted. He compared them with the report prepared by the analysts. Copies had been sent earlier to Washington. The red phone rang. He grabbed it, announced his identity.

'Tremayne here,' the Admiral replied. 'You've seen the latest *Ultra* pics?'

'I was about to call you. They show the *Sverdlov* is already west of Rhodes. That's getting pretty close, Admiral.'

'Which is why I've sent Naples an urgent *Leopard* signal. In short, to move their butts . . .'

Approaching Crete, Hank Tower, commander of the Kidd class destroyer DGG 997 *Spruance*, was feeling frustrated. He was on the bridge when the decoded signal from Washington was handed to him. He scanned it quickly, then called for more speed.

In the engine room the crew looked at each other. *Spruance* was swaying like a ballet dancer in the heavy seas. Normally they would have reduced speed. But orders were orders.

Tower, feet straddled to counter the vessel's motion, stood on the bridge gazing ahead. His frustration sprang from his inability to launch his helicopter in this weather.

At the first sign of a slackening of its force, he would send the machine aloft. That was the way to locate any vessel in the area which had a silhouette even remotely resembling the *Lampedusa*.

48

An Oriental maid showed Buchanan and his assistant into the living-room of Lance Buckmaster's Belgravia apartment. As they entered the room Buckmaster stood up from a Georgian desk and came round it to meet them, his manner affable. He shook hands with Buchanan who introduced his assistant.

'This is Sergeant Warden. He'll take notes of our interview if that's all right with you, sir.'

'Make yourselves at home. Do sit down. Can I offer you a cigarette?'

'Thank you, but neither of us smoke.'

'Jolly good. Neither do I. Goes back to the days when I was with my airborne division. Thank you for agreeing to come here rather than at the Ministry. A hotbed of gossip, any Government department.'

'That's what I thought,' Buchanan agreed as he sat down in a carver chair and crossed his long legs.

'Wouldn't you prefer a more comfortable chair?' Buckmaster suggested.

'This will do me nicely, sir. I know you're a very busy man, so I'll come straight to the point.'

'Not enough people do that. Please carry on.'

Warden, seated in an armchair, his notepad in his lap, was careful to show no expression. This was typical

Buchanan tactics. A gentle opening to relax the target.

'We find ourselves in a bit of a quandary,' Buchanan began. 'We're hoping you'll be able to help us see a little daylight.' He paused. 'The fact is I'm concerned with two murders.'

'Two?' Buckmaster looked puzzled, intrigued. 'How can I possibly help?'

'You haven't asked me which two murders I'm talking about.'

Warden smiled inwardly. It was beginning. Buchanan's tactic of interrogation by psychological attack – disturbing the morale of his opponent. Buckmaster, wearing a hacking jacket and corduroy trousers, was sitting on a chintz-covered couch, legs apart, hands clasped lightly between them. He smiled wolfishly – as much as to say all right, I'll play your little game.

'Tell me, Chief Inspector, which two murders are you talking about?'

'The murder of Edward Doyle, your chief accountant, at the Threadneedle Street headquarters of your company . . .'

'Just hold it there a moment, would you? I understand Ted fell from a window in his office. Poor devil. I heard it could have had something to do with his gambling habits.'

'Gambling habits, sir? What kind of gambling would that be?'

'The gee-gees. Horses. I never knew it while he was in my employ, but apparently he gambled in a big way. And, sadly, usually lost. Most people foolish enough to make that their hobby do lose.'

'Does gambling really fit in with the character of a man who rose to be chief accountant in an international conglomerate as big as World Security?'

Buckmaster waved his hands in a vague gesture. 'I suppose that being concerned with figures he deluded

488

himself that he'd worked out a winning system. I'm just guessing.'

'I'm always interested in guesses. Sometimes they hit the mark. The trouble is we've found no evidence at all that Doyle ever visited a racecourse in his life.'

'That's odd.' Buckmaster frowned as though in recollection. 'I'm sure someone told me something about betting slips being found in his office . . .'

'At his home, sir. Not at his office.'

'Oh, I see. Can't recall who brought the matter up. Maybe my wife. I gather you've interviewed her at Threadneedle Street.'

'What did you think was the significance of Doyle being in possession of betting slips, sir?'

'Well . . .' Buckmaster looked at Warden, then back at Buchanan. 'I assumed the poor chap had got himself in too deep and took the only way out?'

'Suicide? Is that what you thought?'

Warden kept his head down as he scribbled in shorthand. In a brief conversation Buchanan had led the Minister of External Security into the labyrinth of discussing the circumstances leading up to Doyle's death. And this man is a polished political performer he was thinking.

'Well,' Buckmaster said slowly, 'it does seem to follow.'

'You discount then the possibility that Doyle accidentally fell out of his office window. You're saying that in no way could it have been an accident?'

'I can't say I've discounted any possibility. I'm not sure how we reached this point in the conversation.'

'So you haven't discounted the option that Doyle might have been murdered?' A pause. 'Sir?'

'You seem to have forgotten the betting slips you say that you found at his home.'

'No, sir, I haven't forgotten them. There's a difficulty in that direction. A number of betting slips were found in his house tucked under a household article. They were tested

489

for fingerprints. Doyle's fingerprints. There were no fingerprints on those slips. Why would a man carefully wipe old betting slips clean of his fingerprints. Any guesses on that point, sir?'

'I don't quite like the tone of your question.' An edge to his voice now. He sat back and clasped his long jaw in one hand. The blue eyes were like chips of ice.

'To have reached your present position you have to be a man of wide experience and intelligence.' Buchanan paused. 'I simply thought you might be able to help me.'

'I really have no comment.'

Buckmaster relaxed. Warden again kept his expression blank. His chief was on top form. What was coming next?

'Then there's the second murder,' Buchanan went on genially. 'Where you, by your presence at the scene of the crime, seem to be the only link with the Doyle investigation.'

'Which murder is that?'

'The brutal murder of an unknown girl in Tweed's flat at Radnor Walk.'

Buckmaster's jaw muscles tightened. His body stiffened and he stared at the Chief Inspector, who patiently waited for his reaction.

'I understood Chief Inspector Harvey of Special Branch was in charge of that case.'

'Indeed, he is. Quite correct, sir. But informally he has suggested I include that case in my enquiries.' Buchanan reached inside his pocket, produced an envelope and held it out. 'This letter to you from him authorizes me to bring up the Tweed case.'

Buckmaster took the envelope, tossed it on the couch beside him, unread. He sat erect, buttoned up his hacking jacket. Now very much the Minister for External Security, Warden was thinking. Buckmaster's voice was terse, brusque.

'I refuse to discuss any aspect of what happened at

Radnor Walk. A matter of national security. The only officer I'm prepared to talk to is Chief Inspector Harvey – and he already has the meagre information I was able to supply.' He glanced at the red boxes piled on his desk. 'And now, if there's nothing else, I would like to terminate this interview. I expect to be up till midnight going through my despatch boxes.'

Buchanan stood up, followed by Warden. 'I would like to say I appreciate the amount of your valuable time you have given me, sir.'

Buckmaster, also standing, looked at Buchanan with bleak suspicion. Had he detected a note of sarcasm in this too polite police officer? He nodded.

'I'll show you to the door.'

Buchanan waited until his host was reaching for the handle before he spoke again. 'Incidentally, sir, I imagine, as you are going to be working here it will be no inconvenience that we have asked your chauffeur, Hanson, to visit us at the Yard this evening?'

'What on earth for?'

'It concerns Doyle's residence where the betting slips were found. A neighbour opposite, a lady, saw a stranger call at Doyle's house a little while ago. He apparently had a key since he went up to the door, paused, and then went inside.'

'I fail to see how this concerns Hanson.'

'I hadn't quite finished, sir. This stranger, a man, called after Doyle had died. The neighbour proved to be an observant witness, gave us a clear description of the stranger. We showed her half a dozen photographs of various men, one of them Hanson. She immediately picked him out as the man who had called.'

'Where on earth did you find a photo of Hanson?'

'Very straightforward, sir. You're one of the most well-known men in the country. We contacted a photographic library and they came up with several pictures of you

491

arriving at some function – with Hanson standing by the door of your Daimler as you alighted. We blocked out your picture, of course.'

'Obviously a case of mistaken identity.'

'That, sir, is what I wish to check this evening. I won't keep you any longer from your boxes. The work of the Government must go on.'

Warden waited until they were seated inside the unmarked police car parked further down the street. He asked the question as they fastened their seat belts. Buchanan was behind the wheel.

'He road-blocked us on the Tweed business.'

'Which is exactly what I anticipated,' Buchanan remarked as he started the engine and drove away from the kerb, his headlights playing over the snow-streaked street.

'So what was the point?'

'To rattle him. I'm sure he was concealing something from us. His eyes flickered briefly when I mentioned Hanson.'

Alone, Buckmaster walked into his study, closed the sound-proof door and poured himself a stiff Scotch. He felt like a man with a noose tightening round his neck. He swallowed the drink.

First there was Tweed. The agile bastard had so far eluded every effort to eliminate him. He'd check progress on that front in a minute.

Second there was the withdrawal of the Romer loan. He had just managed to cover that by getting Morgan to sell one small subsidiary company at a ridiculously low price. He had never sold before: he had always acquired. It was like losing an arm.

And now there was this smart-alec Buchanan, linking the two cases. He didn't like the sound of Hanson being interviewed. Would the fellow have the sense to say nothing?

The drink helped. He stared at himself in a wall mirror. He looked quite normal, poised, sure of himself. Some of his arrogant self-confidence returned that he would win again. He always won. I've won every battle I've fought, he reminded himself. Nothing's changed: I can do anything.

He sat down at his desk and used his private line to call Morgan in Freiburg. He drummed his fingers on the desk top while he waited. Morgan came on the phone.

'Buckmaster here. Any progress with locating the target?'

'We not only know his whereabouts – he's in Zürich – but we know the exact route he's following when he tries to return by road.'

'If you have to take risks, take them. That consignment must not reach its destination. *Understood?*'

'Fully. Everything has been laid on for his reception . . .'

'Your head's on the block with this one.'

'That doesn't worry me . . .'

'But maybe this will. I've had a visit from a Chief Inspector Buchanan. CID. He asked questions linking the murder at Radnor Walk with Doyle's demise in Threadneedle Street.'

'My God! How could he do that?'

'He's done it, take my word. Oh, there's something else. Apparently he has a witness who alleges she saw Hanson enter Doyle's house – after Doyle's death.'

'I don't like the sound of that. What bloody bad luck . . .'

'So, you see, Morgan, your head really is on the block.'

Morgan began to reply and realized the line had gone dead. He swore as he replaced his own receiver. Buckmaster had gone off the line after delivering the appalling news. Morgan reached for his hip flask, unscrewed the cap, upended the flask and took a heavy slug. The news had unnerved him. He was sweating like a pig. They were

493

closing in on him – would Buckmaster throw him to the wolves if it came to that?

Tweed. He has to be liquidated this time, he told himself. Even if I have to pull the trigger.

Carrying his case, Marler walked into police headquarters in Zürich, announced his identity, said he had an appointment with Arthur Beck. The uniformed police receptionist asked for proof of his identity and Marler produced his passport. His profession was given as Insurance Executive.

He was escorted to a large room with a table in the centre and hard-backed wooden chairs pushed under it. The receptionist said someone would bring him coffee while he waited for Mr Beck.

Marler dumped his case on the spotless floor, lit a king-size cigarette and walked slowly round the room. The walls were painted white. The only furniture was the table and the chairs. The only object on the table top was a heavy glass ash-tray.

Three of the walls were blank. No pictures. On the fourth wall was a large rectangular mirror. Marler stood in front of it and studied the glass. Then he raised his right hand and flapped it in a little wave at the mirror.

On the other side in another room Beck stood alongside Tweed. They had a clear view of Marler. Beck stiffened in surprise when Marler gave his little wave. He looked at Tweed.

'Is that Marler?'

'Definitely.'

'What the devil is he waving at himself for?'

'He's waving at you. He's spotted this is a one-way window. As I said, that's Marler. I'd like to talk to him alone.'

'Be my guest. I'll lock this room and wait upstairs for you with the others . . .'

Tweed walked into the other room and Marler gave him a little salute as a policewoman brought in a tray with coffee and left them alone.

'You really are wicked,' Tweed observed as they sat at the table. 'Beck was startled when you gave your little wave.'

'The whole place screams interrogation room. So why a mirror? It had to be a one-way window for unseen observation. You're not showing signs of wear and tear considering you've been hunted across half Europe.'

'I'm all right. What's happening back at home?'

'I've been putting the wind up Buckmaster. You probably won't approve, but I had a faked picture concocted – showing Buckmaster on a couch with a luscious girl friend. Then I gave it to his wife, Leonora. Should set the cat among the pigeons.'

'I don't disapprove. The man is evil. I know that now.'

'I also had a chat with Chief Inspector Buchanan, the officer investigating the death of Doyle, the World Security Chief Accountant in Threadneedle Street. Told him Buckmaster still has a key to the private elevator up to where Doyle took his dive.'

'How did you find that out?'

'Again, you'll maybe not approve. It came out while I was in bed with the delightful Leonora. Pillow talk.'

'You have been busy . . .'

'Then I called Buchanan again, just after flying out here – and suggested he check the so-called hit-and-run death of Dr Rose. Very convenient. He conducted the post-mortem on the girl found in your bed.'

'You can't put too much pressure on Lance Buckmaster as far as I'm concerned. Anything else?'

'Yes. I may have cleared you of any connection with the girl murdered at Radnor Walk. What's your blood group?'

'A positive.'

'Which is the same as for forty per cent of the

population. I have a photocopy of Dr Rose's post-mortem report, courtesy of Howard. There were blood stains on the sheet – and more traces of blood and skin under one of the girl's fingernails. Her blood group is O positive. Same again as for forty per cent of the population. The punchline is the blood group of the traces under the girl's fingernail. I should have used the singular before. Her index finger. Same as the stain on the sheet. Blood group AB negative. A very *rare* group, the murderer's. My guess is we need to identify the blood groups of Buckmaster and Morgan.'

'Buckmaster's will be recorded at the Ministry of Defence. He's still a reserve officer in the Airborne forces. I have a friend at the MOD. When I get back home . . .'

'*If* you get back. What about Morgan?'

'That may be more difficult, but nothing's impossible . . .'

'Except your reaching London alive. How are you travelling?'

'By road. Now, don't start arguing – I've had enough of that from Paula, Newman *and* Beck.'

'Who's arguing?' Marler tipped ash into the glass bowl. 'I think that may be the safest mode of transport. Depends on the route.'

'That's decided.' Tweed pulled a map out of his pocket and spread it out on the table. 'From here to Basle. Cross into Germany at Basle, then straight up the autobahns at high speed. Later, veer off west through Belgium and arrange for a vessel to cross the Channel.'

Marler studied the route which was marked with a black felt-tip pen. He looked up at Tweed.

'This route has just been worked out?'

'No. I planned it a couple of days ago . . .'

'And told who?' Marler enquired.

'Paula, Newman, Beck and the police escort which will take us through to Basle . . .'

'Then change the route. There could have been a leak.'

'There probably has been. Morgan and Armand Horowitz crossed the frontier at Basle heading towards Freiburg two days ago.'

'I see.' Marler went quiet, blew a smoke ring, studied Tweed. 'You're setting yourself up as a target so they'll come after you. And you're relying on speed to get you through.'

'That and the cooperation of Otto Kuhlmann. I've spoken to him. He's alerting their élite group of counter-terrorist police.'

'You're not going to change your mind, so I won't waste my time. What I'll need is a chopper – preferably a Sikorsky – with a first-rate pilot. I'll also want a sniper-scope rifle.'

'You won't get either from Beck.'

'But I will from Kuhlmann. Then we'll run the gauntlet. It should prove interesting.'

49

8 a.m. The call from Tokyo came through to Buckmaster's Belgravia flat as he was preparing to leave for the Ministry. While he waited for the girl at the other end to put him through to his Far East Managing Director, John Lloyd-Davies, Buckmaster calculated the time difference. It would be 5 p.m., local Tokyo time.

'That you, Buckmaster?' Lloyd-Davies asked in a strained voice.

'Yes. Some problem?'

'You could say that. World Security shares dropped

twenty per cent today on the Tokyo stock-exchange. A tidal wave of selling. No buying.'

'For God's sake, why?'

'Due to strong rumours that World Security is going bust. That its liabilities vastly outweigh its assets. Some problem, as you said.'

'Where are these absurd rumours coming from?'

'I've been trying to track them. Which is why I waited to call you. Top financial consultants are advising clients to get out fast. I haven't traced the source yet. At midday I issued a reassuring statement. It did nothing to stem the panic.'

'Now, listen to me.' Buckmaster gripped the phone tighter. 'I want you to use every contact you have to find out who is behind this. Money, threats – whatever it takes. And report back to me as soon as you find the enemy. Then we can deal with him. That's it.'

Buckmaster put the phone down and stared into space. What would happen when the London market opened? Let alone Wall Street? They were all a lot of sheep. He didn't like the sound of what Lloyd-Davies had said. *A tidal wave of selling . . . It did nothing to stem the panic.*

Picking up the phone again he pressed buttons for the number of his main London broker. Jeff Berners might just be at his office early. He was. Berners answered the call himself, sounded impatient.

'Yes, who is it?'

'Buckmaster. I've just had a call from Tokyo . . .'

'I was about to phone you myself,' Berners broke in. 'You have heard about the big fall? So have we. Here they're already talking about marking down World Security shares by twenty-five per cent . . .'

'That's crazy . . .'

'Purely a precautionary move.' Berners now was soothing. 'Buyers should arrive in droves at that price. At least I hope so . . .'

'You hope so?' shouted Buckmaster. 'We're talking about one of the biggest conglomerates in the world. Quoted on the Tokyo, Sydney, New York, London and Frankfurt exchanges . . .'

'Which could fuel the flames,' Berners warned. 'There have been ugly rumours. One that a major bank in Tokyo is considering withdrawing its loan. Another that Zurcher Kredit in Zürich *have* withdrawn their loan. We called Zurcher Kredit but they wouldn't react, refused to give any comment.'

'Well, there you are.'

'Are we? No Swiss bank ever releases information concerning its transactions. Is it true by any chance?'

'Of course not. I'm surprised you ask me. Where are these rumours coming from?' Buckmaster demanded.

'No one can pinpoint them. There's even a rumour it's a massive bear-raid to force down the price prior to a huge consortium bidding for World Security. That could shove up the price today.'

'Will it do that?'

'You want my frank opinion?'

'For what it's worth.'

Berner's tone hardened. He didn't appreciate the sarcasm. 'People are doing their sums. They calculate you're needing at least five hundred million pounds just to stay afloat.'

Buckmaster felt ice-cold. Where was this precise information coming from? For a moment he was thrown off balance, then he recovered. No hint of his reaction must appear in his response.

'Then they'd damned well better do their sums again.'

'The trouble is,' Berners went on, ignoring the thrust, 'in the market everything is finally based on confidence and on trust. I'll keep you informed of developments . . .'

'Do that thing,' Buckmaster said and ended the conversation.

He sat behind his desk, his mind racing. A couple of minutes later the phone rang again. He snatched up the receiver.

'Yes?'

'Is that Mr Buckmaster? Chief Inspector Buchanan speaking.'

'Yes. What do you want now?'

'Simply to ask you did you ever meet a man called Dr Charles Rose?'

To Buckmaster it felt like a bombardment. His mind raced in a different direction. This was the last question he had expected. Should he deny all knowledge? Just in time he stopped himself falling into the trap.

'The name is familiar. Give me a moment to think. I meet so many people. Yes, it's coming back to me now. This subject does concern national security . . .'

'It also concerns possible murder. A third murder, sir.'

'Would you mind explaining that cryptic remark a little more?'

At the other end of the line Buchanan smiled to himself. He was up against an opponent worthy of his steel. No wonder Buckmaster was feared during debate in the House of Commons, noted for his ability to think on his feet, to slash an antagonist to verbal ribbons.

'Not at all, sir. Dr Rose was the pathologist who examined the body of the young woman found murdered in Tweed's flat. Not long after conducting his post-mortem he walked out of St Thomas's Hospital one dark evening. At his usual time. A great man for precise routine, Dr Rose. He was knocked down and killed in the street by an alleged hit-and-run driver.'

'Alleged?'

'That was what I said, sir. I have reopened the case since I have reason to believe it was cold-blooded murder. And in his appointments book is noted a meeting with you at the Ministry. Does that help your memory?'

'Yes, it does. I remember now. I can't say much about this for obvious reasons – of national security. But Dr Rose came to show me his post-mortem report on the girl found at Radnor Walk. Simple as that.'

'Thank you, sir. And did Dr Rose leave the report with you?'

'Of course not. He took it away with him. The interview couldn't have lasted longer than ten minutes. That's all I can tell you – because that's all there is to tell.'

'You see my problem, sir? I have three deaths to investigate. And the only link between the three is yourself. You were at Radnor Walk. Ted Doyle was your Chief Accountant. And you met Dr Rose.'

'I don't see your problem at all, Buchanan. I repeat what I said to you the last time we met. I am only prepared to discuss these matters with Harvey of the Special Branch. I suggest that from now on you go through the proper channels. Otherwise I may have to complain to the Assistant Commissioner. Do I make my meaning clear?'

'Perfectly, sir. And, of course, it is your privilege and your right to communicate with the AC at any time . . .'

'Don't lecture me,' Buckmaster rasped. 'I probably know the form better than you ever will. And now, if you don't mind, I'd like this line free for an urgent call I'm expecting from Frankfurt.'

'Thank you for your co-operation, sir . . .'

In his office Buchanan put down the phone. He had been talking into the air. Warden looked up from his desk and raised his eyebrows.

'Sounds as though it didn't go too well, sir.'

'On the contrary, Buckmaster is beginning to crack. He could easily have invoked national security to refuse to say a word about Dr Rose. The interesting thing is he went out of his way to explain why Rose came to see him. Which makes me wonder more about our esteemed Minister for External Security.'

'You think you'll break him down in the end?'

'I don't know. But as I've just said, Buckmaster is beginning to crack under the pressure.'

In his study Buckmaster sat with his hands clenched together. The whites of the knuckles showed. It *was* like a bombardment – coming at him from all directions.

He stood up, took the swagger cane he'd used as an officer from a drawer, and walked very erect round the room, slapping his thigh with the cane. During training with the Airborne Division he'd been under live fire. He hadn't flinched from that: he wasn't going to flinch from present difficulties.

The door opened and Leonora walked in. He glared at her. As she'd come in he'd been walking, slapping the cane he still held in his hand. She stared at him with a peculiar expression and then spoke cautiously.

'What are you doing, Lance?'

'Planning on how to conquer the world.'

She sucked in her breath as he continued marching round the room, holding himself ramrod erect. He held his head tilted back as he had when inspecting the troops.

'You're not in the Army now,' she remarked.

He turned on her. His eyes blazed. 'Why don't you knock before you enter my study. I don't want you in here. You're disturbing my planning – my strategic planning. Kindly get to hell out of here!'

She lost colour. She backed away from him. She fiddled for the door handle behind her back, found it, opened the door, backed out and closed it. Outside she leaned against the door and closed her eyes. She was convinced her husband was going mad.

50

Before leaving Zürich, Tweed had a final conference with Beck at police HQ. In the office sat Paula, Newman, Butler, Nield and Marler. Beck had marked the escape route on a large-scale map of Western Europe pinned to a wall. Seated behind the table Tweed looked worried.

'You're not sure this is a good idea now, are you?' Beck remarked.

'On the contrary, I'm more determined than ever to follow the planned route. What's on my mind is the fate of the original crew of the *Lampedusa*. I feel responsible.'

'If I were you, I'd get that out of your mind,' Beck advised. 'You have plenty to concentrate on getting back to London. Everything is organized.' He checked his watch. 'Midnight. You leave in one hour. And Chief Inspector Kuhlmann of the Federal Police has promised full co-operation once you cross into Germany.'

'I'd like a word with Kuhlmann once we're over the frontier,' Marler intervened. 'After all, I am the deception specialist.'

'That can be arranged.' Beck perched his backside on the far end of the table. 'Tweed, you're sure you have enough solid evidence to clear yourself of the accusation of murder and rape in your London apartment?'

'More than enough. Partly thanks to Marler,' he added without elaborating.

'And you think you know who the murderer is?' Beck persisted. 'Buckmaster or Morgan?'

'One of them,' Tweed replied cryptically. 'And I predict

my arrival in London will be the final straw which topples Buckmaster.' He looked at Newman. 'Not that he's in too good a shape now after those phone calls you made all over the world. World Security shares are dropping like the proverbial stone.'

'And I've more calls to make as we head north,' Newman told him. 'It will be a débâcle.'

'You're all assuming Tweed will get there alive,' protested Paula. 'After what happened at Brunni I've no idea what may face us once we arrive in Germany.'

'Not us,' Tweed corrected her. 'Arrangements have been made for you to fly home from Basle under an assumed name . . .'

'Then you can cancel your bloody arrangements. I'm seeing this thing through to the bitter end. You'd have to carry me aboard that plane.'

'Don't push it any more,' Newman warned as Tweed opened his mouth and then closed it without speaking.

'Unless,' Marler drawled, 'you're insinuating Paula would be a handicap on the trip.'

'Blast you both,' Tweed reacted with unaccustomed vehemence.

'Then that's settled,' concluded Paula, and gave him her best smile.

'I feel happier having Paula with us,' Butler remarked. 'A woman often observes something a man misses – she has a good eye for small details.'

'One more thing,' Beck informed them, looking at Paula, Newman, Butler and Nield. 'You're all carrying weapons I supplied. You can keep them while you're still in Switzerland, but before you cross the frontier at Basle you hand all of them back to me.'

Tweed picked up his briefcase and clutched it on his lap. It contained the previous year's appointments book of the call-girl, Sylvia Harman. Beck knew of her existence and had sealed her apartment while his men searched it inch by inch. But Tweed had omitted to tell him about the book. Beck then sprang his surprise.

'If that is all I suggest we leave now. One hour ahead of the planned departure time.'

Tweed was intrigued. Did Beck suspect there was an informant inside his HQ? It had seemed strange he had not suspected the likelihood of a leak. He stood up and Beck led the way downstairs to the cars waiting outside. The others followed, carrying their cases. Tweed's return to England had begun.

Outside the HQ Tweed paused on Lindenhofstrasse before getting into the first of the cars. Paula fumed as he stood there, head cocked to one side. Zürich was very quiet at that hour. What was the unusual sound he had heard? Glancing up, he saw the icicles suspended from the roof gutter. By the light of a street lamp he saw globules of water forming, sliding down the icicles, dropping into the snow below with a soft *plop!* Behind him Beck spoke.

'Yes, the temperature has suddenly risen above zero. The big melt is coming. At last.'

'Which', Marler commented next to him, 'will make driving conditions on the autobahns diabolical if the same thing's happening in Germany.'

'We'll find out when we get there,' Tweed replied and sat in the front passenger seat.

Beck, who was driving him, slipped behind the wheel while Newman took a rear seat alongside an armed detective. As the car started off Newman checked his fully-loaded Magnum inside his hip holster. He could extract it swiftly even inside the car.

Marler took the front passenger seat in the second car and beside him another detective took the wheel. Paula and a third detective sat in the rear. Butler and Nield were inside the last car, one a front seat passenger, the other in the rear, and two detectives accompanied them.

The snow-streaked streets of Zürich were traffic-free as Beck drove out of the city of green spires and ancient buildings. He moved at high speed and followed a devious route towards Basle. Once clear of Zürich, he accelerated, way over the speed limit.

Inside his office at the World Security building in Freiburg, Morgan put down the phone. He shifted his bulk in the chair and gazed at Horowitz with a bland smile.

'My Zürich informant. Tweed & Co left just after midnight. Tweed, his mistress, Newman, three other men, and five detectives. They're coming towards us along the planned route. My informant slipped into Beck's office after they'd gone. And on the wall was a big map with the route marked. Straight up the autobahns from Basle towards Belgium. We're in business.'

'An odd lapse of security, that wall map.'

'Nobody's perfect. And Beck himself is driving the car which has Tweed inside it.'

'And the position at the Basle crossing?' Horowitz enquired.

'Everything's set up. Stieber is waiting there – on the German side, of course. In his Münich film studios van. The police checked him earlier.'

'And left him there?' Horowitz's tone was incredulous.

'Organization.' Morgan waved a stubby-fingered hand, his nails trimmed short. 'Stieber and his driver both have identity cards showing them as members of the Münich film unit. Stieber told the police wallah his van had broken down, that they were waiting for a repair truck. No one's worried.'

'Again, most curious.'

'If you don't like it, I'll handle the job myself,' Morgan snarled.

Horowitz nodded. The pressure was getting to Morgan despite his air of self-confidence. He checked his watch. They would know soon enough now.

It was the middle of the night when Beck stopped the car in an old village near the outskirts of Basle. For the third time during a journey at breakneck speed he took hold of the microphone, used the code signal, *Matterhorn*, and reported his position to Basle HQ.

'I'm going to stretch my legs,' said Tweed. 'You can spare a few minutes?'

'Just a few . . .'

Tweed stepped out into the darkness of a deserted street. Behind him Newman also left the car, the Magnum held by his side. He was followed by the detective, holding a Walther.

It was still cold as Tweed walked up and down in the snow. He looked up at the rooftops of the ancient houses with their dormer windows. Patches of tiles showed where the snow had retreated. He paused. There was a constant drip-drip as the icicles, shorter than in Zürich, sent a constant flow of water droplets into the snow. Underfoot it was soggy – the iron-hard crust had gone. The thaw was speeding up.

'We can provide a hot meal for you at headquarters before we drive to the frontier,' Beck called out.

'Thank you, but I'd sooner keep moving now we've started.'

He got back inside the car with Newman and the detective and Beck sped forward again. He stopped again a little later. Behind them the other two cars pulled up. Beck asked Paula and Newman for their weapons. He made a hand signal out of the window and in the rear car Butler and Nield surrendered their gas- and smoke-pistols.

Beck drove on, crossed a bridge over the Rhine. Within

minutes they had reached the control point between the two countries. Beck stopped his car at the cabin on the Swiss side and a short, stocky, broad-shouldered figure smoking a cigar appeared. Otto Kuhlmann. He shook hands with Tweed as the Englishman climbed out of the car. A detective fetched the cases from the boot.

'Good of you to meet us, Otto,' Tweed said. 'I certainly didn't expect to find you here at this hour. Now! What do we do next?'

'All arranged. We walk across to our frontier post where you see the silver Mercedes waiting.'

'We may be driving into an ambush,' Tweed warned. 'By now I reckon the opposition is desperate.'

'That's been foreseen, anticipated. And I have an account to settle with this World Security gang. One of their trucks once tried to smuggle forbidden high-tech equipment over the border into East Germany. We stopped them, but I could never make the case stick.'

'And you have a long memory,' Newman interjected.

Kuhlmann, an impressive and formidable figure in his dark business suit, grinned at Newman, held out his hand.

'Welcome to the party, Bob. A little while since we last met in Frankfurt. A lot of water has flowed under the bridge since then . . .'

Tweed had thanked Beck and said goodbye while the two men were greeting each other. Then he picked up his case as Paula joined him and they walked towards the Mercedes. Their feet slopped through snow which had become slush. Beyond the Mercedes a large black van was parked well to the side of the road with its rear facing them, a rear with two doors and a porthole window in each door. Tweed noticed by the street lamps it bore in German the legend, *Münich Film Studios Unit*. At intervals on the German sides of the road tall, tough-looking men in camouflage gear carried automatic weapons and watched them coming.

'Who are they?' Paula whispered.

'German anti-terrorist police. We are being received in style.'

Paula shivered. 'Let's get inside the car. It's one of the big jobs.'

She was right. The gleaming vehicle had the capacity to take Tweed, Paula, Newman, Marler, Butler, Nield and one other. Behind them Marler was making his request to Kuhlmann with all the reassurance that it would be granted.

'I'm a marksman. Tweed will confirm my statement. There will be an ambush, maybe more than one. I need a sniperscope rifle and a chopper. Preferably a Sikorsky with an expert pilot. I need to guard this car from the air.'

'You talk big,' Kuhlmann remarked in his gravelly voice. He studied Marler who stared back with his ice-blue eyes. 'OK. I'll oblige you. And with a Sikorsky. But you'll have to wait until we reach Freiburg.'

'Then what are we waiting for?'

Without a glance at the broken-down film-unit van, Kuhlmann ushered his flock inside the Mercedes. Butler and Nield sat on flap seats in the rear, facing Newman and Marler. Tweed ushered Paula into the front passenger seat and waited until Kuhlmann, cigar between his teeth, walked up to him.

'Otto, do you mind if I drive? I've been doing damn-all the past few hours.'

Paula winked at Kuhlmann. 'He just wants to let rip now we're on a German autobahn.'

'Well, I gather he was driving when that articulated truck tried to mow you down when you were last approaching Freiburg. If you'll risk it, I will.'

He went back, opened the rear door and squeezed himself in by Newman's side. Throwing his cigar into the snow, he slammed the door and called out to Tweed.

'I'll guide you. We hit the autobahn soon. Just try and get us there in one piece, there's a good chap . . .'

Morgan put down the phone in his Freiburg office and looked again at Horowitz.

'That was Stieber from his film-unit van. A silver Mercedes, 500 SEL, registration number . . . Headed towards here out from Basle. Tweed's inside it with other passengers. We've got them.'

'Maybe. The petrol tanker is ready?'

'Stationed in a side road just off the autobahn south of Karlsruhe. That where you're going to take them?'

'It's just starting. I'll see how things develop. I never finalize a plan until I have all the data.'

'You'll have a film show soon as Stieber arrives here with his van,' Morgan said jauntily.

Autobahn E 35 stretched ahead in the night endlessly like a huge unrolled carpet, a carpet streaked white and grey in their headlights as Tweed drove at high speed. There was hardly any other traffic. The grey streaks were dangerous – snow had melted, exposing ice below it.

The Mercedes glided through the night and Paula was lulled almost to sleep. She jerked wide awake suddenly as the car swung into a violent skid. Her hands clenched. She glanced at Tweed. His expression was calm as he drove into the skid and the steel barrier loomed up in the glow of the headlamps. Paula closed her eyes, waited for the impact. Tweed slowed, turned the wheel a fraction, skimmed past the barrier and drove on. In the rear Kuhlmann grunted.

'You handled that well. Some of this surface is shot ice.'

'I could have handled it better,' Tweed commented. 'I missed the gleam on the ice. I'll know better next time.'

A large sign appeared in the distance. Kuhlmann leaned forward to see it more clearly.

'You turn off right ahead. Direction Mulheim.'

'We're still south of Freiburg.'

'I said I'd guide you,' Kuhlmann said gently. 'I'm doing just that.'

'I want to be in Belgium before daylight. This is a detour.'

'And you'll see why when you take it.'

Tweed followed directions, took the turn-off for Mulheim. They drove along a deserted road which seemed familiar to Tweed. He waited awhile before he spoke to Kuhlmann.

'Surely we're heading up for Badenweiler Spa, for the Black Forest?'

'Only a short distance. Trust me. I have a little surprise waiting for you, for the opposition.'

Paula, wide awake now, stared ahead. The road was climbing, the snow was thicker on the surface. At least it covered that diabolical ice. Kuhlmann told Tweed to take a side turning to the right and he found himself driving along a road just wide enough for the Mercedes. And still climbing.

'Slow down,' Kuhlmann warned. 'You're coming to a gap in the trees to the left. Take it. And maybe you wouldn't mind slowing down.' He glanced at Newman. 'I didn't know your chief was an ex-racing driver.'

'Got the bit between his teeth,' commented Paula, then she gazed in astonishment as Tweed turned and they entered a vast amphitheatre which was a worked-out limestone quarry. The headlights shone on the walls rising, cliff-like, at the far end. But what held her was the sight of five cars parked in a semi-circular laager-like fashion. Tweed also stared.

Five silver Mercedes, all of them 500 SELs. And they all had the same registration number as the car he was

511

driving. He braked and spoke over his shoulder.

'What on earth is this circus, Otto?'

Kuhlmann chuckled grimly. 'I only had two days to set this up. Getting the cars was easy. Making up the number plates so they all matched the registration of this car was the very devil. But we managed it.'

'I don't quite see the idea,' Paula observed, 'or am I being dim?'

'You saw that Münich film-unit van parked near the border in Basle? That was World Security – filming Tweed's arrival – and this car we got into. I ordered the control police to question the driver superficially and leave it alone.'

'Why?'

'World Security runs its own espionage network. A dismissed employee came to me and spilled the beans. I've been letting them run on a loose rein, waiting my opportunity.' His tone became grim. 'This is it. You get it, Tweed?'

'I think so, but you explain.'

'That film unit will confirm you're travelling in a silver Mercedes with this registration number. They're stopping at nothing to prevent you reaching England alive. How do I know that? They bribed one of my assistants, Kurt Meyer, to give them information. I became suspicious of Meyer. Again I let him run loose for awhile. He used to report from a local public call-box. I had it bugged. Two days ago, when Beck told me you were coming through, I arrested him, put him in solitary.' He glanced at Paula. 'I grilled him myself.'

Paula gave a mock shudder, which was only partly mock. The thought of being cross-examined by Kuhlmann was not a pleasant thought.

'He cracked,' Kuhlmann went on, as though the outcome was the most natural thing in the world. 'Told me about the film van and that a major assault would be made on your way through Germany. So I prepared this.' He

512

waved his cigar at the laager of Mercedes. 'Six cars will travel up the autobahn, all the same make and colour – and all with the same registration number. You, Tweed, will travel in one of them. But which one? They'll have trouble working that out.'

'And who will be inside the other cars?'

'The élite anti-terrorist unit armed to the teeth, all wearing business suits.'

'That reminds me,' said Newman, 'I'd appreciate it if you could loan me a Magnum .45 with spare mags . . .'

'And', Marler chipped in, 'you promised me a Sikorsky and a sniperscope rifle.'

'Waiting for you at the airfield at Freiburg. One of the cars will peel off and take you to the chopper. The pilot knows the plan, will easily catch up with us . . .'

'We'd also like weapons,' Butler suggested in his flat voice. 'Nield and myself. Walthers would suit us fine.'

'That's OK. One of those cars contains an armoury of guns.' He reached a sheaf of papers out of his pocket. 'Just sign these – they're temporary permits to carry weapons. Makes it all legal and above board. I prepared yours, Newman, in advance – and yours, Marler. Beck passed on your request while you were waiting to leave Zürich.' He looked at Butler and Nield. 'You two fill in your names, then sign on the dotted line.' He switched on the overhead light.

'Why are you doing all this for us?' Paula asked. 'And I'd like a Browning automatic . . .'

'Which is waiting for you, again courtesy of Arthur Beck's calling me. Here's your bit of paper. Why am I doing all this? To settle my score with World Security. They're going to attack our convoy, using some of their own personnel. They have some pretty dubious characters on their payroll – but always with no prison records. I want to catch them in the act . . .'

'With Tweed as the target, the tethered goat,' Paula said indignantly.

513

Kuhlmann threw up his hands. 'I thought it was your chief's idea that we do it this way . . .'

'It was,' Tweed said quietly. 'I'm quite satisfied. Which car will I travel in?'

'Second one in the convoy. You can decide who travels with you – on condition you don't drive. Too exposed.'

'I'd like Paula to come with me,' Tweed suggested. 'Then you can organize the rest of the seating arrangements.'

'OK. You sit in the rear with Paula. A couple of my men will occupy the front seats. I'll be in the third car – behind you. Newman can ride with me.'

'That's settled then,' Tweed said impatiently. 'Hadn't we better get the show on the road?'

'Why not?' responded Kuhlmann and opened the car door. 'We should hit the Belgian border before dawn.'

They stepped out into the raw night cold, their feet crunching on stones under the melting snow. In the silence of the darkness they could hear at the end of the quarry the sound of running water sliding down from the top of the cliff. Paula shivered as she glanced round while they approached the cars. The towering walls of the quarry reminded her of an ancient Roman amphitheatre where people died.

51

A short time after Tweed had turned off the autobahn towards Mulheim, Stieber drove his van north to Freiburg. Under the bonnet was a souped-up engine.

Half an hour later Morgan and Horowitz sat together in

the small cinema in the basement at World Security. Stieber sat behind them as the projectionist ran the film taken from the porthole window in one of the rear doors of the van.

Horowitz sat erect, his eyes motionless behind the steel-rimmed spectacles. He studied Tweed closely as he emerged from the Swiss car, ignoring the others. He noted the shoulders hunched against the cold but the head held high, glancing in all directions as he walked slowly through the snow towards the German post. The pause while he stamped snow off his shoes – an opportunity he seized to look straight at the van filming him. Laufenburg all over again – when he had gazed at the house above the Rhine filming his crossing into Switzerland. A reflection from a lamp caught the lenses of his glasses. For a few seconds they were silver, like laser eyes staring at the van. Then the glance swung away in an arc, observing everything at the frontier post. And, by his side, the Grey woman, also glancing all round.

To Horowitz there seemed something implacable in the slow deliberate walk into Germany. This was the man he had hunted across half a continent. Any other target would have been dead long ago.

'That's him,' Stieber whispered excitedly in the dark from a seat behind them.

'Shut your mouth,' Horowitz said with deadly calm. 'I am concentrating . . .'

Still motionless, he watched them approaching a silver Mercedes. 500 SEL. More men followed Tweed and the girl. A flock of them stood round the car as Tweed climbed inside. The registration number was clear – because the car was parked under a street lamp. Why? It would have been so easy to park it in the shadows. Odd. Very odd. Horowitz felt a warning tingle. The rest of the passengers climbed inside the car. One was Robert Newman. Of course . . .

The Mercedes moved off. Past the van. Out of sight.

Horowitz was convinced Tweed had known he was under observation. The whole film clip had the atmosphere of a stage-managed scene enacted for his viewing. The screen flashed white. End of film clip.

Horowitz still sat motionless as the lights came up in the cinema. Morgan stirred beside him, stared at his companion. He dug him gently in the ribs.

'That's it. Now we know the vehicle he's travelling in.'

Horowitz still stared at the blank screen. His voice was detached, as though he gazed into the distance and saw something invisible to Morgan and Stieber. Then he spoke, tersely, in a voice devoid of emotion.

'I need a silver Mercedes. 500 SEL. Like that car.'

'That we can provide,' Morgan said complacently. 'It just so happens we have one in the garage here. It's kept for when Buckmaster visits us. I give it a run now and again to keep the engine tuned up.'

'I'd also have liked the same number plates, but I'd assume there's no time to fake a pair.'

'Not really. We have to leave here at once. Stieber reported he didn't see the car when he was driving the van with that film here. And he can move fast in that van – he suspects they saw him coming, speeded up and took a turn-off. But they'll be back on the autobahn. That map inside Beck's office proves that.'

Horowitz stood up abruptly. 'Take me to the car at once. And your men are already positioned on the autobahn at intervals? And the petrol tanker south of Karlsruhe?'

He was walking towards the exit leading to the garage as he spoke and Morgan, his overfed frame wobbling, had trouble keeping up with him.

'Everything is laid on . . .'

'And your men are carrying no identification, I presume?'

'In the rush I didn't bother. No one in that car will survive the holocaust we've planned.'

'It's your company . . .'

Inside the huge underground garage it was cold and Horowitz slipped into his fur-lined trench coat. As he hurried to the Mercedes he put on his gloves. Reaching it, he scooped up handfuls of frozen snow dropped from the wheels of other cars and carefully smeared it over the front number plate. He repeated the process with the rear plate.

'I'm coming with you?' Morgan suggested.

'No one is coming with me. The keys . . .'

Unlocking the car, he climbed in behind the wheel and Morgan waddled over to open the automatic doors, pressing a button on a wall panel. The huge doors opened slowly with a grinding sound as they broke the ice.

Inside the car Horowitz took from his shoulder holster his Luger, checked the weapon. It was a 9-mm calibre Parabellum, probably the most widely used cartridge of its type. The muzzle had been adapted to take a silencer. Horowitz took the silencer from his pocket, screwed it on, laid the weapon on the seat beside him with spare mags. It had a magazine capacity of eight rounds. One should be enough.

For his steel-rimmed glasses he substituted a pair of horn-rims which altered his appearance. From his pocket he extracted a crumpled black beret and rammed it on his head. The transformation was complete. Without glancing at Morgan, who was running towards a BMW, he drove out, headed for the E 35 autobahn.

As the convoy of six silver Mercedes approached Freiburg the rear car peeled off, driving away up a turn-off leading to the airfield. Inside the car Marler sat in the front next to the detective driver. The other five cars disappeared north towards Karlsruhe.

Reaching the airfield, the car pulled up close to a Sikorsky helicopter with a ladder leading to the main cabin. At the foot of the ladder stood a uniformed policeman carrying an automatic rifle. Marler dived out of the car, thanked the driver, ran towards the guard with his identity card in his hand.

'Marler,' he said, handing the man his card. 'And I'm in one hell of a hurry to take off before someone is killed.'

The guard checked the card with the aid of a pencil flash, handed it back and gestured. Marler ran up the ladder and at the top a burly German in pilot's gear hauled him inside. Marler was talking fast again.

'You have a sniperscope rifle for me?'

'Ready and waiting, sir . . .'

'I have to sight it. Ammo?'

'Incendiary bullets, as requested.'

Marler fed the cartridges into the weapon, asked the pilot, who had retracted the automatic ladder, to leave the door open a moment. He aimed the rifle through the opening, the stock firm against his shoulder. The pilot suddenly pointed.

'There's that wild rabid dog again. The brute's already bitten one of the airport staff. Had to be rushed to hospital. Touch and go whether . . .'

Marler was staring through the night 'scope. Standing in the snow, forelegs apart, was a large mastiff. The 'scope brought the dog's head up close, its mouth smeared with foam, its teeth showing. It began trotting towards the chopper. Marler adjusted the sight, the dog's ugly head and chest filled the 'scope. He pulled the trigger. The report echoed across the airfield. The mastiff disappeared in a bursting cloud of blood, flesh and bone.

'It's been running wild in the woods,' the pilot said. 'I can take off for the autobahn when you're ready '

'How about now?'

*   *   *

Morgan drove the BMW on to the autobahn and headed north. Beside him sat Stieber with a detailed map of the autobahn and the surrounding areas open on his lap. At certain points a cross marked different areas alongside the E 35. These were the carefully chosen ambush areas – where World Security guards waited with various weapons to annihilate the silver Mercedes.

All the waiting ambushers were in radio communication with a control point at Freiburg to co-ordinate the information. Morgan drove at medium speed for two reasons as the occasional flash of distant headlights indicated a vehicle coming towards them on the southbound lanes.

'You did give Horowitz one of those marked maps?' Morgan asked Stieber.

'He has a map with the same markings I have.'

'Good. And keep that radio connection open so we know what is happening.'

One reason Morgan drove at a medium speed was the state of the autobahn. The thaw was continuing. At intervals the streaks of melting snow exposed gleaming patches reflecting in their headlights like glass. Solid ice . . .

The second – and more important reason – he held down speed was he didn't want to run into the holocaust when it happened. He wasn't paid to take risks like that. The head of the Research & Development Division which had planned the ambushes was Stieber. He was an ideal choice for the job. He *enjoyed* his work.

'Shouldn't you step on the gas?' Stieber suggested. 'We're going to miss all the excitement . . .'

'The only thing I may step on is you. Shut up while I drive. It will all happen soon now.'

Inside his silver Mercedes Horowitz drove at high speed along E 35. Under the Luger on the seat beside him was the map with the ambush locations. He drove with great skill, avoiding the deadly ice, hands holding the wheel lightly. Horowitz was quite relaxed: at last he was alone and could handle the situation in his own way.

As at Brunni, he foresaw another débâcle – after all it had been organized by Morgan, a man for whom he had the utmost professional contempt. A con-man, a lackey and lickspittle for his boss, Buckmaster.

Ahead the autobahn followed a great curve, which gave him an excellent view. He sat up straighter. Spread out at intervals round the curve was a convoy of no fewer than five silver Mercedes. For a moment Horowitz was puzzled before he understood the strategy.

Driving with one hand on the wheel, he quickly examined the cars through a small pair of night glasses. His eyes narrowed as he spotted they all had the same registration plate number. He put down the glasses. Clever, very clever. He sensed the hand of Kuhlmann.

In one of those five cars Tweed was riding. *Which* one was the intriguing problem. He watched as they continued driving round the long curve. Car Number Two moved closer to Car Number One. Like a ballet Car Number Three closed up to Car Number Two. The remaining two Mercedes kept their distance at the rear of the convoy. The last Mercedes was a long way back. The rearguard.

The ghost of a smile appeared on Horowitz's normally expressionless face. Tweed was in Car Number Two. First part of the problem solved. Target located. Second part of the problem – how to get alongside Car Number Two.

Horowitz glanced at the map. The first ambush point was about five miles ahead. Horowitz had already worked out his operational plan. The rear car was quite a distance behind the convoy. The first ambush would be launched where the autobahn again followed a long curve. At that point – providing conditions were favourable – he would carry out the first phase of his plan.

* * *

Inside the second Mercedes Tweed sat in the rear seat closest to the steel barrier. Beside him sat Paula, erect, her shoulder bag looped over her left side. In front a detective was driving. In the passenger seat next to him was another detective.

There was so little traffic that the fast-moving convoy was occupying the inside lane. Tweed sat relaxed, eyes half-shut. By contrast Paula was like a coiled spring, staring at the car ahead, turning to check the position of the car behind them.

In the third car Kuhlmann sat beside another detective who was driving. In the rear seats Newman sat next to Butler – who also kept glancing round, a Walther resting in his lap. Newman also appeared to be half-asleep. The steady drumming of the convoy's engines had a hypnotic effect. Butler stirred again.

'Stop shifting about,' Newman suggested.

'I prefer to keep my eyes open, to see what's happening.'

'We'll all know when it happens,' Newman told him.

'That's a fact,' agreed Kuhlmann and bit on his unlit cigar.

At Freiburg Airport Marler was inwardly fuming. Just before take-off they had detected a mechanical fault. Men in overalls were working on the engine, fighting to correct the fault quickly. Outwardly, Marler waited calmly in his seat, staring out of the window at the bleak night. Beside him the pilot rolled cigarettes, placed his latest one inside an ancient tobacco tin. Between his lips dangled an unlit cigarette, tobacco dripping out of the tip.

'It shouldn't be long now,' he remarked.

'When they're ready I'd appreciate it if you move fast.'

'Will do. I've radioed the delay to Kuhlmann. He replied.'

'What did he say?'

'Something unprintable.'

'I can guess.' Marler resisted the temptation to check his watch. When they were airborne, they were airborne. If they were in time.

Morgan kept up his medium speed which would keep him miles behind the silver Mercedes transporting Tweed. There had been only one brief message on the agreed radio band. From Horowitz.

'Preserve radio silence at all costs . . .'

What the hell did that mean? Morgan wondered. It sounded promising – as though Horowitz knew what he was doing. He glanced at Stieber as he began moving round a long curve.

'How far to the first attack point?'

'About twenty miles from here.'

'We should hear something then. I hope. Tweed must be almost there now.'

Horowitz turned the wheel as he began moving round the second long curve. He could see only the last two cars and then the first of these disappeared. He glanced again at the map. The first ambush point was coming up. They might get Tweed at a first attempt, but he doubted it.

He began to put his manoeuvre into operation. Inside the silver Mercedes he saw the blurred outline of a figure glancing back. They'd be puzzled at first by his appearance. The fact that his number plate was obscured wouldn't worry them over much: slush had been whipped up by the wheels for long stretches. He increased speed, closing the gap between himself and the other car.

He lowered the window alongside himself. For two reasons. He had to hear the sounds of the ambush the moment it was launched. The second reason was more deadly. Both cars were moving at speed, which suited Horowitz's purpose. As he froze from the icy air flooding in he listened for the ambush . . .

The first Mercedes in the convoy was a long way round the curve, still in the inner lane and close to the steel barrier. There was no other traffic in sight ahead. The first warning they had that they had run into an ambush came when a rattle of bullets from two Uzi machine-pistols hammered the rear of the car. The driver did the unexpected. Instead of speeding up he slowed down.

'OK, Arber,' he said to the man alongside him. 'Respond.'

Arber lowered the automatic window. The sound of the fusillade had become a cannonade. Beyond the barrier figures clad in Balaclava helmets and ski suits stood behind the barrier, their weapon muzzles aimed. Arber had extracted the pin from a grenade, hurled it. He grabbed the second grenade in his lap, extracted the pin, hurled it. All this in fractions of a second.

The detonation of the grenades murdered the night. The men behind the barrier flung up their arms, fell backwards. The window behind Arber had been lowered. A machine-pistol projected, a hail of answering fire swept along the barrier as more Balaclava-helmeted figures appeared. Like targets in a shooting gallery they collapsed as the bullets ploughed into them. More grenades were thrown from the car. Detonations succeeded each other so one almost merged with another. One attacker held a rocket launcher. His finger was on the trigger when a stream of bullets laced across his chest. He jerked backwards, the launcher pointed skywards, its projectile exploded in the night high above the autobahn. Then silence. The convoy moved on.

In the third car Kuhlmann grinned, spoke to his driver as they sped on.

'The damned fools assumed Tweed was in the first car.

523

Not a bullet hit Tweed's vehicle.' He reached for the phone. 'Thor speaking. Our location is . . . Send the meat wagons. No hurry. Let them bleed . . .'

In the distance Horowitz heard the cannonade, the detonating grenades. This was the moment. He accelerated. Driving with one hand, his other hand rested on the ledge of the open window, holding the Luger. He aimed for the rear tyres of the Mercedes, fired three times. The target car slewed out of control, smashed into the barrier. Metal screamed against metal. The car stopped.

Horowitz rammed his car to an emergency stop, jumped out a few feet ahead of the other vehicle, ran towards it. Behind the windscreen he saw movement. He held the Luger gripped in both hands, fired twice. The windscreen crazed, two bullet holes appeared. In the front seat two detectives sagged, dead.

Horowitz hauled open the rear door. One man was slumped forward, unconscious. The other man moved. Horowitz fired and the movement stopped. He felt the pulse of the slumped man, detected it. Placing the Luger muzzle against his skull he pulled the trigger. The detective jerked convulsively. Once. Seven shots gone. He rammed a fresh mag into the Luger, opened the front door. One man lay back in his seat, a red stain in his forehead. Slight movement from the other man. Horowitz aimed calmly, pulled the trigger twice. He closed both doors, ran back to his own car.

Five minutes later, moving at high speed, he saw the rear of the convoy moving ahead of him. He slowed down, kept the same distance between himself and the fourth car he had observed earlier, settled down to maintain that speed.

Inside the fourth car a detective glanced back through the rear window. He nodded to his companion.

'It's OK. Tail-end Charlie has caught up. Our rear is all right.'

The convoy sped on through the night with Horowitz bringing up the rear. He glanced again at the open map by his side. The main onslaught – the petrol tanker attack – was several miles away yet. That was when, in the confusion, he would complete his mission, would kill Tweed.

The massive petrol-tanker was parked at the side of the slip road leading down to the northbound lanes of the autobahn. The driver sat hunched behind the wheel, his engine ticking over. The tanker was laden to the gills with petrol. On the seat by his side was the radio-control device which was tuned to transmit the beam which would detonate the bomb inside the tanker, a bomb sealed inside a heavy box.

His companion, muffled in a fur coat and hood, stood where he could look down the autobahn. In his gloved hand he held a walkie-talkie ready to warn the driver the target Mercedes was approaching. Through the night-glasses looped round his neck he could see a long way down the straight stretch of the autobahn – far enough to check the registration number.

When the time came he would call the driver, who had his own walkie-talkie. Then he would run back to the juggernaut to take the radio transmitter from the driver. It would be up to the driver to do his job, jump from his cab and clear of the immense mobile bomb.

He saw the lights of a car approaching, pressed the glasses to his eyes. Wrong registration, wrong make of car. Audi. He relaxed, beat his gloved hands round his body to keep the circulation going. They should be here soon now. He hoped.

Inside the second Mercedes Paula was breathing heavily, releasing the tension which had built up during the attack. Beside her Tweed nudged her gently in the ribs.

'You see, they can't even shoot straight,' he commented, recalling General de Gaulle's famous reaction after the assassination attempt in August 1962.

'It was frightening at the time though.'

'Well, that's behind us.'

'What worries me is what may lie ahead of us. They haven't given up yet, I'm sure.'

'On that point, I agree.'

'You really think we'll make it to Belgium in one piece?' Paula asked.

'I believe we will,' Tweed lied. He had grave doubts on that score. 'The unexpected may come to our aid,' he added.

Inside the third Mercedes Kuhlmann sensed the major crisis was close. He picked up the microphone linking him with the other vehicles. 'Kuhlmann here. From now on red alert. Repeat, red alert. And our chopper is grounded. Message ends.'

In the cab of the petrol-tanker the driver would have given anything for a cigarette. Instead he chewed gum. He dare not risk smoking with the cargo of liquid dynamite behind him.

Outside, the lookout, perched at the top of the slip road, half-frozen despite his layers of clothing, pressed his glasses to his eyes once more. He frowned, stared harder, perplexed. In the far distance headlights were approaching. A whole convoy of lights. All silver Mercedes. An awful suspicion entered his mind. He picked up the walkie-talkie.

'Manfred,' he called the driver, 'get ready. They may be coming. Four or five Mercedes. I can't pick up the registration number of the lead car yet. Stand by . . .'

'Can't be the target,' Manfred responded. 'They said only one Mercedes.'

526

'I said hold on! And get ready to move.'

'If you say so, Karl.'

The lookout strained his eyes. The first car was still a good distance away. He held his glasses fixed on it, desperately trying to read the registration plate. Still too far away. The cars were travelling one behind the other, hugging the inner lane next to the barrier.

From his elevated position in the cab Manfred looked beyond the barrier. He couldn't see them, but he knew a group of heavily armed men was waiting. There was no way the men travelling in the Mercedes could survive the weight of the planned assault. He was about to put a fresh stick of chewing gum in his mouth when the voice of Karl came over the walkie-talkie as he ran towards the tanker.

'Get ready to move, Manfred . . .'

Out of breath, he hauled open the door of the cab on the opposite side to the driver. He reached in, grabbed hold of the radio transmitter. He was shutting the door when he yelled at Manfred.

'Move! Go! Go . . .!'

Karl was running back up the slip road to his observation point, slithering on ice, recovering his balance. Behind him he heard the tanker moving down to the autobahn, driving down to position itself at right angles to oncoming traffic. To block the autobahn.

Arriving at the top, again out of breath, he turned the safety catch lever on the radio transmitter. It was now activated. Only one button to press – then the holocaust. Karl raised his glasses again, then stiffened. The cars were still a distance away and the night was oppressive with the silence of the cold. But the silence had been broken. He could hear the chug-chug of a machine in the sky. A helicopter was approaching.

*   *   *

'There's the convoy,' Marler observed as he sat next to the pilot.

He looked down on the autobahn below and counted. Five cars. The correct number. The last car was closing up on the convoy.

Once more Marler raised his own night-glasses. Across his lap rested the sniperscope rifle, fully loaded. The chopper moved ahead of the convoy and suddenly Marler tensed. The pilot glanced at him. Marler had the glass glued to his eyes.

'Trouble?' the pilot enquired through his mike.

'You could say that. A bloody great monster of a petrol-tanker has been parked across the autobahn. And a man is watching from the top of the slip road. Maintain your present height. You see the tanker? Good. Keep us in a hover one hundred yards this side of that tanker. Not an inch closer. Hell is coming . . .'

Marler wrenched off his headset, released his seat belt, moved swiftly back into the main cabin, holding the rifle. Standing with his shoulder pressed against the interior of the fuselage, he opened the door. The Arctic rushed in. Marler peered out backwards. The convoy was approaching. The forward movement of the Sikorsky ceased, the pilot was holding it in a hover. Marler eased his way to the other side of the door, looked forward and down.

The tanker had just stopped moving. It was stationed like a wall across the autobahn. The cab door was open. The driver was climbing out. Marler steadied himself against the fuselage. The pilot was holding the machine almost motionless. Marler raised his rifle, rammed the stock into his shoulder, peered through the sight, his finger on the trigger. The full-bellied side of the tanker jumped into the crosshairs of his weapon. He pulled the trigger. Three times in rapid succession as he sent the incendiary bullets into their target. He sat down in a seat and gripped the arm.

528

A blinding flash. The world came apart. The bomb inside the monster detonated by itself. The tanker disintegrated. Sheets of burning petrol enveloped the fleeing driver. The flaming curtain swept over the barrier where figures stood with Balaclava helmets, weapons at the ready. The detonation had come too early. There was a tremendous roar. The pilot saw the figures behind the barrier running, clothes alight, like weird illuminated ghosts in the night. The blast hit the Sikorsky. The machine wobbled crazily. The pilot gripped his controls, stabilized the machine. A lake of burning petrol spread down one side of the autobahn. The tanker had disappeared.

Inside the third Mercedes Kuhlmann saw the flash, heard the roar, grabbed the phone, shouted the order to the other vehicles.

'Laager. Laager. Laager!'

The drivers performed the previously agreed manoeuvre. The three rear vehicles drove into the next lane, pulled up in a semi-circle. Kuhlmann could see the two cars in front of him. The one carrying Tweed, the car ahead of him, had stopped just in time, short of the inferno flaring in a curtain of flame. Black smoke began to drift up.

Horowitz, in the rear car, reacted instantly when he understood the manoeuvre. He pulled out into the fast lane and past the two vehicles in front of him, stopping alongside the second Mercedes. Confusion. Chaos. The rattle of gunfire. Men shouting. He opened the door of his car, stepped out, the Luger held close to his side. He wrenched open the door of the second Mercedes. In the front two detectives. In the rear on the far side, Tweed, staring back at him. Horowitz's Luger moved in a blur, shot the driver, shot the detective next to him. The driver slumped, injured with a bullet in the shoulder. His companion groaned. A bullet in the ribs. Horowitz noted the girl sitting next to Tweed, aimed the Luger at Tweed. Two more shots echoed inside the car.

A looked of astonishment crossed Horowitz's lean face. Still gripping the Luger, he staggered back. Paula, holding her Browning in both hands, fired a third time. Horowitz was still upright, still moving. He stumbled round the front of the car, silhouetted against the sheet of flame. Newman, standing a few feet in front of his car, fired the Magnum, muzzle aimed at Horowitz. The heavy slug hit him in the right-hand side of his chest, hurled him backwards. He pirouetted like a ballet dancer, fell forward over the barrier and was propelled out of sight.

Newman ran to the barrier – in time to see Horowitz diving head first on to an ice-surfaced lake twenty feet below. As Tweed, Kuhlmann and Paula joined him, he saw the cracking of the ice. Horowitz disappeared through a three-foot-wide hole.

Kuhlmann had been shouting orders, forming his men into an irregular line of attack as they advanced towards the flames, firing with machine pistols at the surviving members of the assault group. He walked rapidly to join Tweed, carrying a powerful flashlight. He shone it down on the icebound lake.

'I don't understand how he was still able to move after I'd fired twice at him,' said Paula.

'He's the most professional assassin in Europe,' Tweed reminded her. 'I once heard of a man with six bullets in him who walked a mile for help.'

'That ice is six inches thick,' Kuhlmann commented. 'He must have gone through a thinner patch. He's still alive.'

Horowitz had drifted up under the ice, seeking the opening. In the glare of the flashlight they clearly saw his hands hammering at the solid surface of his ice tomb, the blurred outline of his head. 'I can't watch this,' said

530

Paula and went back to the car. Horowitz continued bobbing up and down beneath the ice, many feet from where he had dived into the lake. His hands were still beating at the unyielding ceiling above him, more feebly now.

'I'm not getting my feet wet rescuing that,' Kuhlmann remarked. 'For what? The expense of a long trial, a prison sentence, then later he breaks out. No thank you. Tweed, you shouldn't be out here. Newman, escort him back to the car. That's an order.'

Kuhlmann waited by himself, moving the flashlight, until the hands of Horowitz became still. The water beneath the ice shimmered as the corpse slowly sank. Kuhlmann turned back to the cars.

'That's that,' he said to himself.

He walked over to Tweed's car after looking at the dying flames. The firing became desultory, stopped. He bent down to speak to the new driver.

'The fast lane is clear. I'll order another car to lead the way for you. Go slowly until you're past this mess.'

'Same route?' the driver asked.

'Same route. You'll be in Belgium by daybreak. You'd better be.'

He stood up, saw Newman staring skywards to where the chopper hovered over the scene. Newman was making a thumbs-up gesture. Inside the Sikorsky's cabin Marler, watching through his glasses, smiled drily.

'When they start moving follow them. We'll escort them out of Germany.'

531

52

WORLD SECURITY EMPIRE CRUMBLING. SHARES DROP 40%
ON WALL STREET

BUCKMASTER CONGLOMERATE CRASHING. RESIGNATION
OF MINISTER?

MAJOR US BANK CALLS IN WORLD SECURITY LOAN

At 7 a.m. Buckmaster stared at the headlines of the newspapers strewn on the floor of his living-room in Belgravia. He had sent out early for the papers. He ran his hands through his hair. Who the hell had organized this conspiracy? It had to be a conspiracy: he'd organized enough of them in his time.

'I'll still beat them into the ground,' he thought, and then the phone rang. It was Morgan. Calling from Freiburg.

'It went wrong,' Morgan reported. 'The opposition outnumbered us by ten-to-one,' he lied.

'Present location of the target?'

'Last seen heading north along the same route. Middle of the night.'

Buckmaster had always trusted his intuition. 'He went in via Belgium. He'll return that way. Have you someone you can send to conclude negotiations there?'

'Yes. Stieber . . .'

'Then send him. To Brussels. Use the Lear jet. Alert our Belgian organization – to observe and locate. The negotiation must be concluded by Stieber,' he repeated. 'Board the jet yourself, drop off Stieber in Brussels, then fly here . . .'

Buckmaster clasped his hands and stared again at the spread of newspapers. At least he could still take decisions. If Tweed reached London, he was finished. Tweed would only return if – by some unknown means – he had cleared himself. Climax very close.

Tweed abandoned the idea of returning secretly to England by boat. He announced his decision when Newman was driving him into Brussels. He looked at Paula by his side and smiled.

'Remember? This is where it all started?'

'Where I fought you over coming with you.'

'And thank God you did. You saved my life when Horowitz opened that car door. A pro killer to the last, that man.'

'All part of my job,' she said dismissively. 'And how are we going to cross the Channel?'

'By air. I hate the sea. It never stops moving. Bob, the airport is the next stop.'

Marler, sitting alongside Newman, looked over his shoulder. 'Is that wise? Throwing caution to the winds on the home stretch?'

'When I phoned from Aachen I was calling the PM. She has laid on an executive jet for us. Officially, it is to take an EEC Commissioner to London.'

Paula stared at him. 'What's been going on? How could you call the PM when officially you're still a fugitive?'

Tweed lifted the briefcase he was holding in his lap. 'It is all here – the evidence to clear me. The story of Sylvia Harman. Her desk diary you found at her Zürich apartment. The photocopies Bob brought from World Security in Basle.'

'There's something you're not telling us,' she said.

'All will become clear.'

*   *   *

Morgan had disobeyed Buckmaster, had changed his plans. He was waiting near the check-in counters at Brussels Airport. A dozen yards away Stieber sat reading a newspaper. He was waiting for the signal from Morgan warning him that Tweed had arrived.

For Morgan it was desperate measures – a long shot. He had no information from his lookouts in Belgium, all of whom had a photograph of Tweed. He was hoping against hope that Tweed would decide to fly direct to London.

The Lear jet was parked on the tarmac – waiting to take him on to England. The thought of facing Buckmaster and confessing total failure appalled him. He stood close to a bookstall. It was a strategic viewing point: he could see all the check-in counters. He looked at his watch again, then at passengers approaching the counters. No sign of Tweed.

Newman drove along the approach road to the airport. He was worried about one factor: they carried no weapons. At the German frontier Kuhlmann had insisted they surrendered them. Quite correct, but damned inconvenient. He looked in his rear-view mirror.

'Butler and Nield are keeping up with us,' he remarked.

The two men were travelling in another Renault. Kuhlmann had phoned ahead to his opposite number in Brussels, Chief Inspector Benoit, an old friend of Tweed's. The two cars had been waiting at the frontier.

'Benoit is meeting us at the airport,' Tweed informed the others for the first time. 'He wants to wish us *bon voyage*.'

'It will be *bon* when we are airborne,' Newman said grimly as he reached the airport building and pulled in to the kerb.

Tweed carried his own case as he walked inside with Paula close to him, her eyes scanning the concourse. She still thought this was a bad idea but kept her mouth shut. Behind them Newman made a gesture to Butler and Nield to fan out. Unbeknown to Tweed, he had talked to the two men and Marler privately.

Tweed was the only one who showed no signs of tension as he walked across the concourse. A familiar figure appeared by his other side. Benoit. A jovial, portly man in his forties, he had a great beaked nose, light brown hair and shrewd eyes.

'You had a tough time in Germany I hear from Kuhlmann. Welcome to peaceful Belgium.'

'Don't say things like that,' Paula interjected. 'It's tempting fate.'

'My felicitations, Paula,' Benoit replied and then he hugged and kissed her on the cheek.

Tweed had paused near the check-in counters. Benoit turned to explain. He waved towards the counters.

'You need not go near them. I will escort you to the executive jet which has arrived and is waiting to fly you back.'

Morgan nodded to Stieber and moved out of sight behind the bookstall. Stieber looked round, spotted Tweed. Standing still. A perfect target. Holding the newspaper in his left hand he grasped the butt of the Walther inside his raincoat pocket. A range of no more than ten feet. Point-blank . . .

More people were coming in, swirling in a crowd. Outside a jet took off, its engines roaring. Stieber began to pull the weapon out of his pocket. So many people. In the confusion escape should be easy. Everyone would dive for cover. The gun was half-way out of his pocket.

Newman was walking by himself, looking everywhere for danger. He saw a man sitting on a seat. Familiar. Why? Where? A rounded-headed man. It hit him. The night he had driven into Basle past the frontier post. The car waiting. Two men in the front seat. The driver a round-headed man. He moved.

Stieber had the gun almost out of his pocket when an

arm was wrapped round his neck in a hammerlock. Another hand grabbed his gun-hand. There was a struggle as Stieber tried to stand up, to free himself. The gun twisted, was rammed back inside his pocket. His finger pressed the trigger. Another jet roared into the sky, muffled the sound of the shot. He sagged back on the seat.

Newman glanced round. No one was taking any notice. He put his hand round Stieber's neck in a seemingly friendly gesture. His fingers felt for the neck pulse. Nothing. Stieber was dead. In the struggle he had shot himself. Newman eased his body upright, let it flop back against the seat.

Hurrying to a bar, he bought a bottle of Scotch, stripped off the covering, loosened the cap. When he walked back to the seat Stieber was still slumped like a man asleep. Still no one took any notice. Newman uncapped the bottle, placed it carefully upright alongside the corpse, walked away to join Tweed and the others who were following Benoit through an open doorway. Marler caught up with Newman.

'You managed that skilfully. Thought I'd have to lend a hand.'

'You'd have botched it up.'

'Nice to know you have confidence in me, old chum.'

They didn't tell Tweed what had happened at the airport. In mid-air over the Channel Newman and Marler agreed he'd been through enough. Tweed and Paula sat together three rows in front of the two men.

'One thing I ought to tell him now,' Marler said. 'Be back in a minute.'

He made his way along the narrow alley and sat down in the empty seat across from Paula. Tweed had been checking his dossier of evidence, arranging it in sequence. Marler leaned over the aisle.

'You'll have something to add to that once I've visited a certain safety deposit in London. A copy of the post-mortem on Sylvia Harman by Dr Rose. The vital data is, of course, the blood groups.'

'And I have a friend inside the Ministry of Defence who can check the records and give me Buckmaster's blood group in confidence,' Tweed told him.

'And if Buckmaster doesn't have the rare blood group?'

'Then Morgan killed and then raped her. It has to be one or the other of them. They'd never delegate such a grisly task.'

'Have you any idea which of them did it?' Paula asked.

'Yes,' said Tweed, 'I know for a certainty. It all fits in with the *Lampedusa*. That's the key. Now, no more questions.'

Latitude 34. 30. N. Longitude. 27. 20. E. The US missile destroyer *Spruance* was motionless in broad daylight east of Crete. As Hank Tower, commander, studied the silhouette of the *Lampedusa* with the officer who had brought the outline to him, the sea was calm.

A short distance to the north of the destroyer a freighter was continuing on a north-easterly course. When the weather had slackened Tower had launched his helicopter and it was this machine which had located the freighter, *Helvetia*.

'That ship is twin-funnelled,' Tower objected. 'The *Lampedusa* has only one funnel.'

'Agreed, sir. But when you put an arm over the rear funnel and compare the silhouette of that freighter with the silhouette in your hand they match perfectly. I think they've erected a dummy funnel.'

'You just could be right. We'll test them. Give them the order to heave to.'

He waited, staring at the silhouette, comparing it with

537

the freighter, while the signal was sent. There was no response. The freighter proceeded on its course, leaving behind a wake as it increased speed. Tower pursed his lips, gave the next order – to fire a shot across the bows of the *Helvetia*.

Aboard the freighter Singer stared at the destroyer, calculating the distance between the two vessels. He decided he could swim it easily in these calm waters. Below, in the radio cabin, Hoch, the radio op, was gazing out of the porthole. The shot fired across the freighter's bows filled him with hope. He had to leave the *Helvetia*. His only problem was the armed guard who slouched in a chair, pistol in his lap.

The shot across their bows alarmed the guard. He stood up, pushed Hoch aside from the porthole, and peered out himself. He felt he had to go up on deck, to check what was happening. He turned to Hoch, raised the barrel of his pistol, struck Hoch on the temple. At the last second Hoch moved slightly. The barrel grazed his forehead. He collapsed to the floor.

The guard ran out, slamming the door. Hoch waited, heard his running footsteps disappearing along the passageway. He stood up, shook his head, went to the door, opened it and peered in both directions. The passageway was deserted.

The guard ran on to the bridge. Most of the crew were crowded on the foredeck. Captain Hartmann had taken over the wheel from the helmsman. In the distance he could see the heavy bulk of another vessel approaching. The *Sverdlov*. He was going to make a run for it.

The aft deck was empty as Singer climbed the rail, dived into the sea, began swimming with powerful strokes towards the *Spruance*. Behind him on the deck appeared Hoch. The radio op glanced round, saw no one, climbed the rail and dived after Singer.

Hoch also was a good swimmer. For long stretches he

swam underwater before breaking to the surface to take in air. He could see that Singer would arrive first but that did not deter him.

Aboard the *Spruance* a lookout ran up to the bridge, reported to Tower.

'Two men jumped overboard from the freighter. They're swimming towards us, sir.'

'Lower a ladder. Prepare to take them aboard . . .'

On the foredeck of the *Helvetia* Captain Hartmann had lost control of his motley crew. He was concentrating on reaching the *Sverdlov*. All eyes were on the Soviet cruiser. No one noticed the two men swimming in the sea. Singer had reached the ladder, had dragged himself out of the water, was mounting the ladder. Close behind him Hoch surfaced, saw the ladder, took a deep breath for one final effort.

Aboard the *Helvetia* was a seaman called Levitt. Once the skipper of an American freighter, he had lost his ticket for being drunk on duty. He hated the Americans. The shot across their bows had infuriated him. Goddamn Yanks! He'd show them. He whipped off the canvas cover, exposing the machine-gun. Aiming for the *Spruance*, he opened fire, sweeping a hail of bullets along the hull of the destroyer. Hartmann was appalled. He screamed at him but the machine-gun continued its chatter.

Aboard the *Spruance* American seamen ducked. One man fell, laced with bullets. He lay still on the bridge. Singer had reached the deck. He crouched low, saw to his amazement the figure of Hoch scrambling over the side on to the deck. Hoch, who could expose him.

Singer reached inside his shirt, grasped the Luger pistol inside his waterproof holster. He hauled out the gun, aimed it at Hoch, who stared at him in horror. An American officer reacted. Lowering his bullet-shaped head, he ran forward as Singer stood up, hit him in the middle of the back. Singer was thrown forward to the side, slipped on the deck, fell overboard. The officer used his walkie-talkie to call the lookout at the stern.

The engines of the *Spruance* were moving the vessel out of range of the machine-gun. Singer surfaced, saw the hull sliding past him, desperately tried to swim away from the warship. At the stern the lookout peered over, caught a brief glimpse of Singer as he was caught in the undertow and dragged towards the huge slicing propellers. The churning white wake turned crimson for a few fleeting seconds. The lookout saw something like a decapitated head bobbing up and down. It disappeared as he retched over the side.

On the bridge Tower was issuing more orders as his ship put distance between himself and the freighter. His instructions from Naples were specific. If all else failed, in an emergency the *Lampedusa* must be sunk. He gave a fresh order to ready a missile for firing.

Standing with his feet spreadeagled, he watched the *Helvetia* speeding towards the still distant *Sverdlov*. He gave the final order.

A missile *whooshed* into the clear sky, described an arc, fell, and landed square on the freighter amidships. A perfect shot. There was a thunderous boom as the missile exploded. Seconds later the freighter's boilers blew up. Its rear funnel toppled. Tower glanced down at the silhouette he still held. Yes, the so-called *Helvetia* was the *Lampedusa*. He looked up again. The freighter had come apart amidships. The bow upended, slid below the sea out of sight. The stern shattered into a million fragments. A giant column of water soared into the air. Reminded Tower of the geyser, Old Faithful, in Yellowstone National Park. The water seethed and boiled as the relics of the freighter plunged to the bottom of the Mediterranean, taking with it the cargo in the hold. Then the sea began to settle. The crew stood gazing at the place where the *Lampedusa* had floated less than a minute before.

In the distance the *Sverdlov* began to change direction, heading back on a northerly course. Tower gazed at Hoch, brought to him by an officer.

'I'm the only surviver of the original crew of the *Lampedusa*. That man who tried to shoot me and went overboard was Singer. He masterminded the hi-jacking of the ship.'

'Better come below to my cabin, tell me your story . . .'

53

The executive jet was descending towards London Airport. Tweed looked out of the window. It was good to see England again. Most of the snow had gone. Only a north-facing rooftop here and there showed relics of the white blanket which had covered the country.

'You look worried,' Paula commented.

'I am. The big problem is Buckmaster – the national scandal which could break out if he goes down. Imagine the headlines: MINISTER FOR EXTERNAL SECURITY INVOLVED IN WORLD-WIDE FRAUD. Makes me shudder.'

'There has to be a simple solution,' chipped in Marler, who still sat opposite them across the aisle.

'Tell me one,' said Tweed.

'Oh, I didn't say I'd thought of one. I just said there has to be one.'

'Very helpful,' snapped Paula, then stared at Marler. 'And two unsolved murder cases – Sylvia Harman and Ted Doyle, the accountant, from what Benoit told us just before we boarded this jet.'

541

'So where do we go when we touch down? Marler enquired.

'Straight to Park Crescent. To report to Howard. And to the PM.'

'There we go again,' complained Paula. 'I still don't understand your present relationship with the Prime Minister.'

'Cordial,' said Tweed.

'More mystery,' Paula sighed and braced herself for the landing.

Morgan's Lear jet landed half an hour later. His pilot had been given a longer flight path than Tweed's. He walked through Passport Control and Customs without much delay – although the official checking his passport examined every page.

As soon as Morgan had left the official closed his window, picked up a phone and spoke to Jim Corcoran, Chief of Security.

'Gareth Morgan has arrived. He went through Passport Control a couple of minutes ago.'

'Thanks. Excuse the brevity – I have a call to make myself.'

Hanson, the chauffeur, was waiting with the Daimler. Morgan settled himself in the rear seat. He waited until they had left the airport before asking his question.

'Any problems while I was away? With Leonora?'

'Not with Mrs Buckmaster. With myself, sir. I have some bad news. The police have been questioning me. It seems some nosey-parker bitch saw me when I entered Doyle's house to plant those betting slips.'

Morgan leaned forward. 'How the devil could she identify you?'

'I'm still trying to work that out. The police had me in a line-up and the old bag picked me out immediately.'

'We'll get you the best lawyers in the land. You haven't admitted anything, I trust?'

'Simply to deny that I was anywhere near the place. Then I clammed up. It's her word against mine.' He paused. 'I should warn you of something – they have a Chief Inspector Buchanan on the case. He's like a dog with a bone, insists that Ted Doyle was murdered.'

'I've met the flatfoot.' Morgan waved a contemptuous hand to reassure Hanson. 'I can handle him any day of the week. Let's get to Threadneedle Street immediately.'

Tweed opened the door of his office and paused. The room was full of people. Howard sat in the armchair, one elegantly-pressed trouser leg over the arm. Monica sat behind her desk. Two other men sat in hard-backed chairs, swivelled in their seats as he entered, followed by Paula. The significant factor was his own seat behind his desk was unoccupied.

'Welcome home,' Howard began. 'I got your signal from the jet. The PM got her signal, also. She'd like to hear from you when convenient. But first these two gentlemen are anxious to have a word with you. Chief Inspector Buchanan and his assistant, Sergeant Warden. Jim Corcoran informed them you were on your way from the airport – with my permission.'

Tweed nodded at the visitors, took off his coat, which Monica took, and sat behind his desk, slapping his briefcase down on the top. There was an urgent knock on the door and Chief Inspector Harvey of Special Branch appeared.

'I hope I'm not late . . .'

'You are,' Howard told him. He pointed to a chair. 'Sit.'

Tweed took command of the meeting, gazing at Buchanan, who looked as though he had all his marbles.

'Have you identified the dead girl found in my flat?'

'Not yet, sir. In spite of extensive enquiries.'

'Well, I have now . . .'

Tweed emptied his briefcase, arranged Sylvia Harman's diary alongside the pile of photocopies and started talking. He spoke tersely for ten minutes and during that time Buchanan's grey eyes never left his. As he concluded, Tweed pushed the diary, protected inside a cellophane bag, across the desk together with the photocopies.

'When my assistant . . .' He nodded towards Paula seated behind her own desk. '. . . acquired that diary in Zürich she placed it in that bag which was originally wrapped round a new pair of tights. So Harman's fingerprints should be on it.'

'Very helpful, miss.' Buchanan smiled approval at Paula, 'I do have on record the deceased's prints, so comparison should be straightforward.' He paused, looking at Tweed. 'From what you have told me it appears Morgan procured high-class call-girls for Lance Buckmaster. It also seems Sylvia Harman could have been transported quietly to London by this Lear jet. The fact that she was resident in Zürich solves the problem of why we were not able to trace her here.'

'You are the detective,' Tweed replied.

Buchanan stood up. 'I've also been informed Mr Morgan is back in London. With this evidence I think my next visit should be to interview him.'

'You're the detective,' Tweed said again with a smile.

'But what is the motive for all this?' demanded Harvey.

'That comes under the heading of national security,' Tweed replied.

'That simply isn't good enough . . .'

'It's good enough till hell freezes over,' Howard snapped. 'Now I think Tweed has earned a rest. I'll show you gentlemen out.'

'You've made my life very easy,' Buchanan told Tweed and he left the office.

'He said a rest,' Paula reminded Tweed who shook his head.

'It's not all over by a long chalk. Get me Cord Dillon at Langley. Now, please.'

Paula pursed her lips, reached for the phone. A few minutes later she said Dillon was on the line. As soon as the American had identified Tweed he began talking urgently.

'Big news from the Mediterranean. The *Lampedusa* was located just in time. It opened fire on one of our destroyers. The crazy bastards. A Soviet cruiser was heading within a mile of the incident. The destroyer responded, as instructed. A missile sank the *Lampedusa*. The radio op, Hoch, survived. The rest of the original crew were massacred during the hi-jack . . .'

'Oh, no! That's awful, really awful.'

'Fortunes of war.' Dillon sounded laconic. 'What do we do now?'

'Activate Tiger One.' Tweed's voice was decisive. 'Immediately.'

'Will do. I'll send a fuller report from the survivor, Hoch. Stop worrying.'

Tweed put down the phone. Monica and Paula waited. When he didn't say anything, Paula probed.

'Are we allowed to know what Tiger One is?'

'I'm afraid not. At least, not yet.'

IS WORLD SECURITY SOLVENT? SHARES NOSE-DIVE ALL MARKETS

The newspaper headline shrieked at Buckmaster. He paced his living-room. The door opened and Leonora entered, her face grim. She closed the door and gestured at the newspaper on the floor.

'What is going on? I have a right to know. I am the chairman . . .'

Buckmaster lost control. 'You're nothing. You've no right to know anything. Haven't you realized it yet? You're just a figurehead. Someone I put in because a Minister must be seen to be impartial. It's the law that I have to divest direct control of the company when I accepted my Cabinet post. That's all.'

'It's not all.' She clenched her fist. He was in a dangerous mood but she didn't care. 'It was my money which started you in business . . .'

'A feeble pittance!' he shouted at her. 'Since then I've multiplied it millions of times. Built it up into a mammoth.'

'The company is now worth nothing, you idiot. Read the headline again. The shares will soon be worthless. And so will you. And all that will be left will be this apartment and Tavey Grange on Dartmoor.'

'Don't kid yourself,' he sneered. 'This place – and the Grange – are mortgaged to the hilt.'

He regretted the outburst as soon as the words had been uttered. Leonora stared at him in sheer disbelief. She had to get her breath back before she reacted.

'You never told me, you bastard. Well, I can get my own back on you. I may have another chat with that nice detective, Buchanan. About Morgan. He *was* with Doyle later on the night Ted died so mysteriously. I'd forgotten my car keys. I came back up to my office and saw Morgan disappearing inside Ted's office. Very late in the evening.'

'You'll keep your mouth shut,' he said savagely.

'Will I? Don't count on it.' Then she regretted voicing her threat. Buckmaster was advancing on her with a peculiar expression. She backed away, ran to the door, opened it and turned before she slammed it shut.

'Just don't count on my silence any more,' she shrieked.

He heard her running down the staircase, the slam of the front door. Followed by a car engine starting, moving away. He stared once more at the newspaper headline, picked up the phone, dialled.

'Hanson, bring the car round. I want you to drive me to the helipad at Battersea. Call the pilot, tell him to have the chopper ready. He's flying me to Dartmoor.'

Behind his desk in his Threadneedle Street office Morgan sat facing three men. Buchanan, Warden and Harvey. Buchanan had been talking for about fifteen minutes while Morgan listened, his obese figure slumped in his chair.

On the far side of the desk was Sylvia Harman's diary still wrapped in cellophane, the pile of photocopies Buchanan had handed him one by one as he explained what he knew.

What he knew? Buchanan knew everything. Morgan was stunned when Buchanan had gone methodically over the dates marked with an 'M' in the diary – when he had then compared them with the dates of the payments of six thousand francs a time which coincided. Buchanan again sat well back from the desk so he could cross his long legs.

'I have already warned you,' he continued, 'you are not obliged to say anything but anything you do say will be—'

'All right! I've got that. No need to go on about it.'

'I also repeat that if you decide to cooperate by making a statement there is the possibility that may be a point in your favour later. No guarantee, Mr Morgan. I am in no position to guarantee anything.' He paused. 'It is entirely your decision.'

Buchanan said nothing more. He had purposely omitted at this stage the fact that a further examination of Doyle's office had detected Morgan's hand-print on the edge of the window the accountant was supposed to have fallen from by accident. A hand-print which matched several found on Morgan's desk. That could come later. When he was charged with the murder of Edward Doyle.

The silence in the office was heavy, like the oppressiveness before the breaking of a storm. Morgan played with an unlit cigar. He'd been set up, pushed into the front line by Buckmaster. How else could that diary be lying on his desk – together with those photocopies? And instead of the initial 'M' which had been used for camouflage, the initial should read 'B'. It was for Buckmaster he had procured the high-class call-girls. Including Sylvia Harman and her last flight to London aboard the Lear jet.

Morgan lit the cigar, began to talk.

Washington, DC. It was dark, when the massive C-5A transport plane began its take-off from Andrews Air Force Base. The pilot had received the Tiger One signal direct from Cord Dillon. The crew had boarded the plane, surrounded by armed guards.'

The huge machine lumbered down the runway, had almost reached the end when it lifted off. It gained height rapidly, headed out across the Atlantic on a north-easterly course. At fifteen minute intervals the radio operator reported their position by coded signals.

In accord with the very precise time schedule, the C-5A landed at the British airfield, Lyneham, in Wiltshire, just after nightfall. Heavy lifting-gear moved towards the plane and the large rear doors were opened, the ramp dropped. An immense mobile transporter drove close to the ramp and the disembarkation operation began.

The enormous cargo was carefully transferred from the plane to the transporter. Even though Lyneham was an isolated airfield in the middle of the countryside, great canvas screens had been erected round the rear of the aircraft.

During that night many roads in England were closed by police. The explanation given – where inevitable – was that a giant electrical transformer was on the move. But aboard the transporter were heavily armed SAS troops. Other soldiers rode on motor-cycles ahead of and behind the transporter.

It was not possible to move the transporter to its ultimate destination in Yorkshire overnight. So, during daylight hours from the following morning until the next night, the great vehicle was housed in an aircraft hangar on an old wartime airfield.

When night came the transporter resumed its slow journey on the last half of its route. Again roads were sealed off and the vehicle trundled north. Before daylight it arrived at its final destination in Yorkshire.

Top secret signals were immediately despatched to London and Langley confirming its safe arrival. Two men – Tweed and Cord Dillon – breathed sighs of relief.

54

In the underground garage below World Security HQ in Threadneedle Street, Marler had indulged in a little arm-twisting. Literally.

He had pounced on Hanson from behind when the chauffeur got out of the Daimler he had just parked. With one hand over the man's mouth, he used the other hand to bend the arm backwards until it was almost wrenched from its socket. Hanson had moaned with the pain, then heard the whispered question.

'You've got one chance to give the right answer. Make just one small mistake and I'll break every bone in your body. The question is very simple. Where is Lance Buckmaster?'

'Took him to the chopper waiting at Battersea. Ease up a bit, mate, for God's sake . . .'

'Go on.'

'The chopper was flying him down to Tavey Grange, Dartmoor.'

Marler released his grip a little. He waited while Hanson gasped and wheezed before he spoke again.

'Now this conversation is going to remain our little secret, isn't it? If I find you've even hinted to a soul that we had our little talk I'll not only come after you – I'll find you.'

'Don't want any more to do with you,' Hanson had replied.

Marler had left the garage, walked round the corner, climbed behind the wheel of his Porsche, and driven off. Within an hour he was well away from London, driving just within the speed limit to the West Country.

It was when he was bypassing Exeter that he realized most of the country was free of snow but Dartmoor was still in the grip of the freeze. In the distance its high ridges rose like great white waves and not an inch on the moor was freed from the dense blanket. He began climbing, the snow became deeper, the ice-ruts like iron.

Passing through Moretonhampstead, he slowed as the road curved and he skidded. Five minutes later he was moving along the winding drive leading to the Elizabethan turrets and chimneys of Tavey Grange. He pulled up in the courtyard, jumped out and hauled at the bell-pull of the front entrance. José, the butler, opened the door.

'I'm looking for Mr Buckmaster,' Marler said casually. 'I was in this part of the world and thought he might want to have a word with me.'

'You've missed him by five minutes, sir,' José responded. 'He has gone for a drive to Princetown. Said he needed a breath of fresh air. Drove out of here like a madman. Sorry, sir, I shouldn't have said that.'

'Don't worry,' Marler said breezily. 'I didn't hear what you said. And there's no need to leave a message. I must hurry back to London . . .'

Marler retraced his route along the drive, but when he reached the lodge gates he turned left. Towards Princetown, not London. A quarter of a mile away he pulled up briefly. From under his seat he unclipped the Magnum .45, checked that it was fully loaded. It was ironic: he was always joking with Newman about why use that old cannon? He laid the gun on the seat beside him and drove on.

As he climbed high up to the moor he found the snow deeper still, the patches of concealed ice more treacherous. There was no other traffic about and it was bitterly cold. Everywhere it was a white world, a wilderness with the occasional tor rearing up, a white monument.

He slowed down again when he came to the steep curving stretch of road above Shark's Tor. Here the ice was very dangerous. He drove on and still he hadn't passed another car in either direction. The sky was like lead. Was even more snow on the way? Half an hour later he reached the sombre prison-like Princetown.

Driving behind the wheel of his own Porsche, Buckmaster's mind was in a whirl as he drove back into Princetown from Yelverton. He was on his way home. Home? Had he got one anymore? Had he got anything left? The magnitude of his fall from the heights stunned him.

The PM had sent a message saying she wanted to see him. Stuff her! He had had the phones taken off the cradles at Tavey Grange. No way she could communicate with him. He had to work out a fresh plan to beat the bloody lot of them. He had been in tight corners before and fought his way out. What he had done before could be done again.

Driving down the main street of Princetown, past the bleak granite buildings, he peered through his goggles. For a moment he couldn't believe his eyes. A red Porsche coming towards him. It was the registration number which caught his attention. Buckmaster had not built up a world-wide security organization without an exceptional memory for detail. Marler's Porsche!

A whole new stream of thoughts flooded through his mind. Marler. Of course! That was the solution to his problems. As the other vehicle came close he opened the window and waved a defiant hand. Catch me if you can! He'd race Marler back to the Grange!

Marler understood the gesture, gave a little mock salute as the two cars passed each other. Then he swung his car in an illegal U-turn and followed the other Porsche. In his wing mirror Buckmaster saw the manoeuvre and grinned. There had always been something of the schoolboy beneath his ruthless exterior. That was it. Race Marler back. Loser coughed up a bottle of Krug!

Buckmaster was leaving Princetown behind, accelerating, driving up on to the moor as Marler sped forward a hundred yards behind. Buckmaster worked out the plan as he increased speed. Sack Morgan. Throw him into the street. Put Marler in his place. Marler was an expert on security, was just the man for the job. With Marler by his side he'd build a new and bigger empire.

Exhilarated with the idea, he rammed his foot down, racing up on to the heights of the moor. The car skidded on an ice patch. He grinned with excitement, drove with the skid, regained control on the edge of a deep drop. This was the life – took him back to his days with the Airborne Division. He was climbing steeply now and round him spread the empty wilderness. No sign of life. Just the day for a race. Flat out! He sucked in cold air through the open window, drunk with excitement.

Behind him Marler maintained the gap of a hundred yards. Too dangerous for an emergency stop on this surface. He heard the boom-boom of Buckmaster's exhausts. He was increasing speed even more. Marler's lips tightened. He pressed his own foot down. It dawned on him that at any hint that he was closing the gap Buckmaster accelerated even more.

Marler glanced up ahead beyond the two speeding Porsches. A mist like steam was drifting over the moor towards the road. If it reached the road visibility would suddenly drop to nil. Now they were at the top of the moor, coming close to the point where the road dropped suddenly and turned sharply at the same time. He reached for the Magnum, driving with one hand. His own window was open: he had lowered it back in Princetown immediately after the U-turn.

Resting his arm on the ledge of the window, he took aim. At all costs he mustn't hit Buckmaster. And no bullet must dent the car. He timed it carefully as the bend and the drop approached, fired once, then again.

Buckmaster heard the heavy reports of the Magnum, looked in his mirror, saw the hand holding the gun, realized Marler had closed the gap. What the hell was happening? Had Marler gone mad? He'd offered him Howard's head on a plate. A third shot hummed past his window. God! Marler was trying to kill him . . .

He rammed his foot down. He'd out-run him. He could drive faster than any amateur driver in the country. He was on the crest of a hill. A fourth shot winged past his window. He glanced again in the mirror, took his eyes off the road ahead for only a matter of seconds.

Marler had gone stark raving mad. Buckmaster remembered he had a gun in his study. He'd get back to the Grange first, rush upstairs, grab the gun. He remembered he was driving at high speed. He looked ahead. There wasn't anything ahead . . .!

Marler saw the Porsche drive straight off the road and over the edge. He slowed down carefully. Buckmaster's car was leaping into space. The car described an arc, then began its fall. It swung sideways in mid-air, plunged down.

The nose hammered into the summit of Shark's Tor. The impact toppled the car head over heels, cast it out into the abyss. The Porsche dropped like a torpedo heading for its target, reached the rocky gorge below, slammed into the granite and exploded. Fire blazed from the crumpled wreck, was then blotted out by the swirling mist. Marler drove on, past Tavey Grange, through Moretonhampstead – heading for London.

Epilogue

'So *Shockwave* is now in place at Fylingdales in Yorkshire,' Tweed concluded.

Seated in his Park Crescent office were Monica, Paula, Newman and Marler. Tweed had explained how the giant twin computer, the key to SDI, had been flown secretly aboard the US transport plane to Lyneham and then moved north by road.

'I don't understand any of this,' said Paula. 'What was all that business about *Shockwave* being aboard the *Lampedusa*?'

Tweed sighed. 'The key to a highly complex operation approved by the Prime Minister. The original intention was to fly *Shockwave* to Britain. Then Buckmaster intervened, insisted that with so many planes crashing these days sea transport was the safe way to move the computer. Made a very big fuss about the whole affair. Too big a fuss. So we decided to test him.'

'We?' queried Newman.

'The PM and myself. I sensed something was very wrong and I'd been uneasy about Buckmaster since his appointment. He was too good to be true. To my surprise the PM agreed with my plan. She was beginning to have her own doubts about Buckmaster.'

'What plan?' Paula persisted.

'Only five people would know about my plan. The PM, myself and Cord Dillon at Langley. Plus the head of the US Joint Chiefs of Staff, and the President. The Americans were very happy with the idea – they'd been worried stiff about *Shockwave* travelling by sea.'

'But it did,' Paula protested.

'What was loaded aboard the *Lampedusa* was a brilliant mock-up of the real thing. A dummy *Shockwave* constructed in the US by the two British scientists who helped design the real thing. This was the test – the trap, if you like – we prepared for Buckmaster. Only he and I knew the codes for communicating with the ship. On this side of the Atlantic, that is. Had the *Lampedusa* reached Plymouth safely, without interference, then Buckmaster would have been cleared and I would have resigned. Instead it all went horribly wrong. I underestimated Buckmaster badly.'

'I think I see the light,' Newman remarked. 'Do go on.'

'First, Buckmaster, knowing I had the codes, that I would be communicating with the ship, had to get me out of the way – a task he accomplished brilliantly. He framed me with the suspected murder and rape of Sylvia Harman. And he was the man who did the dirty job on the girl. We know that now – and this is highly confidential like the rest. Morgan has talked his head off. Buchanan kindly came here to tell me. It was Morgan who procured call-girls for Buckmaster, who arranged for Sylvia Harman to fly to London by the Lear jet and drove her to my apartment. He told Harman Buckmaster wanted another session with her.'

'And what about the call from Richter, your Freiburg informant?' Paula queried.

'That was Morgan's doing – at Buckmaster's suggestion. To get me away from my flat long enough on the fatal night. They paid poor Richter ten thousand pounds to entice me to the Cheshire Cheese with the excuse of meeting him. Morgan has admitted this. So, I had to run for it – to stay free and try to communicate with Hoch aboard the *Lampedusa*. And while aboard Buckmaster was confident I could have a fatal accident. As I said before, it all went horribly wrong – in every way, I deeply regret.'

'What does that mean?' Newman asked quietly.

'I wrongly assumed that even if the *Lampedusa* was hi-jacked the crew would be put ashore somewhere. Instead they were massacred. I'll have that on my conscience for the rest of my life. I underestimated Buckmaster's ruthlessness.'

'You couldn't have foreseen it,' Paula told him quietly.

'And you did counter-attack,' Newman pointed out. 'Turned the tables on him brilliantly.'

'It's little compensation. Oh, by the way, Kuhlmann is cooperating wonderfully. He's told the press a group of terrorists penetrated World Security in Germany and were out to kill him. My name won't be mentioned. Otto is a good friend.'

'How can you be sure Buckmaster strangled and raped Sylvia Harman?' asked Newman.

'I checked with my friend at the Ministry of Defence. The records show Buckmaster had the rare blood group – AB Negative. The blood group found under Harman's fingernail and the blood stain on the sheet. Morgan's blood group has also been checked. It's O Positive.'

'But won't a lot of this come out at Morgan's trial?' suggested Newman.

'No. Morgan will plead guilty to the murder of Ted Doyle – and get a lesser sentence. It will still be ten years inside, and he has a wife and children. The Crown will accept the plea and no evidence will be offered.'

'And was Dr Rose, the pathologist, murdered?'

'Yes, by Stieber, who flew over here and drove him down in a stolen car. Morgan admitted that, too. Said he was acting on Buckmaster's orders and he, Morgan, only heard about it later. Which I doubt. That won't come out either, now Stieber is dead.'

'Can I ask where that leaves me?' Newman enquired.

'In the clear. No one saw the incident at Brussels Airport. Incredibly, Stieber's body was found only two hours later. It's assumed he committed suicide. His fingerprints were on the gun.'

'And World Security?' Paula asked. 'What's happened to it?'

Tweed picked up a newspaper on his desk. 'It's in the Stop Press. World Security shares have been suspended on the London Stock-Exchange. No more dealings. End of story. And I'd like to thank you all for your support. Without you, I'd never have made it. Maybe you should all go home now, take a well-earned rest.'

He waited while Newman and Paula left the office together. Marler was still sitting in his chair. Tweed stared at him.

'You've had very little – in fact, nothing – to say. Was it very cold on Dartmoor yesterday?'

Marler lit a king-size cigarette, looked at Tweed in surprise. 'I've no idea. It's a week or two since I was down there. I expect all the snow has gone by now.' He stood up, the cigarette tucked in the corner of his mouth at a jaunty angle. 'I think I should push off now, get a bit of shut-eye. Cheers!'

'What was all that about?' asked Monica when they were alone.

'A poor joke on my part.'

Tweed opened the newspaper to the main headline set in large type. It gave him a certain satisfaction.

CABINET MINISTER DIES IN TRAGIC MOTOR ACCIDENT
ON DARTMOOR

LANCE BUCKMASTER NOTED FOR HIS RECKLESS DRIVING

Tweed looked up at Monica. 'Now I want you to take down my letter of resignation to the Prime Minister. I'll sign it immediately and I want it sent to Downing Street by special courier.'

'She'll persuade you to withdraw it.'

'Not this time, Monica.'

THE
GREEK KEY

AUTHOR'S NOTE

This novel is based on facts told to me about a strange and grim murder committed over forty years ago. *That murder remains unsolved to this day.*

It happened in Cairo in 1944 – inside a weird triangular-shaped building near the banks of the River Nile. Not only the building was weird: it housed a mix of army, naval and air force personnel, and secret units whose missions were unknown to the other inhabitants.

The story moves to the present day and all the facts are provided for the reader to identify who was responsible – but I emphasize that the characters portrayed are creatures of the author's imagination and bear no relationship to any living person. Also, the island of Siros – as described – does not exist.

FOR JANE

CONTENTS

Prologue

Cairo, February 1944. Staff-Sergeant Higgins – 'Higgy' to his friends – had no warning this would be the last time he would ascend in the creaking lift climbing slowly to the fourth floor of the Antikhana Building.

At ten in the evening it was silent as a tomb within the walls of the three-sided building. The only sound was the ghostly creak of the old lift as it crawled upwards past deserted landings. Through the iron grille of the cage he could see the stone staircase which rose round the central lift shaft. It felt as though no one else was in the place – no one except the Sudanese receptionist behind his desk on the ground floor.

Not surprising if he was the first to get back, thought Higgy. The few military men who slept there occupied small bedrooms on the rooftop. And they rarely arrived back from drinking and eating in Cairo before eleven. Personally, he liked an early night . . .

He frowned as he slid the door of the cage shut when it had wobbled to a stop. They switched off the lights in the corridors running round the three sides of the building at seven. So where was the glow of light beyond the entrance to the corridor coming from?

He hesitated, listening. Normally he would head straight for one of the three spiral staircases at each corner of the building – the enclosed staircases which led to the rooftop. The light was gleaming from under the closed door at the end of the corridor. The Greek Unit's quarters.

He had no idea what Ionides, who had escaped from

German-occupied Greece, did. Something connected with propaganda, they said. He must have forgotten to turn off the light before leaving for his billet. Or he could just still be working.

Hitching up his khaki drill trousers, he walked quietly along the tiled passage. The first twinge of unease ruffled him when he thought he heard a noise from the room next to the last one. Also part of the Greek Unit's quarters, the two rooms were linked by an inner door. But no light glowed from under this second door. Who would be moving about in the dark?

He paused, grasped the handle, turned it slowly, pushed. The door wouldn't budge, was locked. He stiffened. He'd never known that door to be locked before when one of the Greek Unit was working.

Higgy walked a few paces further and stopped at the second door. Beyond, at the corridor's end, the black hole leading to the spiral staircase gaped. He took a grip on the handle of the door, turned it, entered. He froze.

At the last moment, it occurred to him it might be Ionides' colleague, Gavalas, who was working late. But it was Ionides all right. Except he wasn't all right.

Higgy had his share of battle-hardened courage. An ex-tank commander, he'd seen friends in the desert scorched to death in what they cynically called a 'brew-up'. Not the normal brew-up of tea – the fearsome sight of another tank, hit by a German shell, going up in flames. Locked inside their steel box, few escaped alive.

The office, with barred windows facing the native quarter across the street, looked as though a hurricane had struck it. Drawers were pulled out, contents scattered across the floor. Filing cabinets had been overturned. Crimson splashes smeared the white walls.

The black-haired young Ionides lay amid the carnage,

sprawled on the floor on top of a mess of papers. He was drenched with blood, his dark eyes stared sightless at the ceiling, his head had been almost severed from his neck, his face was slashed brutally, the weathered skin coated with more blood. Blood was everywhere – spattered across the desk where presumably he had been working. The splashes on the walls were more blood.

Higgy shivered. He closed the outer door. Six feet tall, well-built, twenty-eight years old, he stood motionless, gazing at the horror lying a few feet away. Then he remembered the noise he'd heard from the locked room. He stared at the communicating door. God! The maniac who had done this must be inside.

Panic gripped him. His first instinct was to haul open the outer door and run like hell for the roof up the spiral staircase. His throat felt parched. His hands trembled. The silence from the room beyond the communicating door was insidious, made him want to yell.

The silence went on: not a hint of a sound from behind that closed door. Higgy sucked in a deep breath. Had it been imagination, nerves tingling from the empty building? Had he, in fact, really heard anything? He glanced down and saw again the dreadful corpse which had recently been a living man. A black foot-long circular ruler of ebony lay on the floor. He picked it up, took a firmer hold of himself, walked towards the closed communicating door. Still no sound.

He was scared shitless. He was growing more convinced the next room was empty, but if the murderer was still there he wasn't going to let the bastard escape. Ionides was a nice chap, always liked a chat and a joke. Higgy held the ruler like a baton, reached for the door handle with his left hand.

If the killer was inside he was probably holding the knife used to inflict the terrible mutilations Ionides had suffered. The state of the office showed the Greek had fought for

13

his life. No, Higgy thought, should the assassin still be here I'm damned if I'm letting the swine get away.

He opened the door a few inches. The room beyond was dark. He reached his left hand inside, found the light switch, turned it on. Light flooded the second office and he pushed the door wide open, flat against the wall. His right foot tangled with something. A screwed-up bundle, a whole mess of it, and all the sheets were stained a darkish red. Blood.

He took a step inside the office often used by Gavalas. He had heard a rumour that Gavalas had gone on leave. There were no signs of disturbance in this room as far as he was able to see. He gripped the ruler tightly and walked in.

He walked across the empty office which showed no evidence of the ghastly death struggle behind him. He must report this at once. In his dazed state he tried to open the door leading to the corridor without turning the key. *It opened*.

The significance of this hit him like a second shock wave. The door had been locked when he had tried to open it from the corridor. The confirmation that the assassin had been hiding inside the darkened room minutes – moments – after completing his hideous act was too much for Higgy.

He felt his bowels loosening. Throwing open the door, he ran for the nearest toilet, locked the door. Afterwards he was never sure how long he sat on the lavatory.

He went back down through the deserted building by the stone staircase. The lift cage was a potential death-trap. The Sudanese receptionist stifled a yawn as he appeared at the foot of the stairs, gazing at the black ruler Higgy was still holding, sat up straight and adjusted his red fez.

'Who has left the building since I came in here?' Higgy demanded.

14

and whistled down a passing gharry. 'There's your transport home.'

'You've a bloody nerve. I shall complain . . .'

As she strolled back down the steps Partridge was handing a few piastres to the leading urchin. 'Watch this jeep until we get back. If it's OK you get the same again.'

It was a necessary precaution. They could have returned to find the wheels missing. He had heard every word of the conversation between Humble and Mrs Malloy. He passed her on the way up the steps. She gave him a direct look with half-closed eyes and was gone.

'Barmy outfit, this one,' Humble complained as he thumbed the bell. 'Allowing women like that to visit the place. Our first stop is Colonel Grogan. Right tartar from what I hear. Runs this pansy bunch of propagandists.'

'That attractive girl you were talking to . . .' Partridge began.

'Married to some RAF type. Flying Officer Malloy. And she had her eye on you. If you know what I mean.' Humble made a crude gesture with his fingers which Partridge found distasteful.

'I was going to say,' Partridge persisted as Humble pressed the bell again, 'it was odd. She never asked who had been murdered.'

'Who knows what goes through a woman's mind?'

The door was opened by a private in the SIB. 'They're still examining the murder room,' he informed Humble. 'Haven't found anything that helps much yet, sir,' he continued as he escorted them into the lift. 'The body was removed hours ago.'

'I know. You needn't come up with us. Colonel Grogan's on the third floor? We'll find him.'

'Anything from the pathologist yet?' Partridge enquired as the lift began its rheumatic ascent.

'He's been up all night working on the *corpus delicti*. All he'll say so far is that the weapon which carved up Ionides

17

could be a commando-type knife. *Could* be.' he snorted. 'I have yet to get a straight answer from any of those buggers.'

Colonel Grogan's door faced the lift beyond the entrance to the corridor running round the building. Humble knocked on the top panel, a voice rapped out, 'Come in, close the door, you're two minutes late.'

'Accounted for, sir, by the two minutes we had to wait outside to gain admittance to this place.'

'Sit down. This place, as you call it, is one of the most sensitive propaganda centres in Mid-East Command. And who am I talking to?'

Humble introduced himself and his companion, produced his identification, which Grogan glanced at and settled back in his chair. Humble had him weighed up at a glance. A regular soldier, contemptuous of all those 'in for the duration', which appeared to include his visitors.

Grogan, he estimated, would be in his late fifties. His thatch of white hair was trimmed close to his bony skull, his clean-shaven face was craggy, his expression bleak. He sat erect as a poker in his hard-backed chair.

'What do you want?' he demanded.

'Well, sir, we are investigating a particularly horrific murder which took place on these premises . . .'

'Get to the point. I haven't all day.'

'Up to this moment we have interviewed Sergeant Higgins who found the body. Nothing much he could tell us. But I understand that among the units you over-see . . .'

'Command!' Grogan snapped.

'As you say, sir. I understand there is a secret unit led by a Colonel Maurice Barrymore . . .'

'Half-colonel. Temporary appointment. Lieutenant-Colonel Barrymore you must be referring to.'

Oh, my God, Humble thought, no wonder they gave him a desk job a thousand miles behind the lines. A World

War One type. Up boys, and at 'em. Never mind the casualties – take that machine-gun post. He changed tactics.

'I need to interview this Lieutenant-Colonel Barrymore – and his men. I understand they've just returned from some training course. That they've only been back here in Cairo for two days . . .'

'Good luck to you.' Grogan stood up. 'They're waiting for you. Can't imagine why you're interested in them.'

'I don't have to explain my reasons. Sir.'

'Can't imagine why they call you Humble.' Grogan glared. 'Follow me.'

Stiff in his walk, he led the way down the corridor, back straight, the veteran of a thousand inspection parades. Turning along a fresh corridor, he stopped in front of a closed door, opened it and walked in. He made a dismissive gesture towards Humble and Partridge.

'SIB. Over to you.'

Without a glance at them, he walked out, closing the door. The three men waiting in the room stared at their visitors in silence. The windows – again barred – overlooked the front street where the jeep was parked, Partridge noted as Humble made introductions.

'Better sit down, I suppose,' the half-colonel behind a desk suggested. 'Although we can't give you long. We have things to do.'

'So have we, sir,' growled Humble. 'Like investigating a grim murder . . .'

Partridge, seated next to his chief, assessed the three men with interest. Lieutenant-Colonel Barrymore had spoken in a languid voice, was dark-haired with a trim moustache, thin-faced with an aquiline nose. Effortlessly, he carried an aura of authority and command.

The records showed he was only twenty-one years old but from his air of sophistication Partridge would have guessed he was in his thirties. He sat back in a swivel chair,

19

turning a short swagger cane between strong fingers. He pointed with the cane to the two men seated in hard-back chairs on either side of the desk.

'Captain Robson. Company Sergeant Major Kearns. Members of my unit.'

'Which unit is that, Colonel?'

'Classified.' He used the tip of the cane to push a typed sheet of paper across the desk. 'That explains.'

Partridge studied the other two men while Humble scanned the letter. Robson was twenty-two, more heavily built than the lieutenant-colonel. Brown-haired, he also sported a moustache, straggly, and his whole manner was more relaxed. He sat with an arm stretched across the back of his chair and his expression was amiable. He reminded Partridge of a country doctor. Again, he looked older than his years.

Kearns was tall, thin, clean-shaven and hadn't moved a muscle since they entered the room. His brown eyes reminded Partridge of glass marbles. He sat very erect and his expression was bleak, his jaw clenched. All three men had skin tanned the colour of mahogany.

'I can still ask you some questions. I'm going to do just that. It's my job,' snapped Humble, pushing the letter back over the desk-top, the letter from GHQ signed by a general.

'Let's hurry it up, shall we?' Barrymore suggested in his silken tone. 'I'm beginning to get irked.'

'Unfortunately Ionides can no longer be irked. You have met him, of course? All of you? Seeing as you have your unit stationed in the same building?'

Humble's gaze swept over the three men. Nothing changed in Kearns' expression. Barrymore tapped his small white teeth with the tip of his cane. It was Captain Robson who replied.

'Personally speaking, no. I gather he was stuck away up on the next floor. As far as I know I've never set eyes on the chap. Horrible business. Any clues – as to who did it?'

'The investigation is continuing.' Humble turned to Kearns who was studying Partridge like a hangman measuring him for the drop. Only twenty years old. Must be the youngest CSM in the British Army.

'What about you?'

'The same as Captain Robson.' There was a snap in his voice. He'd be a bastard on the parade ground, Humble thought. It was the sheer immobility of Kearns which fascinated Humble. He looked at Barrymore.

'What about you, sir? I've heard there are special units which slip into Greece to help the Resistance there. And Ionides was Greek.'

'Rather an obvious observation. That last remark.' Barrymore made no attempt to conceal the sarcasm. 'No is the answer. And now, I think we've told you all we can. I'd prefer this interview to draw to a close. You've read that letter . . .'

'Which authorizes you not to answer any question affecting military security. No, I haven't quite finished, Colonel Barrymore. I understand the three of you returned to Cairo forty-eight hours ago. That means you were all in the city last night. Where were you between the hours of nine and eleven? Last night. And *that* has nothing to do with military security.'

'If you must know . . .' Barrymore sounded as though he were having trouble stifling a yawn. 'All three of us were getting some well-earned kip aboard a houseboat on the Nile. The location is top secret.'

'Any witnesses to confirm your story?'

Despite his tan, the hint of a flush of blood appeared on Barrymore's face. He stood up and Humble saw for the first time his khaki drill trousers were thrust into the tops of gleaming leather cavalry boots. Walking to the door, he opened it.

'I am not accustomed to being insulted in front of subordinates. May I suggest the interview is concluded? That you both leave now. If you please.'

Humble stood up, nodded to Partridge, and strode out of the room. The door closed behind them as they headed for the lift.

'Botched that one, didn't I?' observed Humble. 'Sprawled right into it. Gave him just the excuse he was looking for to chuck us out. What did you think of them?'

'Funny trio. I couldn't get it out of my mind there was a lot of tension under the surface.'

'Which there would be if they've just returned from some mission to the Greek islands. They're Special Operations Executive – and commandos to boot.'

'SOE? Then that explains . . .'

'It explains a lot,' Humble interjected as they ignored the lift and walked down the staircase. 'It explains why some flaming desk wallah of a general at Grey Pillars provides Barrymore with a letter giving total immunity from questioning. It explains why he could throw me out on my ear. And we can't check their alibi. That houseboat is where the SOE plan operations. It's called *Tara*. Don't know why – but it's off limits even to us.'

Partridge waited until they were settled inside the jeep before he asked his question. First he paid off the chief urchin of the gang guarding the vehicle. 'Not enough!' the urchin screeched. '*Imshi! Yallah!*' Partridge bawled. They ran off, shouting obscenities.

'Did you notice Captain Robson qualified his statement that he'd never met Ionides? *As far as I know I've never set eyes on the chap*.'

'You spotted that, too? You're learning. Gives him an out if we came up with a witness who saw them talking together. Any idea how the murder was done?' he asked as he started the vehicle moving.

'From our visit in the night it seems impossible. The only

22

way out is the front entrance – guarded by the Sudanese receptionist. Our people searched the place from top to bottom. No one there. All windows are barred. You *can* get out on to balconies from certain rooms on the upper floors. But you're thirty feet from the ground. Yet the killer had to be behind that locked door Higgins tried before he went into the next room.'

'And we found traces of blood in the bathroom. My bet is Higgins sat on that lavatory seat quite a long time. I can't say I blame him – but that was when the murderer was cleaning himself up before performing his vanishing trick.'

'Unless the Sudanese receptionist was bribed?'

'I talked with Selim. I've carried out enough interrogations in my time to know he wasn't lying. You know something, Partridge? I've a hunch we're not going to solve this one.'

'This is a bloody waste of time. You do know that?' Humble rapped out as he pulled the jeep into the kerb in front of the Antikhana Building. It was dark, the street was deserted.

Partridge checked his watch. 'Ten o'clock. The exact time Higgins arrived back on the night of the murder. I want to walk right round the outside first. Then go inside – just like Higgins did.'

'You're on your own, laddie. I'll wait here. And watch it at the back. The native quarter . . .'

Partridge jumped down on to the pavement and began walking slowly away from the entrance steps. Although it was dark there was plenty of light from the street lamps. He looked up as he walked, stared at the projecting balconies with their iron grilles.

It was very quiet. The only sound the smack of his shoes on stone. No one about. Probably it had been like this on

23

the night of the murder. He turned the first corner of the building and the side street was a canyon of gloom. He unbuttoned his holster flap, felt the butt of his Service revolver. Butterflies in the stomach. The silence became oppressive, sinister.

He turned the next corner, walking more slowly, trying to make no sound. Across the narrow street to his right loomed the ramshackle tenements of the native quarter. Black as pitch now. He looked up again. The roof of the building was a blurred silhouette against a distant background of star-studded sky. He heard a scuffling sound and his hands were moist. A half-starved cat scuttled across the street.

Completing the circuit, he saw Humble leaning over the wheel, the red glow of a cigarette near his mouth. He mounted the steps, pressed the bell. An SIB sentry opened the right-hand door. Partridge showed his pass, went inside, nodded to the Sudanese behind the desk.

'No one in the building?' he asked the sentry.

'Yes, there is, sir. Colonel Barrymore is still in his office. Professor Guy Seton-Charles is also working late. And Sergeant Higgins is sitting on the staircase.'

'Why?'

'Better, maybe, sir, you ask him that yourself.'

The heavily built ex-tank commander was seated out of sight on the sixth step. Hunched forward, hands tightly clasped, he looked embarrassed and stood up as Partridge appeared.

'Sorry, sir. It's just that I can't go up there alone. I'm waiting for Clanger Wilson, my room-mate.'

'Let's go up together. I'm on the way to the roof myself.' Partridge hastened to put the burly sergeant at his ease. 'Why Clanger?'

'It's his nickname. Nothing malicious. He's always knocking things over. Bit like a bull in a china shop. Everyone likes him. Just a bit of fun. Calling him Clanger.'

'I think you're sensible to wait for company,' Partridge assured him as they climbed the staircase together. 'Think I'd have done the same thing myself in your place. After all, we still have to catch the blighter. Does Colonel Barrymore work this late often?'

'He's still here?' Higgins sounded surprised. 'Never known that to happen before. Not that any of us have a clue what that lot do. We call them the Hush-Hush Boys.'

'Let's look in on him before we go on the roof.'

Partridge opened the door to the office where a light shone from beneath it without knocking. Barrymore was bending over a file behind his desk. He looked up, closed the file quickly and laid a hand flat on it.

'I saw the light,' Partridge explained quickly.

'What the devil do you mean invading my quarters without so much as a warning knock?'

'I've just explained that. I saw the light and thought maybe someone had forgotten to turn it off. And I smell smoke. Is that mineral water, sir?'

A metal wastepaper basket stood by the side of the desk with smoke drifting up from inside. Partridge had pointed to a large glass jug on the desk next to a tumbler. 'Yes. Your powers of detection are extraordinary.' Barrymore noticed Higgins standing in the corridor. He jumped up, strode towards him. 'What are you doing? Snooping around at this hour?'

Barrymore's back was turned when Partridge picked up the jug, doused the papers burning inside the basket. Stooping, he retrieved an intact remnant with a few visible words. *Report on Siros raid.* He turned to face the door. 'Higgins is with me. We were just making our way to the roof.'

'Then kindly make your way.'

As Partridge, cap under his arm, walked back into the corridor Barrymore slammed the door behind him. Going back to the file, he emptied more sheets into the basket and set light to them.

Partridge was walking alongside Higgins towards the corner of the building when a door opened. A man of slim build wearing a pale civilian suit emerged from an office and locked the door. 'Who is this?' Partridge whispered.

'Professor Guy Seton-Charles. Boffin type.'

Twenty-three years old, Partridge recalled from his study of records at GHQ. Rejected for military service on grounds of poor eyesight. The thin-faced man walked towards them hugging a green file under his arm. Everything was thin. Hands, his long studious face. He wore rimless glasses.

'A word with you, sir.' Partridge produced his identity card. 'SIB. We haven't got around to interviewing you yet. What is your precise job here?'

'Difficult to be precise about anything. All problems have shades of meaning. I am concerned with propaganda to the mainland.'

'Mainland?'

'Greece. The authorities are getting it all wrong, of course. The left-wing ELAS *andartes* are the real guerrillas fighting the Germans. The Republican EDES lot are hopeless. But can I convince people here? Even if ELAS are Communist?'

He spoke in a pedantic petulant tone and was obviously launched into a lecture. Partridge stopped him.

'Propaganda? Greece? Then you must have worked with Ionides.'

'Never, my dear chap. No idea why those two – Gavalas and Ionides – were here. Making jobs for themselves, I suspect . . .'

'We must go,' Partridge interjected. 'We'll talk later.' He headed for the end of the corridor. 'Funny type.'

'We've given him a nickname. Cuckoo.' Higgins chuckled.

'I'll lead the way,' Partridge suggested tactfully and began to climb the stone spiral staircase. It was very narrow, curving sharply, and there was no lighting. He felt his way up the wall with one hand, emerging suddenly on to the rooftop.

It was flat, enclosed by a waist-high wall with an iron rail on top. Higgins led the way, heading for one of a row of cabin-like structures erected on the rooftop. Taking out a key, he opened the door, switched on the light and showed Partridge his sleeping quarters. Alongside either wall leading from the door to a window at the far end was a camp bed neatly made up with Army blankets. Higgins indicated the one to his right.

'That's where Clanger sleeps. Luckily we arrived at the unit early enough to grab a cabin. Better than being billeted in Kasr-el-Nil Barracks across the road. No privacy in that madhouse. I'll show you round. Not a great deal to see. Except the Pyramids.'

Partridge made for the side of the roof at the back. Behind him he heard Higgins relocking the cabin door. His macabre experience had shaken the ex-tank commander to the core. Partridge placed a hand on the iron rail perched half a foot above the wall-top, gripped it, tested its strength and peered over. The dark canyon facing the squalid tenements of the native quarter was like an abyss. It was very quiet as Higgins joined him and made his remark.

'I heard you hadn't been out here long, sir. Going into the native quarter is forbidden. For a very good reason. Lord knows how many squaddies have staggered in there dead drunk. They never come out. The body is found days later by Military Police patrols. Throat slit. Wallet gone.'

'So it would take a brave man to go in even stone cold sober?'

'Sober – and armed – he'd probably be all right. Let's look at something more savoury.'

They walked across to the wall overlooking the front

27

entrance. Below, Humble was smoking behind the wheel of his jeep. Higgins pointed south. 'There they are.'

In the far distance, by the light of a waxing moon, Partridge saw the dark silhouettes of the Pyramids of Giza. He pulled at his shirt. He was sweating but the temperature seemed to have dropped suddenly.

'My Gawd! Look at that. Here she comes,' Higgins commented.

What seemed like a black cloud was blotting out the moon, the Pyramids below. Partridge had the impression smoke from a huge forest fire was sweeping into the city. It was a sight which stayed with him for the rest of his life.

'*Khamsin*. Sandstorm. Ever seen one?' asked Higgins. 'You've a treat in store. Inside ten minutes that cloud will blot out Cairo like a London pea-souper. Better get back to your jeep – you'll be lucky to make it back to GHQ . . .'

Humble had the engine running when Partridge ran down the steps of the building. He glared and moved the gears as Partridge jumped aboard.

'I was about to leave without you. *Khamsin* coming.'

'How did you know?' Partridge asked as the jeep rocketed down the deserted streets, exceeding the speed limit.

'That breeze that's flapping your shirt, you stupid bugger. What kept you?'

'I think I know now how the murderer escaped without being seen.'

'Great! And you know who the murderer is?'

'No. No idea . . .'

'Great again! I think my hunch was right. We'll not be solving this one.'

And Humble was right. Up to a point. The case might never have been solved but for a man who hadn't even been born as they raced through the streets. A man called Tweed. Over forty years later.

PART ONE

The Moor of Death

卐卐卐

1

May 1987. It was another rainy day in London. Tweed stood by his first-floor office window gazing across Park Crescent to Regent's Park. Seated behind her desk, his assistant and confidante, Monica, watched the Deputy Director of the Secret Intelligence Service.

'A penny for your thoughts,' she said. 'You're not here – you have that faraway look.'

'Harry Masterson,' he replied. 'Why has he chosen Greece for his holiday? Dammit, he's Sector Chief for South-East Europe. You'd think he'd want to get as far from that part of the world as possible.'

'He does speak fluent Greek – among his other languages.'

'And you saw him in Bond Street the day before he was due to start his leave. With an attractive girl you think was Greek.'

'So, it's simple. Harry is divorced, has lots of girlfriends. This time it's a Greek. Maybe she wanted to go there, felt homesick.'

'I'm not convinced.' Tweed, a compact, clean-shaven man in his forties who wore glasses, sat behind his desk, began cleaning the glasses with a handkerchief. Monica frowned. He often performed that action when he was disturbed. 'Harry can't take a proper holiday,' Tweed continued. 'He once told me he's bored in three days without a problem to get his teeth into. He's been out there for three weeks.'

'And not a word from him, you mean?'

'But there has been a word – if you can call this a word. I got in early this morning. This came in the post.'

Unlocking a drawer, he took out a package shaped like a cigar box. The wrappings were still intact although the package had been opened. Monica stood up, came round and stood by the side of her chief. The address was written in Masterson's clear bold hand. Marked 'Personal'. The stamps were Greek. Tweed lifted off the top packing where he had carefully slit along the edges. Inside was a cigar box.

'From Harry Masterson. I don't like it,' Tweed said grimly. 'It looks like pieces of evidence he's collected about an investigation he's working on. And sent to me in case something happens to him.'

'Aren't you over-reacting? What's inside the box?'

'See for yourself.' Tweed flipped back the lid. 'That girl you saw him with in Bond Street before he left for Athens. Is this her?'

He rummaged among a collection of papers, photographs and a small notebook. Selecting one of the photographs, he placed it on the desk.

'Yes, that's her,' Monica said, studying the picture. 'I'm sure of it. She looks slimmer in a white dress. Good figure. She was wearing a coat when I saw her. I wonder where it was taken? Looks like somewhere in Greece.'

'Look on the back. Zea. Wherever that might be. Notice anything odd about the picture?'

'There are a lot of expensive-looking pleasure craft moored behind her. And beyond, the buildings are stepped up a hill. What's odd?'

'I'm damned sure the girl didn't know her picture was being taken by Harry. She's looking at some book. I think he took it surreptitiously. That's suggestive in itself. I don't think he trusted her . . .'

'Don't use the past tense . . .'

'Come in,' Tweed called out as someone rapped on the

door. A slim, fair-haired man in his early thirties with an air of self-assurance entered. 'Marler, your timing is perfect as always,' Tweed commented. 'You know Greece fairly well.' He handed him the photo. 'Harry Masterson took this picture somewhere in Greece. Any idea of the location?'

Marler examined the print, turned it over, smiled drily. 'It all links up if it's Harry, doesn't it? An attractive female, a small port, very exclusive, millionaires' yachts. Nothing but the best for our high-life Harry. This is the port of Zea. It's along the coast road from the main Piraeus harbour.'

'Why so exclusive?' Tweed asked. 'Apart from the floating palaces? Drug traffickers can afford those boats these days – if they're at the top.'

'Because just behind Zea is the Royal Yacht Club. Nowadays it is officially the Yacht Club since Greece became a republic.' He picked up a magnifying glass from Monica's desk. 'Bet you a fiver some of these still have the initials RYC on their sterns. Are you on?'

'No. I'm fed up with losing money to you.'

'And you would have lost.' Marler was peering through the magnifier. 'Two of the yachts berthed do have those initials. A bit of rather nice snobbery,' he commented in his upper-crust voice. He laid down the glass. 'What's this all in aid of, if I may be so bold?'

'I'm worried stiff about Harry.'

'For what good reasons?'

Marler, dressed in an immaculate pale linen suit, blue-striped shirt, matching blue tie and handmade shoes skilfully weighted in the toecaps – 'useful for kicking your opponent in the balls' – sat down in Tweed's armchair. He lit one of his rare king-size cigarettes. Crossing his legs, the epitome of relaxation, he fixed his blue, ice-cold eyes on Tweed.

'Reason One, why choose part of his working sector for his holiday? Oh yes, I know he likes the sun, but the

33

Caribbean would have served. Reason Two, he always sends a rude postcard. No card. Reason Three, instead he sends this cigar box with stuff which looks to me like clues about an investigation he's conducting. Reason Four, Harry gets bored easily – so if someone has approached him with a problem which intrigues him he'd jump at the chance of occupying himself with it.'

'That the cigar box? May I see?'

'Over to you. See what you make of the contents. I've only had time to skip through them. I find the sending of that sinister.'

'Any note, letter, with it?'

'No. Monica saw him in Bond Street with that girl whose photo you're looking at.'

'When was that?' Marler asked.

'Three weeks ago. The day before he flew to Athens, I assume.'

'You *assume*?' Marler raised an eyebrow. 'These photos are a mix. Some obviously in Greece, some in this country. Don't know where.'

'I do,' said Tweed. 'That one of the outside of The Royal Oak Inn. I recognize it. Winsford. A village on Exmoor. So why do we have Somerset and Greece? Doesn't make sense.'

'Unless he hasn't spent his whole three weeks in Greece. The day he was seen by Monica he could have taken off for Exmoor. Gone on to Greece later. Suggests something the Greek filly told him led him to Somerset. Something he found there led him to Greece. A regular bloodhound, our Harry. Picks up a scent and won't let go.'

'The timing,' Monica agreed, 'suggests it could have been something the Greek girl told him sent him haring off to Somerset.'

'I wonder what,' muttered Tweed, sifting through the non-Greek pictures. 'This looks like Watchet, a tiny port on the Bristol Channel. One of the front, another of the

34

harbour. I remember that line of lampposts along the front
with the small hill at the eastern edge of the harbour.
Dunster High Street, not a doubt. The front entrance to
the Luttrell Arms, leading hotel in Dunster. Another of a
Tudor-style mansion behind a stone wall. Familiar. Near
the Doone Valley if I remember right.'

Marler had emptied the cigar box and was fiddling with
the base of its interior. He raised a thin sheet of wood
pressed down on the base, extracted a folded sheet of
paper.

'Seen this?' he enquired. 'The scene widens. Take a
shufti.'

Tweed studied the opened sheet. Harry's distinctive
writing. *MOD. Brigadier Willie Davies*. Ministry of Defence. Harry had visited the place, presumably before he
flew to Greece, maybe even before he'd driven down to
Somerset. There were two more words written on the sheet
of paper. *Somerset Levels*.

Tweed felt a prickling of the hairs at the back of his
neck, an unreasoned sense of foreboding. He became
aware that Marler and Monica were watching him.

'Something's wrong,' said Monica.

'I hope not.' He passed the sheet to her. 'I don't think
we've told you yet, Marler, that Brigadier Davies is our
most friendly contact at the Ministry of Defence. He's also
a member of the same club as Harry. They were close.'

'Chums, you mean?' Marler enquired. 'As well as a
professional relationship? This business is getting a bit
weird. So many strands. And what the deuce is – are – the
Somerset Levels?'

'One of the most benighted and lonely spots in England.
The area between Taunton and Glastonbury where they
dig peat. In the time of Charles the First the sea used to
flood in. Now they have constructed waterways – they look
like canals. It is like a bleak marshland. I don't understand
any of this – too many strands, as you said.'

35

He stood up and walked over to the window. It had stopped raining. Now they had May sunshine. The pavements were drying out, leaving damp patches. He stood with his hands clasped behind his back. He was, Monica knew, on the verge of taking a decision.

'I want Harry recalled from Greece immediately. Isn't his deputy for Greece, Patterson, at the British Embassy?'

'Yes,' said Monica promptly. 'Harry appointed him a couple of months ago. Patterson speaks Greek and has travelled widely in the archipelago. You're assuming Harry contacted him after he reached Athens.'

'Which he probably didn't,' Marler commented. 'Running his own investigation unofficially, he'd play it close to the chest. Why the MOD? Or again was it something the Greek girl told him? Incidentally, Monica, what made you so sure she *was* Greek?'

'When he stopped me he said something in a foreign language. She looked annoyed. Then Harry said, "The Greeks always have a word for it." Looking back, I almost think he was sending me a signal.'

'Fair do's,' Marler agreed. 'She is Greek.'

'And now,' Tweed said impatiently as he returned to his swivel chair, 'I want that call made to Athens recalling Harry. A direct order. He's to return instantly, the moment they locate him.'

Monica was reaching for her phone when it began to ring as a raven-haired girl with good bone structure came into the office. Marler jumped up, grinned, offered Paula Grey, Tweed's assistant, his chair. He spread his hands, adopted a theatrical pose.

'Lothario offers you his comfortable seat. How is it you look more ravishing every time I see you?'

'Flannel,' rapped back Paula. 'You think I haven't heard all about your women?'

She was crossing her legs when she stiffened. She was looking at Monica who had been talking on the phone. In

36

a broken voice Monica nodded to Tweed to lift his receiver.

'Athens on the line . . . Larry Patterson for you.'

Tweed grabbed up his receiver. It became very silent and still in the office. They watched Tweed whose expression had become poker-faced. In a quiet controlled voice he asked several terse questions, said, 'Yes, of course,' five times, thanked Patterson for calling and replaced the receiver. Leaning across his desk, he clasped his hands, gazed at them and spoke in a monotone.

'There is no easy way to break this type of news. Harry Masterson is dead. He was found today at the base of some cliff called Cape Sounion. I gather it is some distance southeast of Athens. The cliff is very sheer and is three hundred feet high. They will be flying the body home.'

'Oh dear God, no! Not Harry . . .'

It was Monica who burst out like a stricken animal. Her eyes filled with tears. Paula jumped up, put an arm round her and helped her to her feet and out of the room. The silence was oppressive after the click of the closing door.

'Apparently, according to Patterson, he must have slithered over the edge early in the morning,' Tweed continued. 'About nine o'clock a coastguard launch patrolling the area on the lookout for drug smugglers spotted the body on some rocks at the edge of the sea.'

'Balls!' said Marler, his tone harsh. 'Which is what Harry would have said if they'd found me there. I know the area.'

'I'm listening,' said Tweed in the same monotone, twiddling a pencil between his fingers.

'Cape Sounion is about a two-hour drive along the coast road from Athens. It's the southernmost tip of Greece at that point. Perched on the summit of the Cape is the Temple of Poseidon. It's a lonely spot when the tourists aren't there. Beyond the temple the ground is covered with stubby grass which slopes gently towards the brink. You can easily see when you're coming to the end of everything.'

'So?' pressed Tweed.

'Harry had all his marbles – more than most of us. The idea that he slipped over the edge is fatuous.'

'So?' Tweed repeated.

'Harry was murdered. Absolutely no doubt about it. And I would like to know what the hell we are going to do about it.'

2

Action this day. A favourite maxim of Tweed's, borrowed from Winston Churchill.

Tweed had called for the afternoon what he termed a 'war conference'. Inside what Howard, Tweed's chief, insisted on calling the 'boardroom', six people were gathered round a large oblong table.

Like antagonists, Howard was seated at one end of the table, facing Tweed, who occupied the other end. Also present were Paula Grey, sitting on Tweed's right, notebook at the ready. Marler sat next to Bob Newman, foreign correspondent and close confidant of Tweed. Pete Nield, experienced agent, sat opposite Marler and Newman. Already the atmosphere reeked with tension and disagreement.

'Aren't we jumping to a lot of conclusions rather early in the game regarding this dreadful tragedy?' suggested Howard in his slow pontificating voice.

'It's not a game,' Tweed snapped. 'And Masterson's death does not sound like an accident.'

'Hold hard a jiffy . . .' Howard, six feet tall, plump-faced and perfectly tailored in a Chester Barrie navy blue suit, shot his cuffs to expose the gold links.

Oh God, thought Tweed, why did he have to turn up unexpectedly and attend this meeting? He stared hard at Howard as he spoke.

'Well, let's get on with it.'

'I was going to make the point that Patterson is already in place in Athens. He could take a look-see, send us a report. Oh, nothing personal, of course, but why is Mr Newman honouring us with his presence?'

'Because I asked him to. Because he knows Greece. Because he speaks Greek fluently and is flying out there with Marler.'

'Not necessary,' Marler interjected in his clipped tone. 'You know I work on my own . . .'

There was a heavy silence. Tweed kept the silence going while he deliberately arranged the pile of photos in front of him. Newman, in his early forties, well-built, clean-shaven, with thick sandy hair and a strong face, sat watching Tweed with a droll expression.

'I have to say,' Howard continued eventually, 'that I really don't see how Newman, able though he might be, fits in with such an assignment.'

Tweed launched his attack. 'He's fully vetted, as you well know. Patterson has only been in Athens for a short time. Let's get a few opinions.' He addressed Newman. 'Bob, you knew Harry Masterson. Can you see him stumbling off the edge of a cliff?'

'He was sharp as a fox. But I would like to collect a few more facts in Greece. Facts are what I go by.'

'Marler?' Tweed asked.

'So unlikely the idea is ridiculous.'

'Paula?'

'I heard he once left a party half-smashed and walked down the middle of Walton Street balancing a bottle of champagne on his head. The bottle stayed there. Sure-footed as the proverbial goat. Not a chance.'

'Pete?'

39

'Never in a million years.'

'Are you convinced?' Tweed asked Howard. 'If it was murder and we don't act fast the Prime Minister will call us to account.'

'I don't like blackmail,' Howard replied stiffly.

'Who does? You haven't answered the question.'

'Well,' Howard began, his manner breezy, 'first he's a fox, then he's a goat . . .'

'I don't find that the least bit amusing,' Tweed snapped.

'In that case, what do you propose?' Howard's well-fed face was flushed with annoyance. 'And I still maintain Marler could go on his own. Newman is surplus to requirements – I do realize he's rendered valuable service in the past . . .'

'Very generous of you,' Tweed interjected. The trouble was Howard realized Newman was wealthier than he would ever be. The foreign correspondent had made a fortune from his best-selling book, *Kruger: The Computer That Failed*. Tweed spoke decisively.

'Marler and Newman will travel to Greece together Masterson went alone – and see what happened to him.' He glanced at Paula but she was already recording his instructions.

'Marler's deputy, Harris, can take over the German sector in his absence. Agreed, Marler?' He went on as Marler nodded. 'The investigation covers two very different areas. Greece. Dealt with. Newman reports back to me over Patterson's scrambler phone at the Athens Embassy.'

'Why not Marler?' Howard bleated.

Tweed, in full cry, ignored the interruption. 'I shall drive with Paula to Exmoor and check that area. Pete Nield will come with us in a separate car. He will appear not to know us. He will come armed.'

'Why?' demanded Howard.

'Because I don't know what we're walking into. One man has already been murdered.'

'That has yet to be proved,' Howard objected.

'Everyone I asked believes that. I have an open mind but I'm taking no chances. We start tomorrow – before the scent goes cold. The contents of this cigar box Harry posted me will be checked by our experts in the Engine Room in the basement. I want someone to visit Harry's country cottage in Sussex. What was it called?'

'Clematis Cottage, near Apfield,' said Paula, continuing her writing.

'I will contact Jim Corcoran of Airport Security at Heathrow. He'll check the passenger manifests of all flights to Greece over the past three weeks.' Tweed looked briefly at Howard who had lapsed into silence. 'If we can find which flight Masterson used we may find the name of that Greek girl Monica saw him with in Bond Street.' He turned to Paula. 'How is Monica?'

'Harry Butler took her home. He'll pull her round. Should he go down to check Clematis Cottage?'

'Good idea. And tell him to look at a power cruiser moored at a landing stage a few hundred yards south of the cottage. He turns off to the right along the first track.'

'Is that the lot?' Howard enquired with a hint of sarcasm.

'No. We need photos of Harry Masterson run off by the Engine Room urgently this evening. Newman and Marler will need them when they're tracking his movements in Greece. And I want careful blow-ups of the photo of the Greek girl at Zea. Some for Newman and Marler, some for me to take to Somerset.'

'I think I'm going.' Howard stood up. 'I do have other work calling for my attention. I can't rubber-stamp all this in a memo . . .'

'So you'll have a little extra time for that other work calling for your attention.' Tweed smiled. 'Thank you for your cooperation and attendance.'

Howard withdrew, closing the door behind him as

41

though it were made of glass. Round the table there was a sense of relief.

'I have held back two intriguing points,' Tweed told them. 'Harry made a reference to a friend at court at the Ministry of Defence. I hope to visit him before you leave tonight. I can't imagine why Harry went there.'

'And the other point?' asked Marler.

'Endstation.' Tweed looked round the table. 'Like a clue to a crossword puzzle. Mean anything? Suggest anything? The word is written – in Harry's writing – on the back of a British postcard. Just that one word. *Endstation*.'

'Sounds like Cockfosters, the last station on the Piccadilly Underground,' Paula suggested.

'Which doesn't link up with Exmoor – or Greece.'

'The fact that he wrote it on a *British* postcard points to a connection with Somerset,' Newman remarked. 'Harry liked little tricks like that. And he may well have had in mind that cigar box could have been intercepted.'

'So?' enquired Nield.

'He'd write any clue in code. Some puzzle he'd hope Tweed could unravel.'

'Puzzle is the word for what he sent me.' Tweed commented. 'Paula, book tickets for Marler and Newman to fly to Athens tomorrow . . .'

'I've already made a note to do just that . . .'

'But no one moves anywhere, leaves London, until I've seen Brigadier Willie Davies. We need to know why Harry went to the Ministry of Defence.'

Escorted by a male receptionist, Tweed walked down the endless corridor past doors carrying the names of military officers. He clutched in his hand the pass he would have to surrender before being let out of the MOD.

Brigadier Davies, a tall red-faced man with lapel tabs of the same colour, rose from behind his desk as Tweed entered and the door closed behind him. They shook hands.

'Long time no see.' Davies remarked in his crisp staccato voice. 'Take a pew. Long time.' he repeated. sitting down again. 'then we have a queue from your outfit.'

'Harry Masterson, you mean?'

'The great man himself.' Davies tugged at his ginger moustache. ran a hand over thinning hair of the same colour. 'But since you authorized the interview you'll know all about it. Always good for a laugh. Harry. Say anything outrageous.'

'You said I authorized the interview?'

'Course you did.' Davies pushed a sheet of paper with typing across the desk. Tweed glanced at it. A printed heading. General and Cumbria Assurance Company – the cover name for the SIS at Park Crescent. The letter was brief.

Dear Willie – If you could give Harry your cooperation re this one I'd be greatly indebted. At the bottom was Tweed's signature. Forged. Typical of Harry. Tweed thought nostalgically. Break every rule in the book to get what he was after.

'A lot's been happening. My memory must be going.' He phrased the next words carefully. 'The trouble is he took off on a plane without leaving me a report. Just caught his flight after leaving you. I gather. Could you bring me up to date? What he asked. what you told him?'

'Weird case. Going back over forty years.' Davies stood up. extracted a bunch of keys from his pocket and unlocked a green steel cabinet. 'Took me a while to locate the file for Harry.' He grinned as he pulled out a blue file with a red tab attached and handed it to Tweed. 'Still classified.'

Tweed left the file unopened on the desk. The typed inscription on the front in faded letters carried a brief message. *Commando raid on Siros Island, Greece, February, 1944.*

'If you'd bear with me, Willie, I went off abroad as soon as I'd provided the authorization,' he lied glibly. 'It would help if you could tell me what Harry asked you. I'm not sure exactly how much he knew about this business.'

'Oh, he had his facts all lined up.' Davies clasped his hands behind his long neck. 'I'd offer you coffee but why poison a friend? Harry said he first needed details of that four-man commando raid on Siros in February 1944. I expect you know Siros is a large island in the Cyclades, a strategic stepping-stone to Piraeus, the port of Athens. Couriers passed through Siros from Cairo on their way to the mainland to contact the Greek Resistance. Actually, the Resistance was active on the island. German-occupied, of course. And the HQ of the German commander of the Cyclades group. A General Hugo Geiger. All this came from Harry before he looked at that file. And a bit more. I wondered how he'd come about the information.'

'Tell me about the bit more.'

'A four-man commando team made the raid. From Special Operations Executive. Commanded by a Lieutenant-Colonel Barrymore. Had with him a Captain Robson, a CSM called Kearns, and the Greek.'

'The Greek?'

'You didn't know about him? Chap called Andreas Gavalas. He had got out in a motorized caïque, reached Cairo months before. The idea was he knew Siros well. The Resistance lot, by the way, were the Republican crowd EDES. As opposed to ELAS, the Commie faction. Barrymore was taking a fortune in diamonds to hand over to a courier from Athens. Last time Cairo financed them. Turned their cooperation completely to ELAS shortly afterwards. Word was ELAS were doing the real fighting out there against Jerry, even though they were Communists.'

'And that was the extent of Harry's knowledge?'

'No. Weird business. He knew about the tragedy. After

44

they landed on Siros successfully the diamonds were handed to Gavalas to pass on to his Greek contact. The commando team was returning to the beach down a gully and found Gavalas lying dead with a knife stuck in his back.' Davies' expression became grim. 'It was a commando knife.'

'You can't mean that one of . . .'

'The three commandos? No. Barrymore immediately gathered his team together and asked to see their weapons. All of them, including himself, had their knives.'

'Weird, as you say. Why didn't the killer remove the knife?'

'Well, that's something I can understand. Apparently it had been driven into Gavalas with great force. Ever tried to pull out a knife from a dead body? It can take some doing – if it's rammed in deep. Barrymore tried to pull it out and couldn't manage it. So they scarpered pretty damn quick.'

'And Harry explained all this before seeing the file?'

'I think he wanted me to realize he wasn't on a fishing expedition, that he knew a great deal about the murder on Siros.'

'And was it eventually brought home to the killer?'

'Not as far as I know.' Davies made a sweeping gesture with his hand. 'Look at the range of suspects. The EDES section which knew Gavalas was coming. The Germans occupying the island. They patrolled constantly, I gather.'

'And the diamonds had been handed over before the Barrymore team left Gavalas the first time – alive?'

'No, they hadn't.' Davies pursed his lips.

'So the first thing Barrymore would do when he realized Gavalas was dead would be to check for the diamonds.'

'Which he did. They'd vanished.'

'What was a fortune in diamonds worth then? Any data?'

'One hundred thousand pounds. God knows what they'd be worth now. That covers what Harry told me before I searched for the file and he sat in that same chair reading

45

it. His next request was what startled me. Tell you about it when you've scanned the file.' Davies smiled cynically. 'You can't, of course, borrow that file, photograph it, or make a single note. It's the regulations.'

'I know.' Tweed glanced up and caught the cynical smile. He understood. Davies knew Tweed's reputation for a photographic memory. He only had to read a long document once and he had total recall. Every word would be imprinted on his brain.

Five minutes later Tweed pushed the file back across the desk. He sat with hands clasped as he asked the question.

'And what was the request Harry made that startled you?'

'He asked me if I could give him the present whereabouts of Barrymore, Robson and Kearns – if they'd survived. I don't think I can take this any further, Tweed. It involves another department. Better ask Harry when you see him again.'

'Not possible, Willie.' Tweed paused. 'Harry is dead.'

Davies stiffened, his face froze. He opened a drawer, took out an ash tray, a pack of cigarettes and lit one. He dropped the pack back inside the drawer.

'Rarely smoke these days. You tricked me, Tweed. Not like you . . .'

'I thought you might close down on me. It's just possible he was murdered. I've thrown away the rule book. I'm going to find out how he died come hell or high water. You'd do the same thing if our roles were reversed.'

'You're right there,' Davies admitted. 'May I ask where and how?'

'In Greece. He's supposed to have stumbled off a three-hundred-feet cliff a good way south-east of Athens . . .'

'Bloody rubbish. Never!' Davies stubbed out the cigarette, drummed his thick fingers on the desk-top. 'Not

46

Harry. And you won't stop until you've found out what happened.'

'No, I won't.'

Davies stood up, went back to the cabinet, unlocked it, took out a thin blue file and laid it before Tweed. He sat down, lips tightly compressed before he spoke.

'You can look at that appendix to the other file. Same regulations apply . . . Hell, I don't have to tell you. When Harry asked for that information I didn't think I could oblige. I checked with this other department which keeps certain records. You see, Barrymore and Kearns stayed in the Army for a few years after the war. The girl who checks records like that is a tigress. Never gives up. I gave her all three names – Robson and Kearns as well as Barrymore. She located Barrymore easily. Then she obtained a copy of the phone directory of the same area. Came up with all three addresses. Better look in that file.'

A single sheet of paper. Tweed stared, unable to believe it. All the addresses were in Somerset. 'The last two are from the directory,' Davies explained.

'After all these years, they all live in the Exmoor area.'

'Odd, isn't it? Odd, too, that Harry died in Greece – not a hundred miles from the island of Siros from what you've told me.'

Tweed closed the second file, stood up slowly, his mind whirling. He thanked Willie, said they must have a drink soon. At the door he turned before he opened it.

'When I came in you said something about a queue from my outfit.'

Davies was standing close to him, hands thrust in his trouser pockets. He stood thinking for a moment.

'I wasn't too accurate there. You used to be with Scotland Yard. I made a subconscious connection.'

'What are you talking about?'

'A few days after Harry visited me someone else arrived – an ex-Chief Inspector from the Yard called Partridge.'

'Sam Partridge of Homicide? Now retired. I know him.'

'Might as well tell you the lot. Partridge carries no status here, of course. But he's a persuasive sort of chap. And coming so soon after Harry. Well . . . Long and short of it is he also wanted the present whereabouts of Barrymore, Robson and Kearns. I ended up giving him the addresses.'

'May I ask what was his interest?'

'He's still investigating a murder which took place over forty years ago. Never solved. Can't sit at home and cultivate a vegetable patch now he's retired. Very vigorous type.'

'The murder of Gavalas on Siros?'

'No. This is going to shake you. It did me. After Harry. Which is why I coughed up those addresses, I suppose. I'm sure there can't be a connection.'

'A connection between who?'

'The killing of Gavalas on Siros and the murder of some other Greek at the HQ of certain secret units in Cairo. Ionides I think he called him.'

3

'Jim Corcoran came through from Heathrow Airport Security,' Paula reported as Tweed walked into his office. 'We've got the data you need. Corcoran checked the computers. Harry flew out to Athens via Zurich on Swissair Flight 805. Ten days ago.'

'Which gave him about another ten days to poke about on Exmoor before he left. And I know now why he went there.'

'The news is even better. Harry booked two seats aboard the flight in advance. Guess the name of the passenger who sat in the seat next to him.'

'Not in the mood for guessing games. And I've got a mass of my own data to dictate to you . . .'

'A Christina Gavalas sat next to him.'

'My God, it's beginning to link up.'

'How?'

'Exactly how I've no idea. Ready for dictation? File One.'

Tweed stood quite still, eyes half-closed, while he recalled the contents of the Siros file. Paula took it down in her shorthand book, scrawled a fresh heading for File Two, recorded the three addresses Tweed reeled off.

'Two copies only,' he warned. 'One for Newman and Marler. The other for us.'

'Consider it done. Newman and Marler can collect the tickets from Heathrow if they're leaving tomorrow.'

'They are doing just that. I had a word with them on my way in. Let them have the first copy of the Siros file earliest.'

He was sitting behind his desk when the door opened and Monica walked in. She waved reassuring hands as Paula jumped up. 'I'm all right. Better back in the front line than moping at home.' She went to her desk. 'Can I help?'

'Yes,' said Tweed. 'Call the Yard. Superintendent Jack Richardson. Give him my best wishes. I need the home address of Chief Inspector Sam Partridge of Homicide, now retired.'

'Before you phone,' he said as Monica sat behind her desk, 'I want you to react quickly to this question. One possibly important clue from Harry's cigar box. One single word. Ready? *Endstation*.'

'The name of some operation. Codename.'

'Doesn't add up,' Paula intervened. 'It could have been

49

the codename for the raid on Siros. But there's no reference to any codename in the file. Also, Harry wrote it on a *British* postcard. That points to Somerset.'

She turned to Monica. 'Isn't all this pretty painful for you? You knew Harry well. Is it a good idea to come back yet?'

'Anything I can do to track down the swine who killed him. I want to be a part of this. I'll call the Yard.' She reached for the phone.

Tweed was heading for the door. 'Something else to pass on to Newman and Marler. Someone else is taking an interest in the Siros file. Partridge. What's the betting he's in Greece at this moment?'

'Do you think it's a good idea Newman going to Athens with Marler?' Paula asked after Tweed had left the room. 'They seem to fight like cat and dog. Square up to each other on every issue. Bob is early forties, Marler barely thirty.'

'And there, my dear, you have put your finger on it,' Monica assured her. 'They do scrap, I agree. But whereas Marler is quick off the mark, independent-minded – just the way Bob used to be until recently – Bob has become harder, tougher, wary. They could make an ideal combination once they're out there on their own. I think Tweed is banking on that.'

'What changed Bob? Made him a hard man? After all he was an international foreign correspondent. Still is, if a story interests him.'

'Ah, that was his experience behind the lines in East Germany when he went underground with a resistance group. A bitter, grim time, but he came through. Now, I'd better get on . . .'

When Tweed walked briskly back into the room Monica was putting down the phone. She waited until he had sat behind his desk, scribbled a note on his tasks pad.

'Did you know when you were at Scotland Yard they

had a nickname for you? Quicksilver Tweed, they called you, according to Superintendent Richardson . . .'

'A long time ago.' Tweed made a dismissive gesture. 'What about Partridge?'

'I have his phone number at Cheam. Thought I'd call him when you got back.'

'Yes, I'd like to talk to him personally.'

Monica dialled a number. She had a brief conversation with someone, then put her hand over the mouthpiece.

'Partridge isn't there. It's Mrs Partridge . . .'

'I don't know whether you'll remember me,' Tweed began, using his own phone, 'my name is Tweed . . .'

'I know you, it must be years . . .' She had a cultured voice. 'Sam worked with you at the Yard. We met once at a party. I recognize your voice . . .'

'Sorry to bother you, but I need to speak with Sam urgently.'

'He's not here, Mr Tweed. And I've no idea where he is . . .'

Tweed frowned, detected a note of anxiety in her voice now.

'Something wrong, Mrs Partridge? Why don't you know where he is?'

'You know how Sam is. He can't retire gracefully. Too active, restless. He's investigating some old murder case. I am worried. Before he left he said something he's never said to me before.'

'What was that?'

'He warned me never to open the door to strangers. Especially if they looked to be foreigners. He even had a spyglass fitted in the front door before he dashed off.'

'Dashed off where, if I may ask?'

'I've no idea as I said earlier. He packed his own bag. He's taken enough clothes to last him several weeks.'

'What sort of clothes?'

'Some of his old Army khaki drill suits. Plus a lot of

51

normal clothes – the kind of things he wears in this country.'

Tweed paused, wondering how to word it. 'Mrs Partridge, don't be alarmed by my call. It's something I'm working on connected with my insurance job as claims investigator. Wives are pretty clever where their husbands are concerned. They often spot a clue as to what they're up to. Have you any suspicions as to where he might have gone?'

'You're not thinking of another woman?'

Oh Christ, Tweed thought, are all marriages like this? Always the wives not a hundred per cent certain about their menfolk? Mrs Partridge went on talking.

'Sam's not like that. I'd know if it was anything un-toward.'

'I phrased that badly. As you say, Sam is like the Rock of Gibraltar. It's his *destination* I'm interested in. I do need to contact him urgently.'

'Oh, I see what you mean. Sorry, Mr Tweed, I simply haven't a clue as to where he might be.'

'Here or abroad?' Tweed persisted, hating himself.

'I just don't know. He took off two weeks ago and I haven't had a word from him since. Mind you, he warned me that might happen. I just wish I could help . . .'

'That's quite all right. I'm sure you'll hear from Sam soon. By the way, I'd follow his advice. No opening the door to strangers, especially foreigners. I've no idea why he said that – but Sam usually knows what he's talking about. He'll explain it all when he gets back. Take care.'

He put down the phone and stared into the distance. Paula was typing the Siros file out, slim fingers skimming the keys.

'What was all that about?' asked Monica. 'And who is this Partridge character? Where does he fit in?'

'He called on Brigadier Davies after Harry had been there. Wanted the addresses of the three commandos who made up the team which raided Siros. You'll understand that bit when Paula gives you the file for a quick look before it goes to Newman and Marler. Where does Partridge fit in? I wish I knew. It's a peculiar business. Partridge told Davies he was investigating the murder of a Greek called Ionides over forty years ago in Cairo.'

'My God!' Paula paused briefly. 'That makes two murders. And both of them Greeks.'

'And Partridge warned his wife against opening the door to any foreigners. Greeks? Partridge has disappeared off the face of the earth, went off on some trip a fortnight ago. Destination unknown. I've got an awful feeling of presentiment. Harry walked into something too big even for him to handle.'

'But you'll find out what it is,' Monica told him.

'We'll try. Paula and I drive to Somerset tomorrow. You hold the fort. I'll keep in touch – for any messages from Newman.' He clenched his fist on the desk. 'One of us has to come up with something.'

4

'Ten minutes before we land,' said Newman and peered down out of the window of the Swissair DC9 as the plane banked and swung eastwards.

'And we've got damn all to go on,' Marler observed.

From thirty thousand feet Newman stared down as they left the sapphire blue of the Adriatic Sea behind and flew over a landscape of bleak mountains studded with *maquis* – scrub. Savage gulches cleft the terrain between the mountain ridges. A wilderness of rock. They were over Greece. The air was incredibly clear, the sun shining brilliantly.

He felt he could reach down and touch the summits of the highest peaks. He looked at Marler sitting next to him, arms crossed, his face expressionless.

'If I were flying in to follow up a story I'd feel I had more than I normally had. We have to locate Christina Gavalas – the girl Harry flew to Athens with. We have copies of his photo to show round the hotels to find where he stayed. We've got Andreas Gavalas who went with the commando group forty odd years ago to check. We have the island of Siros to visit. We have Nick the Greek . . .'

'Who?'

'A driver who makes his living taking tourists from the Hotel Grande Bretagne on trips in his Mercedes. Nick is an old friend of mine. Very reliable, tough. He knows a lot about what goes on in this country.'

'You make it sound like a piece of cake. Anything else?'

'We have Cape Sounion to visit. I want to look at that cliff where Harry supposedly stumbled over the edge. And we have Chief Inspector Peter Sarris of Homicide in Athens. I once did him a favour – so he owes me one.'

'You know something, Newman?'

'You're going to tell me anyway.'

'I think we've got bugger all. And we should have brought someone to do the legwork.'

'If necessary, I'll do that while you prop up the bar at the Grande Bretagne,' Newman said quietly.

'I think Tweed is rushing it. I like a good basis of solid research.'

'He's moving fast before Howard writes Harry's death off as an accident.'

'I suppose it could have been just that.'

'You're forgetting the cigar box he sent. He knew he was walking a tightrope,' Newman said tersely. 'That he might not be coming back.'

'Trouble is I hardly knew Harry,' Marler reflected, still

54

keeping his voice low. The seats in front of them were unoccupied.

'But I did. And we're starting to descend. End of conversation.'

'Endstation,' Marler responded sardonically.

The big heat hit them like a heavy door as they descended the mobile staircase. Newman looked quickly round. Those bare hills loomed in close to the airport. The light was a glare. Mid-afternoon. Marler made a gesture as they walked towards the airport bus with the other passengers.

'Hardly Heathrow.'

'That has its advantages.'

But Marler had a point, he thought, as they boarded the waiting bus which would take them to the arrivals building which was smaller than any garage at London Airport. They passed the entry checks without any fuss and within minutes climbed inside a yellow taxi.

'Hotel Grande Bretagne,' Newman told the driver in English, 'and we're in a hurry.'

Marler glanced at Newman as they moved off. The driver had not understood the second instruction. That much was clear from his throwaway gesture. Marler marked up a notch in his companion's favour. Newman was concealing the fact that he spoke Greek fluently.

The Grande Bretagne is a solid-looking edifice standing on a corner of Constitution Square – Syntagma as the Greeks call it. The hotel looks as though it has stood there for generations, which it has. Inside they crossed the marble floor to reception.

'We have reservations,' Newman began. 'But first I would like a word with the chief receptionist.'

'You are talking to him, sir,' the man behind the counter informed him in perfect English.

Newman took an envelope from his breast pocket,

extracted a photo of Harry Masterson, laid it on the counter.

'I'm trying to find my stepbrother, Harry Masterson. I understood he stayed here. He may have left by now.'

The receptionist stared at the photo with a blank expression. Then he seemed to seek the right words.

'This, I regret to say, looks very like a man who fell off Cape Sounion to his death recently. There were pictures in the papers. I could be wrong, but they did give the name you mentioned.'

'Can't be the same man,' Newman protested. 'He did stay here?'

'Oh, no sir. I would have remembered. In view of . . .'

'Partridge,' said Marler. 'Does that name ring a bell?'

'Yes, it does, sir.' The receptionist transferred his attention to Marler. 'When I was serving my apprenticeship I went to Britain to learn the language. I was at the Gleneagles Hotel in Scotland. Plenty of partridge shooting up there. Which is probably why I noted this guest's name.'

'May I ask when he was here? Old chum,' Marler said smoothly.

'Let me check.' They waited. A small man wearing the dark suit of a hotel employee was lingering close to the counter – his eyes on the photo of Masterson. Newman stared at him and he wandered away. The receptionist came back.

'I was right. Mr Samuel Partridge?'

'That's him,' said Marler. 'Nice man. Told me he'd probably stay here. Best hotel in Athens.'

'Thank you, sir. Mr Partridge stayed one week. He arrived two weeks ago and then left. For the airport, I seem to remember.' He looked back at Newman. 'But Mr Masterson, no. He did not stay with us. If you would like to register?'

'Certainly.' Newman spoke as he began filling in the form. 'That small man who was standing near the counter. Who is he?'

56

'Oh, one of our temporary employees.' The receptionist made a resigned gesture. 'During the summer season we have to take on temporary staff. Unfortunate, between the two of us. They do not always understand the standards we set here.' He smiled with a certain satisfaction. 'Giorgos will not be with us after September . . .'

After opening his case in his own room, Marler walked along the corridor to Newman's. The foreign correspondent was standing with his hands on his hips, staring out of the window at the view of the distant Parthenon perched on the Acropolis.

'One up to me, I think,' Marler said pointedly as he sat in an armchair. 'Finding that Chief Inspector Partridge has trotted out here to have a look-see.'

'I'll give you that one.' Newman sounded absorbed. 'And Nick the Greek will be here shortly. I got lucky. I had his card in my wallet, the one with his home number he gave me when I was last out here.'

'What's the betting Partridge is now strolling round the island of Siros? You seem somewhat preoccupied.'

'Didn't you spot it?' Newman asked.

'Spot what?'

'One up to me. The receptionist recognized the picture I showed him of Harry because he said he'd seen it in the papers. What I want to know is how did they get that picture? He only became newsworthy when he was a sma-shed-up corpse at the foot of Cape Sounion.'

Giorgos slipped out of the side entrance of the Grande Bretagne, walking through the restaurant. There was no doorman on duty at this exit.

He hurried round to the far side of Syntagma Square where a row of phone boxes stood. Going inside a booth, he dialled a number and waited, tapping thin fingers on the coin box. If he was away too long that sod of a chief

57

receptionist was going to notice his absence from duty. He spoke in Greek when a deep-throated voice answered.

'Giorgos here. I thought you should know two Englishmen have just arrived at the hotel. They are asking questions about Masterson. They have a photograph of him.'

'Another Englishman was there snooping around only two weeks ago. That man Partridge. This is getting dangerous. You have the names of these two new men?'

'No. But I can get them from the records. But only after the chief receptionist has gone off duty.'

'Get them,' the voice rasped.

'It may be late afternoon . . .'

'Get them,' the voice repeated in Greek. 'Call me the moment you have the information. And anything else about these two you can find out. We may have to take drastic action.'

Giorgos was sweating as he hurried towards the restaurant entrance door. And not only with the heat – it was in the high eighties. He was worried the chief receptionist might have sent someone looking for him to carry out some task.

He slowed down as he walked across the entrance and through the doorway leading into the main hall. A tall heavily built man in his forties, clad in a clean white short-sleeved shirt and spotless denims, was approaching the counter from the main entrance. He heard quite clearly what the new arrival said in Greek.

'A Mr Newman is expecting me. He arrived during the past hour or so. Could you tell him I am here?'

'Will do, Nick. It's getting hot early this year. He's in Room . . .'

Giorgos missed hearing the room number but made a mental note of two facts. If this was one of the men he'd phoned about then he already had a name. Newman. He fiddled with a plant in a large holder, moving it a few

inches. The receptionist put down the phone, said something impossible to hear, and Nick headed for the staircase.

Strolling after him, Giorgos mounted the luxuriously
carpeted steps. He had earlier followed the two men after
noting the floor they were making for over the lift bank,
running up the staircase. He had been just in time to see
Newman being shown into his room. Too far along the
corridor to be sure which room. And he hadn't dared to
follow Marler.

The Greek called Nick turned along a corridor, stopped
at a door and knocked. The door opened and Giorgos
clearly heard the voice of the man who had shown the
photograph to reception welcoming him in English. He
retreated back down the staircase, working out an excuse
to ask the question.

'I think I know that man who just arrived, a friend of
one of my cousins.' The chief receptionist stared at him.
'He did my cousin a good turn, if it's the same man.'

'What would the likes of you have to do with Nick? He
drives a Mercedes. Rather out of your class. Don't waste
my time. See that pile of luggage over there? Be ready to
carry it to the cab when it arrives to take our guests to the
airport . . .'

Marler stared straight into Nick's dark eyes as they shook
hands. Firm grip. Hair, streaked with grey, cut short and
trim. A strong face. A firm jaw. A hint of humour at the
corners of the mouth. Marler was good at weighing up a man
quickly. Formidable was the word which came to mind.

'Bob will do the talking,' he said and sat down.

'Take a seat,' suggested Newman. 'We're here about
Harry Masterson who was killed down at Cape Sounion.'

'So, you think he was killed?' Nick sat down, crossed his
powerful legs. 'The papers said it was an accident.'

'One thing while I remember, Nick. Officially I don't

59

speak or understand any Greek on this trip. You think it was an accident?'

'I said the papers did. They think he was drunk. I saw him drunk myself.' Nick smiled drily. 'I drove a friend to the Hilton one evening, carried her bag in for her. Beyond the entrance hall is a large seating area at several levels. A crowd was gathered, watching something. Masterson had perched himself on a rail no wider than my hand, was walking along it like a tightrope walker, a champagne bottle clutched in each hand. A fifteen-feet drop below him. He walked the full length of the rail, then jumped back on to the floor next to the rail on his left. Enough people saw his performance to recall it when the news came through from Cape Sounion a few days later.'

'And he was drunk?' Newman pressed, hardly able to believe it.

'No.' Nick smiled drily again.

'But you said he was.'

'I know enough about drink – and drunks – to recognize the real thing, and when someone is acting being drunk. Masterson was acting. Don't ask me why.'

'He was staying at the Hilton?'

'No idea.'

'And you think his death was an accident?'

'No. I watched his act at the Hilton closely. He was nimble as a goat. A big man but quick on his feet, reflexes as fast as mine. That type doesn't go stumbling over a cliff.'

Newman opened a briefcase, took out a cardboard-backed envelope, extracted three photos of Masterson. He held them while he asked the question.

'I need to know where he stayed. Do you know two men you can trust – really trust?'

'To do what, Mr Newman?'

'Take these photos round hotels in Athens and find out where he stayed. He might have used another name.'

'Yes. They use his name? No? Of course some will

60

recognize him from the pictures in the papers.' Nick was looking at a print Newman had handed him. 'I could do some of the checking myself – divide up the search. It would be quicker.'

'One thing puzzles me.' Newman handed three prints to Nick. 'I really need to find out how his picture got into the press. Doesn't make sense. No one was interested until he became very dead.'

'Yes they were.' Nick clapped his hands together. 'I've just remembered. It happened when Masterson performed his crazy walk with the champagne bottles at the Hilton.'

'What did?'

'They have a creep of a photographer who works the hotel restaurant at night. He was hanging around in the lobby while Masterson did his walk. And he had his camera equipment with him.'

'So what happened?'

'It could have caused a disaster, but Masterson had strong nerves. This stupid photographer took a picture of him with a flashbulb. Masterson wobbled, then recovered his balance and went on. There was a gasp from the people watching.'

'Stupid, as you say.'

'But that is probably where the newspapers got the picture from,' Nick continued. 'All these photographers are after extra income. He took the picture when Masterson was grinning at the crowd – and the picture in the papers was like that. Mind you,' he added grimly, 'that was the only picture he was allowed to take.'

'Somebody stopped him?'

'Yes. Several people protested. The receptionist rushed over and gave the photographer hell. Anything else I can do to help?'

'Drive us to the port of Zea, then on to Cape Sounion.'

'You have the time?' Nick asked. 'Two hours there and back. And it would be best to wait a couple of hours. The traffic.'

'A couple of hours from now then. You still have the Merc?'

'A new one. Parked outside. I'd better go check the meter.'

'Two more things, Nick. Does the name Ionides mean anything?'

'Hardly. It's a common name. I know two. Both shop-keepers. And the other thing?'

'Christina Gavalas,' Marler interjected. 'Does that name mean anything to you?'

'You are joking?' Nick was amused. Marler's expression remained blank. 'You both know Greece. Surely you have heard of Petros Gavalas?'

'You mean the legendary Resistance leader during World War Two?' Newman asked. 'I didn't make the connection.'

'Christina is his granddaughter. She hates him. The Gavalas family is a strange story. Maybe I wait until we drive to Zea and tell you then. If she is concerned in any of this you have big trouble on your hands, my friends.'

5

Leaving the room, closing the door, Nick glanced along the corridor to his right, away from the exit. A small man wearing the black clothes of one of the hotel staff stood making a fuss about closing a window.

Nick looked away quickly, made his way downstairs and out of the hotel to where his Mercedes was parked in the blazing sun. He used a finger to loosen his collar. The heat seemed even worse. Dry and like a burning glass as the sun shone out of a sky as blue as the Mediterranean.

He was polishing the bodywork, which already gleamed like glass, when the small man in black jacket and trousers strolled out of the restaurant exit and round the corner. He was smoking a cigarette as he stood admiring the Mercedes.

'That is a real car. You are taking one of the customers for a drive?'

'Who knows when business will turn up?' Nick stopped polishing and stood facing the little man, the same man who had sneaked up behind him when he first arrived and asked reception to inform Newman he had arrived. Dark eyes too close together between a thin ferret of a nose. A smear of a black moustache above full lecherous lips.

'What is your name – and why aren't you on duty inside the hotel?' Nick demanded.

'I am Giorgos. I am entitled to an afternoon break. You think it is a pleasure working in this heat?'

'Get yourself another job if you are not happy. They pay you, don't they? Now, move away from my car. I am busy even if you can fritter away the day.'

Nick turned his back on the little man, polishing the car as he watched Giorgos walking back up the hill towards the restaurant entrance. In the wing mirror he saw Giorgos pause at the corner, take out a notebook from his pocket and scribble in it before he disappeared. He had recorded the registration number of the Mercedes.

To conceal his action half an hour later, Giorgos waited behind a corner before joining a crowd of pedestrians walking over a street crossing. Nick was still working on his car.

Giorgos made his way along the top side of the square facing the pink-washed building which had once been the

Royal Palace. Now it was the Parliament since Greece had become a republic.

In the centre of Constitution Square is a park filled with a variety of trees and shrubs. Tall railings fence off the park from the pavement beyond. Walking rapidly in the opposite direction from the one he had previously taken, Giorgos slipped inside a phone booth. Again he dialled the same number. Again he had to wait for it to be answered.

He glanced at his watch. His off-duty period was almost over. At least the chief receptionist had gone home, the bullying bastard. The same heavy-timbred voice came on the line.

'Giorgos here. More news. I discovered the names of those two men. Newman and Marler . . .' He spelt them out. 'I think they will be going somewhere in a Mercedes with a Greek driver. The registration number of the car is . . .'

'Any sign of them leaving immediately?' the voice enquired.

'No. The driver is still cleaning the Mercedes. But they may leave at any time. A silver-coloured Mercedes.'

'I can have a car following them in ten minutes.'

'Let us hope they are in time. Oh, there is one more thing.'

'Yes?'

'This is hard work for me. Maybe a little dangerous. More money would be welcome.' Giorgos swallowed, then stiffened. 'Another twenty thousand drachmae would be welcome – if I am to continue this work.'

'Be at your place in the Plaka at nine this evening.' The connection was cut before Giorgos could say 'thank you'.

He was surprised at how easy it had been.

88°F. 31°C. They were driving down Syngrou Avenue, sitting in the back of Nick's silver Mercedes. It was early evening and the scalding sun shone out of the azure sky as clear as a sea without ships. Nick used a handkerchief to wipe sweat off the back of his hand, his forehead.

'Syngrou is the longest avenue in Athens,' he remarked. 'As you can see, it's mainly car showrooms. BMW, the lot.'

Newman glanced back again through the rear window. Marler, wearing the lightweight linen suit he'd changed into, was careful not to look back.

'Some problem?'

'I think we may be followed,' Nick replied.

'The black Mercedes with amber-tinted windows?' Newman suggested.

'That's the joker. We'll know more when we fork for Piraeus. Someone may have been on the lookout for you coming into the city.'

Ruler-straight, Syngrou Avenue, lined with dusty poplar trees, stretched away forever into the distance. Nick maintained the same speed, kept glancing briefly in his rear-view mirror.

'What facts have you to back up that statement?' Marler demanded.

'The fact that one of the temporary staff at Grande Bretagne took an interest in your arrival. Followed us up the stairs when we used the elevator. He was peering round the corner when Mr Newman was shown into his room. The fact that later when I left the room he was hanging around in the corridor, pretending to fool with a window. The fact that he came and tried to get information out of me when I was cleaning the car ready for this trip. The fact that he made a note of my car's registration number. Which may explain that big black Mercedes keeping the same speed and distance behind us now.'

'Any idea who this character might be?' asked Newman.

'Name is Giorgos. Don't know his second name. He's a small creep with a small dark moustache.' Nick made a quick stroke above his upper lip. 'Dark hair. Now, let us see what that black Mercedes does. Here we take the right fork to Piraeus. Left for Cape Sounion.'

He swung the wheel and grinned. 'Still with us. If he stays with us to Zea we shall know.'

'How far from Syntagma to Piraeus?' asked Marler.

'Ten, twelve kilometres. We are entering Piraeus now . . .'

The buildings lining the street were lower than in Athens. Nick pointed out derelict sites between them, the legacy of the wartime bombing of Piraeus. They crossed the main city square with the imposing town hall on their right built like an ancient Greek temple. Then they were swinging round the curve of the waterfront of the main harbour.

They passed large car ferries with their doors open, exposing yawning caverns. Nick slowed down. He gestured towards the vessels.

'The big ferries. They go to Crete and Corfu and Rhodes. The small one is soon sailing for Siros.'

Newman jerked his head. The name of the vessel was clearly marked on its compact stern. *Ulysses.* The last cars and trucks were edging their way up the ramp, forming three rows.

'How long to Siros?' he asked.

'Two hours.'

Marler was staring at the wall of buildings to the left facing the waterfront. Four-storey blocks, they carried names of various shipping lines, most of which he recognized. Watching him in his rear-view mirror, Nick grinned again and gesticulated.

'The headquarters of so many shipping empires. Others have registered in Panama. Some of those big men have yachts which come in to Zea. Petros Gavalas has a small yacht there – what these people would call a rowboat. And still our friends are with us.'

'That black Mercedes?' Newman enquired, careful not to look back.

66

'Yes. And we have made too many turns for it to be a coincidence. Let us see what he does when we turn down to Zea.'

They had left behind the big shipping company buildings. Now they were driving along a narrow street which twisted and turned, following the indentations of the coastline. On the landward side were small old apartment blocks. Freshly painted, they had pots and tubs holding decorative shrubs standing on their balconies.

'It would cost you a fortune to live at Zea,' Nick said. 'Only the very rich have an apartment here . . .'

Staring ahead beyond the windscreen Newman saw a signpost to the right as Nick slowed to a crawl. *Zeas Port*. He turned down a sloping track leading to the sea and along a platform below a high stone wall. The small harbour was crammed with ships moored hull to hull – and each worth hundreds of millions of drachmae. The million-dollar class.

Nick drove along the jetty which curved round the exclusive harbour, protecting it from the sea. Executing a three-point turn, he pointed the car the way they had come. He was parked by the stern of a small yacht, *Venus III*. Jumping out, he opened the rear door.

'This is Gavalas' yacht,' he remarked. 'A very small fish.'

'How could he afford even this?' Newman asked.

'He buys cheap. During the oil crisis he buys it for one tenth of its value from a man who needs cash. Petros is cunning.'

'What happened to the black Mercedes?' Marler enquired, standing by Newman on the jetty.

'It stopped by one of the apartments on the hill, one man got out, carrying a violin case. Then it drove off.'

'Odd that,' Marler observed and lit a cigarette.

'Please?' Nick was puzzled. 'I do not understand.'

'The car follows us from Syntagma. He has no way of

67

knowing where we are going. We arrive here and they drop off one man at an apartment. Some coincidence.'

Newman was running up a flight of steps to a narrow ledge beneath the wall which was now waist-high. The view out over the harbour hit him. The emerald sea, very calm, sparkled with dazzling reflections from the sun. On the far side and further out a fleet of freighters waited, stationary, bows pointed towards the harbour, smoke drifting lazily from their stacks.

'For Christ's sake come down,' Marler called out.

Newman turned, leant his arms on the wall. It was so hot he could barely stand the heat. He stood looking down at the assembled craft. From one of the photographs taken by Masterson this was where he had stood when he took them. On the jetty just about the point where Marler waited.

He recognized the huddle of old apartment blocks, the hills rising behind, bare, mushroom-coloured, flecked with scrub. There had to be something here which would give a clue as to why Masterson had come to Zea. He walked down the steps and spoke to Nick, who was polishing the bonnet of the car.

'There's a whole queue of big ships, mostly freighters, waiting to come in.'

'The cargo docks on the other side,' Nick explained. 'They will be waiting for the signal from Marine Control to berth.'

Newman frowned as he saw Marler staring up at the bridge of the *Venus III*. He followed his gaze and sucked in his breath. Standing by the side of the bridge was a girl with a mane of black glossy hair, centre-parted. She had good bone structure and wore a polka-dot white dress with a thin belt hugging her slim waist. She held her right hand over her thick eyebrows, shielding herself against the sun. It was the girl in the photo Masterson had taken unawares.

Marler stared back with a dry smile. Then he raised his own hand and gave her a mocking little wave. Her mouth twitched. She waved back, then vanished. Nick also stood staring at where she had appeared, the cloth poised above the bonnet.

'Christina Gavalas,' he said in a low voice. 'That is very strange.'

'I want to have a word with her,' Newman said grimly.

A gangplank linked the vessel's stern with the jetty. Newman approached it, followed by Marler at a more leisurely pace. His movements were always slow and deliberate. Except in an emergency.

Newman reached the gangplank when three seamen came round the corner of the deck. They wore white sleeveless sweat shirts, blue pants. In their late twenties they were heavily built and two carried marlinspikes. One of them shouted at Newman in Greek, brandishing his marlinspike.

'What did he say?' Newman asked Nick, although he'd understood every word.

Nick laid a warning hand on Newman's arm. 'He says you are not allowed aboard. This is private property.'

'Tell him to get stuffed. I only wanted to invite the girl to join me for a drink.'

'I think we had better leave,' Nick warned again. He called out in Greek. 'We are just leaving. My passengers were admiring your beautiful boat.'

The Greek waved his marlinspike and the three crewmen walked out of sight. Marler was staring beyond the boats up at the apartment buildings above the small harbour. He saw the sun reflect off something, like one flash of a semaphore.

'Get into the car quick!' he ordered Newman. 'No bloody argument.' He pulled open the rear door and dived inside as Newman joined him. 'Nick,' Marler continued, 'move us out of here fast.'

Nick reacted instantly. For a large man he moved with surprising agility. He was behind the wheel when the shriek of several ships' sirens blasted over the wall. As the noise continued Nick started the engine. There was a heavy *thud*. At the same moment they heard a crackle of glass splintering behind them. The bullet passed between the heads of Marler and Newman, passed on through the open window of the front passenger seat beside Nick.

6

Nick accelerated along the narrow platform, braked, turned up the track leading to the main road. He glanced in the rear-view mirror. Newman and Marler both had their heads turned. The rear window had crazed, had a small hole in it.

'He fired from the top of one of those apartment buildings,' Marler remarked.

'We go up there, yes?' Nick enquired. 'We find the bastard before he can get away?'

'No!' replied Newman. 'Turn left. Head back for the town hall square. Find us somewhere we can talk. And somewhere you can hide the car.'

'I know a bar. Close to it is a bombed site. They will not find the car if I park there.'

'Do it,' said Newman. He turned to Marler. 'Is that why you tried to get me down off the wall?'

'Of course, my dear chap.' Marler was as calm as though he'd experienced an everyday happening. He adjusted the display handkerchief in his breast pocket. 'You normally catch on quicker. You had an absorbed look when you ran

70

up those steps. Stood on that ledge like a target in a shooting gallery. Is it the heat, by any chance?'

His tone was mocking. He reached into his pocket and perched a pair of horn-rimmed glasses on his nose. 'They have seen me once. I don't think they'll recognize me so easily next time.'

'Those glasses make you look exactly like Michael Caine.'

'Flattery will get you nowhere. The lenses are plain glass.'

'You were expecting that shot?'

'Something like it. The black Mercedes follows us. Nick reports they drop one man carrying a violin case, then drive off. A violin case! Not much imagination there. Did they strike you as musical characters? A violin case,' he repeated. 'Just the thing for carrying a dismantled Armalite rifle. You are only alive because he had to assemble his weapon before he used it. I saw the sun flashing off his telescopic sight – which is when I told you to dive into the car. He was a better shot than I'd hoped. Very smart, too.'

'Why do you say that?' Nick asked.

'He had a bit of luck and used it. Those ships' sirens starting up muffled the sound of the shot.'

'They made one huge mistake though,' Newman said.

'Which was?' Marler enquired.

'Firing that shot, of course. Now we *know* someone murdered Harry Masterson.'

The bar was small, located up a side street, was furnished with plastic-topped tables, a plastic-topped counter. Only the floor had a hint of luxury. It was laid from wall to wall with solid marble. Nick had ordered *ouzo* for everyone. Newman asked for a large bottle of mineral water.

'We can't afford to risk dehydration,' he remarked, wiping the back of his neck with a silk handkerchief. 'First

71

things first. That bullet-hole in the rear window of your car could be embarrassing for all of us. Can anything be done about it?'

'You don't want to report the attack to the police?' Nick asked, his broad tanned arms resting on the table-top.

'They could complicate life at this stage. Unless you insist?'

'I have many friends.' Nick drank half his glass of *ouzo*. 'I know a garage mechanic who will fix that overnight. A new window. No questions asked. OK?'

'OK,' agreed Newman. 'I pay the bill, of course. Next – when Christina Gavalas appeared on the deck of *Venus III* you said, "That is very strange." Why?'

Nick paused, refilled their glasses from the jug of *ouzo*. 'It is a bit . . . complex. Is that the word?'

'Tell me, then I'll know.'

'Petros is eighty years old, a ferocious tyrant. Pray you do not meet him. Born in 1907, he married when he was seventeen. His first wife produced two sons – Andreas and Stephen. Twins, but not identical. Andreas and Stephen also married when very young – only eighteen. It was the war in their cases, I suppose. That was in 1943 or 1944. After Andreas was killed on Siros his wife gave birth to Christina – Petros' granddaughter. Do you understand so far?'

'Perfectly,' said Newman. 'Go on.'

'At that time Petros fought with the Communists – the ELAS party. Andreas hated them. He escaped to Cairo, joined the anti-Communist party, EDES. Petros was furious. Called him a traitor. But blood is thicker than water. Petros had a grudging admiration for Andreas. When Andreas was killed in the Siros raid he swore to hunt down his killer. Then came the second tragedy.'

'Which was?'

'The other twin, Stephen, also hated his father and fled to Cairo to join the EDES forces. Then he, too, was

72

murdered. Later *his* wife gave birth also to twins, Dimitrios and Constantine. Again, non-identical. But the strain had run out. They are peasants working on Petros' farm in Devil's Valley.'

'A whole lot of hatred,' Marler observed.

'It gets worse. After the end of the Civil War in Greece between EDES and ELAS – which nearly wrecked my country – in 1950 Petros married again when his first wife died. His second wife produced a son, Anton. Maybe because Petros was then forty-two and his new wife was twenty-eight Anton turned out to be very clever. You see the scope for bitterness in that family?'

'How did Christina react?' Marler asked.

'A magnificent woman now, she is torn between two moods. Greek loyalty to the family – and her detesting Petros who treated her badly. As I told you, it is complex. But that is why I thought it strange to see her on *Venus III*. Petros only keeps the boat so he can watch those millionaires – wait for another to become in desperate need of money. Then maybe he picks up yet another bargain. He owns farms. One near Cape Sounion.'

'So he is rich?' Newman pressed. 'What kind of farms?'

'The one in Devil's Valley is in a remote part of the interior of the peninsula between Athens and Sounion. A dangerous area to explore. He grows figs and olives. His headquarters is an old farmhouse in wild country – reached by a track off the main highway to Sounion. There are even rumours he has a working silver mine. That I don't know about – whether it is working.'

'Let me get this clear,' intervened Marler. 'Petros was a one-time Communist. His son, Andreas, was killed on Siros. OK so far?'

'OK,' Nick agreed.

'And,' Newman suggested, 'this fierce old Petros is a Communist although he's rich?'

'Not any more from what I hear. Petros was sickened of

73

politics by the Civil War. It lasted from 1946 to 1949. A lot of blood was spilt. At the end of it Petros said all politicians could burn in hell. He devoted himself to farming, making money, but he has never forgotten the murder of his sons.'

'How and where was Stephen killed?' Newman asked.

'The rumour is it happened in a street brawl in a native quarter in Alexandria. There are other versions.'

'And Christina wavers between supporting Petros and hating him?'

'So it is told in Athens.'

Marler grunted. 'The only fact that comes out of all this is that Petros – and Christina – could still feel bitter about Andreas' death on Siros. After all, Andreas was her father.'

'That is what I have heard,' Nick agreed. 'And now maybe we should drive back to Athens so I can have the window repaired.' He finished off his *ouzo*, glanced at Newman. 'We forget about Cape Sounion – after what happened at Zea? For today?'

'Back to Athens. Another day we could visit this Petros? I'd like to ask him some questions.'

Nick grinned. 'You have brought some good weapons with you?'

'No. Nothing.'

'You go in Devil's Valley, you go armed. All Petros' men have guns. I said it before. A very dangerous place. You want to come out alive. Back to Athens . . .'

Newman saw the diesel train perched up on an embankment as it headed into Piraeus. He caught glimpses of it between buildings as they left the harbour behind.

'That's the Metro line, is it, Nick?'

'Yes. It starts at the other side of the city. The last stop this way is Piraeus.'

Newman looked at Marler. 'Endstation?'

'Who knows?' Marler adjusted his horn-rimmed glasses, perched his head back and closed his eyes.

Newman stared out of the window as a motorcyclist drew level. The rider, wearing a crash helmet and tinted goggles, turned and stared straight into the car for a few seconds. Then the machine was gone, zooming ahead of them, weaving in and out along the traffic.

'If you don't mind,' Nick suggested as they turned on to Syngrou Avenue, 'I will drop you close to Syntagma Square. That window is conspicuous. I want to get the car inside the garage before a policeman sees it. Then I have another job. I wish to have a word with Giorgos. He will tell me who it is he is working for – who followed us in that black Mercedes.'

'He may not feel like telling you,' Marler suggested.

'I have my own methods of persuasion. I will get his home address from reception. Oh, while I was waiting to take you to Piraeus I contacted my two helpers. Each has a photograph of Masterson. They must have checked with twenty hotels by now. Soon we will know where Mr Masterson stayed. May I drop you here? Only a five-minute walk to Grande Bretagne.'

'That's fine.' Newman had taken out his wallet. 'Time I paid you – for the trip, the repair to the window, and fees for your helpers.'

'Later.' Nick jumped out of the car, opened the rear door. 'You are well organized. Changing your traveller's cheques so quickly.'

He was referring to the regulations which only allow any tourist to bring in three thousand drachmae. Newman had changed cheques for a large sum at the hotel. As they stood on the pavement, the heat still hammering them, he laid a hand on Nick's arm.

'We would like to be there when you question this Giorgos. I have a few questions to put to him myself.'

75

'Late in the evening would be best. He will be relaxed and not expecting a hard time. I call for you at ten o'clock? If I find the time is wrong, I call your room?'

'Ten o'clock. See you then.'

They strolled along the street as Nick drove away. A park stretched away beyond iron railings to their right. Kiosks selling newspapers stood by the railings. People were queuing to buy plastic bottles of mineral water.

A motorcyclist cruised past. Newman frowned, watched the rider sliding in between the slow-moving traffic. The machine disappeared, heading for Syntagma Square.

Arriving at the main entrance to the Grande Bretagne, Newman handed Marler his room key. 'Wait upstairs in my room. I'll be right with you . . .'

Newman followed Marler inside, paused, waited for a brief time, then pushed open the door and peered out into the square. Full of traffic. He scanned the area rapidly. He found what he was looking for further down the hill.

The motorcyclist had parked the machine by a meter, still sat astride it. The same motorcyclist with the orange-coloured crash helmet and tinted glasses who had passed them in Piraeus. Who had later skilfully guided the machine between cars when they were walking.

The rider removed the crash helmet, perched it between the handlebars. She reached up with both hands and draped her waterfall of black glossy hair over her shoulders. Christina Gavalas had arrived. Things were warming up, and not only the temperature. Newman closed the door, went up to his room.

Ten o'clock. On the dot. Nick led the way to his parked car. It had a new rear window. Newman and Marler had dined in the oak-panelled restaurant. It was still daylight as they sat in the back and the Mercedes took off down the hill which was almost traffic-free.

'He lives in the Plaka, this Giorgos,' Nick informed them. 'That is the old quarter of Athens. It spreads out at the foot of the Acropolis, climbs part of the way up the hill.'

'I know,' said Newman. 'Any news about where Masterson stayed?'

'No. It is strange. My helpers have checked all the main hotels. No luck. He must have stayed somewhere. Would he choose some cheap place?'

'Not our Harry,' Newman said positively. 'He liked a bit of luxury. Live high was his motto. Maybe the hotels don't like giving out information about their guests?'

'My helpers are clever. They take round an expensive wristwatch. Say they found it with a credit card in his name. They want to give it back. And they don't read the papers, so they don't know he's dead. They get a reply. No, he didn't stay with us.'

Dusk was falling. The sun had slid down behind the Acropolis. Nick had entered a maze of narrow, twisting streets. There was little space to spare if he met a vehicle coming the other way. Through the open window Newman heard the mournful strains of the *bouzouki* from the open doors of small restaurants and cafés. Sometimes it was Western pop music. Every second door seemed to lead to an eating place. The pavements were crowded with sightseers and customers.

Nick drove into a small square with a muddle of buildings on three sides. The fourth side was open to a large level area littered with stones. The Parthenon Temple, perched on the Acropolis, was an ancient silhouette against the darkening sky.

'Monastiraki Square,' Nick announced. 'We park here and walk back to Giorgos' place. That way we surprise him. And parking is difficult.'

'Damn near impossible,' commented Marler.

Nick led them a short distance along a narrow street,

then he turned up a wide paved alley sloping like a ramp, lined with more eating places, more *bouzouki*. Newman and Marler strolled behind him and suddenly he stopped, held up a hand.

'Something is going on. Look at the crowd. We must be careful.'

'Where does he live?' Newman asked.

'Down that alley to the right. You see that car?'

The police vehicle was empty, parked half on the worn stone pavement. The crowd filled the street, was stationary, was staring down the alley Nick had indicated. They joined the crowd. Newman drew back, mounted the two steps at the entrance to a restaurant to see over the heads. He sucked in his breath.

A macabre sight. Beneath an old metal wall lantern attached to the side of the alley stood a large wine barrel. From the top projected two legs, bent at the knees. The legs were clad in black trousers, which had concertinaed, exposing tanned skin.

'What is it?' Marler asked, perching beside Newman.

'Look for yourself . . .'

Uniformed police swirled in the narrow confines of the alley. Several formed a cordon, holding back the crowd. Two stood on either side of the barrel. As Newman and Marler watched they took hold of the legs, slowly hauled up the rest of the body. Black hair dangled from the upended head.

Nick came close to Newman, whispered, 'I'll get in there. I know a couple of those police. Back in a minute . . .'

As he shouldered his way through the crowd the two policemen laid the body on the stone cobbles carefully, face up. Nick spoke to one of the police in the cordon, was let through, walked up the alley, which was a flight of steps, stopping beside the barrel.

'Looked a trifle queasy,' Marler remarked, and lit a cigarette. 'Did you notice?'

'The body's hair? Lank and dripping. Some liquid dripped off the shoulders when they hauled it out.'

'And since it is a wine barrel one might assume that's what it contains. Wine.'

After a few minutes Nick shook hands with both policemen and pushed his way back through the crowd. He used a handkerchief to wipe sweat off his head as he stood close to them.

'It's Giorgos. He didn't die too easily. They reckon he was grabbed, upended and lowered into that barrel. It is more than half full of wine. They drowned him in it. Held him with his legs kicking, I suppose. Held him upside down until he stopped struggling. Drowned. Then left him like that – legs crooked over the barrel's rim. Someone decided to make an example of him. To keep your mouth shut.'

'They certainly made their point,' Marler observed coolly.

'Let's get out of here,' said Newman.

He felt sick as they made their way back to the car. The shops were still open, shops selling a load of junk as far as Newman could see. Wicker baskets, leather bags, sponges. The shops were crammed between the tavernas. The *bouzouki* music had become louder, reminded Newman of a funeral march. The crowds were denser. Suddenly the Plaka had become a nightmare.

'Back to the hotel, Nick,' he said as they sank into the car. 'Back to civilization and peace.'

Peace was the last thing they found when they returned to the Grande Bretagne.

7

Marler and Nick stood in the corridor while Newman unlocked his door and walked into the room. They followed and Newman stood stock still, his expression grim.

Two men in civilian clothes were searching the room, checking inside drawers, examining the wardrobe. A third man, also in civilian clothes, sat smoking a cigarette. Hawk-nosed, in his thirties, dark-haired, thin and long-legged, his old friend, Chief Inspector Peter Sarris of Homicide, regarded him with no particular expression. He made no attempt to get up, to shake hands. Bad sign.

'May I ask what the hell is going on?' Newman demanded.

'You will all sit down in separate chairs. Not on the couch. No one will speak unless I ask him a question. This is a murder investigation. What is going on?' he continued in the same level tone. 'Surely it is obvious, Bob? We are searching your room. Before you ask, I have a warrant.'

'Best do as His Lordship says,' Newman told his companions.

'No need for sarcasm,' Sarris continued in perfect English.

'I'd have thought there was every need. You expect me to like this? And tell those goons of yours I expect them to replace everything exactly as they find it.'

'Be careful to leave everything neat – the way you find it,' Sarris said in Greek to the two searchers, then switched back to English.

'Only you are permitted to speak, Bob. Where have you just returned from?'

'You know the answer to that question. The Plaka.'

'And how would I know that?' enquired Sarris.

'Because the Volvo police car parked near the alley where Giorgos' body was found had a radio. One of the policemen was staring at me. I'm sure he recognized me. My picture has been in enough newspapers in the past. And my guess is Giorgos had something on him which showed he worked for the Grande Bretagne. One of the uniformed police radioed in to headquarters, reported to you . . .'

'That's enough,' Sarris said quickly. 'I know you are a top foreign correspondent, but you'd have made a good detective.'

'. . . and this is Marler, my assistant, learning his trade . . .' Newman was talking rapidly before he could be stopped. 'My driver Nick I have used on previous visits . . .'

'I said shut up . . .'

'. . . and this afternoon we used him to take us on a peaceful tour round Piraeus and the port of Zea . . .'

'*I said shut up!*' Sarris, livid, was on his feet. He gave the instructions rapidly in Greek to the searchers. 'One of you take the Englishman there to his room. This Greek, Nick, is to be taken immediately to a police car and held at headquarters.' As his men moved, he stood over Newman. 'I have one more word out of you and you will find yourself inside a police cell.'

'On what charge?' Newman enquired amiably.

'Suspicion of accessory to a murder . . .'

'Which one? Harry Masterson's?'

Newman shot out the words as Marler and Nick were bundled out of the room. In time for both to hear what he said. Sarris waited until the door closed and then offered Newman a cigarette, took one himself and sagged back into the same chair.

'Did you have to do that?'

'Do what? I thought you wanted information.'

'You're a bastard.' Sarris spoke in a resigned tone. 'But a clever bastard. When you've finished your cigarette you will have to come to police headquarters.'

'Why waste time? Let's get on with it . . .'

Outside the hotel Sarris was in time to stop Nick being taken away in a police car. 'Where is your own vehicle?' he asked.

'Parked down the hill. The silver Mercedes . . .'

'You will drive it to police headquarters. One of my men will accompany you.'

Sarris drove Newman by himself in an unmarked police car. He began chatting amiably as soon as they drew away from the kerb.

'I have to do this, I'm afraid, Bob. How long is it since you were last here?'

'Two, three years. I'm not sure,' Newman replied vaguely.

'I can see you are going to be difficult to interrogate. Maybe one of your companions will be more forthcoming. You will all be interrogated separately . . .'

'Bully for you . . .'

'A little cooperation would help all round.'

'Not after you searched my room without waiting for me.'

'We have a new police headquarters. Very modern. All the latest equipment.'

'Bully for you . . .'

'It's on Alexandras Avenue. Built about a year ago.'

'You make it sound like the bloody Hilton.'

'There are some similarities. Although not with the Athens Hilton. One of the places your hired snoopers visited when asking where Harry Masterson stayed.'

'Keep talking . . .'

Sarris gave up. Skilfully he drove through the night. Headlights appeared, flashed past them. They were on Alexandras now. Close to the football stadium on the opposite side a small colossus of a building faced with white marble loomed. A very modern rectangular block twelve storeys high it soared up towards the night sky above a vast entrance hall. No premium on space for government buildings in Athens, Newman thought as he followed Sarris inside.

To the left was a reception counter. A uniformed policeman hastily donned his peaked cap. Sarris led Newman to an inner lobby with a bank of four lifts on the right-hand side. His office on the eighth floor overlooked Alexandras. Sarris used an intercom to order coffee.

'Now,' he said, facing the seated Newman across his desk, 'may we start at the beginning?'

'We arrived in Athens . . .'

4 a.m. Sarris in his crumpled shirt-sleeves was showing signs of strain. The ash tray was crammed with his cigarette stubs. Only one of them belonged to Newman.

'So,' Sarris summed up, 'it comes to this. You came here to investigate the accidental death of Harry Masterson, sensing a story. Marler came to learn the ropes, despite his being described on his passport as an insurance executive?'

'I told you. He's fed up with that job. He wants a more adventurous life.'

'The murdered man, Giorgos, took an interest as soon as you arrived at the Grande Bretagne. He saw the photograph you showed the receptionist. Later, he tried to get information from your driver, Nick. You thought he could be a lead. So Nick found out where he lived from reception. You went there with your two companions to question him. You were too late?'

83

'End of story.'

'Bob, you really should have been a barrister. You so neatly make all the facts fit what I know . . .'

'Presumably because they do fit.' Newman drank more coffee. His fifth cup. 'Haven't we just about covered everything – except for what happened to Harry Masterson? An accident, you said.'

'I gave you the official explanation at the moment. He was murdered.'

Newman, cup raised, stared at the Greek. For the first time since the interrogation had begun he was taken aback.

'You change your mind quickly, Peter.'

Sarris stood up, wearily stretched himself, then leaned over the desk, spread both hands flat and stared straight back. His tone changed, became grim, almost spitting out the words.

'You think I have lost my touch? Homicide is my profession, my business. I'm supposed to be able to recognize murder when I see it. You think I park my backside here all day? Let me tell you something. I've visited Cape Sounion. No one with the savvy Masterson had staggers round above that cliff and walks over it. And I met Masterson by chance.'

'When? Where?'

'That night at the Hilton when he pretended to be high as a kite, did his death-defying walk along the rail beyond the entrance hall. I was attending a party. When I walked into the Hilton Masterson was just beginning that charade. I watched him. I tackled him afterwards, asked him what the hell he thought he was doing. Drunk? He was more sober than I am now after all that coffee. I talked with him for maybe ten minutes. He was able, tough, alert and street-wise. And he had the women in the palm of his hand.'

'Women? Any particular woman that night?'

84

'Christina Gavalas couldn't get enough of him. More coffee? You look shaken . . .'

A few minutes later. Sarris stood by the window, had opened the blinds. The first light, the false dawn, was casting a glow over the dead city. The peak of Mount Lycabettus was a massive silhouette in the distance.

'Why?' Newman asked. 'Why the official line that it was an accident?'

'The tourist industry is sacred to Greece, the billions of foreign currency it brings in, a commodity we're a little short of . . .'

'Oh Christ! Not the *Jaws* syndrome again?'

'*Jaws*?'

'The film about a shark off a resort island in America. The mayor didn't want to know about any sharks. Again, it might have frightened the tourists away.'

'Ah, yes, I remember. I see what you mean. Yes, there is a similarity. Murder – especially of an Englishman – would be bad publicity. The British come here like lemmings.'

'So you buried the case?' Newman said bitterly.

'You will apologize for that insult.' Sarris left the window, stormed back to his desk and sat upright in his chair. 'The case is not closed for me. No mealy-mouthed politician gives orders here . . .'

'You have your apology. Unreservedly.'

'It is early in the morning.' Sarris made a resigned gesture. 'We are both fully stretched. But maybe now you understand why I hauled you in? Informers – more than one – had told me men were going round the hotels showing Masterson's photo, asking where he had stayed. I had one in that chair, accused him of being an accessory to murder. He told me Nick was his employer. I phone the Grande Bretagne. They tell me you are the one who hired Nick.

85

Then I get another call from my men in the Plaka, investigating a particularly brutal murder – and he tells me he has recognized you. Now, do you think I do my job?'

'OK, Peter. You move fast. I'll give you that. Ever heard of Petros Gavalas?'

'Why?'

'I did my homework back in London before I came out. You're not the only one who does his job properly.'

'And you found the wolf has his lair north of Cape Sounion – where Masterson was killed?' Sarris had walked over to a filing cabinet. Unlocking it, he sifted through several files, extracted a glossy print from one, laid it on the desk before Newman. 'Petros.'

Newman stared at the print. He had rarely seen a picture which made such impact. A head-and-shoulders photo, the subject gazing away from the camera. An aged, ageless man. Like a prophet from the Old Testament. A great crooked beak of a nose, the eyes large and glowing under thick eyebrows, the face long, terminating in a heavy jaw. A bushy moustache above a thin wide mouth, the lips clamped tight.

'He didn't know his picture was being taken?'

'No,' Sarris admitted. 'We used a telephoto lens from inside an unmarked police van.'

'So he has a track record?'

'No, he hasn't.' Sarris pulled his shirt away from under his left armpit. Despite the open windows beyond the blinds, and a fan whirling overhead, the room was like an oven. The big heat was building up.

'Then why do you have his picture?'

'We think he could be trouble. One day. He has many hectares on his big farm in the wilderness. He rules it like a private kingdom – fief? Is that the word? I thought so. Armed men on horses patrol this kingdom to keep out intruders. They say they carry guns for shooting vermin – birds which feed on the figs. He hates what he calls the

English. Holds them responsible for the death of his son, Andreas, on Siros. An explosive situation.'

'And his granddaughter, Christina, was with Masterson?'

'That night at the Hilton? Yes. I don't know why. Maybe she just fancied him. She is a very beautiful woman. And now, perhaps you should go home with the others.'

Sarris took the photo, put it back in its file, relocked the cabinet. He poured more coffee from a fresh pot brought in by a girl.

'If you believe Masterson was murdered isn't there something you can do about it?'

'What?' Sarris spread his hands. 'I have no evidence. No one saw him at Sounion. The pathologist isn't much help.'

'But what did he say?'

'What I said. He has no evidence. When the coastguard cutter took his body off the rocks at the base of the Cape it was a wreck of smashed bone – smashed almost to a pulp the pathologist told me – showed me. Not a pretty sight. He only had one conclusion. The way the body hit the rocks the stomach was intact – plus its contents. No trace of alcohol. Only mineral water.'

'Time for me to push off.' Newman stood up. 'The others are coming with me?'

'Yes.' Sarris smiled drily. 'Their stories fit what you've told me. You can all go home. Maybe you and Marler should really go home – back to London?'

'You're deporting us?' enquired Newman as he opened the door.

'Wish I could.' Sarris grinned, slapped Newman on the shoulder. 'Take care of yourself. Greece could be bad for your health . . .'

Nick drove his Mercedes along Alexandras as streaks of the real dawn painted the sky with vivid slashes of red and

87

gold. Above a band of black receding night was a curve of pure cerulean, intense as a blue flame, warning that another scorching day was coming.

'Take us somewhere very quiet and lonely, Nick,' said Newman. 'Somewhere we can talk without interruption.'

'Lycabettus,' Nick responded. 'Very high, very lonely – at this hour . . .'

He swung off Alexandras. Soon they were climbing steeply up a road spiralling round the lower slopes of Mount Lycabettus. They drove higher and higher. And as they climbed, below them Athens receded, the view expanded. Newman gazed out of the window. Already the panorama was awe-inspiring. They went on climbing, Nick turning the wheel all the time, negotiating the large car round diabolical hairpin bends, blowing his horn in case a vehicle was coming down. They met no one by the time he stopped at the edge of a precipitous curve.

'End of the road,' Nick said, alighting quickly to open the door, but Newman beat him to it, stepping out and taking a deep breath of fresh clear air. Marler stood on one side, Nick on the other.

'How did you get on, Nick – with their questions?' Newman asked.

'I told the truth.' Nick grinned. 'Some of it. I told them you hired me when you were last here. That explained how you knew me. I told them I drove you to Piraeus to show you the sea, that we looked at the boats at Zea and then drove back. Thank God I had the rear window repaired. It would have been difficult to explain the bullet-hole.'

'I thought of that. Go on.'

'I told them you gave me pictures of Masterson to find out where he'd stayed. That reference you made to him just before we left your room tipped me off I could talk about that. I told them Giorgos was taking too close an interest in our activities, that you wanted to ask him why. So I obtained his address in the Plaka from one of the

88

assistant receptionists – by saying I owed him some money. When we got there we found he was dead. I kept it simple.'

'Which linked up beautifully with what I told Sarris. How did you cope, Marler?'

'I coped. Much the same story Nick told. Kept it simple. I only answered what I was asked. No elaborations. I must say I didn't care too much for your description of me as your assistant.'

'You'll get used to it.' He stared down. 'God, what a view.'

The huge eye of the sun was already glaring down on Athens. A city of white buildings crammed cheek by jowl, spreading out towards the horizon, merging with Piraeus, once a separate port. From that height the immensity of the capital showed dramatically.

In the far distance Newman could pick out a shoehorn-shaped bowl which was the new stadium they had passed on their way into Piraeus. Beyond, the Mediterranean was already a shimmer of hazy blue. It was the sheer *density* of the city of three million inhabitants which astounded Newman.

'Where the devil is the Acropolis?' Marler asked.

'I show you . . .'

Nick ran back to the car, returned with binoculars, focused them. He pointed below into the middle of the endless congestion. 'There. Perched up with the Parthenon on top.'

'Incredible.' Marler gazed at the ancient temple through the glasses as Nick went on talking.

'Most people who first come to Athens think the highest point is the Acropolis. But Mount Lycabettus towers like an old volcano far above anything else. And we are not at the top.'

Newman looked up to where Nick pointed. The mountain soared up further. Perched on its summit was a church with a brown-coloured dome.

'The Church of St George,' Nick explained. 'You can reach it by the funicular at the top of Kolonaki.'

'Kolonaki? I remember that from when I was here before. District for the people with big money?' Marler remarked, handing back the glasses.

'Christina Gavalas has an apartment in Kolonaki,' said Nick.

'The key is somewhere down there,' Newman reflected, gazing down at the vast sprawl. 'The key to who killed Masterson.'

Nick drove them back down another equally hair-raising spiral road into the city. The streets were still quiet. Outside a few shops women were spraying water on the pavements with hosepipes. As soon as their backs were turned the water shrank into damp patches, then evaporated.

'Another hot day coming up,' Nick commented. 'So we all sweat again. Grande Bretagne?'

'You can sweat,' Newman said. 'I'm going to sleep.'

They approached Syntagma Square along Sofias Avenue, a street which Newman remembered ran straight from the Hilton to the square. They would visit the Hilton later.

Nick was stopped by red lights at the entrance to Syntagma and Newman leaned forward, staring through the windscreen. Nick nodded.

'It is the same car . . .'

'With the same registration number . . .'

The black Mercedes with amber-tinted windows was parked across the street from the main entrance to the Grande Bretagne. Behind the tinted glass Newman could see two men sitting in front, two more in the rear seats. Nick parked at the foot of the steps leading up to the hotel. Newman got out slowly, stood upright, stared at the car.

One of the front windows lowered slowly, moved by

automatic control. A head leaned forward, looking direct across the street at Newman. He stood quite still, hands in his jacket pockets.

In real life he looked even more like an Old Testament prophet than in the photo Sarris had showed him. Aged and ageless. The curved beak of the cruel nose. The eyes intense beneath the bushy brows, the craggy forehead. Their eyes clashed over the width of the street. Newman sensed a look of pure hatred, venomous. The window closed slowly, shutting out the gaze of Petros Gavalas. The black Mercedes slid away from the kerb and was gone.

8

Petros Gavalas sat beside the driver, his grandson, in silence as the Mercedes headed down Syngrou Avenue. A very big man, he had pushed his seat back to its fullest extent to give comfortable leg room – so far back that the henchman sitting behind him had cramped knees. As they approached the point where the avenue forked, he spoke in his gravelly voice.

'Dimitrios, take the turn-off to Piraeus.'

'I thought we were returning to the farm . . .'

'Later. I have phone calls to make from the apartment at Zea. You are a fool,' he continued. 'I told you to shoot the driver of their car – to discourage Greeks from helping the English. You missed.'

'But we did not miss with Giorgos,' Dimitrios replied as he turned down the right fork. He chuckled unpleasantly. 'That one had his fill of wine forever.'

'People should not ask for more money than has been agreed. And he was a Greek. He should have known better. He knows now.'

'We are going to kill those two Englishmen?' Dimitrios asked.

'Not yet, cretin.' Petros shifted his bulk: the heat was making him irritable. 'I have already given orders. They will be followed night and day. Let us first see what they are up to. They had better not come near the farm. And they would be most unwise to start asking questions about Andreas. I trust for their sakes they do not go anywhere near Siros.'

'Does it matter? If they do go to Siros?'

It was the wrong thing to say. Petros hit Dimitrios on the arm. He almost swerved off the road. Petros swore at him, turned to glare at his grandson.

'Any English who goes near Siros could be involved in the great betrayal over forty years ago on Siros. Someone will pay for that. With his life . . .'

Marler ran a bath as soon as he entered his room. He stripped off, donned a robe, waited for the bath to fill. He ached in every limb. They'd sat him in a hard-backed chair for the interrogation. Standard procedure . . .

The gentle tapping on the outer locked door startled him. All his mental alarm bells began ringing. He picked up the ebony-backed hairbrush he always packed, held it in his right hand. He opened the door suddenly, leaning against the side wall.

A woman stood in the opening, a woman with a mane of dark glossy hair, a woman in her early forties, a woman clad in tight denims emphasizing her long slim legs and a white blouse unbuttoned at the neck, which exposed the upper half of her full firm breasts. Christina Gavalas.

'Aren't you going to invite me in, Mr Marler?' she

enquired with a slow smile. 'People may talk if they see us standing here together.'

'All right, come in. If you must.'

'Such a warm welcome,' she commented as he closed and locked the door. 'I thought it was time we talked.' She eyed the bed. 'I am a little tired. I don't mind where we talk.'

'That makes two of us.'

Marler stood with his hands on his hips, his mind racing as she unlooped her shoulder bag, dropped it on the dressing table. She reached for the hairbrush he was holding. 'May I? I look a mess.'

She stood in front of the mirror, brushing her hair vigorously, watching him in the mirror. Putting the brush down, she turned, put her arms round his shoulders, clasped her hands behind his neck and kissed him on the mouth, pressing her strong body into his.

'To what do I owe this honour?' Marler enquired as she pulled her head away from his, still grasping his neck. He watched her greenish eyes, his expression bleak and showing no excitement. She arched her thick eyebrows, half-closed her eyes, presenting to him her open front. Marler remained still, without reacting. Let her make the running. Her right hand slid inside his robe, felt his naked chest, moved down.

'I took a fancy to you when I saw you at Zea. I thought that you'd taken a fancy to me. You did wave.'

Her English was perfect. Her technique for rousing a man was good. The roving hand took its time. She gave him her slow smile again. Then she removed the hand, used it to take off her earrings, tossing them on to the dressing table.

'We won't be needing those, will we?'

'If you say so.'

'The cool calm Englishman. I love them . . .'

Standing away from him, still facing him, she undid her

blouse, threw it on the floor. She wore nothing underneath it. She watched for the effect she was creating as she undid her denims, slid them down her legs, threw them on top of the blouse. She kicked off her flat-heeled shoes, shoes fit for running in, for moving around with the least possible noise, Marler noted. He raised both hands, palms towards her, rested them on her bare shoulders and threw her back on the bed. Dropping his robe, he followed her, lying on top of her as she giggled and wriggled.

'My name is Christina,' she said ten minutes later as they lay side by side.

'Christina What?'

Marler lit a cigarette he didn't really want, stared at the ceiling as she pressed against him, the black mane spread over the pillow.

'Does it matter? Tell me something about the man I have just made love with.'

'I am training to be a newspaper reporter. I was in insurance before. Bored the hell out of me.'

'And what story are you working on at the moment?' She snuggled closer, her hand splayed on his flat hard stomach.

'This and that.' He leaned on his elbow, stared down at her and his expression was grim. 'I like to know who I've played with. Christina What?' he repeated.

'Does it matter?' She pouted.

He jumped off the bed, told her to stand up. Puzzled, she got to her feet. She faced him, then gave the same slow smile.

'What is your relationship with Petros?' he demanded. 'Did he send you?'

'Petros? If I am going to be cross-questioned I can get that at police headquarters like you . . .'

She stooped to reach for her clothes. Marler grasped her

94

by her strong pointed chin, stood her erect. 'I answered your question, now you answer mine.'

'I am going . . .'

Marler raised his right hand and hit her hard across the side of her face with the flat of his hand. She reeled under the blow, fell back on the bed. Her eyes blazed. He saw now they were black with greenish flecks. She leapt to her feet. Before she could speak he hit her again on the other side of her face, the blow harder. She now had two red weals. She leapt up again, came for him with clawed hands. She had become a raging wildcat. He grasped both wrists before the fingers tore his face, forced them downwards. She aimed a knee at his groin. He turned sideways, took the thrust on his thigh, dropped both hands suddenly, then hit her with real force. She sagged on to the bed, glaring up at him.

'What is your relationship with Petros Gavalas? You're going to answer before you leave. I didn't invite you here . . .'

'Why don't you go and . . . yourself?'

She no longer spoke her perfect English. She had lapsed into Greek and he realized she was watching him closely. One tough cookie, this girl. She had taken quite a beating but still she was probing.

'I beg your pardon?'

'Nothing,' she replied in English.

She started to get up and he used one hand to push her down on the bed again, digging his fingers into her shoulder. Both their bodies were gleaming with sweat from what they had done together, from the later struggle. The heat was building up in the room and Marler felt parched.

'Can I have a drink?' she asked.

'No. What is your relationship with Petros Gavalas?' he said again.

'I am his granddaughter . . .'

'I know that. It isn't what I meant. And you know that. Did he send you here to extract information from me – by using any method?'

'He wouldn't do that! No Greek would do that to his own kith and kin . . .'

'So you came yourself? Why? Because you love Englishmen? I recall you said that.'

'I hate Englishmen,' she hissed, pulling her hair back from her face. 'I want to get dressed . . .'

'You couldn't wait to get your clothes off when you arrived. If you hate Englishmen why did you take up with Harry Masterson when he arrived?'

'Who?' She drew back as Marler broke loose. Grabbing her by her long hair, he twisted it, pulling her down on the bed as he sat on her stomach, his mouth tight, pinning her down. He jerked her hair and she opened her mouth to scream. His hand clamped flat over her lips, exerting so much pressure she couldn't use her teeth to bite him. Her dark eyes were full of hate.

'Harry Masterson,' he repeated. 'Stop lying. You were seen with him at the Hilton. Other places, too. Now, I'm going to remove my hand. Yell – try to – and I'll knock you out.'

He jumped up suddenly, walked to his jacket, took a cigarette from his pack and lit it. The unexpected change of tactics threw her off balance. She stood up warily, slowly reached for her denims, slid inside them, wriggled herself into them, watching him. Straightening up, she adjusted the slacks, still naked above the waist. She spoke quietly as she made the threat.

'I'm going to accuse you of rape. The Greek police don't like foreign men who rape Greek girls.'

'There's the phone. Call Chief Inspector Sarris. I'm sure he'd enjoy a session with us. That he'll be interested to hear how you gave the signal for a marksman down at Zea to try and kill me. The bullet missed me by inches.'

'What are you talking about? There was no shot. I would have heard it . . .'

Marler was certain that for the first time she was telling the truth. He kept the surprise out of his expression. She reached for her blouse and held it dangling from one hand.

'You might just have managed it,' Marler speculated.

'Managed what?'

'Driven Harry Masterson so crazy over you that he fell for it. When you lured him down to Cape Sounion so he could be killed.'

'No! No! That was something I didn't do. What do you think I am?'

'That's easy to answer.' He pulled his wallet from his jacket. Taking out a sheaf of five-hundred-drachma notes, he looked at her. 'How much? What's your fee? For . . .' He gestured to the bed.

'*You swine! You lousy bastard!*'

'And I have diplomas to prove you're right,' Marler assured her.

She crammed her feet into her shoes, slipped on her blouse, hastily adjusted it. She glanced in the mirror. Her hair was a wild tangle. Marler handed her the brush he had picked up before opening the door earlier. As she used it, brushing her mane vigorously, she again stared at him in the mirror as he donned his bathrobe. This time she had a puzzled expression. His deliberate changes of mood were confusing her. He disappeared into the bathroom, returned holding a glass of water.

'You said you were thirsty. Next time I ask questions please give me answers, then we'll get on fine together.'

She drank the water in two long gulps, handed him the glass. 'I've never met a man like you before. Harry wasn't . . .' She stopped speaking.

'"Harry wasn't like you",' Marler completed for her. 'Tell me – before you go – why did you take up with him?'

97

'He was asking dangerous questions.'

'Such as?'

'About the Greek Key.'

'What's that?'

'Just pray to God you never find out. See you around, Marler.'

'It sounds as though you gave her a rough time. Just like you're giving me one,' Newman grumbled. 'I was fast asleep when you hammered on my door.'

'Thought you'd want to know the latest developments,' Marler replied, unrepentant. 'That you'd rely on your assistant to keep you informed.'

Heavy-eyed, his hair tousled, Newman tied the cord of his dressing gown more tightly, drank some of the coffee Marler had ordered from room service. He pursed his lips as he replayed in his mind Marler's account of his adventure with Christina.

'You have been enjoying yourself,' he said eventually.

'All in the line of duty . . .'

'Don't say that to Tweed. Significant that remark she let slip – "if I am going to be cross-questioned I can get that at police headquarters like you . . ." *Like you*. She knew we had been taken there by Sarris. No motorcyclist with an orange crash helmet followed us that I saw.'

'I thought I caught sight of that black Mercedes when I was taken in the police car,' Marler remarked.

'Did you now?' Newman drank more coffee. 'Then that would prove she *is* working under Petros' orders, that he told her about our visit. Which means she was lying – about acting under Petros' instructions.'

'Oh, she's a lovely little liar. Makes it a way of life.'

'Except on two points, you said. She didn't hear a rifle shot at Zea – which is possible with those ships' sirens blaring. And she wasn't the one who led Masterson down to Cape Sounion. This business is full of twists. And what the blazes is the Greek Key?'

'Maybe it turns the lock to the whole mystery.'

'If we could ever find that key. I'm going back to bed.'

'And our next move is?'

'Keep Nick and his helpers looking for where Masterson stayed. We might start making enquiries about the Greek Key. Someone must know what it is. In short, keep stirring the pot until something rises to the surface. And maybe take a look at Cape Sounion. While we're there we could try to locate old Petros' headquarters in the mountains.'

'Think I've already stirred one pot. It's called Christina Gavalas. I left her not liking us a lot. Which was the object of the exercise.'

'Exercise is the word for what you did.'

'Did you tell Newman everything about Giorgos, Chief?' asked his assistant, Kalos.

'What do you mean, everything?' Sarris demanded.

He stifled a yawn as he gazed down at the traffic jamming up Alexandras. Nine in the morning. It would get worse. He flexed aching hands. He wasn't up to these all-night sessions.

'The knife rammed into his back under the shoulder blade.'

'No, I didn't. We keep that quiet. I kept Newman away from the pathologist. That knife bothers me. Doesn't make sense.'

'The fact that he was drowned in the wine barrel first, then the knife was stuck in later? The lack of blood proves that.'

'Precisely. And it *is* an old British commando knife. The war museum has a specimen. I compared them. The knife in Giorgos is an exact replica. Macabre. Some kind of symbolic gesture?'

'Or something to put us off the real identity of the killer?'

'Could be. I just hope Newman doesn't go poking round in Devil's Valley. Petros Gavalas controls that area like some medieval baron.'

'And what about the number of accidents that have taken place in that area? Hikers and mountaineers who never come back?'

'I've never been able to pin anything on the old villain – but I'm certain his men tossed them over precipices. No one penetrates his territory and survives. He's the old school. Comes from Macedonia. They play rough up there. Yes, I do hope Newman gives that one a miss . . .'

2 p.m. 90°F. 32°C. Newman was freshly shaved, showered, his brain was alert, he had eaten a large lunch in the hotel dining room with Marler and they had returned to his room with Nick who had arrived promptly.

'We're going into action,' Newman rapped out. 'We'll stir the pot, as Marler put it earlier. Not to make it simmer – I want it boiling over.'

'The weather is boiling over already,' Nick remarked as he mopped his forehead.

'We'll drive down towards Cape Sounion,' Newman went on. 'My bet is we'll be followed. That will confirm we are getting somewhere. We'll enquire at the main hotels in the coastal resorts to see if we can find where Masterson holed up. We'll ask openly about the Greek Key . . .'

'What is that?' asked Nick. 'Sounds like a night club . . .'

'That is what we want to find out. And Christina will be in a rage after what happened. She may make a wrong move. Let's get to the car.' He picked up a large plastic bottle of mineral water and they left the room.

Nick ran ahead while Newman and Marler walked down the empty corridor. Newman never used elevators if they

100

could be avoided, if a staircase were available: elevators could become traps.

'You know, Marler, I think we're missing something. Maybe something under our noses.'

'Why the doubts?'

'This mystery is full of twists, unexplained contradictions. Why was Christina aboard that yacht, *Venus III*, *if* she is supposed to hate its owner, her grandfather, Petros? Who is paying for that expensive apartment she has in Kolonaki? We must visit her there.' He corrected himself. '*I* must visit her. She may tell me more than she told you.'

'I whetted your appetite,' Marler said cynically.

'What did Masterson find out that decided someone he had to be murdered? What was the link between him and Christina? Don't forget – they first met in London. Why did Masterson visit the Ministry of Defence to ask about that commando raid on Siros over forty years ago?'

'My head begins to spin . . .'

'I wish we had one man here who is a master when it comes to a manhunt, to untangling a complex web.'

'You mean . . .'

'Tweed. I miss Tweed . . .'

9

A sea of grey unbroken cloud pressed down like a smothering blanket: not a hint of blue anywhere. A fine drizzle like a sea mist covered the desolate landscape, settled on the windscreen of the Mercedes 280E Tweed had borrowed from Newman. He drove slowly along the narrow country road elevated above the grim marshland on either side. Not a soul in sight. At two in the afternoon they had the dreary world to themselves.

'Are we going the right way?' Paula asked as she studied the ordnance survey map. 'I'm lost.' She glanced out of the window, settled in the front passenger seat beside Tweed.

'We're right in the middle of the Somerset Levels, the area Masterson noted down on a scrap of paper in the cigar box he sent from Athens,' Tweed remarked. 'This is where the sea used to flood in centuries ago. Now they cut peat. I want to get the atmosphere of this place.'

He stopped the car, but kept the engine running as he stared around at the bleakness. Paula, dressed in a windcheater and a blouse and pleated skirt, shivered.

'I find this place creepy. Look, there's some kind of a building over there under those willows.'

'One of the farms – the peat-cutting farms.'

Below the road there stretched a ditch full of stagnant water. Paula lowered her window and wrinkled her nose as an odour of decay drifted inside the car. She opened the door, stepped out to take a closer look.

The ditch was coated with an acidic green slime across its surface. Patches of black water showed here and there. In the distance stood the ramshackle building Tweed had called a farm. Its roof slanted at a crooked angle. Smoke curled up from a squat chimney. Another smell assailed her nostrils and again she crinkled them in disgust.

'That's the smell of peat. You can see this side of that farm where they're cutting it. And someone is coming . . .'

Tweed's grip on the wheel tightened as he stopped speaking. Paula turned again to look towards the collection of hovels he had called a farm. Two men were advancing towards them, one walking behind the other along a grassy path leading to where she stood.

Both wore stained old pea-jackets, grubby caps and

muddy corduroy trousers stuffed into the tops of rubber boots. Each carried over his shoulder a long-handled implement. One was some kind of vicious-shaped hoe, the other a long spade more like an iron scoop. Both walked with steady intent, wide shoulders hunched, primitive faces staring at the intruders.

'Get in the car quick!' Tweed snapped.

He had the car moving as she slammed the heavy door and then increased speed. Paula let out her breath, a sigh of relief. Tweed started the windscreen wipers going.

'I didn't like the look of them at all,' Paula said.

'A couple of ugly customers,' Tweed agreed. 'The peat diggers are an enclosed community shut off from the outside world. I know this area well. Went to school at Blundell's near Tiverton. Hated every minute of it – like being in prison. During my spare time I used to cycle for miles – including round here. Pedalled like mad down this miserable road. Even then it frightened me.'

'Why cycle here then?'

'Kid stuff. Got a thrill out of scaring myself. You know something . . .' He glanced across the dank marshlands. 'This would be a good place to hide a body.'

'I'm glad you kept the engine running. There seem to be a lot of willows growing in this wilderness.'

'The other industry here. See those clumps growing by that ditch running away from the road? They're called withies. Shoots from pollarded willows. The osier-workers cut them and make wicker baskets to sell. Chairs, too. They can keep busy all the year round. When they've used up the withies and are waiting for next year's crop they dig up the peat. Goes way back over a couple of centuries. The Victorians were very keen on wickerwork.'

'And where are we?' She was studying the map again. 'I do hate to be lost.'

'Sign of a good navigator. Westonzoyland is probably

the nearest point of civilization. We left the A372 and drove north. We're heading for the A39. We turn left on to that, head for Bridgwater and then west to Dunster via Watchet.'

'Got it. What was in that large package which arrived from Harry this morning with the Athens postmark?'

'Look in the glove compartment. Another mess of clues. And after glancing at them I haven't one. A clue. See what you make of it.'

.She sifted the contents of the reinforced envelope with the address again written in Harry Masterson's distinctive hand. Pulling out something as Tweed switched on the headlights to warn any oncoming vehicle, she examined it and then unfastened a clip, wrapped it round her wrist, closed the clip.

'It's a girl's bracelet. Why would he send that?' she wondered.

'No idea.'

'It's quite beautiful. You've seen the symbol the pendant has been designed as in imitation jewellery?'

'No. I told you I only had time to glance at the contents before we started out from Park Crescent.'

'It's the Greek key.'

Through a hole in the lowering clouds a shaft of sunlight like a searchlight moved across the great sweeping brown ridges in the distance. Tweed nodded towards them as they travelled along a hedge-lined road, approaching a small town.

'Up beyond there is Exmoor. A lonely place for the trio who long ago raided that island of Siros. And why should they all settle in the same area?'

'Let's ask them . . .'

'I intend to. We're close to Dunster now.'

They passed a signpost on their right pointing down a

104

narrow road. *Watchet*. Tweed grunted and Paula looked at him.

'You had a thought.'

'Watchet. I checked it in guide books before we left. My memory was right. It's the only port between here and Land's End. A real port, I mean. In a small way of business. It exports scrap metal and wastepaper to Scandinavia. And, guess where.'

'We turn left soon according to the map. Can't guess.'

'I know where we turn. I remember the road. From Watchet there is the occasional ship plying between the Bristol Channel and Portugal. Turn here . . .'

At The Luttrell Arms Tweed waited until they were settled in their separate rooms before strolling down the staircase to tackle the manager. Each room had its name on the door. Tweed had *Avill*, a large and comfortable room with a door leading to a garden at the back. The manager, a tall, pleasant man clad in black, looked up from behind the reception counter as Tweed placed a photograph on the woodwork.

'Can you do me a favour, please,' Tweed began. 'Has this man stayed here recently?'

The manager stared at the print of Harry Masterson without a change of expression. He looked up at Tweed.

'It is, I am sure you will understand, company policy not to give out information about other guests. If someone came and asked the same question about yourself . . .'

'Special Branch.'

Tweed laid the card forged in the Engine Room basement at Park Crescent alongside the photo. The manager stared at it with curiosity. He had a quiet deliberate voice, the kind of voice used to pacifying impossible guests.

'I have heard about your organization. This is the first time I have met one of you.'

105

'So I would appreciate it if you would answer my questions in confidence. A question of national security.'

'Oh dear.' The manager paused. Tweed replaced the card in his pocket in case anyone came past them. The place seemed deserted. 'I do recognize him,' the manager said eventually. 'He stayed here about three weeks ago . . .'

'For how long?'

Keep them talking – once you've opened their mouths.

'Five days, Mr Tweed.'

'In what name?'

'Harry Masterson. A jolly man. Well-dressed. A joker – made me laugh.'

'And this person?'

Tweed removed Masterson's photograph, replaced it with the blow-up of the picture of Christina Gavalas which had arrived in the cigar box. He watched the manager intently.

'No question of scandal involved, I hope?' ventured the manager.

'I did say in confidence.'

'Of course. Yes, she came with him. They had separate rooms,' he added quickly. 'As a matter of fact, Mr Masterson had the Garden Room, *Avill*, the one you have, the best in the house.'

'And the girl?'

'The same room as your Miss Grey. *Gallox*.'

'Registered in what name?'

'Christina Bland. She wore a wedding ring. You see why I was concerned about a little scandal. Foreign, I thought.'

'Don't be concerned. What did they do while they were here? I realize that's a difficult question – but everyone has to pass this reception area when they come downstairs. Did they spend a lot of time out?'

'A striking couple.' The manager eyed Tweed as though to confirm he was the genuine article. 'Yes, they did go out most of the time. They would have breakfast – I help with that when staff is off duty – and ask for a packed lunch each day. Then we wouldn't see them until long after dinner. We close that front door at eleven and late-nighters have to ring the bell for admittance. Twice I let them in at midnight. I thought maybe they had friends round Exmoor they visited. That's a pure guess. You will keep this between us?'

'You have my word.' Tweed paused, smiled. 'You will keep entirely to yourself the nature of my job?'

'Good Lord, yes, Mr Tweed. The privacy of the guests must be sacred.' He looked embarrassed. 'Yours is, of course, a special case.'

Tweed picked up the second photograph. He put it inside his pocket, turned away, then turned back as though a thought had suddenly struck him.

'In connection with the same investigation, would you happen to know any of these three men? A Lieutenant-Colonel Barrymore, a Captain Robson, a man called Kearns? I do have their addresses. Barrymore, for one, lives at Quarme Manor, Oare.'

The manager took his time fastening up the middle button of his black jacket. Giving himself time to think, Tweed guessed. So I've given him something to think about.

'Again in complete confidence, I assure you.'

'This is a strange business you're investigating, if I may say so.'

'Very strange, very serious, very urgent.'

'Well . . . The three of them are friends. Every Saturday night they dine here. Always the same quiet table at the far end of the dining room. A kind of ritual, I gather.'

'They were here last Saturday? Two nights ago?' Tweed asked quickly.

'Well, no. The colonel is very formal. Always phones himself to book the table in advance. They've missed

107

for three weeks. Probably on holiday. Only my guess, I emphasize.'

'Thank you.' Tweed paused. He looked the manager straight in the eye. 'When you wake tomorrow morning you'll possibly worry about what you've told me. Don't. Worry, I mean. It is Monday. If I am still here next Saturday I shall make a point of dining elsewhere. Then if they come back you won't have me in the room. We do consider people's feelings.'

'So it seems. I thought, if you won't resent it, that your outfit were more aggressive.'

'On the contrary, we find we get the best results by being exceptionally discreet. And the local police shouldn't know I am here. Then we can't have any gossip about my being in the area.' Tweed leaned forward. 'We keep it just between the two of us. So, sleep well.'

'Thank you, sir. And if it's not out of place, I hope you enjoy your stay here. I'm not worrying.'

Tweed went back upstairs and knocked on the door of the room named *Gallox*. 'Who is it?' Paula called out.

'It's me,' said Tweed. She called out again for him to come in.

'Just look at this,' she began as he entered. 'Isn't it marvellous?'

She was sitting on the edge of a huge four-poster bed with a large canopy. It gave the large room a medieval atmosphere. Five feet six tall, the mattress was so high her feet dangled above the floor.

'You should have plenty of room in that,' Tweed observed and sat in an armchair. 'I have just talked with the manager. A tricky conversation. I had to show him my Special Branch card before he'd tell me a thing.'

'I like him. There's something Dickensian about his appearance.'

'And he's a man of great integrity . . .' Tweed told her about their conversation. She listened, watching him,

108

and he knew every word was being imprinted on her memory.

'That's queer,' she commented. 'We thought it peculiar that those three men should end up living in the same part of the country. After all these years they obviously keep in close touch. Why?'

'They could have stayed friends,' Tweed pointed out. 'They were together during the Second World War. Occasionally it does happen. But I think there's more than that to it – the trouble is I can't imagine what.'

'So where do we start?'

'We drive over by the coast road to Quarme Manor. I checked it on the map. Oare is down some side turning. That is after we've had a cream tea at the best place in this village.'

'Why? The manager said they were all away somewhere.'

'I want to see whether Barrymore – for starters – really is away. And if so, where he's gone – if possible . . .'

'This is one hell of a road,' Paula said with feeling.

'Porlock Hill. One of the most diabolical in Britain.'

Tweed was driving up a gradient like the side of a mountain. Added to the incredibly steep angle, the road twisted and turned round blind bends. Added to that, a grey mist was coming in off the moor, coils of sinister grey vapour creeping down the road.

Tweed drove with undipped headlights to warn any oncoming traffic, ready to dip them at the first sign of lights from the opposite direction. Like Tweed, Paula was tilted back in her seat as though inside an aircraft taking off. They passed a road turning off to their right and Tweed nodded towards it.

'That's the toll road, as they call it. That's fun too – it goes down like a water chute slide with a sheer drop on one side towards the sea.'

They had bypassed Minehead before they started the ascent and Paula patted her stomach. 'At least I'm full. That cream tea was fantastic. I'll get fat as a pig. And we're going to miss that turn-off to Oare,' she warned.

They had reached the top of the hill and drove along the level. No other traffic in either direction. The mist was thickening, making it as dark as night. The headlights picked up an inn sign. Culbone Inn.

'I'll check here for that turn-off,' said Tweed, swinging off the main road on to a wide drive.

He returned after a few minutes, climbed back behind the wheel. 'They say it's the next turn-off. A mile or so ahead. Easy to miss. And the road to Oare is very narrow.'

'Sounds great. Just what we need – for a car this size. How big is Oare?'

'Hardly a hamlet. Very spread out, as I remember. Two manor houses. Oare Manor and Quarme Manor, the stately home of Colonel Barrymore.'

'What exactly are we trying to do?' Paula was sat forward, braced against the seat belt, trying to spot the turn-off. At this height the mist was thinning. A chilly sea breeze blew in through her window. She pressed the button to close it.

'It's damn cold. Can I put on the heater?'

'As high as you like.'

Paula glanced at Tweed as she switched on the heater. He seemed impervious to extremes of both cold and heat. He wore a new hacking jacket, a pair of grey flannels, and a deerstalker hat which should have looked slightly ridiculous. But it suited him, gave him a commanding air. He read her thoughts.

'Dressed to merge into the landscape. Wear a London business suit out here and I'd stick out like a sore thumb . . .'

'Stop! You turn off here . . .'

He'd just checked the rear-view mirror, something he

110

did every ten seconds. He swung the wheel and they began to drop downhill. The country lane was so narrow the Mercedes just slid past the grass verges on either side. Beyond them a bank rose, topped with dense hedges. It didn't help visibility as the lane spiralled down steeply, a series of sharp bends. But the mist had evaporated and now they moved through a weird half-light as they dropped and dropped. At the bottom they drove across a gushing ford, reached an intersection. Paula desperately searched the map as Tweed swung right.

'Close to Oare,' he said. 'I remember that ford. From what the publican back at Culbone told me we should soon reach Quarme Manor. On the right somewhere.' The Mercedes was crawling as they navigated the winding lane. Above them in the distance Paula saw great sweeps of the moor, like tidal waves frozen in mid-flight.

'You asked me a few minutes ago what we are trying to do,' Tweed continued. 'We are trying to discover why Harry Masterson came here, what he discovered which led him to fly to Athens. In other words, what is the link between Exmoor and Greece? And who murdered Harry . . .'

He peered through the windscreen, still keeping the Mercedes at crawling pace. 'We have arrived. There is Quarme Manor.'

Paula was alone inside the car. Tweed had driven it into one of the lay-bys carved out of the side of the lane at intervals to allow one vehicle to pass another. He had instructed her to keep all the doors locked while he was away.

'Where are you going?' she had asked.

'To explore round Quarme Manor first, then call to see if anyone is at home . . .'

She sat with the heavy long torch in her lap he always

111

carried when driving. It was still daylight and she could see up on to the moor. She had turned off the heater, opened one window a few inches. Suddenly she stiffened, leaned forward.

She was looking at a ridge behind and overlooking Quarme Manor. It was uncannily silent. The wind had dropped. And despite the fact there was a dense copse of trees huddled round the manor house she hadn't heard the cheep of a single bird.

The horseman was perched on the ridge, silhouetted against the pale grey sky. Even motionless in the saddle, she saw he was a tall man. He held something with a long barrel in front of him, held it across the horse and parallel to the ground. A rifle.

Where the devil was Tweed? She watched the horseman, standing so still he might have been a bronze statue. Could it be Lieutenant-Colonel Barrymore waiting and watching over his property? Then the horseman moved, although his steed remained still.

He raised the rifle to his shoulder. He settled the stock in position and tilted the rifle angle downwards. He was aiming at something – someone – moving inside or just outside the grounds. Oh, my God . . .! Tweed was the target.

She raised the lever which unlocked the door, jumped out into the lane, still grasping the torch. Raising it with both hands like a revolver, she aimed the torch straight at the horseman, pressed on the light. The beam cut through the grey light. She knew it would never reach the horseman but she flashed it on and off time and again.

The horseman shifted in his saddle. The rifle swung in an arc, was now aimed at the car. She ducked down behind the Mercedes, waited for the crack of the shot. Nothing . . . She raised her head, ready to duck again quickly. There was nothing to see. The ridge outline was bare. The horseman had vanished. She had distracted him.

Shaking, she climbed back into the car behind the wheel, closed the door quietly, pressed down the lock.

Leaving the car, Tweed had walked quickly down the deserted lane. Coming closer, he saw Quarme Manor was a large Elizabethan pile built of grey stone with a wing extending forward from either end. The distinctive chimneys festooned the tiled roof. A high stone wall surrounding the place soon hid the house. He came to the entrance. Tall iron grille gates. A name plate. *Quarme Manor.*

No sign of lights. There should be lights if anyone was inside. The two-storeyed mansion was shrouded in gloom – made darker by the copse of trees sheering up inside the wall. Tweed peered through the closed grille gates up the curving drive beyond. A particularly fine example of the Elizabethan period, the mansion stood four square and seemed to grow out of the moor. All the mullion-paned windows with their pointed arches were in darkness.

He walked on along the curving lane, following the line of the wall. The silence was so intense he could almost *hear* it. His rubber-soled handmade shoes made no sound. He came to where the wall turned at a right angle away from the lane, climbing the steep slope towards a ridge behind the manor. A narrow footpath followed the line of the wall. He began climbing.

He had to keep his head down. The path was treacherous with slippery stones concealed beneath brown swathes of last year's dead bracken. He felt damp on his face, squelchy mush underfoot. He paused to stare at a second dense copse of trees – this one outside the wall and beyond the path. Out of the corner of his eye he caught movement. He looked up at the sabre-like cut of the ridge crest. Nothing. He could have sworn something moved.

113

Reaching the point where the wall turned again, running parallel to the front wall alongside the lane, he explored further until he found an opening. The gap was closed off with a single wide grille gate which was padlocked. He bent down.

By the gate the ground was cleared and in the moist earth were clear traces of hoof-marks. A back entrance to Quarme Manor which would take the owner straight on to the moor. And recently someone had ridden a horse here. He peered between the grille bars.

A gravel path led round a spacious lawn with ornamental shrubs arranged here and there. The lawn was cut, the topiary well-trimmed. Such attention cost money. He returned the way he had come.

The left-hand grille gate leading off from the lane opened at a push. His feet crunched as he walked up the drive. Inside the large porch he found an old-fashioned chain-pull bell. He tugged at it, heard it ring inside. A light was switched on, illuminating a diamond-shaped window behind an iron grille in the solid studded door. The lantern suspended over the porch came on. The small window opened. Tweed had a glimpse of a woman's bony face before the window slammed shut. The door was opened half a foot, a chain in place.

'What be it?' the old woman demanded.

'I wish to see Colonel Barrymore . . .'

'He b'aint be available.'

'You mean he is away somewhere?'

'He b'aint be available.'

She repeated the words as though she had been taught to say them by rote. She was tall, late sixties, her grey hair brushed close to the skull, her expression hostile. She was closing the door when Tweed spoke more firmly.

'The colonel will want to see me. When do you expect him to be back?'

'Name?'

'I shall have to tell him you were uncooperative. And he won't like that . . .'

'Phone for appointment . . .'

She was closing the door when they both heard the sound of a car approaching. It stopped outside. A shadowy figure opened both gates after jumping lightly out of the car. Before the headlights blinded him Tweed saw it was a crimson Daimler. Swinging round the short curve, it pulled up for a moment. A face behind the wheel stared out, then the car continued on round the side of the house. To the garage, he assumed.

'This is Colonel Barrymore?' Tweed asked the woman who still stood by the door.

'Better ask him, 'adn't you? Doesn't welcome strangers, you know.'

'It's becoming somewhat apparent,' Tweed remarked drily.

He turned as he heard the crunch of boots on gravel approaching from the side of the mansion. A tall, slim, elegant man in his mid-sixties appeared and stood, studying Tweed with an expression of disdain. Thick black hair was brushed over his high forehead and beneath his aquiline nose he sported a thin dark moustache.

He wore a sheepskin against the night chill and cavalry twill trousers shoved inside riding boots gleaming like glass. How the devil does he drive in those? Tweed wondered. The voice was crisp, offhand, as though addressing a junior subaltern.

'Who are you? If you are selling something you can take your immediate departure. And is that your Mercedes parked in the way down the lane?'

'Which question first?' Tweed asked mildly. 'And my car is in a lay-by. Plenty of room for you to get past even in your Daimler. That's what lay-bys are for . . .'

'I asked that stupid girl to move it and she refused . . .'

'She's not stupid and she's quite right to ignore

115

intimidation.' Tweed produced his card. 'Before you say another word you'd better know who I am. And while we're talking identification, who are you?'

'Colonel Barrymore.'

He moved under the lantern to examine the card, then looked up. 'It's all right, Mrs Atyeo, I'll sort this out myself.' He waited until she had disappeared, then stared at Tweed, handing back the card. 'Special Branch? A bit off the beaten track, aren't you?'

'So is Siros.'

Barrymore stiffened, stood even more erect. He jerked his head. 'Better come inside, I suppose. Just wait in my study until I'm ready to see you.'

By the light of the lantern Tweed saw Barrymore's skin was a tanned mahogany. He stood pulling slowly at one of the kid gloves he was wearing, taking hold of each finger and sliding it slowly half-way off. Even the slightest of the colonel's movements was slow and calculated.

'I'll go and fetch my assistant first,' Tweed said. 'She'll be taking notes . . .'

He was walking away before Barrymore could react. He felt he had left Paula alone in the car quite long enough. She greeted him with relief, told him quickly about the horseman on the ridge.

'That was very bright of you,' he said gratefully. 'To think of shining the torch. Oddly enough, Colonel Barrymore wears riding boots.'

'The man who stopped his Daimler alongside me and rudely told me to push off?'

'The very same gentleman. Surely there was plenty of room for him to pass?'

'Oodles. What do you think of His Lordship?'

'You said it. Let's get back to the manor. We have a right tartar to deal with. Something odd about him. Cold-blooded is the word, I suspect . . .'

116

10

'Go in there. No notes will be taken. I will join you when I can.'

Barrymore turned his back on them and disappeared through a doorway. They were standing in a stone-flagged hall. At the back a huge staircase mounted to the first floor, turning on a landing. Grim-faced, Mrs Atyeo stood holding open a heavy panelled door.

'In 'ere is where 'e wants you.'

'Always wears his riding boots, does he?' Tweed enquired as he walked towards the doorway.

'Part of 'is uniform, 'ain't it? 'E is The Colonel.'

'In capital letters, it appears.'

Tweed entered followed by Paula holding her notebook, the bracelet she had taken out of Masterson's last envelope still dangling from her wrist. Mrs Atyeo's expression changed, became ashen. She was staring at the bracelet and shrank back against the wall to let Paula pass, closing the door behind them.

'Tartar is the word,' Paula commented. 'And for some reason Mrs Atyeo nearly had a fit when she saw this bracelet.'

'I wonder why. Keep wearing it. Sit over there, notebook poised. It puts you offside from the chair behind that desk may put the colonel off balance.'

The study was also a library. Three of the walls were lined with books. The door into the room was cut out of a bookcase wall and lined with green baize on the inside. The fourth wall was occupied by tall mullion-paned

117

windows which overlooked the garden and the distant moor.

'Not very comfortable,' Paula remarked, staring at the tall hard-backed chair behind the desk, the spartan wood-blocks forming the floor, the lack of any soft furnishings and the desk which was a large block of oak. She shifted in her chair, trying to find a less awkward position. Tweed was looking at the books.

'What a man reads can tell you a lot about him. Military history of the Second World War, the campaigns of Wellington, a lot of travel books. None on Greece . . .'

'Prying, are we?'

The soft voice came from the direction of the well-oiled door which had opened silently. Tweed turned slowly and faced the colonel. He wore a dark silk shirt, a regimental tie, his cavalry twill trousers and the riding boots.

Tweed sat down in front of the desk, made no reply as Barrymore crept round the far side and sat upright in his chair, crossing his legs. The man moved like a cat. That was it, Tweed decided: cat-like in his movements and gestures.

'Well?' He waited for Tweed to respond but his visitor sat studying him. He glanced round at Paula. 'I said no notes.'

'And I said Special Branch,' Tweed snapped. 'A statement has to be taken of this conversation. If you object, we can always drive straight to London and conduct the interrogation formally. You know our powers.'

'Get on with it then.'

Barrymore opened a drawer. Taking out a ruler he held it between both hands. As they talked he bent the ruler slowly, then let it revert to its original shape. Substitute for an officer's stick.

'You've got yourself a good suntan, Colonel,' Paula intervened before Tweed began.

'Just back from the Caribbean.' He swivelled his gaze,

118

looking at her shapely crossed legs, her well-formed breasts outlined by her N. Peal cashmere sweater. Her windcheater was draped over the back of her chair. He took his time studying her. 'There are some lovely islands out there,' he went on. 'Not the package-deal spots. Islands with hotels like select clubs. Emphasis on privacy. The last bastions of a civilized holiday. Native servants to attend to your every wish. All the guests vetted. Word of mouth the only *entrée*. None of your wog nonsense like Marbella. You'd like it. I didn't catch your name.'

'Paula Grey.' She clamped her mouth tightly.

'Siros,' Tweed said suddenly. 'During the war you led a raid on the island.'

'Did I?'

'The Ministry of Defence files say you did.'

'Oh, you've been permitted to poke round the MOD?'

'No doors are closed to us. Especially when the murder of a Government employee is involved . . .'

'Which murder?'

The ruler was bent like a bow, close to snapping point. The colonel released the tension, straightened it. His eyes were dark under hooded lids. No trace of expression crossed his tanned face as he watched Tweed.

'The murder of Harry Masterson. You've met him? He was in this area – with a Greek girl.'

'He called here.' Barrymore paused. 'He asked a lot of damn-fool questions. Who was this Greek girl?'

'We're straying. You led the raid on Siros. Tell me what happened – what went wrong? And who came with you?'

'Someone knew we were coming. Cairo was a hotbed of gossip. We were carrying a fortune in diamonds to hand over to the Greek Resistance. To help finance them. Two first-rate men came with me. Captain Oliver Robson and CSM Stuart Kearns. Plus one Greek who knew the island. Andreas Gavalas. His job to hand over the baubles. Someone grabbed them off him. Mission aborted.'

'Haven't you left something out?'

'Probably. Over forty years ago? Is there much more?' He glanced at his watch. 'I've had a long journey. A bath would be welcome.'

He stifled a yawn, hand over mouth. Long slender fingers, more like those of a beautiful woman. Paula was writing shorthand in her book, recording every word. She looked up. Tweed was again waiting. She glanced at a side table near her elbow. A copy of *The Times* lay on it, folded open at the personal advertisements section.

'Andreas Gavalas was murdered,' Tweed said eventually.

'Top secret. They couldn't have let you read that file?'

'That was the most significant incident of the raid. Tell me about it.'

'Unpleasant. One of my few flops. The four-man party got separated. There was an alarm. Someone – forget who – said a German patrol had been spotted. We dived for cover. False alarm. When we found Gavalas he had a knife in his back – the diamonds were gone. We beat a hasty retreat – back to the beach for rendezvous with the motor launch. Then back to Mersa Matruh by night. That's a wog port on the African coast – inside the Gyppo border.'

'I know where Mersa Matruh is. What kind of knife?'

Barrymore slammed down the ruler. 'If you read the file you know. This isn't quiz time. A commando knife – as well you are aware. Embarrassing. I checked both Robson's and Kearns' equipment. Both had their knives. Showed them my own. Any more? I hope not.'

'One final question. Could you please – in a few words – give me your estimate of the characters of Captain Robson and CSM Kearns?'

It was the last question Barrymore had expected. Paula saw the puzzlement in his saturnine face. The colonel steepled his hands, a concentrated look in his dark eyes. Like a man reliving some experience of long ago.

'Robson was seconded from the Medical Corps. Steady as a rock in a tight corner. Cautious. Always looked where he was placing the next footstep. Never panicked. Dour.'

'And Kearns?'

'Courage came to him second nature. Fast on his feet, in his thinking. Could be impulsive. Didn't matter. Had a sixth sense for danger. In an emergency very audacious. Time you went.'

Tweed stood up, showed no sign of resenting the abrupt dismissal. Like the ending of a military inspection. Paula slipped her notebook inside her shoulder bag, walked after Tweed to the door without a glance at Barrymore.

Opening the door, Tweed stood aside and let her walk into the bleak hall. He glanced back. Barrymore sat behind his desk like a statue, hands still steepled, a glazed expression on his long-jawed face. Suddenly he seemed aware they were leaving. He stood up, remained behind the desk, bowed formally, said not another word as Tweed closed the door.

'You'll be leavin' now.'

Mrs Atyeo was waiting in the hall. She unclasped the hands which had rested on her thin waist, went to the front door, drew back bolts, peered through the diamond-shaped window, unleashed the heavy chain, opened it and waited as they filed past her into the night.

They paused under the lantern on the porch as the door was shut behind them. They could hear the bolts sliding back into position, the chain being fixed, a lock turned. The lantern went out, plunging them into darkness. Night had fallen.

Tweed looped Paula's arm through his and they made their way slowly down the drive. He waited until they were inside the car before he sighed and asked the question.

'What was your impression of Barrymore?'

'Nasty piece of work. Like a satyr. Did you notice how he was looking at me? Undressing me with his lecherous

121

eyes. I felt I was naked. Thinks a lot of himself. I can imagine him riding a horse inspecting his troops, riding very slowly along the line with an expression of cynical contempt. And he moves oddly – like a cat. Took those gloves off with a feline grace . . .' She paused and shivered. 'I'm glad you're back with me in the car.'

'You didn't think I'd leave you on your own in a lonely place like this, did you?'

Tweed was watching his wing mirror. Paula froze suddenly and then jerked her head round. A slim hatless man was walking alongside the car from behind them. He leant on the window ledge. She let out her breath, lowered the window. Pete Nield grinned, pulled at his small dark moustache with his index finger.

'How goes the battle?' he enquired.

'Where on earth did you spring from?' she asked.

'Pete has followed us in my Cortina all the way from London. I told you he was coming. He's been parked a short distance behind you ever since I left you.'

'In this road?'

'No,' Nield told her. 'I parked the car beyond a gate leading to a field. Then I sat in a hedge close behind you. I was ready to intervene when that character in the Daimler pulled up by you if he'd tried anything on.'

'But what about in Dunster?'

'Parked the car at the other end of the village. I still have to register at The Luttrell Arms – but I warned them over the phone I'd be late. They won't realize we're together. At the hotel, I mean.'

'You haven't told me what you spotted about the colonel,' Tweed remarked. 'Only that you dislike him. Irrelevant. Pete, get in the back of the car and listen. Now I want both of you to grasp this. Ready, Pete?'

'Jolly comfortable back here. Nice to see how the other half lives.'

'Masterson came down to Exmoor with the Greek girl,

122

Christina. All three men involved in a raid over forty years ago on Siros, a German-occupied Greek island, are living on Exmoor. Harry Masterson, I'm sure, knew that. From Christina . . .'

'Assumption,' interjected Paula.

'Listen! Our main task is to interrogate all three men. And *every* word said by these men is important. One of them may let something slip. There was something very peculiar about that raid on Siros. Now, Paula, you were there when Barrymore gave his version.'

'Well, he was very suntanned,' she said slowly. 'So he could have just come back from Greece . . .'

'Now we're getting warmer. You see, Pete, this Colonel Barrymore has a terse way of speaking. Typical Army officer. But when Paula remarked on his suntan he became positively loquacious – explaining at some length how he'd been to the Caribbean. No specific mention of locales. It was the only time he really opened up.'

'You mean he was lying?' Pete asked.

'Paula, when we get back to London, will type out the transcript of each of the three men's statements – including their description of what happened on Siros. You can read them, decide for yourself.'

'You also asked his opinion of the other two men,' Paula recalled. 'I couldn't see the point.'

'In the end the whole thing may hang on the *psychology* of these three men. Would one of them be capable of murder? And did you notice,' he asked Paula, 'that when I mentioned a murder, Barrymore said, "Which murder?" It sounded to me as though he was thinking of more than *one* murder. Who else could he be thinking of besides Andreas Gavalas who accompanied them on the Siros raid?'

'Harry Masterson?' suggested Nield.

'Or possibly a third murder over forty years ago – mentioned briefly to me at the Ministry of Defence. Back to

123

your car, Pete. We must tackle our next member of the trio.'

'Who is that?' asked Paula as Pete left the Mercedes.

'Captain Oliver Robson. He lives the other side of Oare. I was given directions at that pub at Culbone. Robson calls there for a pint occasionally . . .'

11

After the gloomy Quarme Manor the modern L-shaped bungalow perched on the hillside in the dark looked to be out of another world. Which, Tweed reflected as he stopped the car, in fact it was. A wild leap from the fifteenth century into the twentieth.

The residence was a blaze of lights, standing at the top of a tarred drive above the lane. A wide stone-paved terrace ran the full width of the frontage. Ornamental lanterns were placed at intervals along a stone wall below the terrace, shedding light over the long slope of rough-cut grass to the hedge by the lane. The white-painted gate was open.

Tweed studied the large bungalow carefully. Curtains were drawn back but it was impossible to see inside the picture windows from below. Searchlight beams flooded the night from each corner, illuminating all approaches. He drove in through the entrance slowly, glancing to left and right.

'They'll know we're coming,' he commented.

'They'll hear the car, you mean?' Paula asked.

'No. In each of the gateposts there are photo-electric cells. As we drove through that invitingly open gateway we broke a beam. It will have set off an alarm inside the bungalow.'

'I suppose it's wise to take precautions – living in such an isolated position on the edge of the moor.'

'Including spy cameras projecting from under the eaves? Every possible kind of security measure has been installed. I begin to see something Colonel Barrymore and Captain Robson have in common. When I trudged round Quarme Manor before going up to the front entrance I noticed the high walls were topped with barbed wire. And a straight wire ran beneath it. Electrified, I'm sure. Remember all the security precautions on the front door? Both places are like fortresses.'

'That's what the owners have in common?'

'No. Both of them are scared stiff of dangerous intruders. To an almost pathological extent it appears . . .'

He stopped speaking. He had parked the car at the top of the drive. The front door opened. Framed in the dark opening – the lights inside had been switched off – stood the silhouette of a man. Holding a pump-action shotgun. Aimed at the Mercedes point blank.

'I'll sort him out,' said Tweed.

'God! What a welcome,' whispered Paula. 'Worse than Quarme Manor . . .'

'Good evening.' Tweed had lowered his window. 'We are looking for Captain Robson. It says Endpoint on the name plate.'

'Who are you? What do you want?'

A trace of Scots accent. The voice clear, level in tone, controlled.

'Special Branch. My name is Tweed. We have just called on Colonel Barrymore . . .'

Tweed made it sound as though Barrymore had led them to Endpoint. He waited for a reaction, said no more. Silence is a potent weapon.

'You'd better come in then.' The shotgun was lowered,

still held ready for action as they alighted from the car and walked across the terrace. 'You have some identification?'

'Just about to show you. I'm taking my card out of my pocket . . .'

'It is very lonely out here. There have been two attempts to break in to my home. I'm Robson.'

As he looked at the card, shotgun tucked under his arm, Tweed studied Robson. Medium height, heavily built, but all of it muscle and bone, he was about the same age as Barrymore. And like the colonel his skin was deeply suntanned. The top of his rounded head was covered with an untidy thatch of brown hair and he had a straggly moustache of the same colour. Clad in shirt-sleeves rolled up to the elbows, his shirt was open-necked, but his well-worn grey slacks had a razor-edged crease.

'Better come in, I suppose.' He handed back the card. 'Special Branch? Sure you've got the right man? Let's go and make ourselves comfortable in the sitting room.'

'Oh, this is my assistant, Paula Grey,' Tweed introduced.

'Welcome.'

Robson hardly gave her a glance as he closed the door and walked across a hall towards an open door. A brown-haired woman of about the same age appeared wearing an apron over her dress.

'Who is it, Oliver?'

Tweed detected a note of anxiety in her voice. White-faced, she had an air of bustle. Robson gestured towards her.

'My sister, May. Looks after me. Keeps the place going. Be lost without her. It's all right, May. Barrymore sent them along. We'll chat in the sitting room.'

The moment she entered the hall the warmth hit Paula. Two old-fashioned radiators stood against the painted walls. The sitting room was long and large with a Wilton carpet wall to wall. Cosy-looking armchairs and couches were spread about and a log fire crackled beneath a huge burnished copper hood.

'Do take a pew, anywhere you like. This is my work room, too.'

He sat in an old swivel chair behind a desk with a scruffed top. A tumbler of something which looked like whisky stood next to a pile of newspapers. Robson stood up as they sat down.

'I'm forgetting my manners. What would you like to drink? I can do Scotch, white wine if you prefer . . .'

Paula had sat down close to him near the end of the desk. He stared suddenly as she adjusted the bracelet round her wrist. His right hand jerked, knocking over the tumbler. Liquid ran over the edge of the desk.

'Sorry. Damn careless of me . . .' He opened a drawer, took out a cloth and began mopping up the mess. 'Just back off holiday. Half here, half somewhere else.'

'I guessed that from your suntan,' Tweed remarked. 'You'd hardly have acquired that in this country. Go far?'

'Sailing off Morocco. Agadir and Casablanca. By myself. May can't stand the sea. Stayed back to guard the fort. Drinks?'

Both Tweed and Paula, notebook perched on her lap, asked for wine. Robson poured two glasses of Montrachet. Returning behind his desk, he produced a tobacco pouch and a pipe.

'Fire away.'

'I'm checking details of a murder which took place over forty years ago,' Tweed began. 'During your stint of duty in the Middle East.'

'A long time ago, as you say – that grim business when we made that raid on Siros. Barrymore was in command, but you know that – just coming from his place. Why has it become important now?'

'Because someone else investigating it has just been murdered. Ever met Harry Masterson?'

127

Robson's thumb, tamping tobacco in the bowl, remained poised for a second or two. Paula saw the pause. *Cautious* was a word Barrymore had used, describing Robson.

'Yes, he visited me. Jolly sort of cove. Life and soul of the party type. Asked some rum questions. What on earth is going on? "Just been murdered," you said.'

'That is what I am trying to find out. Could you tell me in your own words what did happen on Siros?'

'Who else's words would I use?' Robson smiled drily.

'And if you don't mind, Miss Grey will record your statement – for the record.'

'Of course not. Certainly she may. Special Branch. You have a system, I suppose. One thing I am entitled to, I assume. A copy of the statement. Siros.' He settled himself at ease in his chair, lit his pipe, watching Tweed from beneath his upswept eyebrows, his light blue eyes thoughtful. What a contrast to Barrymore, Paula thought: he's the soul of relaxation. And his house reflects his informal personality.

'Siros,' Robson repeated, puffed at the pipe, 'the main island in the Cyclades group. Shaped like a boomerang, a huge one. Steep cliffs along the southern coast – rising up to Mount Ida. Same name as the tallest mountain on Crete. No idea why. Siros was the headquarters of General Hugo Geiger, who commanded the German troops occupying the Cyclades . . .'

'Is Geiger still alive?' Tweed interjected.

'No idea. Bit long in the tooth by now if he is. Like our little group. Now . . . The Greek Resistance had made its own HQ on Siros. They thought hiding under the Germans' noses was a smart tactic. We were carrying a fortune in diamonds to hand over to the Resistance . . .'

'Who is "we"?'

'The colonel, of course. Myself. You wouldn't think I was a commando in those days. I'm a doctor. The Resistance lot were short of medical help. Plus CSM

Kearns, stout fellow. Lastly, the Greek, Gavalas. He was to be the contact with his own people. He'd escaped to Cairo. He was the one who carried the diamonds. To cut a long story short, we landed from the motor launch at night on the southern shore, made our way up a difficult defile cut in the mountainside – where the Germans would least expect a landing. It was wild terrain. Someone – can't remember who – sounded the alarm. German patrol. Every man for himself in that situation. We scattered, later reassembled at an agreed rendezvous – and Gavalas was missing.'

'He'd handed over those diamonds?'

'No one knew. Unlikely. That rendezvous was several miles away on the *northern* slopes of Mount Ida. We were still to the south. We started searching for Gavalas. It was pretty dramatic – horrific. Barrymore found him. Dead. A knife sticking out from under his left shoulder blade. And the diamonds had gone. We headed back for the rendezvous with the motor launch due to take us off. Nothing else to do.'

'And the knife?' Tweed prodded gently.

'That made it more horrific. A commando knife. The colonel checked us. We all still had our own knives – including the colonel. Later we wondered whether the knife had been taken off one of the two earlier teams which had perished while raiding Siros.'

'Who by?'

'Could have been one of the Greek Resistance. Even a German soldier. Someone must have had quite a collection. There were six commandos who died on Siros.'

'And the value of those diamonds?' Tweed asked.

'A hundred thousand pounds. Wartime value.' Robson tamped his pipe, glanced at Paula writing in shorthand.

'One more question before we go, if I may. Could you please give me your assessment of the characters and temperaments of Barrymore and Kearns?'

'We make a good team. Kearns has a place on the way to Simonsbath, a stone's throw from here. The colonel is decisive, ice-cold in an emergency. The most controlled man I've ever known. Remarkable. Always ready for any danger, however outlandish. Never lets up his guard.'

'And Kearns?'

'A natural CSM. Very young in those days. Weren't we all? Your legendary man of action. But an excellent planner as well. The two don't usually go together. Could always see three moves ahead in the game. Still can. I think that sums them up. More wine?'

'Thank you, but I think we've taken up enough of your time.' Tweed stood up. 'Could I possibly visit your loo?'

'Of course. Remiss of me not to show you when you arrived.'

When he strolled back into the room Paula had slid her notebook inside her shoulder bag and was standing close to the picture window. Pete Nield would be out there watching and she was trying to signal to him they were leaving. Robson padded across and joined her by the window.

'I'm a lifelong bachelor,' he remarked, fiddling with his dead pipe. 'Not from choice. Once I was madly in love with a débutante. Can you imagine that?'

'Yes, I can. What happened, if I may ask?'

'Why not? It was all a long time ago. I thought my feelings for her were reciprocated. She left me standing at the church. Sounds like an old joke, but it happened. A telegram arrived. *Sorry, Oliver. It won't work. Very sorry. Diana.* And Diana was a Greek goddess in mythology. Went off and married a baronet. Rather put me off women. Present company excluded.'

'It must have been an awful blow.'

'It was a bit. She was a *silly* girl.' He made the comment with such vehemence Paula glanced at him. The eyes were like stones, the mouth twisted in an expression of bitter

130

irony. 'Her baronet hadn't a penny. Had to take a job . . .'

'Thank you for being so helpful,' said Tweed as he returned and stood on the other side of Robson. He tapped the long thin picture window. 'Good view by day, I imagine.'

'Yes, it is. A lookout point over the moor. As to helping you, my pleasure. I'll show you out.'

'You keep your home beautifully warm,' said Paula. It was the first remark which came into her head and she sensed Robson was embarrassed by his display of emotion.

'It has to be oil-fired central heating out here. Tricky during the oil crisis. We practically lived in this room. The log fire . . .'

In the hall the pump-action shotgun was perched in an umbrella stand, the twin barrels pointing at the ceiling. Ready to hand for the next caller, Tweed noted.

The door closed behind them and they climbed into the car. Before starting the engine Tweed looked back at the bungalow, at the security cameras. The viewing screen must be in a room he hadn't seen. 'Something odd about this place,' he said as he reached to turn on the ignition and then leant back. 'Look at the roof, the far end of the long stem on the bungalow. We couldn't see it when we arrived because of the dark and the glare of those searchlights.'

Paula stared through the windscreen. Projecting above the roof of the bungalow rose a wide circular column which reminded her of a lighthouse. Even more so because at the top was a circular rail and behind it the column was made of glass. She expected at any moment to see a slowly revolving light.

'The moon came up while we were inside,' Tweed pointed out. 'Which is why we can see it clearly now. It's like a watch tower. Mind you, when I went to the loo his sister, May, took me the full length of the bungalow behind the sitting room to the main bathroom. On the walls are fishing nets with those glass balls suspended they use to keep nets afloat close to the surface. And fishing rods crossed like swords. Very much a man of the sea, Captain Robson.'

'There's someone inside the lighthouse. I can see his shadow against the moonlight.'

'Time to go.'

'Why did you liken it to a watch tower?' she asked while he drove down the drive and turned back the way they had come along the lane.

'I passed the base of the circular column on the way to the bathroom. It had a curved door, closed. Inside there must be a spiral staircase. Watch tower? Because I think Robson uses it to keep a close eye on the approaches to his home. The ridge along the moor continues from Quarme Manor, runs above Endpoint.'

'They both gave me the impression they're waiting for something dangerous to arrive – Barrymore with that wall and an electrified wire you saw. Now Robson – again with all that expensive security. The kind of thing you expect to see protecting a Beverly Hills mansion.'

'As though they were expecting Nemesis,' said Tweed.

12

Tweed, who had studied the map of Exmoor, drove back the way they had come and then turned on to a country lane leading away from Quarme Manor. Paula watched his expression as the headlight beams followed the twists of the hedge-lined road. The darkness seemed eerie, the moor closing in on all sides.

'Pete is still following us if that's what you're wondering,' she remarked. 'I saw his lights a moment ago behind us.'

'I was wondering about the name of Robson's bungalow. Endpoint.'

'Rather obvious. The lane comes to a full stop below where his bungalow is perched.'

'I noticed that. Something else came back to me. One of those notes Harry Masterson sent back from Athens – wrapped up as a clue only I would understand, he thought. *Endstation.* Close to Endpoint, wouldn't you say?'

'My God! It never occurred to me. Was Harry pointing a finger at Robson?'

'Who knows? It's early days yet.'

'It's getting late nights. Where are we off to now?'

'To pay a call on the third member of the party which raided Siros all those years ago. CSM Kearns. If we can ever find his place in the dark. I've marked where I think it is on that map. Navigate, girl.'

'Maybe he won't welcome a surprise visit at this hour . . .'

'So, maybe we catch him off guard. It's odd the way the three of them live so close together.'

'Perhaps they've remained close friends even after all these years.'

'And you don't sound any more convinced than I am . . .'

It was a difficult drive even when the moon rose, casting a weird light over the landscape. The light became weirder as a mist began creeping down from high up the moor. Behind the phosphorescent glow Paula could still see the ridge crests sweeping across Exmoor like giant waves.

They met no other traffic. They passed no villages. For miles on their way towards Simonsbath they saw not even one isolated dwelling. They were alone in the desolate wilderness as Tweed descended a long curving road, lights undimmed to warn any vehicle approaching from the opposite direction.

'What on earth is that?' Paula asked suddenly.

Lights suddenly appeared further down the slope, lights close together on their right-hand side. Tweed frowned, slowed to a crawl. They were still several miles from Simonsbath from his memory of the map. Woods now lined either side, and the lights gleamed between the tree trunks, flashing on and off as the trunks momentarily obscured them. He stopped the car and stared through the windscreen.

'It's a small estate of modern bungalows. They're crammed pretty close together. Must have been built during the past ten or fifteen years.'

'And I think we may have pulled up just outside CSM Kearns' house,' Paula commented.

To their left inside a gap in the trees stood an old stone two-storey house perched higher up the slope. Surrounded by a high stone wall, there were two six-feet-high solid wooden gates. Tweed reached for his flashlight in the glove compartment, asked Paula to lower her window, switched on the light. A large metal plate carried the name. *Woodside House*. 'This is his place,' he agreed.

He continued to move the light over the solid wooden gates. On the roadside was a grille covering each slab of wood. Reaching over to the rear seat, he grasped a heavy wooden walking stick he had purchased in Dunster. He was never sure afterwards what had made him do this.

'Let's investigate,' he said, switched off the engine and extracted the ignition key.

He locked the car before walking round it to join Paula who stood staring at the gates. Carrying the stick in his right hand, the light in his left, he swivelled the beam to the side of the right-hand gate and saw a bell-push. He pressed firmly with his thumb and they waited.

In the distance beyond the wall there was the sound of

a door being opened, a door which creaked loudly in the heavy silence of the mist-bound night. Footsteps approached with a brisk tread across what sounded like a cobbled yard. Suddenly a ferocious snarl murdered the night, followed by barking.

'My God, what's that?' Paula asked.

'Guard dog.'

'Sounds as though it's short of food – and thinks we'd make a good dinner.'

'Who is it?'

A cultured voice. Terse. Commanding. Talking at them through a small window flap opened in the right-hand gate.

'My name is Tweed. Are you Mr Kearns?'

'Yes. What do you want?'

'Special Branch. I want a talk with you. Now.'

'You have identification?'

'Of course. Wait a minute.' The unseen animal was growling, its claws pawing at the inside of the gate. It couldn't wait to get out. Paula shivered. Tweed produced his card, held it up to the spyhole, shone his torch on it.

'Stand quite still when I open the gate. Move and you'll be torn to pieces.'

'Charming,' Paula mumbled under her breath.

The flap slammed shut. A sound of bolts being withdrawn, the turn of a key and the right-hand gate swung inward. They were still faced with the heavy iron grille. Tactfully, Tweed switched off his light. Also, he wanted to regain his night vision. He felt Paula tense beside him.

The tall figure of a man stood inserting a key into the grille with his left hand. His right gripped a chain holding a huge dog. The creature became excited again, baying and snarling, lunging forward.

'Quiet, Wolf,' the crisp voice commanded. 'Come in. He's harmless . . .'

'You could have fooled me,' Tweed rapped back.

135

'And who is this girl? Not also Special Branch? She can wait in the car.'

'She can come in with me, for God's sake. She's not waiting by herself out here in the middle of nowhere. And she is Special Branch. My assistant, Paula Grey . . .'

As this exchange took place Kearns was closing the grille and the gate, relocking everything. Tweed wandered up the slope paved with stone flags towards the house. Over a hundred years old if it was a day. Paula kept pace, anxious to distance herself from Wolf, which she had now identified as an Alsatian.

'Wait here,' Tweed said as they reached the steps up to the front door. 'Back in a moment.'

He walked swiftly in his rubber-soled shoes round the left side of the stone hulk. At the entrance to a wide passage a horse had recently relieved itself on the stones. Rounding the corner, he was confronted with a stable door, the upper flap open. A horse's head regarded him, poked itself further over the flap and whinnied softly. Tweed held out a hand, stroked its neck. Its smooth hair was wet. It had been ridden hard. And not long ago.

'Leave him alone. What are you poking round here for?'

Kearns' voice was harsh, demanding. He moved as quietly as Tweed. Turning, Tweed smiled apologetically, made a dismissive gesture.

'I'm fond of horses,' he lied. 'That's a very fine animal . . .'

'Come back to the proper entrance.' The Alsatian, snarling like a mad dog, lunged for Tweed, who instinctively raised his walking stick. Held by an expanding lead, it almost reached Tweed and Kearns hauled him back. 'Prowl round here and Wolf will have your guts for garters.' Kearns made the statement in a calm tone.

Tweed followed Kearns at a distance. He switched on the flashlight as though picking his way. To the side of the paved area rough uncut grass and weeds cluttered the earth up to the base of the wall. His beam reflected off something metallic. Pausing, he prodded carefully with the stick. There was a grinding clash of metal. Two sabre-like blades, saw-toothed, sliced across the lower end of his stick. Kearns swung round.

'What the hell do you think you're playing at?'

'You tell me.'

'You just released a trap. We keep chickens and we're plagued with vermin – foxes and such like off the moor. That could have amputated your leg.'

'Let's go inside then. As you suggested . . .'

Inside, a bleak square hall was dimly lit with a forty-watt bulb. The woodblock floor was highly polished, doors led off the hall and a wide oak staircase climbed to a landing before turning to the next flight. From a door at the rear a blonde woman in her thirties appeared smoking a cigarette in an ivory holder.

She had a good figure, wore a powder-blue blouse with a high neck and a classic pleated cream skirt. She watched Tweed with a speculative eye, ignoring Paula. Kearns' mouth tightened.

'My wife, Jill. We have gatecrashers.'

'Would you like some refreshment?' she enquired, still eyeing Tweed. 'Coffee? Maybe something to drink . . .'

Her voice was soft, husky, but Kearns answered for her.

'Not necessary. They won't be staying long. Better come into the mess,' he told Tweed.

'He means the dining room,' Jill explained. She stroked her shoulder-length hair with one hand.

'In here,' Kearns went on. 'Sit down. Both of you.'

The rectangular-shaped dining room was oak-panelled, had an oak dining table and was illuminated by another forty-watt bulb inside an old-fashioned shade suspended high above the table. An atmosphere of spartan gloom pervaded the room. Tweed and Paula sat on chairs at the table while Kearns took up a standing position.

137

'First, I'd like to see your identification again,' he demanded.

Tweed handed him the card and studied their host while he examined the document. Kearns was over six feet tall, a lean and rangy man with a clean-shaven face and strong bone structure. He stood very erect in front of the fireplace which was laid with logs but unlit. Paula suppressed a shiver. It was chilly.

Kearns was in his sixties but he had worn well. His hair was still dark, his complexion was deeply tanned. He carried himself with an air of complete self-assurance and his eyes were like two brown marbles. Never off parade, Tweed thought drily.

He was clad in a pair of dark slacks, sharply creased, and a navy blue polo-necked cashmere sweater. There were traces of dried mud on his dark brown shoes, the only flaw in his otherwise impeccable appearance. He dropped the card on to the table so Tweed had to reach forward to retrieve it.

'Get to the point,' Kearns said.

'I'm investigating an unsolved murder which took place over forty years ago in the Middle East.'

'Oh, that macabre Ionides killing in Cairo. Can't help you. Why bring that up now?'

'Because it may be linked with the recent murder of one of our people. In Greece. At Cape Sounion. Know it?'

'No.'

Kearns stood with his feet slightly apart, hands clasped behind his erect back. He glanced at Paula who was taking notes in her book on the table. She had kept her expression blank during Kearns' reply. This was the first reference to Ionides.

'There are two of you,' Kearns decided. 'Bad tactics to be outnumbered. I also need a witness . . .' He walked quickly to the closed door, opened it, called out. 'Jill, come

138

and join us. Just sit and listen with that remarkable memory of yours. Sit there.' He made brief introductions.

As he returned to his position in front of the fireplace Jill Kearns, still smoking, carrying a porcelain ash tray, sat at the head of the table. She studied Paula, who stared straight back. Hackles rising, Tweed noted.

'Don't see how a recent murder could be linked with the Ionides business,' Kearns resumed.

'Tell me about Ionides. You used the word "macabre".'

'Not much to tell. We had just returned from a mission . . .'

'We?'

'Three-man commando raid on a Greek island. Anti-khana – name of the building in Cairo where Ionides was slaughtered one night – was our official HQ. No one in the place knew what we were really employed for. Propaganda was supposed to be our job. Not even the CO of the building – Colonel Grogan – had a clue about us.'

'Tell me more about Ionides.'

'Some Greek who *was* working on propaganda – printing leaflets to send to the Resistance crowd. Two nights after we got back Ionides was apparently working late, alone in the building – a habit of his. Late one evening someone cut him to pieces. Blood all over the walls. He must have fought for his life – the room was a wreck. Ionides was slashed everywhere. Head pretty near severed from the body. Some maniac must have got in – and out. The Special Investigation Branch – equivalent of your crowd in the Army – never did solve it.'

'Did you ever meet a Harry Masterson?'

'Bluffed his way in here. Bit of a buffoon. Sent him packing.'

'You look very suntanned,' Tweed remarked, switching the topic without warning.

'I should do. Just back from windsurfing in Spain.'

'Your wife kept out of the sun from her appearance . . .'

139

'Didn't come with me. She hates the heat, loves the cold. .s this part of the interrogation? I haven't all night.'

'I have. And we're talking about murder. Maybe three murders. Where had you come back from just before the Ionides killing?'

'I told you. A three-man raid on a Greek island. Siros . . .'

'A:d the names of the other two men?' Tweed interjected quickly.

'The CO, Colonel Barrymore. A Captain Robson, medical officer.'

'And after all these years the three of you all live in the same area. Exmoor. I find that very curious – even strange.'

'Nothing to it. Barrymore and I stayed on in the Army after the war. Same unit. Robson got his demob soon after hostilities ended. Set up in practice as a doctor here. We kept in touch. When Barrymore and I left the Army we weren't sure where to settle. Robson offered to find us property round here. He knew the ropes. Barrymore and I told him what we could afford. Is that all?'

'Not quite. A Greek came with you on the Siros raid.'

'Oh, Gavalas.' Kearns shifted his stance, showed signs of growing boredom, even impatience. 'He was supposed to put us in touch with the Resistance group we landed to meet. Knew them, so he said. I had my doubts. There was a moment when we thought Jerry was near us in force. We scattered. When we met up Gavalas was missing. We found him in a gulch. Obviously he'd hidden there. He was dead. Knifed in the back. Commando knife, too. The colonel sorted that out. Checked that Robson and I had our knives. Showed us his own. Stickler for detail, the colonel. Not that we thought any of us had touched the Greek. Why should we?'

'For a hundred thousand pounds of diamonds that went missing.'

'Obviously taken by the assassin. Siros was crawling with odd characters. Fortunes of war.'

'Misfortunes in this case,' Tweed pointed out. 'For Gavalas. You ride much, Mr Kearns?'

'All of us do. One reason for living on Exmoor. And now . . .'

'Who is "all"?' enquired Paula.

Kearns turned his head as though he'd forgotten her presence and wasn't too pleased about her intervention. He stared at her coldly.

'The colonel and Dr Robson. As I was about to say before you interrupted, is that all?' He stared now at Tweed, looked pointedly at his watch.

'One more question. What odd characters? You just said Siros was crawling with them.'

'Republican Greeks, left-wing Greeks, Royalist Greeks, monks from the monastery. And the German occupation troops. Now . . .' He marched round the table to the door, opened it and went into the hall.

Jill Kearns, who had lit a fresh cigarette, leant across the table to Tweed. 'Are you staying somewhere near?' she whispered.

'Luttrell Arms, Dunster. You can get me there if something's bothering you,' Tweed replied in a low tone. He raised his voice. 'I think we may soon outstay our welcome, Paula.'

In the hall Kearns stood by the open front door. Somewhere close at hand Paula heard Wolf snuffling, growling, scratching at a door. Kearns had handed the dog's chain to Jill when they entered the place.

'Goodbye,' said Kearns stiffly.

'Just before we go,' Tweed persisted amiably, 'please give me your impressions of Colonel Barrymore and Captain Robson.'

Kearns' thin mouth tightened. 'The colonel is a first-rate commander. Can smell trouble a mile off.' He gazed straight at Tweed for a moment. 'Knows at once how to deal with it. No hesitation. Captain Robson was not a regular. More inclined to circle round trouble. Very determined in an emergency.'

'And that estate of new houses just down the road. Seems out of place.'

'Why? Occupied by businessmen, I gather. Probably commute to Taunton or Bristol. Like the country life. How would I know? I'll let you out now . . .'

Tweed and Paula prepared to follow him down the slope. Just before he stepped out Tweed glanced back. Jill Kearns stood watching him, holding her cigarette holder. She nodded at him.

'Goodnight,' said Tweed. 'Sorry to disturb you at this hour.'

'Any disturbance is welcome out in this Godforsaken wilderness.'

Kearns had both the wooden gate and the grille open when they reached him. He stood aside, said not another word as they walked out. The grille slammed shut behind them, followed by the main gate. Standing on the grass verge Tweed heard brisk footsteps retreating back towards the house.

'Well!' Paula blew breath between her teeth. 'That was really something. Imagine living with him.'

They climbed back into the car which was chilly inside. Tweed switched on the heater and tapped his fingers on the wheel before starting the engine. He was gazing at the glow of the estate lights in the mist.

'What was your impression?' Tweed asked as he fired the engine.

'A born CSM. Should still be in the Army, bawling contemptuous commands to his troops. Very self-contained. Could settle anywhere. A bloody iceberg.'

'And his attractive wife, Jill?'

'A manhunter. After more trophies to add to her collection.'

142

'That's pretty catty. Not your usual style . . .'

'I saw the way she watched you while you grilled Kearns.'

'She's a good few years younger than him – and it must get very lonely in that hideous old pile.'

'She's getting to you already.' Paula glanced at Tweed as he let the car cruise downhill. 'You devil, you're teasing me. I agree it can't be much fun married to the perfect CSM.'

'I thought he did that rather well – put on a clever performance. Just stopped short of caricature.'

'Tweed, what are you driving at?'

'Mr Kearns is a great deal more devious than you give him credit for. He was presenting a mask to us.'

'Talking about masks, I wonder about that peculiar little colony of bungalows,' she observed. 'They don't look real. Let's take a closer look. You know, they all look simply too good to be true to me.'

He slowed down even more as they passed the entrance to the estate and Paula counted six bungalows, three on each side of the cul-de-sac. All the dwellings had curtains drawn, lights on behind them. All had the usual status symbols of the upwardly mobile young and ambitious executives. Coach lanterns flanking each porch; more lanterns at the entrance gates to the drives; urn-shaped pots with evergreen shrubs like small exclamation marks.

'Like something out of the Ideal Homes Exhibition they hold at the annual Olympia exhibition in London,' Paula remarked. 'As I said before, they don't look real.'

'And Kearns, who lives on their doorsteps, doesn't seem to know a thing about them. Hard to swallow.'

'Makes sense to me. You said it yourself. He's a self-contained type . . .'

'I also said he was a good actor. What's the matter?'

They had left the bungalow estate behind, the road was now level, winding across the moor, open to it on either side. No hedges. In the moonlight on both sides smooth

143

dark slopes swept up to high ridges silhouetted against the night sky. Paula had stiffened, was staring up to her left.

'There's that ghostly horseman again!'

'Where?' Tweed reduced speed to peer up the slope where transparent veils of pale mist rolled slowly over the moor, assuming strange shapes. Tweed was sceptical. One patch of mist looked like a centaur, then dissolved. 'I don't see any horseman . . .'

'Up there on that dip in the ridge, for God's sake. And he's got his rifle again. He's aiming it . . .'

Everything happened at once. A Cortina came up behind them and overtook, slowing as it pulled in ahead of the Mercedes. 'Pete is still with us,' Tweed remarked. 'I still can't see . . .'

He broke off in mid-sentence. Paula was not given to seeing phantoms as he'd imagined. Perched in a fold between two ridge crests a man on a horse stood still as a statue, rifle raised. Tweed rammed his foot down on the accelerator, turning out to pass the Cortina which had stopped. There was a sharp *crack!* At the same time the sound of splintering glass. Paula jerked her head round.

'Both rear side windows are crazed . . .'

'Bullet,' Tweed said tersely.

He pulled up at a point where two copses of trees shielded the road on either side, forming a shield. In the rear-view mirror he saw Pete Nield crouched behind the parked Cortina, both hands raised, aiming up the slope. The hard detonation of three shots fired in rapid succession echoed through the night. Nield stood up, climbed back behind the wheel, drove forward and stopped alongside the Mercedes. Tweed lowered his window full depth.

'He tried to kill you this time,' Nield remarked. 'How the hell did he make it all the way down here from the Doone Valley?'

'Did you get him?' Tweed asked calmly. Beside him Paula gripped both hands tightly to stop shuddering.

'No. The range of fire was too far for a handgun. Frightened him off before he could try again. Saw him vanish over a cleft in the hills. You didn't answer my question. How could he make it here from the Doone Valley?'

'He'd have to know the country well, have ridden over Exmoor a lot.' Tweed splayed his hands on the wheel. Paula was amazed by his reaction: he was cool as a cucumber. She was still shaking. 'Also there's a moon up,' Tweed went on. 'An experienced rider could have come across country direct while we drove in a half circle slowly.'

'So it could have been either Barrymore or Robson?' Paula suggested. 'Kearns told us they all rode . . .'

'Or even Kearns himself. Time to get back for a late dinner to Dunster.' He glanced at her as he released the hand-brake. 'Don't forget – Kearns is closest and the horse I saw in his table was still saddled up. But the attempt on my life proves that we came to the right place.'

13

The horseman appeared in the middle of the road as they came close to Dunster along a quiet hedge-lined country lane.

He sat motionless on his horse, one hand held up, the other holding the reins. Tweed saw him clearly in his headlights. He turned them from dipped to undipped and the twin glare showed up the waiting man starkly. He lowered his raised hand to shield his eyes.

Pete Nield's Cortina, close behind the Mercedes now,

overtook Tweed's car. Nield drove with one hand on the wheel, his other slipping the .38 Smith & Wesson from his hip holster. Stopping the Cortina, he jumped out of the seat, lifted both hands, gripping the gun, aiming point-blank.

'Don't shoot!'

Tweed had stopped his own vehicle, dived out and ran forward. He stood beside Nield, studying the horseman who remained as still as a bronze statue. Tweed blinked, wondering if his eyes were playing him tricks. Then he spoke briefly to Nield before walking forward.

'You won't need the gun. Incredible. I know who this is . . .'

Standing by the flank of the horse, he extended a hand upwards. The horseman reached down to shake the hand. Both men stared at each other. The horseman was stockily built, in his sixties, sported a brown moustache which matched his thick hair.

'Chief Inspector Sam Partridge,' Tweed said.

'Ex-Chief Inspector. Now retired. You gave me quite a chase over the moors. Where are you staying?'

'Luttrell Arms, Dunster . . .'

'Like me. It's the only decent hostelry for miles. I'll join you there for dinner, if I may. And they know me simply as Mr Partridge. It's only about a mile now. Why don't you drive on and I'll follow?'

'We'll wait for you in the bar,' replied Tweed and went back to his car, waving to Nield to take the wheel of his own vehicle.

'What was all that about?' Paula asked as the horseman turned and began trotting towards Dunster. 'And who is that man? He tried to kill you.'

'There was more than one horseman out on the moor today.' Tweed sat behind the wheel, watching Partridge's retreating figure.

'More than one?'

146

'The man who tried to kill me and that chap. Ex-Chief Inspector Sam Partridge of Homicide. I knew him at the Yard when I served my stint before joining the Service.'

'I don't understand this too well.'

'Neither do I. The long arm of coincidence is stretching itself to breaking point. There has to be some logic in this business somewhere. Partridge called at the Ministry of Defence after Harry Masterson – talked with Brigadier Willie Davies, the chap I went to see.'

'I still don't see . . .'

'When Partridge called at the MOD he told Davies he was still investigating a murder committed over forty years ago. In Cairo. A man called Ionides.'

'In Cairo? But Gavalas was murdered on the island of Siros.'

'Exactly. Odd, isn't it? Two different murders nearly half a century ago. I'm looking into one, Partridge is investigating another. He's staying at The Luttrell Arms.' He switched on the ignition. 'We're meeting Partridge when we get back to the hotel. Should be an interesting conversation, wouldn't you say?'

They sat at a quiet corner table at the far end of the dining room at The Luttrell Arms. Tweed had requested somewhere they could talk on their own. The manager in his dark jacket and trousers had escorted them and whispered to Tweed after pulling out Paula's chair.

'This is the table those three local gentlemen sit at when they meet here every Saturday night.'

'Which three gentlemen?' Paula asked when the manager had gone.

'Barrymore, Robson, Kearns . . .'

Tweed looked across the table at Partridge who sat opposite to him. Paula sat next to Tweed and faced Nield, sitting alongside Partridge. She studied the ex-Scotland

147

Yard man. Beneath his thatch of thick brown hair his face was weatherbeaten, had the ruddy glow of a man who spends a lot of time out of doors. His grey eyes had a steady gaze, his nose was short, almost pugnacious, but his manner and way of talking were gentle. The pursed lips and the strong jaw gave him an obstinate look. Not a man who gives up easily, she decided.

'The three men who are my suspects,' Partridge commented.

'Suspected of what?' Tweed enquired, glancing up from the menu. He noticed Partridge hesitate, glance at Paula and Nield. 'My companions are both fully trustworthy,' he assured him.

'Of the murder of a Greek called Ionides back in 1944 in Cairo.'

'That's a long time ago,' Paula remarked.

'I was hardly out of my teens in those days. For some reason I never understood they attached me to the SIB – Special Investigation Branch,' he explained to Paula. 'Military equivalent to Scotland Yard. I had a fool for a superior – a Captain Humble. Funny name for him – he was anything but humble. Knew it all, so he thought. Knew damn-all from what I could see. He'd been with the police in Manchester before joining the Army . . .'

He paused as the waitress came to take their orders. Paula was studying him again. He wore a hacking jacket, old grey slacks, and by his side on the banquette rested a much-worn check cap. A perfect outfit for merging into the Exmoor landscape. Tweed sipped water and then encouraged Partridge to continue before he could ask what Tweed was doing on Exmoor.

'Tell me a bit more about the murder of this Greek. Ionides, I think you called him.'

'Which wasn't his real name. I'll come to that later.' Partridge rested his elbows on the table and began to talk animatedly. Almost like a man possessed, Tweed noted.

'It was a horrific murder. Took place late one evening after dark in a weird building called the Antikhana. Near the Nile and backing on to a native quarter. Ionides had escaped from German-occupied Greece and was officially working on propaganda fed back into his country. A British sergeant who was billeted on the roof found the body. Blood all over the walls, the furniture, the floor. He had been cut to pieces with a knife. Head almost severed from the body.' Partridge looked at Paula. 'Sorry, don't want to spoil your meal.'

'I have a strong stomach. Do go on.'

'Humble was in charge of the case. Came up with nothing. No one in the building at the time of the murder, apparently. Only one entrance – and a Sudanese receptionist guarded that. Main entrance doors kept locked at night after six. Murder took place somewhere between eight and ten according to the pathologist. So theoretically the murder couldn't have been committed.'

'The windows?' Tweed suggested. 'The murderer could have got out by one of them?'

'Impossible. Bars on all the windows. Security was tight. The case has remained unsolved to this day.'

'So what are you doing prowling round Exmoor?'

Partridge waited while drinks and starters were served. He rapped on the table with his left-hand knuckles, a quiet tattoo. He ignored his soup, started talking again as soon as they were alone again.

'It's a bit complex. Three commandos were based officially inside that building. Two days before the second murder they'd returned from an abortive raid on an island called Siros.'

'Just a moment, Sam,' Tweed interjected, 'you're losing me. You said "the *second* murder" and "*abortive* raid . . ." What was the first murder?'

'The two questions are linked. The raid was abortive because attached to the three-man commando unit was a

149

Greek called Gavalas carrying a fortune in diamonds to hand over to the Resistance on Siros. They were desperately short of funds. On Siros Gavalas was murdered – knifed in the back. The diamonds he was carrying had gone. So, the mission was abortive. Two days later the three commandos were back in Cairo – *before* the murder of Ionides. You see where I'm leading?'

'Never like to assume anything, Sam. You must remember that from our days at the Yard.'

'Humble made a routine investigation of the murder of Ionides and then dropped the case. Something else came up. I was fascinated by the whole thing. The sheer brutality of the killing at the Antikhana. I kept on digging in my spare time. Ever since I've been convinced one of the three commandos was the killer of both men. On Siros, Gavalas. In Cairo, Ionides. The three men were Barrymore, Robson and Kearns.'

Tweed drank the rest of his soup while he thought. Nield, who was keeping quiet, had devoured his shrimp cocktail. Partridge was sipping his soup. Paula watched him as she went on eating her pâté. There were only three other couples eating late dinner.

'Sam,' Tweed began, 'you've spent your life as a detective. So far I haven't heard you produce a shred of evidence to back up this bizarre theory.'

'I told you I went on digging. I bluffed my way into Grey Pillars – as they called GHQ. I checked certain confidential records through a contact there. I found that Stephen Ionides – remember I said earlier it wasn't his correct name – was, in fact, Stephen Gavalas. Brother of Andreas Gavalas.'

14

Three people sat in what was known as the Garden Room – Tweed's bedroom with the door at the far end leading into the hotel's garden. It was elevated one storey above street level and at ten in the evening the curtain was closed over the locked door.

Paula sat in an armchair, her legs crossed, balancing a cup of coffee on her knee. On a couch Nield relaxed, nursing a glass of cognac. Only Tweed sat upright in a hard-backed chair. It helped his concentration.

'I think I'll pop off to bed, get an early night after all that riding,' Partridge had said as they left the dining room.

'So apparently there were two horsemen riding the moor while we were driving round,' Nield observed. 'Partridge was one, and the other is Mr X.'

'I was pretty mad when Partridge said he was the horseman behind Quarme Manor,' Paula reflected. 'Pointing that rifle at you – even if it was unloaded.'

'He used the telescopic sight to find out who I was,' Tweed reminded her. 'Must have had the shock of his life when he saw it was me.'

'But the other horseman near Kearns' place tried to kill you,' Nield pointed out. 'It's Mr X we want to track down.'

'That story about the Gavalas family still carrying on a vendetta worries me,' Tweed said. 'And I don't like the sound of the grandfather, Petros, who – according to Partridge – rules the family with a rod of iron. Sounds like a real ruffian.'

'Would anyone still carry on a vendetta after all these years?' Paula objected.

'The Greeks have a strong family sense. And an equally strong sense of family honour,' Tweed told her. 'According to Partridge two sons of old Petros were murdered. He could still be looking for the killers – or killer. Newman and Marler, who know Greece well, could fill us in on that angle best. Maybe when they return they'll have news.'

'But there is still no news from Athens?' Paula enquired.

'Nothing. I called Monica at Park Crescent while you were tarting yourself up in your room.'

'Tarting?' Paula grinned mischievously. 'Well at least he does notice when I freshen myself up.' Her expression turned serious. 'None of what we've learned gives us any data on poor Harry Masterson . . .'

She broke off as someone knocked tentatively on the door. Nield was on his feet in seconds, gun in hand. 'I'll check that.'

Tweed was also on his feet. 'Crouch behind the bed,' he ordered Paula. Switching off the main light, leaving the room dimly illuminated by table lamps, he moved his chair against the wall and sat down again. Nield approached the door silent as a cat. He stood against the wall to one side, grasped the key in the lock, turned it with great care, took hold of the handle with his left hand, threw it open.

A startled Partridge, still dressed, stood in the doorway. He glanced to his left as Nield slid the gun out of sight. Tweed asked him to come in and Nield closed and relocked the door.

'Very wise,' Partridge commented. 'And sorry to bother you at this hour. But I found things whirling round in my mind, facts I hadn't told you. A man called Harry Masterson was murdered while I was paying a visit to Greece . . .'

'What about this Harry Masterson?' Tweed asked after room service had delivered coffee. It was going to be a long night.

152

'I couldn't find out anything about his background – but I did discover he was squiring Christina Gavalas – that is Petros' granddaughter. Apparently they flew to Athens together. So I began to poke around.'

'Why? If you didn't know this Masterson?'

'Because where he went over the cliff – at a place called Cape Sounion – is close to the entrance to what the locals call Devil's Valley. That's where Petros Gavalas has his farm and his headquarters. It's hidden away in the hills near an abandoned silver mine.'

'Rather a flimsy connection,' Tweed probed.

'You think so? Masterson was with Christina Gavalas – and Cape Sounion was the location of his murder.'

'How do you know Masterson was murdered? Evidence, Sam – have you evidence? Something about the state of the body?'

'No. Just found by a coastguard cutter on the lookout for drug traffickers as it rounded Cape Sounion. Masterson's body was lying on some rocks. He'd plunged down two or three hundred feet.'

'I'm still waiting to hear some evidence,' Tweed insisted.

'Some years ago at a crime seminar in Athens I met a Captain Sarris of Athens Homicide. I visited him on this latest trip. He told me in confidence they couldn't prove anything, but Sarris was convinced it was murder.'

'Why?'

'He'd observed Masterson somewhere. Said he simply wasn't the sort of man to stumble over the edge of a cliff. Do you mind if I light my pipe? After all, you'll be sleeping here . . .'

'Light up! You think better when you're smoking, Sam. I can open the door to the garden later. Anything else?'

'Yes. There's a Greek called Anton riding around on Exmoor – Anton Gavalas, son of Petros. By his second wife. There was a rumour he slipped ashore off a boat from Portugal at Watchet.'

Tweed leaned forward. 'How do you know about this Anton?'

'Sarris told me just before I left to fly home. They keep an eye on the Gavalas family. I visited the harbourmaster down at Watchet. He told me ships do arrive from Portugal delivering cork. They take back wastepaper for recycling – there's a paper mill at Watchet. Then I ran into a roadblock.'

'What kind of a roadblock?'

'The harbourmaster. Got pretty indignant when I suggested maybe someone had slipped ashore without his knowledge. Pointed out his office overlooks the harbour.'

'You still think he came ashore illegally?'

'I phoned Jim Corcoran, Security Chief at London Airport. He checked all the passenger manifests – I'd hinted it might have something to do with drugs. No Anton Gavalas showed up. Maybe he flew in via somewhere like Manchester. Doubtful.'

'How could you know it was Anton?' Tweed pressed.

'Sarris showed me several photos of him.' Partridge looked surprised. 'Thought you'd be ahead of me there.'

'You remember how I used to be.' Tweed waved a dismissive hand. 'A stickler for precise facts. You've seen Anton, then? Here?'

'Riding across Exmoor. Doone Valley area. Using a monocular glass to study Barrymore's place, Quarme Manor. Then on to Dr Robson's bungalow. Same routine there. Later across country to Kearns' place. He knows where those three live.'

'And you know where this Anton is based?'

'No, dammit. And not for want of trying.'

'I'd like his description – unless you have one of those photos.'

'Sarris wouldn't release any.' He closed his eyes, sucked at his pipe. 'Late thirties. Hair black as sin. Small

154

moustache, same colour. Nose of a hawk – like Petros. About five feet six. Nasty piece of work would be my guess. First-rate horseman.'

'And how do you know that?' Tweed went on.

'Followed him. Saw him riding by chance when I was on the moor. Kept well out of sight but one day he caught me. A cunning type. I rode round a big crag and there he was – waiting for me. Asked in a sneering way why I was following him. He speaks perfect English. Sarris told me he'd spent time at a riding school while in Germany. Somewhere in Bavaria. Close to the main railway line between Munich and Lindau on Lake Konstanz – facing Switzerland.'

'What on earth would this Anton be doing prowling round Exmoor?'

'Obviously sent by Petros to locate the three men who took part in that commando raid on Siros. Petros is still seeking vengeance on the man who killed his sons, Stephen and Andreas, all those years ago.'

'And you're doing the same thing, in a way. Still trying to identify the murderer. It's folly, Sam . . .'

'It gives me an interest in my retirement.'

'But it must be costing you a fortune,' Tweed protested. 'Can you afford all this?'

Partridge grinned, sucked noisily at his pipe. 'If I just had my pension, no. That keeps myself and my wife comfortable. We're modest in our life style. You see, an uncle of mine left me a large legacy. Came out of the blue. That finances my hunt. I never could forget that unsolved murder at Antikhana. Haunted me, you might say . . .'

He stopped speaking. Paula had recrossed her legs. She reached down to stroke an itch above her ankle. The bracelet which had remained concealed under the cuff of her cream pleated blouse slid down her wrist. She glanced up. Partridge was gazing fixedly at her wrist, his expression frozen. He realized she was watching him and smiled, looked away.

'I'd forget the whole business, Sam,' Tweed advised.

'I really came to your room to give you this.' Partridge produced a sealed manila envelope from his breast pocket, handed it to Tweed. 'In case I don't wake up one morning that's for you. Inside is the address and key of a safety deposit box. Nearly opposite Harrods in London. Not to be opened while I'm still alive and kicking. Agreed?'

'If you insist . . .'

'I do.' He checked his pipe, which had gone out again, tucked it in a pocket and stood up. 'This time I really am off to bed. Sorry to intrude. But it's been good talking with you – like the old days at the Yard.'

'Just before you go, Sam.' Tweed held up the envelope. 'Give me some idea of what I'd find if I ever visited that safety deposit.' Partridge hesitated, Tweed pressed. 'We worked together once – with Homicide. I'm entitled to an answer.'

'I've been building up a dossier on those three men. All the details are in a notebook inside the safety deposit. I'd like to leave it there.'

'Fair enough . . .'

Pete Nield had been fingering his dark moustache, studying the ex-detective. Now he spoke, his index finger pointed to stress what he said.

'Mr Partridge. On the ridge behind Quarme Manor you said you had used the telescopic sight on your rifle to look at Tweed – which is how you identified him. You also said your rifle was unloaded. Then you told us about following this Anton Gavalas over the moor. Was the Greek armed?'

Partridge turned to face Nield and frowned. 'Yes. He carried a rifle in a scabbard. I saw it clearly through my telescopic sight . . .'

'And your rifle was loaded then – because you felt the Greek was dangerous?'

'As a matter of fact, yes . . .'

156

'Are you still telling me that the rifle you aimed at Tweed was unloaded – knowing you might bump into that Greek again riding the moor?'

'I had the safety catch on.' Partridge paused. 'But you are right. It was loaded. I just thought it embarrassing to let Tweed know . . .'

'It's all right, Sam,' Tweed intervened. 'It's been a long day for you. Better get off to bed now. See you in the morning.'

'Goodnight everyone.'

On this note Partridge left the room. Nield followed him and locked the door. Returning to his chair he sat down and poured fresh coffee which he handed round.

'He's a nice man,' Paula remarked. 'I think he's under great stress.'

'He's also a liar,' Nield told her quietly. 'He lied about his rifle being unloaded when he aimed it at Tweed. Who knows what might have happened if you hadn't flashed your torch, distracted him?'

'Surely you can't suspect Partridge?' Paula said with a note of disbelief.

Nield grinned at her. 'I suspect everyone. Guilty until proven innocent. That's why Tweed employs me. And don't forget by his own admission he was in Cairo when Ionides – Stephen Gavalas – was slashed to pieces.'

'If he was involved he'd never have admitted that,' she objected.

'He's clever enough to know Tweed would find out sooner or later. Maybe he's under stress because *we* have arrived on the scene.'

'I will say that was smart of you to dig out the fact his rifle was loaded.'

'Simple logic. He could have carried night glasses if he just wanted to see what was going on. But no, he has a rifle.'

Paula turned to look at Tweed who had listened to this exchange in silence. He sat with his head rested against the

157

wall, eyes half-closed, miles away. She leaned forward, patted his hand. His eyes snapped fully open.

'A penny for your thoughts. A pound if you push me. And you look worried.'

'I am. About Sam. He's a man with an obsession. The most dangerous state of mind for a detective – or a spy. Fogs the judgement. That's not all.'

'So, tell me . . .'

'All this business about a Greek vendetta. I don't like that one little bit. That old hawk, Petros – he could have brainwashed his whole family into thinking they have one mission in life. To locate and revenge themselves on the man who did kill Andreas and Stephen – *if* it was the same man. And if Sam is right, Petros has harnessed the second generation to his obsession. Hence the arrival of Anton on Exmoor. I sense the kind of man Petros is. He reeks of ferocity and blood.'

'You don't normally use such melodramatic language,' Paula remarked.

'This isn't a normal situation. Not by a long shot. Literally. Someone did take a pot shot at me in the Mercedes a few hours ago. If we're not careful there could be more killings . . .'

'Which reminds me,' Nield suggested. 'In the morning I'll take the Merc to a garage in Minehead, get those windows replaced. I'll tell the mechanic it must have been a wild shot by someone out for sport on the moor.'

'There's a couple of other things, Tweed,' Paula continued. 'I wonder if you noticed Partridge's expression when my bracelet slipped from under my cuff? He stared at the Greek key symbol like a man transfixed.'

'Probably looking at your legs,' Nield joked. 'Enough to transfix any full-blooded male . . .'

'Oh, shut up! The other thing was when we met those three men. Barrymore, Kearns and Robson – all with dark suntans.'

'I did notice,' Tweed agreed. 'And they went to some length to explain where they'd been. Even Barrymore, who wasn't exactly voluble. Interesting that all three said they'd been away to places difficult to check – Morocco and the Caribbean . . .'

'Which, as I said earlier, means one of them could have just returned from Greece where Harry Masterson died.'

'Exactly. And the timing of their absence coincides with when Masterson was killed. Pure speculation, of course.'

'But odd that they should all be away at the same time,' she persisted.

'Now you're reaching,' Nield intervened. 'The month of May – the time when people who are free to go on holiday do. They avoid the crowds.'

'And that's not all,' said Tweed.

'It's enough for me tonight.' Paula stifled a yawn. 'But do tell me what else there is.'

'When we can I want to check Sam's story about Anton Gavalas.'

'How on earth are we going to do that?' she asked, standing up and clearing the coffee cups, arranging them neatly on a tray.

'When we can we visit Watchet. *I* ask the harbourmaster. Was there a ship which berthed from Portugal? *I* carry more clout than Sam, who is now retired. Did he see a man answering the description of Anton coming ashore?'

'Sleep well.' Paula bent down, kissed him on the cheek. 'Forget everything.'

'I'll try.' Tweed smiled grimly. 'I'm expecting developments. Maybe rather unpleasant ones.'

15

The following morning Paula was walking down the old oak staircase when Nield caught up with her. Both had breakfasted with Tweed. Paula had gone to her room to fetch her outdoor clothes, leaving Tweed to linger over his coffee in the dining room.

'I'm off to Minehead to fix the Mercedes,' Nield told her. 'You look thoughtful.'

'It's Tweed. He's worried. He enquired for Partridge before we had breakfast. The manager told him Partridge had early breakfast and had gone off to the stables. He's going to ride over Exmoor again. Tweed wishes he'd leave it alone – or cooperate with us.'

'Independent chap, our Mr Partridge. And, like Tweed said, he's obsessed with a forty-year-old murder. You can't reason with an obsession.'

'I suppose you're right . . .'

She half-opened the door to the dining room, then stopped, paused, and closed it again quietly. Checking the belt of her raincoat, she glanced up at Nield from under her thick eyebrows.

'She doesn't waste much time. I thought she was a manhunter.'

'Who?'

'You'll never guess who's sitting at Tweed's table. Jill, Kearns' ravishing blonde wife. She asked Tweed where he was staying just before we left Woodside House.'

'Tweed will handle her, maybe extract some information.'

'You could be right.' She hesitated. 'Do you mind if I come with you to Minehead, Pete? I can leave a note for Tweed.'

'I'd welcome the company . . .'

Tweed had been sitting quietly, sipping his coffee, sorting out in his mind what he had learned, when Jill Kearns walked into the dining room. Slipping off her suede gloves and her camelhair coat, she'd perched in the chair opposite him.

'I hope I'm not too early for you. Stuart – my husband – went off riding on the moor so it seemed an ideal opportunity to pop over and see you.'

She wore a tight-fitting powder-blue sweater which showed off her well-rounded breasts and had a polo-necked collar. Using both elegant hands she threw her shoulder-length hair over her shoulders, inserted a cigarette in the ivory holder, pausing before she lit it.

'Do you mind? My smoking while you breakfast?'

'Not at all. I'm only drinking coffee.'

'And there's no one else about, so it's an ideal chance for us to get to know each other better.'

'As you say . . .'

Tweed smiled to encourage her. She had excellent bone structure, a well-shaped nose, a full-lipped mouth painted with bright red lipstick. Her eyes were a startling blue beneath blonde arched eyebrows. She radiated animation and he guessed her age at something over thirty. About half Kearns' age. And very sexy.

'Let me tell you something about myself,' she began in the soft, husky voice he remembered well from the previous evening. 'My father was a squadron leader with the RAF in the Mid-East during the war. Stayed on afterwards as an adviser to the Egyptian Government. I was actually born in Cairo.' She cocked her head on one side, staring straight at him. 'Is this all a frightful bore? It must be . . .'

'On the contrary, I'm always interested in the background of a beautiful woman.' She inclined her head, smiled impishly as she acknowledged the compliment. 'Please go on.'

'My mother was Clementine Hamilton. Born in Dublin . . .'

'That name rings a bell.' He waited.

'My brother, David Hamilton, is a Member of Parliament. I was born late. My mother was forty.'

'Was? You mean . . .'

'Both my mother and father are dead. A car crash. They were in a pile-up on the M25 . . .' She hurried on as Tweed began to say something. 'It's all right. It was quite a few years ago. Then I married Stuart – or he married me might be more accurate. His first wife died in a swimming accident. You'll have noticed the difference in age between my husband and myself. I found the younger men callow, quite boring. I didn't know Stuart at all well. He's very handsome – but looks aren't everything.'

'I suppose not,' Tweed commented cautiously.

She reached across the table with her right hand and placed it over his. Her hand was warm, the fingers supple as they entwined Tweed's.

'I need an ally, a confidant, someone I can trust . . .'

'I'm afraid I might not fit the role,' he began.

'Someone right outside this tight social circle on Exmoor. Wait,' she urged as he opened his mouth. 'Please, let me finish. I am becoming frightened. Something is wrong. Help me. Please.'

She released his hand but her eyes held his. Blue? More like *lapis lazuli*. For a moment Tweed was aware of himself standing mentally away from the table, observing his own reactions. The woman was getting to him, exercising all her charm, exerting an almost hypnotic effect.

He drank more coffee, gazed at the base of the inside of the cup. His brain began to tick over again. He chose his words carefully.

'What are you frightened of?'

'The atmosphere. As though something awful is about to happen.' She stubbed her cigarette, fitted a fresh one into the holder, lit it with a gold Dunhill lighter. Tweed reached across to the next table, put a clean cup and saucer in front of her, poured coffee from the pot. She said, 'No, thank you,' when he offered cream and drank half the cup of steaming black coffee. 'Thank you, Tweed. I needed that.' He sensed they were already on intimate terms as he asked the question.

'I'm afraid I don't understand yet – what atmosphere?'

'The moor, for one thing. Being shut up in Woodside at night – cut off from the world by high walls. Like being in prison. My only companion, Wolf, my dog.'

'And for another thing, Mrs Kearns?'

'Jill. Please call me Jill. Then there are Stuart's strange friends. Dr Robson and that Colonel Barrymore. Do you know they were in the same Army unit all those years ago? Now they *still* seem to be in the unit. They meet twice every week. Once here for dinner. On Saturdays. Then for lunch at The Royal Oak in Winsford each Wednesday.'

'Today is Wednesday . . .'

'I know. Which is why Stuart won't be back until late this afternoon at the earliest. So I'm safe. Driving over here in the hope of seeing you. And, Tweed . . .' She leaned close to him and he caught the faintest whiff of perfume. Something expensive. His mind felt dazed. 'They'll all be at The Royal Oak,' she went on in her soft, soothing voice. 'And the weird thing is the colonel – Barrymore – still acts as though he's in command of them. He's creepy. The way he looks at my legs sometimes. I know what he's thinking.'

'Listen to me,' Tweed began briskly. 'Nothing you've

said so far explains why you think something awful – that was the word you used – is going to happen.'

'They've all become so guarded – they seem to have closed ranks against some terrible force they fear is coming. Stuart has those dangerous mantraps concealed all round the house . . .'

'Mantraps?'

'Oh, yes.' She held the holder by the tip and waved it with an elegant gesture. 'He says they're to keep out vermin. I don't believe a word of it. The high walls would do that. Those gates are always kept closed. Stuart stays up half the night, pacing in his study. I can hear him as I lie awake. Now, do you see why I need a friend, an ally?'

'Why choose me? You have your brother David . . .'

'We're not close. He's very busy. I once tried to talk with him and he said it was all imaginings – that I should have married a younger man. We had a bit of a row after that.'

'I still say why me?'

'You're Special Branch.' She paused, her lips parted in a warm smile. 'It's more than that. The moment I saw you I felt that I could trust you. Are you going to turn me down flat?'

'I didn't say that. Can't you get away from Exmoor for a while? Spend a little time with a friend. Say in London?'

'Stuart wouldn't stand for it. He *expects* me to stay at Woodside. I'm his wife . . .'

'So talk to him about it – as you have to me . . .'

She shook her head. Her mass of blonde hair swirled in waves. Tweed wondered what it would be like to run his hand through that jungle of blondeness . . . His mouth tightened. Madness. *I want you to remember one thing, Tweed. Never get mixed up with any woman connected with a case you're working on. That is the road to certain disaster.* His mentor when he'd first joined the Yard.

164

'I can't,' she said vehemently. 'He's closed up inside himself. He always was too self-contained. I realized that after we were married. Too late. Can I come to you if things get worse?'

'If I'm still in Somerset. Why are these three men living so close together? Your husband, Robson and Barrymore.'

'Robson is a doctor. He came out of the Army at the end of the war. They kept in touch. When Stuart and Barrymore retired from the Service Robson helped them find homes. I didn't know any of this until after I was married. I never did like such a peculiar set-up. I'd better go now.'

Tweed stood up promptly, checked his watch. 'Actually, I have an appointment. I can't promise you anything . . .'

She slipped on her coat, left it open, stretching her breasts as she threw back her golden hair over the collar. Walking quickly round the table, she hugged him with both arms, pressed her body close to his and kissed him.

'It's early days for you and me,' she said.

Then she was gone.

The phone was ringing when Tweed returned to his room. He ran, knowing the ringing would stop as he reached for the receiver. He lifted it, said 'Hello.' The manager answered, said there was a call for him.

'That you, Tweed?'

Partridge's voice. Sounded as though he'd been hurrying before he used the phone.

'Yes, Sam.' A click, which told him the manager had put down his instrument. 'I think it's all right to speak now. Where are you?'

'Winsford. You take the road out of Dunster where you met me on horseback. Continue on until you come to a signpost on the right. I'll meet you at The Royal Oak Inn for lunch. 12.30 suit you?'

'I'll be there. Stay off the moor, Sam. We'll cooperate. I can tell you something about Masterson . . .'

'Really?' Still sounded in a rush. 'One thing you should know.' Antikhana. You know where that is? What happened there a long time ago?'

'I'm with you.' Partridge was exercising caution, not trusting the phone. 'Go on . . .'

'I didn't like the look of Selim, the Sudanese on duty the evening it happened. Humble had questioned him. Superficially. I put him through the wringer. He was hiding something. No doubt about it. Selim vanished shortly afterwards. I think someone used a carrot and stick. The carrot, money. The stick, fear. Never seen again. Rumoured he'd gone back to Khartoum. My bet is he ended up floating down the Nile. Must go now . . .'

'Stay off the moor,' Tweed repeated.

'See you for lunch . . .'

The connection was broken. Tweed replaced the receiver slowly. He felt very unhappy about the call. Hands clasped behind his back, he paced the large room. Later he went out into the garden for some fresh air. He stood on a neat lawn, looking at the old castle which perched above the small town at the other end of the High Street. Beyond the wall at the end of the garden green fields stretched away. An atmosphere of pure peace. And the last thing he was experiencing was peace of mind.

Tweed checked his watch again. Fifteen minutes to twelve. He had studied his map of Exmoor, obtained from a newsagent down the High Street. He calculated thirty minutes would be ample time to drive to Winsford. He would give Paula and Nield until noon to get back from Minehead; if they didn't arrive he would leave a note and drive there alone. Someone tapped softly on his door.

'We were quick,' Paula told him as she entered the room followed by Nield. 'Both windows have been replaced.'

'That *was* quick.'

'I found a Mercedes dealer,' Nield explained. 'With a garage next door. I tipped them well before they started. Four men worked on the job. We're off to Watchet now?'

'No. Something came up . . .'

'She certainly did,' Paula commented, teasing him. 'You've come into close combat with the enemy, I see.'

She reached for Tweed's right shoulder, took something between her fingers off his blue bird's-eye suit and held it up. A long blonde hair. 'Good job we didn't get back earlier.'

'Sit,' Tweed commanded. He was irked by his careless-ness. He'd wiped his mouth clean of Jill Kearns' lipstick. He should have checked more thoroughly in the mirror. 'I have a lot to tell – and not much time to tell it. We have to be in Winsford to meet Partridge at 12.30 . . .'

He repeated a concise account of his encounter with Jill Kearns; he had total recall for conversations. Paula and Nield sat and listened while he then went on and told them about the telephone call from Partridge.

'And now you're up to date,' he concluded.

'She doesn't waste much time,' Paula remarked, then clapped her hand to her mouth. 'Sorry, that was pretty catty. She sounds like a very frightened woman. But fright-ened of what exactly?'

'Or a first-rate actress,' Tweed pointed out. 'Sent by Kearns to probe me, find out what I'm really up to.'

'My own thought,' Nield interjected. 'And why should we assume it was Kearns who sent her? If she's having an affair with one of the other two – Barrymore or Robson?'

'You are a couple of cynics,' Paula observed.

'Pete could be right,' Tweed said. 'Someone may have sent her on a fishing expedition.'

'But what was your real impression?' Paula demanded, leaning forward, staring hard at Tweed.

'Not enough data yet. I'm in a neutral zone. And it's time we set off for Winsford. Same procedure, Pete. Paula comes with me in the Merc. You follow in the Cortina. When we get to The Royal Oak, sit at a separate table. You're not with us. Let's move . . .'

'It's Wednesday,' Paula said suddenly. 'That's the day those three – Barrymore, etc., have lunch at The Royal Oak.'

'And that had occurred to me when Partridge suggested meeting me there. No coincidence I'm sure. Sam knows what he's doing. So, when we arrive we don't recognize him unless he comes up to us. It's his game. Let him play it his way.'

Tweed had taken the right-hand turn off the main road to Dulverton, following the signpost to Winsford. The day was overcast and chilly, the winding road ahead deserted. Paula sat beside Tweed, gazing at the huge brown sweeping ridges of Exmoor towering in the distance.

'Look,' she said, 'it's coming back.'

Tweed glanced to his right. Along the high edge of the ridges a wave curled like a surf-crested sea. The mist crept down, blotting out the upper slopes of the moor, advancing remorselessly. Paula shivered. There was something sinister the way the grey vapour swallowed up the moor.

'I hope to God Partridge has reached Winsford,' Tweed remarked. 'Imagine getting lost in that stuff.'

'You would get lost then?'

'Well, it depends. I guess by now he knows Exmoor pretty well. The amount of time he seems to have spent roaming over it. He probably knows which gulches lead down into Winsford. I just don't like the idea of him being up there at all. Let's hope we find him at The Royal Oak, sitting with a pint in front of him. Then I'll feel better.'

Astride his horse Partridge spotted the first wraiths of mist higher up, wraiths which merged into a solid wave of grey as it rolled towards him. Time to head down for Winsford. Turning his horse, he was about to ride down a gully which would take him on to the main road when he saw the second horse.

It stood riderless, reins draped, head down as it nuzzled tufts of grass. The rider lay sprawled on the ground, face down, his head resting on a boulder. His riding cap was askew, tilted no doubt when the animal had thrown him. Or had he been taken ill, fallen from the horse, his head striking the iron-hard boulder?

Partridge gave a quick glance at the mist which was close now. Dismounting, he strode towards the stricken man. It would be the devil of a job getting him down to Winsford. He'd have to try and fold the unconscious man over his own horse. If he was still alive . . .

The thought made him hurry. At the very least he could have cracked his skull – hitting that boulder. Granite. The hardest of rocks. The mist was floating over the sprawled figure when he reached it. The dampness felt cold on his face. He stood astride the figure, stooped to examine it further . . .

You bloody fool! Suddenly Partridge's instinct for danger flared. *Reins draped* . . . No one falling from a horse had time to do that. He was straightening up when the figure came to life. Mist swirled round Partridge's head as hands like a vice gripped his ankles, toppled him face down. He fell heavily, was winded. He ignored the shock. Started to lift himself on his elbows, to whip over and over. He was seconds too late. He felt a dull ache under his left shoulder blade as the knife was driven home. Then he plunged into a bottomless pit of darkness.

'What a lovely-looking place,' said Paula.

They were approaching The Royal Oak after driving past several thatched cottages. The ancient inn had a steep brown thatched roof. The thatch curved round arched windows close to the inn's sign, a painting of an oak tree. Several cars were parked outside.

Winsford was a sprawling village located at a point where several roads met. It nestled snugly below hilly green fields and as they entered the place Paula saw stately evergreen trees shaped like pepperpots. An oasis of civilization amid the grim unseen moor which loomed behind the mist.

'We'll go inside, get a bite to eat,' Tweed said as he parked the car. In his wing mirror he saw Nield's Cortina arrive and stop on the other side of a small green.

Outside, The Royal Oak was freshly painted, its walls a beige colour. Must have stood there for hundreds of years, Tweed thought as he locked the car and walked with Paula. She pulled up her raincoat collar: there was a chill in the air.

Inside, the large, low-ceilinged room stretched away into separate sections with wide openings leading from one to another. The bar was crowded and behind it a giant of a man in an open-necked shirt served drinks and joked with his customers. Mostly locals, Tweed guessed. A log fire crackled and there was an air of animation.

'Where do they all come from?' Paula whispered.

'I expect they ride or drive in from miles around. You've seen some of the lonely places people live in this part of the world.'

'No sign of Partridge,' she whispered again.

'He'll be along. He's a punctual chap . . .'

She gripped his arm. 'Someone else has arrived.'

Kearns strode in as though on parade. Clad in riding gear – pale grey jodhpurs thrust into boots which gleamed, a drab windcheater – he waved his riding crop at the barman. 'What is it today?'

'Hello, sir. Good to see you again. How about a nice chicken and mushroom pie? And your usual double Scotch?'

'That'll do . . .'

'Here's your drink. I'll send over the food. We've kept your table.'

Paula gribbed Tweed's arm again. 'The clan is gathering.'

Oliver Robson, also dressed in riding gear, but scruffily dressed compared with the CSM, appeared, smiling, exchanging words with several people. The barman spotted him at once, called out again over the heads of the crowd.

'Good morning, Doctor. Don't think you got that tan on the moor. Not this year. Nice to see you back . . .'

He repeated the menu and Robson nodded amiably, said he'd have a glass of white wine. His manner was tentative, Paula was thinking. Like a man who was shy. He took the glass and sat down next to Kearns who sat upright, looking everywhere except in the direction of Tweed and Paula. The two men were sitting at a window table where a third chair remained empty.

'Grab that table,' Tweed advised. 'You're hungry?'

'The chicken and mushroom pie smells good,' she replied as a serving woman passed them with a tray. 'And a glass of the white wine. The third member of the club is joining them . . .'

She sat down at a small round table for two after draping her raincoat over the other chair. Barrymore, also wearing riding gear, had stalked in, his manner stiff. The barman greeted him as 'Colonel' and Barrymore nodded when offered food. He took the chair between Kearns and Robson without saying anything and stared around. Like the chairman of the bloody board, Paula thought.

171

Tweed eased his way to the bar, gave his orders, waited while the wine was poured. Something made him glance over his shoulder. Barrymore had moved quickly. He was standing over Paula, a hand on her shoulder as he spoke. Paula gazed up at him, her expression cold, distant.

Turning back to the bar, Tweed paid the bill. Picking up the two glasses he edged his way out of the crowd in time to see Barrymore sitting down again at his own table. Paula's flawless complexion was slightly flushed. He sensed annoyance.

'You have an admirer,' he teased as he seated himself.

'Saucy swine. He had the nerve to invite me over to Quarme Manor. For afternoon tea, and maybe a drink, he said.'

'I'm sure you coped . . .'

'I told him he could phone me at The Luttrell Arms sometime. They serve tea there.' She paused, drank some wine. 'If you think I might get something out of him I'm quite happy to play along.'

'No! On no account are you to be alone with that man. On the other hand, if he does call you at Dunster, take your own decision. But only meet him in a public place. He's still staring at you.'

'I know. Staring at my legs. I was right. He reminds me of a satyr. And Pete is doing his stuff.'

Nield had perched himself on a stool close to the table where the three men sat. He was drinking a half pint of beer, gazing across the room.

'He identified them quickly,' Paula remarked.

'I gave him a verbal description of them. He has sharp hearing. Even with all this babble going on he'll be able to tell us what they were talking about.' Tweed checked his watch. 'Partridge is late. Very out of character.'

'The mist may have delayed him . . .'

'Not like him, not like him at all.'

They had finished their chicken and mushroom pies,

172

eaten some of the inn's excellent French bread, when the commotion started outside. Voices raised, the sound of running feet. Someone shouting. Tweed stood up.

'Back in a minute. I'll just see what's going on . . .'

'You look grim.' She spoke softly. The babble inside the pub was suddenly hushed. People stared out of the windows. Tweed slipped into the street, throwing on his coat as he walked. He paused to get his bearings. Beyond the small green was parked a Land Rover. A police car, its blue light whirling, was close to it. Uniformed policemen were gently pushing back the gathering crowd. Tweed took his card from his pocket, walked across the green. The grass was soggy underfoot. A uniformed inspector held up his hand.

'Please keep back, sir.'

Tweed, his eyes on the long sheath of folded canvas in the back of the Land Rover, showed the card. The inspector, a short and burly man, took the card, stared at it, compared the photograph with its owner, handed it back.

'Special Branch? We don't see much of you in this part of the world. I'm Inspector Farthing.'

'I may be able to help. What is inside that canvas bundle?'

'Something rather shocking. Brought down from the moor by the chap over there with the corduroy cap. A local, Lock. Goes shooting rabbits on the moor. He found the body inside a rock cleft. Pure luck. Rabbit he'd just shot fell inside the cleft. Nothing in the way of identification. No wallet. No letters.'

'Can I have a look?'

'Of course. I hope you have a strong stomach, sir . . .'

Tweed was moving to the back of the Land Rover when Paula joined him. He warned her it might be unpleasant. She bridled.

'Goes with the territory. Don't treat me like a five-year-old.'

173

'It's all right,' Tweed assured Farthing who had laid a hand on Paula's arm. 'She's my assistant.'

He heard a retching sound. Lock, the driver, was stooped over a ditch. Nimbly, Tweed leapt up on to the rear of the vehicle open to the sky. Paula followed. Tweed bent down, folded back one end of the canvas. What remained of the face of Partridge stared up at him, eyes open, sightless. He had been savagely slashed many times with a knife. Folds and slivers of flesh hung in flaps. The nose and eyebrows had almost completely disappeared. The clothes as much as anything identified him for Tweed. Paula sucked in her breath. Plunging both hands inside her windcheater, she clenched them into fists.

'I know this man, can identify him,' Tweed said, folding the canvas gently over the brutally ravaged face. He kept his voice low. Farthing crouched to hear him. The crowd of sightseers was still pushing close to the Land Rover. 'Sam Partridge,' Tweed said. He paused. 'A retired Chief Inspector of Homicide at Scotland Yard.'

'Thank God you were here.' Farthing grunted. 'You don't want to see, but all his fingers are missing. Cut off at the base. I'd say they're at the bottom of some other crevice. And all makers' labels have been ripped off the clothes.'

'Someone took trouble in the hope he wouldn't be found quickly – and by the time he was identification wouldn't be easy.'

Farthing breathed heavily. 'Then this case is going to raise one hell of a stink.'

'I'm sure of it. Can I make a suggestion? People rushed out of The Royal Oak to gawk. But three men are still sitting inside at a window table. Colonel Barrymore, Dr Robson and Stuart Kearns. Send a man in to ask them to come out and look at the corpse . . .'

'Study the reactions of each man,' Tweed whispered to Paula when they had moved to the rear of the crowd.

174

Kearns came out first, strode briskly to the vehicle, climbed into it. Farthing pulled back the canvas, exposed the hideously mutilated face. Kearns stood erect as he gazed down. No trace of emotion showed as he shook his head. 'Never seen him before,' he informed Farthing, jumped down and walked back to the inn.

Robson arrived next and Farthing greeted him more effusively. 'I am glad you were here, Doctor. You're the first medical man to see the victim. He's dead, of course. Do you know him?'

'Let's check before we make assumptions,' Robson replied in a relaxed voice. Tweed could just catch what he said. Robson stooped over the body, felt the pulse at the side of the neck, then nodded. 'He's dead. No doubt about that.'

'An ambulance has been summoned,' Farthing explained. 'But you have given us valuable assistance before. Any idea of the timing of his demise?'

'I could only guess.' Robson frowned. 'Something odd – you see the small amount of blood? Yet the face has been savaged. He was dead before the murderer did that.' His tone was dry and professional as he pulled open the windcheater at the top. 'I suppose you realize the head has almost been severed from the body? Look at that.'

Bile rose in Farthing's mouth as he crouched on his haunches beside Robson. An enormous red gash ran just below the throat, continued out of sight. 'We ought to wait for the forensic team from Taunton before I explore further,' Robson reminded the inspector.

'On the other hand he'll have to be shifted into the ambulance when it arrives,' Farthing pointed out.

'Then we'll go a little further, see if I can find out how he died. Not from that vicious slash across the throat. Again – not enough blood. He was dead when that happened.'

Robson unfolded more canvas to the corpse's waist. Gently he turned the body on its side. The head lolled like

175

the broken neck of a doll. Robson pointed to the back of the windcheater, to a wide rip and crusted blood below the left shoulder blade.

'I would imagine that was the death thrust. He was attacked from behind. A knife was plunged deep upwards, penetrating the heart. That came first.'

He was replacing the body in its original position, folding the canvas back, when the distant sound of a siren came closer. The inspector glanced up. 'Ambulance almost here. Now, Doctor, how long ago?'

'As I said, I can only guess. The Taunton pathologist will be able to give a more accurate diagnosis. During the past two hours I would say. Now, I'd better leave this to you . . .'

He was walking back to The Royal Oak to wash his hands when Colonel Barrymore appeared, strolling towards the crowd, which parted to let him pass through. He levered himself aboard the Land Rover, thrust both hands in his pockets, stared down while Farthing again exposed the face. Ambulance men carrying a stretcher paused behind the vehicle. Tweed stared hard as Barrymore glanced at Partridge's face.

'Must be the work of a lunatic,' he commented sardonically. 'No, I've never seen him.'

Leaping down from the Land Rover, he strolled back to The Royal Oak, presumably to finish his lunch. 'Cold-blooded bastard,' Paula hissed.

'He will have seen a lot of war casualties,' Tweed reminded her.

As they loaded the pathetic canvas bundle aboard a stretcher and carried it to the ambulance Paula stared round. The crowd was dispersing; some heading for The Royal Oak before closing time, others trudging to their homes, while a few men and women stood, unsure what to do next now the show was over.

The quiet country village seemed to have taken on a

macabre atmosphere. She looked up towards the overcast sky, a threatening gloomy pall; towards the moor where the mist was slowly retreating, exposing the sweep of the grim brown ridges. Somewhere up there a frightful murder had taken place. She hated the moor now and turned to Tweed.

'What do we do next? Did you notice anything about the way those three men reacted to looking at poor Partridge?'

'I noticed the absence of something.'

'Don't start talking to me in riddles.' She played with the bracelet composed of Greek key symbols. 'The murder of Partridge is reminiscent of what we heard about that other horrific murder of the Greek in Cairo during the war.'

'Which reminds me of something I should tell Farthing . . .'

He caught up with the inspector who was just about to climb into his car. Farthing looked at him with an impatient expression.

'Bringing those three chaps out of The Royal Oak didn't get us far. What was all that about?'

'They're all locals. I thought they might have seen Partridge. But there's something else you ought to do. Have you a notebook? Good. Note this down.' He gave Partridge's description of Anton Gavalas, spelt his name. 'I should put out an all points for him. Partridge told me he saw him riding all over Exmoor. And there was one occasion when the Greek confronted him, accused Partridge of following him.'

'We'll check . . .' Farthing held a microphone from the radio car in his hand and studied the description he'd noted down.

'I'll be at The Luttrell Arms in Dunster if the CID man put in charge of the case from Taunton wants to talk with me.'

'Roger . . .'

Farthing was issuing an all points bulletin for Gavalas as Tweed and Paula walked back to the Mercedes. Nield strolled out of The Royal Oak towards the Cortina.

Tweed drove back at speed to Dunster, overtaking the ambulance, his expression grim. Paula glanced at him, laid a gentle hand on his arm. He showed no emotion but she sensed he was concealing a feeling of deep shock.

'You're upset, aren't you?'

'I worked with Sam at the Yard once. He was a good friend and my mentor. I learned a lot from him. Facts, he used to say, concentrate on *facts*. Then the solution will come sooner or later. He was generous with professional advice. Not always the case. Now I have to hunt down the man – or men – who killed Sam and Harry Masterson. Whatever it takes.'

She was disturbed. She had never heard him express himself with such vehemence; almost as though he were prepared to throw away the rule book. 'I have a feeling this is important.' She dangled her bracelet. 'Harry wouldn't have sent this Greek key bracelet unless it pointed to something. I wish we knew what it means.'

It began to rain. Tweed turned on the windscreen wipers. The moor was lost in a veil of fine drizzle, disappearing like a monster retreating to its lair, Paula thought. A beastly day – in every way. Wet, chilly, a nightmare day. Tweed made the remark as they reached Dunster.

He turned into the High Street, the cobbled areas like sweating stones. No one about; people were huddled indoors. He swung the Mercedes into one of the parking spaces opposite the hotel.

'You could be right,' he muttered. 'Maybe the answer lies not here but in Greece. Let's hope Newman and Marler get lucky.'

PART TWO

Devil's Valley

𖼄𖼄𖼄

16

11 a.m. 104°F. 40°C. The heat scorched them like a burning glass. The cloudless sky above the ferry was a molten blue. Newman lifted his hand, wiped his forehead. He was dripping with sweat. His shirt was sodden. The car ferry bound for Siros edged away from its berth at Piraeus, turned slowly through ninety degrees, headed out into the gulf.

Newman stood at the bow of the vessel, elevated above the car deck and below the bridge. The ferry to Siros was small compared with the giant five-deckers which plied between Piraeus and Crete and Rhodes. Below the bridge and stretching to the stern, trucks and cars were parked three abreast, filling the ferry which was open to the sky.

Nick had had to back the Mercedes on to the ferry up the ramp so, like the other vehicles, he faced the ramp for ultimate disembarkation at Siros. Marler, wearing an open-necked shirt loose outside his khaki drill trousers, appeared alongside Newman and grinned.

'Enjoying the weather, old chap? A super day for the trip.'

'If you say so, and not so much of the old chap.'

'Just an expression, old boy. Don't mind me . . .'

'I won't.'

Marler, damn him, looked as cool as a cucumber. Resting his hands on the rail, Marler stared ahead at the millpond sea where the sun reflected like wavelets of mercury. Newman had earlier rested his own hands briefly on that rail. Very briefly. Like touching a red-hot iron.

'What's the object of our trip to Siros?' Marler enquired. 'That is, assuming I'm permitted to be put in the picture.'

'No need for sarcasm,' Newman growled.

'Irony, not sarcasm. Big difference. Why the change of plan at a moment's notice? Sort of thing Tweed would do. We were going to check out Cape Sounion where Harry Masterson took his dive.'

'You have such a subtle turn of phrase, Marler. The enemy – whoever they may be – would expect us to follow Masterson's trail. Instead we're going to Siros – where over forty years ago a man called Gavalas was murdered during a commando raid. I want to see the place where it happened.'

'You think there's a link with Masterson's death?'

'Tweed said it was a possibility. And that commando raid came up in conversation when Harry visited that chap at the MOD.'

'And how on earth are we going to find the spot where Gavalas was killed on Siros?'

'Nick. He knows the island well, has friends there. But we'll have to watch ourselves every step of the way . . .'

'Which is why, I suppose, you had Nick kit us up?'

'That's why,' Newman agreed. He tilted his wide-brimmed straw hat to shield his eyes. Marler, who seemed impervious to the torrid heat, was hatless, his fair hair gleaming in the sunlight. 'Watch it,' Newman warned, 'Nick's coming.'

'It's very hot,' Nick complained as he hauled himself up the companionway leading from the car deck and stood mopping his neck with a large handkerchief which was already limp with moisture. 'You can get a drink inside. The only way to avoid dehydration. I came up for a breath of air. There isn't any.'

'Join us,' Newman suggested.

'No.' Nick shook his head. 'I'll get a bottle of orange juice, take it back. I'd better stay with the Merc. You know why . . .'

Ten minutes later Newman stood alone on the bow deck, a fresh bottle of orange juice in his hand. Four more unopened bottles stood on a nearby seat. He'd have drunk gallons of the stuff by the time they reached Siros, two hours' sailing time away. *You know why . . .* He recalled Nick's words.

It was Newman's idea that they travel to Siros armed. He had not forgotten the bullet fired at them at the port of Zea. And Siros, he suspected, was a sensitive area for someone. He felt confident they had slipped the leash by boarding the ferry at the last moment, but he was not a man to take unnecessary chances.

Hence the guns and ammo Nick had obtained from God knew where. A sniperscope rifle for Marler, one of Europe's top marksmen; a Lee Enfield .303 rifle for himself; a Smith & Wesson .38 revolver for Nick. And all concealed, carefully taped to the underside of the chassis of the Mercedes. Which was why Nick was staying down on the car deck. To keep an eye on the car and its hidden cargo.

An hour later the ferry was moving at speed across the surface of the incredible sapphire blue of the Mediterranean. It almost hurt Newman's eyes to stare at it as he maintained his vigil, thinking, planning his moves when they landed. Over to the port side he made out the tip of Cape Sounion where Masterson had died. He raised the field glasses looped round his neck and focused them.

Perched at its summit the near-intact temple of Poseidon, guardian of the sea, came up in the lenses. A vision of perfection. Newman sighed, dropped the glasses, looked ahead. He'd liked Masterson.

Passing the Cape, the ferry headed south-east direct for the Cyclades group of islands. Siros was the closest of the group but was still out of sight. Peace, perfect peace, Newman thought as the ferry ploughed on through a shimmering heat haze. Probably their tour of Siros would also be peaceful, quite uneventful.

Deep in the heart of Devil's Valley, not twenty miles north of Cape Sounion, Petros Gavalas sat on the veranda of his headquarters farm. He had just put down the telephone. A summer hum of insects drifting above the grass was the only sound.

The farm was huddled under a looming limestone crag, almost hidden from the air, nestled in a wide defile between scrub-studded hills rising like cliffs. Shifting in his cane seat, Petros yelled his instruction hoarsely in Greek.

'Dimitrios! Christina! Get out here fast. And tell Constantine to be ready to take off in the helicopter. Come on! You should be here now, damn you!'

He waited until his two grandchildren stood before him. Christina, clad in tight-fitting denims and a flowered blouse, looked down at him, took a cigarette out of her mouth and ran a hand through her long dark hair.

'Was that Anton?' she enquired anxiously. 'He is on his way back from England?'

'No. And Anton can look after himself. He has a job to do. So have both of you.'

He studied the thin-faced Dimitrios, who often acted as his driver. Forty-four years old, he had Petros' dark eyes, his cruel mouth. With more training, another five years, Dimitrios might become as ruthless as Petros himself, although the old man doubted it. He twisted his hawk-nosed profile, stared hard at Christina.

'That Englishman, Marler, you got information from. Did you sleep with him, you whore?'

'Of course not,' she lied smoothly, refusing to lose her temper with the old bastard. God, she thought, he's still living in 1947. The world has changed since then. But he'll never know it. Petros leaned towards her, reached out a

184

gnarled hand to grasp her arm, to twist it. She was too quick for him: she stepped out of his reach.

'I told you once. That's enough,' she snapped. 'What job? Who phoned you?'

'Pavlos – from Piraeus.' Petros slumped in his chair with disgust. 'He had trouble getting through on the phone. Nothing works in this country any more. Since the colonels went . . .'

'Don't start that again,' she rapped back. 'What has happened?'

'Oh, nothing much.' He made a sarcastic gesture with his hands. 'Just that the two English – Newman and your Marler – are at this moment aboard a ferry bound for Siros. The chopper will get you to Siros ahead of them. The ferry left Piraeus at eleven this morning and arrives soon after one o'clock. It is now noon – so move your leaden feet. Christina, you will stay out of sight. If Dimitrios decides, you can meet your Marler and lure him into a trap.'

'He is not my Marler. You have said that twice. Say it a third time and I will not go . . .'

'You try to disobey me?' Petros heaved himself out of the chair, clenched his fist and moved towards her. 'I will beat you until you cannot move . . .'

'No more!' she shouted back. From the sheath attached to her belt she whipped out a long-bladed knife and waved it in front of her. 'Come one step nearer and I'll cut you open . . .'

Petros stood stunned. He couldn't believe what was happening. A woman was threatening him. Aware that Dimitrios was watching him closely, that he must not lose face to a mere female, he changed tactics. Slapping his thigh, he raised his large head, roared with laughter, then gestured at Dimitrios.

'You see! She is a true Gavalas. A real spitfire, my little Christina.' He turned back to her. 'Use that knife to cut

185

open this Marler and I will buy you a beautiful dress from Kolonaki. Now, off you go! You are armed, Dimitrios?'

'Constantine has loaded shotguns and rifles aboard the chopper. He guessed it was an emergency . . .'

'Then what are you waiting for? If those two English go near where my son, Andreas, was killed in the war – you kill them.'

He stopped speaking as the sound of a helicopter's rotors starting up drowned all further conversation. He sank back into his chair as Dimitrios and Christina ran off round the side of the house. *Stephen and Andreas, vengeance for your deaths will be mine*, he said to himself. He felt great satisfaction.

He had four descendants – Dimitrios, Constantine, Christina and Anton. He believed all shared his obsession that the killers must be dealt with. He had dinned the idea into them since childhood and worried only about Christina. Women should not think – only obey.

Petros looked around the front of the farm while he waited to see the machine take off for Siros. It was a large building. The veranda ran thirty feet along the front. The once-white walls were grey with dirt. In places they sagged, were held up by huge beams of wood which served as props. Many tiles on the roof were broken. Petros never spent money on repairs unless he simply had to.

This meanness had helped make him rich. Money in the bank. That was *power*. And he owned a second farm way up north in Macedonia. A farm which boasted many scores of head of cattle. They provided the milk the tourists loved. And for making the cheese the tourists staying at the great hotels also loved. Goat's milk, which Petros preferred, was not liked by the visitors bloated with money.

The Sikorsky was airborne, flew along the front of the farm as it gained height. The pilot, Constantine, waved. Petros waved back. They would do the job. And the sight of the Sikorsky made him feel good. War surplus bought by another farmer at a knock-down price.

Petros had coveted the Sikorsky. One night during a heatwave summer he had led his grandsons to the farmer's fields. They had used flaming torches to set fire to his crops. He had been ruined. Only then had Petros approached him with an offer for the Sikorsky – an offer which would not have bought a second-hand car. Desperate for money, the farmer had sold him the machine. I'm a good business-man, Petros told himself. Now I wait, see what happens on Siros.

Aboard the ferry Nick sat behind the wheel of the Mercedes and started up his engine. They were coming in to Siros, the ramp would soon be lowered. Newman stood on the bow deck as the ferry began turning slowly through a half-circle, ready to berth stern first. Alongside him stood Marler, lighting one of his king-size cigarettes.

'Pretty-looking place,' he drawled.

Newman was carefully scanning the waterfront with his glasses, searching for any sign of a reception committee. The island was mountainous, one limestone giant rearing in the distance. Mount Ida, he assumed. The lower slopes were arid, studded with more scrub.

He blinked. The small port of Siros was crammed with stark white-walled two-storey houses. Huddled together and piled up the hill, they glared beneath the burning sun. The shallow-sloped red-tiled rooftops were stepped up the incline. He followed the route of several narrow walled roads which appeared to zigzag upwards. A rabbit warren.

The harbour was sickle-shaped, enclosed by two curving jetties. Inside the entrance a small fleet of fishing vessels and motorized caïques were moored. Along one jetty wall the golden strands of scores of fishing nets hung drying. The tavernas and shops lining the waterfront had a sleepy look.

'It's a working port,' Newman remarked, lowering his glasses. 'Not many tourists find their way here would be my guess. And I still wonder about that chopper which flew over us earlier.'

'Could have landed anywhere,' Marler replied off-handedly. 'I think we'd better join Nick . . .'

There was a bump as the stern touched shore by a stone causeway. The ramp was lowered, vehicles began moving off as Newman ran down the companionway, then slowed his pace. It was like moving inside a red-hot oven.

'You take it easy in Greece, old boy,' Marler needled him, strolling down the steps.

'And you don't let on I speak Greek,' Newman warned. 'That way we may hear something interesting.'

'Sir!' As Newman looked over his shoulder Marler gave a mock salute.

Cocky bastard, Newman thought, then quenched his irritation. He had better watch himself in this inferno. Nick had driven the Mercedes off and was waiting on the waterfront. Small boys were dancing round the gleaming car, touching it and then jumping back as Nick shouted at them.

'Where to first?' Newman asked, climbing in beside Nick while Marler settled himself in a rear seat.

'To meet my friend, Spyros. I sent him a radio message from Athens. He lives high up here in Siros . . .'

The car was moving, turning away from the waterfront into one of the narrow side streets. Almost immediately the street was climbing, twisting round narrow corners over the paved surface. On both sides they were hemmed in by the clean whitewashed walls as they ascended the labyrinth. Sweat started pouring down Newman's back. The tunnel-like streets, the blinding glare off the white walls – every-

188

thing intensified the hellish heat despite the fact that Nick had opened all the windows.

'Where is everyone?' Newman asked. 'We haven't seen a soul.'

'Indoors. Resting,' Nick replied. 'Even for Siros today is very hot. It helps. If we see someone out we must wonder why. Who they are. Did you see that old Sikorsky with the blurred markings which flew over the ferry?'

'What about it?' Newman asked, glancing at Marler, who looked damnably cool and relaxed as he lolled in his seat.

'A woman passenger wearing dark glasses and a scarf over her hair was checking the ferry through binoculars. I think she was trying to find someone. Maybe us?'

'Cross that bridge when we come to it,' Marler responded.

'This is a good place to stop,' Nick went on. 'Then I can get the guns from under the car . . .'

He had reached a tortuous turn and pulled up half-way round so they had a view both down and up the street which was still deserted. Sliding under the car, he was less than a minute before he handed Marler his sniperscope rifle, followed by Newman's weapon. Scrambling out from under the car, he glanced round as he dumped a hip holster with his revolver on the front passenger seat.

'It's all right,' Newman assured him, 'we watched both up and down the street while you were under the car.'

Nick strapped on the holster while Marler raised his rifle and peered through the sniperscope at a fisherman walking slowly along a jetty far below. Nick slipped on a lightweight linen jacket he kept slung from a hook behind the driving seat. He left it open and grinned at Newman.

'It will be hot wearing this – but it conceals what I carry. You hide your rifles under that travelling rug rolled up on the floor in the back.'

'And now?' Newman asked.

'We meet Spyros who is waiting at the top. He will take us to Mount Ida — to the place where the Greek was murdered during the war . . .'

'They have disappeared,' said Dimitrios. 'One moment the Mercedes is driving up towards us, then it vanishes. What kind of a trick is this?'

'They're probably parked at the corner of the road down there. Where it turns a sharp bend. That church dome hides it from us,' concluded Christina.

She sounded thoroughly rebellious. She shook her dark mane, exasperated with her cousins' slave-like obedience to Petros.

Constantine shrugged his shoulders, irked by her attitude. This was not women's work. Like Dimitrios he was thin and bony and he sported a moustache which curved round the ends of his slit of a mouth. He looked after his moustache proudly: it had made him a big hit with the girls, really rolled them over. On their backs.

They were perched on the roughcast terrace of a house overlooking the port of Siros. Through his binoculars Dimitrios had observed Newman, Marler and Nick coming ashore from the ferry. It was Christina who had earlier confirmed they were aboard when Constantine had overflown the ferry.

The house belonged to Petros and was empty. Today was Wednesday. On each Monday a local woman came to clean up the place. Parked in front of the house was a battered Cadillac, paint peeling from its bodywork. Petros had bought it for a song from a man in need of money. The weapons transported aboard the helicopter were stowed inside the Cadillac. Shrubs sprouting blood-red flowers decorated the terrace in large Ali Baba pots. Christina put on her dark glasses, lit a cigarette.

'You won't need to use the guns,' she told them.

'We use them if they go near Mount Ida,' Constantine snapped at her. 'You remember what Petros ordered?'

'Ordered! You are like a couple of puppets he dangles at the end of a string. Harm the Englishmen and everything goes wrong. The police will hunt you down. Sarris himself might come. He only waits for his chance to put you all inside for ever. Then what happens to me? If necessary I will handle Marler, lead him and the others away from where it happened . . .'

Constantine grinned unpleasantly, made an obscene gesture. 'Ah! You and Marler. Petros was right. You will do as we tell you to do . . .'

His left hand gripped her arm. He froze. Her free hand had whipped out the knife from the sheath attached to her belt. He felt its point tickle his throat. Her black eyes blazed with fury.

'Let me go or I'll rip your throat open. God knows how many women you have had, you fornicator . . .'

He released her, stepped back carefully. The fear was written large on his face as she followed him and his back pressed into the terrace wall. It was only as high as his hips and there was a long drop to the paved street below. She rested the point of the knife against his breast bone. He breathed heavily. She was strong; if she pushed the knife a couple of inches more . . .

'You will never use that filthy gesture in front of me again,' she told him. 'You will not use the guns. We will find some other way of diverting them. You understand?'

'Yes, Christina. For God's sake . . .'

She sheathed the knife suddenly, turned away. Her expression was contemptuous. As she had always suspected Constantine was a coward. Dimitrios, careful not to interfere – he had previous experience of Christina's temper – stood staring through his binoculars. He lowered them quickly.

'You were right,' he told her. 'They had hidden behind

191

that corner. Why? Could they have spotted us? Impossible. They are driving this way. We must leave in the Cadillac quickly before they arrive, drive up towards Ida and see what they do next . . .'

Nick turned yet another sharp-angled bend in the zigzag road which went up and up. Newman glanced out of the window on his side. Nick was a superb driver: he had missed scraping the wall of a house by inches. They were very high up now and Newman caught glimpses of the sea which was an incredible mixture of brilliant colours – sapphire, turquoise, *lapis lazuli*. No picture postcard had ever captured this. The car slowed and stopped.

'Spyros,' said Nick.

An old hunchback, clad in peasant clothes and with a face like a wrinkled walnut under his wide-brimmed straw hat, sat perched outside a house. He was whittling a piece of wood with a knife. He stood up, adjusted the angle of his hat, opened the rear door of the car and joined Marler.

Nick drove on as he made introductions. 'Spyros. Sitting next to you is Marler. My other friend is Bob Newman.'

'I am pleased to meet both of you,' Spyros replied in English and with quaint old-world courtesy. 'You take the next fork to the right when we leave Siros port and climb the mountain.'

He opened the cloth he had used to wrap the piece of wood and the knife and continued whittling, careful to keep the pieces carved off on the cloth. Marler stared at the wood. It was beginning to take the shape of a madonna. Spyros kept glancing up as he worked, checking their position.

They emerged from the labyrinth of the port of Siros suddenly. Ahead the road was no longer paved. A track of white dust, it snaked up the mountain which rose sheer above them. Before long they were driving along a ledge just wide enough to take the Mercedes. On Nick's side rose a sheer wall of limestone. Newman peered out on his side and the mountain fell away into a deep precipice. Far below a grove of olive trees spread their stunted branches. Beyond the grove the sea spread into the distance, ink blue.

'You're sure the Merc can get all the way?' Newman enquired in what he hoped was a casual tone.

'Spyros would not have let us come if it was not possible.'

'Good for Spyros . . .'

Newman glanced down again and began to feel the symptoms of vertigo. He averted his gaze, forced himself to concentrate on the track ahead spiralling up and round the mountain. At several points there were tracks leading off through gulches in the mountain. Newman would have given anything to tell Nick to turn into one of the gulches – away from the hideous precipice which was growing deeper and deeper. Had the old Greek sensed his fear? Still whittling at the wood, he said suddenly, 'We are very close now. The country will open out. We shall leave the abyss.'

'And then?' Newman prodded.

'We shall be at the place where Andreas Gavalas died over forty years ago.'

The Cadillac, driven by Dimitrios, had taken the other route on the far side of the mountain. Hidden inside a copse of olive trees, they had seen Nick heading up the seaward road.

'They are going where they shouldn't,' Dimitrios said. 'So, we get there first and wait for them . . .'

He had driven like a madman up the curving road with Constantine beside him, a rifle and shotgun resting in his lap. In the back of the car Christina sat tense and silent.

To her left the ground sloped away steeply but not precipitously. In the distance she could see the white-walled houses of Siros port – looking like a child's model.

'We turn here,' Dimitrios said and swung off the road inside a deep-walled gulch which snaked between lofty heights of limestone. The wheels bumped over rocks, shaking the vehicle.

'Why?' demanded Christina.

'We are now ahead of them,' Dimitrios condescended to explain. 'We will check to see they are going all the way. Then, if they are, we turn round here and go on up the mountain. There is a place where we can look down on them, see what they do.'

He had stopped at a point where the track widened and turned the Cadillac so it faced the way they had come. He had concealed the car out of sight of the gap at the end of the gulch. Daylight showed and way beyond it the intense blue of the sea.

'A place where you can look down on them?' Christina queried. 'You are taking your guns with you? Why?' Her hand clawed at Dimitrios' shirt collar as he was alighting. 'What are you planning to do?'

'You heard what Petros ordered. To shoot them if necessary. Now let go, you treacherous cat. At the end is the other road. We shall see their car pass if they have come this far.'

As Spyros had predicted, they had left the abyss behind. Ahead, below the sheer wall of the mountain, an area of flat scrubland stretched before them. Nick stopped the car, Newman stepped out, stretched and took another swig from the plastic bottle of mineral water. They had six unopened bottles: dehydration, as Nick was never tired of warning, was the greatest danger. Newman grimaced after drinking, replaced the cap. The liquid was tepid, tasteless.

The plateau of arid scrubland projected out from the mountain wall, then sloped steeply downwards. A wide deep parched gully led its winding way towards the distant sea. Its surface was cluttered with limestone boulders and pebbles. In winter, Newman guessed, it would be a gushing torrent. Now it was bone dry.

'Where?' asked Marler in his direct way.

Spyros pointed to the gully with his knife. The rocky gulch lay about two hundred yards away. Shielding his eyes, Marler gazed up at the towering mountain above them.

'What in Hades is that?'

Newman stared up. At the summit of Mount Ida, clinging to the edge of the rock, was perched a huddle of ancient buildings. Built of solid stone, one shallow-roofed building was hanging above another, perched at different levels and all joined in one complex.

'The monastery of Mount Ida,' Spyros told them. 'From there you see all over the island. During the war the German general, Hugo Geiger, established a lookout unit. He respected the monks. He said someone should live in peace in this frightful war.'

'Where?' Marler repeated again. 'Where exactly did this Andreas Gavalas die?'

'Inside the gully.' Spyros pointed the knife. 'I will show you the place . . .'

'Not yet.' Marler placed a hand on the old man's shoulder as he began to walk out into the open. 'Everyone back inside the car,' Marler continued, reaching inside for his rifle. He pocketed the sniperscope sight, picked up several spare magazines. 'Go on, get in quick,' he ordered. 'The lot of you.'

'May I ask why?' Newman enquired.

'You may. A mile or so back coming up the mountain I glanced down one of those side tracks leading into a gulch. I saw movement, a man watching. He dodged back out of sight. Before you venture into the open I'm going up there.'

He looked up the mountain which was fractured with deep fissures, some wide enough to allow passage for one man. Newman sucked in his breath at the prospect, thinking of the vertigo.

'You stay in the back, Bob,' Marler instructed. 'On this side of the car. Keep an eye on me. When I wave my rifle you can go into the open. Only then.'

He looped the rifle over his shoulder, wriggled his feet in his rubber-soled calf-skinned shoes to test their ankle support. 'If I'd known I'd have brought climbing boots. Can't be helped. I'll cope.'

'Watch it – for God's sake,' Newman warned.

'And I never knew you cared . . .'

Typical of Marler to mock just before he was attempting a climb fraught with risk, Newman thought. They settled in the car and Newman peered up. Marler was already a good twenty feet up a narrow fissure, finding a foothold on one side, then on the other.

17

'We climb up here. It looks straight down on the place,' said Dimitrios as he switched off the engine.

He had turned off the mountain road, backing the Cadillac into a cul-de-sac. Christina peered through the rear window. At the end of the cul-de-sac a wide defile led upwards between rocky walls. A primitive staircase carved out of the rock led out of sight.

'What is this? Where does it lead to?' she demanded.

'The monks made it ages ago.' Dimitrios grinned as

he gripped his rifle, opened the door and slipped out. Constantine joined him with his shotgun. Dimitrios thrust his head in through the rear window. 'Christina, you wait here. We're going up to a high point which overlooks the place. You hear shots, we will be back soon after. Then we drive back.'

'I told you, Dimitrios . . .'

They were gone, climbing the rough-hewn steps rapidly, Dimitrios in the lead. They disappeared round a corner. She climbed out of the car, left the door open, ran back on to the mountain road. From the view ahead she knew roughly where she was. She began running, jogging at a steady trot up the road.

She wore a lightweight jump suit and trainer shoes. As she ran she hauled her dark glasses out of her pocket, perched them on her nose. The stupid cold-blooded bastards. They liked their work: Petros had trained them well. They were true grandsons of the sadistic old ruffian.

Ten minutes later she was still running uphill, pacing herself. She was close to where the mountain ended, where the ground became flat, spreading out towards the sea on the other side of Ida. Pray God she got there in time . . .

Dimitrios crouched down, settled himself in the nest between massive boulders. He perched his rifle in the cleft of a rock, looked along the sight. Three men were alighting from the Mercedes parked at the edge of the plateau. Beside him Constantine aimed his shotgun.

They were positioned seventy feet above the three men. Both of the Greeks were excellent shots. The place Dimitrios had chosen was a meditation point used by the monks. High above them reared the overhanging monastery. Dimitrios glanced up once, then down again. He was satisfied no one looking down from the summit of Mount Ida would ever see them. An overhang of rock almost completely obscured the view from that height. The over-hang was two hundred feet above where they waited.

'Let them get well out into the open,' Dimitrios warned his brother. 'Then there is nowhere to hide. We can pick them off one by one.'

'Which shall I aim for?' Constantine asked.

'You don't. Leave it to me. If one dashes back for the car, he's your dead meat for today. Any minute now . . .'

'Andreas was found lying dead somewhere near the top of that gully,' Spyros explained.

Newman led the way, avoiding the numerous sharp rocks which littered the ground, often almost hidden by scrub grass. The heat beat down on the back of his neck. He tied a handkerchief round it as he walked. It was very still and silent at this height. No screech of gulls. A stillness which was uncanny – and unsettling. He was the first one to hear the sound of running feet approaching.

Breathing heavily, Christina appeared round the side of the mountain, saw them, increased her pace until she reached them. Holding his rifle loosely in his right hand, Newman stopped and waited, suspicious. What the hell was such an attractive girl doing up here in the wilderness? He didn't like questions to which he had no answer. Nick stepped forward.

'This is Christina Gavalas,' he informed Newman.

'Introduce me. Who is he? Quickly!' Christina demanded.

She was panting from her exertions, her breasts heaving under the jump suit. Newman was careful to keep his eyes on hers. They glowed with life. And she was the enemy.

'Robert Newman,' Nick replied. 'The foreign correspondent . . .'

'And where is Marler?' Christina asked anxiously.

'Oh, he's gone to deal with a call of nature,' Newman told her easily. 'What are you doing up . . .'

'You are in great danger. There are men up the mountain with guns . . .'

She broke off as a man appeared from the direction she had come. At least six feet tall, he was clothed in a black robe and wore a black cylindrical hat. A priest. Member of the Greek Orthodox Church, Newman realized. His face was lined with age but he was erect, his movements brisk. He spoke in English.

'Welcome to Mount Ida. You wish to see the monastery? I fear the lady cannot enter.'

Newman took a quick decision. The priest, he estimated, was in his late seventies. Had probably spent all his life in this part of the world. Including the period of German wartime occupation.

'We are looking for the place where – over forty years ago – a Greek citizen called Andreas Gavalas died.'

'Was murdered,' the priest corrected him gravely, stroking his black beard. 'I was here when it happened.'

'You mean you saw what actually took place?' Newman concealed his excitement. 'You know who killed Andreas?'

'Damn that priest. He will have to take his chance.' Dimitrios carefully aimed his rifle at Newman's chest. 'Bull's-eye,' he gloated.

Constantine knocked the rifle barrel upwards. By some miracle Dimitrios avoided pulling the trigger. He glared furiously at his brother. 'Cretin! Why did you do that? Do it again and I will break your arm . . .'

'There is a priest down there,' Constantine protested.

'So? Since when did you go religious? Petros is an atheist – he brought us up to regard the whole Church as a swindle on the people. What does one less priest matter?'

'And Christina is down there. Are you mad? If your aim is bad you could hit *her* . . .'

'Since when was my aim bad?' He glanced down. 'Now look what you've done. They have started walking towards the gully – the place Petros said they must not reach.'

'The problem is solved then. Forget it.'

'No, I will not forget it.' Dimitrios grinned evilly, hoisted his rifle and tapped Constantine's jaw gently with the heavy butt. 'Interfere again and you'll need a new jaw. You understand? No distractions this time. A moving target? Bull's-eye. Again . . .'

He repositioned the rifle, rested it firmly in a cleft in the rock, thrust the butt firmly against his shoulder, lined up the sight, took the first pressure. One final squeeze . . .

The bullet slammed into the rock less than an inch from the hand on the trigger. A rock splinter cut Dimitrios' cheekbone. His rifle jerked up. This time it fired. The shot winged into the sky. A second bullet slammed into the rock between the two brothers crouched less than half a foot from each other. The third bullet struck Constantine's shotgun. He let go, yelled. The weapon dropped out of sight over the brink. They were scrambling out of the nest when a fresh bullet nicked the heel of Dimitrios' shoe. He jumped with sheer fright.

A hundred feet above them, perched on a ledge protruding from the mountain wall, Marler reloaded. He aimed down in seconds, pulled the trigger. The fifth bullet ripped a shard of cloth from Dimitrios' right shoulder. Before he followed Constantine, who was scrambling back towards the staircase, he risked a glance upwards.

He saw Marler on the ledge and beneath the huge overhang of rock. Constantine looked back, saw the few seconds when his brother was glancing up.

'Come on!' he yelled. 'He missed five times. He'll kill you with his next shot . . .'

'Stupid cretin!' Dimitrios yelled back as he also began to run. 'He aimed to miss . . .' Dimitrios was enough of a marksman to recognize shooting superior to his own. Feeling safe as he ran out of sight of the ledge, he jumped with fright again as a fusillade of bullets peppered the rock walls on all sides, showering him with sharp splinters. How could this be?

'Shoot the bastards!' Christina urged Newman viciously.

Newman was standing, legs braced apart, rifle aimed up at the mountain as he continued shooting at the fleeing figures still in view from below. Christina, eyes blazing, stared up at Marler, now edging his way back along the ledge – at her hated cousins disappearing from sight down the staircase. Newman smiled, lowered his rifle, reloaded.

'You're one lousy shot,' she informed him, her hand pressed into her hip.

'You think so?' He smiled again. 'I aimed to miss – just as Marler did. There's been enough killing. And we don't want to start up a fresh vendetta with your lovely family.'

'Blessed be the merciful,' said the priest.

'I don't know about that, Father.' Newman grinned again. 'I might agree – so long as the merciful are alive. Which isn't often the case if you read history. Now, where was Andreas Gavalas murdered? And what did you see?'

The priest led them to the gully wending its way down to the sea. Near the top, where tufts of bleached grass stood at the edge of the dried-up watercourse, he pointed. A smooth-sided cleft large enough to hide a man. This had been Andreas' temporary grave. The priest, taking a 'walk of solitude', had discovered the body by accident.

The hilt of a knife had protruded from beneath the left

shoulder blade and the man was dead. Hurrying back towards the monastery for help, the priest had met several monks who had accompanied him back to the cleft. The body had vanished.

The priest had reported the incident to General Geiger, the German commander-in-chief. Geiger had checked with the only patrol in the vicinity. Later he had told the priest he was satisfied his men had no knowledge of what had happened.

'Then who took away the body?' Newman asked. 'And did you see the British raiding party approaching up the gully after landing from the sea?'

'Yes. I saw them from the monastery. Perhaps that is why my steps led me this way. Presumptuous curiosity. Not a virtue.'

'How many men in the raiding party?' Newman persisted.

'Four. I watched them through field glasses before starting on my walk down here.'

'Four Greeks, you mean?' Newman asked casually.

'No. Three British soldiers and one man dressed in peasant garb. I presume that was Andreas Gavalas who knew the island. I knew they were British because they wore green camouflage raincoats.'

'Surely they would have been seen by that German lookout unit I heard was established in the monastery?' Newman suggested. 'If you saw them coming, the Germans must have done?'

'The British were clever – and lucky. They landed when a thick winter sea mist was covering this area. When I saw them through my field glasses the mist had parted for a short time. At that moment the watchguard unit was being replaced by new men coming on duty.'

'And have you ever heard a whisper as to who might have removed Andreas' body?'

The priest pulled at his beard, his eyes avoided

Newman's. 'It is a mystery,' he eventually replied. 'And now I must return if you will excuse me.'

'The whole business is peculiar,' Newman responded.

He stared round the scrub-covered platform. Very little cover for a raiding party which must have relied on the mist to reach the shelter of the mountain. Doubtless Andreas had known ways of penetrating the fastness. Marler was walking towards them at a jaunty pace, rifle propped over his shoulder, as Newman stared once again upwards. What a life – confined most of your days inside that fortress-like complex perched half-way to the sky. A large bird, probably an eagle, drifted off a tongue of rock and circled them high up.

'Can you take me back to Athens in that car?' Christina asked Newman. 'My cousins drove me up here in an old Cadillac. I have been abandoned.'

'All the way to Athens?' Newman queried in surprise.

'I'm not going back to the Devil's Valley – to where Petros is waiting to beat hell out of me. I've finished with that life.' She moved closer to him, her eyes enormous. 'I will pay for my passage. The last ferry leaves in two hours. You will take me? Please.'

'And how will you pay me?' Newman enquired ironically, expecting a certain answer. She had lowered her voice so only he could hear her.

'With information. About Harry Masterson.'

'You just bought yourself a one-way ticket.'

Marler arrived, brushed dirt off his jacket, grinned at Christina. 'You get around, little lady.'

She walked slowly up to him, a half-smile on her face. 'We met earlier, you may recall . . .'

'How could I forget?' He smiled sardonically.

'I do not forget either. I have something for you, Marler. A keepsake. Is that not the right word?'

She was still smiling when her right hand whipped up, palm open, and hit him with all her considerable force

203

across the face. The blow jerked his head sideways. She smiled again, watching the red weal which had appeared across his cheek.

'Now we are quits. Is that not the right phrase?' She turned to Newman. 'Now, I am ready when you are.'

The priest had lingered with Spyros a few yards away, as though reluctant to leave. His expression was a study in indecision. He seemed to make up his mind suddenly and walked to within a few feet of Newman. He took a deep breath before he uttered the words and then walked rapidly away towards the mountain.

'The disappearance of that body. There was something else on the island when it vanished. I suggest you look in that direction. I refer to the Greek Key.'

18

Nick drove the Mercedes back along the far side of the mountain, much to Newman's relief when he saw the ground beyond the brink sloped away gradually. It had been his idea to use this route after talking with Christina.

'Those two hard cases, Dimitrios and Constantine,' he pointed out to Marler before they started back, 'will travel in their Cadillac to Siros port. Then they'll ditch the car and fly back in their chopper. They landed on open ground just outside Siros according to Christina. They came here in that machine which overflew our ferry.'

'What's the plan?' Marler demanded.

'If we can catch up with that Cadillac I'd like a few words with them – and I guess you would. This time with our fists. Petros has to be discouraged from sending his jackals

204

after us. I don't want to spend the rest of our time in Greece looking over our shoulders. When we get back to Athens *I* want a quiet talk with Christina on her own. I'm sure she has more information.'

'Why not me? I've known the girl a bit longer . . .'

'Oh, yes!' Newman's tone was ironical. 'You got to know her so well she pasted you one.'

'It was the only way I could hope to get her to talk . . .'

'It was the only way *you* thought you could get her to talk – and she didn't.'

'It's just possible you could be right,' Marler admitted reluctantly. He felt his face. 'She's a beauty but she packs a rare punch . . .'

'Which you richly deserved. Let's get over to the car.'

'May I enquire what is the next object of the exercise with her?'

'Christina met Harry Masterson in London, probably pointed him to Exmoor and those three ex-commandos. Why? Only she can tell me. So, old boy,' Newman went on, mimicking Marler, 'I'd appreciate it if from now on you leave the beauty to me. And on the way back we'd better assume those two thugs may be waiting to ambush us.'

They arranged the seating to anticipate the worst. Marler, loaded rifle across his lap, sat in front next to Nick. In the rear they placed Newman, Christina – sitting in the middle – and Spyros occupied the other corner. The hunchback was apologetic as Nick drove away from the plateau, heading for the far side of the mountain.

'I was not a great help to you, Mr Newman. The priest told you everything.'

'Everything? Are you sure about that? Who took away Andreas' body? And what is the Greek Key?'

'Don't ask me that.' The hunchback shuddered, clasped his veined hands tightly. 'I know nothing about such things.'

205

'But I do.' Christina pressed her shoulder against Newman, turned and gazed at him. 'Maybe later, when we are alone, the two of us should talk.'

'I'd welcome that.' Newman stared back at her. 'You speak very good English.'

'That was my mother's doing. I was lucky enough to be well-educated. And sometimes I think that is why my cousins – and Petros – hate me. They are still men of the soil. They think like peasants, behave like them. My mother was left money by a distant relative. She banked it secretly. Petros was furious. One night she packed me off to Zurich. To a school. I found I was good at languages. As well as Greek I speak German and English. I took a law degree. Then I made a mistake.'

'Which was?'

'I came back for my mother's funeral. Petros insisted I must pay my respects by staying in Devil's Valley for a time. Like a fool I agreed. Time went by. They all made me think their way. Now I have had enough of them for two lifetimes. We will talk later.'

Spyros had produced something from under his floppy jacket. Newman heard a strange sound, glanced across Christina. Spyros was clicking a length of black worry beads. His expression was anxious. Newman looked out of the window. The view was spectacular: a vast panorama stretching all the way down across the island to the sickle-shaped harbour.

There was tension inside the car. As they approached each bend Marler leaned forward, gripping his rifle, alert for any sign of the Gavalas brothers. He had warned Nick to be ready for an emergency stop at any second. Nick kept wiping a hand dry, then grasping the wheel tightly, staring ahead while he crawled round the bends.

The worry beads stopped clicking. Newman remained quite still. Spyros leaned forward, staring in his direction. Newman went on gazing out of the window as the car continued its steep and tortuous descent. Now he could pick out individual boats berthed in Siros harbour.

'My cousin, Sarantis, is an archaeologist,' Spyros began. 'Is that the right word?'

'He goes on excavations – digging up ancient sites. A lot of them round the Plaka district in Athens,' Newman encouraged him.

'That is so. But Sarantis likes places where there are few of his kind. Like Cape Sounion. The Temple of Poseidon.'

'Sensible chap.' Newman forced himself to stay relaxed. 'So what about Sarantis?'

'He is very old. Like me. But he has a wonderful memory for faces. He was near Cape Sounion when the Englishman, Masterson, was thrown from the cliff not many weeks past.'

'He saw it happen?'

'No. But he did see the two men who went to the temple shortly before the killing.'

'*Two* men? You are sure? You did say he was very old,' Newman reminded him gently.

'Eighty years. He recognized Masterson from the pictures later in the papers – the man thrown from the cliff, he said.'

'And the second man,' Newman probed. 'He could describe him? How does he know Masterson was thrown off – if he didn't see it happen?'

'I think he did, but he felt it was dangerous to admit that. He has a good memory for faces,' Spyros repeated, in the manner of the old.

'He described this second man to you?' Newman enquired.

'No. But you could ask him. He would tell you. He likes the English. Treat him gently, please. He is frightened by what he saw at Cape Sounion.'

'You have his address in Athens?'

'Athens? He lives here on Siros. In a house near the top

207

of the port. We could see him before you take the ferry back to Athens.'

'Let's do that,' Newman agreed. 'Maybe we've stumbled on just what we've been seeking. By pure chance – coming to Siros. I have experienced that when I was a foreign correspondent,' he told Marler, who was watching him in the rear-view mirror. 'A stroke of luck when you least expect it. And it opens up a whole new picture – maybe leading all the way back to Exmoor.'

'Sounds just a shade too easy to me,' Marler commented, switching his gaze to the view beyond the windscreen.

Approaching the outskirts of the port, Nick spoke in Greek to Spyros who gabbled vehemently in reply. Newman was watching the view out of his window, apparently taking no interest in the conversation, his expression blank as he absorbed every word of what was being said. Spyros was having second thoughts about mentioning Sarantis; Nick was reassuring him.

Driving down a narrow paved street, closed in again by the glaring white walls of the stone houses, Nick swung off the street up a curving walled ramp. The house was isolated from the town, grey shutters masked the windows, the brilliant red front door was closed. Marler leapt out of the car, gripping his rifle, and poked his head in the rear window to speak to Spyros.

'Is there a rear way out of this place?' he asked urgently.

Newman noticed he had released the safety catch on his rifle. He was tense, quick-moving. Spyros looked up at him and gestured.

'Round the other side. There is a terrace leading to a door. A flight of steps runs down into the street.'

'What's the matter?' asked Newman as he also left the Mercedes holding his own rifle.

'Something not quite right here,' Marler said tersely.

208

'What makes you think that?'

'Sixth sense.' Marler spoke to Spyros again. 'This Sarantis. Does he live alone? Any wife, servants?'

'No. By himself. A woman comes in each day . . .'

'Will she be here now?'

Marler was firing the questions. Frequently he glanced at the closed shutters. He frowned as he glanced up at the flat roof. 'Any way to get up there?' he demanded before Spyros answered his first question. Nick, who had switched off the engine, had caught the atmosphere, stood near the front of the car, his right hand under his loose jacket, close to the revolver.

'The woman comes only in the mornings,' Spyros replied. 'And round that corner there is a flight of steps leading to the roof . . .'

'I'll take the roof,' Marler snapped. 'Bob, you take the rear door. Nick, wait by the front door here . . .'

'You wait in the car with Spyros,' Newman warned Christina and ran after Marler.

'The front door is ajar,' Newman warned Nick. 'Synchronize our watches. OK? Eighty seconds from now we both go in. Caution is the word . . .'

Newman ran round the side of the house. Marler was taking the steps to the roof two at a time. The terrace widened overlooking the deserted street. Siesta time. Probably all day. The heat burned his back. The grey shutters were closed over the windows at the back. Newman arrived at a door painted a bright blue.

This door was half-open. Somewhere out of sight further down the street a car started up, sped away. Could mean nothing. He checked his watch. Thirty seconds to go. He stood to one side of the doorway, listening. The sound of the car departing had vanished. A heavy heat-laden silence descended on the terrace. No sound of movement inside the single-storey house. He had the feeling the place was empty. So why were both doors open?

209

Ten seconds. He took a firm grasp on his rifle, held it at waist level. Raising his right foot he kicked the door wide open, darted inside, pressed his body against a wall.

A drop of at least twenty degrees. Positively cool compared with outside. He was inside a large L-shaped living room. A lot of soft furnishing: armchairs, couches. An arched fireplace took up most of the opposite wall. His eyes swivelled, getting accustomed to the dim light. A desk pushed up against the right-hand wall. Its surface littered with papers. He could hear Nick prowling round out of sight. His eyes were fixed on the desk area.

A chair was overturned. The body of an old man lay sprawled on the tiled floor. He lay very still on his back, his eyes staring at the roughcast ceiling. His right hand stretched out, clawed except for the index finger pointing towards Newman as though in a gesture of protest. Nick appeared, gun in hand, followed by Marler who moved with the silence of a cat.

'Anyone in the place?' Newman asked. Both shook their heads. 'Get Spyros. Warn him. I think we're too late . . .'

'Dead as a dodo,' Marler pronounced in a neutral tone.

He was crouched over the body, had checked the neck pulse. He remained crouched on his haunches, his forehead wrinkled as he looked round. Newman was standing gazing down at the old man. He pointed to a scrape mark on the tiles close to the desk.

'Difficult to say what happened,' he commented. 'That looks like the scrape of his shoe. He could have stood up, slipped, cracked the back of his skull. No, I don't think so. Look at his wrist. It's been broken . . .'

'Which could have happened when he slipped. This floor is very highly polished. Makes for accidents.'

'And he broke his arm as well?' queried Newman.

He could now see the arm was turned at an unnatural

angle – it was fractured close to the elbow. He looked up as Spyros entered, followed by Nick and Christina. Spyros walked slowly to the body and his voice quavered.

'Is he . . .'

'I'm afraid so,' Newman told him. 'He is dead. Who is it?'

'My old friend, Sarantis . . . my oldest friend . . .'

Tears ran down his weathered cheeks. Christina wrapped an arm round his shoulders, hugged him. Taking out a handkerchief she wiped his face, whispering to him in Greek. She led him to one of the couches where he sagged, then looked up at her.

'You are very kind – all of you,' he said in English. 'I will be all right now.'

'I'll take up guard on the roof,' Marler said crisply. 'Keep a lookout. I don't think we should linger here very long.'

Then he was gone. Christina disappeared briefly, returned with a glass of water. Spyros accepted it gratefully, gulped down the contents. Christina, her expression grim, walked over and stared at the body. Her voice was harsh.

'Another killing?' she demanded. 'They tried to make him talk?'

'Who?' Newman enquired, propping his rifle more securely inside an armchair.

'Dimitrios and Constantine, of course.'

'Why "of course"?'

'Because of this.' Stooping, she pulled out a handkerchief from under the body. It was brightly coloured with a diamond-shaped design. On a cream area it was discoloured with something dark reddish which looked like dried blood to Newman. 'Dimitrios has a handkerchief like this,' she said coldly. 'The rotten swine.'

'Is that the only handkerchief of that kind in Greece?' Newman asked.

'Well, no. You can buy them in the shops in Athens . . .'

211

'Then you can't be sure. Give it to me. Nothing must be disturbed.'

Newman tucked the handkerchief back under the body in the same position she had dragged it from. He checked his watch. Spyros sat very still, staring at Sarantis as though wishing to imprint on his mind this last memory of his friend. A great mistake, Newman thought: and made by so many people.

'They were here,' Christina insisted. 'How did he die?'

'Painfully,' Nick whispered so Spyros shouldn't hear. 'His wrist was broken, then his arm. The shock could have killed him . . .'

'You see!' Christina protested to Newman. 'Sarantis worked up on that platform where we were. They wanted to extract information from him, the brutes . . .'

'We don't know who "they" were,' Newman insisted. 'We don't even know there were two of them . . .'

'Yes we do,' she hissed. Nick nodded as she went on. 'Go in the kitchen. There are the remains of a quick meal – *two* plates on the table, two dirty knives, two pieces of half-eaten cheese and two hunks of bread. Two wine glasses . . .'

Marler appeared, rifle held in both hands. 'I really think we should get away from this place.'

'My own thought,' Newman agreed. He looked at Spyros. 'When I first arrived at the back door I heard a car disappearing towards the port. What time is the next ferry?'

Spyros checked his watch. 'An extra one left about one half hour ago. Today there are a lot of trucks bringing supplies to Siros. You can catch the last ferry for Athens if you leave now. About one half hour for you to drive to the ferry. Then about one quarter of an hour before it leaves.'

'Time for a quick snack at a taverna on the waterfront,' Marler said firmly. 'I'm famished.'

'We inform the police?' asked Christina.

212

'Not from Siros,' Newman replied. 'We get caught up in this and it could take days, even weeks. We might even be suspected. I don't want to move Sarantis – but we haven't seen the condition of the back of his skull. He could have been hit over the head.' He looked at Spyros. 'Do you think you could keep quiet until the police arrive on their own? Even then, you'd be better to stay out of the whole tragedy. For your own sake.'

'I prefer to mourn in silence . . .'

'Then we'll drop you off at your house. I don't think you'll be bothered. Only that priest knows we were on Siros. I doubt if the police will go all the way up to Mount Ida. Let's move . . .'

'And the police?' Christina persisted.

'I'll make an anonymous call to headquarters from Athens,' Newman replied vaguely. 'We have things to talk about – you and I – when we get back to the city.'

19

Room 318 at the Athens Hilton had a spectacular view from the balcony across the city. In the distance the Parthenon perched on the summit of the Acropolis was silhouetted against a clear evening sky. Her arms folded, Christina stood on the balcony alongside Newman.

'It is very beautiful,' she said, 'especially when you think of man's age-long struggle to become civilized. Two steps forward, one step backward. You know they're going to come looking for me,' she added quietly. 'My horrible family. Petros will see to that.'

'Which is why I brought you here instead of the Grande

213

Bretagne. And you registered under an assumed name.'

'They will still track me down. They will tour the hotels. A few drachmae will change hands. They have photos they can show a bellboy, a reception clerk.'

'When you arrived dressed so differently? Wearing those huge dark glasses and your hair concealed under a scarf.'

'Maybe you're right, Bob. I wish I could feel as carefree as those people by the pool.'

She looked down to where guests sprawled round the large swimming pool, the water a deep turquoise in the sunlight. Even with the air-conditioning going full blast the large double room behind them was heavy with heat. Newman watched her while she gazed at the pool.

On their return to Piraeus aboard the ferry, Nick had driven them to Kolonaki, the Mayfair and Park Avenue of Athens rolled into one. He had left Newman and Christina there while he took Marler back to the Grande Bretagne. Christina had bought herself several new outfits and nightwear because all her clothes were at Petros' farm. Newman had paid with traveller's cheques and she'd made him promise to accept payment from her.

'I can go to the bank in the morning,' she had insisted. 'My mother left me all the money left her by her relative. There was quite a large sum even after paying for my education . . .'

Newman had braced himself for an ordeal. A woman buying clothes would take forever. He found he was wrong. Christina was decisive, could look quickly at a dozen outfits in her size, pick out one immediately, try it on in minutes, then buy it. They came closer together during the shopping expedition. Newman was always consulted as to whether he liked what she'd chosen. Twice he shook his head and she looked for something else.

Now she was kitted out with one evening dress and an adequate wardrobe for daytime. When she changed out of her jump suit she gave it to him, he rolled it up, took it outside the hotel and rammed it inside a litter bin. They would be looking for her dressed in that.

'Are we having dinner together?' she asked as they stood on the balcony. 'Or is that too forward of me?'

'The nicest possible way to put it. I've been hoping you would join me. We'll try the Ta Nissia here.'

'Super!' Her eyes glowed. 'Now, you've appointed yourself my bodyguard. Can you read a magazine or something while I take a bath?'

'Take your time . . .'

He was sitting by the large picture window spanning the end of the room when someone tapped on the door. He walked rapidly and quietly to the door. Leaving it on the chain, he opened it and Marler waved a hand through the gap.

'Embarrassing moment?' he drawled. 'I can come back. Give you another hour with her?'

'Shut up and come in. She's taking a bath before we have dinner downstairs.'

'The balcony,' Marler said tersely.

He waited until they were outside, then slid the door closed and lit a cigarette. 'No sign of the enemy at the Grande Bretagne yet. And,' he forestalled Newman, 'I wasn't followed. Do you realize you may be walking into a lethal trap?'

'What the hell does that mean?'

'Strikes me you're getting pretty cosy with Christina. That's OK as far as I'm concerned . . .'

'Oh, how very kind,' Newman interrupted ironically. 'Nice to have the Marler *Good Housekeeping* seal of approval . . .'

'Let me finish. It could be a set-up – organized by Petros to lure you into a trap. All this stuff she's been handing out about hating them, that they'll come after her. Has she had a chance to use a phone since you left us?'

215

'As a matter of fact, no.' Newman held up a hand. 'And before you waste any more breath, did you really think the idea hadn't occurred to me? If it is a trap I'll be walking into it with my eyes wide open – to see where it leads. Tweed has used the tactic very successfully himself in the past.'

'Pardon me for being alive.' Marler gazed down at the illuminated swimming pool. 'Plenty of talent down there. Look at that brown beauty sprawled on the grass. And, while we're on the subject, I did as you suggested. Called in at the British Embassy and contacted Patterson. Bit of a drip, but after seeing my identification he let me call Tweed on scrambler. You have to call him back when you can. Sometime tonight. Remember we are two hours ahead of London.'

'That means my going to the Embassy . . .'

'It's on Sofias Avenue – a ten-minute walk along it from here.'

'I know that, too. The point is Christina must be guarded during my absence. You're elected.'

'We need to fix a time, then. There's a large hall outside this room with armchairs. I can sit there – but I need to know when to be here.'

'Be downstairs by the bank of lifts at ten forty-five. When you see me leave you come straight up . . .'

'Ten forty-five? My, we are looking forward to an athletic evening.'

Newman punched him hard on the arm. 'Just piss off, Marler – and before you go, you told Tweed about our trip to Siros?'

'Of course. He said it was as he'd thought before I called – that the solution to Masterson's death lies out here in Greece.' Marler held up a warning finger. 'Don't forget, the last Englishman who got pally with the glamorous Christina was Harry Masterson. And he ended up as a pancake at the foot of Cape Sounion.'

'Again, your subtle turn of phrase. I liked Harry. Now, Marler, just piss off . . .'

Petros sat in his cane chair on the veranda of the farmhouse in Devil's Valley. His shirt front was open, exposing the hair on his barrel-like chest. Across his lap rested a shot-gun. The sun had sunk behind the cliff-like wall of the mountainside to the west. The valley was dark with shadows like blue smoke.

His son and two grandsons stood outside the veranda, keeping their distance, showing their respect. Anton was the most confident. Still wearing his dark blue English business suit, he had loosened his tie and unbuttoned the collar at the neck.

Compared with his two nephews, Dimitrios and Constantine, who were clad in shabby peasant garb, Anton was small and dapper. He smoked a cigarette while he waited for Petros to speak – something the other two would not have dared do. Petros leaned forward.

'Anton is smart,' he began, his voice grating. 'He has just returned from England and the English don't even know he was there.'

'But Passport Control . . .' Dimitrios began.

'Tell me, tell these simple-minded cretins how you did it,' Petros suggested.

'It was easy. Just like that.' Anton snapped his fingers. 'An English gesture,' he lectured his nephews with a superior smile which infuriated them. 'You are right, Dimitrios. I was able to enter England without any check by Passport Control.' He paused. It amused him that he had fooled Petros, an old brigand – an illiterate who couldn't speak a word of English. Well-educated – at Petros' expense – he secretly despised his father. 'I think it would be unwise to reveal my route – it could be given away by Dimitrios in one of his drunken stupors.'

217

'Now, listen to me, all of you,' Petros growled. 'I taught you, since you were mere children, family honour demands that we revenge ourselves on the killers who dishonoured our family name. Your father, Dimitrios and Constantine, was Stephen, my son who was murdered in Egypt during the war. Christina's father, Andreas, was murdered on Siros. Not that she cares . . .'

'We know this,' Dimitrios muttered in a feeble show of defiance, but Petros heard him.

'Silence! Both of you are in disgrace. You blundered badly on Siros today. More of that later.' He sank back and the chair creaked. Hooding his eyes like a hawk, he spoke again.

'Anton. Tell us what you found in England. Make it brief.'

'There is a lonely area called Exmoor. Also a place like here called the Doone Valley. The three men who went with Andreas on a commando raid to Siros – Barrymore, Kearns and Robson – live close together on that moor. Which is strange. They are not related . . .'

'Tell them about the places where they live,' Petros prodded.

'Each house is well-defended. Like small castles expecting an invasion. One has television cameras watching all approaches. Another is guarded by a fierce dog called Wolf. The third has tall walls topped with barbed wire and a single separate wire. I was suspicious. I scaled a wall carrying a cat. I dropped the cat on the single wire. There was a flash. It screamed, died. Electrified. They are afraid – after all this time . . .'

'How did you find these three men?' asked Dimitrios.

'Christina went to England and used a newspaper advertisement which attracted the attention of a Harry Masterson . . .'

'That's enough,' Petros interrupted, eyes wide open. 'No need to give details. But which of the three is guilty, has our blood on his hands? Or were all three involved in both murders?'

'I don't know.' Anton made a resigned gesture with his manicured hands – hands which contrasted with the roughness of his nephews' who, Petros reflected, were poles apart. 'I made discreet enquiries in the pubs on Exmoor,' Anton continued. 'The three men meet twice every week – for lunch in one place, for dinner in another.' His manner changed, became more nervous as he talked more quickly. 'Then there was the strange incident of the murder of the Englishman, Partridge, on the moor.'

'Partridge, did you say?' asked Dimitrios, quick to sense Anton's change of mood. 'We know an Englishman of that name was poking round Athens, asking questions. That he later visited Siros.'

Anton looked at Petros before replying. The old patriarch nodded agreement for him to continue. 'It was the same man. There was an old picture of him in a newspaper reporting the murder. It is worrying – the report said he was a detective for most of his life with Scotland Yard. The Homicide Branch.'

'There was a man of that name in Cairo when Stephen was killed,' Petros reminded him. 'We found out later. He was one of the military detectives who supposedly investigated Stephen's death. Very young, he was. Is Partridge a common English name?'

'Not as far as I know,' Anton replied. He hurried on. 'That is why I returned here quickly. They were hunting for the killer.'

'And why should they think it was you?' demanded Dimitrios.

Anton hesitated again, looking at Petros. The old man frowned. It was a good question. 'Answer Dimitrios,' he ordered.

'I happened to be riding on a different part of the moor when he was killed,' Anton replied. 'Watching the homes of the three men who were the commandos.'

'I see.' Petros frowned and Anton shuffled his feet.

The old man turned on the two brothers, determined to humiliate them, to exert his authority. 'Now, tell us what a mess you made of things on Siros today. Describe in detail. Anton should know what fools his nephews can be . . .'

Petros sat staring into the distance while Dimitrios recalled the day's events. It was when he came to describe their visit to the home of Sarantis, the archaeologist, that he transferred his gaze to Dimitrios who seemed uncomfortable.

'Constantine,' he broke in suddenly, 'do you agree with all that Dimitrios has said?'

'Yes.' The more passive brother paused. 'We tried to make him talk, to tell us what he knew about where Andreas died. We broke his wrist, then his arm. The old fool slipped on the polished floor, fell over backwards and cracked his skull on the tiles.'

'Go on.'

'We decided to leave quickly aboard the chopper. We knew you would not want us to be tangled up with a police investigation . . .'

'So, you leave in the kitchen the cutlery and things you used to eat a quick meal. With your fingerprints on them, of course.'

'No, Petros! We wiped everything clean. Knives, the glasses. We would have put them away but we were afraid someone would arrive.'

'You ate when you first questioned him, then took him into the living room to apply more pressure?'

'That is how it happened.'

'I wonder whether to believe you.' He was silent for a moment. 'And these two Englishmen Christina reported on – Newman and Marler. You fouled that up as well. No information from Sarantis.' He raised his voice to a shout. 'Do I have to be everywhere to make sure you do the right thing? All of you, get out of my sight. No, wait!

Christina has disappeared. Last seen with those English.'
His tone was venomous. 'Tomorrow you go to Athens,
find her. Do not let her see you. Follow her and tell me
what she does, where she goes. Later I decide what to do
about her. Now, go! Prepare the meal. If you can do that
properly . . .'

Petros sat alone on the veranda, a grim smile of satisfaction
on his lined face. Frequently it was necessary to crack the
whip to remind his family who was the chief. He looked
up as Anton appeared and spoke, his voice low.
　'While I have been away, Papa, has anyone been seen
near the silver mine?'
　'No.' He smiled bleakly. 'You worry too much. Leave
me alone. I have to think.'
　Despite the mild rebuke, Petros approved: it showed
Anton was using his brain. At least one of the litter had
turned out well. Odd it should be his second wife's only
son. The wife who had died from overwork like the first –
driven on by Petros' insistence they run the farm. Early
in Anton's childhood Petros had realized he was the bright
one. How he had scrimped and saved to educate the
boy.
　While Dimitrios and Constantine had worked in the
fields, Anton had been sent to a select school near Berne
in Switzerland – away from the fleshpots of Athens. A
school where discipline was strong, where he had learned
to speak English and German.
　But Petros had taken the precaution of bringing him
home during the holidays for Petros' own kind of discipline.
He had hammered into the boy's head that his half-
brothers, Andreas and Stephen, had been murdered – that
the family must take their revenge. A cloud of poisonous
hatred hung over Devil's Valley.
　It had been a long struggle. First the Civil War from

221

1946 to 1949 between the Communists and the anti-Communists. Breaking out soon after World War Two had ended, it had gone on until the Communist guerrillas were defeated. So many wasted years.

Only recently had Petros been able to devote all his efforts to his vendetta. He had reached the stage where he was quite unable to realize it had become an obsession, filling his every waking moment. A stray thought crossed his mind. The Communists.

Why – after all these years – had the Russian, Oleg Savinkov, reappeared in Athens? He was one of the old school, a Stalinist. And the new man, Gorbachev, was a very different leader, they said. Savinkov, once called The Executioner, did not fit the new pattern Petros heard about in the cafés of the village he visited. To play checkers, to listen to the gossip. Above all to get the first hint of a farmer in trouble. Someone whose land or stock he might buy for a pittance.

Why had Savinkov changed his name to Florakis? The Russian did speak Greek fluently. And he had bought a small farm adjacent to Petros on the coast. But why had he made a point of meeting him when Petros was sitting alone in a café? The Russian had handed him an envelope crammed with drachmae. A large sum – so large Petros, greedy for money, had not accepted at once.

'What do you expect me to do for this?' he had asked bluntly.

'Only one thing – which fits in with your own purposes. You make sure no Englishmen visit the island of Siros and poke around up near Mount Ida.'

'You expect me to kill them?' Petros had demanded.

'It is up to you.' Savinkov had shrugged. 'Maybe you rough them up a bit. You could sabotage their car – the mountain roads are dangerous.'

'And how do I get in touch with you?' Petros had asked, testing Savinkov. 'Walk across to your farm?'

'Never. And you know me only as Florakis. That is why I am paying you . . .'

Since then Petros had kept the money inside the same envelope in his Athens bank. For Petros this was an act of unprecedented willpower. But one day he might wish to sever all connection with the man who had appeared like a ghost. Then he would throw the money back at him.

But why, he asked himself for the twentieth time, should Savinkov take an interest in the murder of Andreas all those years ago?

20

Inside a first-floor room above a taverna in the Plaka, the sole occupant, Oleg Savinkov, was also reflecting on the past. A wiry thin-faced man in his sixties, with blank grey eyes, he sat at a table in his shirt-sleeves and mopped beads of perspiration from his forehead.

The evening heat confined by the rabbit warren of narrow twisting streets was ferocious. He drank more mineral water; years ago he had stopped drinking any kind of alcohol. Years ago . . . In 1946 he had been a young man of twenty, known and feared in Greece as The Russian – or The Executioner. Sent to Greece by Stalin personally because of his talent – his talent for assassination.

1946. Stalin had agreed at Yalta that Greece should come within the British sphere of influence. But when the Greek Communist ELAS movement rose up in revolt and looked like taking over the strategic country – with its

223

potential great Russian naval base at Piraeus – Stalin quietly betrayed his promise.

Savinkov had been smuggled into Greece from Bulgaria. His mission had been brutally simple: to assassinate all the leaders of the Greek right-wing EDES movement fighting the Communists. He had succeeded – up to a point. Five top EDES leaders fell victims to his high-powered rifle. Hence his nicknames – The Russian and The Executioner.

But he had failed to take out the chief EDES leaders. Enough remained at the head of their troops to defeat the Communist uprising eventually. Savinkov had decided wisely not to return to Russia: Stalin demanded one hundred per cent success.

By this time Savinkov had learned Greek fluently and he merged with the landscape, working on a remote farm in Macedonia. The years passed and he seemed to have become the forgotten man. That was until he received discreet word from the Soviet Embassy that someone important wished to meet him.

The visit of General Lucharsky, a Deputy Chief of the Soviet General Staff, to Greece was never reported in the press. By 1986 Savinkov was settled in the Cape Sounion area, owning a small farm growing figs and olives. He had saved money, obtained from a small bank a mortgage to buy the property. He had applied for the loan in the name of Stavros Florakis. Over the years he had obtained sufficient forged papers to establish a new identity as a Greek citizen.

Here he had taken a risk. After some hesitation he had contacted one of the Communist ELAS leaders who had gone underground, the man with whose group he was working when the whole revolt fell apart. It was a greater risk than he realized since this benefactor kept a discreet and distant line of communication open with the Soviet Embassy in Athens. But this man had seen no reason to inform on Savinkov – his own relations with the Russians had been precarious. Until 1986 . . .

Florakis-Savinkov drank more mineral water. He wouldn't sleep, he knew. The oppressive heat would last all night long. Plus the babble of voices and *bouzouki* playing which drifted upwards through the dense humidity and through the open window.

1986. He had been visited at his farm late one evening by the ELAS leader who had provided him with the papers of a Greek citizen. The man's arrival had been a shock – it was Savinkov's first intimation that he had been watched, that they knew where he was.

He had been invited to meet an 'important visitor' to Athens. That was after he had been asked a number of questions about his reaction to the change of leadership in Russia. Savinkov had been frank – thinking that if he was candid the invitation which worried him might be withdrawn.

No, he did not approve of Gorbachev's *glasnost*. This was not the real Communism he had risked his life for during the Civil War. It was a dangerous departure from Lenin's creed, and so on. To his surprise an appointment had been made for that same evening. His visitor would drive him to Athens.

His destination turned out to be the Hilton Hotel. He was escorted to a room on the second floor where a man wearing a lightweight grey business suit had opened the door and ushered him inside. Tall and lean with the face of a fox, he wore a pair of dark glasses and offered Savinkov vodka. He refused, mentioned that he had not touched alcohol for forty years.

'I am Colonel Gerasimov of the GRU,' his host said as they sat facing each other across a small round table.

General Lucharsky was confident his deception would

225

never be penetrated. His photograph had never appeared in a newspaper and the general public abroad didn't know of his existence. He was weighing up his guest as he poured himself a glass of the vodka, a fact Savinkov was aware of. Mention of the GRU had reassured him – as intended – since it was a GRU colonel who had accompanied him to the Bulgarian border in 1946.

'We are very worried about General Secretary Gorbachev and his crazy *glasnost*,' Lucharsky commented.

He had no doubts about coming straight to the point: Doganis, who had brought Savinkov to him, would have checked his outlook. And for a man of sixty-one Savinkov looked very fit – more like forty. Already Lucharsky was fairly sure they had selected the right man.

'He is ruining Lenin's work,' Savinkov agreed, 'but why am I here?'

He spoke slowly. It was many years since he had conversed in his native language. But he had taken the precaution of reading novels in Russian and he found the language coming back fast.

'You were once trained as a radio operator,' Lucharsky said. 'Is that not so?'

'Yes. Before I came to Greece to do a job in 1946 . . .'

'To kill reactionary Greek leaders.' Lucharsky leaned forward. 'We need a liaison man who can communicate by radio in English. I understand you are fluent in that language?'

'I learned it in the days when I served as a waiter in hotels here to make money to buy my farm. I keep it up by talking with English people during the tourist season . . .'

'Good. You are just the man we need.' Lucharsky smiled. His wide mouth made him look even foxier. A conspirator type, Savinkov was thinking. 'You will have to operate the latest type of transceiver. Doganis will train you in the use of the instrument, will give you the codes, the wavebands, the times for transmission. England, you see, is two hours behind Greece.'

England? Savinkov was startled. In the old days he used to think very fast and he found his brain moving into high gear again. The man watching him from behind the tinted glasses would be in his forties. He would show him he was not dealing with some dumb peasant.

'There could be a technical problem. Transmitting over that distance.'

'Doganis tells me you have high mountains, very lonely, near your farm. You could use one of your donkeys to take the transceiver to a peak. From there transmission will be top-class.'

'Yes, it would.' They had thought this out very carefully. Which gave Savinkov confidence. But he needed to know exactly what he was doing – and why. He sat up straight, staring at the glasses.

'In the old days I never operated in the dark. I must know what this is all about, Colonel.'

'An independent type. Good,' Lucharsky repeated. 'Really I have already told you. Gorbachev must be removed before he can do any more damage. There is a group inside Russia – high up – which is determined to replace him by a correct type of leader. The trouble is we have to be very careful. He has ears everywhere – inside Russia. So we have reactivated an organization outside the motherland. Partly here in Greece, partly in England. You will be the link. Doganis will deliver the messages you must send. At other times our associate in England will send you signals at certain times arranged in advance. That's it. And Doganis is your sole contact. Never go near the Soviet Embassy here.'

'Who am I communicating with in England?'

'The codename is La Jolla – a small place in America.

227

Doganis will explain everything. Oh, by the way, when you leave here he will drive you to a room we have rented for you over a taverna in the Plaka. I think that is all.' Lucharsky glanced at his watch.

'I don't see how this is going to bring down Gorbachev. And I will be risking my freedom. Greek counter-intelligence could trap me and I would be a spy.'

'You are right.' Lucharsky pursed his thin lips. They had reported Savinkov was intelligent and self-reliant. A thought occurred to him. 'You are not married, we know. What do you do for a woman when you need one? Any permanent girlfriend?'

'None. I would have had to entrust her with my secret. If we had quarrelled one day she might have betrayed me. I have an old woman who comes daily to the farm to cook for me and two men who work on the land. When I need a woman I go into the city here and pick one up. Always a different one. That way, no complications.'

'You are very well organized. And now you will excuse me?'

'I still don't see how you are going to replace Gorbachev – even operating a group safely from outside.'

This was the crunch. By now Lucharsky had made up his mind – time had not eroded Savinkov's training, his reliability, his faith in the cause. Lucharsky waved a hand as though swatting a fly.

'If necessary we await our opportunity – preferably when he is abroad – and kill him. You object to that?'

'Why should I? In the past I have killed enemies of the cause.'

Doganis had been waiting for him outside the room and had led him to a Citroën parked in front of the taxi rank outside the hotel. It had been a baking evening as Savinkov stared at the car.

'What happened to the Peugeot you drove me to Athens in?'

'We change cars. Frequently. It is good security. Get in. Now we will go to the Plaka. Inside the locked boot there is an old suitcase. Inside that is the transceiver. You start training tonight . . .'

And, Savinkov thought as he poured yet more mineral water, it was inside this room a year ago that Doganis had produced from a worn, shabby suitcase a superb large transceiver. They had practised half the night, Savinkov tapping the key while the machine was switched off. He had been surprised how quickly he had mastered the machine – so different from the one he had used in 1946.

Later that week Doganis had again visited his farm and the training had continued until Savinkov could operate it blindfold. His greatest shock had come that first evening here in this room when he had tackled Doganis about the clandestine organization working outside Russia.

'Colonel Gerasimov told me they have reactivated an organization – an apparatus – outside the motherland. What does that mean? I do need to know what I am doing,' he concluded aggressively.

'You might as well know. We may have to send a stranger to you with a message. This will identify him. The apparatus which has come alive again is the Greek Key.'

21

Newman escorted Christina through the large bar at the Hilton and down the staircase leading to the Ta Nissia, the main restaurant. It was located at a lower level from the vast entrance hall paved with solid marble. Christina paused at the bottom step and grasped Newman's arm.

'Oh, look, that tempts my taste buds madly.'

Facing them was a vast open fireplace and over the fire spits revolved slowly, cooking the food. The lower spit supported a whole roasting pig. On the long spit above it chickens were turning slowly and an appetising aroma drifted towards them.

'No need to consult the menu,' Newman joked. 'I've reserved a corner table . . .' He gave his name to the maitre d' who escorted them past a huge cold buffet table into a spacious room shut off from the outside world.

They settled themselves at the table and Newman sat alongside Christina on a red velvet banquette, his back to the wall so he could watch the whole room. He glanced at her as she studied the menu. 'You're looking superb in that dress, what there is of it. It suits your figure.'

She glanced at him wickedly. 'Maybe a little too revealing.'

'I'm happy.'

It was the one item of clothing they had purchased in Kolonaki she had not allowed him to see. A strapless, low-cut dress of black velvet, it hugged her closely. 'You'll have to be careful not to drop anything down the front,' he remarked, with a quick look at the upper half of her well-formed breasts.

'You would think of that.' She giggled. 'I've decided. No starter. Spit-roast chicken for me. And it's nice to have a man who's so well-organized.' She nodded towards the ice bucket where a bottle of champagne rested half-concealed beneath a white napkin.

'Veuve Cliquot.' He looked at the waiter standing to take their orders. 'We'll start on the champagne right away – and we can order now . . .'

She waited until they were alone. 'Are these the opening moves in an attempted seduction?'

'You brought the subject up.' He lowered his glass. 'First I need to hear all about Harry Masterson.'

'I thought there'd be a catch.' She sighed. 'What do you want to know?'

'Everything. From the very beginning. How you met him would be a good opening.'

'I like this place. It's the first time I've been here. Silly, isn't it?' She gave him a bewitching smile. 'I suppose it is because I live here. A strange room, very cleverly designed.'

He looked round. The walls were constructed of very solid rough brown stone. Set back into the walls at intervals were alcoves containing Greek pottery – beautifully shaped vases and jugs. A soft glow illuminated the room and the windows were high up and recessed into the solid stone. At 8 p.m. there were only a few tables taken, but more guests were filtering in. Newman refilled their glasses.

'Now, about Harry Masterson,' he said firmly.

'What a persistent man you are. Well, it's a long story . . .'

'We have all evening.'

'Petros still had me under his thumb. He persuaded me it was my duty to help find who killed Andreas and Stephen. We Greeks call it *philotimo*, a matter of family honour.'

'Go on.'

'He went about it deviously – like he does everything. I had to fly to Zurich. There I stayed overnight and bought a return air ticket to London. I'd flown to Zurich by Swissair. I used British Airways to fly on to London. When I got there I stayed at the Strand Palace. I then inserted a personal advertisement in *The Times* newspaper.' She paused. 'Petros had written the words. The advertisement read, *Will anyone interested in the Greek Key and who knows about Antikhana please contact me. Irene.*'

Newman sipped champagne to conceal the shock he had

received. Harry Masterson had been Tweed's sector chief for the Balkans, and that zone included Greece. Newman was also recalling that among the items Masterson had posted back to Tweed was a bracelet – a bracelet from which was suspended a symbol. The Greek key.

'What happened next?' he enquired amiably.

'Petros thought I might be contacted by one of three men – the men who were part of the commando raid on Siros when Andreas was murdered. A Colonel Barrymore, Captain Robson and Kearns, a company sergeant major. Whoever answered the advertisement was likely to be the murderer. So Petros thought. He felt sure they would have to find out who was enquiring after all these years.'

'I don't understand the Greek key bit.'

'I'm not talking about that. Too dangerous. For you . . .'

'There's no limit on danger.'

'Don't you want to know who got in touch with the phone number I put in the advertisement?' she asked.

'Go on,' he repeated, confident he already knew the answer.

'Harry Masterson. I was very taken aback. Then I thought it could be one of the three men using a false name. Especially because of the precautions he told me to take when he arranged to meet me.'

'What precautions?'

'I had to meet him at a certain place in Lincoln's Inn – where all the British lawyers are. It frightened me when I arrived at eleven in the morning. No one about. All those ancient courtyards. I thought it was a trap. I'd armed myself with an aerosol. He was very clever. The appointment was for the same morning he phoned. I only had less than an hour to get there.'

Yes, very clever, Newman thought. So typical of Harry – to select a rendezvous where he could watch her approach,

232

make sure no one was following her. A thought occurred to him.

'How would he know it was you?'

'On the phone he asked me where I was and to give a description of myself, what I would be wearing. I waited for ten minutes and decided no one was coming. At that moment he came round a corner. Again he was clever. I realized he couldn't be one of the three men – he was too young. But I thought one of them might have sent him. He took me a short walk to a public place in Fleet Street, The Cheshire Cheese pub. Lots of people about. I felt safe then.'

She paused and drank half a glass of champagne. The restaurant was filling up. As he listened Newman kept a check on the new faces; for one especially. The face of Petros. He'd recognize him: from the picture Sarris, the police chief, had shown him; and even more from that moment he had spotted Petros inside the black Mercedes when they had returned early in the morning from police HQ.

'We're inside The Cheshire Cheese,' he reminded her after their meals of spit-roasted chicken had been served.

'Harry had a way with women. I felt he was OK but I still asked who he was, what he did. He said he was with Special Branch, the British secret police. I asked him to prove it and he showed me a card with his photograph. I found myself telling him about the murders of Andreas and Stephen, why I'd come to London, about Barrymore, Kearns and Robson. He said he had ways of tracing them. I couldn't believe my luck. I asked him what his interest was.'

'And he told you?' Newman was intrigued to learn what piece of fiction Harry had invented to cover that question.

'He said it might just link up with a case he had investigated and never solved. We arranged to meet the following day after he'd made certain enquiries. I've no idea where he went . . .'

I have, thought Newman. To pump Brigadier Willie Davies at the Ministry of Defence. He let her eat her meal while he traced in his mind what had happened. It was all becoming horribly clear now – the tragedy of Harry Masterson.

Harry had been given a month's leave. Unmarried, Harry detested holidays, got bored within twenty-four hours. He'd seen the advertisement Christina had placed in *The Times* and reacted to it for a lark – anything to occupy his time.

The moment he'd met Christina he'd been hooked – but cautious – by her story, by Christina herself. Harry liked the ladies. He had still kept up his guard by pretending to be a Special Branch officer. That had impressed Christina, had given her confidence he could help her. But at any time Harry could pull out, pleading call of duty with another case.

'What happened next?' he asked as she pushed her empty plate to one side. 'And we need more champagne . . .' He mimed the request to their waiter.

'When he arrived next morning at the Strand Palace he was carrying a small case. He told me to pack, that we were going on a journey, that he'd traced not only Barrymore, but Kearns and Robson, too. I was shaken to the core. He said we had to drive to the West Country, to a place called Exmoor . . .'

She went on to explain how they had put up at a hotel in Dunster near the coast. Harry had then driven off to visit the three men now he knew their addresses.

'He made appointments?' Newman asked.

'No, he was devious. He phoned each of the three men and said he was making an enquiry on behalf of the Ministry

234

of Defence, that he would be with them shortly. Then he put the phone down before they could ask any questions. That way he knew they'd be where they lived when he arrived.'

'You'd told him everything you knew about the two murders – one in Cairo, one on Siros? And about Petros' vendetta?'

'Yes.' She smiled ruefully. 'Harry could get any secret out of a woman. I told him more than I intended to.'

'So what happened after he'd seen the ex-commandos?'

'He was suspicious of one of them. He wouldn't tell me which one. He told each of them the identity of the murderer was now known, that he was on his way to Athens to check with the chief of police. He thought the guilty one would follow us.'

Oh God, Newman realized, and he succeeded. At the cost of his own life. No back-up. That had been Harry's fatal blunder. But he had always been a lone wolf, brimming with self-confidence. Had he left behind a clue?

'Did he say anything about how the three men received him?'

'He was very amusing about Colonel Barrymore who tried to treat him like a common soldier. They had a violent argument. Harry ended up by telling him that if they'd had many colonels like him they would have lost the war. Then we flew out here.'

'What came next?'

'I don't really know.' For the first time she sounded depressed. 'We booked in at the Astir Palace at Vouliagmeni. That's a sea resort on the way to Cape Sounion . . .' Which is why we weren't able to locate where he stayed, Newman thought grimly. She continued as he watched her closely. 'He said he was going to see Chief Inspector Sarris. I don't know whether he ever did. He changed his mind a lot.' She sipped more champagne and leaned against him. 'I'm getting a bit tiddly. Lovely.'

He changed his mind a lot. Newman knew why Harry had done that: to keep Christina off balance in case she was passing on information to someone. He had never completely let down his guard with her.

'Then what happened?' Newman prodded.

'He told me over early breakfast one morning he was visiting Devil's Valley. He wouldn't say why. I'd told him about the silver mine. I think he was going to try and find it. I feel awful about that. I may be responsible for what happened to him.'

'What silver mine?'

'It's near the top of a mountain in Devil's Valley. Nobody has worked it for years. It's abandoned – but Petros forbids anyone to go near it. I don't know why. He has even told his shepherds who work near it to shoot anyone they see prowling in that area.'

'Which is against the law,' Newman remarked.

'Petros makes his own law. Harry was intrigued by that silver mine – why it was forbidden territory. I've never been near the place.' She shuddered, drank more champagne.

'So, when Harry set out on his last journey that morning he was trying to locate this abandoned mine. Any idea what the place is like?'

'Dimitrios once told me something when he was drunk. The shaft is still open. It goes down a long way, a vertical drop with the old cage which took down miners still suspended at the top. It sounded horribly sinister to me. But at the last minute before he left Harry changed his mind again. He received a phone call when he was getting ready to leave his bedroom. He said he might go first to Cape Sounion to meet the Englishman.'

'What Englishman? What time in the morning was this?'

Newman was watching her closely. Was she spinning him an elaborate yarn? Setting the same trap for him she'd set for Harry? She was such a beauty with her mane of black glossy hair; by the light of the single lighted candle on their table her bare shoulders gleamed. A girl to dazzle any man.

'We'd had breakfast at six,' she continued. 'Neither of us could sleep that night. The phone call must have come through before seven in the morning. Harry went up to his room to take it. He looked pleased when he came back, said his ruse had worked. I presume he meant telling those three ex-commandos he was flying to Greece while we were on Exmoor. The caller had disguised his voice but Harry was sure he knew who it was. He wouldn't give me even a hint. Said it was dangerous . . .'

And it had been dangerous, Newman reflected grimly. It had ended in Harry's death. But what she had told him was confusing. Had Harry tried to locate the silver mine first before going on to Cape Sounion?

'Christina, did Harry know the exact location of the worked-out silver mine?'

'Yes. He had a map of the area he bought in Athens. He asked me to mark its precise location on the map, which I did. Afterwards I wished I hadn't done that. Harry could be very persuasive.'

'So can I.' He produced a large-scale map he'd purchased of the huge peninsular area stretching between Athens and Cape Sounion. 'Mark the location for me.'

She pushed back her empty plate, clasped her hands in her lap, turned to face him. 'No. The last time I did that a man died. I'm growing fond of you, Bob . . .'

'Cut that out,' he said brutally. 'Mark the bloody map. Now!'

'It's your funeral.' Her eyes flashed. 'And don't ever use that tone to me again.' She spread out the map, took the pen he offered, studied the map, then drew a cross at the top of a mountain.

'Petros is crazy,' she warned. 'You'd be crazy too if you went anywhere near Devil's Valley.'

237

'When was the last time you saw Harry? Alive, I mean,' he persisted, his voice cold.

'You bastard . . .' Her voice trembled. She was on the verge of tears. 'When he left the breakfast room and went straight to his hired car . . .' She fiddled in her envelope-shaped handbag for a handkerchief.

He put an arm round her back, rested his hand on her shoulder. 'No need to get uptight, Christina. But I knew Harry well. I have to know everything he did – planned to do. What about a spot of dessert? The strawberry gâteau looks pretty good – forget about your figure for tonight, even if I can't . . .'

'Flattery could get you somewhere.' She recovered her poise as he squeezed her shoulder. 'And I'd love some gâteau. And more champagne.'

He waited until dessert was served, until she was tucking into the huge quantity with gusto. 'To sum up,' he began, 'you went to London at Petros' command, inserted the advertisement, made contact with Harry. OK so far?'

'On the nose,' she assured him and winked.

'He drove you to Exmoor, after tracing Barrymore, Robson and Kearns. He went to see each man, told them he was flying soon to Greece. You arrived with him. What was your mood about the mission Petros had sent you on when you got back here?'

'Bloody bolshie. I'd had Petros up to here. The trip to London – and spending time with Harry – had snapped any bonds with Petros. I didn't care any more who had killed Stephen, Andreas. I'd never even known them. I was worried about Harry. Now I'm worried about you. If it's not a secret, what are you going to do next? Please . . .'

She laid a hand on his arm. Then she waited until he turned towards her and kissed him full on the mouth. 'Please,' she repeated. 'I've been honest with you.'

'Fair enough. I'm going to phone a man in London I

238

know after I've packed you off to bed. And Marler will stand guard. Outside your room.'

'Who are you phoning?' she pressed.

'My editor,' he lied. 'I am a foreign correspondent. Remember?'

22

Newman arrived at the British Embassy at eleven, well after dark. The large villa on Sofias Avenue was surrounded by a stone wall, looming up behind a Turkish-style church. Patterson, his contact, was a pain in the neck.

Impatiently, Newman waited in the hall as the round-faced man in his forties carefully examined his press card and then his passport. A typical bureaucrat, Newman thought: inflated with a sense of his own importance. Smooth-faced, he turned the passport pages with irritating slowness.

'For God's sake,' Newman snapped. 'You knew I was coming. Tweed warned you.'

'It is my responsibility who uses the phone,' Patterson responded in his bland voice.

'It's just a phone . . .'

'It's the scrambler,' Patterson reminded him pompously. 'I have to log all calls, be very careful who uses it. You have no diplomatic status . . .'

'*You* won't have any if I report you're obstructing me. You're on probation, don't forget.'

The blow struck home. Patterson's well-padded face flushed, he ran a manicured hand over his slick black hair. 'No need to be rude,' he bleated.

'Just realistic. Let's get on with it. Now. Tweed is waiting. Or have you forgotten London is two hours behind us? He likes to get home early to work on files,' Newman lied.

The phone was in a small room in the basement. A table, chairs pushed under it, the phone with the red button the only object on the table top. Newman sat down, reached for the phone, then looked up at Patterson who still stood waiting.

'Piss off, there's a good chap. This is confidential. Leave the card and passport on the table. Shut the door on your way out.'

Pressing the red button, he dialled Park Crescent. Paula came on the line within seconds. She sounded relieved to hear his voice.

'We wondered what the devil was happening to you . . .'

'Nice to be loved. Tweed about? I'm on scrambler from the Embassy in Athens.'

'He's here. Take care . . .'

Tweed sounded as fresh as sea air at nine in the evening. Newman plunged straight into a terse report of what had taken place since his arrival. Tweed listened without interrupting. At the end of five minutes Newman concluded his story.

'That brings you up to date. Doesn't really take us any further as to who killed Harry.'

'It might have done. You have a pipeline into this weird Gavalas clan – Christina. Whether she can be trusted is for you to assess. What do you think?'

'I'm leaning to the idea she has broken with the whole crew. But only leaning – she's pretty street-wise and could be a first-rate actress. Pity Harry hadn't told her who the mysterious Englishman who phoned him was. Could it have been one of the commando trio?'

'Yes. All three I visited had just returned from separate holidays abroad. All had a deep suntan – which they could

240

have picked up in Greece. The timing is right, too. One of them could have been out there at exactly the time Masterson was killed. I have the feeling the solution lies in Greece. That raid on Siros all those years ago. What intrigues me is the missing body – who took the dead Andreas away from that gulch? And why? I may fly out to join you when the right moment comes. What's your next move?'

'To explore that old silver mine in Devil's Valley. Something very strange about that – the way Petros takes such precautions to keep strangers away from the place . . .'

'Don't!' Tweed's tone was sharp. 'I don't like the sound of Mr Petros one bit. We may do it together later. You need plenty of back-up to go into a place like that. Harry Butler and Pete Nield would be useful. Plus Marler. At the moment Butler and Nield are on Exmoor, nosing around and picking up gossip about Barrymore, Kearns and Robson. How are you finding Marler?' Tweed asked casually.

'A pain. But I can handle him. One thing I will give him – he's a good man to go into the jungle with. I'll keep you in touch . . .'

'Don't go.' A pause. 'At this stage it seems like a vendetta directed by Petros against whoever killed his two sons, Andreas and Stephen. His main suspects being on Exmoor. Is that how you see it?'

'With the little data we have to go on yet, yes. Especially now you've told me about this Anton character. Christina hasn't mentioned him, which I find odd. Butler and Nield are on the lookout for Anton, too, I assume?'

'Anton has disappeared. I suspect he's flown by some secret route back to Greece. He didn't pass through London Airport – I've had the security chief there check the passenger manifests.'

'But it backs up the vendetta theory.' Newman paused and Tweed said nothing. 'Or is there something more?'

'I think this business could be much bigger, far more

serious than we realize. I can't figure out the link between Exmoor and Greece.'

'There has to be one?'

'If there isn't, then we're wasting our time. But who pushed Masterson over a Greek cliff?' Tweed paused again. 'After he'd visited Exmoor. We're missing something . . .'

Florakis – Oleg Savinkov, The Executioner – crouched at the top of the mountain above his farm. It was 2 a.m. and earlier he had received a coded signal he suspected emanated from inside the Soviet Embassy in Athens.

His suspicions were correct. But he would have been surprised had he known the hand which tapped out the message was that of Colonel Rykovsky, military attaché. Rykovsky had waited until the Embassy staff had gone home: hence the arrangement made via Doganis for Savinkov to be ready to receive the signal at two in the morning.

Savinkov had placed the powerful transceiver given to him in a small depression at the mountain summit. The telescopic aerial was extended as he checked his watch by the light of a pencil torch. Time to retransmit the message to England. And for that elevation was needed to cover the long distance.

His bony face was tense with concentration as he sent out the call signal, received immediate acknowledgement. He began tapping out the coded message, keeping an eye on his watch as he operated. Three minutes was the maximum agreed time for any transmission.

It was unlikely Greek counter-espionage would have detector vans as far south as this remote wilderness, but Doganis had emphasized the importance of security.

'Take no chances. You are the linchpin of the whole operation.'

'What operation?' Savinkov had asked.

'I don't know, but it's big, very big. It could change the whole course of history. That's all I've been told.'

The words echoed in Savinkov's brain as he completed tapping out the signal. He felt excited as he depressed the aerial, lifted the heavy transceiver back inside the shabby suitcase. It was a long climb back down the mountain to the farm but he would be there long before daylight.

One thousand six hundred-odd miles to the north-west another hand on Exmoor was already beginning the task of decoding the signal which had just come in from Greece. The unbreakable one-time code had been used, the novel the series of numbers referred to was Sinclair Lewis' *Main Street*. Half an hour later the message was decoded, written on the pad which had a sheet of protective plastic beneath the sheet to avoid any risk of an impression of the wording reproducing itself on the sheet beneath the plastic.

All equipment and preparations should be made immediately. Possible that target will land in Britain on way to or when returning from Washington summit. Potential timing September or October this year. The Greek Key.

23

'Gorbachev must go, he is destroying the military supremacy we have taken so many years to build up. His crazy *glasnost* will be the ruin of the Soviet state,' General Lucharsky said vehemently.

By which he meant the power of the Red Army, his faithful aide, Colonel Volkov, thought as they strolled side

by side in full uniform in the Moscow park. Children played
ball games on the grass in the warmth of the sunlight round
them as they followed one of the many twisting paths.

Lucharsky had chosen the park for this conversation
because it was impossible for them to be overheard. He
walked very erect, hands clasped behind him, head bowed
in thought. Volkov asked the question tentatively. He was
not sure Lucharsky wanted to reveal details of the plan but
his curiosity drove him on.

'How can we ever hope to achieve his replacement? The
Politburo is now packed with a majority in his favour . . .'

'Ligachev,' the General said tersely. 'He is Number Two.
He does not agree with the new madness. Once Gorbachev
has been removed he will take over and the yes-men in the
Politburo will swing behind him.'

'But how can the present General Secretary be removed?'

'He can be killed.'

The cold-blooded audacity of the statement astounded
Volkov and he was silent for a few minutes as they continued their stroll. Lucharsky took off his peaked cap and
ran his hand through his blond hair, enjoying the feel of
the sun on his forehead.

'But it must be done outside Russia,' Lucharsky continued, 'at a suitable moment. I set the wheels in motion
when I made my unofficial visit to Greece. There are plenty
of hard men in the Politburo who will welcome a return to
the good old days. Fortunately, Comrade Gorbachev is
playing into our hands. He agrees we must do everything
possible to spread our influence in the Mediterranean. But
by peaceful means. You, Comrade, have been chosen to
follow up my visit to Athens. Like me, you will travel there
in civilian clothes – on an unofficial visit. We are offering
the Greek government special trade concessions. While
you are there you will carry verbal orders from me to
Colonel Rykovsky, the military attaché at the Athens

244

Embassy. I will give you those orders just before you fly to Athens via Zurich.'

'Why Greece? What is happening there?'

Lucharsky changed direction, headed for a path which twisted through a wooded area of birch trees. He had spotted two men in plain clothes who had KGB written all over them. One had a pair of field glasses slung round his neck. He might be a lip-reader. They entered the wood.

'Because,' Lucharsky explained, 'it is too dangerous to plan a coup inside the motherland. Gorbachev is no fool. He knows he faces opposition and has eyes and ears everywhere. We must not underestimate him. So, we have reactivated an organization outside Russia, one which has not operated for years. It is composed of men who worked for Stalin, who have been forgotten. Shadow men.'

'And Greece is this base?'

'One of them,' Lucharsky replied enigmatically. 'We are using the KGB cell system. Only what you need to know is told to you. There is great dissatisfaction inside the Red Army, as you know. When Gorbachev has gone the Army will again wield all the power it once did after Stalin died.'

'But you implied this organization outside the motherland is made up of Stalinists,' Volkov reminded him. He was bewildered.

'So it is. We use them, then discard them. They may well be the scapegoat for the assassination of Comrade Mikhail if that proves necessary.'

'You mean they do the job for us and then we accuse them of being responsible?'

'Possibly. It would be better if we could spread rumours once Gorbachev has gone that he was the victim of hard-liners inside the Pentagon. We will play our cards as the game progresses. We wait for our opportunity – which may come within a few months. Our only chance to liquidate the mad dog is while he is outside Russia. There our allies can operate more safely.'

245

'I am at your service, Comrade General,' Volkov, a round-faced ball of a man replied.

'Who knows?' Lucharsky commented, adjusting his cap to a more jaunty angle. 'It might end up in promotion for you.'

Always dangle the carrot in front of the donkey, he thought. No point in explaining that those who helped would also have to be eliminated when the coup succeeded.

Inside his office at Park Crescent Tweed sat behind his desk staring into the distance. The desk-top was covered with neat piles of documents which he had just examined for the third time. The items Masterson had posted him from Greece and the notebook of Partridge he had collected from the safety deposit in Knightsbridge.

Paula sat at her desk checking through a file. Every now and again she glanced up at her chief. In another corner Monica bent her head over a card index, her dark hair tied behind her neck in a bun.

'Are we getting anywhere?' Paula ventured. 'After that phone call from Bob last night?'

'Listen, both of you.' Tweed sat upright in his swivel chair, hands clasped in his lap, his eyes alert behind his glasses. 'Let's go over what we have briefly. Damn all, as far as I can see.'

'Maybe more than we know,' Paula suggested. 'Basically it all appears to have started with two murders a long way off and a long time ago. Andreas Gavalas on Siros Island, Stephen Ionides – now revealed as Stephen Gavalas. Someone is trying to bury both killings.' She caught Monica's expression. 'Sorry – that sounded a bit callous . . .'

'But it may be true,' Tweed agreed. 'Go on.'

He was, Monica realized, conducting in reverse an exercise he'd often carried out with her. At a certain point of an operation he would sum up the main points, using

246

Monica to bounce off his ideas, to test their relevance.

With Paula he was listening to how she saw the situation – seeking a key element they had overlooked. Something simple; maybe a factor which didn't fit what they knew. Paula went on.

'We have met Barrymore, Robson and Kearns – the three men who were with Andreas when he was killed. The same three men were back in Cairo when Stephen was brutally murdered at the Antikhana Building. Both victims were brothers. It really stretches the long arm of coincidence to breaking-point – that the commando trio were in the vicinity of two murders. OK so far?'

'Go on . . .' Tweed had relaxed, listening with his eyes closed as he visualized what she was saying.

'Now we have two odd complications – which don't link up with what I've said so far. The mysterious disappearance of Andreas' body from Siros the night he was killed. And the arrival of Anton Gavalas on Exmoor making enquiries about the ex-commandos.'

'Something else odd about Anton,' Tweed pointed out. 'The way he vanished without leaving a trace of the route he used. We checked with the harbourmaster at Watchet. No ship left for anywhere when Anton pulled off his vanishing act.'

'Anything in Partridge's notebook?' Paula asked.

'Yes. According to Partridge Anton is well-educated and speaks fluent English. Yet Newman told me his nephews – Dimitrios and Constantine – are peasant types. And what game is Anton playing? In his notebook Partridge records Anton is a lone wolf with plenty of money at his disposal. Newman also said Christina hadn't mentioned Anton. They seem to want him to be the invisible man.' He paused and Monica asked who 'they' were.

'That is what we need to find out. Anton could be acting independently of old Petros. This vendetta business is complex, reeks of a long and dangerous hatred. You know,

247

I'm getting the impression someone is using the vendetta as a smokescreen – to hide something far more deadly. And who killed Masterson?'

It was Saturday night at The Luttrell Arms in Dunster. They always dined together on Saturdays. At the corner table at the far end of the dining room Colonel Barrymore occupied a seat facing the room with his back to the wall. Dr Robson sat beside him while Kearns was seated opposite the two men. They were at the coffee stage.

'Another large Scotch,' Robson called out.

'Of course, sir. Coming right away,' the manager assured him as he passed their table.

'Pushing the boat out a bit, aren't we?' Barrymore commented in a supercilious tone, glancing at his companion.

Robson's complexion had lost most of its suntan and was now a ruddy colour like a setting sunset. It was his fourth double plus several glasses of Beaujolais. He stroked his thatch of brown hair, pulled at his straggle of a moustache, grinned amiably. As usual he was in high good humour.

'Thought we were here to enjoy the evening. Ever known me to be half seas over?'

'There's always a first time,' Barrymore continued in a lofty tone. 'And we have serious business to discuss. See that chap with the dark moustache, black hair, a hearing aid? Caught him watching Quarme Manor this morning. I challenged him.'

'You did?' Robson sounded amused and Barrymore glared at him. 'Where was he?'

'Up on the ridge behind the manor. Riding a horse.'

'Free country – in case you've forgotten.' He chuckled. His blue eyes lit up as his drink arrived. 'Thank you.' Lifting the glass, he swallowed half the contents. 'That's better.' He turned to Barrymore. 'So what happened when you *challenged* the chappie? Sounds like the corporal of the guard.' He grinned at Kearns who stared back, blank-faced, ramrod-backed.

'Had the insolence to tell me he was bird-watching,' Barrymore continued. 'Hence the field glasses trained on Quarme Manor. Rode off pretty sharp, I can tell you.' His tone changed, became silky. 'Gentlemen, I smell trouble. There was the Greek you encountered, Kearns.'

'And how can you be sure he was Greek?' Robson chaffed the ex-CSM. 'Wearing his *Evzone* outfit, was he?'

'No laughing matter,' Barrymore snapped. 'Tell him,' he ordered Kearns.

'Well, sir,' Kearns began, gazing at the colonel, 'his appearance for one thing. Olive-skinned, the facial bone structure. I've seen enough of them to recognize the breed. When I spoke to him he replied in English but with a slight accent. Greek.'

'Not Bulgarian or Yugoslav?' Robson enquired. He grinned again, drank more whisky. 'Would you know the difference?'

'Yes, I think I would,' Kearns responded stiffly.

'And what was he doing? More bird-watching?'

'Said he was on holiday, that he liked wild places. Asked me the way to the nearest pub. Told him Simonsbath, miles away from where we met. To test him. Later I saw him riding down a gully towards Winsford. Which *was* the way to the nearest pub. See what I mean, sir?'

'He knew the moor, tried to pretend he didn't. That's what I want to talk about. The enemy could be closing in. Need to take more precautions.'

Barrymore sipped his cognac and Robson glanced at the balloon glass. 'Time I had one of those . . .'

Pete Nield, sitting with Harry Butler three tables away, adjusted his earpiece. A snappy dresser, he wore a navy blue business suit and a large jewelled tie-pin in his pale red tie. The tie-pin, shaped like a flower, was a directional microphone. The wire attached to it behind his striped

249

shirt led to the miniaturized tape recorder in his jacket pocket. He spooned more fruit salad into his mouth as he listened.

Harry Butler, heavily built and clean-shaven, was dressed informally in a tweed sports jacket with leather elbow patches and a pair of grey slacks. He leaned over to whisper in Nield's 'good' ear.

'Reception OK?'

'Picking up every word,' Nield replied in an undertone and fingered his neat moustache.

The Engine Room wizards at Park Crescent had excelled themselves. Despite the presence of people at four other tables the directional mike was recording every word of the conversation at Barrymore's table. It had been easy for Nield to 'point' the microphone in the correct direction. A man fiddling with his tie-pin attracted no attention . . .

'You're not going to have a cognac on top of all you've had?' Barrymore enquired sardonically. 'You do have to drive home.'

'I'll get there.' Robson grinned again. 'I always do.' He signalled to the manager, pointing to the colonel's glass and then himself. The manager smiled, acknowledging the request. 'The other chappie,' Robson continued, 'the bigger one with the thin one you *challenged* . . .' His tone was mocking. 'Was he on the moor as well?'

'Never seen him before. As I was saying . . .'

'Had the thin one that hearing aid when you met him?' Robson persisted with the geniality of a man who has imbibed well.

Barrymore frowned, trying to recall the scene. 'Don't think he had. But he wouldn't need it, would he? Not out on the moor. Now, for the third time, I think we should review our defences. Too many people poking around. There was that Tweed who barged in on us all.'

'Special Branch,' Kearns remarked. 'I thought that rather strange. Despite the yarn he spun. Seemed to me he had an ulterior motive for calling on me. That man worried me.'

'Oh, just one of the horde of bureaucrats justifying his fat salary at the expense of the taxpayer.' Barrymore waved a languid hand. 'Wish I'd had him in the battalion. He'd have had to jump to it.'

'I suspect, sir,' Kearns persisted quietly, 'Tweed has had a spell in the Army. Something about his manner. And he'd done his homework. Knew about the raid on Siros. And the murder of that Greek chap, Ionides, at the Antikhana . . .'

'Hardly relevant.' Barrymore made a dismissive gesture.

'Are you certain, sir? Did anything strike you as weird about that body they brought down off the moor at Winsford?'

'Should it have?' The colonel was clipping the tip from a cigar. He lit it with a bookmatch as Kearns continued.

'The savagery of the attack.' Kearns paused. 'He was slashed to pieces. Just like Ionides all those years ago.' He turned his attention to Robson. 'You examined the body inside the Land Rover. Surely I have a point?'

'Somebody had really done a job on the poor chap. A broad-bladed knife would be my guess. Mind you, it was a brief examination.' Robson's tone suddenly sounded sober, professional. 'Fail to see the connection with Ionides.' He drank more of his large cognac. 'Thought we were assembled here to enjoy ourselves.' He chuckled. 'But you Army types never slough off your skin.'

'The fact remains,' Barrymore intervened irritably, 'we now have possible enemies on two fronts. The Greeks and this Special Branch lot. I just hope to God it isn't the Greek Key.'

'After all these years?' Robson scoffed and grinned. 'Come off it. Not like you to suffer an attack of nerves, Barrymore.'

'I never suffer an attack of nerves, as you put it,' the

colonel replied coolly. 'I'm just saying we should look to our defences. Just in case.'

'Put up more barbed wire,' Robson joked. 'Lay a mine-field round Quarme Manor.' He hiccuped. 'Call out the guard!'

'I'm serious,' Barrymore said coldly.

'I fear you are. As for me, business as usual. Carry on with my local practice. Did you know the local paper is doing an article on me? *The Only Doctor in the Country who Rides to See Patients* will be the headline. Rather good.'

'Jill has gone up to London,' Kearns said suddenly.

'Why?' Barrymore demanded.

'To pick up a few things from the shops she said.'

'You should have stopped her.' Barrymore sounded angry.

'Well, sir, that isn't the easiest thing in the world . . .'

'You made the mistake of marrying a younger woman,' the colonel told him brutally. 'Wives should be kept under heel. In the Army they knew their place . . .'

At his table Pete Nield finished his coffee, glanced round the dining room. A couple was just leaving. Which left only the trio at the end of the room and his table occupied. He leaned close to Butler.

'Time to go, wouldn't you say? We're going to look conspicuous.'

'Agreed. Let's move the feet now.'

Nield waited until they were in the deserted hall and suggested a breath of fresh air. They wandered out under the ancient portal into a deserted High Street. Opposite the entrance the old Yarn Market with its many-sided roof was shrouded in shadow. A moon cast a pale glow over the silence. Barrymore's Daimler was parked across the road.

'How's the recording?' Butler enquired, thrusting his hands into his trouser pockets.

'Let's check. Inside the Yarn Market would be a good place . . .'

Taking the recorder out of his pocket, Nield turned the volume to 'low' as they stood under the roof. He pressed the button which reversed the tape. Then he switched on the sound and together they listened.

Another large Scotch . . . Of course, sir. Coming right away . . . Pushing the boat out a bit, aren't we . . .

Nield switched off. He gazed through one of the arched openings to the far end of the town. The eerie silhouette of the brooding castle loomed above the buildings. The sudden silence of night was uncanny.

'Perfect,' Butler commented. 'The voice tone is good. You can tell who is talking.'

'I think I ought to drive up to London tonight,' Nield suggested. 'Then Tweed can hear the tape in the morning. I can drive back here tomorrow if that's OK.'

'Do it,' Butler agreed. 'While you're away I think I'll keep an eye on the colonel.'

'Why choose him?'

'Sixth sense. As Tweed would say . . .'

24

Three people were seated round Tweed's desk as he listened to the tape for the third time. Monica sat crouched forward, her head turned to one side, her forehead crinkled with concentration.

Paula sat upright, notebook in her lap as she made notes. On the third replay she ignored the notebook, staring out of the window as she visualized the faces of the three men whose conversation was reeling out as they had talked over dinner at The Luttrell Arms.

Tweed was the most relaxed. He sat back in the swivel chair, his hands resting on the desk-top, no particular expression on his face. He glanced at Pete Nield, seated behind Paula's desk, who was smoking a cigarette while he watched the others. The recording ended, Tweed switched off the machine.

'Very interesting, most revealing. What they said. And the relationship between those three men.'

'The reference to the Greek Key?' Paula suggested.

'That possibly, but something else. Pete, describe to me how they were seated. You came in with Harry to find them starting dinner?'

'No. We carefully did it the other way round – to avoid calling attention to ourselves. Harry asked one of the staff when they normally arrived for their weekly dinner. So we were at our table when they came in. Other tables were occupied with guests so we merged with the background.'

'And how were they seated in relationship to the two of you?' Tweed repeated.

Paula looked puzzled. She couldn't fathom the reason behind the question.

'They came into the dining room about ten minutes later,' explained Nield. 'They walked past us. We had our backs towards them as they entered. You know the corner table where they sit?' Tweed nodded and Nield went on. 'Barrymore and Robson faced us. Kearns had his back to us the whole time. Which is why his voice comes across quieter.'

'I thought it was like that. Something said in their conversation could be very significant. I may have the lead I've been waiting for.'

'And you wouldn't care to tell us what that is?' Paula enquired.

254

'Not for the moment. In case I'm wrong.' Tweed smiled. 'Listen to the tape on your own a few times. You might get it.'

Paula glanced down at her notes, then clenched her fists with a gesture of frustration. 'You'll drive me crazy with your hints one of these days.'

Monica nodded sympathetically. 'I know just what you mean. He's been doing it with me for years.'

'If you agree,' Nield said, 'I plan to drive straight back to join Butler again on Exmoor. Have there been any developments at this end?'

'Bob Newman called from Athens . . .' Tweed gave him a concise account of their conversation, picking out the main elements of the data Newman had passed on. 'Does anyone spot something odd about what he told me? Bearing in mind the clear description he gave of the topography of where Andreas Gavalas was killed?'

Three blank faces stared back at him. Paula pursed her full lips and sighed. 'Here we go again – more mysterious hints. I give up.'

'I have two questions I'd dearly love answers to,' Tweed told them as he perched his elbows on the desk. 'The raid on Siros. The three-man commando team – with Andreas – land on a hostile coast. They make their way up a twisting gulch. That gulch is overlooked by a monastery perched on Mount Ida like the nest of an eagle. The Germans have established a permanently manned lookout post on top of that monastery looking straight down the gulch. Why, then, in heaven's name, did the raiding party choose that point to climb up the island? There must have been scores of other places safer for them to choose.'

'Does sound very strange,' Paula agreed. 'Plus the fact that the body went missing.'

'My second question,' Tweed went on, 'is what happened to the cache of diamonds Andreas was carrying to hand over to Greek Resistance fighters on Siros? In those days they were worth about one hundred thousand pounds – so Brigadier Willie Davies at the MOD told me.'

'Stolen by the man who murdered Andreas,' Paula said promptly. 'Maybe we're dealing with a case of simple robbery.'

'I don't think so,' Tweed objected. 'And I've been to see a leading diamond merchant in Hatton Garden I know. I asked him what a parcel of diamonds worth a hundred thousand back in 1944 would be worth today. I got a shock.' He paused, looked round. 'Any estimates? No? My contact could only make a rough guess. Something in the region of one million pounds sterling.'

There was a stunned silence in his office. Nield screwed up his eyes, thinking hard. Paula crossed her legs, tapped her pen against her teeth, then reacted.

'So we may be looking for something – or someone – showing signs of great wealth? What about Barrymore and Quarme Manor?'

Tweed shook his head. 'He bought it years ago. Probably for a song.'

'He has a Daimler,' Paula persisted.

'An old job,' Nield interjected. 'Looks glitzy but wouldn't fetch all that much. A cool million? The only thing I've seen in the area is that modern little estate of de luxe bungalows near Kearns' place . . .'

'We're looking for something pointing to one of those three men we've listened to on the tape,' Paula objected.

Tweed was hardly listening. 'That business of where they landed on Siros. And the missing body. The priest told Newman they had asked the commander of the German occupation troops about Andreas. None of his patrols knew a thing. And Geiger was convinced they were telling the truth. So who else on the island could have spirited away the body? There's only one answer.'

'Which is?' Paula asked.

'It had to be some of the Greek Resistance people. But which lot? And why on earth would they do that? Now our next job is to pay a visit to Guy Seton-Charles. You come with me, Paula.'

'And who might he be?' she enquired.

'A name in Partridge's notebook. A professor of Greek Studies at Bristol University. The intriguing fact is he was based in the Antikhana Building at the time of Ionides' murder.'

'How could he help?' Paula persisted. 'After all this time?'

'That's what I want to find out.' Tweed swung in his chair to face Nield. 'You come with us to Bristol in a separate car – then later return to Exmoor to provide Butler with back-up. I want those three men to be aware of your presence. It will put pressure on them, may force one of them to make a wrong move.'

'You've used that tactic before,' Monica commented. 'And it worked. You're doing the same thing with this Seton-Charles, aren't you?'

'Partridge found out something,' Tweed remarked sombrely. 'I am certain he was murdered because he approached the wrong man. Which man?'

The timing was better than Tweed could have hoped for. He was approaching Professor Seton-Charles' room when the door opened and a brunette in her early twenties rushed out. She was in such a rush she almost collided with Paula who was walking alongside Tweed. The door automatically closed behind her on spring-loaded hinges. Very slim, her intelligent face flushed, she stopped abruptly, clutching a green folder.

'I'm dreadfully sorry. I could have knocked you down.'

'I'm pretty sturdy . . .' Paula began, and smiled.

257

'You look really upset,' Tweed said quickly. 'Professor in a bad mood?'

'The sarcastic bastard! I'm not attending any more classes he takes . . .' The girl flushed again. 'Oh, Lord, I'm sorry. Are you friends of his . . .'

'Hardly.' Tweed acted on instinct. 'We've come to investigate him. Special Branch. What's the matter with him?' he asked persuasively.

'Everything! He's a bloody Trotskyite. Tries to brainwash us . . .' She paused. 'God, I'm saying all the wrong things.'

'Don't worry, we won't quote you.' He squeezed her arm. 'Do me a favour. We were never here. Agreed?'

'My pleasure. I'd better push off now.' She turned back for a last word. 'And I can keep my mouth shut. Give him hell.'

Tweed waited until she had disappeared round a corner at the end of the corridor. Then he knocked on the door which carried a name in gilt lettering. *Prof. Guy Seton-Charles*. The door opened swiftly. A man started talking and then stopped when he saw them.

'That's my last word, Louise. You have an IQ of minus . . .'

'Special Branch.' Tweed showed his card. 'You're alone. Good. May we come in . . .' He was walking forward as he spoke while the man backed away and Paula followed, closing the door. 'You are Professor Seton-Charles? This is Miss Grey, my assistant, who will take notes during the interview.'

'Interview about what?'

'The unsolved murder of a Greek called Ionides in Cairo over forty years ago. We can sit round that table. If anyone arrives to interrupt the interview please tell them you're busy, get rid of them.'

Tweed was at his most officious. He fetched two fold-up chairs from several rows arranged beyond the table. The

258

room was furnished starkly; walls bare, painted off-white; the table for the lecturer to sit behind and address his class; windows on the far wall which looked out on to a roughcast concrete wall.

Guy Seton-Charles was a slimly built man in his early sixties, Tweed estimated. His face was plump and pale, and perched on his Roman nose was a pair of rimless glasses. The eyes which stared at them were cold and bleak and wary. He had thinning brown hair, was clean-shaven, his mouth was pouched in a superior expression. Prototype of the self-conscious intellectual, Tweed decided.

He was dressed informally in a loose-fitting check sports jacket, a cream shirt, a blue woollen tie and baggy grey slacks. Not a man who gave much attention to his personal appearance.

'This is an unwarranted invasion of privacy,' Seton-Charles protested in a high-pitched voice.

'Oh, I can get a warrant,' Tweed assured him, 'but then we'd have to hold the interview in London at headquarters. Might not be possible to avoid a certain amount of publicity . . .'

'There's going to be publicity,' the Professor spluttered. 'I can promise you that . . .'

'About a murder investigation in which you might be involved? No skin off my nose.' Tweed was seated on one of the fold-up chairs. He pointed to the chair behind the desk. 'Unless you want to sit down and hear why we are here. Make up your mind.'

'Murder investigation? About Ionides? You're a bit late in the day, aren't you?'

His tone was truculent, sneering, but Tweed noted he had sat in his chair, a significant concession. He frowned as Paula sat in the other chair, produced her notebook, rested it on her lap and waited, pen poised.

'Is she going to record my answers? A bit bureaucratic and official.'

259

'Oh, it's official.' Tweed's expression was grim.

'All about a forty-year-old murder?'

'Which may be directly linked with two more very recent murders.'

Behind the rimless glasses Seton-Charles' greenish eyes flickered. Tweed had the impression he was thrown off balance. He recovered quickly.

'Which murders? If I am permitted to ask. It all sounds so melodramatic.' A tinge of sarcasm in his voice now.

'We may come to that later. Let's go back to Greece – and Cairo during the war. You had a job and an office inside the Antikhana as a young man. Why weren't you in the Forces?'

'Didn't pass the physical, if you must know. My eyesight.'

'What was your job? Start talking, Professor. I'm a very good listener. It's your job – talking.'

'Even as a young man I had an interest in Greece. It's my subject,' he added pedantically. 'They said I could do my bit for the war effort by going to the Mid-East. I was packed off aboard a troopship round the Cape and landed up in Cairo. My job was to create propaganda to encourage the Greek Resistance . . .'

'Which side?' Tweed snapped.

'Oh, you know about that battle in high places? The SOE lot – Special Operations Executive – in Cairo had a fetish for backing the right-wing crowd. Wanted to bring back the King after the Germans were defeated. Wrong side altogether. The EDES people. The London end were brighter – possibly as a result of reading my reports.' He preened himself with a knowing smile. 'It was the ELAS organization who were killing Germans by the score . . .'

'The Communists, you mean,' Tweed interjected. 'After Russia had been attacked by Hitler, of course.'

'No need to be snide . . .'

'Merely stating a fact. You supported the idea of switching the airdrop of arms to the Communists. That right?'

'Yes. As I told you, they were really fighting the enemy – and London agreed. Churchill himself took the decision, so I heard. Killing Germans was his main aim in life in those days . . .'

'And Ionides was the man you worked closely with,' Tweed guessed.

'I wrote the text for leaflets in English. Ionides translated them into perfect Greek. I wasn't up to that then. I didn't know him at all well. We worked through secretaries. Hardly ever spoke a word to him. Very close-mouthed, our Mr Ionides.'

'Who do you think killed him so savagely? And why?'

'No idea. My billet was an apartment in another part of Cairo. I wasn't there the night it happened.'

'Quite so.' Tweed gazed at the concrete wall beyond the window, switched the topic suddenly. 'Where do you live, Professor?'

'You do jump about . . .'

'Just answer the question, please.'

'I bought a bungalow on a new estate near Simonsbath on Exmoor. Rather exclusive . . .'

'You work here in Bristol, yet you live on Exmoor?' Tweed's tone expressed disbelief. 'Why?'

Seton-Charles sighed heavily as though his patience was wearing thin. He spoke as though explaining a simple point to a child. 'With the motorway a lot of people commute between a home on Exmoor and Bristol. Businessmen as well as university professors, amazing as it may seem. My hobby is walking. I like the open country, the moor. Would you like a list of some other people who live exactly as I do? Your assistant could take down names, help to fill out your report.'

'Might be helpful,' Tweed agreed equably. 'Plus the occupation or profession of everyone living on that bungalow estate.'

Seton-Charles' expression went blank. Something like venom flashed behind the glasses, then disappeared. Tweed was puzzled so he kept silent, forcing the other man to react.

'I don't know anyone on the estate,' the Professor snapped. 'I keep to myself. I take students' papers home to work on. Any free time I walk the moors, as I've already told you. I was referring to the *bourgeoisie* who live in luxury pads near Taunton.'

'That bungalow you live in must have cost a packet,' Tweed observed in the same level tone.

'I have a huge mortgage, if it's any concern of yours. The colonel was very helpful.'

'The colonel?'

Tweed was careful not to look at Paula. He sensed she had frozen, pen poised in mid-air. Only for seconds then she relaxed as Tweed waited again. Seton-Charles was answering more slowly.

'Colonel Winterton. He owned the land the estate was built on – had some old barns pulled down. That was why he was permitted to build. With a restriction the houses should be one storey high.'

'Where can I find this Winterton?'

'No idea. I never met him. I dealt with his staff at an office he had in Taunton. It was a package deal – he arranged the mortgages where required. He was fussy about who he sold the properties to. You had to qualify.'

'How?' Tweed pressed.

'I don't know about the others. When he heard I was a professor in Greek Studies he accepted me. I think the other residents are brokers, solicitors – boring things like that. They leave for work before me, I get back when they've got home. We don't mix.'

'So you could give me the address of Winterton's office based in Taunton? I'd like that.'

'You're welcome to it. Except it's no longer there.'

262

'What do you mean? Stop playing the half-smart intellectual with me.'

'You don't know everything . . .' Seton-Charles paused. Paula could have sworn he changed like a chameleon, then recovered, changed back again. Something about the cold glint in the eyes. 'Once he'd sold all the properties he closed down the office and the whole outfit vanished.'

'Vanished?' Tweed's tone was sharp. 'Explain that.'

'The staff weren't local. They disappeared. The rumour was that Winterton pocketed his profits and went to live abroad.'

'The whole outfit didn't vanish,' Tweed objected. 'Who do you pay your mortgage interest and repayments to?'

'Oh, we found out that was handled by the Pitlochry Insurance Company. Winterton had simply acted as middleman, taken his commission. That's it. End of the trail.'

Was there a smug note in Seton-Charles' voice? Paula couldn't be certain. He sat behind the table, smooth-skinned hands linked together. Like a man satisfied he had closed all the loopholes.

'You visit Greece frequently?' Tweed said suddenly.

'I go to Athens spasmodically.' He was frowning as though he hadn't expected this thrust. 'I have links with the university there. Take seminars . . .'

'Your last visit was when?'

'A few weeks ago. I thought we started out with the murder of Ionides over forty years ago.'

'We did.' Tweed stood up. 'Which makes a good point at which to end our first interview.'

'Our *first* interview?'

'That's what I said,' Tweed replied and walked out.

They waited in the Mercedes loaned by Newman, waited in the car park. Tweed sat behind the wheel, Paula stirred restlessly beside him. There was no one else about and they were hedged in by cars on either side.

'What do you think of him?' Paula asked. 'And why did you insult him with that half-smart intellectual crack? Not your normal style.'

'To rattle him. I think it worked. *You don't know everything.* He got that far and stopped what he had been going on to say. Something funny about that new estate of bungalows near where Kearns lives. And Pete Nield, who often hits the nail on the head, remarked that estate was the only thing he'd seen on Exmoor worth a cool million. Something like that.'

'Where is Pete? He followed us down here from Park Crescent as you suggested, then dropped out of sight.'

'He's parked in the Cortina up the road. Again as I suggested. I want to see if Seton-Charles takes the bait.'

'Don't understand.' She gave a rueful smile. 'Par for the course – working with you. I still don't see why there should be something funny about the bungalow estate.'

'There may not be – but Seton-Charles is an experienced lecturer, used to fielding the sort of questions I threw at him. He answered fairly tersely, then went out of his way to explain a lot about the estate. I don't think he liked my asking where he lived. Now, who have we here?'

'Professor Seton-Charles – and in one devil of a hurry.'

In the distance the Professor was wending his way among the army of parked vehicles. He carried a briefcase and his hair was flurried in a breeze. For a man in his sixties he moved with great agility.

'Maybe it has worked,' Tweed commented. 'Pressure. Everyone remembers the last thing you say. I mentioned this was the first interview, suggesting I'd be back. One odd thing about our conversation. He only made a brief comment on my reference to two more recent murders. The *absence* of something so often goes unnoticed.'

'Well I didn't notice it, but I was taking notes. Are you going all mysterious on me again?'

'The absence of any later comment by the Professor. You'd expect almost anyone to come back to that – to ask again what I'd been talking about. Whose murders? He didn't . . .'

'He's getting into a Volvo station wagon. Do we follow?'

'No, too obvious . . .'

'He's a professor. His mind will probably be miles away while he's driving.'

'Seton-Charles,' Tweed told her, 'has a mind like a steel trap. He may have nothing to do with what we're looking for, but he has to be checked out. And carefully . . .'

Tweed waited until the Volvo was moving towards the exit, then turned on his ignition. He drove out of the slot slowly, turned into the main aisle as Seton-Charles shot at speed for the exit. 'Speedy Gonzalez,' Paula commented. Tweed arrived at the exit seconds after the Volvo had swung left. Perching with the nose of the Mercedes at the exit, he flashed his lights. Seconds later Nield drove past the exit, following the Volvo in Tweed's Cortina.

'There, it worked,' Tweed said with some satisfaction.

'You arranged with Pete to park outside?'

'Yes. I foresaw I might get lucky, pressure Seton-Charles into leaving. Pete will see where he heads for, who he meets, and report back to me.' He checked his watch. 'Three o'clock – we can make Park Crescent by early evening. We'll be driving into London when the commuters are pouring out.'

'Pressure all round,' Paula remarked as they left the car park. 'Butler and Nield showing themselves to the ex-commando trio. After Nield has tracked Seton-Charles. You think we're getting somewhere?'

'Time will tell. I'm waiting for someone to crack. Here – or in Greece.'

Monica looked up as they entered Tweed's office. 'Nield called ten minutes ago . . .' The phone started ringing. 'Maybe that's him.' A brief exchange, she nodded towards Tweed's phone.

'Just got in, Pete,' Tweed said. 'Any news?'

'Subject drives straight back to Exmoor, makes a call from a public box near Simonsbath. Which is strange.'

'Why?'

'He has a phone in his bungalow. They have overhead wires out here. A three-minute call – and he checks his watch.'

'And then?'

'Drives back to the estate and into his garage. He has one of those electronic devices so you can open it from inside the car. Something else odd I noticed. Perched on the roof of his bungalow is one of the most complex aerial systems I've ever seen – plus a satellite dish. A whole mess of technical gear. Change of subject. Gossip in the pubs reports a dog ferreting on Exmoor came home with Partridge's wallet in its mouth. A hundred pounds, all in tenners, intact. Banknote numbers in sequence. That's it.'

'You've done well. Get back to Butler in Dunster. Start a campaign of harassing all three men. Put on the pressure – but from a distance. And watch your backs.'

'Will do. 'Bye, Chief.'

Tweed put down the receiver, jumped up from his desk and began pacing the office as he rubbed his hands with satisfaction.

'Things are moving. It worked, Paula. Seton-Charles called someone from a public booth. Reporting my interrogation of him, I'm sure. We're on the right track.'

'At last,' said Monica.

'And I want you to call Inspector Farthing of Dunster police,' he told her. 'Partridge's wallet has been found. I'd like a list of everything inside that wallet. Someone may just have made the fatal mistake I've been waiting for.'

At the summit of the mountain where he used his transceiver Florakis-Savinkov completed sending the latest coded message to England. The pace was hotting up. Earlier he had been instructed to receive the signals from Athens weekly. Now it was twice a week. The radio traffic was increasing.

He was about to sign off when he was amazed to receive an order given in clear English. He blinked as he recorded the message. *From now on call sign changed to Colonel Winter.*

25

Newman was in shirt-sleeves as he drove along the coast road which twisted and turned and was empty of other traffic. It was twilight time, the most torrid period of the day as the earth gave up its heat and the atmosphere was cloying and humid. Nick sat beside him with a worried frown; beyond him the Mediterranean was indigo, a smooth sheet of water stretching away towards the hulk of a huge rock rearing up out of the water.

In the distance a toy-like temple perched at the summit of a cliff was silhouetted against a purple sky: the pencil-thin columns of the Temple of Poseidon where Harry Masterson had died. In the rear of the car Christina pulled at the tops of her slacks thrust inside climbing boots. She was perspiring all over. It had been one hell of a hot day and her nerves were twanging at what they planned to do.

'Tell me when to stop,' Newman called over his shoulder. 'We must be near now.'

'Round the next two bends. That structure we're passing is on the land of a farmer called Florakis. He sold it to a developer.'

Newman glanced at the ruin-like structure on the landward side. In the half-light it looked like an abandoned building site, as though the developer had run out of money.

'What is that place?' he asked.

'The beginning of a new hotel complex,' Nick replied. 'They are spoiling the whole coast with new tourist developments.'

The structure had a weird skeletal look. Two storeys high, it consisted of a steel framework for several buildings and he could see right through it to the hillside beyond, like staring through the bones of a Martian-type skeleton eroded by time.

'I still don't like the idea of you going with Christina into Devil's Valley,' Nick said for the second time. 'Petros has armed shepherds patrolling the area night and day. They all carry rifles. Tourists, amateur mountaineers who have gone in there never came out. They had "accidents". They fell over precipices, God knows what. I must warn you . . .'

'Thanks, Nick. You have warned me. You've done all you can.'

'Then stay away from that old silver mine. Please.'

'Of course. The idea never entered my head.'

Christina bit her knuckles to stop herself protesting. Newman *was* going into Devil's Valley with the sole idea of locating the silver mine. He had concealed his plan from Marler as well as from Nick. At first she demurred at his suggestion to act as his guide into the Valley. But he had the map she had marked when they had dinner at the Hilton two weeks ago.

'Stop the car round the next bend,' she called out. 'You can park it well off the road on a flat area. It is part of Florakis' land but farmers go to bed early because they rise at dawn.'

Newman pulled in, turned the car in a wide half-circle so it faced the way they had come. He switched off the engine. A brooding silence fell over the mountains which rose close to the road. In the back Christina shivered at the lack of sound. A moon was rising, casting a pale illumination over the arid mountain slopes, the still, endless sea.

'Nick,' Newman told him, 'I think the car would be concealed much better if you drove it back to that building site.' He looked at Christina who had climbed out and was standing alongside him. 'We could find that on the way back easily with the moon up, I assume?'

'Yes. It would be a good landmark . . .'

'And exactly where do we go to find the entrance to Devil's Valley?'

'Straight up that gulch. It's on Florakis' land but only for a short distance. I can show you on the map.'

Newman slipped on his sports jacket, took a pencil torch attached to the breast pocket, shielded it with his hand and opened the map. Christina traced the route up the gulch, showed where it led to the entrance to Devil's Valley. Newman held his hand so Nick couldn't see the cross which marked the silver mine.

'We'd better get moving,' he said. He checked his watch. Well after ten o'clock. He opened the glove compartment, took out Nick's revolver, slid it inside his hip holster, pocketed spare ammo. 'You won't fall asleep?' he asked Nick. 'We'll be away for some time.'

269

'Not me. I can stay awake all night. And I'll drive back to the hotel development and wait for you there.'

'See you. The rifle is in the back -- just in case.'

'It will be in my hands until you return,' Nick promised.

Parked in the shadows of the steel framework, Nick was careful. He smoked the cigarette inside his cupped hand. The headlights of the car approaching from the Athens direction appeared only five minutes after he had arrived. He stubbed out the cigarette. It was the first vehicle he had seen for over an hour.

The headlights swung over the building site as the car slowed. They swept over his Mercedes. He opened the door, took a firmer grip on the rifle, the muzzle aimed through the gap. The car was stopping.

It backed slowly, very slowly. For the second time the headlights played over the Mercedes, for a longer period. Nick sat very still, raised the muzzle slightly, slipped off the safety catch. The car had stopped now. The headlights stayed on, beamed at an angle beyond his own vehicle, glaring on the building site, which took on a surrealist quality in the dazzle.

Nick had acute hearing. He listened in the heavy silence -- for the opening of a car door, the crunch of feet on the loose stones covering the ground. Nothing. The silence grew heavier. Sweat began trickling down his neck. He sat immobile as a Greek statue. Nothing. The driver couldn't be a ghost . . .

'Hello, Nick. I could have shot you rather dead.'

Marler's voice, speaking through the open passenger seat window. How the hell could a man move so silently?

'Come on, Nick, where have they gone? Newman and Christina? I followed you from Athens, so where are they? Exploring Devil's Valley?'

Nick reached for the bottle of mineral water, took a long swig. He was in a state of shock. And couldn't decide whether to tell Marler the truth. Marler seemed to read his mind as he leant an elbow on the open window.

'Loyalty is a virtue. Especially for a Greek. I know that. I also know you wouldn't want something to happen to Newman – something fatal. The last man who made friends with Christina ended up at the bottom of a cliff. She's all Gavalas. So, tell me – Newman needs back-up. Desperately. We're talking about Devil's Valley.'

'Christina is guiding him to the entrance to the Valley. He is going to find the old silver mine. I know it. He said he wasn't but I know he was. They went up a gulch two bends further down the road.'

'Show me. And mark the location of that silver mine.'

Marler dropped a large-scale map of the area into Nick's lap. 'I don't know the exact location of the mine . . .' Nick protested.

'Do the best you can. Hurry. I'm driving my car alongside yours. Back in a minute . . .'

He parked his vehicle a few feet away from Nick's, doused the lights and walked to the boot. He appeared at Nick's window and the Greek stared. Marler wore mountaineer boots, had a long loop of rope coiled over one shoulder, an Armalite rifle over the other.

'You came equipped?' Nick said.

'I saw Newman and Christina buying boots in a shop. I guessed the rest. I'm a good guesser. Marked the map yet?'

He studied the map Nick had marked by the overhead light. He nodded, took the map, refolded it, shoved it inside his pocket.

'I'm off on my travels now. See you.'

'It could be dangerous . . .'

'I agree. For anyone I meet up there.'

* * *

Newman led the way up the gulch with Christina close behind. The moonlight helped. He was careful where he placed his feet: the gulch was littered with loose rocks. Sound carried a long way at night. He was relieved to hear no sound from Christina as she plodded up behind him. Which is why he heard the faint tumble of stones slithering.

He stopped, turned, grasped Christina by the arm, raised one finger to his lips. Unlike some women she didn't ask questions: she simply raised one thick eyebrow. He crouched down behind a boulder, pressing her down, and her shoulder rested against his.

'Someone else on the mountain,' he whispered.

'I didn't hear anything – and I have good hearing . . .'

Another slither of stones. One came over the side of the gulch and touched Newman's right boot. Christina nodded. Newman had been right. Someone was approaching and very close.

They were crouched behind the large boulder at a point where the gulch began to turn sharply above them to the left. Whoever was on the prowl couldn't be descending the gulch, thank God, Newman thought. For the stone to have slithered from immediately above them the intruder had to be moving higher up the slope. Could he see down inside the gulch? Newman slipped the revolver out of the holster and Christina gripped his other arm. He looked up and froze. He hardly dared breathe. He held his body tense – for fear of dislodging even a pebble.

Along the crest of the ridge above, the silhouette of a man was moving. In the moonlight Newman could clearly see the bony profile, the prominent nose, the sunken cheeks beneath prominent cheekbones, the curve of the mouth. Over one shoulder was looped a rifle. He was carrying something in the other hand – something heavy. Newman frowned and then felt his right leg begin to cramp. He gritted his teeth.

Christina, hunched beside him, kept perfectly still.

272

Newman was staring at the heavy bag the man was carrying as he climbed the mountain – he knew it was heavy from the way the figure sagged to one side. But it wasn't a bag. It was rectangular-shaped, like a metal box. Newman was certain it was a high-powered transceiver – and that size meant it was capable of transmitting over long distance. The silhouette disappeared behind the ridge.

'That was Florakis,' Christina whispered. 'Someone pointed him out to me in the Plaka.'

'You're sure? In this light . . .'

'Positive. I could see his profile clearly. And he is walking on his own land. What on earth can he be doing at this time of night?'

'No idea,' Newman lied. 'Let's get moving. How much further to Devil's Valley?'

'We're nearly there. Another hundred feet up this gulch and we cross the pass. Then it's downhill . . .'

They climbed higher up the gulch inside its shadow, the ground levelled out and Christina pointed. Beyond, a track descended into an arid steep-sided valley, the slopes studded with scrub. The crest of the far side was lower and, following the line of her extended arm, Newman saw a weird structure perched on the crest. It looked like a large shack, but there were no walls. Between the supporting pillars at each corner there was open space and moonlit sky beyond the apertures.

'The old silver mine,' Christina said. 'A track from that huddle of boulders down there leads straight up to it. Mules used to bring the ore from the mine down that track years ago.'

'You know your way back?' Newman enquired casually.

'I know every inch of this country. As a child I used to roam all over it. I liked to go down that gulch so I could cross the highway and swim in the sea.'

'Sorry about this. It's for your own good . . .' Newman swung round and clipped her on the jaw. He caught her as

273

she sagged and laid her carefully on the ground, placing her head on a soft tuft of grass as a pillow. He checked her pulse, found it was regular. Taking out the note he had prepared earlier, he tucked it inside the top of her slacks. Then he hoisted the rifle on his shoulder and started the descent, heading for the silver mine.

'There is someone coming up the track,' said Dimitrios and he slipped the safety catch off his rifle.

'You are imagining it,' objected Constantine. 'You see ghosts everywhere. Because of what is in the mine . . .'

'Someone is climbing that track,' Dimitrios insisted. 'I tell you I saw something move.'

'Now he says he *saw* something,' Constantine scoffed. 'In the past tense. Sure, he saw something move – a goat, maybe?'

Petros had sent them out as he did regularly – as another form of discipline, of keeping them under his thick thumb. And forcing them to stay up all night in the open toughened them. Petros had a dozen reasons for exerting his authority.

'Tonight you will go up and guard the mine,' he had ordered. 'One day there will be an intruder. Too many have been poking their snouts into my valley. And all accursed English. First there was Partridge – and he gave you the slip. Then came Masterson. Now we have more. This Newman, this Marler. Why so many so suddenly? Am I the only one who can scent danger? You go tonight . . .'

So they had climbed to the summit of the ridge close to where the mine reared up like a hideous eyeless monument. Constantine peered over the edge to where he could see stretches of the track as it mounted up to a point a quarter of a mile from where they waited.

Parts of the track were clearly illuminated by the moon; other parts were obscured by overhangs of rock, by the blackest of shadows. He could see nothing. From his ragged jacket pocket he pulled the bottle of *ouzo*. He handed it towards Dimitrios as he sneered at his brother.

'Drink some. It will steady the nerves of an old woman . . .'

'You talk to me like that and I break your scrawny neck, wring it like a chicken's.'

But Dimitrios snatched the bottle, tore out the cork and upended it. The liquid gurgled down his throat. That was better. He recorked the bottle, looked at Constantine and stiffened.

'What is it, cretin?'

'There is someone down there now coming up the track – a man with a rifle. A well-built man used to rough country.'

'Where?'

Dimitrios peered over the edge, saw nothing – only the wending track which came and went. Into the moonlight. Back into the shadows. He leaned over further, his mouth a thin slit, shoved the bottle into his own jacket, rested both hands on the rock, still staring down.

'Now you see ghosts.' He glanced at his brother. 'What are you doing?'

Constantine, always the quieter, the calmer of the two brothers, was checking his shotgun. He nodded with satisfaction. Then looked at Dimitrios.

'Inside ten minutes he will appear at the top of the track. We move now to that point. That is where we prepare the ambush.'

'And we drop the body down the mine . . .'

Marler had taken a short cut from the hotel site where Nick was waiting with the parked cars. He had scaled the almost sheer face of the mountain, working his way up a chimney hollowed out of the limestone. The map had shown him he would reach the pass far more quickly

275

than by following the route Newman and Christina had taken.

Now he heaved himself over the top and the pass was thirty feet below. He descended rapidly, reached the entrance to the pass, stopped, head cocked to one side. The rope was again looped over one shoulder, the rifle over the other. Someone was coming. He heard the stealthy movement of feet padding among the bed of pebbles. A thick needle-shaped column of rock rose up near the track. He slipped behind it.

Christina was in a cold fury. Her jaw was sore, but that was nothing. When she regained consciousness she had found the note tucked inside the top of her slacks. Its message was clear – to the point. *Christina, this expedition is too dangerous for me to take you any further. Sorry for the tap on the chin. Go straight back to Nick. I'll join you there. Later. Bob.*

The stupid swine. She could have helped him find the mine, showed him where to veer off the track so he reached it more quickly. She *knew* the country. He didn't. And her sharp eyes could have spotted any shepherd guards lurking . . .

The arm came round the back of her neck, lifted her off her feet. She used her elbows to thud into the midriff of her attacker, her feet to kick back at his shins. She wriggled like a snake and the pressure on her throat increased. The voice whispered in her ear.

'Don't want to strangle you. Relax. Go limp. I'll let you go. Be quiet. There may be others about. Ready?'

Marler's voice. She stopped struggling. He released her. She turned round. His expression was bleak. She swung her right hand with the speed of a striking snake. The flat of her hand slapped hard into the side of his face. His head didn't move.

'Make you feel better? Jezebel . . .'

'Why call me that, you bastard?'

276

'Because you've just led Newman into another trap – the way you did with Masterson . . .'

'You bloody idiot!' She waved Newman's note at him. 'Better read that. He socked me one, left me behind because he was worried about me . . .'

'Worried you'd betray him . . .'

'Read the bloody note.'

He shrugged, took the note, read it, then looked at her. 'OK. Tell me where he's gone.'

'To the silver mine. The crazy idiot. He's a suicide case.'

'Hardly. At least I hope not. Care to tell me exactly where this mine is?'

'You can see it from the end of the pass. I'll show you . . .'

Her long legs covered the ground in minutes. Marler had collected the rifle and rope he had left behind the needle of rock and hurried to catch up with her. At the end of the pass again she pointed, indicating the position of the silver mine. Marler frowned, then turned to her. She waited, hands on her hips, her expression contemptuous, eyes flashing. He lifted a hand and his slim fingers closed round her chin. She gritted her teeth, determined not to wince. The gentle way he handled her was a surprise. He turned her chin to examine it by the light of the moon.

'Sorry. I was checking to see how hard he'd hit you. Scarcely a bruise. Just enough to put you out. How long ago do you think he left you?'

She looked at her watch. 'I checked it just before we got here. I must have been out cold ten minutes. No more than fifteen.'

'Then I have to hurry. Anything you can tell me to help?'

She repeated what she had told Newman. She pointed out where the track ran up to the mine. But this time she tried to show where Marler could veer off three-quarters of the way up, cutting across direct to a point just below the mine.

277

'Got it,' Marler said. 'Do me a favour. Go back to Nick. I think I can make it faster on my own. And I don't want to have to worry about you.'

'I'm popular with the men tonight, aren't I? Marler, why are you waiting? Get there fast . . .'

Newman had caught the faintest hint of movement high up and out of the corner of his eye. Imagination? He remembered the man he'd only known as Sarge. The time when he'd trained with the SAS – the Special Air Service – Britain's élite strike force, so he could write a series of articles on them. Sarge had put him through the full course. And he'd survived it. Just.

If you even suspect you've seen something, heard something, smelt something – *assume the worst*. You've been seen. Sarge, the toughest man Newman had ever known, the sergeant who'd put him through his paces, had said something else. Get inside the enemy's mind. Sit in *his* chair. What would you do *if you were him*? Out-think the bastard . . .

Newman moved into the shadows out of the moonlight. He paused, took out the compact pair of night glasses he'd bought in Athens. His mouth was parched with thirst, with fear. His boots, his clothes, were coated with limestone dust from his journey up the track. Slinging the glasses from his neck, he took the opportunity to relieve himself against a rock. Then he took a swig from the small bottle of mineral water in his pocket. Now . . .

He leant against the side of the rock and raised the glasses, aiming them where he thought he'd seen something move at the top of the ridge to the right of the track. He moved the glasses slowly, scanning the whole ridge. He stopped. Silhouetted against the night sky was the outline of a man, a man peering over a rock parapet. Got you. He held the glasses very still. No doubt about it. One of the shepherd guards. And he held the high ground. Time to rethink.

Assume the worst. He'd been spotted. Coming up the track. So what would the enemy do? Wait for him where the track emerged at the top. The solution? Get off the track. Move up to the left. However rough the going. Head diagonally straight for the mine. He put the glasses back into his pocket. Began climbing higher, so long as he kept in the shadow. He nearly missed the defile spiralling up to his left.

It looked pretty steep, but rock projections formed a kind of ladder. He entered the defile, felt safe from observation. It was exactly like climbing a ladder. He placed his boots on each projection, hauled himself higher and higher. He began to feel the strain on his calf muscles. He was sweating litres with the effort. Keep going. He must be close to the top.

His head and shoulders projected above the defile without warning. He remained perfectly still. Listening. Sniffing. For the smell of a mule. The shepherd might well be patrolling on an animal. He turned his head very slowly. He had emerged just below the crest of the ridge. Keep below it. That was the mistake the shepherd had made. He could see the spectral outline of the mine. No more than a hundred yards to his left.

No sign or sound of anyone else. He rubbed the calves of both legs. No time to get cramp. He hefted the Smith & Wesson out of the holster, moved towards the mine in a crouch, placing his feet carefully. The ground was powdered dust. Easy to slip on. The mine came closer.

'The bastard has tricked us.'

Dimitrios stood at the top of a huge crag which gave him a view of the whole length of the ridge. Below him

Constantine waited, gripping his shotgun. Dimitrios clambered down and joined his brother.

'What do you mean?' Constantine asked.

'I saw him moving. He's nearly reached the mine. We'll have to hurry. He left the track, came up a different way.'

'Then let's get moving. If we lose him Petros will go mad.'

'Petros is mad. Maybe we don't tell him what happened. That shaft goes down forever. Who is to know? So long as you keep your big mouth shut. I lead, you follow. We've got him cornered.'

Newman approached the weird structure cautiously. There could be another guard hidden and waiting. Resisting the temptation to peer inside the shaft, he crawled slowly round, pausing at each of the four corners. The structure reminded him of a ruined Greek temple constructed of rusting iron. He peered round the final corner. Nothing.

He had completed one circuit round the mine. He chose the side furthest away from the head of the track, from where he had seen the immobile silhouette on the ridge. Straightening up, he looked into the mine.

No cage. Christina had said there was a cage at the top. But she had never been up here. Someone must have told her about a cage, had lied. He was looking down into an immense bucket made of iron. It was suspended by a chain windlass coiled at the top. He switched on his pencil torch, his hand well below the surface of the mine. At its base he saw remnants of ore. He thought his light reflected off veins of silver, but it could have been his imagination.

Newman was baffled. Why should Petros make such a fuss about no one going near the mine? Between the huge bucket – large enough to hide a crouching man – and the side of the shaft was a wide gap. He shone the torch down the shaft. The light penetrated only a short distance into bottomless blackness. A musty aroma drifted up to his nostrils. He swivelled the light and saw a huge chain dangling beneath the bucket. And something else he couldn't identify . . .

He heard the shuffle of feet hurrying across rock-strewn ground. He peered through the aperture and saw two men coming, still several hundred yards away. From the direction of the track. They dropped out of view, presumably into a dip in the ground. But he had seen the long barrels perched over their shoulders. Men with rifles. He glanced round quickly.

No cover. Anywhere. The ridge behind him was open, as exposed as the slope which fell away from it. And they could out-range him with those rifles. A handgun was useless except for closer quarters. He went very cold, thinking. He leaned over into the mine, took hold of the rim of the bucket, tried to move it. The bucket was so heavy he couldn't shift it a centimetre. He flashed his light on to the windlass chain holding it. The links in the chain were enormous. He recalled it had been built to hold God knew what tonnage of ore.

He slipped on the pair of gloves he had used when scaling the defile. Without them his hands would have been bloodied raw – clutching at razor-edged rocks to heave himself upwards. He gave one more brief glance to where he'd seen the two men approaching. Any moment now and they would climb up out of the dip into view. He lowered himself into the shaft, hanging on to the rim of the bucket. It remained immovable as the Rock of Gibraltar. Now for the tricky part.

Engulfed in the darkness of the shaft, he held on to the rim with his left hand, felt down with his right for the dangling chain attached to the base of the bucket. He was just able to clutch it. Every muscle in his body strained as he jerked the chain with all his strength, testing it. It held. He took a deep breath, let go of the rim and fell. He whipped his right hand round the huge chain a second before the full weight of his body pulled at him. Now he had two hands gripping the length of chain which continued at least seven feet below him. He could tell that because he'd used both feet to get a hold on the chain lower down. His right foot rested on one of the enormous links. His left foot slipped, dangled in space. He forced it upwards, felt for a foothold, found it opposite the other foot and hung there suspended. The bucket had still not moved. But something light but unyielding had brushed his face. He couldn't identify it. He took another chance.

Holding on with his right hand, he felt for his pencil torch with his left. Sweating like a bull, he switched it on. He estimated the two men would not yet have arrived in the vicinity of the mine. What he saw by the light so frightened him he nearly lost his grip.

Suspended by a separate chain from beneath the bucket was a man-sized skeleton. The skull was inches from Newman's cheek. A gibbering skull with one eye intact.

Inside the gloves his hands were suddenly greasy with sweat. He gripped the chain more tightly, scared stiff his hands would slip out of them, plunging him down the shaft. The eye twitched and Newman nearly had a bowel movement. Then he saw it was an insect perched in the hollow eye socket, something like a praying mantis. The light had disturbed it. The insect twitched again, then flew upwards. Newman switched off the torch, rammed it in his pocket, gripped the chain with his free hand. Just in time. The strain on his right hand was becoming unendurable.

In the brief seconds while the light had been on he noticed the skeleton was wired together, which explained how it could hang there. Jesus! What a companion to hang suspended next to. Newman concentrated on securing his grip with his hands, his feet. Then he heard movement at the top of the mine.

Two voices. Talking excitedly. Leaning over to peer down into the shaft. Now they were moving round as though to get a better view. Still chattering.

Then the beam of a powerful flashlight shone down into the darkness. The light swung slowly, probing the shadows. The angle of the light changed, penetrated deeper. Newman looked down and cursed inwardly. The flashlight was shining on the lower part of his dangling legs, illuminating them from the knees downwards. More chatter. Then silence. Followed by a metallic click. Newman recognized the sound. The release of a safety catch. The flashlight beam remained very steady now, shining on his legs. He realized his teeth were clenched tightly. The bastards were going to shoot him in the legs. Not one damned thing he could do. Except wait for the impact, the slipping of his hands from the chain, the plunge down the shaft until his body smashed against the base, however far that might be . . .

Marler, smaller than either man, held the rifle at a horizontal angle, level with his nose. He swung the butt to his left. It smashed into the back of Dimitrios' skull. He was collapsing when Constantine began to turn round. Marler reversed the swing and the barrel thudded with all his strength against Constantine's forehead. The Greek sagged to the ground, dropping his shotgun. Dimitrios' flashlight had vanished down the mine.

Marler leaned over, switched on his own flashlight. He called down. 'Anyone at home?'

'Me, for God's sake. Hanging on to a chain under the bucket.'

'Hang about. I need a minute. You can last that out?'

'What the hell can you do?'

283

'Haul you up.' As he had started talking Marler had picked up the looped rope he had laid quietly on the ground before creeping up behind the two Greeks. He was creating a large loop with a slipknot. He tested the knot, then picked his flashlight off the parapet, shone it down.

'I'm lowering a rope with a big loop. Plus a slipknot. I can see your lower legs. Can you slide them inside the loop? I'll haul it up slowly. You have to get it round your chest, under your armpits. Think you can manage that simple exercise?'

'Give it a go. Soon as you're ready. I have company . . .'

Marler ignored the cryptic remark, held the torch in his right hand, lowered the loop with his left. When it was level with Newman's dangling feet he had to swing it away from the wall of the shaft. Newman saw what he was doing in the beam of the flashlight, waited for what he hoped was the right moment and swung his feet off the chain. Marler jerked the loop up and it ringed Newman's legs. He warned that the light would go out and took the rope in both hands. He hauled it up slowly and Newman called out that it was sliding up over his body.

'Tell me when it's under your arms, there's a good chap . . .'

'Now . . .'

'Tricky bit coming,' Marler called out. 'I need both hands to haul you up. When you let go you'll swing against the side of the shaft. Try and cushion yourself. Piece of cake. If you're lucky.'

'Thanks for the vote of confidence . . .'

Marler had his feet and knees braced against the side of the mine. He had knotted the rope in a few places to ward off as much rope burn on his hands as possible. And Newman weighed a few more pounds than he did. He called down that he was OK and waited for the considerable increase in weight. Newman called back that he was letting go.

The rope had slid up under his armpits, the loop had tightened. He let go of the chain and swung outwards, his right hand palm up. It slammed into the wall. His hand stung horribly from the impact. For a moment he hadn't the strength to call up.

'OK to haul you in? Tell me, for Pete's sake,' Marler rasped.

The weight was greater than he'd expected. His knees were pulverized with the pressure against the side of the mine. Newman said something he couldn't catch. Can't mess around any longer, Marler told himself and began to haul up the excruciating weight.

Newman came up facing the curve of the wall, hands pressed into it to steady his ascent. His head appeared over the top, Marler arched his body backwards, gave one last heave. Newman's hands scrabbled at the edge of the mine, then he came over the top like a cork out of a bottle and flopped on the ground beside the two unconscious Greeks.

'This one with the shotgun was going to pepper you,' Marler remarked as he stooped over the unconscious Greek. 'I heard the charming conversation when I came up behind them. Relieved to be back in the land of the living?'

'You could say that. Who are these two jokers?' Newman eased his back up, rested it against the side of the mine, took off his gloves and flexed his aching fingers. 'Did you do a real job on them – or will they come round? If so, maybe I'd better put a bullet in their skulls.'

'Tweed said you'd become a hard man after that trip behind the lines in East Germany.' As he spoke he was searching the Greeks. He pulled out a bottle, uncapped it, sniffed, used his handkerchief to wipe the top and handed it to Newman.

'You need a pick-me-up. Drink. *Ouzo.*'

'Thanks.' Newman upended the bottle, swallowed, choked a little. He took another swig when he'd recovered. His whole body was aching. Legs, arms, hands, shoulders. 'Who are the bastards?' he asked again.

Marler was scanning a photo he'd taken from a grubby envelope. 'This one, as I thought, is Dimitrios. Taken with a girlfriend. Rather crudely erotic. I was pretty sure I recognized him from our little escapade on Siros. The other is Constantine. Meet the Gavalas brothers.'

'Let's hope I don't – on the streets of Athens. For their sake.'

'Feeling better? You have a hike. Back down the track to where Nick is waiting with the cars.'

Newman forced himself to stand, supporting himself with a hand on the wall of the mine. He drank a little more *ouzo*. Marler took the bottle off him.

'That's enough. We don't want you drunk. I'll be ready to go in a minute.'

Marler was emptying the rifle. He threw the cartridges down the slope, then held the rifle poised over the well. 'Might interest you to listen to this . . .' He let go and the rifle plunged down past the bucket into the black hole. Newman waited and his hand tightened on the wall. Seconds passed before they both heard the faintest of thuds. Marler looked at him.

'You could have sprained an ankle if you'd gone down there.'

'Ended up as a jelly. Safe to leave these two thugs?'

Marler was stooping over the Greeks, lifting an eyelid of both men. He straightened up. 'Out for the count for a while yet. Maybe I split a skull.' He emptied the shotgun, sent it down after the rifle. Dimitrios was wearing a sheathed knife under his jacket. Marler was about to toss it into the well when Newman stopped him.

'Let me look at that.'

He held the knife up to the moonlight and his voice was

grim. 'This is a standard-issue commando knife. I'd like to know how he got hold of that.' He dropped it inside the well. 'While I remember, thanks for saving my life . . .'

'All part of the Austin Reed service. You're an idiot, you know that? Coming up here by yourself. I followed you from Athens. Had an idea what you were up to, you crazy loon.'

'You could be right. Let's make with the feet. But I discovered the secret of the mine.'

'That's what I like. A bit of melodrama. Back to the track . . .'

26

Florakis lowered the transceiver into the cavity, concealed it with a flat rock, picked up the shotgun he had left inside the cavity before climbing the mountain. The transceiver was heavy. Now to investigate the two cars parked on his land down by the hotel site . . .

Dawn was breaking over the Mediterranean shore, flooding the unruffled sea with a variety of fantastic colours. Behind the wheel of his Mercedes Nick sat smoking another cigarette. The ash tray was crammed with stubs. Disgusting. He hauled it out from under the spring clip, stepped out of the car, then reached back in for his rifle. You never knew.

Christina was curled up on the back seat like a cat, fast asleep. Nick walked quietly across to a pile of rocks, lifted a few and emptied the ash tray, then replaced the stones. Crouched over, he froze. Someone was approaching from behind the steel framework. He remained crouched, aimed the rifle.

Florakis came round the corner, shotgun held in both hands. He stopped abruptly when he saw Nick, who straightened up, rifle still pointed. 'Good morning to you,' Nick called out in Greek.

'What are you doing on my land?' snapped Florakis.

'Parking off the road. You see any damage we've done?'

'We?'

Christina had woken, had heard the exchange. Running her hands through her mane, she sat up and looked out of the open window. Florakis glanced in her direction, grinned lewdly and turned his attention back to Nick.

'I charge a fee for screwing on my land . . .'

'Watch your mouth,' Nick responded sharply. 'Who the hell are you?'

'Stavros Florakis. I own this land,' he repeated. 'I'm telling you to shove off now before I blow a hole in you . . .'

'Keep very still,' Nick warned. 'You forgot your back.'

Florakis stiffened as he felt the muzzle of Marler's rifle press into the nape of his neck. Marler nodded again at Nick, who understood. 'Place that shotgun carefully on the ground, step over it towards me. A dozen paces will do, then stop.'

Florakis bent forward, laid the weapon down, did as Nick had ordered. He stood in the open as Newman walked past him, keeping out of Nick's line of fire. He went towards the Mercedes and called out to Christina. 'Give me the mineral water. I'm parched.'

He drank from the bottle, turned round, leaned against the car. He smiled as Florakis stared back bleakly. Yes, Newman thought, this is the man we saw on our way up the gulch, the man carrying a heavy transceiver.

'What's his name?' he called out to Nick. 'I couldn't quite get it.'

'Stavros Florakis. He owns Greece,' Nick replied in English.

A tough, wiry individual, Newman was thinking. Self-contained. A typical Greek shepherd. Except that he carried a transceiver up the mountain. The lined face suggested he was in his sixties. Newman's mind wandered. In his sixties. Weren't they all – Barrymore, Kearns and Robson. And Tweed had rabbited on about the missing link with Greece – between Athens and Exmoor. So, during World War Two Florakis would have been about twenty. Old enough to be in the Resistance. Which one? The instinct which had made him one of the world's best foreign correspondents was working again.

He took out his handkerchief, wiped the mouth of the bottle, turned as though to say something to Christina, and wiped the rest of the bottle clean. He turned round and smiled.

'Nick, I think we ought to apologize for trespassing on Mr Florakis' land.' He began to walk towards the Greek, holding the bottle by the neck, still smiling. 'It's thirsty weather. As a token of our regret I'd like to offer him a drink. Translate for me.'

Nothing in Florakis' neutral expression showed he'd understood every word Newman had said. He listened patiently as Nick spoke in Greek. Florakis was nervous: all these people appearing, seeing him out and about at dawn. The last thing he wanted was any talk of his nocturnal activities to reach Athens.

Newman extended the bottle, holding it by the neck. Florakis was also bone dry: he had forgotten to bring his water bottle. He nodded his thanks, grasped the bottle, took a good long drink, handed it back to Newman, who again grasped it by the neck and wandered back to the car.

'Nick,' he called over his shoulder as he reached the car, 'let him know we're leaving now. That if we come this way again we'll park elsewhere.'

While Nick translated Newman leaned in the window. 'Christina,' he whispered, 'give me that paper bag the bottle came in.' He slid the bottle inside the bag, holding it by the neck, then he pressed the top of the paper bag inside the neck and capped it. He now had Florakis' fingerprints.

'What was all that business about the bottle?' asked Christina as Nick drove them at speed back along the coast road to Athens.

Newman sat beside her in the rear of the Mercedes while Marler followed close behind in his own car. Newman was staring out of the window as the sun came up from behind the mountains and bathed the Mediterranean in its fierce light. The sea was now a smooth sheet of pure mother-of-pearl. An amazing country.

'Just fooling around,' he replied.

'And how was the fooling around in Devil's Valley? Marler did find you. Did you find the mine? And thanks for the sock on the jaw. I love you too.'

'Quiz time,' Newman said jocularly. 'So many questions.' He looked at her chin. 'No sign of a bruise. Just a gentle tap. Marvellous, isn't it? You save a girl from what could be a death-trap and she hates your guts.'

She looped her arm inside his, nestled against him so he could feel the firmness of her breast pressing into his body. 'Don't remember saying anything about hating your guts. And you evaded answering my questions.'

'I do believe I did.'

He looked out of the window again. They were covering the distance to Athens, seventy kilometres from Cape Sounion, in record time. They passed a hotel at the edge of the shore and tourists were walking the beach, swimming in the placid water.

'They make use of every minute,' he called out to Nick.

'They know what they do,' he replied. 'Later in the morning no feet will be able to touch that beach. The sand will be so hot it will burn them like a red-hot stove. They'll retire to their rooms, lie on their beds and sweat it out with nothing on.'

'What a lovely idea,' Christina whispered. 'Maybe we could lie on my bed at the Hilton with nothing on, sweat it out?'

'I'm dumping you there,' Newman said abruptly. 'Nick, make for the Hilton. Then have breakfast with Christina. When she goes to her room would you please sit in the lobby outside to guard her till I get back? A large tip will be my thanks.'

'Forget the tip, I take care of her.'

'Thanks a lot,' Christina snapped, her eyes flashing. She pulled away from him and stared out of her window.

'I have business to attend to, an editor to keep quiet,' Newman told her. 'And you may be in even greater danger now after what has happened. And don't ask me what.'

'Did you tell Christina about the skeleton?' Marler asked as he drove away from the Hilton.

'Nary a word. Nor about the mine . . .'

'Which means you're getting smart. *You* don't trust her.'

'Can it, Marler. Information like that is dangerous. You do realize who that skeleton is?'

'I think so. You tell me.'

'The missing Andreas. My guess is Petros was on Siros when the commando raid took place. He took the body of his son. He's stark raving mad. He must have had it buried, then after the war the bones were removed to Devil's Valley. Wired together – hidden in the mine. You know Greece well. Tell me again about *philotimo*.'

'And you're sure this is a smart move – what we're doing

now? Driving to police headquarters to see Chief Inspector Sarris?'

'I want Florakis' fingerprints checked against their records. Look, a sixty-year-old Greek, tough as they come, lugs a transceiver up a mountain. He's gaining altitude. That suggests long-distance transmission. Who is he contacting? So secretly? I've had this lucky break before as a correspondent. You are working on one thing, you stumble across something much bigger. Yes, I think it's a smart move.'

Very little traffic at seven in the morning. They were coming close to Alexandras Avenue below the soaring peak of Mount Lycabettus. Close to the new police headquarters.

'*Philotimo*,' Marler began, 'is the Greek code of ethics which rules family life. No one must dishonour the family. If they do, the disgrace must be wiped out. In extreme cases by killing the culprit. Even if it is a member of that family. Only then can the family have peace of mind. Petros is just the type of man to be soaked in the creed – in the crudest and most old-fashioned way. Just the man to go to extreme lengths.'

'Just the man to go right over the edge,' Newman commented. 'I think Petros is taking the attitude Andreas cannot be finally buried until his murderer is identified and executed. Petros is crazy as a coot. Revenge is the most self-destructive force that can take hold of a man.'

'And this is the main reason we're going to see friend Sarris?'

'No. I want the fingerprints on this bottle checked. We may have stumbled into something even more diabolical than Petros' desire for revenge.'

The Thin Man. The hawk-nosed, dark-haired Sarris sat listening behind his desk. His eyes never left Newman's.

He smoked one cigarette after another. But he listened without interruption.

'That's it,' Newman ended, his voice hoarse from talking, from his ordeal at the mine. 'The skeleton at the mine, the bottle on your desk with Florakis' fingerprints. The transceiver I saw Florakis carrying up the mountain.'

'Petros has committed no crime,' Sarris responded, stubbing a cigarette. 'Yet. Funny you should come to me with this news of a possible transceiver . . .'

'Possible?'

'You have no proof that was the object Florakis carried. But, as I say, it is funny you come to me at this moment. Have you ever noticed weeks, months, can go by with no clues in a case? Then, bingo! Within hours the clues pour in.'

'What are you talking about? I'm damned tired.'

'Have more coffee.' Sarris poured as he went on. 'A friend of mine is what you call in England . . . a radio ham. Is that right?'

'Yes. An amateur radio operator. Sometimes they're helpful – pick up Mayday calls over long distances. That sort of thing.'

'My friend picked up something strange on the airwaves. Someone transmitting a series of numbers – sounds like a coded signal. At the end there are a few words in English – from the man receiving the coded signal.' Sarris leaned forward. 'So maybe the operator sending the coded signal was transmitting to England.'

'A big assumption,' Newman objected. 'English is a universal language these days . . .'

'Judge for yourself. My friend has a tape recorder. He recorded the entire signal. You might like to hear it . . .'

Sarris pressed a lever on his intercom, spoke rapidly in Greek, sat back, lit a fresh cigarette. 'The cassette will be here in a moment.'

He was wearing a pale linen suit and even at that early

hour he looked alert. He watched his two visitors until a uniformed policeman brought in a cassette. Sarris picked up the cassette, inserted it inside a machine on a side table. 'Listen,' he commanded.

The cassette reeled out a string of pure gibberish for Newman. He glanced at Marler who was staring out of the window, showing no apparent interest in the proceedings. Sarris was checking his watch. After two and a half minutes he raised a warning hand.

The gibberish stopped. There was a pause. Then it came through loud and clear. In English. *From now on call sign changed to Colonel Winter*. Staring at Newman, Sarris switched off the machine.

'You have heard of this Colonel Winter?'

'No. Doesn't mean a thing to me.'

'Pity. I am thinking of informing the Drug Squad. The traffickers are becoming very sophisticated. Using coded radio signals to warn of a shipment on its way. The Drug Squad has radio detector vans. Maybe they'll send a couple down to Cape Sounion, try to get a fix on this Florakis.'

'And the fingerprints on that bottle?'

'We'll check them through our records. That could take time.'

'You can isolate Florakis' prints? I gave you that postcard I showed Christina while we were driving back. You've taken my prints. The card gives you Christina's. Eliminate hers and mine and you're left with Florakis.'

'I had worked that out for myself.' Sarris rose from behind his desk. 'Thank you for the information. Now I expect you'll want to get back to the Grande Bretagne, have a shave, some breakfast, then maybe some sleep. You've been up all night.'

'I had hoped for more from you,' Newman said as he stood up.

'I gave you the radio signal – which may link up with Florakis.' He paused. 'I will give you something more. I said earlier all the clues seemed to pour in at once. Yesterday we had a woman here with a weird story. A Mrs Florakis. About sixty and recently she took a bus tour to Cape Sounion. A widow, by the way. Married very young.' He smiled thinly. 'I see I have your attention?'

'Go on.'

'Her husband, Stavros Florakis, was killed in 1947 during the Civil War. In a battle with the Communist ELAS forces. It so happened a woman friend saw him die near Salonika. This woman also saw the Communists search the body, take his papers, then they incinerated the corpse. Something Mrs Florakis never understood. Still intrigued?'

'Stop tantalizing. You sound like my editor.'

'As I said, Mrs Florakis takes this bus tour. The bus stops off the road close to a new hotel building site. To let them get a good view of Poseidon. A man appears with a shotgun. He threatens the driver, tells him to get off his land. The bus driver argues. Mrs Florakis then hears the man with the shotgun shout, "I am Stavros Florakis. I own this land and you are trespassing." She gets a good view of this man. She gets a shock. He is not a bit like her husband. Then she remembers what happened to him. All this flashes through her mind in a few seconds. Then the bus moves off. She tells her story to me very clearly, but I am not impressed. We get so many crazies wandering in here. For good public relations I let her make a formal statement, which we filed. Now you tell me something that makes me think maybe I was wrong.'

'Florakis is an impostor,' Newman observed. 'So who is he?'

'Maybe – just maybe – the fingerprints you cleverly obtained can unlock his true identity.' He shook hands with Newman and Marler. 'Let us keep in touch, gentlemen . . .'

* * *

295

'So that covers what Newman told me, Kalos,' Sarris concluded as he clasped his hands behind his neck and relaxed in his chair. 'What do you make of it all?'

Kalos, his trusted assistant, was very different physically from his chief. Small and stocky, with thick legs and arms, he had a long head and intelligent eyes. In his early forties, he had been passed over for promotion several times but bore no grudge. It was Sarris' private opinion that it was Kalos' lack of height which had held him back. Most unfair, and Sarris had done his best to help him up the ladder. But who said life was fair?

'We've had a lucky break again,' Kalos decided. 'We ignored the Florakis woman – but she may have fingered the key link in the organization the Drug Squad is trying to locate. With no success. Unless it's political,' he mused. 'Not drugs.'

Sarris sat up straight. 'What does that mean?'

'My mind roams.' Kalos smiled drily. 'As you know there are people higher up who don't approve of a man who lets his mind roam. Never get fixated on one theory. My inflexible maxim, and stuff them upstairs.'

'You said unless it's political. Please elaborate.'

'Last year,' Kalos began, fitting his bulk inside the arms of a chrome-plated chair, 'a so-called Colonel Gerasimov visited us from Moscow. We were asked to guard him like royalty – but discreetly with plain-clothes operatives. He spent very little of his visit at the Soviet Embassy, a lot of it at the Hilton. He had three rooms booked and switched from one to another. I got curious and had him secretly photographed . . .'

'Without my permission,' Sarris chided him.

'You know me. When I visited Belgrade unofficially about this drugs problem I showed that picture to a Yugoslav – a Croat called Pavelic in the security services. I got him drunk and showed him the picture. He laughed when I said it was a photo of Colonel Gerasimov of the

GRU. He told me it was General Lucharsky, a Deputy Chief of the Soviet General Staff.'

'I remember. Do continue,' Sarris urged him with a quizzical smile.

'Yugoslavia is sensitive to power movements inside the Kremlin. Gorbachev suits the Belgrade Government fine. Pavelic, though, is a hardliner. He told me Lucharsky was "one of ours".'

'You didn't tell me that bit,' Sarris snapped.

'Why raise hares? You were up to your eyes in work. While in Athens the man at the Soviet Embassy Lucharsky spent most time with was Colonel Rykovsky, the military attaché. And an expert in communications.'

'How do you know that?'

'The Greek cleaning woman they employ when their menial staff is on holiday happens to clean my apartment.'

'Purely by chance, of course?' Sarris was leaning forward now, taking in every word. 'You do realize you are far exceeding the scope of your duties, my friend?'

'I like to know what is really going on.' Kalos ran a stubby finger round his open-necked collar and smiled drily again. 'It is hardly likely to affect my promotion prospects. And now we hear a Colonel Volkov will soon visit us from Moscow. Odd.'

'Why?'

'Pavelic, the Croat, was *very* drunk when we talked alone. He said to me, "I would not be surprised if you receive another visitor in Athens one of these days. Lucharsky's aide and confidant. A Colonel Volkov. Another sound man." Translation – another hardliner. These are not pro-Gorbachev men. So why do they travel to Athens, I wonder?'

Sarris sat thinking. Yugoslavia was a 'federation' of six different nationalities. A racial mix, and not all of them loving each other. Croatia, the Yugoslav state in the north, was the most rebellious, the most pro-Russian, the one

297

closest to the real hard men in the Kremlin. Gorbachev's opponents.

'This is all speculation,' he suggested, testing his assistant.

Kalos ran a hand over the thin brown stubble which covered the dome of his head. 'You are right. Up to now. There is one more thing. When off duty I often amuse myself by following the military attaché, Colonel Rykovsky. He likes wandering inside the Plaka. He thinks he has lost anyone who might just be tailing him. Then he meets and spends time with Doganis.'

'Doganis?'

'A leading member of the Greek Key.'

27

'Where to now?' Marler asked as they climbed into his car.

'British Embassy. I'll rout that fat slob, Patterson, out of bed if necessary.'

'Be it on your own head.' Marler nodded towards the clock on the dashboard. 'Eight in the morning here is six o'clock back in London. Who will be at Park Crescent apart from the guard?'

'Tweed would be my bet. I think he's reached the camp bed stage by now.'

They both knew what that meant. Tweed started investigating a fresh case slowly. Then the tempo built up. He unfolded the camp bed kept in his office and took up a permanent vigil at his desk, often working well into the night.

At the Embassy on Sofias Avenue Patterson greeted

them in his shirt-sleeves, unshaven, sullen. He let them inside the hall without a word. No one else was about as Newman rubbed both hands together vigorously.

'The scrambler phone. It's an emergency.'

'When isn't it? And you might have shaved before invading the precincts of Her Majesty's Embassy.'

Ye Gods! Newman thought. How bloody pompous can you get? He grinned at Patterson. 'You look pretty rough yourself. Late night on the town?'

'I don't indulge. Like some people. I'll unlock the door – you know the drill. He can't come with you.' He jerked his thumb at Marler.

Marler said nothing. He produced his Secret Service card, held it under Patterson's nose, withdrew it when Patterson reached for it. The official bit his lip, made no further comment, produced a bunch of keys and unlocked the door leading to the basement. Newman ran down the steps after switching on the light.

Marler pulled out a chair as Newman sat down and pulled the phone towards him. Upstairs Patterson slammed the door shut with great force. Newman pressed the red button, dialled the Park Crescent number.

'Who is calling?' Tweed's voice, very alert.

'Newman here. Sorry to call at this hour.'

'That's all right. Very glad to hear from you. I was worrying. I slept here, got up with the dawn. Paula's here – she couldn't sleep and has just arrived. In case you need data taking down. Now, I'm listening . . .'

He listened without saying a word for ten minutes as Newman reported everything that had happened since they last spoke – including the trip into Devil's Valley and how Marler had saved his life. Glancing across the table he saw Marler spread his hands in a *What the hell* gesture.

'You shouldn't have gone in alone,' Tweed told him.

'I know that now. OK, I'll behave in future. Nowhere tricky without my chaperon. Now you know the lot.'

299

'And maybe we've come a long way – with the information you've given me and what I've gleaned at this end. A lot more of the pieces in my hands. Now I have to try and fit them together. I'd better warn you, I'll be phoning Peter Sarris to try and stop him taking any action. Yet. I'll cover you. What's the next move you plan?'

'Grilling Christina again about her relationship and movements with Masterson. That's what I came out for – to find out what really happened to Masterson. It looks like the Greeks to me. Petros and his vendetta. He's mad as a hatter.'

'And dangerous. Tread carefully. He'll be turning Athens upside down to locate Christina. But don't be too sure you've got to the bottom of anything. Someone may be using Petros as a gigantic smokescreen – to divert our attention.'

'From what?' Newman asked.

'I don't know. Just a sixth sense. There are some pretty peculiar characters involved. Including a Professor Guy Seton-Charles. At the moment he's in the West Country, holds a position at Bristol University. But he takes seminars at the university in Athens. Greek Studies.'

'Description?'

'Early sixties, looks younger. Slim build. Clean-shaven, thinning brown hair, Roman nose. About five feet eight. Intellectual type. Conceited manner. Most distinctive feature the rimless glasses he wears. Informal dress.'

'I'll recognize him. Early sixties again. So many of them are. Barrymore, Robson, Kearns, Florakis . . .'

'Which could be significant. Takes them back to World War Two – where all this started, I suspect. Another point about this Seton-Charles. He was stationed in the Antikhana Building in Cairo at the time of the Ionides murder.'

'A pattern is beginning to form,' Newman suggested.

'Yes, but it's like a kaleidoscope. New events shake it

up, give a fresh picture. One more thing before I go. And warn Marler – he can be impulsive. Petros is a very dangerous man. That crazy business about the skeleton in the mine. I'm sure you're right. It is the remains of Andreas. Watch your step, both of you. And has something else struck you just before I go?'

'I expect not, since you phrase it like that.'

'From your description Florakis' land adjoins Petros' – that is a strange coincidence. Might be worth following up. But cautiously. Keep in touch . . .'

As Tweed put down the phone the door opened and Monica came in. She greeted Paula, took off her raincoat, said she would be making coffee for everyone. Tweed waited until she returned with the tray and asked for black coffee. He was still working on automatic pilot, struggling to throw off the remnants of sleep.

'I woke early,' Monica said as she filled their cups. 'It was all going round and round in my head.'

'I can give you more – enough to make your head spin. Newman just called . . .'

He gave them both a concise résumé of the data Newman had provided. The two women listened intently. Paula made a few notes in her book. Monica absorbed it in her encyclopaedic memory. Tweed leaned back in his chair as he concluded.

'So what do you make of all that?'

'Florakis seems to be the key,' Paula said promptly. 'You've been looking for a link between Greece and England. The fact that he appears to be sending coded signals to somewhere here may be the missing link. That reference to Colonel Winter intrigues me. Colonel Barrymore?'

'Not necessarily . . .'

'But the thing I got from that tape recording Pete made

of the conversation at The Luttrell Arms was Barrymore still treats his two companions as though he's in charge.'

'Colonel Winterton,' said Monica. 'The man Seton-Charles told you had handled the property transactions for that bungalow estate near Kearns' house. Colonel Winterton, who disappeared once all the properties were sold. The Invisible Man.'

'Have you contacted Pitlochry Insurance then?' Tweed enquired. 'They were the outfit which actually loaned the mortgages.'

'I managed to get through after you left yesterday afternoon. I had trouble getting the manager to part with the information. I used our General & Cumbria Insurance cover to get him to open up. Said we'd had an enquiry from a Colonel Winterton about a property deal, that he'd given Pitlochry as a reference and . . .' She began choking. 'Coffee . . . went down the wrong way.'

Paula jumped up, accompanied her to the ladies' room. Tweed sat thinking. The plate at the front entrance read General & Cumbria Insurance Co. The cover had worked well. They pretended to be a specialized company dealing with top security protection for private individuals of great wealth. Officially, they also dealt with kidnapping insurance, negotiating with the kidnappers if a client was snatched. This explained all the trips abroad made by Tweed and his sector chiefs. They were even a member of the insurance industry's association – to complete the cover. Monica came back with Paula, dabbing at her mouth with a handkerchief.

'I'm all right now,' she said, sitting down behind her desk. 'I was telling you about Pitlochry. The manager said they'd found Colonel Winterton sound and businesslike. He confirmed that Winterton had simply acted as a middle-man between clients buying those bungalows and Pitlochry supplying the mortgages.'

'He met him?'

'No, that was the odd thing. Odd to me. All the trans-actions were carried out by correspondence from the Taunton office and Winterton on the phone.'

'Did you manage to get any idea how he sounded?'

'Yes, by cracking a joke. Winterton had a very upper crust way of talking. Very much the colonel addressing the battalion – the manager's phrase.'

'Any forwarding address?'

'None. No one at Pitlochry has any idea where he is nowadays.'

'The Invisible Man,' said Paula.

'Another cul-de-sac,' Tweed remarked. 'Which reminds me – we still have no idea what Masterson meant by his note referring to *Endstation*. I feel certain that's a major pointer – either here or in Greece. Masterson was the cleverest interrogator I ever met. He was trying to tell me something. But what?'

'Dead end for the moment,' Paula said briskly. 'But I've come up with something.' There was a note of triumph in her tone which made Tweed and Monica stare at her. 'I didn't tell you while we were there. I thought I'd follow something up for myself.'

'Which was?' asked Tweed.

'You remember the evening we visited Colonel Barry-more when you interviewed him? I was sitting to one side. He had his copy of *The Times* folded back to the personal advertisement section. I memorized the date. Yesterday I went off to Wapping, checked their files. What do you think I found?'

'She's playing you at your own game,' Monica said and chuckled. 'Teasing you.'

'So I'll play along. What did you find?'

'An advertisement placed at the time Christina Gavalas was in England, the time when Harry Masterson was going around with her over here. The advertisement was this.' She read from a small pocket diary. '*Will anyone interested*

303

in the Greek Key and knows about Antikhana please contact me. Irene. It gives a phone number for contact. I phoned the number. Turned out to be the Strand Palace. I phoned the hotel, said I was the sister of Christina Gavalas. Had she stayed at the hotel? They wouldn't play. So I jumped in a taxi and went down to the Strand. I sexed up the reservations clerk – naughty of me, I think he thought he had a date. He looked up their records. Christina stayed there at the relevant time.'

'But Irene is the wrong name,' Monica observed.

'I think she did that to protect herself. Not knowing who would come looking for her.'

'I agree,' Tweed said. 'Type out that ad with the date and add it to the file. You did a good job. Actually,' he admitted, 'I knew about the advertisement. Newman told me over the phone that Christina had explained to him during dinner that was how she met Masterson. He saw the ad and contacted her.'

'Thanks a lot!' Paula threw down her pencil. 'So I wasted my time.'

'Hardly. I didn't spot that newspaper in Barrymore's study – which shows he was interested. And in the near future I think you and I should drive down again to Exmoor to see how Butler and Nield are getting on. We know more than we did last time.'

He stopped as the phone rang. Monica grabbed her receiver and spoke briefly. Putting her hand over the mouthpiece she looked at Tweed.

'Talk of the devil. Pete Nield on the phone for you.'

'Sorry to phone you so early. I called on the off chance,' Nield explained. 'I'm talking from a public box. We put the pressure on and guess what's happened. The hunters have become the hunted. Harry and I are being watched by Barrymore and Kearns.'

'What do you mean?' Tweed's tone was sharp, alarmed.

'We each took one of them in turn and let them spot us

– riding on the moor. Now when we get up there they appear out of nowhere and stalk us! It's uncanny . . .'

'They know the moor better than you'll ever do. What was their routine before they turned the tables on you?'

'Robson rode to see patients during the day. He can go for ages without food or drink. His patients are scattered over a large area. Evenings he has a meal, presumably prepared by his sister. Then he retires up to that conning tower place and reads. After dark he draws the curtains. Goes to bed late.'

'And Kearns?'

'He rides the moor a lot. His wife, Jill, never appears. She hasn't been seen by either of us. Maybe he locks her up. As for Kearns, he rides up to the summit of Dunkery Beacon. Stays up there at night. God knows what he's doing. Can't get close enough. Weird bloke. A solitary.'

'Dunkery Beacon? That's the highest point on Exmoor . . .'

'That's right. Like to know about Barrymore?'

'Of course.'

'He's about one hundred feet from where I'm talking. Inside a newspaper shop that opens early. He's standing by the window, half-pretending to read a paper. But he's watching me. He came into the village on a horse tethered further down the High Street. He's also got a rifle in a scabbard attached to the saddle.'

Tweed thought quickly. 'Now listen to me. Butler is inside The Luttrell Arms? Good. This is what you do. The unexpected. You vanish. Pay your bills. Then both of you drive to Taunton. The colonel can't follow you on a horse. Hire fresh cars in Taunton. Quite different models. Book into the main hotel in Taunton, using assumed names. Change your clothes – buy new ones which completely change your appearance. Then switch your attentions to Professor Guy Seton-Charles. Track him night and day. Don't let him know you're on his tail. You can pick him

305

up tomorrow morning at his bungalow on that estate. Understood?'

'Will do.'

'And let Monica know the name of your new hotel, how we can contact you. Now, move!'

Tweed slammed down the phone. He started cleaning his glasses on his handkerchief. Monica watched, winked at Paula. She recognized the signs.

'Something has happened?' she ventured.

'Yes. The pressure worked . . .' He told them what had happened. 'Maybe crisis time is approaching.'

'And the object of the new exercise is?' Paula asked.

'To throw Barrymore and Kearns off balance. One moment they're being tracked by Butler and Nield. Suddenly the trackers disappear. I'll bet for the next week Barrymore and Kearns scour the moors looking for them, wondering where the devil they've gone. Also I'm pulling Butler and Nield out of the firing line. Maybe literally.'

'Don't follow,' Paula said.

'I didn't like the sound of the rifle Barrymore is carrying. You get shooting accidents on moors. And no one can prove it wasn't just that. And it's psychological warfare.'

'Don't follow that,' Paula said.

'We'll leave Exmoor alone for a week. Just when the hunters think they've scared off the opposition you and I arrive – asking more questions.'

They had breakfast brought in by the day guard, George. Sandwiches and coffee which they consumed at their desks. It was ten o'clock when Tweed asked Monica to put in a call to Chief Inspector Sarris of Athens Homicide.

'I met him once at a security conference in Geneva. He's very bright, but I have to try and stop him doing something. The timing is wrong. If he's not there, ask for Kalos . . .' Tweed spelt it out for her. 'He is Sarris' clever assistant.

Has a mind like a computer – especially where Greek history is concerned.'

Tweed returned to studying the file headed *Ionides*. Monica reported all the lines to Greece were busy. 'Probably travel agents booking holidays. I'll keep trying.'

'Fair enough. Meantime, try Brown's Hotel again. In Dunster I made an arrangement with Jill Kearns that if she came up to London we'd meet. I said I'd keep in touch with the hotel so I'd know when she was here.'

'I'm calling daily. She wasn't there yesterday . . .'

'Nield told me she's disappeared from Exmoor, that they haven't seen her for some time. Try now . . .'

'She's on the line,' Monica told him a few minutes later.

'Tweed here. When did you arrive?'

'Darling, how absolutely marvellous to hear your voice. So reassuring. I'm on my own. God, am I glad to be back in civilization. I was going out of my mind on that dreadful moor.'

'Can we meet today?' Tweed asked, stemming the flood.

'You asked me when I arrived. Late yesterday. Just in time to have tea. It's out of this world, tea at Brown's. Why don't we do that?'

'Good idea. I could get there about three-thirty. Would that suit you?'

'Gorgeous. I'll count the minutes. Don't be late. They have the most scrumptious strawberry cake. But it goes quickly. Oh,' she added as an afterthought, 'I'll have something interesting to tell you. Not over the phone, darling.'

'Three-thirty then. Goodbye . . .'

Tweed put down the phone as though it were hot. He sighed, took out his handkerchief, mopped his forehead in mock horror. 'Good job you didn't take that conversation down.'

'She's very attractive,' Paula said in a thoughtful tone.

'Swarms all over you.' He looked at Monica. 'But you did tape-record the conversation I had with Nield?'

'Yes, I saw you nod twice. It's recorded for all time. Want to hear it played back?'

'Later. Something Nield said was significant and now it's gone. I was concentrating on getting them out of Dunster. Damned if I can remember what it was. You listen to it, Paula. See whether something strikes you. Monica, try Peter Sarris again.'

'Chief Inspector Sarris? London calling. Mr Tweed of Special Branch would like a word with you . . .'

Tweed spent little time over exchanging greetings. 'Robert Newman, the foreign correspondent, has told me of his conversation with you, Peter. He's fully vetted . . .'

'He works for you these days?' Sarris enquired.

'No, he doesn't. But when he's after a story and comes across something he feels affects national security he tells me.' That covered Newman. 'I have a big favour to ask you. Hold off any action on this character Stavros Florakis. Give him enough rope and he'll hang himself. I'm at the early stages of the investigation.'

'What investigation is that? If I may ask.'

'You may. I'm investigating the death of one of my top men – Harry Masterson. Can't tell you what it's about yet. Point is Florakis' farm is close to Cape Sounion where Masterson died in suspicious circumstances.'

'Official verdict is an accident.'

'And the unofficial? I'm on scrambler.'

'So am I,' Sarris assured him. 'We had it installed when drugs became a major problem. Unofficially? I'm only expressing my personal opinion. There are people higher up who wouldn't like this . . .'

'Don't worry. This chat is totally confidential.'

'Masterson was murdered. I went to the Cape myself,

308

looked over the ground. No sane man could have stumbled over the edge. And Masterson was very sane – I saw him once at the Hilton. So, you want me to hold off the cavalry?'

'Please. We're at an early stage, Peter. I'm not sure at which end the key lies yet – yours or mine. Talking about keys, have you ever heard of the Greek Key?'

Sarris hesitated. Only for a second or two, but Tweed caught it.

'Doesn't mean a thing to me. Will we be seeing you out here?' he continued.

'Hard to say just now. How is Kalos? I remember him well at that security conference in Geneva. You have a clever assistant there.'

'Ah, but you are shrewder than some people here on the higher floors.' Sarris hesitated, this time for longer. Tweed waited, sensing the Greek was making up his mind about something. 'It is interesting you mentioned Kalos. He has made an important discovery. As you may know, Newman obtained Florakis' fingerprints. We were putting them through the computer. Kalos – as always – went his own way. He checked back through a card index of old records going back to 1946.'

'Sounds like Kalos,' Tweed commented.

'He came up trumps. An hour ago we were comparing the fingerprints of Stavros Florakis with another set under the magnifier. They matched.'

'Who is he really?' Tweed kept the excitement out of his voice.

'A certain Oleg Savinkov. Sent in by Stalin to murder leaders of EDES, the right-wing group fighting the Communists during the Civil War. Are you with me?'

'I have read about it. Go on.'

'Savinkov was nicknamed The Executioner, sometimes The Russian. So what is he doing as an impostor back in Greece? Someone has reactivated him. Can't be

309

Gorbachev. He's in the détente business. You still want me to hold off the dogs?'

'More than ever. And I will definitely be flying to Greece as soon as I can . . .'

28

Newman knew there was something wrong the moment he stepped out of the elevator on Christina's floor. Nick was sitting in an armchair on guard. He was smoking a cigarette and the ash tray on the marble-topped table was filled with discarded butts.

But it was Nick's reaction as soon as the elevator doors opened which warned Newman. Nick stood up abruptly and his right hand slid inside his jacket towards the Smith & Wesson revolver Newman had returned to him. When he saw who it was Nick converted the movement into scratching his armpit.

'Is she safe?' Newman asked.

'OK. But we have a problem, a crisis. Anton, one of her relatives, has arrived. He came up to this floor, then wandered off down that corridor when he saw me. Later he came back and went down into the lobby again. Could still be there.'

'A good moment for me to have a little talk with Christina.'

'Maybe not. She's very touchy. Like a bomb that could blow up in your face. It's Anton that did it. I told her. Felt I had to . . .'

'You did right.'

Newman went to her door, rapped in the special way

310

they had agreed. She opened the door after removing the chain and Newman realized she was in a bad mood. Her eyes looked larger than ever, she didn't smile, she turned her back on him and walked towards the balcony, arms folded under her breasts.

'Anton is here. They've found me,' she snapped before he could say a word.

'You haven't told me about Anton. Talk. And keep away from the balcony. If he's by the pool he could see you.'

'What difference does it make? He knows I'm here.'

· 'We'll handle that.' He took hold of her by the shoulders and turned her round, sat her down on the edge of the bed. 'Stay put.' He lifted the half-empty glass on the table, sipped it. 'Champagne. Bit early in the day.'

'I needed something to settle my nerves. The bottle's in the fridge. Fill it up for me.'

'Anything the lady wants, the lady gets.'

'Anything?' she asked as he brought back the refilled glass, handed it to her. She was wearing a cream blouse with the top three buttons undone. She wore no bra.

'Not that now,' he said. 'I have questions to ask.'

'Your eyes said something different.'

He moved away to a chair. She also wore a short pleated cream skirt. Her legs were stunning. Get your mind on the business in hand, he told himself.

'Stop it,' he snapped. 'Tell me about Anton. The full *curriculum vitae*. That means his life from the day he was born.'

'I know. I'm not illiterate – like Dimitrios and Constantine.' She sipped her champagne. 'Nor is Anton. He is Petros' son by his second wife – who was worked to death like the first wife. That makes Anton, six years younger than me, my uncle, for God's sake. Petros spotted he was bright. He spent money on his education, every drachma that was available.'

'What kind of education?'

'A good school in Athens. Anton was always top of the class. So he went on to a school in Switzerland. As well as Greek, he can speak German and English fluently. He's a natural linguist. An expert horseman – he learned to ride in Germany, then went on to Vienna for dressage. Petros wanted a gentleman in the family, someone who could mix at all levels of society. He's also a crack shot with any kind of rifle or handgun.'

'Where did he learn that? In Devil's Valley?'

'You're joking. When he came back here Dimitrios and Constantine hated him. The one thing they could do to make him look useless was to shoot. Anton flew to England, joined a shooting club. When he came back he could make Dimitrios and Constantine look like children with guns.'

'Happy families. How old is he?'

'Thirty-eight. He looks ten years younger. He dresses smartly. Oh, I've left a bit out. When he came back from Geneva he had a spell at Athens University. He came under the influence of an English professor. He still attends his seminars when this professor comes here in summer.'

'You know the name of this professor?'

She screwed up her thick eyebrows. 'A double-barrelled name. I met him once. Didn't like him. He reeks with conceit and self-satisfaction. But he's clever.'

'Try and think of his name.'

'Got it. Guy Seton-Charles . . .'

Newman had a word with Nick, who went straight down to the lobby by elevator. Returning to the bedroom, he found Christina sitting in front of the dressing table, brushing her hair. A bottle of mineral water and a glass stood next to her cosmetics.

'I've sobered up,' she announced. 'I drank two glasses of water. Do you think this is a good idea – my going down to the lobby with you if Anton is still there?'

'Part of the plan. If he's hanging about I want him to see you. And I want to see him – so I'll know him in future.'

'He's the most dangerous of my relatives. Because I'm well-educated too he resents me. And he has pots of money of his own. Money is power he says.'

'Where does it come from?'

'He runs a chain of shops in Athens and Salonika. They sell expensive television, video and radio equipment. Imported, of course. We Greeks don't make anything – except silverware. Anton is clever technically, too. He can build the most complicated high-powered radio equipment.'

'That's interesting,' Newman commented to himself. He went to the door as he heard the agreed rapping signal. It was Nick.

'Anton is still here. He's strolling round the lobby below the elevators. With a bit of luck we could see him by looking down. Without him seeing us.'

'That's not the idea. Come with us. Ready, Christina?'

'If you insist.'

They crossed the first-floor lobby. Nick had pressed the button, the elevator doors opened and they stepped inside. Newman gave Christina's arm a squeeze as the elevator descended. She made a moue, stiffened herself, stood erect.

'To hell with Anton,' she said.

'That's my girl,' Newman responded.

They stepped out into the main entrance hall. Below them, beyond a waist-high wall, was a deep well, a large reception area approached by steps from the even vaster marble-floored hall leading to the street. 'Over to your left, behind the pillar,' Nick whispered.

313

Several couples occupied some of the spacious couches at the lower level. A small man stepped from behind a pillar, lifted a small object to his eyes, held it there, then replaced it in his pocket.

Marler sat in an armchair at the lower level. He had a newspaper in front of his face. He dropped the paper, stood up, wandered over to where Anton was lighting a cigarette. Marler brushed past him, looking the other way. 'Excuse me,' he said in English and walked on a few paces. He took the camera he'd filched from Anton's pocket, fiddled with it, snapped it closed again and tucked it down inside the side of his slacks.

Anton still stood by the pillar. A small compact man wearing an expensive lightweight blue suit which Marler suspected was made of silk. He had a blue-striped shirt and a pale blue tie. Very dressy, Mr Anton. His pale face was plump and his black hair was brushed back over his high forehead. No parting.

As Marler approached he was feeling in his jacket pocket. He looked up, put out a hand to detain Marler, who stepped behind the pillar. 'A word with you,' Anton said, following the Englishman. 'You've just stolen my camera.' His right hand gripped Marler's arm and there was strength in the hand.

Marler wrenched his arm loose, shook himself, his expression bleak. 'Don't do that again.' He glanced down on the floor, pointed. 'Your bloody camera is down there. You dropped it, you stupid little man.'

Anton stooped with agility, retrieved the camera. As he stood up Marler hit him hard on the jaw with his clenched fist. No one sitting in the reception area could see behind the pillar. Anton sagged, the back of his head caught the pillar, he lay on the ground.

Marler hurried to the steps, ran up to the higher level where Newman waited with Christina and Nick. 'He's out cold. Time to move her. I'll inform the reception desk . . .'

314

'Nick, go out to the car. Be ready to drive us to the Grande Bretagne . . .'

Newman grasped Christina by the arm, guided her into a waiting elevator, pressed the button. As it ascended he talked fast. 'You kept most of your case packed as I suggested?'

'Yes. I can dump my cosmetic stuff inside in its sachet and be ready in two minutes.'

'Make it one . . .'

In the main lobby Marler was talking to the chief receptionist. 'A chap has collapsed behind a pillar down there. Just keeled over. May have had a heart attack.' He waited until the receptionist phoned for a doctor and rushed off, then asked a girl for the bill for Christina's room.

'Everything's paid up,' he announced as Newman emerged from an elevator, carrying a bag with Christina by his side. Behind him he heard the same girl receptionist call out. 'Phone for you, Mr Newman . . .'

'Take Christina to the car,' Newman ordered Marler. 'I'll be with you in a minute. God knows who this could be.' The girl behind the counter handed him the phone.

'Tweed here, Bob. There's an emergency. Call me back safely within the hour. No later . . .'

'Thanks a bundle.' Newman lowered his voice. 'We have a crisis at this end. I'll call back.' He slammed down the phone.

Nick was waiting outside at the end of a queue of taxis. He opened the rear door of his Mercedes and Christina dived in, followed by Newman. As Nick dumped her bag inside the boot Marler appeared at the rear window. 'Follow us to the Grande Bretagne,' Newman told him. 'Reserve a room for Christina in the name of Mrs Charles. Take over. Nick will be taking me back to the Embassy.'

'Will do.'

Nick turned into the traffic. Christina was producing a large silk scarf from her handbag. She carefully wrapped

315

it round her hair so it was concealed. Next she donned a pair of dark wrap-round glasses, then looked at Newman.

'Do I pass inspection?'

'Unrecognizable.' Newman felt relieved. Everyone was getting into the swing of quick escapes. And Nick was driving a devious route to the Grande Bretagne. Christina looped her arm inside Newman's and snuggled up against him as he glanced through the rear window. Marler was close behind.

'How the devil did Anton find me?' Christina wondered.

'Probably by showing a photograph of you to a member of the sfaff short of folding money . . .'

'But I arrived at the Hilton disguised.'

'And then paraded yourself on the balcony. There were loads of staff serving drinks to the sun-worshippers round that pool. I should have thought of that. I should also have thought of telling you to wear your scarf and glasses when we had dinner at the Ta Nissia restaurant. We'll be more careful at the Grande Bretagne.'

'And maybe,' Nick called over his shoulder, 'I should park this car at the Astir Palace across the road from the Grande Bretagne. They'll have the registration number by now. It means booking a room . . .'

'Book one. In a different name. Buy a case and a few clothes, including one of those peaked caps the Germans like to wear. We want to sink out of sight – and that includes you. And sleep in the Astir Palace room, if that's OK. Then you're available on the dot when we need you. Unless your wife would object?'

'Glad to see the back of me.' Nick grinned. 'Sorry about the traffic snarl-up, but no one can follow us into this.'

They had arrived at Omonia Square, the Piccadilly Circus or Times Square of Athens. Everywhere intersecting roads converged, the traffic was solid. The square was surrounded with second-class hotels, department stores. Nick tapped his hand on the wheel as he waited.

'Refugees from abroad flock to this area. The police don't mind. They know where to look if they're after someone. Miracles will never cease. We're on the move again . . .'

On the veranda of his farm deep inside Devil's Valley Petros was lecturing his two grandsons viciously. He gestured with a heavy fly-swatter as they stood in front of him.

'You, Dimitrios, are telling me again that several men crept up behind you that night at the mine, then clubbed both of you. Is that still your story?'

'It is the way it happened . . .'

'Liar! Cheat!' Petros moved with savage speed. The end of the fly-swatter whacked Dimitrios across the back of his left hand. Reinforced with leather, the swatter brought up an ugly weal. And Petros was still sitting in his chair. 'You lie in your teeth,' he snarled.

'It was like that . . .' Constantine began, then stopped when Petros turned to him. He braced himself for the blow but Petros relaxed in his chair, studying the end of the fly-swatter as he talked in a calm tone.

'You were both staring down inside the mine. You saw the legs of a man protruding from under the bucket. Had you shot him without hesitation – as I would – you would have turned round and seen the single man coming up behind you, the man one of you probably glimpsed before he knocked you both out. Clumsy fools.'

'Why do you say that?' Dimitrios ventured. He sucked his injured hand.

'Because I know the mine, know that for hundreds of yards it is surrounded with loose rock chippings. One man trained in field warfare, one very clever man, might make his way silently across those rocks without making a sound. One man,' he repeated. 'I refuse to believe that several

317

men managed it. You are covering up for your idiocy. It was a trap, you realize that?'

'A trap?' Constantine sounded genuinely puzzled.

'Of course. One man – the man inside the mine – lets you see him. He leads you to the mine. His companion then creeps up behind you both. Constantine, you said you saw a rifle barrel just before it struck you. He did it like this.' Holding the fly-swatter by the middle of the handle, Petros swung it first one way, then the other. 'Were they the English?' he growled. 'You saw one man coming up the track.'

'Too far away to see him at all clearly,' Dimitrios broke in before Constantine could reply. It was a relief to be able to tell the truth.

'And you did a lousy job of not finding Christina,' Petros sneered. He was enjoying himself, taking them down a peg, showing who was boss.

'We did our best,' Dimitrios protested. 'So many hotels . . .'

'Oho! Your best. Your worst, you mean. You walk into the Hilton and try to bribe the chief receptionist! He knows it is not worth risking his fat salary to give out information. I would have gone after the menials – people like yourselves. A chambermaid, a cleaner. Someone who needs the money, someone who goes into every bedroom. Well, at least Anton is now looking. He will find her.'

'We could go back, try again,' Constantine suggested eagerly.

'Now you grovel.' Petros spat beyond the veranda. They took all the insults he heaped on them, he was thinking. It was a tribute to the power of his personality. His huge body emanated physical magnetism. He waved towards the scrub-studded mountains.

'Get out there in the sun. Tend the sheep. Make sure the other shepherds are not sleeping behind rocks. If you catch one, kick hell out of him.' He paused. 'That was curious that you should see Florakis climbing a mountain

318

at that hour. Keep an eye on him, too. Report to me when you find out what he is up to.' Petros could not resist one last dig. 'And forget about Christina – let Anton find her. Anton has brains.'

When Dimitrios and Constantine had left the farm, climbing up the track even a goat might find trouble negotiating, kicking up limestone dust which filled their nostrils, sweating in the afternoon sun, Petros remained on the veranda. His leonine head sunk on his barrel-like chest, he remained awake, thinking.

Always the hated English. Newman and Marler – those were the two English Giorgos had reported as registering at the Grande Bretagne. Giorgos who had ended rammed inside a cask of wine upside down in the Plaka.

Without any formal education, Petros possessed a native cunning, the devious mind of a peasant which sometimes could out-think the well-educated. Newman and Marler who had seduced Christina into joining them. They had been sent by whichever of the three men had killed Andreas on Siros all those years ago.

Which one? Colonel Barrymore, Captain Robson or Company Sergeant Major Kearns? Could all three be involved in the bestial murders? Because later – when the war was over – Petros had visited Cairo to learn what he could of the murder of his other son, Stephen, masquerading as Ionides. An Egyptian who worked as a cleaner at the Antikhana Building had told him. The same three men had been based in the building. In some way one of them had penetrated Ionides' real identity, had discovered he was the brother of Andreas.

Which one? Petros asked himself the question he had pondered a thousand times. Now Anton – clever Anton – had located them at some place called Exmoor. Why were they all living so close together?

319

It didn't matter! Petros heaved himself out of the chair, went into the farmhouse, returned with the box he kept hidden. He opened it. Inside, wrapped in newspaper, was the commando knife, the knife he had used all his strength to heave out of Andreas' back. The knife he would one day use to kill the murderer of his two sons.

Dapper and assured, despite his experience, Anton thanked the chief receptionist and walked out of the Hilton. The doctor they had summoned had been a nuisance. Anton had assured him he'd fainted, caught his jaw against the side of the pillar. He had also handled the chief receptionist cleverly. Just before he left he made the remark casually.

'It was the heat. I must have fainted just before my friends left the hotel . . .' He described Christina, Newman and Marler. 'Did they say which hotel they were moving to? Maybe not – as they left in a rush.'

'No, they didn't. As you say, they were in a hurry,' the chief receptionist had replied.

Which confirmed Anton's suspicions. He shrugged as he walked into the blazing heat, hardly noticing the change in temperature. He had found her once, he would find her again. But first there was more urgent business to attend to. He checked his watch – he was late for his appointment.

Let the bastard wait. He would be so relieved when he saw Anton arrive. He ignored the taxis. Their drivers had good memories. He made his way over the complicated crossing and walked briskly down Avenue Sofias towards Syntagma Square where the Grande Bretagne was located.

Anton smiled to himself as he thought how livid Petros would be if he knew where he was going, who he was going to meet and why. The old ruffian was living in the past.

Had no idea of what was really going on in the world. Wouldn't he be surprised one day when he found Anton was a Cabinet Minister? The Ministry of the Interior for preference. There you had real power.

Half an hour later he was walking through the maze of alleys and streets which made up the honeycomb of the Plaka. Was the plan already beginning to work? Sooner or later the man he was going to see would have to tell him what was happening. The clod who was still important to Anton. For the present. The man called Doganis. The Athens chief of the Greek Key.

'You're late,' Doganis greeted him. 'Why?'

Anton sat in a rush-covered chair in the room above a taverna, took his time about lighting a cigarette. He disliked this hulking brute but was astute enough to conceal his distaste. Doganis, a man in his sixties, was heavily built with broad shoulders and a large head of greying hair. His hooded eyes regarded Anton with a cold expression.

Anton studied his chief, careful to betray nothing of the contempt he felt. The huge soft hands holding a circular ebony ruler, the sagging jowls, the barrel-like stomach. Out of condition, out of touch with the modern world. One of the Old Guard. A gross monument of the Civil War days.

Doganis was also studying the dapper Anton. Ambitious, ruthless. A young upstart who had to be kept in his place. Dressed like a gigolo. Doganis had been ordered to tell him the next move in the operation; personally he thought it premature.

'You are going back to England soon,' he informed him. 'You'll be taking letters to Captain Robson, Sergeant Major Kearns and Colonel Barrymore. Two of the letters will be meaningless. The third you will have the honour of delivering to Jupiter.'

'Jupiter? Who is that?'

'The man who is reactivating the organization. Do not ask who he is.'

'Jupiter is a Roman god, not a Greek,' Anton remarked, feeling his way.

'Which confuses the issue, protects his identity. You travel to England again in a few weeks' time – after we have received an important visitor from abroad.' Doganis paused. At least they hadn't told him to reveal yet to Anton that the visitor was Colonel Volkov, aide to General Lucharsky. 'You can travel there by the secret route again, I assume? Again there must be no record of your visit to England.'

'It worked before, it will work again,' Anton told him boldly. 'You do your job, I'll do mine . . .'

There was a sudden cracking sound. Anton stared. Doganis, who constantly held something in his restless hands, had split the ebony ruler in two in his fury.

Anton was astounded. The grotesque obese Doganis he had put down as effete had enormous strength in his apparently flabby hands. Strangler's hands. Doganis pointed the jagged end of one half of the ruler at him. His voice was more sinister for its soft tone.

'Listen to me, Gavalas. We have laid a tremendous responsibility on your immature shoulders. I have only to report you have lost my confidence and you are dead in twenty-four hours. You have displayed arrogance. I find that disturbing.'

Anton swallowed. The room was dimly illuminated by an oil lamp on a side table. Doganis' huge shadow suddenly seemed to fill the room. He forced himself to speak respectfully. 'I apologize, Comrade. I wished to assure you all will go well.'

'And remember this,' Doganis continued, ignoring the apology, 'I may introduce you to our visitor. He may wish to brief you himself. Treat him with reverence. Phone me daily from a public call box.' He changed the subject without warning, watching the other man closely. 'Is everything quiet down at Cape Sounion? No sign of anyone becoming curious about Florakis?'

'No sign at all,' Anton assured him.

'You replied too quickly. What about Petros?'

'He is still planning his mad revenge on the English murderers of his two sons. He thinks of nothing else.'

'Useful. He will divert the attention of those two Englishmen, Newman and Marler. Go now. Your future depends on obedience to the cause.'

Anton stood up quickly, glad to leave the presence of this man who now frightened him. He hurried down the narrow staircase leading direct to the street. He paused before he walked into the deserted street.

He did not see the small stocky man with a stubble of brown hair waiting in the shadow of a doorway across the street. For the simple reason that Kalos did not want to be seen. Kalos wore a stained old jacket and baggy trousers. He raised the camera with the infra-red lens and snapped off three shots. Anton turned left and walked rapidly away.

I'm lucky, thought Kalos. Whoever he is left the building when the tourists and the locals are eating and drinking inside the tavernas. He already had inside his camera two shots of Doganis. At least he had known this senior member of the Greek Key.

Kalos had waited over an hour outside the apartment Doganis rented in the Plaka, then had followed him to this new rendezvous above a taverna. Maybe Sarris would identify the younger man who had just left after spending half an hour with Doganis. The Greek Key was apparently recruiting younger members. A bad sign. And Kalos wondered who, where, and how they were finding fresh recruits.

323

29

'Bob, what crisis?' Tweed asked. 'Where are you talking from?'

'The Embassy. On scrambler phone. Now, you listen . . .' Newman explained tersely what had happened. He was alone in the basement room: Patterson had pushed off after unlocking the door.

'So your main task,' Tweed said, 'is to guard Christina, hide her away from Petros . . .'

'Our main objective is to find out who killed Masterson. And the last person we've found yet who saw him alive is Christina. It may be significant that Petros – through Anton – is doing his damnedest to track her down. What's your problem?'

'*Your* problem now,' Tweed told him. 'I had Butler and Nield on Exmoor, tailing Professor Guy Seton-Charles. An hour ago I had an emergency call from Butler. He was at London Airport. Seton-Charles suddenly took off. Left his bungalow with a case, drove a devious route to the airport . . .'

'Devious?'

'He took the main road to London, then cut off down a side turning. Nield followed him and Butler cruised on along the highway. Later Butler saw Seton-Charles come back down a slip road. From that point Butler and Nield leapfrogged so the target wouldn't spot them. At London Airport Nield stood behind Seton-Charles as he booked a first-class return to Athens. He's in mid-air now. British Airways flight 456, departed London 2.35 p.m., arrives at

Athens 8 p.m. Both local times. Can you get to the airport and track him? Remember his description?'

'Perfectly. And I've loads of time.'

'I need to know who he *contacts*. Something very funny about the professor.'

'Leave it to me . . .'

The BA flight from London touched down at Athens Airport at 8 p.m. Newman, lounging in a seat near the exit, spotted him at once – Seton-Charles wore a light-weight linen suit crumpled from sitting inside the aircraft. The professor climbed into a taxi. Newman got inside the next taxi.

'I'm a detective,' he told the driver. 'Don't lose that taxi – and here's a thousand drachmae as a tip.'

'What has he done?' asked the Greek.

'That's what I'm trying to find out . . .'

Settling back in his seat, Newman took off his jacket, mopped his forehead. The interior of the vehicle was like a sweat box. He recalled a headline blazoned on a newsstand. *Killer Heatwave Hits Greece*. And the character who wrote that one up wasn't joking, he thought.

Half an hour later, after passing between endless rows of white-walled two-storeyed houses backed by arid hillsides, they entered the city. Seton-Charles' taxi pulled up outside its destination. The occupant got out, paid off the driver and without a backward glance carried his bag inside the Hilton Hotel.

Tweed had phoned Jill Kearns at Brown's Hotel an hour before he was due to have tea with her. He had explained something urgent had come up, an emergency he had to cope with personally. Would she forgive him? Could they make a fresh date for tea in a couple of days' time?

Jill had shown no signs of resentment, said she certainly understood he had a difficult job. She would look forward even more to their being together now she would have to wait a little longer to see him. He put down the phone and looked at Monica.

'She's still keen to see me. Meantime we'll see where she goes, how she spends her time, who she meets. I fixed this up while you were out.'

'Fixed up what?'

'At this moment Paula is sitting in the lobby of Brown's. Jill can't get out of either the Albemarle Street or the Dover Street exit without Paula spotting her. When she leaves, Paula follows.'

'Paula will recognize her?'

'You've forgotten.' Tweed relaxed in his chair, pleased with the way things were developing. 'Paula,' he reminded her, 'was with me when I visited Kearns on Exmoor at his horrible old house near that bungalow estate where Seton-Charles lives. Jill sat in the room during my interview with Kearns – as did Paula. They sat within six feet of each other.'

'Is this Jill bright?'

'A very attractive blonde, in her thirties, and very bright.'

'Then she may well spot Paula following her,' Monica objected.

'You think so? Before Paula left here she altered her hair style. I loaned her a pair of glasses with blank lenses. It's amazing how a pair of glasses alters a person's appearance. On top of that she left early enough to call at Simpsons in Piccadilly – to do some shopping.'

'What shopping? You can be so exasperating. You're enjoying keeping me in suspense.'

'She went to buy a white raincoat, one with a large collar which buttons up to the neck. You may have observed it is drizzling on and off. In that outfit Jill will never recognize her.'

'And what's your motive in this devious – typically devious, if I may say . . .'

'You just did.' Tweed grinned.

'Devious ploy I was going to say if you'd let me finish just one sentence.'

'I'm suspicious of the glamorous Jill Kearns. She may be acting on her husband's instructions. I'm giving her enough rope – two days of it – to hang herself.'

'You don't trust anyone, do you?'

'Especially not attractive blondes who flatter me, try to make out they think I'm the cat's whiskers.'

'Maybe for her you are.' Monica doodled on her note-pad. 'She may be just what you need . . .'

She stopped speaking, feeling she'd gone too far. Tweed's wife had left him several years ago, had walked out to take up living with a Greek shipping magnate. Last heard of in Rio. Tweed showed no sign of having heard her.

'Now we're on our own, let's check the facts we have so far, what we're doing. I'm a good listener as you know.'

He relaxed in his chair, hands clasped in his lap, eyes half-shut. Monica began her survey of recent events, reciting from memory.

'Object of the exercise – to track down the killer of Harry Masterson . . .'

'I'm going to get that bastard,' Tweed said half to himself.

Monica paused, surprised by the vehemence of his tone, then went on. 'Harry was going on holiday, bored stiff with the idea. He sees the ad Christina Gavalas placed in *The Times*, signing herself Irene. Intriguing reference to the Greek Key, which is a mystery to us still. Christina tells the story of the murder of Andreas and Stephen during the war. Harry gets interested, fools her into thinking he's a detective. Together they visit Exmoor. OK so far?'

327

'Go on.'

'Harry visits each of the three men, one of whom the Gavalas family is convinced is the murderer. Robson, Barrymore and Kearns. Harry is probably the shrewdest interrogator we've ever had – so maybe he spots the bad apple. He then, God save his soul, lays a trap. He tells each of the three he's flying to Greece. Which he then does with Christina. Harry is killed at Cape Sounion.'

'And,' Tweed added, 'by the time Paula and I do the same run Harry did – visit those three on Exmoor – they've all been on holiday and have suntans. Which means one of them could have been to Greece while Harry was there.'

'What I just can't see is who could have tricked Harry and pushed him over that three-hundred-feet cliff.' Monica shivered. 'The big question is who could have gained Harry's trust?'

'Christina is the obvious answer. The obvious is often correct.'

'There is an alternative,' Monica mused. 'Someone else Harry had no reason to fear but who got the better of him.'

Tweed opened his eyes. 'That's a new idea you have there. Someone he met in Greece?'

'Doesn't seem likely,' Monica disagreed. 'Next thing, Newman and Marler go out to Greece, make contact with Christina, who seems to have changed sides. But that could be another ploy, this time to trap Newman. That woman worries me. I sense she's clever.'

'Not clever enough to fool Newman,' Tweed assured her.

'She may have fooled Harry. I gather she's very attractive.'

'Harry,' Tweed recalled, 'was a great one for the girls. After his wife divorced him because he wasn't home every night, Harry made hay, was a devil with women.'

'Bob Newman is single again,' Monica reminded him.

'After that brutal murder of his French wife in the Baltic.'

'No woman ever fooled Bob,' Tweed insisted. 'He might *pretend* to go all starry-eyed over someone like Christina – but he'd be fooling her. Go on with your summary.'

'Newman and Marler contact Christina. They hear about this old villain, Petros – òbsessed with tracking down his sons' killers over forty years afterwards. An impossible mission . . .'

'Theoretically,' Tweed interjected. 'But his son, Anton, does find his way to Exmoor – and locates all three ex-commandos. Petros must be a man with a deep peasant cunning. Obsessed, I agree. An impossible mission? Maybe not. And those three on Exmoor are scared of something. Look how Paula and I found all three were living inside fortresses. As I said to Paula, they're like men waiting for Nemesis.'

'Next development,' Monica continued, 'we get all this weird data from Newman. And weird it is – Andreas' skeleton hanging inside that old silver mine. Macabre. Petros is obsessed.'

'No proof it is Andreas. Probable, yes. Certain, no.'

'Plus the strange trip to the island of Siros. Dimitrios and Constantine – according to Christina – tried to shoot Newman. And,' she pressed on, 'this is the hairbrained place where the three commandos landed – with a German lookout point perched in that monastery above them. Back to the present day, we have the murder of Giorgos – who worked for the Grande Bretagne and spied on Newman and Marler. Also macabre – ending head down in a cask.'

'I think the solution lies in Greece.' Tweed, suddenly alert, walked over to the window and gazed towards the trees of distant Regent's Park.

'Looks like it,' Monica agreed. 'That's further reinforced by this peculiar Seton-Charles character hurtling off to Athens. That might mean nothing – except for the devious route he took to London Airport. Harry and Pete handled that cleverly. But what do they do now?'

'They're already doing it. While you were out when Butler called from London Airport I sent them both back to cover Exmoor. Robson, Barrymore and Kearns are still holed up there. Change of tactics again. Butler and Nield will have gone back to checking on that curious trio. Later, I'll fly out to Greece. I want to question Petros.'

'That could be dangerous. Newman nearly got killed venturing into Devil's Valley.'

'Sometimes you have to take chances.' He was pacing restlessly. 'Harry was murdered at Cape Sounion. That's close to this Devil's Valley. And some swine murdered Sam Partridge on Exmoor. That Greek, Anton, was floating about when it happened. Two scores I have to settle. Someone is going to pay the price.'

Monica again was disturbed by the ferocity of his language, his bitter tone. She spoke quietly.

'Be careful. Don't get obsessed – like old Petros. You're losing your normal sense of detachment. You always said that was the fatal mistake . . .'

'Stop nagging me, woman.' Tweed stared at her. 'I'll work it out in my own way without your advice . . .'

He stopped, appalled at Monica's expression. She looked like a woman who had been whipped across the face. In all their long relationship he had never spoken to her like that.

'I'm dreadfully sorry,' he apologized. 'I do rely on your judgement – maybe more than you've ever realized. I feel like a man walking in a fog, a tired man,' he admitted. He stuffed his briefcase with tape recordings and files. 'I think I'll spend a couple of days in my flat, sitting in an armchair, thinking. I need something to happen which points the way.'

'It always does.' Monica smiled. 'Now you're following your usual method. Don't worry. You're under pressure.

I'm amazed you haven't blown your top before. And there's a lot of personal feelings you've had to grapple with. Go home, get some rest – or would you like some coffee first?'

Tweed said thank you but he wanted to get straight off. He put on his shabby Burberry, squeezed her shoulder and walked out with his briefcase. Monica stood up, went to the window to watch him walk round Park Crescent through the net curtains. She was frightened. Tweed was acting like a man obsessed with his problems.

He left the building. He paused on the front steps to button up the raincoat, glancing all round the Crescent in case there were hostile watchers. Then he headed for the taxi rank.

On the way he passed a newspaper seller with a poster propped against the garden railings. Tweed didn't even notice it – he was thinking about Monica. It read, *Reagan–Gorbachev Summit in Washington?*

30

'I'm scared stiff. I need someone to confide in.' Jill Kearns laid a hand on Tweed's knee. It was two days later.

Tea at Brown's. Tweed looked round the room, admired the wooden wall panelling, the moulded ceiling. The atmosphere of the place created an air of intimacy. Especially when you were with a woman.

They sat at a table in an arched alcove at the end of the lounge. Behind them was a fireplace and they were isolated from the other guests taking tea. He twisted round in his deep armchair to look at Jill. She was worth the effort.

She had twirled her blonde hair into a single long plait looped over her shoulder. And she was dressed for London. A pair of tight-fitting leather trousers thrust into boots which displayed her well-shaped legs. She also wore a tunic of some black material splashed with vivid-coloured oriental flowers. Tweed drank some tea before replying.

'What exactly is worrying you?'

'Stuart, for one thing . . .'

'And for another?'

Tweed helped himself to a scrambled egg roll, bit off half of it. On the table in front of them stood a four-tier stand of some of the best food he'd ever enjoyed. The lowest tier had delicate little sandwiches with the crusts removed; on the second and third tiers were selections of bread and more sandwiches. Logically, the top tier held a variety of cakes, including some chocolate eclairs. You worked your way up.

'The company he keeps,' Jill replied, squeezing his leg. She used the other hand to eat and drink. The room was full of couples and quartets whose conversation muffled what Jill was saying. 'Those two men, Captain – Dr – Robson, and Colonel Barrymore. The colonel gives me the creeps.'

'Why?'

'He seems to mesmerize my husband and Robson. You'd think they were all still in the Army and Barrymore was their CO – the way he talks to them. Loathsome sarcastic bastard.'

'I take it you don't like him . . .'

'Don't make fun of me.' She looped her hand round his left hand he'd rested on the arm of the chair. 'You'll help me, won't you, Tweed? I wish I could get you on the telephone. Give me your number. It would be nice if we could have dinner. More cosy.'

All in a rush. She'll proposition me soon, Tweed thought. I wish to God I knew what she's really up to. He asked a question to throw her off balance.

'How do you know all this – how Barrymore talks to them? I thought they met by themselves for dinner once a week at The Luttrell Arms.'

'Sometimes they come over to our place and talk half the night in the study. I eavesdrop.'

'A bit naughty, that.' He smiled to take the sting out of the comment.

'You've got a lovely smile,' she said.

'You overheard something that frightened you,' he probed.

Outwardly impassive, Tweed wasn't feeling too comfortable. A woman had come in and sat down at a small table at the side of the room. She had folded her raincoat and parked it on the other chair. She was watching them briefly over the top of her glasses with a cynical expression. Paula. She hadn't, he knew, missed the fact that Jill was clasping his hand.

'Stuart is reinforcing the defences, as he put it. He's even laid some of those beastly steel-teethed traps outside the walls of our house. Barrymore advised that. They're all strengthening their security. Just as though they were expecting a raid.'

'Perhaps they are. By who?'

She hesitated, pushed two fingers under his shirt cuff. 'I've no idea. I feel like a prisoner.'

'You escaped for now. You're sitting here, in the middle of London. Not on Exmoor.' He poured more tea and she leaned over to hold the teapot lid in place, her breasts brushing his arm. 'You're confiding in me, as you put it, although I can't imagine why.'

She released her hand, flopped back in her armchair, her long leather-clad legs stretched out in front of her. Paula raised her glasses higher up the bridge of her nose, adjusted her beret and looked away. Tweed wished she'd stop sending signals.

'Because,' Jill said, 'you put the wind up all three when

333

you came to see them. I heard Stuart talking to Barrymore on the phone after you'd left. He was agitated. He started to say "This man Tweed is dangerous," then he slammed the door of his study and I couldn't catch any more. If you can put the wind up those three you're the man for me, my ally.'

She remained flopped in the chair but still looked elegant as she spoke in a coaxing tone.

'What about dinner here tonight? Say eight o'clock. And you haven't given me your phone number yet.'

'Can't do that – give you a number. Security. What I can do is to have you called daily in case you've got a message for me . . .'

'And dinner?'

'I expect to be working till midnight. Dinner will be sandwiches at my desk. Sorry.'

'If you agreed to dinner . . .' She crossed her legs and watched him through her lashes. 'I might have more news to pass on to you.'

'I can't promise to be an ally,' he warned. 'And if you've really more to tell me, do it now.' He decided an eclair was pushing it and took another scrambled egg roll.

She took a pack of cigarettes from her large handbag, extracted a king-size cigarette when he shook his head, and lit it with a gold-plated lighter. In the mellow light her beautiful bone structure stood out clearly. He was tempted to change his mind, to say he could make it for dinner. She's a devil, he was thinking. Blowing out a stream of smoke, she smiled.

'I can read your mind, Tweed. You're reconsidering your decision about dinner.'

There was an aura about her which drew him to her. In her thirties, he reflected. Not such a huge difference in their ages. He drank half a cup of strong tea to get a grip on himself.

'How long have you and Stuart been married?'

334

'Ten long years. Oh, it was fun to start with. He's a good-looking bastard. I met him soon after he'd left the Army – at a party in Taunton. He had a sense of humour in those days. Then he became cold – and spent more time with Barrymore and Robson. That's when he started turning the house into the Tower of London – like the others. I could leave him any day now for the right man.'

'That might be traumatic . . .'

'No more traumatic than the way we live now. At nights he spends half his time riding over the moor up to Dunkery Beacon. He's not back by midnight.' She looked at him with a certain expression. 'So I make a point of pretending to be fast asleep when my lord and master rolls in.'

'Dunkery Beacon? That's the highest point on Exmoor. And it's pretty rough country. How does he manage in the dark?'

'He doesn't.' She leaned forward to straighten his tie. 'He only goes up there half the month – not before there's a half moon waxing. I spend my evenings watching the television rubbish. I lead the most exciting life.'

'At least he seems generous,' Tweed remarked. 'Your clothes, that lighter . . .'

'Paid for out of a big legacy my favourite uncle left me.'

Tweed checked his watch. 'Sorry, but I have to go . . .'

She sat up straight and her face was close to his. 'All right, I'll tell you. One night when the three of them were talking they left the study door open a bit. A few nights ago. I crept down the stairs. Do you want to know what I heard?'

'Up to you.'

'My reward for telling is you have dinner with me soon. Promise?'

'I'll think about it.'

'The trouble was I only heard a bit. Then one of the

335

treads on the staircase creaked. Barrymore came to the door and slammed it shut. I froze, still as a mouse.'

'Did he see you?' Tweed kept the anxiety out of his voice.

'I'm not sure. Before that happened Robson said they'd better watch out. He sensed that the Greek Key might arrive soon on Exmoor, that he'd heard Petros – I think that was the name – was looking for them . . .'

Tweed was getting anxious: it was after 7 p.m. and there was still no sign of Paula. Monica, who worked all hours, saw him check his watch.

'She'll be all right. Paula can look after herself.'

The phone rang, she picked it up, spoke briefly. She nodded towards Tweed's phone.

'It's Harry Butler. Says it's an emergency. Not like him . . .'

Tweed lifted the receiver. 'Hello, Harry. Where are you calling from?'

'From a public phone box in Minehead on the coast. We're staying at a tiny place called Porlock Weir, also on the coast. End of the road. Literally. It stops there. I decided we needed a new base. Not Dunster, not Taunton. Porlock Weir is tucked away. Has a toy harbour for boats. The only way west is to walk along the rocky shore. I can hear the tide coming in at night. High tide around midnight. Got a pencil handy? Good. We're staying at The Anchor Hotel. I'm in Room Three, Pete has Room Two. Telephone number is 0643 862753. Got it?'

'Yes. Something's happened?'

'The ex-commando lot have disappeared. All three. Robson, Kearns and Barrymore. They've left Exmoor . . .'

'How do you know that?' Tweed felt a chill creeping up his spine.

'I took Barrymore and Robson's residences – because

they're close together. Pete watched Kearns. We kept in contact with our car radios. Careful what we said. Not a sign of them. I decided to use bull-at-gate method.'

'What did you do next?'

'Called at each address after buying new outfits. Country stuff. Pete shaved off his moustache – after a lot of pressure from me. I wore a polo-necked sweater and a pair of tinted glasses. Not foolproof, but if one of them opened the door we'd know at least they were there.'

'And the result?'

'At Quarme Manor that old bat of a housekeeper, Mrs Atyeo, tells me the Colonel is not at home. Can't say when he'll be back. I chatted her up, but let's skip that. So I drove on to Captain Robson at his posh bungalow. His sister – when I coax her – says her brother is away in London. Pete had a rougher time at CSM Kearns' place. No answer to the bell-push so he scrambles over the gate. The dog comes at him – ruddy Alsatian type. Pete coped, bashed the beast on the nose with the barrel of his gun. They don't like that – a hefty bonk on the nose. Pete prowled round the place. It was after dark. No lights. No one home. That's it. They've gone. To London maybe. Robson could have lied to his sister. We feel we should have seen one of them go.'

'Not necessarily. Harry, both of you stay on at The Anchor – and pick up any gossip on the three men. Call Monica if there's a fresh twist. In any case, call daily. Take care.'

Tweed sat staring into the distance after putting down the phone. Monica watched him as she removed the cassette which had recorded Butler's conversation.

'He said something which triggered off a memory,' Tweed told her after a few minutes. 'Can't put my finger on it. We'll play it back later, see if I can spot what it was.'

He walked over to the wall where three maps had been

337

attached – maps carrying flags with names. A map of Exmoor. A map of the Greek area stretching from Athens to Cape Sounion. And a map of Athens which Monica had obtained.

On the Exmoor map flags with names located the homes of Barrymore, Robson and Kearns, the bungalow estate, Professor Seton-Charles' residence, The Royal Oak at Winsford and The Luttrell Arms – the two places where the trio met weekly for lunch or dinner. One flag pressed in close to Winsford carried the name Sam Partridge. Tweed picked up two more from a tray on a table and wrote Butler and Nield on each. He pressed these in over Porlock Weir.

The map of Greece carried fewer flags. One for Petros in Devil's Valley, another close by for Florakis. A third, perched at the edge of Cape Sounion, carried what amounted to an obituary. Harry Masterson.

The street plan of Athens was becoming crowded. At the corner of Syntagma Square where the Grande Bretagne was situated, three more names: Christina Gavalas, Newman, Marler. At the other end of Avenue Sofias a flag for Professor Seton-Charles at the Hilton. And, finally, at the police headquarters building on Alexandras, Peter Sarris and Kalos.

'Who is Kalos?' Monica asked.

'The Dormouse.'

'Sorry? Did I hear you aright?'

'You did. I met Kalos, Sarris' loyal assistant, at the security conference in Geneva. A small, stocky chap with a stubble of light brown hair peppered over his head. I nicknamed him The Dormouse – because that's what he looks like. We got on well together. When I go to Athens he's the man I'm hoping will tell me anything they know. Sarris is more cautious. Another reason for my respecting The Dormouse is his uncanny ability to track a suspect while merging with his background. Sarris told me that.'

'Maybe you'd better fly to Greece soon,' Monica suggested.

'All in good time.' He looked at the wall maps again. 'At least we have our forces well distributed – Newman and Marler in Greece, Butler and Nield on Exmoor. There's a name missing.'

'Who's that?'

'Anton. Trouble is he's a will o' the wisp. First he was back in Greece, then he slips into this country by some unknown means before slipping out again. I'd like to know how he managed that.'

After parking his car at The Anchor Butler went for a walk westward along the coast. It was dark and he passed several isolated cottages with lights burning inside. To his right he could hear the slap of the incoming sea hitting the rocks. He turned round, went back to The Anchor and into the bar. Nield was chatting to the barman, a young chap who polished glasses as he talked.

'They have a ghost prowling the beaches at night,' Nield said to Harry, who ordered half a pint. 'Meet John, the barman. Local.'

'Not exactly a ghost,' John told Butler as he served him. 'A few weeks ago the old crone, Mrs Larcombe – lives in the end cottage – swears she saw flashing lights out at sea. Then another light flashing further west along the coast. Can't take her seriously.'

'Bats in the belfry?' suggested Butler, only half-listening.

'Hardly. Sharp as a tack. Local nosey parker. It was about the time that Portuguese ship, *Oporto*, was due to berth at Watchet.'

Butler frowned. 'Surely not at night – no ship could get inside Watchet except in broad daylight.'

'They said it missed the tide, had to heave to offshore all night.'

Butler nodded, said to Nield he was hungry. Time for dinner.

Paula arrived back at nine o'clock. She took off her raincoat, sagged into the secretarial chair behind her desk, kicked off her shoes. Monica said she was making coffee. Paula grinned. 'Bless you.' Tweed leaned back in his chair, studying her.

'You look all in – and you're still wearing those glasses.'

'So I am. I'd forgotten them. Thank the Lord I was wearing my flatties. That Jill Kearns has the stamina of a goat.' Waiting until Monica had left the room, she looked at Tweed quizzically. 'I'm sure you could have ended up in bed with her. She's ravishing. And she's after you. You do know that?'

'The thought crossed my mind. Don't push it. Give me a report. About her movements.'

'Window-shopping for three days. Didn't buy a thing. Went all over the West End . . .'

'She didn't spot you?'

'Of course not. I wore that beret I had on in Brown's, took it off from time to time. Switched round my reversible raincoat – every conceivable variation . . .'

'But did she at any time use a public call box?' Tweed asked.

'Definitely not. This evening she had early dinner – at Brown's. Then went up to her room. I thought it was time to return. To report to "Sir",' she added with mock solemnity.

'And that's it?' Tweed sounded disappointed.

'Except I found out she always stays at Brown's when she comes to town.'

'How did you discover that?'

'I chatted up the hall porter.' She looked at Monica who had come back with a tray. 'You're an angel.' She drank half her cup of black coffee, then gazed at Tweed. 'Now, what did you find – apart from the fact that Jill has wandering fingers?'

Tweed gave her a concise summary of his conversation with Jill. 'Well, did you notice anything interesting or significant she told me?'

'Robson's reference to the Greek Key,' Paula said promptly. 'I also spotted it's the first time we've heard any of the Exmoor trio mention Petros – linking him to the Greek Key. Surely that is significant?'

Tweed pursed his lips. 'Significant of what? But Robson seems to have changed his mind. On Nield's tape – recorded during their dinner talk that night at The Luttrell Arms – Robson scoffed at Barrymore's mention of the Greek Key.'

'And now he's linked Petros with it – whatever "it" may be.'

'So I simply must confront Petros – interrogate him – sooner or later.' He caught Monica's dubious glance and looked away. 'I have something else to do urgently. Monica, try and get Jill at Brown's for me. She could be in great danger.'

'Why?' asked Paula.

'She always stays at Brown's – you just told me. They'll know that on Exmoor and I've just heard all three ex-commandos have disappeared. That they may have come to London . . .'

He broke off as Monica signalled she had Jill on the line. He took a deep breath and began talking. She must pack at once, book a room at the Stafford Hotel in St James's Place, pay her bill and take a taxi there. Yes, tonight. At once. He put the phone down and sighed with relief.

'Thank God for a woman who does what you ask without questions.'

'Proves what I said earlier,' Paula remarked and winked at Tweed.

341

He turned to Monica. 'Could you play back that recorded talk I had on the phone from Minehead with Butler? Paula, listen carefully to what he says.'

Paula rested her elbow on her desk, cupped her chin in her hand, concentrated. Butler's cool voice came through loud and clear. As the tape ended Tweed asked his question. 'Anything strike you as interesting – bearing in mind that jumble of clues Masterson sent me in a cigar box from Athens?'

'Nothing. I must be thick. And I'm tired and hungry. So what did I miss?'

'Probably nothing, as you said. It was a wisp of an idea I had. I wanted to see if it hit you in the same way. And I'm taking you out to dinner. Monica has stuffed herself with sandwiches – fortunately.'

'Wild exaggeration,' Monica protested. 'But I have eaten. And why "fortunately"?'

'Because I want to locate Barrymore, Robson and Kearns. May, Robson's sister, let slip he'd gone to London. Start phoning hotels. Those three will be together.'

'What makes you so sure?' Paula asked. 'Before I pop along to the bathroom to fix my face. I feel a wreck.'

'Because those three have stuck together for years – trapped by the past and their fear it may come back. They're haunted men.'

'The two murders forty years ago? You think they were all involved?'

'I doubt that,' Tweed replied. 'Put yourself in their places. I suspect two out of three are wondering which of them committed the murders. I also suspect the guilty man is cleverly manipulating the other two. Listen again sometime to the tape recorded by Nield at The Luttrell Arms. Now, hurry up – I have a raging appetite too!'

He went on talking as he put on his Burberry after Paula had gone to the washroom.

'We'll wait a week or two longer before I fly to Greece – wait and see if anything breaks. Newman and Marler will be pretty active out there. Their rooting around may provoke someone to make a false move, to surface. There's something going on we've missed. I sense it.'

'Take-off time coming,' Monica observed. 'Your usual method. First gathering all the data – which can take ages. Suddenly it will be all action. I'm starting already. What kind of hotel might those ex-commandos be staying at?'

'Not Claridge's or The Ritz.' Tweed had his eyes half-closed as he thought. 'One of them stole the present-day equivalent of a million pounds in diamonds after killing Andreas. So he won't throw it around, show he's loaded. Try the hotels in the medium-priced range. Maybe somewhere in Kensington.'

'You don't ask much, do you?' She was reaching for the yellow pages when Paula reappeared. 'This job could take forever.'

'You may get lucky. We must try,' Tweed said as he opened the door for Paula. 'One more point. From now on we'll codename the murderer Winterton, the ghost who sold those bungalows on Exmoor.'

31

Moscow. General Lucharsky was walking in the park again with his aide, Colonel Volkov. Both men wore civilian clothes and Volkov had to quicken his pace to keep up with the long strides Lucharsky was taking. The sunlight cast thin shadows from the trunks of birch trees. Mothers pushed prams with babies along the lower path as

Lucharsky headed for a dense copse of trees, mounting a curving path.

'You leave for Athens tomorrow,' he reminded Volkov.

'I am fully prepared, Comrade General . . .'

'I should hope so,' Lucharsky snapped as they entered the copse. 'Everything depends on your passing on the verbal orders to Colonel Rykovsky, to Doganis and Anton, the Greeks. Events are moving quickly. I hear the Gorbachev–Reagan summit will take place in Washington. More important, the British Prime Minister has invited the General Secretary to land in England en route for America. A stroke of incredible luck.'

'What is the position now?' Volkov enquired.

'Gorbachev has gone too far. He is signing a treaty in Washington for the withdrawal of intermediate missiles from Europe. If we let him do that he will go on for more disarmament. The Red Army's power will fade instead of growing. And we have some powerful allies. Elements high up in the KGB are worried. They yearn for the return of the days of Brezhnev.'

'So it is something drastic?' Volkov suggested as he pushed aside foliage from his pasty plump face. The path they were following was getting overgrown, was rarely used.

'Gorbachev will be assassinated,' Lucharsky announced in his calm clipped voice. 'The Troika took the decision last night.'

'That will be difficult, and who will take over? What is this Troika?'

'A lot of questions, Comrade. First, you remember that document I handed you yesterday when I was wearing gloves? An incriminating document.'

'Yes.' Volkov felt a chill crawl up his spine despite the humid heat which enveloped Moscow that day.

'I put it in your safe after you had read it. I locked the safe and said I would keep the key. You do recall this?'

Lucharsky asked in a mocking tone which had reduced subordinates to jelly. 'I only check your memory because you had drunk a lot of vodka.'

'At your urging . . .'

'I am a good host, although I stick to mineral water since the new General Secretary's expression of dislike for hard drinking. That document – locked away in your own safe – carries only your fingerprints. You would be shot within a week if that document was placed before the Politburo.'

'Why do you threaten me, Comrade?'

'Just in case you thought you could obtain swift promotion by betraying the Troika which, officially, does not exist.' Lucharsky stopped, faced his companion, gave him a Siberian smile. 'Of course we know you would never dream of betraying us. Now, you asked certain questions. Who will take over from Gorbachev? Answer: Yigor Ligachev, his Number Two in the Politburo. He has openly disagreed with *perestroika* and *glasnost*. He does not know what we plan, but once the seat is vacant he will be compelled to become the new General Secretary.'

'And the Troika?'

'The three-man council of high-ranking Red Army officers who have decided Gorbachev must be removed. I am their liaison with the men in the field who will do the job.'

Which was a lie. No point in letting Volkov know that Lucharsky was the top man among the three generals who made up the Troika.

'But who will carry out the assassination?' pressed Volkov, anxious to know the plan would really work.

Lucharsky folded his arms, swung again on his heels, staring through the foliage which surrounded them. On no account must they be observed. And Volkov's anxieties were transparently clear to the General. He must reassure him for the moment.

'The assassination will apparently be carried out by two Arab fundamentalists. Those fanatics are capable of any

345

mad action. And relations between Moscow and Iran are deteriorating. That way we avoid any danger of a confrontation with the Americans – in case rumours spread it was the work of the CIA. We need the time to establish Ligachev in power, to turn back the clock to Lenin's age. To renew the great military build-up.'

'Arab fundamentalists? That is clever,' Volkov agreed.

'So tomorrow you travel with the instructions inside your head to Athens,' said Lucharsky, resuming his walk over the path encumbered with undergrowth. 'Doganis is controlling the operation – although he doesn't know what is really involved.'

'And what does he think he's getting out of all this?'

'A shrewd question, Comrade. We have hinted at support for a new Communist uprising in Greece. Doganis sees himself as a future Prime Minister. It won't happen that way, of course.'

'But, Comrade, I speak no Greek,' Volkov protested.

'Which is why you are chosen. While at the London Embassy you perfected your English. Doganis speaks the same language.'

'Everything has been thought of,' Volkov remarked, impressed by the efficiency of the planning. Then something struck him. 'I don't see how British security – which is good – will be penetrated? What weapons will be used?'

'No more questions.' Lucharsky increased his pace. 'But I can tell you the special weapons needed are at this moment on their way to their destination. Now I leave you, as last time. Go to your mistress's apartment. That gives you a reason for sneaking into Moscow if you are recognized. Give me five minutes to get back to my car.'

He turned round before leaving the copse, stood looking down at Volkov. 'And don't forget that document plastered with your fingerprints, locked away in your own safe. The KGB would not treat you with kid gloves – not after reading that document. *Bon voyage*, Comrade . . .'

Lucharsky emerged cautiously from the trees, standing to glance round like a man enjoying the warmth of the sunshine. Then he hurried back to his car parked in a deserted side street. It stood outside the block which contained the apartment of a well-known general he knew to be on holiday at a Black Sea resort. A further precaution – just in case a KGB patrol noted down the registration number.

Once inside the Chaika, Lucharsky took a pouch from his pocket, selected a specially designed tool. It took him only five minutes to turn back the odometer fifty kilometres. His chauffeur logged all journeys and recorded the precise distance. There was now no record he had ever made this trip from the barracks.

Everything has been thought of. Volkov didn't know the half of it. Lucharsky had earlier decided that after Gorbachev had been eliminated all his collaborating subordinates would go the same way. Rykovsky and Volkov would die in a helicopter crash over the Caspian Sea. Florakis would be ordered to take out Doganis and the other members of the Greek Key. Then Lucharsky would send someone from Moscow to liquidate Florakis.

Yes, everything had been thought of.

Kalos took the call at police headquarters the following day when Sarris was absent from his office. It came from the chief of security at Athens Airport.

'That you, Kalos? Stefanides here. Your target just arrived. Colonel Volkov. In person.'

'Hold him till I get there. Make out you've received threats against Russian personnel. That you're bringing in a bullet-proof limo from Athens. I'll fix that before I leave. Hold him.'

'Will do. See you . . .'

Kalos followed the limo, driving an unmarked police car

347

himself. It took forty minutes to reach the airport. Damned hot, Kalos thought as they arrived. Late afternoon. Like a furnace. He watched Stefanides escorting a stocky man clad in a pale grey lightweight suit to the limo. He had thick black hair, was clean-shaven, a pair of large rimless glasses very like those Corbachev wore. In many ways he was like a pocket version of the General Secretary. And his face was pasty and plump – making him stand out as a new arrival. An easy man to follow.

Kalos watched a porter dump two suitcases in the boot, started his own engine as the boot was slammed shut. The limo glided away along the main road into Athens. Kalos followed.

Destination: the Soviet Embassy. As Kalos had expected. He parked the Saab behind another car, settled down to wait. Kalos was good at waiting. He watched Volkov disappear inside the building, followed by the chauffeur carrying the bags. Ages would now pass while Volkov conferred with Colonel Rykovsky.

Kalos radioed in to his assistant at police headquarters that he was on surveillance, that it might take all night. There was no request for information as to where he was. Surveillance meant secrecy. And he didn't want Sarris to know what he was up to. Yet.

Twenty minutes later Kalos had a surprise. Two men emerged and started walking down the street towards him on the far side. Volkov had changed into a linen suit, wore a straw hat. The glasses and the walk confirmed to Kalos it was Volkov. They were smarter than he'd anticipated. Never underestimate the enemy: Sarris' favourite maxim.

The second man, also short but slimmer, wore a similar linen suit and a peaked cap favoured by German students. A beak of a nose with a dark smear of a moustache, neatly trimmed, a man who made quick gestures with his hands. Colonel Rykovsky.

They hailed a passing taxi, climbed inside. Kalos waited until he saw the taxi moving in his wing mirror, did an illegal U-turn, tracked the taxi. In Omonia Square they paid off the taxi, gazed into a department store's windows. Not normal behaviour. Kalos felt a glow of satisfaction as he pulled into a parking slot which a woman had just vacated.

The two Russians moved slowly along the pavement, stopping to stare inside another window. Rykovsky glanced over his shoulder, scanning the street. Kalos was slumped behind the wheel, eyes almost closed. A taxi stopped, dropped a fare and both Russians moved.

As Volkov climbed into the rear Rykovsky gave the driver his instructions and followed his companion. The taxi pulled out into a gap in the traffic. Kalos grinned to himself as he turned out, one vehicle behind the taxi. Who were they going to meet so secretly was the $60,000 question.

Inside ten minutes the taxi entered the Plaka, driving slowly, wending its way amid the labyrinth of twisting streets. The two Russians alighted outside a taverna. *Papadedes*. That made sense, Kalos thought, as he watched the couple disappear up a staircase alongside the taverna. Papa made a nice income on the side out of that first-floor room sealed off from the taverna.

He rented it out at exorbitant prices to Athenian businessmen who took their mistresses there. The room was nicely furnished, including one of those sofas you could convert into a bed. Papa also supplied his clients with drinks – at only four times the price charged in the taverna.

Kalos turned into a side street, parked his car on the one-man wide pavement and the cobbled street. He felt in his pocket. Yes, he had the compact Voigtlander camera he always carried. He got out, took up a position in a doorway where he could see the staircase entrance.

Something serious was going on. Why couldn't they have had their meeting inside the Soviet Embassy? That puzzled Kalos. And he was damn sure Volkov had disguised himself. OK, it was pretty warm. And the Russian had just flown in from Moscow. But that straw hat had been well pulled down over his face – and they'd spent very little time outside.

He was about to light a cigarette when he stiffened, reached for his camera, the unlit cigarette clamped between his lips. A tall heavily built figure was strolling towards the taverna. The Fat Man. An open-necked shirt, clothes hanging loosely from his body. Doganis. Senior member of the committee that controlled the Greek Key.

Kalos raised his camera, cupped inside his hand, waited. Doganis stopped suddenly, turned on the pavement, a woman collided with his huge bulk. He ignored her as he glanced down the street the way he'd come. Then he plodded on in his large trainer shoes, paused again to look back in front of the staircase entrance as though not sure of his whereabouts. Kalos took three quick shots as the Greek swivelled his outsize head. Full-face, profile – and behind him the name over the taverna. Then Doganis vanished. He'd slipped up the staircase towards the room where the Russians had gone. For a large man he moved with great agility.

Kalos pocketed the camera and frowned. He was disturbed. This looked even more serious than he'd suspected.

Inside the expensively furnished room Doganis stood gazing at the two Russians who sat at a highly polished English antique round table. A tray – brought up by a waiter from the taverna before anyone had arrived – stood on the table.

350

Two bottles of vodka, three cut glasses. Both men had a glass in front of them.

Doganis nodded to himself. Free of the anti-alcohol restrictions imposed by Gorbachev, they were indulging themselves. The slim supercilious Colonel Rykovsky stood up to make introductions. Doganis shook hands with Volkov, squeezing his hand in a vice-like grip. The Russian had trouble avoiding grimacing at the pressure.

'Vodka?' Rykovsky offered.

Doganis shook his head, lowered his bulk into the third chair at the table. He wanted a clear head dealing with these goddamn Russians who had let down Greece in 1946 during the Civil War: they had not supplied the weapons needed. Later the US President, Truman, had sent a military mission, arms by the ton. That was what had defeated them. Rykovsky remained on his feet, downed the full glass of vodka, and explained.

'I am leaving you now with Colonel Volkov,' he continued, speaking in English. 'He has a long message to give you. It must be transmitted by Florakis to Jupiter tonight. The first part, that is. The signal is so long it has to be divided into three parts – sent on three successive nights. You have a good memory?'

'You know I have,' Doganis growled, his large paws clasped on the table-top. 'Get on with it.'

'Volkov will tell you where one section ends, the next begins. When he has passed on the complete message Volkov will leave. Give him five minutes. Then go yourself, drive at once down to Cape Sounion. Florakis will be expecting you. I have already phoned him. I am now returning to the Embassy to call him and confirm you are coming. He will wait for you at that site where they are constructing a new hotel complex. You know it?'

'I do.'

'They have stopped work on it for the moment. Something to do with waiting for fresh materials.' Rykovsky waved an elegant hand. 'The main point is the complex is deserted. When you get back to Athens, call me at the Embassy. Use your normal codename. Simply tell me you have found a further supply of mineral water – despite the shortage owing to this infernal heatwave. Remember, all calls are monitored, recorded . . .'

'I know that.'

'And get down to Cape Sounion as soon as you can. Florakis will need time to code the message. Understood?'

'Yes.'

Rykovsky told Volkov he would see him back at the Embassy later. He was leaving when he turned back.

'Doganis, you do have transport to drive to Sounion?'

'My car is parked a quarter of a mile away. I know what I am doing.'

Rykovsky nodded, bit his lip, decided to say no more. The Greeks were a touchy lot. He was glad to get out of the room. Doganis was glad to see him go. He turned to Volkov. 'I am listening.'

The stocky Volkov knocked back another glass of vodka, saw the Greek's expression and refrained from refilling his glass.

'This is the message. I will say it slowly. There is a lot to remember. The first part concerns furniture vans . . .'

Kalos took two photographs of Rykovsky as he hovered at the exit from the staircase, looking to left and right. The Russian then walked briskly away to the left. Doubtless searching for a taxi. In his notebook Kalos noted down the precise time, as he had done when Doganis had arrived.

He was growing more puzzled. That left the gross pig, Doganis, upstairs with the new arrival to Athens, Volkov. Most peculiar. It was half an hour later before a second figure appeared. Volkov. He walked straight into the street in the same direction, straw hat rammed down concealing

352

the upper half of his face. He stopped suddenly, lifted the hat as he stared round. Kalos took two more shots, waited until Volkov had disappeared, noted down the time. He had been precisely thirty minutes alone with Doganis. Most mysterious.

Unless he had been passing detailed instructions to Doganis – but why had Rykovsky not remained present? My God, Kalos was thinking: maybe Moscow doesn't even trust Rykovsky to hear what Volkov was saying. The cell system – carried to these lengths! The instructions must be incredibly secret.

Five minutes later, exactly, Doganis stood at the exit, lounging against the side, lighting a cigarette, scanning the street. A real professional, the overweight slug. Kalos risked it, took another photograph. Without a glance in his direction, Doganis walked off.

Kalos memorized the time, ran to his car, backed it into the main street, crawled after Doganis. That had been a difficult decision Kalos had wrestled with. Who to follow? Since they had met so furtively, he'd decided the Russians would probably return to the Embassy. You're my meat, he thought as he trailed after Doganis.

Kalos found he could drop back well behind his target. Among the tourists and locals crowding the Plaka Doganis loomed up among the other heads like a bear lumbering forward. He had parked his battered old Renault on an open stretch of ground. Kalos waited until he had eased his bulk behind the wheel and started moving. Then he followed him.

'Repeat the whole message back to me. Indicate where one section stops, another begins,' said Doganis.

'Get stuffed. I've memorized it perfectly,' Florakis snapped.

'Prove it.'

'I said get stuffed . . .'

The two men sat in the front seats of Doganis' Renault parked in the shade thrown by the skeletal structure of the new hotel complex. Florakis, wearing his shepherd's garb, cast a sneering glance at the bloated jelly beside him, reached for the door handle.

'I said prove it,' Doganis said in a quiet voice. 'That comes from the top. I have to tell them you've really grasped the message.'

'Play with yourself, you overblown melon . . .'

Doganis grasped Florakis by his arm below the elbow. He squeezed as Florakis swore and struggled to get free. There was a brief tussle, then Florakis' face twisted in agony. He was staggered by the strength of that fat man who he'd imagined was soft as a jelly. Doganis, with no expression, began to bend the arm. Florakis stifled a scream of pain.

'Now, let's try again, shall we?' Doganis suggested, releasing his grip.

'You stupid bastard,' railed Florakis. 'There's no feeling in my arm. And I have to tap out your bloody signal . . .'

'You're right-handed,' Doganis said mildly, gazing out of the window where an opening in the building structure framed the sizzling blue of the sea. 'I remembered that when I twisted your left arm. In any case, you'll be OK by nightfall when you do the job. Going to repeat the message? Word by word?'

'Blast you! Yes . . .' Florakis took a hold of himself, let his rage evaporate, then began reciting carefully.

'That's pretty good,' Doganis said fifteen minutes later. 'One more thing before you ride your donkey back to that cesspit you call a farm.'

'What's that?' Florakis asked sullenly.

'In future don't ever again forget I'm the boss. Now push off. I'll give you ten minutes to get clear before I drive back to Athens . . .'

Behind a boulder a short distance up the arid hillside under the scorching sun Kalos was watching. He peered through the field glasses he'd taken from his glove compartment. He'd followed Doganis all the way from Athens, keeping well back when he realized his quarry was taking the coast road.

He'd crested a hill with a clear view of the Temple of Poseidon atop Cape Sounion when he saw the Renault swing off the road behind the building site. Immediately he'd turned off the main road himself, jouncing over the rough ground into one of the many gulches which ended near the coastal highway. Parking his car well inside the gulch, he had climbed high enough to stare down at the site.

His glasses had brought up clearly the two men seated inside the stationary car. Kalos had recognized Florakis and he recalled finding the fingerprints which exposed Florakis' real identity. Oleg Savinkov: The Russian, The Executioner of the Civil War.

He waited until Doganis had driven over the crest on his way back towards Athens, then drove after him. He didn't expect to discover any new twist but he followed Doganis all the way back to the city. His eyes narrowed as he grasped that Doganis was heading back into the Plaka. He was even more startled when Doganis parked his car on the same open space and got out, then checked his watch and waited, lighting a cheroot. Kalos parked illegally in a one-way street and waited.

Thirty minutes passed before Doganis made his way on foot to the same street where he had arrived earlier in the day. Kalos guessed his destination was the room over Papadedes taverna and watched him disappear inside the entrance to the staircase.

Kalos parked his own vehicle in the side street he had used before. Standing in the doorway, he saw Colonel Volkov arrive five minutes later. He noted down the time below his record of Doganis' entering the building.

Very curious. This meeting was taking place without the presence of Rykovsky. He blinked and only took his camera out in time when a third figure walked down the street, paused by the entrance, glanced confidently around and vanished inside.

He wrote down the arrival time of Anton Gavalas. What the hell was going on?

32

'This is political dynamite,' Sarris snapped, staring at his assistant. He waved the file containing Kalos' report. 'We have to bury it. You want us both to lose our jobs?'

Kalos ran a hand over his stubble of hair, unperturbed by his chief's outburst. He clasped his hands and spoke with great deliberation, gazing out of the window where night was falling over Mount Lycabettus.

'Point One. We know Doganis is the most powerful figure on the so-called committee running the Greek Key. An organization of fanatical Communists which has lain fallow for a long time. In that file there is photographic proof that Doganis met with Colonel Rykovsky and the new man from Moscow, Colonel Volkov . . .'

'That's what I'm talking about,' Sarris protested. 'Our government hopes for closer relations with Russia now Gorbachev has proclaimed his policy of *glasnost* . . .'

'These people are not *glasnost*,' Kalos interjected in the same calm tone. 'They are hardliners – anti-Gorbachev. That swine, Pavelic the Croat, said as much to me when I was in Belgrade. He also let drop the name General Luch-arsky – who visited us last year as Colonel Gerasimov of the GRU. I stole his photograph from Pavelic's file when he was dead drunk. I followed him to the Hilton Hotel where he interviewed Florakis.'

'And now you've put Lucharsky in your report! I hadn't finished when you interrupted me. I don't make our government's policy. I think they may be a bit over-hopeful . . .'

'To the point of idiocy,' Kalos commented.

'Keep quiet. Our government hopes for more trade with Moscow. Maybe even sophisticated military equipment to make our army stronger than the Turks . . .'

'It won't happen. Let me go on,' persisted Kalos. 'Point Two. Rykovsky leaves Doganis alone with Volkov – which suggests even he is not permitted to hear some highly secret message from Moscow – from Lucharsky, maybe. Point Three. After that meeting I follow Doganis. To where? Another subversive rendezvous – this time with Oleg Savinkov, alias Florakis. Peter, this is a conspiracy I have uncovered.'

'That's an assumption . . .'

'And there is more – also backed up with photographic evidence in that file. Doganis drives back to Athens, to the same rendezvous in the Plaka. What happens now? Colonel Volkov arrives on his own – again Rykovsky is not privy to this clandestine meeting. Who else arrives? Anton Gavalas. Where does he fit in? He's supposed to be helping his crazy father – to locate the man who committed two murders over forty years ago. I repeat, it is a deadly conspiracy.'

'And I repeat I cannot show this to the Minister. He will blow his top.' Sarris softened his tone. 'Kalos, you know I'm right. If I thought there was the slightest chance the Minister would let us follow this up I'd hand him the file.'

'You're the boss.'

Kalos sat, motionless, still gazing out of the window. He

357

knew Sarris had judged the situation correctly. He was frustrated beyond belief. Sarris rose from behind his desk, took the report out of the file, separated the photographs.

'Kalos, I'm sorry about this. It really is to protect you as well as me.'

He went over to the shredding machine. Kalos watched impassively as Sarris fed in the photographs, then the typed sheets Kalos had produced on his own typewriter. A mess of shredded fragments showered into the plastic bag. The job done, Sarris sat behind his desk.

'I had no choice. Forgive me.'

'You are ordering me to cease my investigations?'

Sarris chewed his lower lip. 'I don't recall saying that. And you have an excellent memory. Just be careful, for God's sake. For ours . . .'

Kalos nodded, left the room and went back to his own office. He locked the door, went to his desk, unlocked a lower drawer and took out the duplicate file of the report Sarris had destroyed. There were also copies of the photographs: Kalos had developed them himself in his own darkroom in his apartment on the edge of the Plaka.

With the file tucked under his arm, he crouched down and turned the numbered combination on the door of his safe. Opening it, he used a screwdriver to prise open the slim secret drawer at the bottom. Dropping the file inside, he closed the drawer, shut the safe, spun the combination lock.

As he straightened up he thought how curious it was that Sarris had not asked him for the negatives: Sarris, who never missed a trick.

After witnessing the meeting between Doganis and Anton Gavalas, Kalos had again been faced with a difficult decision. Which of the two men to follow? They had left the building separately: Doganis had emerged first. Kalos let him go.

358

Ten minutes later Anton had appeared. Kalos had followed him. He was surprised when his quarry took a taxi which dropped him outside the Astir Palace Hotel on Sofias Avenue, only a short distance from the Grande Bretagne.

There was nothing else he could do about that so he returned to present his report to Sarris.

Inside his room Anton sat on the bed and dialled the number of Petros' farm in Devil's Valley. He had to wait some time before they made the connection with that remote area.

'Anton here . . .'

'You have found Christina?' growled Petros.

'Found her and lost her . . .' Anton explained briefly his experience earlier that day at the Hilton. He expected Petros to explode. Instead the old man said he needed a minute to think. Anton jumped in quickly.

'Isn't it time I returned to England? We should know what the commando killers are doing on Exmoor. This time I may find out whether all three were guilty – or whether it was only one of them.' He went on talking quickly. 'I have ideas for harassing them. As I told you, they already live in terror. They've barricaded themselves in their homes like men scared witless.'

'But we must find Christina . . .'

'Let those lazy sons-of-bitches Dimitrios and Constantine come back to Athens. She's here somewhere. All the idiots have to do is to bribe cleaning women, show them her photograph. Not approach the chief receptionist like that cretin, Dimitrios, did. Which is more important?' he pressed on. 'Tracking down Christina or tracking down the killer of your sons? I could be in England in a few days. This time I will be more aggressive.'

The word 'aggressive' decided Petros. He liked the sound of that. It appealed to his temperament. It was how he went about problems.

'Very well,' he said. 'When will you leave? You have plenty of clothes?'

'Probably tomorrow. And I packed a case before I came to Athens. In any case, I have money. Keep Dimitrios and Constantine down there for two days, then kick their asses, send them, tell them they can't come back until they've found her.'

Splendid, Petros thought. Anton was becoming more like himself every day. Very aggressive.

'You can use the special route to England you mentioned?'

'Absolutely.' Anton was standing up now, his voice vibrant with confidence. 'Don't worry if I'm away for a while. This time the job must be done . . .'

Anton put down the phone, realized he was sweating profusely. It wasn't the heat – although the room felt like an oven. He had managed to persuade Petros, the old fool, to agree. Now he was ready to carry out the orders Volkov had passed to him.

Anton was pleased so much responsibility had been heaped on him. It augured well for the future. He saw a top Cabinet post in a Greek Communist government in his grasp. Who knew? Maybe one day he would be Prime Minister.

Extracting a Swissair timetable from his case, he sat down, checked flight times. Flight SR 303 left Athens at 5 p.m., arrived at Zurich 6.45 p.m., local time. He needed a late flight: there was some more work to do before he left Athens in the morning. He turned the pages.

From Zurich another non-stop flight, SR 690, departed Zurich at 12.10 p.m., reaching Lisbon in Portugal at 1.55 p.m. Again local times. That meant spending only one night in Zurich. He always stayed at top hotels: with luck he'd find some willing married woman on her own to spend the night with.

Anton was careful with women. The married ones, away

from their husbands and out for a fling, were safest. No comebacks. No risk of some annoying entanglement. He checked the dates in his diary. His memory had served him well.

The freighter, *Oporto*, was not due to sail for several days. Then it would leave Portugal with its holds full of cork, bound for the Somerset port of Watchet. Later it would return with a load of wastepaper.

Plenty of time to get in touch with the skipper, Gomez. To warn him this time there would be a special cargo as well as himself. And to call Jupiter at the agreed time to have someone ready for the rendezvous at sea. The phone number, he felt sure, was a public phone booth. Most important of all, time for him to contact the arms dealer in Lisbon, to collect from him the special weapons which would go aboard the *Oporto*.

Anton called room service. 'Send me up a double Scotch. No ice. No lemon. Plus a bottle of mineral water.'

He sat down, tired from the concentration. Now the only remaining task was to contact Professor Seton-Charles at his seminar at the Hilton in the morning. He'd go along as a student. Pass on the instruction Volkov had given him for the Professor.

33

Seton-Charles had held three seminars for Greek students over a period of two weeks. Newman and Marler had taken it in turns to monitor his movements. The seminars were held in a conference room inside the Hilton. They were advertised on a board in the vast lobby, giving the whole

361

two-week programme. Subject: The Greek Civil War, 1946–1949.

The tension was rising between Newman and Marler. Security on Christina had been tightened up to the hilt: they had learned from their experience at the Hilton. Well-disguised, a scarf concealing her hair and wearing her outsize tinted glasses, she had registered as Mrs Irene Charles at the Grande Bretagne.

Booked into a suite, she stayed there. All meals were sent up by room service. Newman kept her supplied with books and magazines. 'This is marvellous, Bob,' she told him one day. 'The first real rest I've had in years – and I'm reading like mad . . .'

To keep up their watch on Seton-Charles, Newman and Marler had very little sleep. They exchanged surveillance duty at the Hilton; one staying with Christina, the other eating and keeping an eye open at the Hilton. Marler complained after a few days of this ritual.

'I feel locked in. I'd like to be outside, trying to find more data on what happened to Harry Masterson. Maybe take a trip to Cape Sounion, see what's going on down there.'

'Feeling the heat?' Newman grinned as he used a sodden handkerchief to mop his neck.

'No. You're the one who can't stand it. Doesn't affect me.'

'I can stand the waiting better than you can,' Newman told him. 'We're doing what Tweed asked. Checking on Seton-Charles and guarding Christina.'

'And as far as we can tell the Professor hasn't gone outside the Hilton. Which is pretty weird. Maybe he uses the phone in his room.'

'Not for any calls we'd want to know about. He'll know they'd go through the hotel switchboard.'

'So maybe he sneaks out in the middle of the night.'

'I have a feeling any message will be smuggled to him

362

by someone attending one of those seminars. Probably he doesn't like the heat. He looks the type. I saw him go outside once and he came straight in again, glad to return to the air-conditioning. Patience, Marler.'

'You know where you can stuff that. As for waiting, you spent your life waiting as a foreign correspondent. Mostly holding up bars, from what I've heard.'

'Which shows your ignorance,' Newman rapped back. 'I was moving about, searching for fresh contacts. Time you got back to the Hilton. Don't fall asleep . . .'

'Up yours, chum.'

They had been drinking mineral water at the Grande Bretagne bar. It was eleven at night: Newman had come back sometime after he'd seen Seton-Charles go up to bed. He mopped his sticky hands when Marler left. It was going to be another torrid night.

They had booked two rooms at the Hilton. Whoever was on duty stayed up until he was pretty sure Seton-Charles had retired for the night. He then waited another two hours, sitting in the lobby. Just on the off-chance S-C reappeared. Then he went to his room, set the alarm for five o'clock. After taking a shower, he put out his outfit to wear in the morning. Which meant the man on duty fell into bed at about 2 a.m. For three hours of sleep. No wonder the relationship – never good at the best of times – was growing strained.

It was Newman who spotted Anton Gavalas attending the final seminar eleven days later.

Christina had shown him a group photograph. Petros flanked by his family at the farm, occupying the central position, sitting on the veranda.

'Looking like God Almighty,' Christina had remarked venomously. 'Dimitrios and Constantine are there – on either side. As you see, I'm relegated to the outside – the proper position for a female. And that . . .' She had pointed to a slim man standing with his hand on Petros' shoulder. '. . . is Anton. Petros' favourite, the smooth bastard.'

Newman borrowed the photograph. He showed it to Marler at the first opportunity, pointing out Anton.

'Cocky-looking sod,' was Marler's only comment.

Eleven days later Newman was 'on duty' at the Hilton. He had eaten breakfast in the ground-floor restaurant, sitting four tables away from Seton-Charles who was looking limp from the heatwave.

Now he sat in the lobby on a couch close to the entrance to the conference room where the third and final seminar was taking place in half an hour's time. Newman wore a short-sleeved shirt, open-necked, a pair of loud check slacks. He was smoking a cigar, reading the *New York Times*. He looked like one of the many American tourists staying at the hotel.

Students – men and girls – began arriving, standing round, chatting. Age range: sixteen to twenty-five, Newman estimated. Some carried briefcases, others clutched files. Newman stretched out his legs, crossed them at the ankles. He wore green socks decorated with white diamonds, a pair of loafers.

Seton-Charles arrived in his shirt-sleeves, a pair of creaseless powder-blue slacks. Newman puffed at his cigar, glanced up as he turned to a fresh page. For a moment he glanced at the Professor, who looked down at him. Behind the rimless glasses perched on his Roman nose eyes as hard as diamonds skimmed over the seated man. Newman had a shock.

This was the first time they had looked straight at each other. The first time Newman had noticed those eyes. You're a cold-blooded bastard, he thought.

Then Seton-Charles was leading the students inside the conference room. Like a shepherd leading lambs to the slaughter. Why had that thought entered Newman's mind? He settled down, then glanced up again as a latecomer arrived, hurrying inside the conference room. Newman froze inside as the slim, smartly dressed man passed him. Anton Gavalas . . .

He stood up and wandered to a seat on the far side of the lobby. Startled as he was by Anton's appearance, Newman still noticed what else was going on.

A moment after the Greek had disappeared he observed a man who had been lingering outside the entrance come into the hotel. A small stocky man who reminded him of a dormouse. The newcomer also took a seat against the wall, settled himself, crossed his fat legs and began reading a Greek newspaper.

Newman forgot about him as he sat down to wait. He'd have given a lot to be an invisible witness to what was happening inside the conference room.

When Anton walked into the seminar the students were sitting down in the rows of chairs facing the dais where the Professor stood behind a table, arranging papers in neat piles. He paused, Seton-Charles looked up, Anton walked across the room and mounted the dais.

'Good morning,' he whispered. 'Jupiter has sent me with information . . .'

He had been going to say 'instructions', but then he looked at the eyes behind the rimless glasses. No sign of recognition. Ice-cold, they seemed to assess him at a glance. Anton began to wonder how high up in the power structure this man might be.

'Take a seat in the back row. Record a few things in this notebook. Make sure you're still here when the last student has left.'

The back row was empty. Anton sat down, perched the notebook he had been given on his knee, took out his gold Parker pen and listened as Seton-Charles began to lecture.

Seton-Charles was a natural orator, reminding Anton of newsreels he'd seen of Hitler. He started slowly, then worked himself up to a pitch of fanaticism, waving his arms. When he stopped the students applauded vigorously, then filed out. Anton pretended to make more notes until they were alone.

He stood up, approached Seton-Charles, who was gathering up his papers and stuffing them into a file. Again Anton mounted the dais. The Professor's hair was dishevelled from his oration and he was sweating profusely from his efforts and the heat.

'Yes?' he said without looking up.

Anton felt it was important to address this man respectfully. 'You are requested to catch Swissair flight 303 today to fly to Zurich. It departs at 5 p.m. Then tomorrow you fly on to London and return to Exmoor. That is the message.'

'That means they have managed it,' Seton-Charles said, half to himself.

He looked up and stared at Anton as though photographing his appearance on his memory. Anton felt he dare not ask what they had managed, who they were.

'So you are not surprised, I shall be on the same flight,' he explained.

'I shan't even notice you. Hadn't you better go now? At once . . .'

Anton flushed at the tone of curt dismissal. Without another word he left the room. His feelings were a mixture of fury and fear.

In the lobby Newman watched Anton leave. He wished he could have followed him. But his task was to keep up the watch on Seton-Charles. Tweed had made that very clear.

Newman observed the quick short steps Anton took as he crossed the marble floor and left the hotel.

He lowered his eyes to his newspaper when out of the corner of his eye he saw movement. The dormouse-like man had folded his newspaper, shoved it inside his pocket and was also leaving. It looked very much as though he had Anton Gavalas under surveillance.

Outside the Hilton Anton climbed into a cab, slammed the door. Kalos ran to his Saab parked a few yards away and dived behind the wheel after unlocking the door with one deft movement.

He followed the taxi into the traffic, his bead-like little eyes gleaming with interest. The route was back along Sofias Avenue, past the British Embassy, and round Syntagma Square. The taxi returned to the opposite side of Sofias and Anton paid the driver, disappearing inside the Astir Palace Hotel. The same place where Kalos had followed Anton after his rendezvous at Papadedes.

Several days earlier Kalos had decided a piece was missing from his report. He had phoned the Astir Palace and obtained confirmation that Anton *was* registered at that hotel. He could hardly use a false name: he was too well known in Athens.

Since then Kalos had endured a long vigil patiently. Anton had stayed inside day and night – until this morning. Now a fresh link was established – of a sort. Anton had a connection with one of the students attending the seminars; maybe even with the crazy-looking Professor Seton-Charles. The latter seemed unlikely.

Parking his car, Kalos wandered into the vestibule of the modern-looking hotel, a black glass block which did not fit in with the more traditional surrounding architecture. He arrived in time to hear Anton giving the receptionist instructions in Greek.

'I shall want my bill ready immediately after lunch. Then

you must arrange a car to get me to the airport by 3.30 p.m. The car must not be late.'

'Of course not, Mr Gavalas,' the receptionist assured him. 'I will deal with everything myself . . .'

He tailed off. His guest had walked away, was heading for the elevators. Kalos pursed his lips, wondering where Anton was flying to. Well, he would be there in good time to find that out.

In his room Anton called room service, ordered a large Scotch. The plane was leaving at 5 p.m. but he had deliberately arranged to arrive at the airport very early. The last thing he wanted was to bump into Seton-Charles.

Anton, a ruthless, hard man, had met some tough characters during his wanderings as a youth. But there was something about the Professor which disturbed him. The man reminded him of a cobra.

In the late afternoon Newman was driving a hired car towards the airport. He had seen Seton-Charles collect a travel folder from the reception desk in mid-morning. The Professor had returned to his room, reappearing for lunch. When he stepped out of the elevator he was carrying a case which he deposited with reception.

Newman had phoned Marler, phrasing his message carefully over the hotel phone. 'I'm tied up. Urgent business suddenly cropped up. Be with you this evening. Can you hang on there?'

'My pleasure . . .'

Arriving at the airport, Newman parked two vehicles behind the taxi Seton-Charles was travelling in. He stood behind him in the queue for checking in, heard the Professor being booked aboard Swissair flight 303 to Zurich, left the queue. Tweed must be informed at once.

Leaning against a wall, Kalos watched, took a quick picture of Newman. Earlier he had done the same thing when Anton arrived. Anton was flying to Zurich. Why? He waited until the queue had evaporated, approached the check-in girl.

'That Englishman with the thinning brown hair, rimless glasses. Where is he flying to?'

'I'm afraid we can't give out information . . .'

Kalos placed his police identity card in front of her, waited.

'Oh, I suppose that's different.' She hesitated, Kalos waited.

'He's a Professor Seton-Charles,' she said. 'First-class seat on Swissair flight 303. Departs 5 p.m., arrives Zurich 6.45 p.m.'

'Thank you,' said Kalos. ─

He thought about what he had learned as he drove back to police headquarters. Anton had arrived three-quarters of an hour ahead of Seton-Charles. A trick. Kalos was certain the two men were collaborators: they had taken the precaution of not appearing to know each other. They'd sit in different sections of the plane to keep up the masquerade. But Anton had attended the Professor's seminar.

He tapped his fingers on the wheel as he waited at a red traffic light. What the hell could he do now to find out where they had gone? Then he had an idea. Switzerland . . .

Arriving in his office, Kalos locked the door before he made the call to Berne, capital of Switzerland – and head-quarters of the Federal Police. He was lucky. Arthur Beck, chief of the organization, was in his office.

Kalos spoke tersely, explained what had happened, gave details of the flight. He described both Anton and Seton-Charles. Could Beck help?

'Something to do with drugs?' Beck enquired, still speaking in English.

369

'Could be,' Kalos replied non-committally.

'I'll go myself,' Beck decided. 'Anything to help Peter Sarris. I have time to get a chopper from the local airport, Belp, fly to Kloten Airport outside Zurich. I'll be there to watch the passengers disembarking. Which is most important?'

'Anton,' Kalos said after a moment's thought. 'Maybe you will call me back. Sarris is up to his ears.'

'Consider it done,' Beck replied and broke the connection.

Kalos put down the phone. Sarris had no idea what he'd started, and Kalos had no intention of letting him know. If it all blew up in his face, Sarris could disclaim all knowledge of what his assistant had been up to. As he began to record the latest details in his secret file Kalos was worried. Had he been right to give Beck priority in watching Anton?

34

'Newman here, speaking on the Embassy phone. Can you hear me?'

'Very clearly, Bob,' Tweed assured him. 'What's happened?'

'Seton-Charles is on his way back to England. At least, I assume he is . . .' He gave an account of his recent discoveries, including the appearance of Anton.

'You're probably right,' Tweed agreed. 'He's a devious so-and-so. Remember how he tried to make sure he wasn't followed to London Airport on his way out. My guess is he'll catch another flight back here tomorrow. At least that means you only have to guard Christina. One of you can start poking around again. How are you and Marler getting on?'

'Like two long-lost brothers.' He nearly added, 'who hate the sight of each other,' but kept his mouth shut. 'First I'm going to have another talk with Christina about Anton. Do you really need both of us to stay on in this inferno?'

'Yes. If you can stand the heat.' Tweed paused. 'You see, when the right moment arrives I'm flying out there. I may need back-up. I must grill that scoundrel, Petros.'

'Be it on your own head. He's got armed shepherds patrolling the whole area.'

'We'll cope. Keep in touch . . .'

Tweed sat back and looked at Monica and Paula. 'One bit of good news. Anton still seems to be floating round Athens. I didn't like the idea of that Greek on the prowl over here. And Seton-Charles is probably on his way back to Exmoor. I sense things are hotting up. Monica, warn Butler at Porlock Weir about the Professor possibly returning. Maybe at long last we're getting somewhere.'

The grim news reached them the following day.

In her room at the Stafford Hotel Jill Kearns checked herself in the mirror. Her bedside clock registered 6.25 a.m. She eyed herself critically, fiddled with her single golden plait. That would have to do. And how many people would be about at this hour? Not the point, she thought: never appear in public except at your best.

She was wearing a form-fitting pale green sweater, a white pleated skirt and flat-heeled shoes. Just the outfit for her early morning walk before breakfast.

A girl of firm routines, she always walked on the moor every morning before breakfast. Always left the house at precisely 6.30 a.m. Stuart, for some unknown reason, found her routine irritating. 'Should be in the bloody Army,' he'd told her. He never accompanied her; at least he hadn't for the last few years.

She said 'Good morning' to the hall porter and went out of the hotel, turning left into St James's Place. No one else about, thank God. It was a fresh morning, was going to be one of those rare fine days with the sun shining and the warmth on your face.

Reaching the end of the deserted street, she came out into St James's Street. Again no one in sight. Only a Jaguar parked by the kerb a score of yards further down the street, facing her way, the engine ticking over. She took a deep breath and made for the pedestrian crossing.

She was half-way across it when she heard the Jag coming. It had started moving the moment she stepped off the pavement. She glanced to her right, then froze in horror. The car was driving straight at her.

She began to run, taking a diagonal course to cross the whole street. Glancing again over her shoulder as she reached a point just midway across where a side street opposite entered from St James's Square, she had a glimpse of the driver behind the tinted glass.

He wore a chauffeur's cap pulled well down over his head and a pair of tinted goggles like motorbike riders affected. She ran faster, thanking her lucky stars she was wearing her flat-heeled shoes. The Jag was turning now, coming at tremendous speed.

The radiator slammed into her, lifted her whole body and threw it against the railings of a basement area on the far side of the street. She twisted under the immense impact. Then her lifeless body lay sagged against the railings. Blood from her smashed jaw flowed down over her green sweater, spreading like a lake.

The Jaguar picked up more speed, vanished in the distance as it turned into St James's Square. Suddenly it was very quiet.

35

'You're not going to like this.' Monica, who had rushed into Tweed's office, paused for breath. In her hands she clutched a copy of the *Evening Standard*.

'You're back early from lunch,' said Tweed as Paula jerked her head up from the file she was studying.

'It's awful,' Monica went on, sinking into her seat. 'I know how you liked her.'

'What is it?' Tweed asked, very alert.

'It's in the stop press. A Mrs Stuart Kearns, staying at the Stafford Hotel, was killed by a hit-and-run driver early this morning.'

'Show me.' Tweed's tone was bleak. He read the item, looked at Monica. 'Let's get this in the right sequence. Which hotel did you track those three down to? Something like a theatre.'

'Barrymore, Kearns and Robson are staying at the Lyceum Hotel. A modest place just off the Strand, close to Trafalgar Square.'

'And it says here the so-called accident occurred in St James's Street. Not very far from the Lyceum. Phone up the place. I want to know if they're still there.'

He stood up, shoved his hands inside his jacket pockets, began pacing up and down close to the window, his brow furrowed.

'They've checked out,' Monica told him as she put down the phone. 'All three left mid-morning. No forwarding address.'

'Get Chief Superintendent Walton of Special Branch. Urgently.'

'Why did you say "so-called accident"?' enquired Paula.

'Because I don't believe it. Jill Kearns had all her marbles. That newspaper item says it happened before seven in the morning. How much traffic is about at that hour?'

He broke off to take the call. 'That you, Bill? Tweed here.'

'You on scrambler? Good.' Walton's voice was its normal buoyant tone. 'Are you still forging my Special Branch identity cards in that Engine Room? I don't know why I let you get away with it.'

'You supplied the original model for copying,' Tweed reminded him. 'We agreed total secrecy could only be maintained if we did the job. And if anyone queries one they'll be put through to you.'

'Someone has queried one,' Walton warned him. 'Recently. A Colonel Barrymore. I told him you belonged to my department, that he'd better answer any questions you put to him. Very supercilious, he was. Plummy-voiced type. Now, what can I do for you?'

'Early this morning a Mrs Stuart Kearns, staying at the Stafford Hotel, was killed by an alleged hit-and-run driver. There's a stop press in the *Standard*. I think it was murder. I'm going to give you details of three possible suspects. They were staying last night at the Lyceum Hotel off the Strand. I'd like you to phone Chief Inspector Jarvis of Homicide at the Yard. Warn him, but don't mention me.'

'Why not?' Walton enquired. 'You and Bernard were pals during your old days at the Yard.'

'Because I need to maintain a low profile. Here are the details, including the addresses of the three men. Incidentally, they've left the Lyceum . . .'

He read out where Barrymore, Robson and Kearns lived on Exmoor. Walton said OK, he'd call the Yard. Say he'd had a tip from a very reliable source. And they must have lunch one day.

'What are you up to?' asked Paula when Tweed had finished the call.

'Pressure. I want maximum pressure put on those three. It's possible one – or all – of them will break. Though I doubt it.'

'You really think they ran down poor Jill?'

Tweed began cleaning his glasses with his handkerchief. 'It's a long coincidence. The morning Jill is killed the three of them are staying at a hotel about half a mile away.'

'But you moved her to the Stafford for safety – and they only knew she always stayed at Brown's. How could any of them have found her?'

'I'm afraid I blundered. I may even be responsible for her death. By mistake, anyway. I think she was being watched during that afternoon I went to Brown's for tea. Someone got frightened of what she might have told me. I suspect I was followed when I walked up Albemarle Street and didn't notice.'

'That's ridiculous,' burst out Monica. 'You always check . . .'

'On the other hand,' Paula said quietly, 'I was following her for three days. I could have been spotted. And I was with Tweed when he visited all three men on Exmoor.'

'Pure surmise.'

Tweed dismissed the idea with a wave of his hand. Secretly he was pretty sure she was right. But it was not something he wanted on Paula's conscience.

'Then,' Paula continued, 'they would have seen her change her hotel to the Stafford. And I bet that was a morning habit of hers on Exmoor. To stroll over the moor. Always at the same time.'

'Forget it!' Tweed snapped. 'We have to decide what to do next.'

'What do you suggest?' asked Monica.

375

She sensed an atmosphere of depression in the room. Worse, a mood of guilt that one – or both – of her colleagues had caused the killing of Jill Kearns. Paula had sunk into a brooding silence, so unlike her normal buoyancy. It was Tweed who changed the mood.

'We take action. Monica, call The Anchor at Porlock Weir. Tell Butler – or Nield – to call me back urgently. He'll know what that means – use a public phone box. I want to find out if Barrymore and Co. have returned to Exmoor. Then we'll move.'

'How?' asked Paula, lifting her head.

'You and I will drive down there at once. Partridge was murdered on Exmoor while those three were there. Jill was murdered in London – while they were here. I'm going to ask each of them a lot of tough questions.'

Monica was already dialling The Anchor. She spoke for a short time, then put down the phone. 'Both of them are out,' she told Tweed.

'Keep trying at intervals until you get one of them. I want to be at their throats before they've had time to settle in.'

Monica nodded. Again she didn't like the vehemence with which Tweed had spoken. If he'd still been a Chief Superintendent at Scotland Yard in Homicide, they'd have taken him off the case. Too much personal involvement.

Zurich. Arthur Beck could pass in the street for any profession. Except that of Chief of Federal Police. In his mid-forties, he wore a light blue business suit, a cream shirt, a blue tie which carried a kingfisher emblem woven into the fabric. Plump-faced, his most prominent feature was his alert grey eyes beneath thick dark brows the same colour as his hair.

He sat alone in an office at Zurich police headquarters with a window overlooking the River Limmat, the university perched on the hill rising steeply from the opposite shore. Lifting the phone, he dialled Kalos' number. The Greek answered quickly.

'Beck here. I have some data on your Anton Gavalas. Ready?'

'That was quick. It was only yesterday. Go ahead.'

'Anton disembarked from the Athens flight, caught a taxi to the Hotel Schweizerhof which faces the main station. He had early dinner, then wandered down the Bahnhof-strasse to the lake. He sat on a seat watching the boats come and go. No one approached him. He made no phone calls from the hotel – I found that out after he'd left.'

'Left for where?'

'Let me tell you in my own way,' the Swiss said precisely. 'I checked with the porter after he'd returned from his walk. He went straight to bed. This morning he has a leisurely breakfast. Again, no one approached him. Then he leaves by cab for Kloten Airport, where he arrived. A model citizen, Mr Anton Gavalas. Always well-dressed. Walking down the Bahnhofstrasse he could be mistaken for a Swiss – except for his dark suntan.'

'What happened next?' Kalos asked.

'He produces a first-class ticket, checks in his luggage for the SR 690 flight bound for Lisbon . . .'

'Lisbon?' Kalos sounded surprised.

'Lisbon in Portugal,' Beck continued genially. 'The 12.10 p.m. that reaches Lisbon at 1.55 p.m. That's Portuguese time. Which means you can alert someone in Lisbon to meet the flight if you wish. End of report.'

'I'm very grateful.' Kalos paused. 'It almost sounds as though you followed him everywhere yourself.'

'But I did. My dear Kalos, when you're trapped behind a desk in Berne most of the time, reading files, it does you good to get out on the streets again. Stops you getting rusty – your mind going to sleep.' He added the last bit in case Kalos' English was not up to the colloquialism.

377

'I really am grateful,' Kalos repeated. 'I owe you one.'

'Indeed you do. But that's for the future. Good hunting . . .'

In his Athens office Kalos put down the phone and mopped his forehead. The heatwave was getting worse. There was a real shortage of mineral water.

Lisbon? Kalos was baffled. He added the data to his secret file. What could the connection be? And he had no way of checking, no link with Portugal he could use without Sarris' cooperation.

36

Anton landed at Portela Airport, changed a sum of Swiss franc high-denomination banknotes into escudos, the local currency. He never used traveller's cheques while moving about secretly: they left a trail which could be followed. Inside the taxi he opened his case, used the raised lid to conceal what he was doing from the driver.

Inside the suitcase was an executive case crammed with Swiss banknotes. He had been handed this by a woman who visited his room at the Schweizerhof in Zurich. An incident Arthur Beck had no chance of observing; the woman had reserved her own room at the hotel for the night.

Anton collected the equivalent of £5,000 in escudos, tucked the bundle into an envelope. He then counted out the equivalent of £10,000 in Swiss banknotes, transferred them to a second envelope and put them in another pocket. When he closed the lid, the executive case contained £100,000 in Swiss notes. He looked out of the window.

Lisbon was a galaxy of colour-washed houses: pink, blue, green and all of them pastel shades. The side streets were narrow and twisting. He paid off the driver outside the Ritz Hotel.

Speaking perfect English, he registered under the name Hunter, using the forged passport Doganis had supplied for his previous trip. The Portuguese were strict about examining passports. Inside his room he checked the time and ordered mineral water from room service. He would need a clear head for coping with the arms dealer.

He ate a quick dinner in the restaurant, keeping an eye on the time. It was still light when he took a taxi to Cascais, a resort and fishing village on the coast. The air was sultry, but nothing compared with the burning heat of Greece. He paid off the taxi on the promenade, found a cheap clothing shop and bought a large fisherman's pullover, a pair of trousers. His feet were shod in trainer's shoes which fitted him comfortably. Footwear was important: you never knew when you would have to move fast.

Checking the time again, he walked along the front, the package of wrapped clothes under one arm, the other holding the executive case which was well-worn and had a grubby look. He found a *fado* café which was crowded, went inside, sat at a table and ordered a glass of wine which he paid for.

He drank half the glass, asked the waiter for the washroom, disappeared inside it. He locked the door of the cubicle, undid the parcel. Within a minute he had pulled the trousers up over his own pair and donned the turtle-necked pullover. Flushing the toilet, he stuffed the wrappings behind it and walked out carrying the case.

He made a point of finishing the glass of wine, standing at the table as people pushed past him. The place was a babble of voices with a background of mournful *fado* music.

Personally, Anton preferred the *bouzouki*. He checked the time once more.

He walked along the front and it was dark now. Lights sparkled in the clear air, the Atlantic rolled in, threw its gentle waves on the shore. Carlos, a gnarled wiry fisherman, was waiting with his boat moored, a lamp shining in the tiny wheelhouse.

'Mr Hunter,' he greeted, 'my wife had your phone message, passed it to me.' Clambering ashore, he pointed. 'Everything is with us when you need.'

He was pointing at a donkey cart half-filled with hay, a donkey between the shafts and fastened to them with traces. Anton frowned, put his free hand on the animal's shoulders. The head peered round.

'She has to carry a weight,' he commented. 'And also stay by herself for some time.'

'She is good. You take the cart. Look at wheels. She carries weight. When you come back I take you with cargo to *Oporto*.'

'The freighter is at the harbour now? Gomez is expecting me?'

'All is ready, Mr Hunter. We take cargo aboard in the night. The *Oporto* sails when the sun rises. One day from this day. Sails for England.'

'Here you are, Carlos. I'll be back later.' Anton handed him the envelope containing £5,000 in escudos. 'Don't open that envelope until you're inside the wheelhouse. And turn down the lamp.'

'I'll do that. All the time God gives us. I nearly do not know you in those clothes . . .'

Anton led the donkey cart along the front back the way he had come. He had no trouble controlling the animal. He'd had a lot of experience in handling the creatures on Petros' farm. The main thing was that it was docile.

From the cafés he was passing came more *fado* music, the voices of men and women who had consumed large

380

quantities of wine. It was not a night when anyone was interested in what was happening on the deserted front. Arriving at a narrow side street, he guided the donkey across the road, parked it outside a shop which sold swimwear and which was closed. Just beyond was the entrance to the dimly lit Rua Garrett. The address Volkov had given him.

He left the bright lights and plunged into Stygian darkness as he picked his way over the uneven cobbles of Rua Garrett. One place was still open, double doors thrown back. He strolled past it, glancing inside. A big place with a cracked concrete floor – a service garage on one side, a ship's chandler on the other.

His glance showed him a gloomy cavern lit by oil lamps. On the garage side a car was perched on an elevated platform about a foot above a service pit. He walked in when he was satisfied only one person was inside.

'Mr Gallagher?'

'That's me. What do you want?'

'I've come to collect the merchandise, the type with a sting in its tail.'

'So, you're the one? Brought the money?'

'Of course.'

Gallagher was six feet tall and broad-shouldered. He spoke with an American accent. In his late thirties, his manner was offhand and he moved silently. Like a big cat. Anton studied the insolent expression, the restless eyes. The arms dealer was not a man Anton liked the look of. Still, he had come prepared.

Gallagher held out a large hand. He made the universal gesture with thumb and forefinger.

'I'd like to see the colour of your money first.'

'That is reasonable.'

'Wait! We need a little privacy for our business transaction.'

He walked over to the wall, pressed a switch and the

381

double doors closed automatically. The place was not so down at heel as Anton had thought. Sealed inside the cavern, the stench of petrol and oil grew stronger. Anton laid his case on the table, unlocked it, raised the lid and stood back. While Gallagher walked back to the case and picked up bundles at random, riffling through the banknotes, Anton hoisted his pullover a little higher.

'Just how much is here?' Gallagher demanded.

He had the flattened nose of an ex-boxer, a mass of untidy hair the colour of ripened wheat, a hard jaw. His pale eyes watched Anton, waiting for an answer.

'One hundred thousand pounds in Swiss francs. The agreed price in the agreed currency. For three Stingers. Plus six missiles.'

'Price just went up,' Gallagher informed him. 'Law of supply and demand. Been a heavy call for Stingers. IRA, Angolan rebels, Iranian nutcases. People like that. £145,000 is the going rate. Take it or leave it.'

'But the price was agreed,' Anton protested coldly. Volkov had been very clear on that. 'Your reputation rests on keeping to a deal once concluded.'

'Grow up, buddy boy. I said the going rate is the price. You can't raise it? Get lost.'

'I didn't say I hadn't got that much,' Anton replied. 'Since you insist, I'll pay it. But first I want to see the weapons.'

'You need to go to the bank?' Gallagher pressed, arms folded. 'Or is it in there?' He nodded towards the case Anton had shut and relocked. 'You came ready for the bad news? *I heard it on the grapevine*,' he sang the old melody and then laughed.

'I hid more money in the Rua Garrett earlier,' Anton told him. 'You'll never find it – but it's within a hundred yards of where you're standing. Now, show me the weapons.'

'Good to do business with a gentleman.' Gallagher grinned and walked back to the bank of switches and buttons on the wall. He pressed one and the elevated platform supporting the car rose up four more feet. The arms dealer lowered himself into the pit, pressed a switch which illuminated the darkness. Against one wall was a large canvas bundle. He unstrapped it, rolled back the canvas with care, exposing three Stingers and six missiles. He looked up.

'Satisfied?'

'Bring one up, plus one missile. No – take the middle ones in each case.'

'Leery sort of bastard, aren't you?'

Gallagher placed a Stinger and a missile on the garage floor, hauled himself up. 'Show you how it works.' He grinned again. 'You get value for money here. It's shoulder-launched by one man. Weighs only thirty pounds. It has a hundred per cent hit rate – mainly due to its infra-red heat-seeking system, plus its amazingly accurate aiming system. You fire in the direction of the aircraft and leave it to do the rest – home in on the target. God knows how many Soviet fighters it's wiped out back in Afghanistan. Take hold of it.'

Anton balanced the weight in both hands, surprised at its lightness. It looked like a mobile telescope with a wide muzzle at the front tapering to a slimmer barrel resting on his shoulder. To his right as he held it was a large rectangular plate. He peered through the aiming system.

'This is how you load it,' Gallagher said, inserting a missile. 'Don't pull the trigger or we'll both end up as red goulash.'

'I want a demonstration,' Anton remarked as he handed back the weapon. 'Don't argue. For £145,000 I'm entitled to check the damned thing works . . .'

Gallagher had driven them in his Volvo station wagon into the hills. Leaving Rua Garrett, Anton had noted the donkey still stood patiently with the cart where he had parked it; it looked as though it would stay there all night.

Gallagher pulled up at a lonely spot overlooking the sea. Getting out, he grasped the Stinger and the single missile concealed under a travelling rug. They picked their way past a cactus grove and Gallagher halted at the top of a cliff. Out at sea a lone fishing vessel was returning to port, navigation lights twinkling. Gallagher handed weapon and missile to Anton.

'There's your target. There's always one comes crawling back late.'

'I don't understand.'

'That fishing vessel. Get on with it. It's about two miles away. How far will your target be in the air?'

'Less than two miles. I still don't understand . . .'

'Oh, for Christ's sake! The missile is heat-seeking. That boat has a boiler in the engine room. Aim straight for it.'

'Won't there be an enquiry?' Anton inserted the missile, raised the Stinger, cuddling it into his shoulder. 'The police might start searching – when they realize what did it.'

'Except they won't. A month ago a similar fishing vessel blew up – the boilers they use are ancient as these hills. It will be recorded as another case of inefficient maintenance. They don't bother that much round here.'

Anton aimed at a point well below the wheelhouse. He squeezed the trigger, the missile left the launcher, curved in a low arc above the Atlantic at such speed he didn't see its flight. A dull boom echoed in the humid night. The fishing vessel turned into a pillar of flame after a brief flash. The flame died fast.

Lowering the Stinger, Anton gazed at the smooth surface of the sea. The fishing vessel had vanished. He lifted the Stinger, peered through the aiming device. He could see no trace of any wreckage.

'Satisfied?' Gallagher demanded. 'If so, let's get back to the garage.'

'How many in the crew?'

'Roughly half a dozen. Plenty more where they came from . . .'

'Drop me at the entrance to the Rua Garrett,' Anton told the arms dealer as they drove along the front. 'I have to bring my transport.'

'That the transport?' Gallagher enquired as Anton, carrying his executive case, alighted by the donkey cart. 'You'll get a long way with that. And I bet I know where you hid the balance of the money. In that mess of a hillside at the end of the street.'

'And you could search for years and never find it. See you at the garage. Don't wrap the merchandise until I'm there.'

'Anything you say, buddy boy . . .'

I don't think he's American at all, Anton was thinking as he led the donkey cart into the side street, following the Volvo. Under the accent, the over-use of American slang, he had detected traces of some unidentifiable Mittel-European language.

He left the donkey cart outside the open garage doors. Inside Gallagher had lowered the elevated car back over the pit. A careful man, Mr Gallagher. Anton continued down the dark tunnel of the narrow street.

He'd noticed when he first arrived that at the end the street stopped where a steep hill rose, its slopes covered with undergrowth and trees. He found a narrow path twisting up and followed it a short distance. Crouching down, he unlocked the case, lifted the lid.

He took a number of bundles of banknotes and stuffed them inside his pockets until his pullover bulged in an ugly manner. This would appear to be the extra money. He locked the case, made his way back down the tortuous path, walked back to the garage.

'Looks like you're going to have a baby,' Gallagher commented.

He stood by the control panel, pressed one switch, watched the garage doors slowly close, pressed another and the platform elevated above the service pit. Anton put the case down on a table, hoisted his pullover a few inches as he asked the question casually.

'Supposing I want to come back and ask you a question tomorrow. About the operation of the Stingers. You'll be here?'

'No. Anything you want to ask, ask now.' He lowered himself into the pit. 'I'll be away for a week in another country. A fresh deal.'

'Your regular customers – for servicing cars – will be pleased.'

'They know me. The doors are closed, I'm not here. Give me a hand. Take these, put them on that big table, the one with the sheet of canvas.'

When the three launchers and five missiles were laid on the top of the table, Gallagher hauled himself out of the pit. He towered over Anton. He spent the next ten minutes working rapidly, wrapping each launcher and missile in polythene sheets; then he arranged them on the large canvas already spread out. Rolling up the canvas, he fetched some straps and began securing the bundle. 'You can start relieving yourself of that money,' he suggested.

Anton pulled out the bundles of banknotes, laid them in stacks on the table-top. Gallagher was fastening the last strap when the Greek stepped back to pick up the case he'd stowed under the table. Gallagher had his back to him, stooped over the canvas-wrapped weapons.

Anton took out a handkerchief, blew his nose, kept the handkerchief in his hand, grasped the handle of the commando knife inside its sheath fastened to the belt under his pullover. He drew it out, stepped forward and rammed it with all his strength into Gallagher just below the left shoulder blade. Gallagher gasped, made a muted gurgling sound and slumped forward across the table.

'You really should keep to an agreed price,' Anton said.

Anton used two of the straps as makeshift handles to carry the canvas bundle to the donkey cart. At that, he staggered under the weight which must have been between a hundred and fifty and two hundred pounds. And Anton kept himself fit.

He dropped it into the cart and moved the hay to conceal the weapons. He hauled large handfuls close to the bundle, which caused it to sink, then dumped the hay on top. It took him a good five minutes to complete the job. Returning to the garage, he repacked the stacks of banknotes in the case, locked it and buried it under the hay.

Half an hour later he was leading the donkey along the deserted front. The cafés and discotheques were going full blast. From open windows the sound of guitars being strummed, of girls singing *fado*, drifted. At least it guaranteed an empty waterfront.

He had acted quickly clearing up the garage behind closed doors. Gallagher's dead body had been heaved into the pit. Anton had found an oil-stained canvas sheet to cover the corpse. Then he had pressed the button and lowered the elevated platform. He had doused the three oil lamps. Fortunately the control panel was near the doors: he had pressed the switch and dived into the street before they closed.

Carlos leapt on to the jetty when he arrived. Between them they lowered the weapons into his fishing boat. The Portuguese hid them under a pile of fishing nets. He wiped his hands on his trousers and looked at Anton, who asked the question.

'What about the donkey and the cart?'

'Will wait until I return from the *Oporto*. Then I go home. I saw a fishing boat out there die.'

'Sorry?'

'It blew up. Boom! They do not take care with boilers. I am careful. It is my living . . .'

'Has the coastguard gone out?'

It was an important question. Anton was thinking police launches might be prowling around.

'No.' Carlos spread his hands. 'They will not make the hurry. Maybe when the sun rises. Are we good to leave for the *Oporto*?'

'As soon as you can get under way . . .'

Anton felt relieved as he saw the shoreline receding. It would be a week before anyone started worrying about Gallagher's closed garage. That had been a bit of luck. As the boat chugged steadily towards the main harbour Anton wiped his forehead. They were away.

Gomez, skipper of the freighter *Oporto*, was well-organized. A short fat jolly man, he helped to bring the canvas-wrapped cargo aboard up a gangway lowered on the far side from the jetty where his ship was moored. Anton waited until Carlos was guiding his fishing vessel back to Cascais, then handed Gomez the envelope containing £10,000 in Swiss banknotes.

'The same amount as before. Where is the crew?'

'Below decks. I invented work for them when I saw Carlos coming. What they don't see, they don't know. Better I hide this in a safe place?'

'Very safe.' He knew Gomez would assume he was smuggling drugs. 'When do you sail? I have to complete some business.'

'At dawn the day after tomorrow.' He checked his watch. 'It is eleven-thirty. Yes, not tomorrow, the day after. That is OK?'

'Perfectly.' Anton, holding his executive case, decided to take it with him. He had to return to The Ritz, act normally, sleep there, have breakfast, then pay his bill. 'I would prefer it if I could slip aboard tomorrow and stay under cover until you sail.'

'What time? Your cabin is ready now.'

'Probably about midday. You can time arrival at our destination as you did when you took me before? At eleven o'clock at night? Again someone will be waiting to take me ashore.'

'There is a problem.' Gomez, his weatherbeaten face making him look more like sixty than forty, scratched his head. 'Last time I told the harbourmaster at Watchet we had engine trouble. Ah! I have it. This time, after you leave us, we will steam back a way down the Bristol Channel, turn round, and berth during the morning.'

'I'm counting on you.'

'Of course. You will be put ashore at Porlock Weir just as you were before.'

37

'I've never seen anything like this place,' Tweed said as they walked out of The Anchor. He had Paula on one side, Butler on the other. 'It's fascinating. A tiny world on its own.'

Tweed had driven down with Paula to Porlock Weir after he had warned Butler they were coming. 'Book us two rooms at The Anchor,' he had told Butler. 'I want to avoid The Luttrell Arms in Dunster this time. The idea is to surprise Barrymore and Co. You said they've all returned to Exmoor?'

Butler had confirmed the three men had arrived back the previous day. As they left The Anchor after a satisfying lunch he explained.

'Nield and I each have our own hired cars. We spent our time touring the whole area, checking for any sign of life at their residences. We split up, went to pubs to catch any gossip. It's common knowledge the three men took a trip away from Exmoor. You can't go to the loo down here without everyone knowing. Nield is out having another look-see.'

They crossed a narrow wired-fenced footbridge over seventeen-feet lock gates. A notice warned, *Closed Spring Tide*. Tweed paused, gazing at the oyster-shaped harbour behind the gates. Low tide. The harbour was a basin of sodden mud. A trickle of water ran under the footbridge out of the basin. Expensive power cruisers, moored to buoys, heeled over at drunken angles.

No one else was about as they followed a footpath past a small row of three terraced houses; all of them old, one with a thatched roof. Beyond, a shoal of pebbles led steeply down to a calm grey sea. Tweed stopped, taking in the atmosphere.

He looked back at the gabled hotel which was combined with The Ship Inn. Gulls drifted in the overcast sky, crying mournfully. Behind the coast the hillside, covered with dense trees, climbed. To the west the rocky coast stretched away and everywhere was a feeling of desolation.

'A quiet hideaway,' Tweed commented. 'Like the end of the world.'

'That reminds me.' Paula sounded excited as she delved inside her handbag. 'I found this in a pocket in my suitcase when I was packing to come down here. A brochure I picked up at The Luttrell Arms.'

She handed him a coloured brochure headed *Take*

the West Somerset Railway to Minehead. Below was a picture of an old-fashioned steam train. He opened it up and looked at the map inside as Butler peered over his shoulder.

The steam train started at Minehead, ran along the coast through the port of Watchet and later turned inland over the Quantock Hills, ending at Taunton. It began running on 29 March and shut down for winter on 29 October.

'*Endstation*,' said Paula. 'That clue Masterson gave you inside the cigar box he posted from Athens. He was drawing your attention to that old privately run railway.'

'And which is *Endstation*?' Tweed asked. 'Minehead or Taunton?'

'No idea. Don't you think I'm right?'

'Maybe.' Tweed folded up the brochure, handed it back to her. 'Hang on to it. It goes through Watchet, I see. The port where Anton probably came ashore from that Portuguese freighter.'

'Except he didn't,' Butler said. 'I checked that out. A two-storey building looking straight down on the harbour there is Customs and the harbourmaster. I followed him into a pub and got chatting. Told him a cock-and-bull story about how a friend had boasted he'd come ashore from that freighter without being spotted. The harbourmaster said bullshit. They keep a sharp lookout for suspicious characters trying to sneak ashore. It's this drugs problem. He was a solid ex-seaman type. Said it was impossible. I believe him.'

'Another theory gone down the drain. Let's wander west along the coast a bit. Looks pretty lonely.'

Butler led the way back across the footbridge and they walked down a road a short distance. It stopped abruptly and they had to pick their way across a treacherous surface of pebbles and small rocks.

'It really is the end of the world out here,' Tweed remarked.

'Maybe that's what Masterson meant when he wrote *Endstation*,' Butler suggested. Wearing a thick woollen pullover as protection against the damp sea mist drifting in, he walked with his hands inside his trouser pockets. 'There's an old dear back in one of those cottages who says she's seen ghosts – and lights flashing late at night. The barman told me so I called on her. A Mrs Larcombe. In her late seventies, but sharp as a tack.'

'I don't think you're right,' Paula objected. '*Endstation* is one of those two terminal stations on that railway – Taunton or Minehead.'

'What's got into him?' Butler asked her.

Tweed was striding ahead, peering at the ground, his Burberry collar buttoned to the neck. He seemed totally absorbed in his thoughts.

Paula told Butler about the death of Jill Kearns. He listened as she explained Monica's anxiety about Tweed becoming obsessed. 'And now his mind is full of three deaths,' she went on. 'Masterson's, of course, and Sam Partridge and Jill.'

'Don't see how they link up. One in Greece, one on Exmoor, one in London.'

'That's what he's trying to do – link them all together. Drop the subject, he's coming back . . .'

'I found traces of a wheeled vehicle,' Tweed announced. 'In a patch where sand showed.'

'No vehicle would cross that terrain,' commented Butler.

'And on the way back, could we call on Mrs Larcombe if she's at home? I'd like a word with her . . .'

The cottage was built of stone, roofed with red tiles mellowed by the years. Swagged lace curtains draped the windows, the front garden was barely three feet wide but the lavender borders were trimmed and there was not a weed in sight.

Approaching the cottage, Tweed noted there was an end window facing west where he had walked. Butler raised the highly polished brass knocker shaped like a dolphin and rapped it twice. A nameboard on the picket gate carried the legend *Dolphin Cottage*.

A tall sharp-faced woman opened the door. Her nose was prominent, she was long-jawed, her eyes alert, her mass of hair grey neatly brushed. Butler spoke to her for a moment, then gestured for Tweed and Paula to enter. Mrs Larcombe led them into what she called 'the parlour', invited them to sit down and Butler made the introductions.

'What can I do for you, Mr Tweed?' she asked, seating herself in a chintz-covered armchair.

'I'm in insurance. No, I'm not trying to sell you any policy. I'm Chief Claims Investigator for my company. A holidaymaker called Burns disappeared here a few weeks ago. Last seen late at night walking that way.' He twisted in his chair, pointed west. 'We've had a claim on the basis presumed dead. Since no body has been found I'm puzzled.'

'Funny goings-on round here.' Her eyes glistened, bird-like. 'No one believes me. They think I'm seeing ghosts. I know what I saw and heard.' She sat more erect.

'Could you tell me a little more?' Tweed asked quietly.

'It would be a few weeks ago – about the time your Mr Burns disappeared. Can't fix it exactly. Yes, I can. About the time the Customs at Watchet practically took that Portuguese freighter apart. Didn't find anything except a lot of cork. The rumour was it was carrying drugs.'

'What did you see and hear?'

'Close to midnight it was. I don't sleep well. I was looking out of my bedroom window which faces the way you pointed. I saw a light flashing out at sea. Like someone signalling. Then another light flashing from the shore. There was a ship at sea, a fairish way out.'

'You had your bedroom light on?' Tweed enquired.

'No, I didn't. I'd got out of bed in the dark and put on my dressing gown. I know where all the furniture is. I had the window open. It was a sticky night.'

'This ship you saw – it had navigation lights? Which is how you came to see it?'

'No, it didn't. But my sight is very good. No glasses, as you see. I saw it as a vague silhouette. I thought that was funny. What you've just mentioned. No navigation lights.'

'And that was all?'

She stiffened. She wore an old-fashioned black dress with a lace collar pinned with a brooch. 'You don't believe me?'

'Yes, I do. Because your night vision would be good – since you hadn't put a light on. Was there something else?'

'I went back to bed, leaving the window open for some air. I fell asleep quickly. Then I was wakened by a noise. I felt fuddled but I got up again. It was the engine noise of some vehicle approaching – from the same direction. I thought that funny. No cars drive over those pebbles. By the time I got to the window it was passing my gate. No lights. I ran to the front window because the noise stopped. I was worried – it sounded to have stopped by my front gate. I made a racket opening the front window – the thing sticks. As I looked out the engine started and the vehicle disappeared towards Porlock.'

'Without lights?' Tweed asked gently.

'No. As it passed the harbour the lights came on. The red ones at the back and dimmed headlights in front. Then it was gone.' She leaned forward, her eyes shrewd. 'Could it have been your Mr Burns?'

'Possibly,' said Tweed. 'No way of telling for sure. Could you describe what sort of vehicle it was? Even in the dark?'

'An odd-looking beast.' She frowned with concentration. 'High up off the ground. Behind the cab it was squarish. At a guess, canvas-covered.'

'Colour?'

'Couldn't tell.'

'White or cream?' Tweed suggested.

'Definitely not. It would have shown up more. A darkish colour. No idea who was driving – I was looking down on it, you see.'

Tweed stood up, took his glasses case out of his pocket, fumbled, dropped it on the dark floral-patterned carpet. The room was dim. He put his hand behind him, stopped Paula searching for it. He almost knocked over a vase of dried flowers. Mrs Larcombe stepped forward, took hold of the case, handed it to him.

'You'll be lost without this.'

'Thank you. And thank you for giving us your time. Your help is greatly appreciated.'

'*You* do believe me then?' Mrs Larcombe asked as she stood up to see them out.

'Oh, yes, I believe you.'

'Well, I'm glad someone doesn't think I've lost my marbles . . .'

Paula waited until they were walking back to The Anchor before asking the question. 'What was that business about your glasses case? There was no need to take it out of your pocket.'

'A final test on her eyesight. My case is dark-coloured. Even I couldn't see where it had dropped – it merged with the carpet. Mrs Larcombe has exceptional eyesight.'

'What do you think she saw then?'

'Some kind of covered jeep or four-wheel-drive vehicle which could negotiate that pebble ground easily. Now I'm phoning Colonel Barrymore. He's first on the list for some hard interrogation. His reaction to my calling him will be interesting.'

Inside his room at The Anchor Paula looked out of the window while Tweed made his call. She had a view down over the road which ended a short distance to the west, and the harbour with the dried-up channel where the sea would come flooding in.

Tweed's conversation with Barrymore was brief. He spoke tersely and concluded by saying, 'Then I will call you back within the hour.'

'He says he has to try and cancel an appointment,' Tweed told her. 'I think he's up to something. Let's have some coffee sent up and review what we've discovered. Butler is taking a well-earned rest . . .'

He called back exactly one hour later. This time the conversation was longer. Tweed's manner was even more abrupt. He closed by saying, 'Very well, if you insist. It will save me time.'

He looked grim as he replaced the receiver. 'I was right – he was up to something. He's phoned Robson and Kearns and invited them to join him at Quarme Manor. We'll be confronted by the three of them.'

'Including Kearns? But surely he must be distraught so soon after the death of his wife?'

'We'll see, won't we?'

38

Colonel Barrymore did not bother to receive them. When they arrived at Quarme Manor the door was unchained and opened by Mrs Atyeo. She ushered them into the hall and then indicated the door to the study.

'They'se waitin' for you in there.'

'Thank you,' Tweed said pleasantly. Followed by Paula, he opened the door without knocking. They were seated round a large oak table in the bay window. Barrymore,

Kearns and Robson. The colonel had his back to the window with Robson at his left and Kearns on his right. Tweed instantly realized that the seating arrangement forced Paula and himself to face the light while the others had their back to it. An old tactic. Barrymore remained seated, launched his onslaught as soon as they were inside the room.

'I see you've brought that girl again. This time I won't have her taking notes. You sit there and there.'

'Paula Grey is my assistant,' Tweed rapped back. 'She will take notes of the entire interrogation.' He sat down and dropped his bomb. 'Now we are investigating four murders which may all have security implications.'

'Four? What on earth are you talking about?' Barrymore demanded in his most commanding voice.

'One, Ionides at the Antikhana during the war.' Tweed waited to see if anyone would correct him, say 'Gavalas'. Three blank faces stared back at him. 'Two, Andreas Gavalas on Siros when you made your commando raid. Three, ex-Chief Inspector Partridge here on Exmoor.' He paused.

Paula was watching Kearns. He sat very stiffly, motionless, and his face was drained of colour, chalk-white. Tweed turned to him.

'Four, your wife, Jill. My condolences.'

'She was knocked down by some hit-and-run bastard,' Barrymore protested. 'And that's pretty bad form to raise the subject – to call it murder is madness.'

'Then why is Scotland Yard investigating it as a case of murder?'

'How do you know that?' Barrymore snapped.

'I have contacts. I'm Special Branch. You know that. You checked up on the phone with my chief, Walton.'

Robson, wearing a loose-fitting brown shirt, a plain brown tie, the knot slack below his throat, and an old check sports jacket, stirred. He turned to face Barrymore.

'You didn't tell me that.'

'Must have slipped my mind,' the colonel replied curtly.

Robson tugged at his straggly moustache, turned back to face Tweed. His pale blue eyes studied him for a moment.

'What makes you think Jill was murdered?'

'A cleaning woman inside one of the St James's Street clubs saw a Jaguar waiting by the kerb with its engine running. The moment Jill started to cross the street the man behind the wheel headed straight for her. Cold-blooded murder.'

Tweed waited again. Before leaving London he had changed his mind, had phoned Chief Inspector Jarvis in charge of the case. No description of the driver worth a damn. The silence inside the room became oppressive.

Paula was studying Kearns. He sat like a statue. Not a blink of an eyelid at Tweed's statement. Years of iron self-discipline as a CSM, she thought. Never show your emotions however tough the situation. She felt Tweed was treating him inconsiderately.

'Why have you come to see us?' Robson asked, leaning forward, gazing at Tweed as though deciding on a diagnosis.

'Because you're all suspects, of course . . .'

'How dare you!' Barrymore burst out. 'Are you accusing us? And what evidence have you to base that slanderous statement on? I want an answer.'

'I'll give you one. You were all members of the commando raid on Siros. Andreas Gavalas was murdered. A fortune in diamonds he was carrying for the Greek Resistance was stolen. You were all based at the Antikhana Building in Cairo. You had returned from the raid. Ionides was murdered. You were all here on Exmoor a good few weeks ago. Partridge was murdered. You were all staying in London at the Lyceum Hotel – only a short distance from St James's Street. Jill Kearns was murdered. How much more coincidence do you think I can swallow?'

Robson laid a restraining hand on Barrymore's arm. He asked the question in the manner of a doctor enquiring about a patient's symptoms.

'Why do you think that Jill was murdered?'

'Because someone who knew she always stayed at Brown's saw me having tea with her. Whoever it was became worried she might tell me too much.'

'Stretching it a bit, aren't you?'

'Possibly. Until I link it up with the fact you must all have known she made a habit of staying at Brown's, that she made a habit of going out for a walk at that time every single day of her life. The killer followed her to the Stafford where I asked her to go, hoping to ensure her safety. Where were you all at 6.30 a.m. that fatal morning?'

Barrymore opened his mouth to protest. 'What damned impudence. I'll see you in hell before . . .'

'Best to reply,' Robson intervened. 'We all got up early – the habit of a lifetime. Goes back to Army days. By early I mean about 5.30 a.m. None of us have breakfast. There were tea-making facilities in the bedrooms. I spent my time packing, then studied some medical journals. No one to verify that.' His smile was wintry. 'Barrymore had gone for a walk – I know that because I went to his room and there was no reply. Kearns was also out walking. It was a fine day. Doesn't help a lot, does it?'

'Not a lot,' Tweed agreed. 'You were out for a walk, Barrymore?'

'You heard what Captain Robson said. I'm getting a trifle fed up with you . . .'

'And I'm fed up with the fact that my old friend, Sam Partridge, was foully murdered,' blazed Tweed. 'I'll move heaven and earth to find out who did that.'

Paula glanced at Tweed in surprise. She'd never known such an outburst during an interrogation. Then she saw the supercilious smile of satisfaction on Barrymore's face. He'd needled Tweed. She glanced back as Tweed began cleaning his glasses on his handkerchief and nearly sucked in her breath. Tweed had put on an act. She tensed: she was witnessing a duel between Tweed and the three men. Kearns spoke for the first time.

'That cleaning woman. Did she get a description of the driver? And what about tracing the owner of the Jaguar?'

'Stolen from outside a night club near the Lyceum Hotel where you stayed. Some fool of a yuppie got drunk, left the keys in the ignition, was persuaded to walk back to his flat in case he was stopped by the police.'

Tweed stood up and Paula closed her notebook, which carried a complete record of the conversation. Barrymore remained seated, his voice sardonic.

'You know your own way out. Mrs Atyeo will be waiting to lock up after you leave the premises. Don't come back.'

Tweed sat behind the wheel of the Mercedes where he had parked it in a lay-by twenty yards or so away before arriving at Quarme Manor. Butler, who had followed them from Porlock Weir, then waited, parked behind the Mercedes, appeared at Tweed's window.

'Next move?' he enquired.

'I want to ask Robson something on his own. His Saab is in the courtyard. Let's hope he comes out soon. You wait here. Then if Barrymore appears, follow him.'

'There's a better place for me to wait. I can back my car just a short distance and into a field. That way I won't be conspicuous if he comes this way.' Butler paused. 'Is it a good idea my leaving you? I'm the one with the gun.'

'It's broad daylight still. Not to worry. You back your car – and where is Nield?'

'No idea. We'll see him sometime at The Anchor when he's good and ready. Does Barrymore know where you're staying?'

'No. I said I'd phone him back when he wanted to call me.'

Paula stretched her arms to ease the tension out of herself as Butler left them. 'Did you get anything out of that interview? It was a bit fraught at times.'

'Two things you might have noticed. The absence of one of them asking a question. And someone else did say something.'

'And now you're going to leave me dangling. I'll ask you again. You think they're all in it together? Or just one of them?'

'Just one.'

'I'm too smart to ask which. Lord, it's getting darker.'

Earlier there had been hazy sunshine during their drive to the Manor. Now low heavy clouds were rolling in, obscuring the crests and higher slopes of the moor. It began to spot with rain on the windscreen. Then the Saab came out, turned in the other direction and drove off.

'We've got him,' said Tweed and followed as the Saab vanished round a bend. He drove slowly and when they reached Endpoint Robson had disappeared. The Saab was parked just below the terrace and Tweed gazed towards the Doone Valley. When he got out he stretched his legs, pacing up and down.

'Time to beard the lion in his den,' he remarked and they walked up the steep drive. It was very quiet, a silence Tweed felt pressing down on him. Then he stopped. The drive continued round the right-hand side of the bungalow. Parked next to the end of the building was a canvas-covered four-wheel-drive vehicle. Dark-coloured.

Robson's sister, May, opened the door, welcomed them inside and showed them into the sitting room. She asked them to sit down.

'Oliver is writing out his medical records in the conning tower. I'll just fetch him.'

'Conning tower?' Tweed asked.

'Well, I think it looks more like a lighthouse – the tower at the end. But Oliver calls it the conning tower. Back in just a minute.'

Her thick hair seemed even greyer in the daylight. She wore a flowered print dress over her ample form. On this second visit Tweed noticed she had the same pale blue eyes as her brother, eyes which had a remoteness about them.

Robson appeared quickly, gave his shy smile. He took out his pipe as he sat down and began to fill it with tobacco from an old leather pouch.

'Something else?' he enquired.

'Yes. Sorry to trouble you again – but it was Barrymore's idea I met all three of you at his place. Going back to that morning at the Lyceum Hotel, you said you went along to the colonel's room and he was out for a walk. How did you know he was out?'

'First there was a *Do Not Disturb* notice hanging from the handle of his door. He always does that when he goes out – very security conscious, our CO. That way any burglar will assume someone is sleeping inside. Don't bother myself.'

'You said "first". What else was there?' Tweed persisted.

'I wanted to ask him something. So I banged on his door to make sure. He's a light sleeper, like most Army types. He was definitely not there. You sound like a detective.' He smiled to take any sting out of his remark.

'I used to be one.' Tweed paused. 'With Homicide at the Yard.' Robson nodded and puffed at his pipe as Tweed continued. 'What did the three of you do the night before in the evening – after you'd arrived at the Lyceum?'

'Barrymore had some business to transact. Kearns and I went to Rules for dinner. The colonel joined us later.'

'And after your meal you did what?'

402

'Kearns and I went back to the hotel. Barrymore went for a walk. Said he felt like a breath of fresh air. He's a keep fit sort of chap.'

Tweed stood up. 'Well, thank you. Sorry to disturb your work.'

'That's all right. Do you mind if May shows you out? I've quite a workload to get through. There's a bug going round and I've been rushed off my feet. I make quick notes after seeing a patient. Then when I get the time I make a proper record. Ah, here is May.'

'I was going to ask if anyone would like coffee?' she said.

'They're just leaving. Perhaps you'd show them out . . .'

She accompanied them to the front door, Tweed said 'Goodbye,' and she closed the door.

Tweed walked down the steps off the terrace and strolled round to the end of the bungalow. Paula followed as he stood looking at the four-wheel-drive vehicle. Along the bodywork of the passenger seat side at the front was painted a word. *Renegade*.

'Can't be the same one,' Paula whispered. 'Mrs Larcombe would have noticed that word. It's in huge letters and painted white.'

'No, she wouldn't have done,' he observed, 'it's painted on the far side – the wrong side when she looked out of her window.'

'Can I help you?'

It was May who stood just behind them. Neither had heard her approach on the tarred drive. Tweed smiled and indicated the vehicle. 'We were just admiring it. In bad weather it must be a godsend.'

'Oh, that isn't Oliver's. He borrows it from Mr Kearns.'

39

Inside the isolated public call box near Simonsbath Seton-Charles pulled at his lips with his thumb and forefinger. He was waiting for the phone to ring, had been waiting a good ten minutes. Jupiter insisted he arrived in good time.

His car was parked off the road amid a clump of trees: an empty car left in the middle of nowhere in full view could attract attention. He looked round through the windows for the fifth time. The deserted road spiralled away up on to the moor. Mist curled down over the ridges. If the call didn't come soon it was going to be a difficult drive back to his bungalow.

He shivered. The chill seemed to penetrate the box. He felt the cold after his stay in Athens. He grabbed the phone when it began to ring.

'Clement here,' he said. 'Speaking from . . .' He gave the number of the call box, reversing the last two digits.

The voice began speaking immediately, the tone clipped, the accent upper-crust. No time wasted on greetings. Straight into the instructions.

'We need two furniture vans for the move. In Norwich there's a firm called Camelford Removals. Just gone bankrupt. Selling everything off. Purchase two vehicles, large ones. Pay in cash to save time. Store them in the barn at Cherry Farm in Hampshire. Make sure the doors are double padlocked. Two sets of keys. I want you to drive there tonight after dark. Put up at a hotel in Norwich.'

'I can't drive two vans back myself . . .'

'Think, man. Store one in a garage in the Norwich

area tomorrow. Drive the other to Cherry Farm. With a motorbike inside. Use the bike to get back to Norwich. Then drive the second van back to the farm. The bike is expendable. I want both vehicles at the farm two days from now. Camelford Removals' address is . . . Got it?'

'Yes,' said Seton-Charles. 'You're sure the vans will still be available? Not already sold?'

'My dear chap, the advertisement said they have six vans they want to shift. Bound to be at least two left, providing you're in Norwich first thing tomorrow. That's it . . .'

The connection was broken. Seton-Charles hurried back to his Volvo station wagon, backed it on to the road, started driving for his home on the bungalow estate.

He had no idea of the identity of the man who had called him. He thought the codename Jupiter rather pretentious, but driving along he realized Jupiter was a first-rate organizer. Now he'd drive to Norwich during the late evening, find a hotel. He'd have to park his Volvo in a lock-up, buy a second-hand motorcycle.

When he'd purchased the two furniture vans he'd park the motorbike inside one, then drive it to Cherry Farm, an uninhabited farmhouse he'd visited earlier. Next he'd ride the bike back to Norwich, collect the second van, drive it to the farm. Finally, he could use the bike to ride back again to Norwich to pick up his Volvo. The bike would be dumped in some convenient wood. Job done.

But what could Jupiter want with a couple of furniture vans? He couldn't even guess. But the operation – whatever it might be – was under way. And there had been a hint of urgency in the way he'd been given his instructions.

'Do go easy on Kearns,' Paula said as Tweed parked the Mercedes just short of Woodside House. 'Remember, his wife has just been killed.' She looked up. 'Good Lord, it's Pete.'

Nield leant on the edge of Tweed's window. He looked very tired. He winked at Paula and then spoke to Tweed.

'It's a small world, as they say. Seton-Charles has come back from Greece. I've been checking for days. He's just returned to that bungalow of his at the end of the cul-de-sac after making a covert phone call.'

'Covert?'

'I saw his Volvo parked outside his bungalow so I hung around. He has his own phone, as you know. So what does he do? Drives to a public call box near Simonsbath.'

'A long call?' Tweed asked.

'Let me tell it my way. I follow him. He hides his Volvo in some trees, walks into the box, then waits at least ten minutes.'

'That sounds like a professional. He has an arrangement to be at a certain call box at a specific time. Go on.'

'The phone rings. He snatches it. Conversation lasts precisely ninety seconds. Then he drives back here. His car is inside his garage. What do you think?'

'He bears watching.' Tweed looked closely at Nield. 'You've had a long day, I'd say.'

'Bit frayed. I could do with a sit-down and a half pint.'

'Then drive back to The Anchor now. If Seton-Charles put his car away it doesn't look as though he's going anywhere tonight. We'll see you for dinner. Go and relax.'

'Thanks. You're still prowling?'

'We're calling on friend Kearns. If he's home.'

'He is. I saw him ride in on his horse a while ago. I'll get moving . . .'

'Wait for that beastly dog to appear,' Paula said as Tweed pressed the bell-push beside the gates.

A light came on over the distant porch. Kearns came out slowly. He was carrying a heavy stick. He shone a

406

flashlight and the powerful beam reached the gate, blinding Paula. Tweed half-shut his eyes.

'No dog,' Paula whispered. 'Funny.'

'It's you,' Kearns greeted them. 'I suppose you'd better come in. I'd like it kept brief, whatever it is.'

'Of course,' replied Tweed.

They followed him carefully up the centre of the path, keeping clear of the rough grass and the mantraps it concealed. Kearns led them into the dimly lit hall. Outside it was twilight; dusk was gathering over the moors. Paula dropped her handbag, scrabbled on the floor and picked it up.

Tweed hardly noticed: he was thinking Kearns was getting careless about security. The inner heavy wooden slab doors had been open when they arrived; only the grille gates were closed. Where was the dog?

There was a sudden ferocious snarl from behind a closed door as Kearns passed it. A heavy thud, as though the Alsatian had hurled its bulk against the far side. Kearns hammered a clenched fist against the door.

'Shut it!' he growled.

The first sign of tension – of emotion – he had shown. He took them into the same dining room with the oak table and the panelled walls. Again the lighting was dim. White-faced, Kearns sat at the opposite side, gestured for them to join him on the far side.

'What is it now?' he demanded.

'I know this is a grim time for you,' Tweed began, 'but we need as much information as we can get about your wife's murder. And memory has a habit of fading fast . . .'

'You are convinced it was murder?' Kearns asked, his large hands clenched, the knuckles showing white. His brown marble-like eyes stared at Tweed.

'Yes, I think it was. It's not much consolation – but since the Yard is also convinced they'll do their best to hunt down the killer. An ordinary hit-and-run driver who's probably never caught can cause even more anguish.' He looked round the room. 'The place looks well looked after. Have you got someone in to help?'

'I've done it myself.' Kearns stiffened his back. 'I don't want any other woman inside the house now Jill's gone.'

'I understand. Incidentally, at Quarme Manor I gathered you went for an early morning walk the day you left the Lyceum Hotel. So did Barrymore – on his own. Did you by chance see him while you were out?'

'Strangely enough, no.'

'Why "strangely"?'

'Because,' Kearns explained, 'he always walks in St James's Park when we're in town. Which is where I went. No one else about at that hour. I didn't see any trace of him.'

'One more question, then we'll leave you in peace. I called in on Dr Robson while I was on my way here. He had a four-wheel-drive vehicle parked by the side of his bungalow. It's got the word *Renegade* painted on the side opposite to the driver's seat. Said he'd borrowed it from you.'

'That's right. But it isn't mine. I borrow it from a chap called Foster. Stockbroker type. Lives in the bungalow nearest the main road – on the left as you face the cul-de-sac. We do a lot of that on Exmoor – exchange things on loan. It saves money.'

'How old would this Foster be?' asked Tweed.

Kearns looked surprised at the question, but answered. 'I'd say about forty. Like most of them on that estate.'

'And when did they all move into those bungalows?'

'Fifteen years ago.'

Tweed stood up. 'Thank you for bearing with me. You have some friends you can talk to? I know myself what it's like – stuck on your own in a house when your wife is gone.'

Paula glanced quickly at him. She realized Tweed was

408

recalling the time when his own wife had left him for a Greek shipping magnate.

'Oh, yes. In Winsford,' Kearns replied. 'I'll survive. Let me show you out.'

As they crossed the hall they heard the Alsatian. Now it was moaning and whining behind the closed door. Tweed thought that it sounded as if it were mourning the death of its mistress.

It was dark as Kearns used his flashlight to guide them to the exit. He said 'Goodnight', locked the grille gates and walked slowly back to the house. Tweed and Paula returned to the car. He sank behind the wheel, took a packet out of the glove compartment and smoked one of his rare cigarettes. Paula kept silent for a few minutes before she spoke.

'You're ruminating.'

'A lot to think about. That four-wheel-drive vehicle, *Renegade*. First it seems to belong to Robson, then Kearns and now this man, Foster. The question is, who drove it along the coast near Porlock Weir about midnight? No way of telling.'

'So we can't pursue that line of enquiry – assuming that it's worth pursuing.'

'Then there's the weird psychological set-up between the three men – Robson, Barrymore and Kearns. That must be quite something.'

'I'm not following you.'

'Use your imagination. Three men take part in that commando raid on Siros all those years ago. Andreas Gavalas is murdered with a commando knife. One of them did it . . .'

'But Barrymore checked their weapons after they found the body.'

'So, the killer carried an extra knife, knowing what he was going to do in advance. A hundred thousand pounds' worth of diamonds – now worth a million – went missing.

409

When Barrymore and Kearns leave the Army they settle on Exmoor, close to Robson – who found accommodation for them. I don't think the three of them conspired to murder Andreas. Just one of them.'

'I'm being dim – what about the psychological set-up?'

'It's diabolical, like something out of a Tennessee Williams play. Nobody knows who did it. But two out of the three *know* they didn't. So two of them who are innocent must have wondered all these years which man was a murderer. That makes for almost unbearable tension.'

'So why stay together?'

'That's the truly diabolical part. There's another factor locking them together – fear of Petros and the Gavalas clan coming to Exmoor for revenge. They're trying to protect one another.'

'You're right,' Paula said slowly, 'it's a macabre relationship.'

'Let's get moving.' Tweed shook himself alert. 'I want to take a quick look at that bungalow estate down the road.'

He parked near the bottom of the hill with the engine still running. In the night they had a good view of the six bungalows with whitewashed walls, three on either side of the cul-de-sac. Curtains were closed. Behind them lights shone. The coach lamps in the porches were all lit. No sign of life.

Each dwelling had a low wall, also whitewashed, bordering a trim lawn inside. All the gardens had the grass cut. No cars were parked either in the road or on a drive. All neatly tucked away inside the garages attached to the bungalows. On the roofs of five of them were the same conventional television masts. Only Seton-Charles had the complex structure with a satellite dish.

'I tell you again,' Paula said, 'it doesn't look real. If robots walked out I'd hardly be surprised.'

'Best get back to The Anchor . . .'

He was releasing the brake after moving the gear into drive when she touched his arm. He put the brake back on and turned to her.

'What is it?'

'This.' She was holding a small white stick she'd taken out of her handbag. 'Remember when we arrived at Kearns' place – I pretended to be clumsy and dropped my handbag on the floor. I'd seen this on the woodblocks.'

'What is it?'

'I'm pretty sure it's French chalk. Let me test it.' She held the stick, rubbed it on the cuff of her cotton blouse. A white mark appeared. She brushed at it with her fingers and it vanished. Opening the glove flap, she balanced the makeshift shelf on her knee, rubbed the stick across it. The substance appeared as small grains of powder. She bent forward, sniffed at it. 'No smell.' Moistening her index finger, she dabbed it in the powder, tasted it. 'No taste. It is French chalk.'

'I fail to see the significance.'

'You know I make some of my dresses. I use it for marking. And there's another purpose it could be used for.'

'Now you're keeping me dangling.'

'Kearns' complexion – normally ruddy when the suntan has worn off – is white. We put it down to grief. I think he used this stick of French chalk to alter his complexion, to simulate grief. It must have dropped out of his pocket. I think he used it to touch up the effect just before he appeared at the door. There is a mirror in the hall. And I noticed traces of white powder on his jacket lapel.'

'My God!' said Tweed. 'And Howard still thinks I'm wrong to introduce women into the Service.'

411

40

They arrived back at The Anchor and found Butler and Nield having a drink in the bar. Nield sat at the corner table with his head leant against the wall, his eyes half-closed. It was early for business: they had the place to themselves.

'Don't get up,' Paula said as Nield stirred. 'You look all in.'

'Application to the job in hand.' Nield smiled. 'Your boss expects non-stop action,' he said as Tweed arrived with the drinks: mineral water for himself, a glass of white wine for Paula. 'I've been driving over those moors until they seem to start moving.'

'Application!' Butler snorted and drank from his half-pint glass. 'That's what we're here for.' He lowered his voice, speaking to Tweed, who sat next to him. 'Barrymore left Quarme Manor soon after you'd gone. Drove into Minehead. Made a call from a public box. Funny thing to do – he has his phone at home.'

'How long a call?'

'Between one and two minutes. I was going to time it but found my watch had stopped. Then he drives straight back to Quarme Manor.'

'Odd,' Tweed agreed. He looked round the table. 'Does anyone know whether Jill Kearns used to take that Alsatian when she went for her early morning walk on the moor?'

'I do,' Nield said. 'The answer is yes. Came out in a chat I had with the barman over there. She was well-known for those walks. Always started at 6.30 a.m. on the dot. The dog always went with her. For protection as much as company, I imagine. A lonely place, the moor.'

'That means the dog was pining for her,' Tweed remarked. 'And why am I worried about Mrs Larcombe down the road? Something she said. It will come back to me. What is it?'

Paula plucked at his sleeve. 'Look outside.' He twisted round, gazed out of the window. Two men and two girls clad in denims and windcheaters were getting out of a Land Rover covered with a canvas roof. They walked off towards the harbour. 'You see,' she said, 'another of those vehicles.'

Butler nodded. 'Four-wheel drives? They're pretty common – Pete and I have seen a number while we've driven around.'

'And there,' said Tweed, 'goes another theory I had. Every time I think I've got somewhere it turns into a dead end.'

'Like Porlock Weir,' Paula chimed in and sipped more wine.

'One thing I'd like you to do,' Tweed said to Nield, 'is check on the inhabitants of that bungalow estate near Kearns' place. Any titbit you can pick up.'

'First target the electoral register,' Nield replied. 'Then go on from there.'

'Why the interest?' Paula asked.

'Two remarks you made. That it didn't look real. And that you almost expected robots to emerge. Incidentally, the pathologist at Taunton told me Partridge was killed by someone who knew just where to insert the knife. Another thing, Pete,' he went on, 'I need to know whether Kearns still takes those night rides up to the summit of Dunkery Beacon . . .'

'Certainly not at the moment. Only when there's enough moonlight to see his way. Tricky riding those moors at

413

night even for a really experienced horseman.' He drank more beer. 'Well, that should keep my days filled.'

'There's more for you.' Tweed smiled at Nield's expression. 'You'll cope. I'd like you sometime – in daylight – to get up to the top of Dunkery Beacon and poke around up there. With Butler's help you'll manage. Plus, of course, keeping an eye on the other two. I wouldn't want you to have time on your hands, to get bored.' He finished his mineral water and stood up. 'I fancy a breath of fresh air. Want to come, Paula?'

'Lovely idea. Help to work up an appetite for dinner. That remark you made about the pathologist's comment again points the finger at the commandos.'

'Any news from Greece?' Tweed asked Butler as he donned his Burberry. 'You check regularly?'

'As you requested. Not a word. Monica didn't seem worried. She said Newman only calls when he has something solid. Same with Marler.'

'See you.' Tweed nodded to the barman, opened the door, paused. 'Pretty blustery out there.' He took his old waterproof hat off a peg and rammed it over his head. Paula wrapped a scarf round hers.

'Gale warnings round all coasts,' the barman called out.

'Which means a sleepless night,' Tweed remarked to Paula. 'Our bedroom windows both face the front.'

'Harry and Pete will be OK. Theirs face the back. I'm OK . . .'

The wind hit them as they plodded west along the road and then over the track which was still moist from the morning tide. To their right they could hear the crash of the sea against the rocky shoal. Spume, caught by the wind, blew off the wave crests and they felt it on their faces as they walked against the nor'wester.

'Are we staying here long?' Paula asked, her mouth close to his ear.

'I haven't decided. We may push off back to London

within a day or two. I've stirred up those three ex-commandos again. One of them may be nudged into making a wrong move. I'm stumped, Paula. And this doesn't seem the right place for any funny goings-on. That vehicle Mrs Larcombe saw would have to drive on through Porlock village even before it could turn up Porlock Hill. Too much risk of being seen.'

'That's not so. Harry told me about the toll road.'

'Told you what?'

'A very lonely road which turns up the hill just outside Porlock Weir. Apparently it turns up and joins the main road to Culbone. Sheer drop on one side. Harry's point was, that is the direct route to Quarme Manor and Endpoint – even on to our Mr Kearns' place. You take the first left off the main road like we did during our last visit. No one would see you driving that route late at night.'

'I've had enough of this,' said Tweed. 'We'll turn back.'

The wind was hammering them, making it difficult to walk over the sliding pebbles. They reached the track and were hurrying towards The Anchor when Tweed grabbed Paula's arm.

'Let me take a quick look at the harbourmaster's office. It has a notice behind the window.'

He took out a pencil torch, went close up to the deserted building. He shone the beam on the cardboard clock with adjustable hands. *High Tide 10.50 p.m.* The sea was already surging inside the channel which fed the harbour.

'I hope we decide to go back to London,' said Paula. 'If it's going on like this.'

Arriving back in the bar, they hung up their raincoats and got rid of their headgear. Butler and Nield sat at the same table. Tweed offered drinks.

'Not for me,' said Butler. 'I'll stick with this half pint – you may want to send me off somewhere.'

'I'll have a second,' Nield decided. 'I'm not going anywhere. Except to bed after a good dinner.'

'Harry,' Tweed said as he sat down, after calling out the order to the barman, 'have you shown Masterson's photograph to the barman here?'

'No. You told us to keep quiet about him – unless a lead turned up. It didn't.'

Tweed pulled an envelope from his breast pocket, extracted the matt print inside. When the barman arrived with Nield's drink he tapped the print.

'Recognize him? A friend of mine. Said he might stay here a few days. I owe him twenty pounds he lent me when I found I'd left my wallet behind. Can't trace him.'

The barman took hold of the print, studied it with half-closed eyes. He pursed his lips. 'You couldn't add a pair of tinted glasses? And a yachting cap – one of those peaked efforts with gold braid.'

Tweed took back the print, handed it to Paula. 'You're the artist.' She opened her handbag, delved inside, her hand came out holding a felt-tip pen. She frowned for a moment, then started working. She added tinted glasses and a yachting cap. Tweed was startled: it was just the type of gear Masterson would go for. He handed it again to the barman.

'Yes, that's him. Came in here half a dozen times. Thought I knew him when you showed me it first time. Now I'm sure. Had a whizz of a girl with him. Long dark hair and eyes a man could drown in. Spoke good English, but she looked foreign.'

'How long ago was this?' Tweed asked quietly.

'Seems like months ago. A lot of weeks anyway. It's coming back to me. Engaging sort of guy. I remember him asking about the colonel. Did he come in here? I said now and again. Mostly in the evenings.' He handed back the print.

'The colonel?' Tweed queried.

'Yes. Colonel Barrymore. Lives over at Quarme Manor near the Doone Valley. Gloomy old place.'

416

'Thank you,' said Tweed, and gave him a pound coin.

Paula crossed her legs. She swung one foot up and down. Studying the mud on her shoe, she asked the question.

'Does that mean we'll be staying?'

'I'll sleep on it.'

The *Oporto* mounted a huge wave, the deck tilting at a steep angle. Even in the dark Anton, clinging to the rail, could see its foaming crest. Knowing what was coming, he tightened his grip. The freighter hovered on the crest, then plunged downwards into the chasm. All around him Anton could see giant walls of water which seemed about to overwhelm the vessel. The plunge continued, as though it was heading for the bottom of the ocean. It was pitching and tossing at the same time.

The wind tore at his sodden windcheater, threatening to rip it off his body, howling in his ears. He had just returned from a perilous trip to the hold crammed with baled cork. Twice each day he checked the canvas-covered Stingers, tucked away by Gomez next to the bulkhead.

Anton had taken the precaution of tucking a thread of cotton pulled from a shirt under one of the straps. If anyone fooled around with his precious cargo he would know. The cotton thread was still in position when he made his recent check. As the *Oporto* regained its equilibrium in the trough, Anton ran up to the bridge before it started climbing another mountain.

He opened the door to the wheelhouse and the wind snatched it from his grasp. It took all his strength to pull the door shut. Behind his wheel, Gomez glanced round, his expression impassive as always despite the fury of the storm. Anton hung on to a side rail, ignoring the mate who understood no English.

'Where are we?' he asked.

'Just abreast of Ushant in France. To the east.' Gomez

made a quick gesture to his right, then grabbed at the wheel.

The freighter was heading downwards again, its bow flooded with teeming sea. Anton thanked God he was a good sailor. But the view from the bridge was terrifying. An army of tidal-size waves moved towards them from all directions.

'Are we keeping to schedule?' he asked anxiously. 'I mean with this storm.'

'We shall be heaving to off Porlock Weir two days from now. On schedule.' Gomez gave him an evil grin, showing the gold in his teeth. 'If we survive . . .'

Seton-Charles looked like anything but a professor in Greek Studies as he drove back to the Victorian bed-and-breakfast boarding house in Norwich close to midnight. He wore a boiler suit used for gardening. Before leaving his bungalow he had smeared the overalls with a mixture of oil and grease.

He had decided to leave for Norwich early and had driven off ten minutes after Tweed and Paula made their way back to Porlock Weir from Kearns' house. Now he would be in Norwich, ready to visit Camelford Removals, first thing the following day.

Well along the A303 he had seen a truck drivers' café and had pulled in alongside a giant twelve-wheeler. Inside the café he ordered a mug of steaming tea and sat down at a table close to the door. The place was full of drivers, some chatting, others slumped over their own mugs. A juke box playing pop records had added to the noise and the place was filled with blue smoke.

After drinking half the mug of tea, Seton-Charles had left. On his way out he paused to button up his suit at the neck. He eyed the row of caps hanging from wooden hooks. He took a cap with a plastic peak and walked out.

He didn't try it on until he reached a lay-by well clear of the café. It fitted well enough. And for the rimless glasses he normally wore he had substituted his spare pair of horn-rims.

After reserving a room for the night at the boarding house, he ordered a plate of fish and chips and another mug of tea at a cheap café. While he ate he studied the town map he had bought from a newsagent. He decided to take a look at Camelford Removals. He parked the Volvo round the corner from the warehouse, surprised to see lights inside. The figure of a man was silhouetted against a grimy window.

'I've come to take a look at a couple of furniture vans,' he informed a short middle-aged man who introduced himself as Mr Latimer, owner of the bankrupt business. 'They mayn't be what I'm after, but I come on spec . . .'

He slurred his vowels and spoke with a coarse accent. Latimer showed him the four vans still for sale. Seton-Charles chose the two largest, then began haggling over the price, which was expected. He bargained carefully: not offering too little but refusing to agree to Latimer's first price.

They compromised and Seton-Charles pulled a bundle of well-used fifty-pound notes from a pocket in his stained overalls. He paid the agreed deposit and Latimer held several of the notes up to the naked light bulb suspended over a roughened table.

'Done,' he had said. 'You'll collect soon? Pay the balance before you drive them away?'

'Only way to do business. Night . . .'

As he settled between grubby sheets that night Seton-Charles was satisfied. Within two days he'd have both vans hidden away in the barn at Cherry Farm. Although God knew what Jupiter wanted them for.

41

At the Grande Bretagne Newman had caught on to the game Christina was playing. She was holding back on supplying more information to keep him there as a protector against Petros and the Gavalas family. He was on the verge of threatening to leave – to force her hand – when something happened that decided him to be patient a little longer.

The killer heatwave had broken. It was a mere 80°F. September temperature. Marler arrived at 9 a.m. in Newman's room, sprawled on a sofa. He lit a cigarette.

'Well,' said Newman, 'get on with it. What's happened?'

'Patience, chum. You know I've been paying frequent visits to the Cape Sounion area. Object of the exercise to keep an eye on Florakis traipsing up the mountain at night with that transmitter.'

'You're sure it is a transmitter?'

'Absolutely. Took a pair of high-powered night glasses with me. Spent night after night watching him. It's stopped.'

'What has?'

'Do listen. Florakis has stopped making his excursions with the jolly old transmitter. I realized something last night – out of the blue, so to speak. It coincides with no moon.'

'You mean he only transmits when there's a moon? Doesn't make sense.'

'Transmits for about two weeks – when the moon's waxing and waning. Only possible explanation? It's important to the man he's transmitting to. Something else happened. Equally important. Tweed wants to interview friend Petros, I believe?'

'Yes he does. When he can get out here . . .'

'Better make it soon. That snide Dimitrios spotted me watching by the sea shore. Crept up on me. Thought I must be deaf and blind. Put down his rifle, came up behind me, grabbed hold of me. Thought he was going to throttle me, silly ass.'

'So why not tell me what happened next?' Newman asked in a resigned tone.

'Just going to. He ended up flat on the ground, arms pinned to his sides, my knee in his groin. He gave me a splendid opportunity to get him talking. He talked.'

'And how did you accomplish that feat?'

'As I said, we were by the edge. No one about. Still dark. I dragged him to the water's edge. Goes down deep there. Held his head under water three times. He thought I was going to drown him. Which I would have done if he hadn't opened his mouth.'

'Get on with it,' Newman snapped. 'What did you learn?'

'Within two weeks Petros is leaving Devil's Valley. He's owner of a cattle farm in the far north. Macedonia. Tweed would have trouble finding him there. Two weeks,' Marler repeated. 'Up to Tweed, wouldn't you say?'

'I'll call him from the Embassy. But first I'm going back for a word with Christina. You made Dimitrios talk. I'm going to do the same job on her about Anton.' A thought occurred to him as he grasped the door handle. 'Surely you've blown it. Dimitrios will go straight back to Petros and tell him what happened?'

'Doubt that. I warned him. If I heard he'd said anything the next time I saw him would be the last. For him. And he's going to keep quiet for another reason. If he told Petros he'd spilt the beans the old man would kill him.

You'll want me to guard Christina when you go to the Embassy, I take it?'

'I'll want you to do just that. Stay with her.'

'Hurry it up, then. I'm short of sleep.'

Christina had just finished drying her washed mane when Newman entered her room. She threw it back over her shoulders.

'How do I look?'

'Never mind that.' His voice was harsh. 'Marler and I will be leaving if you don't start telling me everything you know about Anton. You're on your own.'

'No!' She was appalled. 'Petros will find me. He'll kill me.'

'That's your problem. A family tiff . . .'

'Tiff! Don't you realize yet what he's like?'

'Start telling me then.' Newman perched on the edge of the bed. He folded his arms and stared out of the window, not looking at her as she slumped into a chair.

'I'm frightened. I've told you so much about them already. If Anton found out he'd be even worse than Petros. Anton is cruel.'

'I'm still waiting.' He looked at his wristwatch. 'But not for long.'

'You're a bastard . . .'

'I have diplomas to prove it. Stop stalling.'

She sat down in a large armchair, curled herself inside it like a cat, exposing her long legs. He made a point of not admiring them as she began.

'Anton is one of those people who can do anything. An expert at scuba-diving. Good with boats. Anything mechanical. He can design and build a word processor, a video recorder, a transceiver. And repair them if they break down. He's experienced with hydraulics. He got an estimate for a lift to be installed in his warehouse at Piraeus, thought it too much – so he built the damned thing himself. He's a good horse rider, but I told you that . . .' Once started, she didn't stop. 'He's an expert on handguns and rifles. A crack shot with both. Won some kind of trophy once at Bisley in England. For God's sake, isn't that enough? Oh, and he's a hell-raiser with the women. I think I told you that before.'

'A bit of an all-rounder,' Newman mused.

'He's also good at carpentry. Very good.'

'Carpentry?'

'Building anything out of wood. He made all the furniture for his room at the farm in Devil's Valley. That's the only decently furnished room. The rest is a slum.'

'Why didn't you tell me this before? People must know his many talents.'

'No, not many. He's very secretive. He likes his image of playboy. It amuses him to fool people. I loathe him – and I've never understood him. One more thing, he can fly any kind of light aircraft. Cessnas, Pipers, etc. He belonged to a flying club, then resigned once he'd mastered flying. Said he was bored with it. I think he craves excitement, new worlds to conquer. And he's very ambitious – to become one of the most important men in Greece. I really think I've given you the lot.' She watched him through her eyelashes. 'Do I still get protection?'

'You do. For as long as we can manage it. I have to go out for a short time. Marler will stay with you.'

'He'd better keep his distance,' she said viciously and picked up a hairbrush, 'or I'll crack his skull with this.'

'Argue it out with him while I'm gone.' Newman grinned. 'All I think he wants is kip – sleep. Alone . . .'

Tweed put down his office phone after asking Newman to call him daily. He sat for a few minutes, thinking. Paula and Monica were careful to keep quiet while they worked.

'Paula,' he announced, 'we have to fly to Greece – and soon. Inside the next couple of weeks. Monica, book a couple of first-class return tickets via Zurich. Open date. Bob has just told me Petros is leaving Devil's Valley for some other farm he has up in Macedonia. No one knows the territory up there. Marler and Newman do know Devil's Valley. I need to interrogate the old villain. He's crazed with a lust for vengeance. I want to find out whether he had Masterson killed.'

'How will you go about it?' Paula asked.

'I shall go into Devil's Valley with someone who speaks Greek as an interpreter. I'll grill him at his farm – the only way to get at him. He never comes to Athens – or rarely – so Newman said.'

'That could be dangerous,' Paula protested. 'He sounds mad as a hatter. And Newman told us earlier the area is crawling with armed shepherds.'

'We'll cross that bridge when we come to it.'

'I don't like it,' Paula insisted.

'No one asked you to.' He regretted the words as soon as he had spoken. 'I'm sorry, that was rude. I'm confused about this whole business. There seems no rhyme or reason to it. Unless the whole thing revolves round Petros.'

'You could ask Peter Sarris for help,' Paula suggested.

Tweed shook his head. 'No police until we know what we're getting into. We'll rely on our own resources.' He looked at Monica who had just made the phone call. 'All fixed up?'

'Two open date return tickets via Zurich booked.'

'Is this why we returned here so quickly from Porlock Weir?' enquired Paula.

'Yes. I felt I was getting out of touch with the position in Greece. Butler and Nield can keep a watch on any developments on Exmoor. You have your bag packed, Paula? Good. I may decide to leave suddenly for Athens.'

'Why go via Zurich?' Monica asked. 'Instead of flying direct?'

'I want to consult Arthur Beck. We'll call him before we leave. He often knows what's going on. And there are direct flights to Athens from Zurich.' He paused. 'So there are also flights direct from Athens to Zurich.'

'Oh Lord!' Monica groaned. 'He's being enigmatic again.'

Midnight. The storm had abated when the *Oporto* was rounding the tip of Cornwall. The sea now was just choppy as the vessel hove to west of Porlock Weir. On deck on the starboard side Anton held the flashlight and directed the coded signal towards the distant shore. Then he waited.

Gomez stood alongside him close to the gangway which had been lowered over the side. At the foot of the steps waves lapped over the metal platform. The canvas-wrapped Stingers, recovered from the hold, lay at Anton's feet. He wore a waterproof windcheater, thick seaman's trousers tucked inside rubber boots and over this gear a dark green oilskin. His suitcase was protected with another oilskin lashed round it with rope.

'You will need luck to make contact a second time,' Gomez commented.

'The crew are all below decks?' enquired Anton.

'As arranged – except for a lookout who can be trusted.' In the dark he smiled. 'He has been paid to be trusted . . . Look. Over there.'

Anton had already seen the light flashing its return signal from the shore. He checked the number of flashes, then sent a brief final signal, acknowledging, and rammed the flashlight inside a pocket of the oilskin.

'Now we have to wait. But not for long, I suspect . . .'

He was right. As the freighter rocked slowly under the

surge of the sea the sound of an engine approaching reached his acute hearing. The night was moonless but soon both could see the white wake of the small boat. Anton reached down and hauled up with both hands the heavy weight of the canvas bundle. Gomez picked up the suitcase with one hand; with the other he raised a pair of night glasses to his eyes, leaning against the rail as he scanned the shoreline. They were two miles out. To the east he picked out the lights of Porlock Weir. He lowered the glasses.

'Be very careful when you go down the gangway. The steps will be slippery. You are carrying a heavy weight.'

'I'll be all right. And when I've left you're turning round and sailing out to sea, ready to come back tomorrow?'

'Do not worry. No one will know we arrived off England earlier.'

The small grey-coloured motorboat, powered by an outboard at its stern, was close. Gomez could make out the figure of the solitary man aboard. As before, he wore a Balaclava helmet under a dark green oilskin. He cut the power, the boat glided forward, bumped against the platform. Balaclava hurled up a mooring rope. Gomez caught it with his free hand, the glasses looped round his neck, made the rope fast to the rail.

Anton stood on the top platform, slowly went down, step by step. He rested the bundle on the rails on either side, letting them take the weight, sliding it down. The moored boat ground up against the *Oporto*'s hull, made a grating sound. Anton was half-way down when the sea lifted the freighter, then dropped it. Anton lost his grip, the bundle tumbled down the remaining steps, landed on the lower platform. He swore in Greek, grabbing the rails to recover his balance.

Balaclava leant forward, took hold of the cargo, heaved it up and lowered it quickly inside the boat. Anton stepped off the platform and joined him. Gomez called down, dropped the mooring rope he had untied and Balaclava hauled it in, dripping, looped round the handle of Anton's suitcase.

Anton sat down as his companion started up the outboard, grabbed the tiller and guided the boat away from the *Oporto*. He was just in time. A large wave lifted the boat, would have hurled it against the freighter, but Balaclava had steered the boat round. He headed for the distant shore.

The motorboat was coming in close to the rock-strewn coast. Behind it cliffs loomed, hiding them from the mainland. Anton was careful not to stare at the eyes which looked out through the slit in the Balaclava helmet.

He had no idea of the identity of his companion. When he had landed on his previous trip to Exmoor the same man had met him, wearing the same gear. Because of the loose flapping oilskin he wore it was impossible for Anton to guess Balaclava's height, build or age. Only the voice was distinctive. Upper-crust, clipped. On the rare occasions when he spoke.

As they approached the shore, the boat pitching and tossing, the engine was cut out. Balaclava crouched over the tiller, peering ahead, steering the craft towards a slope. There was a grinding sound as the keel rode up over rocks and pebbles, stopped.

'Take the weapons, put them in the vehicle.'

Anton heaved up the bundle, stepped out of the boat and staggered to the canvas-covered four-wheel-drive vehicle parked close to the shoreline. He used his shoulder to ease up the flap at the rear, hoisted the bundle higher, lowered it inside on top of a pile of coiled ropes. The wind whipped at his oilskin, blew it round his legs as he let the flap drop and went back for his case.

Balaclava had taken an axe attached to the side and began hammering at the deck. The axe was heavy, its blade honed like a razor. As he worked chips of wood flew up and he protected his eyes by holding one arm across them. He paused as Anton lifted out his case, turned to him.

'The sea goes down a hundred feet here. We have to lose this boat. Don't stand there watching me – keep an eye out along the shore.'

The axe began to sweep down again in thudding arcs. Inside a few minutes the boat was holed. Balaclava went on working, enlarging the gaping cavity. He was only satisfied when the hole was a foot wide, then he hurled the axe into the waves and returned to the vehicle. Climbing into the rear, he shifted the Stingers and covered them with the mass of rope. Jumping back on to the shore he gestured Anton to join him.

'We want to heave the boat over the edge. Give me a hand . . .'

They stood near the bow on either side and pushed with all their strength. The boat slid slowly backwards, the outboard poised over the edge. They straightened up, stretching their strained arms, took hold of the boat again. One more prolonged heave and the boat was floating. It filled rapidly with water, drifting just offshore. Then it went down stern first. The bow hovered above the surface, disappeared.

Balaclava strode towards the vehicle, climbed in behind the wheel and Anton sat beside him. They drove off without lights, heading away from the sea, bumping and jostling over the rough terrain.

The driver switched on his lights as they reached the track past the cottages. He never gave a glance at the darkened dwelling where Mrs Larcombe had talked with Tweed. He drove on along the road at higher speed, passing The Anchor Hotel, continuing towards Porlock.

Reaching the toll road, he swung the vehicle up the steep

curving slope. At the top he turned right again along the coast road. Beyond Culbone he turned left off the main road down on to the winding country lane which eventually led to the Doone Valley. For the first time he broke his long silence.

'Here is the key to the small house where you spend the night. It is unoccupied. And here is a pencil flashlight so you can find your way round it. The electricity is cut off. You will find canned meat, a tin opener, a loaf of bread, butter, knife, two bottles of mineral water inside a brown paper parcel in a downstairs room. Also a sleeping bag. The place is unfurnished. We'll park the vehicle in a garage alongside. But take the weapons into the house. Sleep with them by your side. And here is a sheathed knife for protection – to be used only in an emergency.'

Anton took the weapon. 'This is a commando knife,' he commented. 'I brought a couple with me . . .'

'Listen!' Balaclava was concentrating on negotiating the road which dropped as it twisted between high hedges. 'Keep that knife. Now, in the morning you take the weapons to Cherry Farm. You remember how to get there from the drive we took last time?'

'Yes. It's near Liphook in Hampshire.'

Balaclava stopped the vehicle at a bend where he could see in both directions, pulled an ordnance survey map from the door's pocket. 'Use the flashlight and show me the location of Cherry Farm. Your route is marked part of the way in pen – driving along side roads. That way you should avoid all police patrol cars.'

Anton unfolded the map, studied it with the aid of the light. He pointed to an area. 'The track to it turns off about here.'

'Good. Keep the map. Burn it when you get there. And you've plenty to keep you occupied when you do get there. You will find you have company. You give him the password – Sandpiper.'

'What does he say in return?' Anton asked.

'Nothing.' Balaclava chuckled, a hard cynical sound. 'You'll recognize him. Tomorrow morning you drive this contraption to Taunton.' He hauled a slim folder from the same pocket. 'I've marked on this with a light pencil cross the car park where you leave this vehicle about ten in the morning. You park at the very back where there's a thick hedge. Hide the cargo under that hedge while you're away hiring a car from Barton's – they are marked with a pencilled circle. And here is a driving licence in the name of Partridge for hiring the car. Drive it to the car park. Collect the cargo. Then head for Cherry Farm. You leave this vehicle in the car park and you must be on your way by eleven o'clock. I will have the vehicle collected. Understood.'

'Let me check this.' Anton was studying the street plan of Taunton with the aid of the flashlight. He found the cross and the circle. 'All clear. But why can't I drive straight on to Cherry Farm now? Or am I dropping you somewhere?'

'Of course not. I have transport waiting not far from the house where you spend the night. And travelling at night is dangerous. You could be stopped and checked by a patrol car. You should have thought of that yourself.'

'You are right,' Anton agreed quickly. There was something in Balaclava's manner, in his contemptuous tone, which frightened him.

'Needless to say, you burn the Taunton map soon after you have left Taunton behind. Now listen carefully. I said earlier you will have plenty to occupy you at Cherry Farm. Something that will test your skills as a carpenter and hydraulics expert. So *listen*. There are two furniture vans at the farm. This is what you have to do . . .'

By early afternoon the following day Anton was driving his hired Austin Metro close to Liphook in Hampshire.

The Stingers and missiles were in the boot, concealed under a load of groceries he had bought in Glastonbury.

On both sides of the country road the flat fields stretched away beyond low hedges. The sun was shining and he hadn't passed another vehicle for several miles. He drove round a bend and slowed his speed, recognizing he was very close. Anton had the most retentive memory for routes and geography. Across the road were freshly fallen leaves. Autumn was coming. Soon September would become October.

He stopped the car alongside a closed gate with a gravel track beyond. He sat listening for several minutes, listening for the sound of the distant approach of any more traffic. Nothing. He got out, opened the gate which carried the legend *Cherry Farm* in white paint. Driving up the track a few yards, he stopped the car again, got out and went back to close the gate. Attention to detail.

The field alongside the track was spongy grass. As he drove further he passed large lakes, the product of rain which had fallen three days earlier. Poor agricultural land. He followed the curve of the track and Cherry Farm came into view.

A long low two-storey building made of brick with a tiled roof, it had two squat chimney stacks and a large barn to the right of the farmhouse. The place had a deserted look and he drove slowly, his eyes scanning the whole area in search of a sign of life.

Beyond the large barn stood two long sheds with corrugated iron roofs. The doors to both were closed. As he drove closer he saw the farm had an abandoned look. Undergrowth was smothering the tiny garden in front. Ivy creeper sprawled up the brickwork like a giant spider, its tentacles crawling over the closed shutters.

Had something gone wrong? Where was the man he was supposed to meet? He drove on round the back of the farmhouse, parked the car in a muddy yard, switched off

431

the engine and listened again. There is no silence more eèrie than that of a deserted countryside.

Anton remained behind the wheel, checked the knife in the sheath attached to his belt. No cattle, no sheep. No animals of any kind. More lakes standing in the soggy field behind the farm. No birds chattered or wheeled in the clear blue sky. Then the back door opened. Seton-Charles came out to meet him. Anton hid his astonishment.

'Sandpiper,' he said.

'You have the weapons? Good. We'll get them to their hiding-place inside the house. Then drive your car and park it inside the first shed beyond the barn. There are doors at this end . . '

Seton-Charles stood in the kitchen, watching Anton through his rimless glasses as the Greek ate ham sand-wiches, drank mineral water. Seated at the table, Anton ignored the Professor. There was a distinct sense of unease between the two men. It had been different in Athens when Seton-Charles had lectured him at the university. Anton finished his meal, decided to establish his authority from the beginning.

'I'm in charge here. You know that?'

'So I was informed.' Seton-Charles' tone expressed no enthusiasm for the arrangement. He leaned against the dresser, folded his arms. 'What role are you playing here?'

'You leave this farm from time to time?' Anton asked cautiously.

'Not without your permission. I prepare the meals from now on. I give you any help you may need with your work. What work?'

'Communications,' Anton persisted. 'How do we keep in touch with Jupiter?'

'We don't. There is a phone in the hall. He calls us. We

432

make no calls, have no contact with the outside world. You buy fresh food supplies in Liphook when we need them.'

'And might anyone come poking around here?'

'No. Haven't you seen the state of the farm? The land is useless, waterlogged half the time. The next farm is miles away. Now, if you don't mind, I'd like some idea on what I'm supposed to help you with. The two furniture vans are hidden inside the huge barn, one behind the other.'

Satisfied with the security, Anton dabbed at his mouth with a silk handkerchief. He twisted round in his chair to stare hard at the Professor.

'You saw the short planks of wood still in the boot? I bought them at a timberyard on the way. You've seen the two boxes on the floor here?'

'Yes.' Seton-Charles stared down at the containers, made of heavy wood and like tool boxes. The lids were open. Inside one was a collection of wires, steel slides and other electrical-type equipment. The second box looked like a carpenter's and was crammed with planes, saws, screwdrivers and other tools. 'What are you up to?' he asked.

'A complex operation. Each of those furniture vans has to be fitted with a large sliding panel in the roof – electrically operated. The hydraulics will be difficult. And inside each van I'll be building a platform with steps – the platform top to be about three feet below the roof, fitted with a chair I'll clamp to the platform.' Anton grinned. 'Guess what all that is for?'

'I'm not in the guessing game,' Seton-Charles said coldly.

'We're in the business of building two mobile rocket launchers.'

PART THREE

The Greek Key

42

'We're coming in to land,' said Paula and gripped Tweed's arm. 'This is the bit I never like.'

'Look at the view over there out of the starboard windows,' he suggested and squeezed her hand.

They were aboard Swissair flight 801, approaching Zurich's airport, Kloten. The machine was banking and Paula saw framed in a window the magnificent sweep of the Bernese Oberland range, its peaks snow-capped. She sucked in her breath as she watched the mountain summits silhouetted against a backdrop of cloudless azure sky.

Tweed had taken one of his snap decisions. They had left London Airport at 9.30 a.m. and were due to arrive at 12.05 p.m. Before leaving Tweed had phoned Federal police chief Arthur Beck, an old friend. Beck was meeting them at Kloten. What worried Tweed was the closeness of their connection with the Swissair flight taking them on to Athens.

Flight 302, bound for Athens, departed from Kloten at 12.30 p.m. It gave them no time at all to check in on the fresh flight and Tweed needed time to consult with Beck. As the plane descended he laid his hand over Paula's and she turned and smiled.

'I'm OK now. Just a brief fit of nerves. Do you think Monica has got through to Newman, warning him we're coming?'

'It all depends on how early Newman makes *his* daily call to her. At least we know where to find him. The Grande Bretagne . . .'

Paula hardly realized the plane had landed as it skimmed along the runway. Beck was waiting for them at Passport Control. He wore civilian clothes and a Tyrolean hat with a little feather in the hat band, dressed like a man on holiday. The grey eyes under the thick brows gleamed as he spotted Paula. He took her arm.

'Welcome to Zurich, Paula.' He kissed her on the cheek. 'We bypass all the checks.' He looked over his shoulder as he led her to a side door which a guard unlocked. 'You'd better come too, Tweed. We have time to talk.'

Tweed smiled to himself. Beck had developed a soft spot for Paula when they'd met previously in Geneva. And he had organized their arrival so no one would notice them. He followed Paula along a corridor and into a starkly furnished room with maps on the walls.

'Thank you,' said Paula as Beck pulled out a chair for her from under a table. 'But what about our cases? Shouldn't I go to the carousel?'

'All taken care of, my dear. I phoned Jim Corcoran, security boss at London Airport. When you checked in a special small red label was attached to your luggage and Tweed's. Two of my men are at the carousel now, collecting your things.'

'Am I permitted to join you?' Tweed enquired mischievously.

'As a special favour, my friend. This is Kloten security chief's office I have borrowed. As you see, there is coffee and sandwiches. You would like some, Paula? Good.'

On the table was an electric warmer with a transparent flask of coffee perched on it. Sandwiches wrapped in cling-film. A telephone with a red button. Tweed sat down and stared at the instrument as Beck spoke while he poured coffee.

'Monica called you from London, spoke to the security chief and left a message. Can you call her urgently?'

Tweed looked at a clock attached to the wall with a red

438

second hand sweeping the dial. 'We're going to miss our flight we're booked on for Athens. It leaves at 12.30 as I told you.'

'So . . .' Beck waved a hand. 'It has been delayed. A bomb hoax. All passengers have to identify their luggage laid out on the tarmac before they board. That takes time.' He smiled. 'One of the advantages of being Chief of Police.' He sat next to Paula as he addressed Tweed. 'So, make your call, then we can talk.'

I should have guessed he'd tie it all up for us, Tweed thought. He reached for the phone, pressed the scrambler button, dialled Park Crescent. Beck and Paula talked in whispers while Tweed was calling London. She liked the Swiss: he had a wicked sense of humour. She put her hand over her mouth to suppress laughter and then noticed Tweed's expression as he replaced the receiver.

'Is something wrong?'

'Later,' he replied and looked at Beck. 'Greece. Have you heard anything unusual on the grapevine?'

'No. Unless this comes under the heading of unusual . . .' For five minutes he recounted his two conversations with Kalos. He recalled how he had followed his quarry, kept an eye on him while he had spent a night at the Schweizerhof and then boarded a plane for Lisbon the following day.

'Lisbon?' Tweed's expression was grim. 'Are you sure, Arthur?'

'Of course I'm sure. I followed him myself to the airport. Later I checked with the pilot that he was on board. He was.'

'Sorry. That was a silly question. How long ago?'

'Ten days from today.'

'Hell's teeth.' Tweed stood up, began pacing the room. 'And I was congratulating myself that he was safely back in Athens. I'm getting this all wrong.' He looked at Paula. 'I said the solution lay in Greece, not Exmoor. Maybe it's the other way round.'

'Do we go on?' Paula asked.

'Yes. And we'd better hurry.'

'Might be as well,' Beck agreed. 'The baggage check should just about be over. You'll have to identify your own stuff. It will be all that's left on the tarmac . . .'

He hugged Paula, shook hands with Tweed. 'Anything more I can do to help – you give me a call.'

'You've helped a lot already,' Tweed assured him and they followed the Swiss to the aircraft.

They had eaten lunch. The plane was thirty thousand feet up and well south over the Adriatic Sea before Paula asked the question.

'You had bad news when you talked with Monica?'

'It's getting worse. Like the Klein problem we faced last year, the body count is rising. Butler called Monica. You remember that nice sharp old lady, Mrs Larcombe, we called on at Porlock Weir? This morning a neighbour noticed she hadn't taken her milk in. She started worrying, called the police. They found the front door unlocked and Mrs Larcombe battered to death.'

'Oh, that's awful. She was so bright for her age. Bright for any age. What do they think happened?'

'The *police* think some drunken youths called, pushed open the door when she reacted to the ringing of the bell, attacked her and walked off with fifty pounds she always kept in ready cash under her mattress. They found two empty beer cans in the front garden. No fingerprints.'

'I did catch your emphasis on "police". What do you think?'

'I'm convinced it was staged. Drunken youths don't remember to wipe beer cans clean of fingerprints. Something bothered me about what she said to us and I couldn't recall it afterwards. Now I can.'

'What was it?'

'When that four-wheel-drive vehicle stopped outside her house at midnight she opened the front window. She said that window *creaked*. My guess is the driver heard that creak. And no one believed her when she said she saw flashing lights out at sea and up the coast. She saw them all right.'

'I still don't follow,' Paula commented.

'That was the first run – bringing something, or someone – landed on the coast. There must have been a second run last night, an important one. They couldn't risk her seeing them – so they called on her, she opened the door, and that was it. The fact that she opened the door is significant.'

'Someone she knew?'

'I think so. She was a shrewd careful woman. And I noticed she had one of those spyglass things in her front door. She could see who was there before she opened it. Yes, someone she knew – or knew of. A respected citizen.'

'What a brutal thing to do.' Paula shivered. 'To kill an old lady like that just on the off-chance she looked out of her window at the wrong moment.'

'But we are dealing with a ruthless killer. Look at the score – Sam Partridge, Jill Kearns and now Mrs Larcombe. The stakes must be very high.'

He peered out of the window. The air was crystal clear, without a cloud. He looked down on the intense blue of the Adriatic. A tiny blur of white on the blue located the wake of a ship moving south: the ship was invisible.

'When we get to Athens,' he went on, 'someone must go to the Embassy to call Monica. I want her to contact Roberts of Lloyd's of London, get him to check the shipping register.'

'Why?'

'Remember what Beck told us about Anton. He took a flight from Zurich to Lisbon. Roberts can check the

441

movements of any vessel sailing from Lisbon about ten days ago – a vessel bound for Watchet on the Somerset coast. The killing of Mrs Larcombe backs up a vague theory I'd developed – that the way Anton slipped in without any record was that he came ashore from some vessel during the night. Hence those flashing lights Mrs Larcombe really did see.' He grunted. 'And now he may be back on Exmoor again. I don't like that at all. Monica must warn Butler.'

'And you think Jill was killed because she knew too much?'

'I have another idea about that. She may have been run down simply to divert our attention away from Exmoor to London.'

'That would be too horrible,' Paula protested.

'I said we're up against a ruthless killer.' He looked round the interior of the aircraft. They were travelling first-class and the section was three-quarters empty, which enabled them to talk freely. He peered out of the window again, checked his watch, settled himself back in his seat. 'Less than one hour to Athens. I have the feeling we're going to stir up a hornet's nest.'

The heat hit Tweed like a hammer as he emerged from the aircraft on to the mobile staircase. He walked down the steps and, with Paula by his side, made for the main building.

'God!' said Paula. 'It's baking and you don't like the heat.'

'So it's a good job you reminded me to wear my safari jacket and tropical drill trousers. Now, let's get the show on the road . . .'

Newman was waiting for them in the reception hall. He grinned as he came forward, shook hands with Tweed, hugged Paula, took her case.

'I phoned Monica early and she told me your flight details. I have a car outside. Straight to the Grande Bretagne? Marler is there, looking after Christina.'

'Straight to the Grande Bretagne,' Tweed replied. 'Sarris must not know I'm in town. We have to organize an expedition into Devil's Valley. I must see Petros, cross-examine him.'

'That will have to be planned carefully,' Newman remarked as he sat behind the wheel and drove off after storing their cases in the boot. He sensed tension in Tweed, that he was in one hell of a hurry.

Forty minutes later they were sitting in the room Newman had booked for Tweed. Newman relayed to him all the details about Anton he'd extracted from Christina. As he listened, sipping mineral water in his shirt-sleeves, Tweed's expression became grimmer.

'A man of many talents,' he commented as Newman concluded his report. 'And now I'm sure he's returned to England.' He told Newman the news Beck and Monica had given him in Zurich. 'I don't like the sound of any of this. But when can we get down to Devil's Valley? Tomorrow?'

'That's pushing it. You'll need protection – and an interpreter. Petros doesn't speak English, you don't speak Greek. I think we have just the man. Nick the Greek, our driver. I've kept him on ice. He's holed up at the Astir Palace just across the square. He's even protested about the extra fee I pay him, saying he's doing nothing for it. Do you want to talk with Christina?'

'Yes.' He looked at Paula.

She shook her head, smiled impishly. 'Better you see her on your own. I'll cramp your style. I bet you have her eating out of your hand.'

'I doubt that.' Tweed finished off his second glass of mineral water. 'But one-to-one conversations normally get off the ground better.'

'Especially when you're with an attractive girl,' Paula went on.

'Oh, do shut up.' Tweed put on his jacket. 'Just going to the bathroom. Back in a minute . . .'

Paula waited until he reached the door, then called out. 'Don't forget to comb your hair!' Tweed gave her a glare and vanished.

'You do twist his tail,' Newman commented.

She became serious. 'I'm trying to relax him. I'm really worried about him. He's got the bit between his teeth over this business. He's become obsessed.'

'Can you explain that quickly? I'll be taking him along soon to Christina.'

'It started with Masterson's death. You can't kill one of Tweed's sector chiefs and expect him to shrug it off like Howard might. Then Jill Kearns – and he took a fancy to her – was murdered in London. Before that his old friend Sam Partridge was killed on Exmoor. And now an old lady in her seventies, a Mrs Larcombe, he interviewed has been battered to death at Porlock Weir. That was the last straw, I suspect. All the killings could be linked. If he decides Petros is in some way responsible I don't know what he'll do. Which is why I'm petrified about this Devil's Valley visit. Tweed has lost his sense of detachment.'

'Thanks for telling me. I'll bear it in mind. Now I must call someone.'

Newman went to the phone, dialled a number, perched on the edge of the bed. 'That you, Nick? Can you get over here for a talk? In about five minutes? Good. My room. See you . . .'

Tweed came out of the bathroom as he put down the phone. 'We'll be having a conference about the trip to Devil's Valley while you talk with Christina,' he told Tweed. 'Nick, Marler and myself.'

'The sooner the better. I'm ready for Christina. What about you, Paula? Going to peek at the shops?'

444

'She'll be joining us,' Newman said firmly. He seemed to have taken command of the situation, noted Paula. Noted it with relief.

Newman escorted Tweed to another room on the same floor. When he rapped on the door in a certain sequence it was opened by Marler. He gazed at Tweed, then at Newman.

'You might have told me he was coming. About time,' he continued, looking at Tweed. 'Glad to have you on board. We need to take some action.'

'You'll get all you can handle soon,' Newman promised him. 'Be a good chap, push off to my room. Here's the key. Tweed wants to talk with Christina.'

As Marler left he walked into the room, followed by Tweed, and introduced him to Christina. 'My Editor-in-Chief . . .'

Christina was sitting on a sofa, her back propped against one end, her long legs stretched out. She wore a low-cut emerald green dress, strapless, and backless to the lower part of her spine. She put down the book she was reading and stared at Tweed with her large eyes as Newman left the room, assessing him. Then she swung her legs off the sofa and sat with them crossed, one bare arm rested along the top of the sofa.

'Do sit down. Pull up a chair close to me. You look like a man who can take care of himself.'

'I've survived so far.' Tweed moved a chair, sat down so their knees were almost touching. She was a woman who liked close combat, who liked to touch a man if he passed inspection. Tweed had a feeling he'd done just that. And he wanted her to talk. She asked him if he'd like a drink. He said mineral water would be fine. She reached out to a table standing at the end of the sofa, poured him a glass from a collection of bottles, then she helped herself to a glass of white wine. She raised her glass.

'Here's to us.'

'To us . . .'

'And you're not an editor.' She peered at him over the rim and sipped some wine. 'You have the eyes of a policeman. They're nice eyes.'

'I was once a policeman.' He had decided frankness – up to a point – was his best tactic with this shrewd and glamorous creature. 'What can you tell me about the Greek Key? I need your help. Very badly. A lot of people have already died here and in England. I suspect more may die unless I find out what is going on.' He took off his glasses, laid them on the table. 'I need all the help I can get.'

'Will Newman or Marler be coming back?' She watched him through half-closed eyes.

'Not unless I summon them. I wasn't thinking of doing so.'

He had trouble keeping his eyes off her beautifully moulded shoulders. The dress fitted her snugly; her well-rounded breasts projected against the cloth. She leaned forward and kissed him full on the mouth.

'That was for starters, Tweed.'

'The Greek Key?'

'A group of the most dangerous men in Greece. Shadow men who operate in the dark. The police can't find them. They live secret lives. Does that sound melodramatic?'

'Yes. But it sounds just what I'm looking for. Tell me more.'

'So you don't really need your glasses to see?'

'Only long distance. When I'm driving. Times like that. Then I forget I'm wearing them. Tell me more,' he repeated.

'I've told you too much already. You want to get me killed?'

'No. I'd go a long way to prevent that. Is Anton a member?'

She blinked, lowered her eyes. He could have sworn the suggestion came to her as a great shock. That she was

446

thinking back over incidents she had observed – trying to link them up with his question.

'I never thought of that.' She opened her full red lips and ran the tip of her tongue along her lower lip. 'I can trust you?'

'You must decide that for yourself.'

'When my mother sent me to the university – she's dead, Petros killed her with overwork on the farm – there was an English professor, Guy Seton-Charles.'

'What about him?' Tweed asked in the same quiet tone.

'There were rumours. He came to lecture from England each year. Behind his back they called him The Recruiter.'

'Who were "they"?' His voice was very soft now, careful not to disturb her mood.

'You will protect me?' She leaned close again and her eyes were enormous. She slowly removed her earclips, placed them on the table.

'Yes,' he said. 'Providing you do exactly what I tell you when the time comes.'

'You're a nice man. Some of the students who attended the Seton-Charles lectures stopped going to them.'

'Who was he recruiting for?'

'The Greek Key.' Her smooth-skinned face was almost touching his and he caught a waft of perfume. He told himself to move back but he was frightened of breaking the spell. 'I asked what it was and they wouldn't tell me. You asked me if Anton was a member. He attended the lectures and finished the course. After that he was a changed man.'

'Changed in what way?'

'He used to lay women like rows of beans. He still kept his playboy image outwardly – but he seemed to have become colder, more purposeful – dedicated. That's it. *Dedicated.*'

'Dedicated to what?'

'I don't know. Really, I don't, Tweed. As though he'd found some mission in life. Almost like a religious conversion. But he's an agnostic. That's all I can say.'

Tweed eased his chair away. He stood up. Christina also stood up and walked towards him. He had a curious gleam in his eyes. He saw his glasses still on the table, picked them up. Before he could put them on she grasped him.

'Let's do it. Now.'

He sighed, shook his head. 'Christina, I said I would protect you. I will. But I can't if we get involved with each other. I must go. Pack your things ready for a quick departure. All except your night things.'

'I have to say thank you.'

She pressed herself against him, kissed him again.

'You'll be leaving tomorrow,' he told her.

'Unless Dimitrios or Constantine or Anton reach me tonight.'

'Which do you fear most?'

'Anton. Of course . . .'

'He is no longer in Greece. And you will continue to be with someone until you leave. It may be a woman.'

'What use will she be? In an emergency?'

'More deadly than a man. I must go. Lock the door and only open it for the special knock. You do have confidence in me?'

'Completely.' She ran her hands through her hair. 'We will meet again?'

'If possible. It depends on how things develop . . .'

He waited outside the closed door until he heard her lock it. His hands were wet with perspiration. And not from the heat.

Four people sat round a table in Newman's room. Newman himself, Nick the Greek, Paula and Marler. Two litre bottles of mineral water stood on the table with four

448

glasses. The bottles were almost empty. Tweed was introduced to Nick who clasped his hand in a firm grip and gazed straight at him. Tweed liked what he saw.

'Bob,' he said, 'take Paula along to Christina and introduce her. I want you to stay with her, Paula. Only open the door to the special knock Bob will demonstrate.'

Paula looked amused as she stood up and smoothed down her skirt. She stood close and whispered. 'Better go into the bathroom and comb your hair again. Clean up your mouth at the same time.'

Newman had reached the door with Paula when Tweed stopped them. 'Wait a moment.' He looked at Nick. 'I understand you can find weapons. We'll all be away when we go to Devil's Valley. Paula should have some protection. A small handgun. Can you obtain one for her?'

Nick, still seated, rolled up his left trouser leg and revealed the holster strapped to it. He pulled out a small gun, a .32 Browning automatic. He showed it to Paula.

'Do you know this gun?'

'Yes. It's a Browning. I've practised with it. That would do nicely.'

'And spare mags.' Nick handed her the gun and hauled the mags out of his pocket.

Paula dropped the mags into her handbag. She examined the Browning, released the magazine from the butt, made sure there was no bullet up the spout, all the time holding the weapon pointed at the wall. Nick watched with approval as she rammed the mag home again, dropped the weapon inside her handbag.

'You know the gun,' he said.

Tweed laid a hand on her shoulder. 'Only to be used in extreme emergency – if Christina's or your own life is in danger. You have no permit to use that in Greece. But if push comes to shove I'll square it with Peter Sarris. Take care.'

'And *you* take care,' she said vehemently. 'This whole secret expedition to Devil's Valley is madness . . .'

'Now go along with Bob and make friends with Christina.'

When they had gone he excused himself. Inside the bathroom he checked his appearance in the mirror. He should have done that before he'd left Christina. His hair was mussed up; traces of lipstick showed on his mouth. Christina had deliberately let him go like that – knowing there was another woman with him. Just to show Paula. Women! Thank God he'd kept control of himself.

He had a wash, used a tissue to clean off the lipstick. When he had combed his hair he went back into the bedroom.

'What's the plan?' he asked, sitting down at the table.

'She's quite a girl, Christina,' Marler remarked cynically.

'Don't you start.' Tweed jabbed his index finger at Marler. 'I said what's the plan?'

'Crack of dawn tomorrow we start out,' Marler began in a languid tone. 'We drive to the entrance near Cape Sounion. You go in on foot with Nick. He speaks Greek, he's the interpreter, and he knows the way. And we've devised back-up . . .'

Marler explained the details and Tweed listened in silence. He nodded when Marler had finished. 'You've been out here a while. You know what you're doing. At least, I hope so. I approve the plan.'

'It will be tricky – the timing,' Nick interjected. 'Dangerous, too.' He was looking at Tweed. 'What type of gun would you like? I can get most . . .'

'I never carry a gun.'

Tweed stood up. 'I have to attend to something now.' Newman came back into the room, using his key to unlock the door. 'I'm off to the Embassy,' Tweed told him. 'I have to talk to Monica, get her to contact Roberts at

450

Lloyd's. And warn Butler Anton is probably back on his patch.'

'I'll come with you,' said Nick. 'We pass the Astir Palace on the way to the Embassy. I can pick up another Browning from under my car in the garage.'

'I can go alone. I know the way. I studied a street plan of Athens before I left London. No one will recognize me.'

'I'm coming with you,' Nick persisted. 'Petros could have men watching this hotel. They would see you arrive with Newman and make the connection.'

'You're right. Thank you.'

Tweed cursed himself inwardly for not thinking of that. Maybe the heat was getting to him. They were crossing the road to the Astir Palace when Nick made the remark.

'It will be touch and go whether we survive in Devil's Valley.'

43

Dawn was breaking over the Temple of Poseidon when the two cars pulled off the coast road close to the skeletal hotel building site. Nick drove the Mercedes with Tweed beside him. Behind them Newman drove a hired Peugeot with Marler as his passenger.

'I'll drive,' he'd told Marler when they started from Athens in the dark. 'We want to get there in one piece.'

'I was a racing driver once,' Marler informed him.

'I know. You must have been a menace to the other contestants. I don't want to end up in the sea . . .'

Tweed stepped out of the Mercedes and stretched. He was wearing a pair of mountaineer boots purchased in

Kolonaki. He'd worn them for the rest of the previous day to break them in.

Nick lifted up the travelling rug on the rear seat, took hold of the twin-barrelled shotgun. He had a fresh Browning strapped to his leg, a .38 Smith & Wesson in a hip holster under his loose jacket.

'A walking armoury,' Tweed had joked.

'We'll need it,' Nick had replied without a smile.

While Nick was collecting the weapon, locking the car, Tweed gazed at the fantastic colours of sky and sea. A spectrum of rose pink, cobalt and sapphire sea. An incredible sight you wouldn't find anywhere else in the world.

'Ready?' asked Nick.

'On a job like this the thing is get moving. No palaver.'

Nick led the way behind the complex and they plunged into the wilderness of limestone bluffs looming above donkey trails which twisted and climbed. There was no sound once they'd left behind the screech of the gulls over the sea which soon vanished from view. Nick placed his feet carefully, treading wherever possible on tufts of grass to deaden the sound of his footfalls. Behind him Tweed followed suit, watching for any sign of human life.

He wore a wide-brimmed straw hat, his safari jacket, tropical drill trousers tucked into the tops of his boots. Despite Nick's long sloping strides, Tweed had no trouble keeping up with him. In London he'd taken to rising very early, walking two miles round the deserted streets every day. At the weekends he drove down to Surrey, parked his Cortina and climbed the North Downs. He was in better shape than for years.

They crossed the pass and began to descend into Devil's Valley. The tortuous path twisted as it dropped rapidly round boulders of limestone. Both Nick and Tweed carried water bottles slung over their shoulders. Nick carried the shotgun in his left hand and paused as he came to each man-high boulder. He peered round it cautiously, waved to Tweed to proceed, and walked on.

The sun was climbing in a clear turquoise sky. Already it was becoming very hot: the heat from the previous day had never dissipated during the night. As they progressed deep inside the valley Tweed cast frequent glances up at the ridges enclosing them to east and west. No sign of movement. Only the occasional sheep came into view, head down as it searched for nourishment among the scrub grass.

Tweed saw a weird squat structure perched on the ridge against the eastern skyline. He guessed it was the abandoned silver mine where Newman had had his nightmare experience. They arrived at the base of the valley and the path ran to left and to right. Nick paused, drank from his water bottle, wiped sweat off his forehead. Tweed wrapped a large silk handkerchief round his own neck to mop up the sweat.

'What's that thing?' Tweed asked, pointing to a crumbling high building. A series of chutes ran at angles and all the metal was rusty. The derelict structure stood at the foot of a path climbing up the eastern slope.

'The old ore-crushing plant where they extracted the silver,' Nick explained. 'Hasn't been used for years. Donkey trains brought down the ore. Have you noticed how quiet it is? And no sign of anyone.'

It was the first conversation they had had since they started out. They had agreed in the car they wouldn't speak during the descent into the valley. Nick had explained that voices carried a long distance.

'Well, isn't that our good luck?' Tweed commented and drank from his own water bottle.

'It's too quiet. And I have not seen one single shepherd. That I do not like.'

'Why not?'

'It is almost as though they know we are coming. Fifteen more minutes' walk along this path to the left and we see Petros' farmhouse . . .'

It was creepy. Despite the glare of the sun burning down Tweed found the silence unnerving. Now they had to pick their way among a bed of stones and rocks and he realized they were walking along the path of a stream. In winter it would be a gushing flood.

Tweed paused to glance round. Dante's Inferno. That was what it reminded him of. The deep valley, the mountains closing in, the heat trapped in the wide gulch they were moving through. It was the sheer aridity of the slopes which appalled him. Scrub, nothing but scrub.

By now his boots and clothes were coated with fine limestone dust. It clung to his wet face. Nick turned and walked back to him. He scanned the slopes and shook his head.

'Maybe we should go back,' he suggested.

'Why?' asked Tweed.

'Look at that flock of sheep grazing high up on the mountain. No shepherd. There should be a shepherd. Something's wrong.'

'How many shepherds has Petros?'

'Between twelve and fifteen. It is a big farm. And all those men are armed.'

'I'm not turning back now. I have to see Petros. Let's keep moving.'

Nick shrugged. 'OK. Petros' farm is round the next bend. We approach very cautiously . . .'

The long tumbledown building with a veranda stretching its full frontage came into view. Nick stopped abruptly. The desert-like atmosphere was transformed. Tweed gazed at the olive groves climbing up behind the farmhouse, small stunted trees with tortured twisted trunks. On the empty veranda stood a large wickerwork chair. Tweed noticed the cushions were depressed – as though someone had sat there recently. The silence was even more oppressive.

'I am responsible for your safety,' said Nick. 'I think that we should turn back at once. We are walking into a trap.'

When Newman had introduced Paula to Christina the previous day and left them alone the atmosphere had been frigid. Christina eyed Paula up and down, lit a cigarette and then asked her casually, 'You're Tweed's woman?'

Paula tensed, then relaxed. 'Not in the sense you mean.' She decided she'd start as she meant to go on. 'Let's get one thing straight between us. I'm here to protect you. Just like Newman and Marler were. We're going to be penned up inside this room. Even at night because I'll be sleeping in the other bed. We'll use room service for all meals, including breakfast. Two women cramped together like that is a recipe for an explosion. There won't be one. Now, shall we start all over again?'

By the following morning they were chatting like old friends. It was Christina who brought up the subject when the waiter had taken their breakfast things away.

'Have they gone into Devil's Valley?'

'I think they're somewhere in Athens. On some checking job.'

Christina sat close to Paula, laid a hand on her arm. 'I can tell you are fond of Tweed. I like him myself. If he's gone into Devil's Valley he'll be killed. Petros hates what he calls English. He thinks an Englishman killed both his sons during the war.'

'Tweed can look after himself . . .'

'Then that *is* where he has gone?'

Paula bit her lip. She'd been indiscreet: Christina was quick. And very worried. Which increased the anxiety

Paula was feeling. Christina gripped Paula more firmly, her tone emphatic.

'I know the area. Petros and his men know every inch of that Godforsaken wilderness. Even if they've all gone – Tweed, Newman and Marler – they won't survive. Your friends are committing suicide. Their bodies will never be found. They'll be dropped down the old silver mine shaft . . .'

'Don't.' Paula began to feel sick. Christina had conjured up such a vivid picture. 'I didn't say that's where they were going.'

'But it is, isn't it? You said Tweed can look after himself. Petros is crazy. He has no mercy, no feelings. He lives only for revenge. Don't you understand? He's obsessed.'

Obsessed. Paula was shaken. Tweed, also, she felt was obsessed. What would happen when the two men confronted each other? She got up out of her chair, began to pace round the room. I'm doing what Tweed does, she suddenly thought.

'You have to do something,' Christina insisted. 'Now.'

Paula stopped by the telephone and smiled. 'I think I'm going to do something which will lose me my job.'

'Do you mind? If it saves Tweed – and the others?'

Paula checked the phone book, picked up the receiver, dialled police headquarters, asked for Captain Peter Sarris.

Keeping well away from the farmhouse which was overshadowed by a limestone crag, Tweed walked slowly forward over the dusty ground. Nick walked alongside, gripping his shotgun in both hands, the muzzle parallel with the earth.

'You interpret for me,' Tweed said. 'I'll try to make it a quickfire conversation.'

'With who?'

'I sense there are people here – all around us . . .'

He stopped speaking as a large tall man emerged from

456

the farmhouse. He had a hooked nose and thick eyebrows, a lined face. For a man of eighty his movements were vigorous. He carried a double-barrelled shotgun similar to Nick's and was followed by two much younger men. From Newman's description they were Dimitrios and Constantine. Both carried rifles.

'I am Petros,' the old man announced as he descended the steps. 'Bring me a chair, Dimitrios,' he ordered.

Nick translated as Dimitrios carried the wicker chair into the sun. Petros sat in the chair, crossed his legs, laid the gun over his lap, the barrel aimed at Tweed's stomach. The safety catch was on. Seated in the open, Petros reminded Tweed of an Old Testament patriarch. His presence radiated authority and domination.

Dimitrios padded well to the right while Constantine also came into the open, taking up a position on the left – making it impossible for Nick to cover both men. He aimed his gun direct at the old man's chest.

'You were expected,' Petros said, and grinned.

'My name is Tweed. I hold a senior position in the British Special Branch. That is our version of a secret police force. I am investigating the deaths of Andreas and Stephen Gavalas, among others.'

'Listen to him!' Petros threw back his great head and roared with laughter. 'He expects me to believe his lies.' His manner changed, became menacing. 'The main thing is you are English. I hate all English. You made a big mistake coming here, a fatal mistake.'

'You are blind, old man? You can't see my friend has a gun aimed at you point-blank?'

'At the first sign of movement you are both dead. *You* must be blind. Have you overlooked Dimitrios and Constantine?'

Tweed had not overlooked them. They stood, feet slightly apart. Dimitrios had his rifle aimed at Tweed, Constantine aimed his weapon at Nick. Sweat was running down Tweed's neck into the already sodden handkerchief. More sweat trickled from his armpits. But inside he was as cold as ice as he held the old man's eyes.

'There have been more murders. One of my men, Harry Masterson, came here. He ended up at the foot of Cape Sounion. Don't say you've never heard of him. It was in the papers. You were responsible for his murder?'

Petros' eyes gleamed, locked on Tweed's. He patted his shotgun, as though to check it was there. There was pure hatred in the dark eyes.

'No,' he said eventually, 'I know nothing about that. He must have been the man who came into Devil's Valley by night weeks ago. We couldn't find him. You should have asked Florakis.' He waved his left hand towards the western ridge. 'He owns a scrap of land over there, two hundred hectares or so.'

'You call that a scrap of land?' Keep him talking, Tweed was thinking.

'I own two thousand hectares here.' Petros made a grand gesture. 'Another thousand in Macedonia. If I had killed your man I would tell you. Why not? You will not leave here alive . . .'

'You are a member of the Greek Key?'

Petros scowled, screwed up his thick eyebrows. 'You know too much, Mr Tweed. Yes, during the Civil War I was a member. But when I found they were controlled by Moscow I left them. You think I want some commissar telling me what to do?'

'So you won't like the idea that Anton is a member?'

'You lie!' Petros' face was distorted with fury. He uncrossed his legs and his shotgun barrel shifted, pointing into space. 'You dare to say that to me, English? Your time has come. I will listen to no more of your filthy accusations. You are at the end of your life . . .'

*   *   *

458

Tweed said the first thing that came into his head, something which would distract the old ruffian. 'You know about those diamonds which were taken from Andreas' dead body on Siros? A fortune.'

He reached up, removed his hat, scratched at his head, smoothed down his hair. 'Order your grandsons to freeze.' Nick translated rapidly.

The first shot hit the ground between Petros' splayed feet, kicked up a puff of dust. The second bullet struck within inches of Dimitros. The third a foot behind Constantine. Petros' gnarled hands gripped the sides of his chair. He sat motionless.

On the top of the eastern ridge Marler squinted through his telescopic sight, the crosshairs centred on Dimitrios' chest. At the summit of the western ridge Newman held his own rifle, aimed at Constantine. The telescopic sight brought up the Greek so close he felt he could reach out and touch him.

Tweed put his hat back on his head. There was a dry smile on his face. 'You really think I'd wander into this place without protection? My men are marksmen, as you may have realized. They could have killed both Dimitrios and Constantine – their bodies would be lying in the dust. Had you moved, Nick would have shot you dead. Who would have carried out your mission of vengeance? If anyone attempts to move they will be shot. Now, can we continue?'

'You are a brave man.' Petros spoke slowly, glancing up at the ridge crests. 'You are also a clever man. OK. Talk.'

'Let's talk about Anton. He went to England many weeks ago by a secret route. You sent him, I suspect. His mission? To locate three men. Colonel Barrymore, Captain Robson and CSM Kearns, the same three men who accompanied Andreas on the fatal raid on Siros. Am I right?'

Petros drew a hand across the grey stubble of his unshaven face and stared at Tweed. It was a long minute before he replied. Tweed could feel the furnace-like heat radiating up from the ground.

'You are right,' Petros told him. 'That was the first stage in my plan to kill the man responsible.'

'You know which one did it? Anton found these men?'

'We don't know which one. Yes, he found them. All living so close together. I thought that strange.'

'Then Anton returned, told you what he had discovered. But it took you only part of the way. Because you still didn't know who murdered Andreas on Siros, stole the diamonds, then returned to Cairo and killed Stephen, masquerading as Ionides? The killer must somehow have found out his real identity. That worried him sufficiently for him to decide Stephen also must die. Why was Stephen living in Cairo under an assumed name?'

Tweed waited while Nick translated. He was trying to keep his questions short, to encourage Petros to continue the conversation, but he had to extract the whole story.

'You are right,' Petros said again. 'About Anton's first trip to England. And the rest. The EDES mob sent Stephen to Cairo as a spy. They gave him false papers under the name Ionides.'

'Maybe it was the right-wing EDES which killed Andreas?' Tweed pressed on.

'No. They had their headquarters on Siros, under the nose of the German commanding general, Geiger. They wanted the diamonds. They would never have killed one of their own.'

'What about the Germans? Maybe one of them did the job, found the diamonds, took them?'

'I thought of that.' Petros paused. 'This will sound peculiar. I arranged a truce with General Geiger. He agreed. He did not want a bloodbath. A Greek killed in battle is one thing. But killed by a German soldier who steals from him, that is another. We met under a flag of

460

truce. He was a reasonable man. He said he knew which patrols were near the area that night. He would question them himself. I knew I could trust him. Later he sent me a message. Only one patrol was near the place where we found Andreas. None of them had even discovered the body.'

'So that leaves the three commandos?'

'Yes. Now, I think we end this . . .'

'Wait! Anton is now in England again. Did you send him – or was it his idea? Did he persuade you it would be a good idea?'

For the first time Tweed saw doubt in Petros' expression. The old man stirred uncomfortably, looked away from Tweed towards the farmhouse and beyond.

'It was his idea,' he said slowly. 'He pressed hard for me to agree. Mr Tweed, do not remove your hat again. Do not make the signal a second time. Look behind the farmhouse . . .'

Tweed turned his head. Then he knew the reason for the absence of shepherds when they had made their tortuous way into Devil's Valley. A group of about a dozen men in shepherd's clothes stood scattered above the farmhouse, concealed beneath the overhang of the crag where neither Marler nor Newman could possibly see them. He had been out-manoeuvred.

'I have only told you all this because I knew you would never leave this place alive,' Petros told him. 'You see they are all armed.' He stabbed a finger at Nick. 'Now you are marked for the first shots. As you drop I shall move very quickly – which I can – inside the house. Away from your marksmen who will not react until you make the signal. Then it will be too late. So, Mr Tweed, you should never have come here . . .'

'Keep him talking for just a minute,' Nick whispered in English.

Tweed did not ask why. 'You haven't asked about

461

Christina. I know where she is. She is under my care. And not in Greece.'

The fury returned. The hands clutched at the chair. 'You hold her as a hostage? I do not believe it. I would do that, but you are not such a man . . .'

'A different subject,' said Tweed, seeking the maximum distraction, 'Why did you wait for so many years before trying to locate the three commandos? It doesn't make sense.'

Petros' eyes seemed to start out of his head. His right hand clenched the chair as he spat out the words. A streak of near-madness glittered in his expression. Obsessed, Tweed thought – I'm facing a man obsessed . . .

'First there was the Civil War . . . then the years of work to make money, to build up the farm . . . you need money to conduct a manhunt. I had my family to bring up. The years passed quickly, too quickly. And all that time the thought never left my head. I must track down the killer of my sons. I live with that each day. That is what keeps me going. *Revenge*. And now your time is up . . .'

Marler was a long way below the eastern crest where he had shot from. He knew he was taking a desperate gamble – that he was leaving one flank unguarded. But he had heard the tumble of rocks sliding, which meant someone was moving beneath the overhanging crag protecting the farm.

He knew he had assessed the geography correctly: Newman, perched high on the western ridge, couldn't possibly see beneath the great crag. As he made his rapid descent, his rifle looped across his back, he was helped by his small stature, by his slim build, by the fact that he was moving down the sandy bed of a dried-up stream – which enabled him to move silently.

He avoided shifting even the smallest pebble which might

give away his presence. His small feet skipped down the twisting bed. Then he slowed down, peered round the precipitous wall of the crag. The roof of the farm lay below. Under the shelter of the crag stood a group of shepherds, well spaced out, each holding a rifle or shotgun to his shoulder. Marler unlooped his own weapon.

Tweed could now hear the sounds which Nick's acute ears had picked up. The putt-putt beat of helicopter motors approaching fast. The machines appeared suddenly and at the same moment. One Alouette came over the western ridge, the second appeared over the eastern crest. Police choppers.

Petros stared upwards, exposing his thick neck. The chopper which flew in from the west was already dropping. Sarris was behind the swivel-mounted machine-gun, the glasses he had used looped round his neck. The window was open. A policeman beside him used an amplified loudhailer to shout the message in Greek.

'Drop your weapons or we open fire . . .'

A shepherd concealed behind a large boulder raised his rifle. He aimed for the pilot's cabin. There was a single report. The shepherd crumpled, shot in the back. Marler switched to another target. The shepherds panicked, hoisted their rifles to shoot at the chopper. Sarris' machine-gun began its deadly chatter, sweeping across those at the highest level. Shepherds threw up their hands, sagged to the ground.

'Run, Tweed . . .'

Nick darted forward, rammed the muzzle of his shotgun under Petros' jaw, shouted at him to get inside the house. The old man jumped out of his chair, fled for the veranda. Tweed was already running towards the house. On the western crest Newman saw one shepherd aiming his rifle over the rooftop at the running figure. He squeezed the

463

trigger. The shepherd dropped his weapon, took two paces forward, fell flat on his face.

Both Alouettes had landed. Uniformed police holding guns dropped to the ground, ducked under the whirling rotors, spread out, surrounded the farm. Sarris strode up the steps and into the farmhouse. Tweed held an axe he had snatched from the kitchen wall.

'Better late than never,' said Sarris.

44

They drove along Alexandras Avenue and pulled up outside police headquarters. Sarris had driven Tweed back from the helipad where the chopper landed after flying them from Devil's Valley. In the rear seats were Newman and Marler. Nick was driving his Mercedes back on his own; a uniformed policeman was bringing back Marler's hired Peugeot. Sarris switched off the engine, lit a cigarette.

'What was that business about the missing commando daggers at Petros' farmhouse?' Tweed asked.

'Six of them,' said Sarris, 'all collected from British commandos the Germans captured raiding the Cyclades islands. General Geiger apparently kept them as trophies. One night Petros and some *andartes* broke into his villa, walked off with them. Petros has kept them in a glass case at the farm.'

'I heard your conversation with him in Greek,' Newman commented. 'The old maniac used to gaze at them every evening before he went to bed – to remind himself of his mission of vengeance. I'd say there were five, not six, in Geiger's villa. The sixth could have been the knife which killed Andreas. It was Petros' lot who found the body and removed it – and remember the knife was still sticking in Andreas' back.'

'But how did you know Petros had this macabre collection?' Tweed asked.

'I had one of his shepherds in my pay. He's the man who dropped flat and survived when I opened fire. I had to twist Petros' arm to find out what happened when I noticed the case was empty.'

'And what did happen?' Tweed pressed. 'I have a reason for asking.'

'Petros eventually admitted they disappeared many weeks ago – about the time Anton left for his first trip to England.'

'Which *may* explain who killed Sam Partridge,' Tweed remarked.

'Why the doubt?' asked Marler.

'Because the three men on Exmoor would also have access to the weapon – when they were in the Army. We still don't know who the killer is. What will happen to Petros?' he asked Sarris.

'He'll end up behind bars. Maybe in a padded cell. Now, was your crazy expedition worthwhile?'

'Yes. I'm convinced Petros had nothing to do with the killing of Masterson. Which is why I came here. I also believe Petros was kept alive by his dream of vengeance, that he might never have taken any real action. The dream would have gone.'

Sarris opened the door. 'Let's go to my office, get a drink. I'm parched.' He looked at Tweed as he climbed out of the car. 'There's someone waiting to see you. And you'd better say thanks to her very nicely.'

Tweed asked the question suddenly, hoping to catch Sarris off balance. 'What precisely is the Greek Key?'

'It's an ancient symbol. You must know it. You see it used on embroideries, it appears in the friezes of temples.'

'Freeze is the word – what you all do when the phrase is mentioned.'

Tweed followed Sarris inside the building while Newman and Marler brought up the rear. They waited and then stepped inside an elevator. When they walked into the office Paula, who had been reading a magazine, dropped it and rushed to Tweed, hugging him.

'God! You're crazy,' she exploded. 'I warned you. Sarris sent a radio report from the chopper. You walked into an ambush.' She released him, stood back, spoke in a solemn voice. 'And I know I disobeyed your instructions. So I expect to be sacked.'

'Stuff and nonsense. I owe you my life.' Tweed sank into a chair while Sarris ordered coffee and mineral water over his intercom. 'But where is Christina? Is she on her own?'

'Of course not!' Sarris snapped. 'Paula phoned me. Before I drove to the helipad I left orders for a plain-clothes man to go to the Grande Bretagne to guard Christina – so Paula could come here.' He looked at Newman and Marler who had also sat down. 'Officially you were not involved. Which is why I've confiscated your rifles. They'll get lost. I won't ask how you obtained them.'

'That's big of you,' said Newman. 'Considering Marler shot down a shepherd who was aiming his rifle at the cabin of that chopper you were flying in. You could be cold meat on a slab now.'

Sarris grinned, looked at Tweed. 'Is he always so independent and aggressive?'

'Yes,' Marler interjected. 'A pain in the arse. But we did hold the situation until you arrived.'

'I think you all went mad,' Paula said and sipped at the cup of coffee served by a uniformed policeman. She was watching Tweed: there had been a major change in his mood and manner. The vehemence and tension seemed to have drained out of him.

A man came in and Tweed looked up. The Dormouse.

He stood up, smiled and shook hands. 'Good to see you again.'

'I would suggest,' Sarris began, 'that Kalos takes you for a ride away from here. That you ask him the question you put to me downstairs. I'd like the rest of you to stay while we cook up an official report, something that will make my superiors happy. The truth – but maybe not the whole truth . . .'

The Dormouse drove Tweed to the Plaka. He apologized for the transport, his battered old Saab. 'No one notices it,' he explained, 'which is why I favour it. Now the question.'

'What is the Greek Key?'

'I'll tell you when we reach my flat – that and a lot more. It's politically sensitive, which is why Sarris suggested we get out of police headquarters.' He manoeuvred the vehicle carefully inside the labyrinth, stopped outside a taverna, his engine still running. 'See that – Papadedes. Note the entrance to the staircase alongside – Papadedes hires out the room upstairs to men taking a woman up there. But other people have used that room. I will tell you in my flat.'

He parked the car inside a narrow alley climbing steeply up towards a hilltop. His flat was above a shop selling baskets and leather handbags to tourists. Tweed settled himself in an armchair after a good wash in a tiny bathroom. He felt more civilized after getting rid of the mixture of dried sweat and dust.

Kalos fussed about, making coffee. He placed the cup on a small round table next to the chair, produced a tin jug and two glasses. '*Retsina*,' he explained. 'If you do not like it leave it. And here is mineral water. Some bread with a little cheese – made from cow's milk. I do not think goat's milk cheese would appeal.'

'Very good of you, Kalos.' Tweed sipped at the

467

retsina. It tasted resinous. 'I like it. Now, can we talk?'

'The Greek Key,' Kalos began, settling himself in another armchair, 'is a highly secret underground organization of hardline Communists. It is run by a committee but the man who counts is Doganis, in his sixties . . .'

'Ah,' said Tweed, 'another man in his sixties. So he goes back also to the Second World War.'

'That is true.' Kalos leaned forward, tapped Tweed on the knee. 'And these are very hard men indeed. They are bitter because they just failed to take over Greece during the Civil War. We were saved by the American President, Truman. He sent a military mission, tons of arms. Now they have surfaced again. They are anti-Gorbachev.'

Tweed stiffened, put down his glass. 'Their activities are confined to Greece?'

'I don't think so. From the records, during the Second World War there were strong rumours the real controller of the Greek Key was an Englishman based in Cairo. Let me tell you what I have discovered.' He took a file from his briefcase. 'This is my secret report. You can read it later. Now, we start with the clandestine visit of General Lucharsky to Athens . . .'

Tweed ate the bread and cheese, listened grimly as The Dormouse described what he had found out. Lucharsky . . . Colonel Rykovsky. The arrival later of Lucharsky's aide, Colonel Volkov . . . the link with Doganis . . . Florakis, alias Oleg Savinkov, The Executioner . . . Pavelic, the Croat hardliner who had provided Kalos with secret information while drunk . . .

'This Pavelic,' Tweed said eventually, 'he is in touch with Moscow?'

'He boasted he had underground links with the hardliners inside Russia who hate and fear Gorbachev's reforms – that Gorbachev would not last much longer.'

Tweed recalled that Marler had seen Florakis carrying

a modern transceiver up a mountain on his land. The Dormouse listened with a gleam in his beady eyes.

'Who is he transmitting to?'

Tweed opened up, telling him about the three ex-commandos living on Exmoor; the long-ago murders in Cairo, on Siros; about the killing of Sam Partridge – who had been in Cairo as a very young man; the killing of Jill Kearns and Mrs Larcombe and the story the old lady had told Tweed.

Kalos nodded. 'We have uncovered a major conspiracy controlled by the hardline anti-Gorbachev faction in Moscow. I just cannot see where it leads.' He handed his file to Tweed. 'I would like you to read that – it includes times and photographs of the conspirators . . .'

Tweed read the file, automatically memorizing every detail. He studied the photos. Kalos sat with his hands clasped in his ample lap, waited patiently. When Tweed had finished he handed back the file.

'My God, it looks far worse than I ever dreamed. Could you get me copies of those prints?'

Kalos delved into his file, produced a large envelope which he passed to Tweed. 'I anticipated your request. I made copies myself in my own darkroom. All the dates are written on the back. I have signed my name and used a police headquarters rubber stamp. Sarris knows nothing of this. He destroyed the original file in my presence.'

'Sarris is involved?' Tweed asked.

A shake of the stubble-covered head. 'I'm sure he guessed I had already prepared a duplicate file. It was significant he did not ask for the negatives of those prints. Sarris would never forget a point like that. Except deliberately. We understand one another. Why do you think he suggested I took you away from HQ for a talk?'

'Of course.' Tweed smiled. 'It is just that I have a habit of trusting no one.'

'A very good habit. What are you going to do now? You

believe one of those three ex-commandos is the real head of the Greek Key?'

'I do now.'

'But which one? You have interviewed them all twice. Surely one of them let something slip? You are known for your flair for interrogation.'

'I think I know who it is.' Tweed paused. 'The devil of it is I have no proof.'

'And this Professor Seton-Charles you mentioned. The Recruiter, as Christina called him when talking with Newman. He too is involved?'

'Up to his ruddy neck would be my guess. Again, no proof. You asked me what I'm going to do. I'm very grateful to you, Kalos, for your cooperation. What you've dug up all on your own has filled in a lot of gaps. I am returning to England as rapidly as possible. The solution lies there.'

'Let me phone Sarris, see where they all are.' Kalos picked up the phone, dialled, spoke in Greek, waited, then spoke again at greater length. He put down the phone. 'Sarris tells me they are all at the Grande Bretagne, waiting for you. I hinted you may be leaving. He thinks that a good idea – after your experience in Devil's Valley. He looks forward to seeing you again.'

Tweed stood up. 'Thank you once more for everything. I am sure we will meet again.'

'There is always a next time in our work. I will drive you to the hotel.' The Dormouse smiled shyly. 'It has been a great pleasure to deal with you. I suppose you realize you may not have much time left to stop whatever is planned? They have been working on it for over a year.'

'That's what worries me. *I* don't think we have much time left. One more thing, could you leave Florakis alone? He sounds like the communications link. I don't want that disturbed.'

470

'I can persuade Sarris to agree to that. Now, as you say, you are short of time . . .'

They were all waiting for him in Newman's room: Newman himself, Marler and Nick. Newman told him Paula was still guarding Christina in her room.

'You see,' Nick intervened, 'I noticed at the farm that Dimitrios and Constantine were missing. I checked the bodies myself. I think they are in Athens, searching for Christina. It may be days before they hear Petros has been arrested. Sarris said he was keeping it out of the papers.'

'We are all leaving by a Swissair flight tomorrow,' Tweed told them. 'It leaves at 5 p.m., arrives at Zurich at 6.45 p.m. We stopped in the square on the way back and I bought tickets for everyone.' He dropped a folder on the table. 'Better collect your tickets now.'

'Why Zurich?' Newman asked. 'Why not a direct flight home?'

'Because we are taking Christina with us. I promised her protection. She will stay with our friend in Switzerland until this is all over.'

'May I make a suggestion?' said Nick.

'Go ahead.'

'You may well need strong protection until you have safely left Greece. If you take a taxi with Christina and Paula to the airport, Newman and Marler could follow close behind in the hired Peugeot the police returned.'

'That's good thinking,' agreed Tweed.

'But in case of emergency none of you is armed. Sarris took your rifles, as he took my shotgun. But I was not searched – I think that was deliberate.' He opened his jacket, took it off, exposing the hip holster carrying his .38 Smith & Wesson. Unfastening the holster, he laid it on the table. Pulling up his trouser leg, he unstrapped the holster containing a small Browning automatic, laid that on the

471

table. Then he emptied his jacket pockets of spare magazines and looked at Marler and Newman.

'Take your choice.'

'But we'll never get through airport security,' Newman pointed out.

'Yes you will. Because I will drive ahead to the airport to make sure it is safe. If I am standing leaning against my car when Tweed's taxi arrives, all is well. I then go to the men's room, followed by Newman and Marler. They hand the guns back to me.'

'Very bright,' Tweed agreed again.

Marler grabbed the Browning before Newman could object, saying he was smaller and wasn't going to lug the heavier Smith & Wesson about. Newman grimaced.

'Trust him to find the easy way.' He looked at Nick. 'You said you were running low on petrol.'

Nick jumped up. 'So I go and fill her up now. Do it at once is my maxim. I will be back later.'

Newman waited until they were alone. 'Tweed, shouldn't someone go to the Embassy, call Beck, warn him we're coming?'

'I was about to do that myself . . .'

'I feel like a walk. Give me his Berne number and I'll make the call.'

Tweed took out the pad he always carried with a sheet of plastic to stop the imprint of what he wrote being reproduced on the sheet underneath. He wrote down Beck's number from memory, gave it to Newman. After studying it for a few moments, Newman held the sheet over an ash tray, set light to it.

'I'm on my way . . .'

Tweed was left alone with Marler, who ran his hand through his fair hair before asking his question.

'What about Andreas' skeleton hanging inside that silver mine?'

'It *was* Andreas. Sarris told me he had questioned Petros

after I told him about its existence before we left the farm. Petros admitted he had kept the skeleton until he had administered justice – his phrase – to the murderer of his sons. Sarris sent a couple of men up to find the skeleton. I suppose it will be buried in due course. The whole episode shows Petros was crazy with his obsession.'

'And you're no further for'ard with who killed Masterson?'

'Yes, I am. After cross-examining Petros before the choppers arrived I'm convinced he told the truth. He had nothing to do with Masterson's death. So we're looking for someone else – which is what I came here to find out.'

'Any ideas?'

Despite their ordeal in Devil's Valley Marler looked fresh and ready for anything. He had cleaned himself up in the bathroom and emerged a new man.

'A lot,' said Tweed. 'I've been fed a whole load of new information. The trouble will be checking it out – and I'm not sure how much time we've got. You'll all be chasing your tails when we get back home. But Zurich comes first. Not that I expect it will be anything but a stopover . . .'

Beck met them at Zurich the following evening and they travelled from Kloten Airport to the Hotel Schweizerhof in two unmarked limousines. Inside the second car Christina was escorted by a plain-clothes policeman.

'She will be taken into the mountains,' Beck explained when they assembled in Tweed's corner room overlooking the Bahnhofstrasse and the main station. 'In a house near Santis,' he went on. 'Is there someone who needs smoke in their eyes? I didn't see anyone following us from the airport.'

'No. Just keep her out of harm's way,' Tweed replied. 'I'll give you a call when I'm sure the coast is clear. And we'll pay the expenses.'

473

'Oh, there will be a bill.' Beck smiled and sat down as Tweed gestured towards a chair. 'I have news. Is it for your ears only?'

'Everyone here knows what's going on.'

Tweed waved a hand, embracing Newman, Paula and Marler. When they arrived Christina had said she'd be taking a bath. She had been quite happy that Gustav, her guard, should stay in her room and drink coffee.

'I realized Anton Gavalas was important to you,' Beck began. He had chosen a chair next to Paula. 'I checked with Interpol in Paris, asked them whether anything unusual had happened in Lisbon. It has.' His voice became grave. 'And about just the time Anton was in the Portuguese capital. A murder.'

'God! Who was it this time?' Tweed asked.

'An unsavoury international arms dealer who went by the name of Gallagher. He ran a garage, apparently – as a cover for his real activities. He had been watched as he travelled all over Europe. No evidence. He was found stabbed in a service pit in his garage. Could there be a link with Anton?'

'Any idea what kind of knife was used?'

'Yes. It was left in the body. People don't realize it can be very difficult to withdraw the weapon if it is driven in deep. This one was. A British commando-type knife.'

'That sounds like Anton.'

'There is more. Some guesswork . . .' Beck waved a dismissive hand. 'But the dates are right. Anton stayed one night at The Ritz. The following day a Portuguese freighter carrying a consignment of cork for England sailed. The *Oporto*. After a few days it arrives at some port called Watchet in Somerset, unloads the cork, takes on board a cargo of wastepaper. Is this relevant?'

'More so than you might ever dream,' Tweed urged him on grimly.

'The *Oporto* had been shadowed by French aircraft.

French Intelligence, the *Direction de la Surveillance du Territoire*, had discovered the *Oporto* had visited Tripoli in Libya before arriving in Lisbon. Their aircraft lost it because of a storm and only picked it up again after it had left Britain and was sailing apparently back to Lisbon. Another storm drove it close to Brest. They sent out cutters and boarded it in French territorial waters. Anyone losing interest?'

'I'm fascinated,' said Paula. 'You're leading up to something.'

'I enjoy a little drama – as Tweed here sometimes does. They found in the hold an armoury of Sam missile launchers, missiles, hundreds of rifles and forty thousand rounds of ammunition. At the time there was an Irish fishing boat near Brest. Fodder for the IRA. Paris is certain of it.'

'I don't like the sound of this,' Tweed commented.

'Then you won't like the rest much. The DST interrogated Gomez, the *Oporto*'s captain. He wouldn't give any information. But a member of the crew he had rebuked did talk. He said before the ship reached Watchet it heaved to and someone carrying a large bundle was off-loaded into a waiting motorboat. The craft then headed for the British shore.'

'Did he recognize – I mean, see – anyone in the motorboat he could describe?'

'No. He was concealed behind the bridge and frightened of being found. End of story.'

'Or the beginning,' said Tweed. 'Sam missile launchers. That frightens me. What *was* landed on that remote stretch of Somerset coastline? And why? For what purpose? Those are the questions we must find answers to. And the solution lies back home in England.'

45

London. As soon as Tweed arrived back at Park Crescent
he worried away like a beaver at the problem. He assembled all his helpers in his room, issued a whole series
of instructions.

Newman, Marler, Paula and Monica were there. Everyone had to know what the others were doing. The Director,
Howard, back from a long holiday, lounged in a chair,
listening. He made a typical comment as he brushed imaginary specks of dust off his immaculate navy blue suit.

'This is costing us a fortune. Your trip to Athens
alone . . .'

'Are you saying we are wasting our time?' Tweed enquired.

Paula sat behind her desk watching Tweed. He had lost
his earlier manner of a man obsessed: seeing Petros had
cured him of that. It was now the normal Tweed: calm,
dogged, speaking in a controlled tone. Paula felt enormously relieved.

'No,' Howard replied. 'Not after hearing all the details.
I don't like that business Kalos told you about General
Lucharsky, Colonels Rykovsky and Volkov – above all the
connection with Doganis. It does sound as though the
hardline faction inside Russia – the anti-Gorbachev lot –
has succeeded in establishing a power base outside Russia.'

'And that base is over here. All we have to do is to find
it.'

'You make it sound so easy,' Howard observed.

'What gets me,' Paula persisted, 'is how they were able

476

to do that under our noses.' She frowned. 'Unless it was set up a long time ago and has recently been activated.'

'Monica,' said Tweed, 'double-check with Roberts, our man at Lloyd's. I want all details of the movements of that Portuguese vessel, the *Oporto*. Paula, drive down to Exmoor with Newman. Find out on the spot whether Butler and Nield have discovered anything more about movements in that area. Especially about Anton – and Seton-Charles, who seems to have vanished off the face of the earth. Marler, Interpol have persuaded Lisbon to send me that knife used to kill Gallagher. It's arriving at London Airport aboard this flight.' He gave him a sheet of paper. 'In the custody of the pilot of the plane. Bring it back here. I want to check if it really is a commando-type weapon.'

'We stay at The Anchor at Porlock Weir?' Paula suggested as she took from a cupboard the small case she kept packed for emergency trips.

'It's out of the way, a good place to stay under cover. And you can check on Mrs Larcombe's murder. Bob, you get out of the car short of the hotel, register as though you don't know Paula. It can come in useful to have a secret reserve.'

'And I'll have my Mercedes back, thank you very much.'

'Goody,' said Paula. 'I'll get to drive it. At ninety down the motorway,' she joked.

Tweed gave her a look as she left with Newman. Marler raised himself slowly from his chair. 'I'd better push off to the airport before you think of something else . . .'

'Just like old times,' Monica said when Marler had gone. 'It's all go – the way I like it.' She reached for the phone to call Lloyd's. 'Do you really think Anton is back in this country?'

'He's somewhere over here. What I'd like to know is what he's doing,' Tweed answered sombrely.

* * *

It was raining heavily at Cherry Farm in Hampshire. Anton could hear it beating down on the roof of the huge barn where he was working. Perfect weather: it kept potential snoopers indoors. Inside the second furniture van, parked behind the other vehicle, he turned round as Seton-Charles appeared and climbed up the lowered tailboard.

'How are you progressing?' the Professor asked.

'I will show you. We are far advanced.'

Anton moved a tool box on the floor among the straw, used his screwdriver to lever up the hinged floorboards. Beneath was the secret compartment he had constructed to store the Stinger launchers and the missiles.

Seton-Charles gazed round the interior of the huge vehicle. At the front, behind the driver's cab – shut off from the interior – Anton had erected a wooden platform, railed, and with steps leading up to it. A special wooden chair he had designed with an adjustable back was clamped to the platform floor.

Anton inserted a missile into the launcher, carried the weapon up to the platform, and sat in the chair. Reaching down, he depressed a switch. There was the faint sound of electrical machinery on the move. A large panel in the van's roof slid open, exposing the roof of the barn six feet above the top of the van.

He settled himself into the chair, raised the launcher, the stock pressed firmly into his shoulder. The Greek swivelled the weapon through an arc.

'Imagine open sky, a plane approaching three thousand feet up. I press the trigger, the heat-seaking device homes on the target. *Boom!* No plane. Satisfied?'

He didn't give a damn whether his companion was satisfied or not. The main thing was *he* knew it would work. He climbed back down the steps, detached the missile, wrapped it separately in a polythene sheet, did the same thing with the launcher, made sure they were safely tucked away and closed the floorboards. Then he rubbed dirt over the joins, moved straw over the compartment.

'Now I have to do the same job with the other van. It all takes time.'

'Maybe I could help by going in to Liphook and fetching the new food supplies?' Seton-Charles suggested.

He was getting housebound. Anton had not allowed him to leave the farm since he had arrived. The Greek shook his head. He had grown a thick moustache; he wore a greasy boiler suit and wore the type of cap affected by the average farm worker. His British boots were smeared with caked mud.

'I get the food,' Anton told him. 'You said Liphook. Do you not realize I buy each time from a different town? Where is your sense of security?'

'I am sorry. That was a foolish mistake . . .'

'Which could have been fatal. Let us go into the farm-house – I want to check the two rooms we have prepared for the prisoners. They will be brought here within the next few weeks . . .'

They entered the farm by the back door: Anton insisted that they never used the front entrance which was kept permanently locked. He led the way up the old staircase and along the corridor to the two rooms facing the back. They were separated by the bathroom.

Each door had two locks and a bolt Anton had fixed. In each door was a spyhole with a cap which closed down over it on the outside. They could look in but an occupant could not see out. He opened the first door, walked inside. The room was starkly furnished.

An iron bedstead screwed to the floor over which was spread a straw-filled palliasse and two blankets. An Elsan bucket in the corner for the performance of natural func-tions. Anton told Seton-Charles to operate the light switch which he had installed in the corridor. He walked over to the windows he had double glazed. No way of breaking out there – especially as the shutters were closed and padlocked on the outside.

'Who are these prisoners?' Seton-Charles asked.

'Just two men.' Anton continued as though talking to himself. 'I must remember no pork. Lamb and chicken is their diet – and somewhere I will find Turkish coffee. In a supermarket in Winchester, probably.' He looked round. 'Yes, all is ready for our visitors.'

'I would like to know what is going on,' Seton-Charles protested.

'Patience. In the meantime, when you are not helping me as labourer you can study your Greek books. Jupiter stressed in his last call you must remain here.' Anton grinned unpleasantly. 'And do you think you would sleep well at night if you upset Jupiter?'

Paula and Newman stayed for several weeks at The Anchor. When Newman phoned Tweed from a public call box one evening Tweed said he wanted them both to remain there until recalled. They were to explore the whole area, to listen to gossip in pubs, to try and find the route Anton used to *leave* the country.

'I don't think he boarded a ship the way he probably came in,' Tweed said. 'We've been very busy here, contacting every airport in the country. No passenger manifest shows that he left by a scheduled flight. And remember, Christina told you he was a pilot, experienced with flying light aircraft . . .'

When he put down the phone Monica queried his decision.

'You have a lot of people in one area. Paula, Newman, Butler and Nield. Isn't that overkill?'

'I'm deliberately saturating that district. I feel it in my bones the solution lies on Exmoor.'

'Anything interesting from Bob? I know it's on the tape I can listen to, but I find your comments more informative.'

'Everything seems normal. Dr Robson visits his patients

– riding his horse. He works long hours. Barrymore makes infrequent phone calls from the phone box in Minehead.'

'Isn't that peculiar? Surely you said he has a phone of his own at Quarme Manor?'

'Apparently it often goes on the blink, as Newman expressed it. Something to do with the overhead wires getting blown down. It's the stormy season down there. Gale Force Ten and heavy seas.'

'What about Kearns?'

'He leads a strange life. When there's a moon he rides up to Dunkery Beacon, stays there a while. Butler has watched him through night glasses. He sits on his horse, still as a statue. Then he disappears for a while before riding back to his house.'

'Makes sense to me,' said Monica. 'The poor man has lost his wife. He just wants to be on his own. And he's trying to keep his sanity by maintaining old habits.'

'Another funny development – Paula found this out from lunching in pubs on Exmoor. Kearns doesn't meet his chums Barrymore and Robson any more. No Saturday night dinners at The Luttrell Arms, no Wednesday lunches at The Royal Oak, Winsford. He has cut himself off from them completely.'

'You can't tell how grief will affect people.'

'It's a very major change in relationships,' Tweed pointed out. 'For years those three acted as though they were still members of an Army unit. Kearns walking away is bound to affect the other two, Barrymore and Robson. Psychologically, I mean. We are still seeing the thing develop.'

'You'll get there in the end,' Monica encouraged him.

Tweed took from a drawer the commando knife which had killed Gallagher in Lisbon. That had been a frustrating exercise. At the last moment the Portuguese police chief had refused to send the weapon direct to London: Marler had arrived at London Airport several weeks before, only to find the pilot had nothing for him.

The knife had been ultimately despatched to Interpol in Paris. Which was the correct procedure. Tweed's friend, Pierre Loriot, had immediately flown it to London, but it had all taken precious time. Then there was the report from Lloyd's of London on the *Oporto*.

The typed document had confirmed all Tweed had been previously told. The vessel's clandestine call at Tripoli in Libya. Its voyage from Tripoli back to Lisbon – the arrival at that port coinciding with Anton flying from Zurich to the Portuguese capital. The shadowing of the vessel by French aircraft, culminating in its seizure after leaving Somerset off the port of Brest. The discovery of the large armoury of weapons which, Paris was certain, was destined for the IRA. Another dead end, as Tweed termed it, leading them nowhere further.

It was now November. Rain fell in a slanting downpour outside as Tweed put the weapon back in the drawer.

'I'm missing something,' he said. 'I feel it is under my nose and I can't see it. Get out all those tapes of phone conversations. I want to listen to them again. With a fresh ear.'

The dacha was located in the hills north-east of Moscow. There was a colony of them nearby where the bigwigs relaxed in summer, but this one was isolated. It was used for high-security military conferences in the hot season.

General Lucharsky stopped the Chaika a few hundred yards away from the shuttered building, switched off the engine, walked the rest of the way. His gleaming fur-lined boots crunched in the crisp hard snow; there had been a light fall the previous night. The temperature was eight degrees below freezing and he pulled up his military great-coat collar, revelling in the invigorating air.

The building was made of timber. Steps led up to the veranda overhung by the projecting roof. The place was surrounded with birch woods flaked with white. Sunlight reflected off the snow crystals. Lucharsky climbed the steps, stood by the front door and looked around. He listened carefully and heard nothing in the heavy silence. He had not been followed. He rapped on the heavy door four times slowly.

When the door opened two men, also wearing the uniforms of generals, appeared. Lucharsky put a finger to his lips. With a swift gesture he indicated that they should follow him. He led the way back down the steps and into the woods. His arm brushed a branch and crusted snow fell on it.

'Why could we not stay in the dacha?' asked a short stocky general with stubby legs and thick eyebrows under his peaked cap. General Budienny.

'Because it may be wired for sound,' Lucharsky told him contemptuously. He towered over both his companions. 'Out here no one can hear us.'

He stopped inside a hollow encircled with trees. The Troika was assembled. Lucharsky kicked snow off his boots before continuing. The third man, an expert on armoured divisions, listened.

'The plan is proceeding,' Lucharsky informed them. 'I have now heard Gorbachev will land in Britain at the invitation of British Prime Minister Thatcher. We have him.'

'On the way to or back from the Washington summit?' asked Budienny.

'En route to Washington. Except his plane will never land. In one piece, that is. The missiles are in place.'

'How do you know where he will land? London Airport?' persisted Budienny.

'We don't know yet.' Lucharsky waved a gloved hand. 'It makes no difference. The missiles are located in a central

483

position close to many airfields – including RAF military bases. They are mobile. Can be moved to the correct area as soon as we get the precise data.'

'How do you know all this?'

Lucharsky sighed. 'We have direct communication with the man who will control the operation. By radio. A complex route. But coded signals are received by one of our men at the Black Sea naval base of Novorossiisk. He is an excellent radio operator and brings me the signals regularly to Moscow.'

'Routine is dangerous,' Budienny objected. 'And our necks are on the block.'

Lucharsky sighed again, his expression saturnine. 'Since that naval base is so important a courier flies frequently to Moscow to report on progress about enlarging it. Our man is that courier. And before you suggest he could be searched he carries the messages verbally in his head, then tells me.' His tone became mocking. 'If your fears are now allayed perhaps I can proceed? The plan has taken on new dimensions.'

'What are those?'

'As Number Two in the Politburo, Ligachev – who has openly disagreed with Gorbachev's so-called reforms – will automatically become General Secretary. He knows nothing, of course, of what we plan.'

'But what are these new dimensions?' Budienny repeated.

'Once Ligachev is in power the real hardline element inside the Politburo will take over. Those men Gorbachev has not yet got rid of. Then next year, in 1988, we launch the limited attack.'

'Attack?' Budienny's eyes gleamed.

'We manufacture a border incident – as Hitler did against Poland in 1939. Our armies, brought close to the western frontier at night when the American satellites are blind, invade West Germany. We outnumber NATO enormously with our tanks. With our artillery and our air force. We shall reach the Rhine in three days.'

'That means World War Three,' Budienny objected.

'No. We stop at the Rhine. We announce we are going no further. The Americans will be in the middle of their presidential election. Everything will be in confusion in Washington. You think they will want a conventional *limited* war – a three-day coup – to turn nuclear? To risk New York, Chicago and Los Angeles become incinerated ash-heaps? Then we have in our hands the Ruhr, the great German powerhouse of armament production. We become the greatest power on earth.'

'And who will bring down Gorbachev's plane over Britain?'

'I told you before.' Lucharsky clapped his gloves together without making a sound. 'Shi-ite Muslims. They will end Gorbachev's regime of anti-Leninist idiocy . . .'

46

At Cherry Farm Anton stood inside the second furniture van and surveyed his workmanship. He wore his boiler suit and his cap: he had developed the habit of wearing it all the time except when he went to bed. In the little spare time left over he had visited pubs some distance away, drinking beer while he listened to the locals' chatter. Anton could now talk with the accent of a working man. Holding a power tool in his right hand he turned to Seton-Charles.

'Well, you have seen the second demonstration. The sliding panel works, as it does in the other van.'

The two men stood close together; space was cramped.

Near the driver's cab Anton had erected another platform with steps leading up to it; a chair with an adjustable back was clamped to the floor below the sliding panel.

But the rear part of the van was crammed almost roof-high with old furniture – as was the van behind them. To leave the van they had to squeeze past the projecting legs of tables and a large wardrobe among other items. This was a precaution Jupiter had insisted on when he had given instructions to Anton after his landing on the coast.

'Then, if by chance you are stopped,' Balaclava had explained, 'the police will see a van stacked with furniture which will hide the launch platform . . .'

Before starting work on the rear van Anton had visited various furniture auctions, storing the junk he had purchased in the front van. Seton-Charles had studied the stack of local newspapers Anton had bought all over Hampshire, looking for furniture auctions. He had been surprised and pleased at how many there were.

'Let me see the panel open again,' Seton-Charles suggested. 'I want to be sure it works every time.'

Anton shook his head. 'The generator makes a noise. I tested it several times while you were inside the farm, keeping a lookout for snoopers. God, I've driven a long way, buying everything I needed from different shops. No one will have a clue about what we were constructing.'

'But why does each van need a small generator to operate the panel,' asked Seton-Charles, whose knowledge of mechanical problems was zero. 'Surely you could have used the power from the van's engine.'

'Which shows how much you know. For one thing the van will be stationary when we launch the missiles, the engine turned off. The driver will warn us over his walkie-talkie when the plane is in view. Only then do we open the panel.'

'It seems very well organized,' Seton-Charles agreed. 'That smell of fresh paint is turning my stomach. Was it really necessary to change the name on the outside?'

'Again, Jupiter's orders. We don't want any connection with Camelford Removals, the bankrupt outfit in Norwich you bought them from. Now we are Smith's Removals of Birmingham. There are two such firms in the city.'

Anton had spent hours with a paintbrush, first obliterating the old names, waiting for the paint to dry, then substituting the new names. But Seton-Charles had a point: the barn, with its doors closed at both ends, reeked of the stench.

'Tonight we'll open the rear doors of the barn after dark, let the smell out,' he decided. 'We'll take it in turns to stand guard while those doors are open. Later I'll rub dirt over the fresh paint . . .'

He stopped speaking as the phone extension he had rigged up from the farmhouse began ringing. He sent Seton-Charles back to the farmhouse, picked up the phone.

'Alfred Moss speaking.'

'Are both containers ready yet?'

The same supercilious, upper-crust voice Anton disliked. Like a commander giving orders to lowly subordinates. He took a deep breath.

'Yes. They are ready to move to the port.'

'Your two guests will be arriving today. Noon at the arranged meeting place. Foster and Saunders will be travelling with them. I must go. My garden is being ruined by magpies and goldcrests. I'd like to convert the place into a closed circuit. Don't be late . . .'

Anton put down the phone and swore in Greek. Arrogant bastard. But he was clever. In a few words – seemingly innocent if overheard – he'd conveyed a lot.

The two men who were bringing the prisoners to the lonely crossroads were called Foster and Saunders. They would give the password *magpies*. Anton would reply with *goldcrests*. He ran to the doors, opened one, closed it, snapped the padlock shut on the outside, ran into the

487

farmhouse. Seton-Charles stood in the kitchen, waiting for the news.

'I have to leave at once. I'll come back with the prisoners. Be ready to open the shed doors . . .'

'Is it wise to keep on using the same Austin Metro you hired in Taunton? We've had it for weeks. And what about payment to Barton?'

'Jupiter arranges fresh payments in cash. It's risky changing cars, using that driving licence. I must be off . . .'

Driving at a modest pace along a winding country road, Anton reflected on the past. He kept a close eye on the dashboard clock, but he didn't want to arrive early. Hanging about – even in the middle of nowhere – was dangerous. A police patrol car might become interested.

He was thinking about Petros and his lust for revenge. Anton had never shared his father's one-track outlook on life. He had simply gone along with him for years; originally to make sure the money for his education was forthcoming. He had played up to the old man like mad. Later he had borrowed from him to help set up his chain of radio, television and video shops. Then he had met the man who had changed his life. Professor Guy Seton-Charles.

Anton had attended the first lecture at Athens University out of sheer curiosity. More intelligent – and cynical – than the other students, it had not taken him long to see through the professor. Under the guise of lecturing on Greek Studies, it had soon become apparent to Anton this was a course in political indoctrination. In the Communist creed.

In his turn, Seton-Charles had spotted Anton as the cleverest, most cold-blooded and ambitious of his students. Just the material he was looking for. They had formed an alliance rather than a friendship. Anton had decided the West was on its way out; the future belonged to Russia.

So convincingly did he appear to embrace Communism

he was in due course invited to join the Greek Key as a junior member. The fact that his father, Petros, had supported the Greek Key during the war helped. Anton simply saw it as the quickest route to power in Greece. That was until Gorbachev replaced Brezhnev. *Glasnost? Perestroika?* This was no route to a Communist takeover of Greece.

Recruited to the inner councils – after expressing his anti-Gorbachev sentiments – Anton had become a trusted member of the conspiracy. And then there was the detail of Petros' collection of British commando knives. It was Doganis who had suggested how these might come in useful when he learned of their existence.

'Steal them,' he advised Anton, before his first trip to England. 'You may have to kill someone. You could do that? Good. If it comes to that, use one of those daggers. It will confuse any investigation. The English are poking around still trying to find out who killed Andreas Gavalas. Use one of those daggers and they will go back over forty years, ignoring the present. An excellent smoke-screen . . .'

Anton glanced at the clock again, increased speed. When he arrived at the crossroads a Ford station wagon was pulled up inside the trees. A man dressed in a smart blue navy pinstripe suit appeared. He wore pigskin gloves. Anton noticed they were soiled, which did not go with the smartness of the rest of his appearance. He pulled up, switched off his engine, looked round and listened. The only sound was the crunch of the man's shoes on a gravel track where the Ford was standing.

'Excuse me,' the man said, standing by Anton's open window, 'I'm looking for the Magpie Inn.'

'I can tell you how to get to the Goldcrest Inn.'

'Thank God. Oh, my name's Foster. It's been a fraught business. We have them in the back of the station wagon. Hands bound behind their backs, ankles tied, their mouths taped, eyes blindfolded. Saunders is over there and will help. How are you going to move the merchandise?'

'Under the travelling rugs in the back of *my* car. One on top of the other . . .'

Seton-Charles ran out as Anton arrived back at Cherry Farm. The Greek lifted the corner of a rug and exposed the two captive Shi-ite Muslims dressed in prison garb. They untied the rope round the ankles of one man, manoeuvred him out of the car. When he tried to struggle they frogmarched him inside the farmhouse, up the stairs and into the prepared room.

'Dump him on the bed,' Anton ordered. 'He'll be safe while we get the other one inside . . .'

Five minutes later they had both men in their separate rooms. Anton held a Luger pistol while Seton-Charles tore off the tape and removed the blindfold. The Shi-ite blinked in the unaccustomed daylight and glared. Anton gestured towards the canvas sack he had dragged up the stairs. From its open end protruded the head of a slaughtered pig taken from the chest freezer in one of the sheds.

'Any trouble with you and I kill you, then you'll be buried in a grave with this pig.'

'No! No! No . . .!'

Anton watched the man's terrified expression. It had worked. The only form of intimidation which would quell a Shi-ite. The Muslim religion regarded the pig as the most unclean and horrific of animals. Anton waited behind the pig lying on the landing floor while Seton-Charles released the prisoner's hands. The Shi-ite rubbed his wrists to get the circulation going and all the time he stared at the pig's head as though hypnotized.

Anton waited until Seton-Charles had left the room, then threw inside a bundle of clothes: three suits in different sizes, underwear, shirts, socks and shoes.

'You get out of that prison garb, choose the clothes which fit you best, wrap the others in a bundle. We'll collect them when we feed you. Put your prison stuff with the bundle.' He aimed the Luger at the trembling Shi-ite's head. 'If you try to get away I will shoot you dead. Then you will share eternity with a pig.'

Seton-Charles closed, double-locked, bolted the door. 'Let's hope one of those suits fits him.'

'One will fit well enough. A man escaped from prison doesn't always have the right clothes to wear. Now haul the pig sack along to the other room and we'll repeat the process . . .'

He watched as Seton-Charles heaved the heavy sack along the corridor, his rimless glasses perched on his nose. Anton had been careful not to comment on the fact, but he had been surprised at how useful the professor had been. He was stronger physically than the Greek had realized. He had proved a useful workmate during the conversion of the vans, handing up tools to Anton on the platform, finding the right screws, and a psychological change had taken place in the relationship of the two men.

Seton-Charles now accepted Anton was boss and he prepared good meals for them. Something I might have foreseen, Anton thought: the professor was a bachelor who lived alone. looked after himself and was fastidious in his habits. They paused in front of the second reinforced door.

'That latest phone call I had from Jupiter,' Anton told him. 'We've reached the stage of closed circuit.'

'What's that?'

'We stay under very close cover. We don't leave the farm for anything unless it's essential.'

'Then the operation must be close?'

'Soon,' Anton assured him, 'it has to be soon.'

47

Tweed had 'broken silence'.

He had sent out a general alert all over Europe to counter-espionage chiefs, to his personal underground network of informants. The message was always the same.

Any data on past and present movements of Anton Gavalas, citizen of Greece. Suspected member of hardline Communist group the Greek Key. Also identical data on Professor Guy Seton-Charles, British citizen, Professor of Greek Studies at Bristol University, England, and Athens University, Greece. Data required extreme urgency. Tweed.

Copies of a photograph of Anton – made from the print inside the file Kalos had provided for Tweed – accompanied the request. But only a word description of Seton-Charles was sent. Tweed realized they had made a bad mistake in not photographing the professor.

Howard wandered into Tweed's office a week after the messages had been sent. It was his blue pinstripe suit day. He perched his buttocks on the edge of Tweed's desk, adjusted his tie, smiled at Monica who was stunned by such amiability.

'Any progress from the boys abroad?' he enquired.

Tweed winced inwardly at the phraseology. 'Nothing that gives us any kind of lead. Later this afternoon I have a meeting with the Prime Minister. I thought it was time she knew about this business.'

He waited for the explosion of outrage. It didn't come. Instead, Howard ran his fingers over his plump pink face and nodded approval. 'I was just coming in to suggest maybe we ought to let her know. Frankly, I'm surprised you didn't seek an earlier conference.'

'No hard facts to go on. Ever since Masterson was killed it's been like seeing shadowy figures in the mists of Exmoor. You aren't sure whether you actually saw anything or not. It may be a tricky interview. She *does* like facts. Oh, Paula is on her way here, driving up from Somerset. I just hope she gets here before I leave for Downing Street.'

'And why is the delightful Paula driving back to London? She could have reported over the phone from that public call box in Minehead.'

'She said she had information she'd sooner give me face to face.'

'Sounds intriguing. I suppose you couldn't record her report so I could play it back later?'

'I'll do that.'

Howard glanced at the machine on Tweed's desk, the neat piles of cassettes. 'You've been listening to those things yet again? The tapes of Butler's phoned reports and that clandestine job Nield did during dinner at The Luttrell Arms? You still think you've spotted which one of the three is the killer?'

'Yes.' Tweed stood up, began pacing slowly. 'But no proof. In case anything happens to me I typed out a secret report which is inside a sealed envelope in the safe.'

Howard stood up, pulled down his jacket at the back. 'Damned if I could point the finger at any of them. And God knows I've listened to them often enough. Why be so cryptic?'

'Because I could be wrong. The main thing at the moment is two people have gone missing. Anton Gavalas. I checked with Sarris and there's no sign he has returned to Greece. Then Guy Seton-Charles has vanished off the face of the earth. He'd accumulated several months' leave, so Bristol University informed us. He said he was going abroad. No trace of him on any airline passenger manifest.

And he always flew everywhere – again according to Bristol.'

'So, we're up the proverbial gum tree. Good luck with the PM.'

On this encouraging note Howard left the office. Monica stopped studying her file. 'He's also worried. Like you are. And although I hate Howard's guts, his instinct is sometimes very sound. I wish you hadn't said that thing about in case anything happens to you. It's tempting fate.'

'Don't be so superstitious,' Tweed chided.

Monica slammed her pencil down on her desk. 'Have we got one damn thing to go on after all this effort?'

'Two things. When I was interviewing old Petros at his farm he mentioned there had been rumours during the Second World War that the Greek Key was controlled by an Englishman in Cairo.'

'Seton-Charles was in Cairo . . .'

'So were the three commandos. The second thing also came from Greece. Kalos told me a radio ham – a friend of Sarris' – had picked up a coded message. At the end there was an instruction in English. *From now on the call sign is changed to Colonel Winter*. History can be changed by such chance happenings.'

Paula arrived early when Tweed and Monica were standing by the window, drinking tea. She was behind the wheel of Newman's Mercedes. As she parked by the kerb further along the Crescent Tweed saw the automatic radio aerial retracting, sliding down inside the rear. He frowned, held his cup in mid-air.

'What is it?' asked Monica.

'Nothing. Just an idea.'

'She's made very good time. And she seems to be in a rush – she's almost running. And her clothes!'

Paula was wearing a pair of tight blue denims and a windcheater. An outfit neither of them had ever seen her adopt before. Paula was classic pleated skirts and blouse with a well-fitting jacket. She disappeared inside the entrance below them.

'I'll make her coffee,' Monica decided. 'She's had quite a long drive. Back in a minute. And I think something's wrong.'

Tweed had his back to the window when there was a knock on his door, he called, 'Come in,' and Paula appeared, carrying in one hand her briefcase, in the other her small travelling case.

'What's the matter?' he asked, coming forward.

'Does there have to be something?' she asked, went to her desk and dumped two cases. Her voice was cool, too cool. She turned, leaning against the desk, and smiled wanly as he gave her a hug, kissed her on the cheek. She was a shade too controlled.

She took off her gloves slowly, placed one neatly on top of the other. Then she folded her arms, tilted her chin in the defiant look he knew so well. She was white-faced and there were dark circles under her eyes.

'I drove like a bat out of hell to get here.' She smiled again at his expression. 'But within the speed limit all the way.'

'What's the matter?' he repeated.

'You really are the most perceptive man.' She paused. 'It's good to be back.' Another pause. 'I've just shot two men.'

Tweed concealed the jolt he'd felt. 'Why not sit down and tell me about it? Monica is coming with coffee. The Browning automatic I sent down by courier was for you then? Not for Newman or Marler, as I thought?'

'They've given me hell, those two.' She sat down, crossed

495

her legs. 'I gave them hell back. Am I – or am I not – a fully-fledged member of this outfit?'

'Very fledged.' He smiled and drew a chair close to her. 'I have always shown you that's the way I feel, surely?'

'Yes. *You* have. Want to hear about my target-shooting – with live targets?'

Her voice was steady but Tweed sensed tension under the surface. He fetched a bottle of cognac and a glass from a cupboard, poured a hefty snifter. 'Get that down inside yourself.'

'Thanks.' She held the balloon glass in both hands to drink – to stop the glass shaking, Tweed suspected. 'My, that's made a difference.' She relaxed against the chair-back, her normal colour started to return. 'I hardly know where to start. I suppose it was Marler who saved my life. He arrived soon after I did.'

'Because I decided we needed every possible person down there. Exmoor is a vast territory to cover. And why not start at the beginning? When you'd arrived with Newman at Porlock Weir . . .'

Monica had phoned ahead and there were two rooms reserved for them when Newman and Paula carried their cases into The Anchor. They reached Porlock Weir in the early evening – Newman had encountered heavy sea mist drifting across the road. The moor was blotted out.

They had a conference with Butler and Nield over dinner and divided up duties. Newman took charge, made the suggestion. The dining room was almost empty so they could talk easily.

'We have three people to watch – Robson, Barrymore and Kearns. Nield, you take Robson. I'll keep an eye on Barrymore. That leaves Butler for Kearns . . .'

'No go,' Butler informed him. 'Tweed has given me the

job of checking out the people who live on that bungalow estate near Kearns' place.'

'And I'd like to help Harry, if he doesn't mind,' Paula said. 'I was the one who thought there was something odd about the place.'

'Be my guest,' replied Butler with enthusiasm. 'I've been helping Nield watch the three commando types. The electoral register in Taunton is our first check,' he told Paula.

'Then I'll have to take on both Barrymore and Kearns,' Newman decided. He grinned at Paula. 'You're just about as bloody . . . independent as Marler.'

'You were going to say bloody-minded,' Paula told him. 'Maybe I am. Do I get the order of the boot?'

'I'll overlook it this time. Eat your dinner, it's getting cold . . .'

The problem solved itself the following day when Marler turned up at The Anchor, sent down by Tweed. Secretly Newman had been relieved the previous evening: Paula would have protection, working with Butler. He was careful not to point this out to Paula.

While Paula and Butler visited Taunton, Newman gave Marler the task of shadowing Kearns in his hired Peugeot. Apart from Newman, they all travelled in hired cars. It took a week for Butler and Paula to come up with a list of names of the owners of the bungalows on the estate. Once she had the names Paula took to visiting The Royal Oak at Winsford where she was soon firm friends with the heavily built barman. She always arrived before the crowd at lunchtime, always came alone.

Bit by bit she told Jack, the barman, about herself. 'I'm recovering from an illness – convalescent leave they call it, the insurance company I work for. And when I was a kid I used to come down to Taunton to visit relatives . . .'

Her psychology was shrewd: country folk liked to know who they were talking to. Gradually she extracted from

Jack information about the occupants of the bungalow estate. The one day she avoided was Wednesday: she had seen Barrymore and Robson lunching at their usual table. They were still keeping up the ritual meetings, but Kearns was not there with them. She checked his absence on two Wednesdays before avoiding that day.

'Thinkin' of buyin' one of those bungalows when it comes on the market?' Jack commented to her one day. 'You'll be lucky. A funny set-up that lot, you mark my words.'

'Funny in what way?' she asked.

'Ever 'eard of a bungalow estate put up fifteen years ago and not one of the original owners has moved? Six bungalows there are. Six men. You'd think at least one would have moved on. New job, somethin' like that. Not a bit of it. They're all still there. And keeps themselves to themselves.'

'You mean you've never met one of them?'

'Now I didn't say that, did I, miss? One of them came in here soon after they'd all moved in. Chap called Foster. Didn't take to 'im. Drank gin and tonics while he chatted. La-di-dah type.'

'What did he chat about? It sounds like a mystery. I love mysteries,' Paula glowed.

'Said he was an investment counsellor, whatever that might be. Works in Bristol. His wife has some big job overseas. Never seen 'er. Said his friend, Saunders, also had his wife abroad. Some job with the UN in New York. Funny sort of married life. Wouldn't suit me – visiting the missus once or twice a year.'

'You mean the wives never come here?'

'That's about the long and short of it. Then there's the crank. Professor Guy Seton-Charles. Bachelor. Something to do with Bristol University. In summer they mows their lawns at the weekends. That's about all you see of 'em. Stuffy lot, if you ask me.'

Paula swallowed a piece of her chicken and mushroom

pie, the day's speciality chalked up on a blackboard. She sipped at her glass of white wine. Jack was polishing yet another glass until it came up gleaming like silver crystal.

'I heard there was a Mr Simon Morle living in one of the bungalows,' she said casually.

'Maybe. I wouldn't know. They're there and yet they're not there.' People were beginning to fill up the tables. He turned to another customer. 'What can I get you, sir?'

That was the night they had the most almighty row back at The Anchor.

They were all assembled for dinner at their usual table. Paula sat between Newman and Marler. Butler and Nield faced them, and Nield, inadvertently, lit the fuse.

'Saw you today, Paula. I was tracking Robson when he tried to call on Kearns. Got no joy. I thought Kearns must be out. Robson pressed the gate bell several times, no one came out, so he pushed off. I had wondered whether Kearns was ill.'

'I think he is,' Paula replied. '*I* saw Robson call, then drive off. A few minutes later Dr Underwood – we met him in the bar if you remember – called. Kearns came out and let him in.'

'What did you mean, Pete?' Marler asked. 'You said you saw Paula. Driving along the road?'

'No. Parked in her hired Renault inside a gateway overlooking that bungalow colony – and Kearns' place.'

Marler turned to Paula. 'What the devil were you doing there?'

'Observing that bungalow estate. You can look down on it. It's odd – one woman seems to clean the lot. Furtively.'

'How do you mean?' Nield enquired.

'She always slips in by the back doors. She has a key to each of them. I've used night glasses to watch her after dark . . .'

499

'*After dark?*' Marler's tone expressed incredulity. 'How long have you been keeping up this vigil?'

'For about two weeks.'

'You do realize it's only a matter of time before you're spotted,' Marler persisted in a cold voice. 'It's madness.'

'I have already realized that.' She said the words deliberately, disliking his tone. 'I saw the solution today. There's a riding stable near Dunster which hires out horses. In future I'll ride – which means I can get on the moor, check the area from different angles.'

'You bloody well won't . . .'

'Partridge used a horse,' she snapped. 'For the same reason, I suspect. He could see more from a horse.'

'And look where it got him.' Marler leaned his long white face – his Grecian suntan had long since faded – close to hers. 'It got him a knife in the back. You should be armed. You shouldn't be doing it at all.'

'No one's going to stop me,' she said icily, staring hard at Marler. 'If you feel that way, get me a weapon . . .'

It was Newman who calmed the atmosphere. He knew Paula was seething at the unspoken suggestion that she couldn't take care of herself. He remembered times when Tweed had put her in the front line to toughen her up. Standing up, he said he was driving into Minehead to call Tweed, to ask him to send a Browning automatic with spare magazines by motorbike courier. While he was away the rest of the meal was eaten in silence.

The following morning after breakfast Newman tapped on Paula's door. Inside he handed her a Browning and spare mags.

'So, I've come of age,' she said and smiled drily.

'How are you going to carry it on a horse – so it's easy to get at in an emergency?'

She produced a makeshift but neat holster made of blue denim and took hold of the Browning where she had laid it on a table. Releasing the magazine inside the butt, she checked to make sure there wasn't a bullet up the spout, pushed the mag back inside the gun and slipped it inside the holster. Two straps of the same material were attached to it.

She was wearing tight denims thrust inside riding boots and a padded windcheater. All purchased the previous day. Then she strapped the holster to her right upper leg close to her crotch. Parading round the room, she made a gesture with her slim hand.

'I'm on a horse. You meet me. Would you notice it?'

'No. It blends in perfectly. How on earth did you make that holster?'

'By staying up half the night. I cut material from the bottom of my jeans – tucked inside my boots you can't see where I took it from. Then a lot of careful sewing.' She came close to him, kissed him on the cheek. 'I expected you to flare up like Marler last night. Thanks for your vote of confidence.'

Newman shrugged, grinned. 'You are one of the team. Marler's got a short fuse. What did that cleaning woman you saw down at the estate look like?'

'Middle-aged. Medium height. About a hundred and twenty pounds. Grey hair tied back in a bun. I've got several photographs of her. I was carrying my camera with the telephoto lens. Should we send the film to Tweed?'

'Let me have it. Maybe in a few days one of us will have to go up to London. You'd finished the film?'

She handed him the spool. 'Yes. And I've a fresh one in the camera. The one you're holding has pictures of all the men living there. Plus pictures of the bungalows. Including Seton-Charles' place with that weird complex of TV aerials attached to his chimney.'

She hid the Browning with its holster and the mags at the bottom of the wardrobe, then picked up neat rows of shoes and spread them over the gun. Straightening up, she looked at Newman.

'After that row at dinner last night I feel like a walk along the coast. I didn't get much sleep and I'm feeling restless.'

'Let's go . . .'

It was dark but the gale had slackened to a strong breeze as they strolled along the track westward. Paula glanced at the cottage where Mrs Larcombe had lived, then looked away. Newman was careful not to refer to it.

'What are the others doing?' she asked as they picked their way across the pebbles.

'We're keeping up the watch on the commandos. Kearns appears to have recovered, but he's limping a bit. Maybe he twisted his ankle. Butler followed one of the men who live in those bungalows to the Somerset and Cornwall Bank in Bristol. Watched him draw about a thousand pounds in fifties. He's reported it to Tweed who has now started a discreet check on where that money comes from.'

'Anything new on the commandos?'

'Not really, blast it. Robson still rides to see his patients at all hours. He has one old duck who delights in using her bedside phone and calling him out late at night. Lives in a creepy old mansion near Dulverton. Barrymore is still making calls from that public box in Minehead. Kearns has no help in his house – looks after the place himself, does his own cooking. Army type, I suppose . . .'

He stopped speaking as Paula grasped his arm. They were some distance west of Porlock Weir, walking close to towering cliffs. 'I heard something funny, a sinister noise,' Paula whispered.

Then Newman heard it. A crumbling sound, the noise of grinding rocks. He looked above them, grabbed Paula's hand, shouted at her to run. They headed for the sea. Behind them the sound increased, grew to a rumbling roar. At the water's edge Newman turned and Paula swung round with him. She gazed, appalled.

By the light of the rising moon they saw a gigantic slab

of cliff sliding down from the summit, a slab which broke into smaller pieces as it rolled towards the beach. Enormous boulders bounded downwards towards where they stood, their backs to the sea. The boulders lost momentum, came to rest two dozen yards away. A sudden silence descended. Paula shivered, huddled closer to Newman.

'It's OK,' he said. 'That's it.'

'My God, if we hadn't run we'd have been under that.'

She pointed towards a dark mass of rocks piled up the height of a two-storey house. They were making their way back, keeping to the edge of the sea, when Paula pointed again.

'Who can that be?'

In the distance, close to the track, a man on horseback was riding away from them. Hunched forward, close to the horse's head, it was impossible to make out his shape, guess his height. He reached the track and the horse broke into a gallop. When they arrived back at The Anchor there · was no sign of any horseman and they hurried inside to report the landslip.

The violent incident took place next day.

48

Grey mist was curling over the high crests as Paula rode her horse over the high ground behind the bungalow estate. It lay about two hundred yards below her and from this angle she was able to observe features she had not seen before.

Behind the end of the cul-de-sac a path led down into a dip invisible from the road. An old barn-like structure huddled in the dip, a building with half-doors. Both upper halves were open and two horses' heads peered out. This was her first realization that someone living on the estate rode the moors.

She saw movement, the opening of a back door in Seton-Charles' bungalow. Lifting her glasses looped round her neck, she focused. It was the grey-haired cleaning woman, carrying a mop and a plastic bucket. Paula remained perfectly still: people rarely looked *upwards*.

The woman opened a gate in the back garden fence, walked into the next garden. She put down mop and bucket, fiddled with a bunch of keys, inserted one in the rear door of the bungalow and disappeared inside with her cleaning equipment.

Paula dropped her glasses, rode on, slowly circling the estate. As usual, no sign of cars. They had probably all driven off to their jobs. The cars she had seen earlier, arriving back in the evenings, were Jags and Fords. No Mercedes or Rolls-Royces, but the cars they drove still cost money. There seemed to be no shortage of that commodity.

She had watched them at weekends cutting their lawns with power mowers, big machines which did the job quickly. It was late November and she gave a little shiver: the cold clamminess of the approaching mist rolling down the slopes was making itself felt.

She kept moving slowly, like a rider out for a gentle morning bit of exercise. For the moment she was sheltered from the estate by a gorse-covered ridge. She guided her mount up the side and perched on a small rocky hilltop which gave a bird's-eye view. The two horsemen seemed to appear out of nowhere.

One moment she was alone on the hilltop, the next moment they rode out from behind a concealed ridge and confronted her. They stopped about two dozen feet away, staring at her. She noticed several things as she casually dropped her right hand over the holster.

They were experienced riders: neither had his feet inside the stirrups. Probably because they had mounted their horses in a hurry. She recognized their mounts as the horses which had peered over the half-doors. One man was tall, lean-faced and with jet-black hair. His cheekbones were prominent, almost Slavic. The other was short and heavily-built with an ugly round face and a mean mouth.

Both were in their forties, she estimated. Both wore windcheaters and slacks thrust into riding boots. The Slavic-faced man raised a hand, unzipped the front of his windcheater, left it open. The ugly man began guiding his horse, took up a position on her right side. She responded by turning her own horse.

'I like to face strangers,' she informed them and smiled.

'Why are you spying on us?' Slav-Face demanded.

'It's normal to introduce yourself in this part of the world,' she replied. 'I'm Paula . . .'

'And I'm Norton. Now, I'll ask you again – why are you spying on us?'

His right hand slipped inside his windcheater, emerged holding a gun. A 9mm Walther automatic as far as Paula could tell. She froze. The weapon was aimed point-blank between her breasts. Paula glanced to her left. A ridge higher than the hilltop masked the road. No help from that direction – even if Nield came driving along.

'This is moorland open to the public,' she snapped. 'You think you own Exmoor?'

'Gutsy, eh?' Norton commented. 'Now answer the question.'

'I ride all over the place. I don't know what you're talking about. And it's illegal to threaten someone with a weapon in this country.'

'She says it's illegal, Morle,' Norton said to his companion, still staring at Paula. 'She says she doesn't know what I'm talking about.'

His voice was cultured; high falutin' some would have called it. Almost a caricature of Marler's drawling way of speaking, but with an underlying sneer. Norton and Morle. Paula recalled the names she'd recorded while Butler examined the electoral register. These were two of them: she had all five names in her head.

'So if she doesn't know what I'm talking about,' Norton continued, 'how come she's been sitting in a parked car up the road day after day, watching the bungalows through field glasses?' He still held the gun levelled at her. 'I think maybe we will continue this discussion inside my bungalow, have a real cosy chat.'

Paula had been frightened when the two men first appeared. Now she remembered Newman putting her through her paces at a quiet spot on the North Downs. And he'd gone through the Special Air Services course before writing an article on the SAS. *Faced with a gunman there's always something you can do – say – to distract him, if you're armed* . . . And now, unsure of survival, she had gone as cold as ice.

'So you've confused me with someone else,' she said. 'Parked in a car, my foot. A horse is my form of transport here. You can tell the difference between a horse and a car? This is not very encouraging – when Foster asked me if I could take on the job of helping clean the bungalows.'

'He did what?' Norton's forehead crinkled with puzzlement. He turned to Morle. 'Do you know anything about this? He must be clean out of his . . .'

As he spoke the gun sagged, the muzzle aimed at the ground. It took seconds for Paula to haul the Browning from the holster, to grasp the butt in both hands, to aim it. Norton saw movement out of the corner of his eye. He began to lift his own gun. Paula fired twice. Norton slumped, was falling from his horse, when Morle ripped down his zipper, shoved his hand inside, began to haul out a gun. Paula had swivelled the Browning, her knees clamped to her horse to hold it steady. Twice more she fired.

Morle grabbed at his saddle with one hand, slowly toppled. A loud explosion echoed. Paula thought she was hit. Then she saw Norton had pulled the trigger in a reflex action as he hit the ground. The bullet winged across the moor.

The men's two horses galloped off in panicky freedom. Paula's mount threatened to rise up on its hindlegs. She pressed a firm hand on its neck, made soothing noises, dismounted, trailed the reins and approached Norton, still gripping her Browning. He lay unconscious, his fingers had dropped the gun. She bent down, felt his neck pulse. It beat steadily. Blood oozed from his right shoulder.

Standing up, she ran across to examine Morle. He also was unconscious. A red stain spread across his slacks close to his left hip. Again she checked the pulse. Again she felt its regular beat. Thank God, she thought and stood up, deciding what to do.

Two minutes later she was riding fast along the track which led to Exford, a four-mile trek. She left the horse at the riding stables she had hired it from. Nothing more to pay. Walking along the road, she entered the field where she had parked her Renault, got behind the wheel.

She drove across country, turned on to the A396 and arrived via Minehead at Porlock Weir half an hour later. To her infinite relief Newman and Marler had just returned to The Anchor.

Tweed drank three cups of coffee while he listened to Paula's story in his Park Crescent office. She spoke tersely, with not a wasted word. On his desk lay the sheet of handwritten names she had given him – the occupants of the six bungalows. He already knew them from the earlier report Butler had given him on the phone. He squeezed

507

her hand as she concluded her account, stood up and went back behind his desk.

'So Newman and Marler cleaned up the mess,' he said.

'They were marvellous. I wondered if they'd say I'd made a mistake stopping at the first public phone box on my way back to Porlock Weir. That was when I phoned the police, refused to give a name and told them there'd been a shooting incident near the bungalow estate close to Simonsbath. That they'd better send an ambulance. I felt I couldn't just leave them there. Marler said he'd have done just that . . .'

'Marler would,' Tweed commented drily.

'But Bob said I'd done the right thing. He took the Browning, spare mags and my makeshift holster. They were going to end up in the sea. Bob also said it was lucky Norton's gun went off by chance. That would confuse the police investigation.'

'Eat your ham sandwiches,' said Monica. 'You need something inside you.'

'Now you mention it, I'm famished.' She devoured one sandwich and Tweed waited, glancing at his watch. 'Am I holding you up?' she asked.

'No. Our tame accountant is due soon. Butler reported that he had followed Foster twice to the Somerset and Cornwall Bank in Bristol. He saw him draw about a thousand pounds in cash each time. He heard the teller address him as Mr Foster. Perry has the details and is in the Engine Room phoning God knows who to trace where that money came from. It's so often the money which helps us find out who people really are.'

'Well, there is something wrong about that bungalow estate. I said it was funny when we first saw it,' Paula said defiantly.

Tweed nodded. He understood her attitude. She was bound to suffer a reaction from the experience sooner or later. And the sooner the better.

'It's the first time I've shot anyone,' Paula went on and sank her teeth into a fresh sandwich.

'They're only injured,' Tweed assured her. 'Newman drove over to the estate after you'd left in the Mercedes. He arrived as they were carting those two thugs into an ambulance. He showed his old press card and they recognized the name. He called the hospital later.'

Tweed omitted to tell her Norton was in a coma, that Morle was still unconscious. Police were waiting by their bedsides ready to take statements.

'More alarming,' he went on, switching her mind to another topic, 'Marler arrived at the estate and flourished his fake Special Branch card, so the police let him in. The bungalows are all empty. The cars have gone. Most sinister of all, they can find not a single fingerprint. Everything has been wiped clean. You were so right about that estate.'

'What does that mean – no fingerprints?' Paula asked.

'I think you discovered the secret base of sleepers established fifteen years ago by the Englishman who controls the Greek Key. A base which was recently activated – and has now been evacuated – thanks to your encounter with Norton and Morle. We have now made copies in the Engine Room of those photos you took – and circulated them to every police force in the country. We also have their names.' He glanced down at the list on his desk.

Foster, Saunders, Norton, Morle, Sully.

'Anything else?'

'Yes. Before I sent out the European alert I circulated the registration number of Seton-Charles' Volvo station wagon over here. And Newman visited Bristol University with a police artist. They used several students to build an Identikit picture of the professor. Copies of that have gone out.'

'Will anyone take much notice?'

'I think so,' Tweed said grimly. 'I named him suspected terrorist planner. Highly dangerous.'

509

'Talking of terrorists,' Monica chimed in, 'there's an interesting story I cut from a recent copy of *The Times*. Two Shi-ite Muslim killers were air-lifted by a chopper from Gartree Prison exercise yard. Most audacious. They killed an Iraqi diplomat.'

Tweed wasn't listening. Paula had remembered a further incident.

'There was a big landslip when Bob and I were walking from The Anchor one night along the coast . . .' She described the experience. 'They've put up a big notice. *Warning. Keep clear. Danger of cliff falls.*'

The phone rang. Monica answered, looked up at Tweed. 'Perry is ready to emerge from the basement with his report on the Foster bank account.'

'Tell him to come up.'

Perry was a small, precise, neatly dressed man who wore pince-nez. Monica thought he was a giggle but he had a shrewd financial brain. Clutching a blue file, he sat on the edge of a chair facing Tweed. He glanced at Monica and Paula.

'This is highly confidential.'

Tweed compressed his lips. 'You should realize by now Paula and Monica know more about what's going on than you ever will.'

'Then I will commence.'

He opened his fat file but Tweed glanced at his watch. He had to leave soon for his appointment with the PM. And now Paula had brought information – facts – which made his interview well worthwhile.

'Just tell me in a few words what you've found out.'

'Very well, but I think you should read the file later. The enquiry took longer than I expected. It is a devious trail – and I had to get Walton, head of Special Branch, to vouch for me before the bank manager in Bristol would talk. Then I had to use your name for Europe . . .'

'I know. Chief Inspector Kuhlmann of Wiesbaden in

510

Germany called me. So did Beck in Zurich. Do get on with it.'

'Foster originally had twenty thousand pounds in his Bristol account. He's closed it now. The money was telexed from the Deutsche Bank in Frankfurt. They received it from the Zürcher Kredit Bank in Zurich. That's the end of the road.'

'What does that mean?'

'Zürcher Kredit received the funds from Liechtenstein. That's an iron door no one can open. Not much help, is it?'

'On the contrary, it fits into the pattern which is appearing so rapidly at last. Thank you, Perry. Yes, I suppose you'd better leave the file.'

He waited until they were alone. 'A secret Soviet base is set up fifteen years ago – in hardline Brezhnev's time – at that bungalow estate. It's screaming at us now. Those five men in their early forties would be in their mid-twenties when they slipped into this country. They'd have identities cooked up at Moscow Centre's Documents Section. A Colonel Winterton – whom no one ever met – bought a piece of land with an old house on it. Marler found that out from pub gossip. He had the house knocked down, the six bungalows built in its place. All ready for the *Spetsnaz* unit to move in . . .'

'*Spetsnaz?*' Monica queried.

'You know – élite Soviet troops equivalent to our SAS. Trained to merge into the landscape of a foreign country. They were probably originally intended to assassinate specific key figures in the defence of this country. The leader of the Greek Key, an Englishman living on Exmoor, was their commander.'

'I know what they are,' Monica protested, 'but surely you're reaching, as the Americans would say. Guessing . . .'

'I'd sooner say I'm deducing the solution from clues now in our hands. They always kept to themselves. Foster visited The Royal Oak and chatted to the barman. Luckily barmen have good memories. Foster makes a point of telling him two wives have jobs abroad – which makes the place sound more natural, as opposed to six bachelors, including Seton-Charles. Having fed the barman that much – knowing it would be spread round the district – Foster never goes back there again. Paula finds one woman is cleaning all six bungalows . . .'

'In her forties, too, I'd say,' Paula interjected.

'That's very peculiar,' Tweed continued. 'Six men, all strangers apparently when they buy their bungalows, use the same woman. In England? Not likely. Now Perry tells us Foster draws large sums from a fund which originated in Liechtenstein. So we can't trace where the money came from. Now we hear they've all disappeared, leaving not one fingerprint behind. Everything those men did is shrouded in secrecy. Except the two in hospital. It stinks of *Spetsnaz*.'

'And it wasn't due to the shooting incident Paula was involved in,' Monica stated. 'How do I know that? Because I know how long it takes to clean my flat. To erase all fingerprints from six bungalows must have taken days of meticulous work by that woman. They were leaving anyway. Doesn't that mean an operation is imminent?'

'It means we have very little time left to trace them,' Tweed said grimly. 'And I have very little time to keep my appointment with the PM.'

'Anything more we can do?' asked Monica as he put on his Burberry. It was typical November weather outside, a heavy drizzle.

'Only wait. And hope. We've thrown out across the country all the information we hold. I'm off.'

'One other thing while I remember,' Paula said. 'Nield heard this in a pub. Kearns' dog kept on moping and whining for Jill. He shot it recently and buried it in the garden at the back of his house. Put up a wooden cross inscribed, *In loving memory of Jill*.'

'Damn!' Tweed hardly heard her as the phone began ringing and Monica picked it up. 'I can't talk to anyone . . .'

'It's Marler. Says it's very urgent.'

'Make it quick,' Tweed said after grabbing the receiver.

'Newman visited the hospital after hearing Morle was talking. Arrived, found Morle had a serious case of fever, high temperature. The policeman told Bob what Morle had mumbled. One word over and over. Then Newman heard it. Stinger. The police chap thought he was talking about the drink. *Stinger*. Do you get it?'

'Yes.' Tweed found he was gripping the receiver tightly. He said thank you and put down the phone.

'Bad news?' Paula asked.

'The worst. Now we know what Anton brought ashore. Stinger rocket launchers and missiles. God help us.'

He ran down the steps to the ground floor, forced himself to pause at the exit, glance round. Across the road stood the usual news seller. He stopped briefly to buy an *Evening Standard*. And this time he stared at the poster summarizing the main news.

Gorbachev To Meet Thatcher At Brize Norton En Route Washington.

49

Jupiter lay very still in bed inside his house on Exmoor. In the dark he ticked off in his mind the list of tasks dealt with. Everyone was now in place. It was 30 November: Gorbachev would land at Brize Norton on Monday 7 December.

Land? He would be blown to pieces in mid-air. The meeting with the British Prime Minister would never take place. Within days, Yigor Ligachev, Number Two in the Politburo, would take over as the new General Secretary. Ligachev had no time or sympathy with *glasnost*, with *perestroika*, and all the other nonsense. He had openly said so.

Jupiter had been trained as a youth in the hardline school. The world must be made safe for Lenin's Marxist principles. Only the Red Army could achieve the final victory. And I, he thought, will have contributed an essential role to that eventual victory I won't live to see. The Red Flag flying over Buckingham Palace, the White House in Washington. No, that would take more years than I have.

He smiled as he thought of the final signal he had transmitted to Greece. He had changed the scenario. The weak link was Florakis. It was ironic – that Florakis would pass on to Doganis the signal tomorrow, signing his own death warrant. *Closed circuit.*

Driving along the coast road to Cape Sounion just before dawn, Doganis hunched his huge, seemingly flabby bulk over the wheel. It suited him to be up early: he no longer slept well and woke with his brain churning with excitement. Everything had gone so well. Using Petros' insane lust for revenge as a smokescreen had completely foiled the opposition. He pulled up close to the hotel site, leaving his engine running.

'I have a fresh signal,' the lean-faced Florakis said as he got into the passenger seat. 'But why do I need the transceiver?'

'Put it in the boot,' Doganis ordered.

He waited until they were driving along the winding highway before he answered. Florakis glanced at Doganis who stared straight ahead: he disliked him intensely, this mountain of flesh, gone to seed. He should keep fit, an activity Florakis prided himself on.

'We are moving the location where you transmit from,' Doganis informed him. 'It is dangerous to transmit from the same area too frequently. You said it was a short message. Two words. What are they?'

'Closed circuit. That was all. Then he signed off.'

I guessed right, Doganis thought. And the timing is correct. Soon the operation will be accomplished. Unlike Florakis, he knew this would be the last signal. He went on talking as he drove closer and closer to Cape Sounion. And his own timing was correct – it was still half an hour before dawn.

'In future you will transmit from the summit of Cape Sounion. There is no one about at 2 a.m. I will show you the ideal place I have found – a dip in the ground beyond the temple.'

He stopped the car at the entrance to the track leading up from the highway. He told Florakis to fetch the transceiver. Inwardly Florakis sneered at this; the flabby bastard hadn't even the strength to lug the transceiver uphill.

They walked in silence past the restaurant and hotel which showed no lights. Then they climbed the twisting rocky path to the summit. Doganis wheezed, apparently with the effort. They reached the elegant Temple of Poseidon, its columns silhouetted in the dark.

Doganis led the way past it and down the slope towards the cliff edge. The ground was covered with scrubby grass and Doganis stopped at the edge of a bowl. He pointed one thick finger.

'That is the place. You make all future transmissions from here . . .'

'I see. But why bring the transceiver? I am not going to use it now.'

'Because you will not need it any more.'

515

Doganis raised his huge hands, clamped them round the throat of Florakis. The Greek was taken by surprise, but not frightened. Doganis had gone mad – even to imagine he could cope with a man of Florakis' strength. He tried to knee Doganis in the groin, but the attacker had turned sideways and the blow struck his thigh. Florakis felt a flash of fear. It had been like hitting the leg of an elephant. The pressure on his windpipe increased. Lights appeared before his eyes. Doganis' face seemed enormous as he began to bend Florakis whose back arched in a bow. If the process continued his back would be broken. Panic took hold. He kicked futilely with his right foot at Doganis' leg. It felt like striking ebony. Then he sagged, lost consciousness as Doganis went on strangling him.

Satisfied that he had done the job, Doganis let him slump to the ground. They were perched on top of the slope. Doganis used one foot to lever the prostrate corpse. It began to roll. The momentum increased. Like a broken rag doll Florakis vanished over the edge of the cliff. Doganis grunted with satisfaction, flexed his hands.

'I am arresting you for cold-blooded murder,' a quiet voice said behind him.

The Dormouse stood about two dozen feet away, further along the top of the ridge where it curved inland. He stood, a tiny figure, with his hands clasped behind his back, staring at Doganis, at the sea behind him which stretched away like a sheet of black steel. Stood as though about to make a speech.

'You came alone?'

Doganis could hardly believe it, looked round for re-inforcements.

The plump tiny figure looked so absurd. There was no sign of anyone else.

'Yes,' said Kalos. 'I have been watching your apartment

516

in the Plaka for days – and nights. I followed you in my Saab without lights. You were so intent on your murderous plan you never dreamed you might be followed.'

'And you think *you* are going to arrest *me*?'

Doganis began to move slowly towards Kalos who remained quite still. Hands still clasped behind his back as Doganis crept along the ridge, padding silently.

'Is this the way you killed the Englishman, Harry Masterson?' he asked.

'Yes. You might as well know it since you will end as food for the fishes. Masterson was also deceived like Florakis – by thinking I was a fat weak slob. I told him I could show him where the leader of the Greek Key lived. He was making too many enquiries about us. He was confident he could handle me. And he was stronger than Florakis.'

'Stay where you are,' Kalos ordered. 'Do not take one more step towards me. I have handcuffs behind my back. I am taking you in.'

Doganis continued his ape-like progress. A sound came from inside him, a rumbling noise which was his version of a chuckle. He raised both hands, ready to grasp this doll round the throat. He would be able to lift him off his feet, throw him over . . .

Kalos brought both hands from behind his back. They held the 9mm Walther automatic he had extracted from the holster strapped to the middle of his back. He fired once, aiming to disable. The bullet struck Doganis in the left shoulder. He stopped. Then he came on again. Kalos fired again. At the thigh. Still Doganis moved forward like an enraged bull elephant. Kalos shifted his aim, shot him through the heart.

Doganis slumped slowly to the ground on the seaward side of the ridge, on to the slope. Like Florakis, his huge bulk began to roll. He caught a medium-sized boulder a glancing blow and the loosened boulder also started to roll. Kalos stood watching as Doganis' body reached a steeper section of slope, picking up speed. The gross corpse shot over the brink, dropped out of sight to fall three hundred feet, followed by the boulder.

He walked over to the transceiver Doganis had intended hurling off the cliff. He embraced its sides with both hands, his gun slid back inside his holster, and staggered back to his Saab, preserving Florakis' fingerprints on the handle.

50

Three men paced the snow-bound barracks square south-west of Moscow. In the centre of the group strode General Lucharsky, flanked by the other two members of the Troika. Their boots crunched the hard snow and they had the square to themselves: all officers and men were moving out aboard military transport for the annual manoeuvres in the Ukraine which would be watched by Lucharsky.

The timing suited Lucharsky admirably. He would be out of the way when the imminent crisis broke. His companions waited for him to speak. He kept them waiting. An assertion of his authority. A bitter wind whipped at his white bony face.

'Everything is prepared,' he said eventually. 'We are so far advanced radio communications are being cut. The weak links in the Greek Key are being eliminated. It all depends now on Jupiter in England.'

'Gorbachev has played into our hands,' commented General Budienny. 'Thank God he is landing in England. But British security is very good. Is Jupiter better?'

'The commander of the *Spetsnaz* unit which has been

activated is an ex-soldier in the British Army. A formidable man. He will find a way. Meantime, General Budienny, your armoured division will remain here ready to seal off Moscow should a crisis arise.' He stopped and stared hard at the stocky, wide-shouldered general. 'But on no account must you move unless you receive a direct order from Yigor Ligachev to preserve stability.'

'Of course not, Comrade General. My division has always had to stand by for that role – even under Brezhnev.'

Lucharsky resumed his walk in the square where they could not possibly be overheard. 'And the one general who might rebel because he is a *glasnost* enthusiast will be taking part in the Ukraine manoeuvres. At the slightest sign of resistance on his part I will have him arrested. So what can possibly go wrong?'

'You were worried at one time when your KGB associate warned you the British agent, Tweed, was in Greece.'

'Until I heard he was concentrating on that crazy old idiot, Petros. Then I knew he had taken the bait – incensed by the killing of his sector chief, Masterson, which is why I ordered Masterson's liquidation. You can forget Tweed. He is confused, like a ship without a rudder, sailing round in circles.'

Snow had begun to fall again, heavy flakes which drifted down out of the pewter sky. Lucharsky paused, bent down, scooped up some in his gloved hand and rubbed it on his face.

'That helps the brain to become alert, Comrades. The first snow of winter – the winter which will descend on *glasnost* and freeze it to death.'

1 December. Tweed had not returned to his office the previous day. He had to wait at Downing Street to see the PM. And when he did meet her the meeting had lasted far longer than he had anticipated.

Now he was walking in Regent's Park with Paula. The

wind was biting and he wore his British warm topcoat. Paula clutched her own coat collar at the neck as they made their way across the deserted open spaces.

'Let us go back to the beginning,' Tweed said. 'I still have the worrying feeling I have missed something.'

'You've done everything you can,' she assured him. 'It is a matter of waiting for a break.'

'But we have so little time left. Gorbachev lands at Brize Norton on Monday 7 December. That leaves only six days. So, recall how it all started for me.'

She summarized the early events and Tweed listened in silence. 'Then,' she went on, 'there was the murder of Sam Partridge on Exmoor. You had to identify him for that local policeman . . .'

She broke off as he stopped, gripped her arm. 'That's it. Why did I have to identify him?'

'Because his wallet was missing. And later discovered with plenty of money inside it – by a dog ferreting in the Doone Valley.'

'So robbery was certainly not involved.'

'They were new notes. The numbers ran in sequence,' Paula reminded him. 'No thief with half a brain would risk spending them.'

'Back to the office.' Tweed's tone was firm. 'I want to see the list Marler sent us of what was in that wallet. *Something* was missing.'

'Sam's driving licence.' Tweed's voice held a note of triumph as he sat behind his desk and studied the list. 'It wasn't in his wallet. That's what is missing. And he drove down to Somerset. He told me he parked his car in the street at Dunster.'

'Then why hasn't someone reported its presence – parked there all this time?' Monica objected.

'Because someone – maybe Winterton himself – drove

it away and parked it in some hidden place on Exmoor. Maybe an abandoned building. They didn't want the car – they're using the licence. Which means they probably hired a car on the strength of Partridge's driving licence.' He scribbled on his desk pad, tore off the sheet. 'Paula, here's his address. Call the Vehicle Registration people in Swansea immediately. Find out the licence number.'

'Which could take God knows how long. They don't move fast,' Paula warned.

'Tell them you're Special Branch.' He produced his card. 'And tell them I need a reply within one hour. That we are searching for an escaped terrorist. Dammit, they're using computers. Within one hour . . .'

It was one hour and ten minutes later when Vehicle Registration phoned back with the number. Tweed called the Commissioner of Police, identified himself, gave him the number. He had hardly put down the phone when it rang again. Newman reporting from Exmoor. No change in the situation.

Tweed explained what he wanted, gave him the licence number and urgent instructions. 'I want all four of you on this. Divide up the area into sectors. Then drive round to every place where you can hire a car. Show them the number. If someone used the licence to hire a car their records will show it. I need any information you can get within twenty-four hours.'

'We have as long as that?' Newman asked cynically.

'Quicker if you can.'

At Cherry Farm the balance of power had changed, much to Anton's chagrin. It had started with a phone call from Jupiter. He told Anton in his cryptic way that three more guests would be arriving. Foster, Saunders and Sully.

At the appointed time Anton drove the grey Austin Metro Seton-Charles had hired in Taunton weeks before to the crossroads where he had taken delivery of the Shi-ite prisoners. A Ford station wagon and a Vauxhall Cavalier stood parked alongside each other on the verge. The lean-faced smartly dressed Foster he had met before came towards him.

'Tawny Owl,' Foster greeted him.

'Night Heron,' Anton replied, wondering why Jupiter had thought it necessary for them to exchange agreed codewords when he knew Foster. There were two men in the Vauxhall who waited inside until Anton led the way, driving at the head of the convoy back to Cherry Farm. He didn't like the look of any of them. They had the smell of hardbitten professionals, almost as though they had undergone military training.

Foster introduced his companions after his two cars were hidden in the second shed. In the large kitchen at the back Seton-Charles examined the new arrivals through his rimless glasses. He also did not like what he saw. Foster, quick-moving and quick-talking, wasted no time.

'This is Saunders, my second-in-command. If I'm absent you take orders from him. This is Sully. We've brought our own food supplies. Sully will cook for the three of us . . .'

'Seton-Charles has been doing the cooking,' Anton interrupted. 'He can do the meals for all of us.'

'I said Sully will cook for us. You two look after yourselves. Now, where are the Stingers, the mobile launching platforms?'

Anton took them upstairs into the bedroom he occupied, opened a cupboard. Over his left arm was looped the handle of a walking stick with a hardened tip. He used both hands to push his clothes, suspended from a rod, to each side. Foster grunted.

'We'll need a better place than this in case a patrol car comes poking around.'

'Will we?' Anton snapped. 'Then find them yourself.'

522

Foster dropped to his knees, crawled inside, felt around the wooden planked floor. Anton looked at Seton-Charles, raised his eyebrows. *Bighead* his gesture conveyed. Sully, smaller, slimly built and also very fit-looking like the others, caught the expression.

'We can do without the sarcasm,' he growled.

Foster hammered hard at the back of the cupboard with his knuckles, expecting a hollow sound. He gritted his teeth – he had almost broken his knuckles on solid wood. He crawled out of the cupboard, stood up.

'All right, I can't find them,' he said and his tone was more polite.

Anton stepped inside, pressed hard with the tip of the stick on a knot of wood in a corner. There was a loud *click*. The rear panel opened inwards a few inches and Anton pushed it wide open, held it, revealing the compartment beyond with a long canvas bundle on the floor.

'You hold the panel open,' he warned. 'There is a spring-loaded hinge which closes it automatically. You haul that out . . .'

They stood inside the front furniture van after squeezing past the auction junk Anton had purchased. Seton-Charles had been told to stay in the farmhouse to keep watch. Holding a launcher with a missile inserted under one arm, Anton mounted the steps to the platform, followed by Foster and his two companions.

Anton settled himself in the chair, pressed the switch and the panel in the roof slid back. Foster stared, glanced at Sully and Saunders who also gazed up. 'Who created all this?' asked Foster.

'I did,' said Anton.

'Jesus, I'm impressed. The other van the same?'

'A replica of this one . . .'

There was an argument about who would drive each

523

van, who would use the launchers. Anton refused to give way. 'I've been trained in the weapon's use by the arms dealer. I'm firing one of the launchers. Who the hell drives is your problem.'

Foster compromised. He and Anton would fire the launchers; the vans would be driven by Saunders and Sully. He asked about communication and Anton produced a walkie-talkie from a leather sheath attached to the platform. 'The driver has his own, tells the launcher when the target is in sight. Anything else?'

Foster asked about the Shi-ite prisoners who would be left dead inside the vans, their hands pressed on the launchers to leave fingerprints. Anton told him about the dead pig he was using to keep them passive. Foster nodded. 'Except when it is on view,' Anton continued, 'I keep it in the chest freezer in the shed. I rigged up a generator to power the freezer.' Foster nodded again, then raised the delicate topic.

'You heard from Jupiter that before we leave nothing must be left to show we were here?'

'Yes. When the call was finished I asked Seton-Charles to dig a grave in the field at the back for the pig.'

'You know what will occupy this grave?' Foster asked quietly.

'Look, I've just told you.' Anton stared at Foster, who stared back with a poker-faced expression. Was he grasping what he'd been told, the Greek began to wonder. Maybe this cold-faced man wasn't too bright? 'It will be occupied by the pig,' Anton repeated.

'Together with Seton-Charles. He's expendable.'

2 December. An atmosphere of tension was building up inside Tweed's office at Park Crescent. There had been no further reaction to the long list of enquiries they had sent out. No one had called about Anton's photo or the

Identikit picture of Seton-Charles which had been widely circulated.

None of the four men scouring Exmoor had reported back on the phone. Tweed, Monica and Paula spent their time listening once more to the tapes of the conversations recorded. They reread the files, including the report Newman had dictated about their visit to Greece. They searched desperately for something they had overlooked. Late in the evening Monica brought more coffee and asked her question again.

'Can't you tell us anything about your interview with the PM?'

'At a certain stage – closer to 7 December when Gorbachev will land at Brize Norton – I shall recall Newman, Marler, Butler and Nield from Exmoor. They must stay there a day or so yet in the hope they find two things – if Sam Partridge's driving licence was used to hire a car in the area, and the route used by Anton to leave the country secretly. When they arrive back we hold a meeting. Then you will hear what has been decided.' He paused. 'I can tell you the PM was convinced I am right, that we have her full support to indent for any weapons we may need. And that two Westland helicopters have been put at our disposal. At my suggestion they are being equipped with swivel-mounted machine-guns and the words "Traffic Control" are being painted on the fuselages. They are at a private airfield called Fairoaks near Woking in Surrey.'

'What's the idea?' Paula asked.

'I should give the credit to Newman. He phoned me in the middle of the night and I outlined the situation. He knows what's coming. So does Marler. Newman made those suggestions.'

Paula glanced at the camp bed made up in the corner. 'So you didn't get an undisturbed night's rest.'

'I don't expect any of us will during the next five days . . .'

He stopped speaking as Howard strolled into the room and sat down in the armchair. He carried a sheaf of photoprints.

'No developments yet, I assume? It's a tense time.'

'Nothing,' Tweed replied. 'And there's always tension at this stage.'

'As you know,' Howard remarked, 'I'm a bit of a car buff. It struck me that that *Spetsnaz* unit Paula uncovered must have moved to a new base prepared in advance.'

'I agree.' Tweed wondered what he was getting at.

'We know Foster has a Ford station wagon, Saunders a Vauxhall Cavalier, Seton-Charles a Volvo station wagon – from the information supplied by Vehicle Registration at Swansea. Sully left his Jag behind in the bungalow garage, so we can forget that. It occurred to me they won't dare hire fresh cars – they'd have to show their driving licences. With me so far?'

'So far, yes.'

'That means they'll have to use the same transport to move about. But they may respray their vehicles to disguise them.'

'Highly possible,' Tweed agreed.

'So I have used photographs of those three cars and traced them on a sheet of paper. But I filled the colours in with a solid black. Then I had these photocopies made. If we're looking for those cars from a chopper and use these photocopies we won't be fooled by any change of colour. They're all fairly common makes of car. We'll spot them by their shapes.'

He reached forward, dumped the photocopies on Tweed's desk and sat back again. Tweed studied the copies.

'I think this is a clever idea,' he decided. 'Everyone involved in the search will have a copy.'

'Then I need one,' said Howard and took back a copy.

'What for?' asked Tweed.

'Because I'll be in one of those choppers. You can ride in the other machine.' He raised a hand as Tweed started to protest. 'Don't argue. I'm good at spotting cars. And if you tell the PM I'll never speak to you again.' He stood up. 'So that's settled. I'm fed up with fighting the war from behind my desk with paper darts.' He glanced at Monica's stupefied expression as he left. 'And better give Monica a brandy. Looks like she needs it.'

'My God!' Monica burst out when Howard had gone. 'I'd never have believed it.'

'You always did underestimate Howard,' Tweed told her, and then the phone began ringing.

There was dead silence as Monica grabbed the receiver. She listened, looked at Tweed. 'It's for you. Peter Sarris. Athens.'

Tweed greeted the Greek police chief, then kept silent for five minutes. Gradually he hunched closer to the phone. When he put it down he stared bleakly into the distance for a long minute before speaking.

'It's very close,' he said gravely. 'Doganis strangled Florakis on Cape Sounion, sent his body over the cliff. He didn't know Kalos was following him. Doganis admitted he'd killed Harry Masterson. Apparently he's as strong as an ox. Kalos had to shoot him.'

'What does it mean?' Paula asked.

'It means the Soviet hardliners back in Russia – probably led by General Lucharsky – are wiping their tracks clean. Killing off anyone who could betray them. 7 December is definitely zero hour. Pray for a break soon.'

527

51

Friday, 4 December. At Cherry Farm the atmosphere was strained and becoming worse. Five men were living in close proximity inside the farmhouse. Anton had agreed with Foster's decision that no one must appear outside. The temperature was low and a biting wind swept across the waterlogged fields and rattled the closed shutters.

The Shi-ite Muslims, shivering with cold, had complained they were freezing. They were given extra underclothes and left to cope. Conditions were little better for their five captors. There was a tantalising pile of logs on one side of the large fireplace in the living room. No fire could be lit: smoke from the chimney would show a passer-by the place was inhabited.

There was no electricity, no gas, no water. All services had been cut off from the supposedly abandoned farm. Seton-Charles cooked a meal for himself at midday using Calor gas for the stove – an item he had bought on his way back from Norwich. He had very little left.

In the living room Anton and Foster pored over two ordnance survey maps, planning out the route to the general area of Brize Norton. Saunders and Sully stood behind them as they crouched over the table. They all wore extra clothes brought with them: woollen pullovers and two pairs of socks.

'Transport,' Anton said suddenly. 'We've talked about it but taken no decision. I'll drive the Austin Metro and park it so we can get away afterwards, then get inside the furniture van.'

'It's a risk, I agree,' said Foster. 'And I'll take the Ford station wagon – again a risk. But not so risky as trying to hire different vehicles. We'd have to show our driving licences. The Vauxhall can stay here.'

'What is the escape route?' Anton demanded. He stood with his arms folded. 'You fobbed me off before but I want to know now before we talk any more about routes.'

Foster compressed his thin lips. 'Very well. We're close to doing the job. Afterwards we abandon the vans, then drive back to Exmoor. We leave the way you came in – by motorboat from the beach at Porlock Weir. A ship will be waiting for us outside the three-mile limit. An East German freighter. The East Germans are not nearly so keen on *glasnost* as Gorbachev.'

'Another point – I'd like to discuss it with you alone.'

'Really?' Foster's cold grey eyes narrowed. 'Let's go take a breath of fresh air.'

The air outside the back of the farmhouse was more than fresh: it was bitter. Foster thrust his hands inside his jacket pockets. Until he was twenty-five years old he had been used to the razor-edged wind sweeping across the Russian Steppes. Fifteen years in England had made him more susceptible to the cold.

'What is it?' he demanded.

'I have decided I can't shoot Seton-Charles. Killing that arms dealer in Lisbon was child's play. He was a stranger. Seton-Charles introduced new opportunities into my life. I don't like him – but he's become a part of my life.'

Foster stood more erect, held himself stiffly as he stared hard at Anton, reassessing him. Anton forced himself to gaze back but inwardly he felt nervous. Suddenly he felt the force of the *Spetsnaz* leader's personality.

'That calls for a change of plan,' Foster informed him, his tone grating. 'I have been watching Seton-Charles. I thought he was no more than a theorist. He is dedicated – more dedicated than you will ever be. He will drive one of the furniture vans, Sully the other. That leaves Saunders and myself to operate the launchers.'

'But I can do that,' Anton protested. 'What would I do?'

'You drive the escape vehicle. When we met the second time at the crossroads and drove back here a Post Office van overtook us. He passes along the road at the end of the track every day, Sully tells me. First time early in the morning.'

'That's right. Seton-Charles told me. What's the idea?'

'On the morning of Monday 7 December, we stop the driver, seize his vehicle. No one notices a Royal Mail van.'

'What do we do with the driver?' Anton asked.

'Kill him, dump the body in that grave Seton-Charles dug. I'll do the job.' Foster's lip curled. 'I don't think you're up to it.'

'But I can fire one of the launchers . . .'

'But you won't. You've trained us. The Stinger is a weapon it is easy to use. Now, you can stay out here while your balls freeze – assuming you have any. I'm going inside to look at those maps again. Saunders and I are going to reconnoitre the route to Brize Norton.'

He walked inside the farmhouse, closing the door quietly. Anton shivered in the wind. The look in Foster's eyes, his manner, had frightened him. But he had to admit Foster was well-organized: they had brought with them three pairs of the type of overalls worn by furniture removal men. They had spent time rubbing dirt into them, crumpling them to take away the appearance of new garments.

Anton went back inside to find Foster and Saunders bent over the maps. Foster was tracing a route with a pencil, careful not to touch the maps. He looked up as Anton returned.

'And we'll be taking your Austin Metro for the reconnaissance – no one will know about that vehicle.'

*   *   *

530

Friday, 4 December. It was late afternoon when the call came through to Park Crescent from Newman. Monica told Tweed he was on the line and pressed the recording button.

'I've found out Sam Partridge's driving licence was used to hire a car. Weeks ago – and the car is still on hire. Someone with an upper-crust voice phones Barton's – the car hire outfit – and an envelope of money to extend the hire is pushed in the letter box at night. Barton's is in Taunton. The car is a blue Austin Metro, registration number . . . God, I called at enough places before I found the right one.'

'Good work, Bob. We'll circulate that car's details immediately. Now, can you contact the others within the hour? I want everyone back here tonight. It's an emergency.'

'I'm calling from the Minehead phone box. Couldn't find an empty one in Taunton – so I drove back here like a bat. Butler and Nield happen to be at The Anchor now. We'll be on our way within half an hour. Don't go, Marler has news for you. Here he is . . .'

'I know how Anton slipped out of the country,' Marler drawled. 'Got back here to find Newman monopolizing this box. Anton is an expert pilot of small aircraft. Remember – Christina told Newman. Dunkeswell Airport, a small private airfield south-east of Tiverton. He flew out in a Cessna.'

'You're sure? There's a manifest to prove it?'

'Like hell there is. I identified myself to a pilot, showed him Anton's photo, told him he was a leading terrorist. He went as white as a sheet. I had to exert a little pressure – you don't want to hear about that. Briefly, Anton paid this pilot a large sum in cash . . .'

'To fly him back to Lisbon?'

'Not quite. Anton insisted on flying the Cessna himself. Took the pilot along as passenger. The pilot flew the

531

machine back to Dunkeswell. The controller of the airfield was away, doesn't know what happened.'

'Another question answered. You're coming back to London. A disaster is imminent.'

'If weapons are in order,' Marler responded, 'I'd like a rifle with a telescopic sight. See you . . .'

On her other phone Monica was finishing giving details of the Austin Metro to the Commissioner of Police. She put down the phone, her eyes gleaming with excitement.

'It's all happening at once. Like it so often does.'

'And these things come in threes,' said Paula.

The call from Norwich came at 7 p.m.

Waiting for Newman and his three companions to arrive, Tweed had a meal of ham sandwiches, followed by fruit, with Paula and Monica. Extra camp beds had been erected in the office next door where the two women slept overnight. They were all beginning to feel housebound when the phone rang.

Monica frowned as she answered the call, listened, asked several questions, then put her hand over the mouthpiece.

'It's Norwich police headquarters. A Constable Fox. Calling in reply to our circulating Seton-Charles' Volvo description and registration number. Sounds tentative. He's called the General & Cumbria Assurance cover number we used.'

Tweed picked up his phone, asked how he could help.

'Constable Fox speaking, sir. In response to your enquiry re the Volvo station wagon.' The youthful voice hesitated. 'My inspector wasn't sure I should call. I keep a careful record in my notebook of even trivial incidents. You never can tell when the information may be needed.'

'Very sensible,' Tweed encouraged him. 'Do go on.'

'Back in October late one night. I can give you the date

532

in a minute. Left my notebook in my tunic pocket. As I was saying, I was on duty and I saw this Volvo park near a corner. A man got out and walked round to a furniture removal firm selling off bankrupt stock. It was eleven at night so I was curious. Especially as he could have parked in front of the warehouse. Am I wasting your time, sir?'

'Please go on.'

'There were lights in the warehouse so I thought I'd better check. This chap goes inside after Latimer answers the door.'

'Latimer?'

'The proprietor of the firm selling off the vans, Camelford Removals. When I saw it was Latimer I thought it must be OK, so I pushed off. Then the next morning I was walking near the same area when I saw the Volvo driver pass me behind the wheel of one of the furniture vans. Trouble is his description does not tally with your Identikit. He wore horn-rims and an old cap.'

'But the registration of the Volvo is the same as the one we sent out?'

'Quite definitely. I checked that in my notebook.'

'Could you contact this Latimer, persuade him to wait until I arrive? He'll be paid for his trouble. And can you wait for me at the station until I arrive? It will be after ten.'

'I'm on night duty again. And behind enquiries counter tonight. Latimer practically lives at the warehouse. I can phone him.'

'My name is Tweed. I'm coming. Your recording of trivial events could end up in promotion. I'm leaving London now . . .'

As Tweed had guessed, Constable Fox was in his early twenties. A thin, pale-faced man, he had an earnest manner

533

and blushed when he was introduced to Paula. Tweed was careful to show him his Special Branch card. Fox took the card, studied the photograph inside the plastic guard, stared carefully at Tweed and handed it back. He was carrying the Identikit picture of Seton-Charles in an envelope.

Outside police headquarters he opened the rear door of the Cortina for Paula, closed it, then joined Tweed in the front.

'Latimer is waiting for us, sir. I didn't give him any idea who was coming.'

'Very sensible,' said Tweed again, then concentrated on Fox's directions. They reached the furniture warehouse in a few minutes and a short middle-aged man opened the door as they pulled up. 'That's Latimer,' Fox whispered.

Tweed introduced himself and Paula, showed his card, and with only a cursory glance Latimer invited them inside. They sat round a rough-surfaced wooden table and Latimer drank tea from a tin mug. Tweed took the envelope from Fox, extracted the Identikit picture and pushed it in front of him. 'Is that the man who bought a furniture van from you?'

'Two vans. No, it doesn't look like him. He wore horn-rimmed glasses, not rimless, and a driver's cap.'

Tweed looked at Paula, pushed the Identikit towards her. 'You are the artist. Mr Latimer, please describe as best you can the type of glasses, the kind of cap. Miss Grey will convert the picture under your guidance . . .'

He changed places so Paula sat next to Latimer. She produced a small clipboard and a felt-tip pen from her capacious shoulder bag and worked on the picture, altering it from Latimer's instructions. Then she pushed the picture in front of him.

'That's the chap. Magic it is, the way you did that. I've a good memory for faces. No doubt about it.'

'You said he bought two vans. He had someone with him?' Tweed enquired.

'No. Collected them both himself, one by one. Both the same day. Was gone about eight hours before he came back for the second job. Twin vans, they was. Only one left now.'

'He spoke with an educated accent?' Paula enquired.

'No. Workingman's lingo.' Latimer scratched his head. 'Mind you, it didn't sound it came natural to him.'

'He paid by cheque?' Tweed probed.

'No. Cash. Fifties. I held them up to check them. You can't be too careful these days. Funny sort of bloke. And that cap didn't fit him too well.'

'You said you had only one van left,' Tweed reminded him. 'Is that the same as the two you sold to this man?'

'Came from exactly the same stable. Want to see it?'

'Yes, please.' Tweed looked at Paula. 'Did you bring your camera?'

'Always carry it. Plus flashbulbs . . .'

They were there another half hour. Paula took pictures of the van from different angles. Tweed then persuaded Latimer to drive the furniture van into the street, deserted at that hour. Paula peered out from a top-floor window in the warehouse, looking down on the van with her camera. In the street below Tweed saw three flashbulbs go off. Then Paula waved her hand.

Latimer backed the van further away, stopped it at the entrance to another street, presenting her with a sideways angle. Three more flashbulbs went off. Tweed told Latimer he could drive the vehicle back into the warehouse.

'What's this all about?' he asked as he climbed down from the cab.

'A gang of very dangerous terrorists. Now, I want to pay you for your time.'

'On the house, Guv. If it's bleedin' terrorists I'm 'appy

to oblige. Shoot the bastards when you catch up with 'em.'

'Thank you for your cooperation. I'll bear your advice in mind. Now,' he said to Paula who had reappeared with Fox, 'we have to get moving. And Constable Fox, I'll be recommending your work to your inspector when this is all over . . .'

It was 2 a.m. when Tweed and Paula arrived back at Park Crescent. All the lights were on in the building behind closed blinds. They went straight down into the Engine Room in the basement where the staff were waiting. Paula handed one of the technicians her film, Tweed told him to develop and print immediately, then to produce two dozen copies.

His office was full of people when he opened the door. A large table had been moved in and round it sat Howard, Newman, Marler, Butler and Nield. The remnants of a meal were on the table and Monica was pouring more coffee. Marler sat smoking one of his king-size cigarettes.

'Any joy?' he enquired.

Tweed explained what they had learned as Paula took a spare seat at the table. Most of his listeners looked weary except for Howard and Marler who appeared fresh and alert. Howard raised the query.

'What on earth would they need two furniture vans for?'

'Remember the Stingers,' Marler told him. 'That reference to them we got from Morle rambling in high fever. Those vans are mobile rocket launcher platforms. Who notices a furniture van? It stops, they drop the tailboard and fire the missiles from the rear opening.'

'Oh my God!' Howard was appalled. 'Hadn't we better contact the PM?'

'And alert the SAS?' Newman suggested.

'We're on our own,' Tweed said quietly. 'SAS teams are guarding the Brize Norton perimeter. The PM calls us her private insurance policy. And while I remember, each one of you must carry one of these cards. Force Z is what she's termed us – Z for zero hour.' He dropped a pile of fresh identity cards he'd collected from the Engine Room on the table. 'Sort them out. Each carries an individual photograph. Including one for you, Howard – if you still insist on coming.'

'I do.'

'All security personnel at Brize Norton have been informed about Force Z. If you run into one of them you'd better speak quickly, then show the card.'

'How the hell do we go about this?' Howard demanded.

In reply, Tweed walked across to a wall map he had pinned up. It covered Oxfordshire, Wiltshire, Berkshire, Hampshire and London Airport. A tiny village called Liphook came just within the large circle he drew with a felt-tip pen.

'We have to think ourselves into the mind of Winterton.' He glanced at Howard. 'That is the codeword for the Englishman directing this operation.'

'Who is Robson, Barrymore or Kearns, you still think?' Paula asked.

'Yes. Based on the fact that Petros heard during World War Two that the Greek Key was controlled by an Englishman located in Cairo. The fact that the *Oporto* seaman who talked saw Anton being taken ashore near Porlock Weir by a man disguised with a Balaclava. The facts which came out of the tape recording Nield made of their conversation at The Luttrell Arms. The fact that the secret *Spetsnaz* base was situated on Exmoor. The fact that the murders of Andreas and Stephen Gavalas took place when those three men were nearby. The fact that Partridge and Mrs Larcombe were murdered on Exmoor. The fact that when Jill Kearns was run down in London those three men were staying at a hotel not a quarter of a mile away.'

'I get the point,' Paula agreed. 'But now you've withdrawn everyone from Exmoor. Shouldn't someone be keeping an eye on those men now we're so close to the climax?'

'Yes. And you're elected.'

There were protests at the idea. From Howard. From Paula. 'I want to be in at the finish,' she objected. 'I believe I have contributed to the investigation . . .'

'Agreed,' said Tweed. 'You were the first one who spotted – and persisted – something was wrong with that bungalow estate. To mention only one thing. But from what Newman told me on the phone all three men are still on Exmoor . . .'

'It's too dangerous,' Newman snapped. 'She's already had her taste of gunpowder confronting Norton and Morle. And Winterton may have left the area by now.'

'He hasn't.' Tweed was emphatic. 'I haven't had time to tell you – but the Chief Inspector at Taunton has set up roadblocks on every route east out of the area. Barrymore, Robson and our friend, Kearns, are well-known. If one of them – Winterton – tries to leave Exmoor I'll know within minutes.'

'So that explains why we were stopped by the police near to Glastonbury,' Newman commented.

'And Paula will again be armed.' Tweed took a Browning automatic and spare mags from a desk drawer, placed them in front of her. 'Now, are you happier?' he asked her. 'Your job is to see which of the three makes a move.'

'I'll settle for that.'

'Good. Now maybe we can get on. I've tried to think myself inside Winterton's mind. He would know in advance there was a good chance Gorbachev would land in Britain

538

to meet the PM – he would have found that out from Moscow, I'm sure. The hardline faction is there. He knows Gorbachev is coming, but where will he land? London Airport? Possible, but unlikely. Lyneham Air Force Base in Wiltshire? A good bet. Brize Norton in Oxfordshire? Another good bet – because security would be easier to set up rather than at London Airport. Makes sense?'

'Yes,' said Marler. 'How does he go on from there?'

'He sets up an advance base . . .' Tweed went to the wall map and waved his hand round the circle he had drawn. '. . . somewhere inside this area. This gives swift access to whichever landing point is chosen. The furniture vans will be hidden there. But I don't think we'll see them from the air until Gorbachev's aircraft is approaching Brize Norton on this coming Monday. Today is already early Saturday . . .'

'Surely as soon as daylight comes,' Howard intervened, 'we can fly over the area in the choppers. We might just see something.'

'No go,' Monica informed him. 'I called Fairoaks Airfield where the machines are being equipped and repainted. They said Sunday morning was the earliest they could be serviceable.'

'So we wait until Sunday,' Tweed announced. 'In any case, most of you look as though you could do with a good rest. I want you on top form when we fly in those choppers. Anything else?'

'Bob,' Paula suggested, 'could I use your Mercedes? I'll drive down there as soon as this meeting breaks up. Then I can grab a few hours' sleep at The Luttrell Arms and start searching. God knows, I'm familiar with Exmoor by now.'

'As a very special favour.' Newman stifled a yawn. 'Yes.'

'I don't think we should all be airborne.' Butler spoke for the first time. 'Nield and I were talking about that – after Monica explained what she knew of your plan. We'd both like motorcycles, equipped with radio so we can contact you in the chopper.'

'I'll think about that.' Tweed checked his watch. 'Now, if there's nothing else . . .'

'Weapons,' said Marler. 'What's available? We'll need a variety as I see it.'

'Everything you want. The PM gave me *carte blanche*. An armoured car is delivering an arsenal and standing by at Fairoaks. You'll get your rifle with telescopic sights. Handguns. Grenades. Take your pick when the time comes.'

'One final point,' said Paula. 'You still think you know the identity of Winterton?'

'Yes. But no evidence. And I expect him to stay in the background during the operation. On Exmoor. Maybe you'll spot who he is.'

Paula said nothing. She opened her hand and a stick of French chalk rolled on the table.

52

Saturday, 5 December. It was after midnight when Foster took Anton into his bedroom at Cherry Farm, closed the door. Fatigue was registered on the faces of both men and tempers were getting short.

'Those Shi-ite prisoners are getting restless,' Foster opened with. 'What did you tell them they were here for?'

'That they were hostages for an exchange of two men kidnapped in Beirut. That negotiations were proceeding but they took time. They think we're British Government agents. You'd best leave them to me.'

'With pleasure. I have enough on my hands. Practising

weapon drill for one thing. It's Saturday and everyone is feeling the strain. Today we keep under cover. Get some rest. We have to be on top form tomorrow and Monday.'

'Tomorrow is Sunday. What happens then?'

'We do a trial run. Saunders and I found two perfect places to hide the furniture vans as close to Brize Norton as we need to be. Your turn to empty the Elsan buckets. Do it before you go to bed . . .'

He stopped as he heard the phone ring downstairs. Automatically Anton turned towards the door. Foster pushed him out of the way. 'I'm taking all calls now.'

He hurried down the creaking wooden staircase into the hall where the phone was perched on a table. He lifted the receiver and gave the agreed false number. The familiar cold distant voice spoke.

'Is everything ready for the Monday conference? All delegates fully briefed?'

'Yes. We've checked the conference site. I'm double-checking it tomorrow, Sunday, to make sure nothing has been overlooked.'

'I should hope not at this stage. You'll give me a report when we meet? That's all.'

Foster put down the phone, knowing that would be the last call he would receive from Jupiter. The reference to 'when we meet' was a hint they would meet aboard the East German freighter, *Stralsund*, which would be waiting for them at the mouth of the Bristol Channel. Only then, after all these years, Foster thought, will I know who has been controlling us on Exmoor.

'Any crisis?' asked Anton, who stood at the foot of the stairs.

The question confirmed to Foster he had been right to stop Anton operating one of the two precious launchers. He was growing more nervous by the hour. Foster glanced at the phone.

'How is the bill for the calls made on this phone paid

541

for? You said earlier you had a phone booth you called at certain times.'

'All taken care of by Jupiter. A local solicitor in Taunton receives the bills, pays for them from a large sum Jupiter sent him in cash after instructing him over the phone.'

Foster was satisfied: it was tiny details like this which could upset all their plans. Jupiter never seemed to miss a trick. Anton was still standing by the staircase.

'What is it?' Foster snapped. 'Time we all got some sleep.'

'That Post Office van . . .'

'Don't shit yourself. I'll kill the driver. You can just bury him. And dump the Elsan closets we've been using for lavatories on top of the body. We leave this place neat and tidy. Don't forget to keep your gloves on – no fingerprints.'

'The Post Office van,' Anton began again. 'If you'd listened I was going to say it's a long drive to Porlock Weir. We'll need to top up the tank with petrol . . .'

'And we still have plenty of the stuff left in spare cans in the boots of the two cars we came here in. And also dump all our sleeping bags in that grave. Now, push off . . .'

He called after Anton as he was mounting the stairs. 'How much mineral water left?'

'A dozen litre bottles. I have kept a watch on supplies,' Anton rapped back.

'Good for you.' Foster's mind was checking other details. They would take the oil stoves and lamps which had provided heat and illumination with them. They could be thrown into ditches one by one on their way to Brize Norton. He went upstairs, nodded to Saunders who sat in a wicker armchair in the corridor where the Shi-ites were imprisoned. Saunders had a Luger lying in his lap. Any trouble in that direction and he'd crack their skulls with the Luger barrel, which was their ultimate fate anyway.

It was Foster's turn on the duty detail to watch the approach to the farm from the front window. Later in the night Seton-Charles and Sully would take over. Rest for everyone. Sunday would be a busy day – making the trial run to Brize Norton.

In Tweed's office at 3 a.m. everyone had left to get sleep except for Monica, Tweed and Butler. Newman had remarked that Butler had had more sleep than any of them, so he could make the report on Exmoor. With a cup of black coffee in front of him, Butler spoke tersely.

'You'd almost think they were setting out to look normal. Dr Robson still rides the moor at all hours to see patients. One old semi-invalid lady at Dulverton is always calling him in the middle of the night to her decrepit mansion. He goes . . .'

'How does she call him? Do you know?'

'By phone. She has an extension by her bedside upstairs. Barrymore drives into Minehead after dark to call someone from that public box we use. Pub gossip has it his housekeeper, Mrs Atyeo, is threatening to walk out on him. No one knows why – she's been there for years. Kearns still goes riding during the night. Nield was driving along that lane which leads to the Doone Valley after dark. He noticed Kearns' horse tethered beneath some trees at a lonely spot midway between Quarme Manor and Endpoint.'

'So Kearns could have been calling on Robson or Barrymore?'

'That's what Pete said. He didn't hang around – he'd have been seen. Barrymore and Robson still have lunch together at The Royal Oak each Wednesday. Dinner together every Saturday at The Luttrell Arms. Oh, and one night Marler was trying to follow Kearns on his horse riding up to Dunkery Beacon. Near the summit Marler heard a single loud explosion – a cracking sound like a grenade detonating. He couldn't find out what had been going on.'

'Unless Kearns was destroying something,' Tweed

suggested. 'I think you'd better get some shut-eye, Harry. There's a camp bed for you. Second door on the right when you leave here . . .'

For the next half hour Tweed was on the phone. He called Frankfurt, where Marler's deputy was standing in while his sector chief was away. He called Vienna and spoke with Masterson's deputy to check the Balkan sector. He called Berne and spoke with Guy Dalby about the situation in the Mediterranean. Finally, he called Erich Lindemann in Copenhagen, the sector chief for Scandinavia.

'All quiet,' he commented as he put down the phone. 'Except in Vienna where they report extensive military manoeuvres in the Ukraine. Under the command of General Lucharsky. Which they always carry out at this time of the year.'

He stretched his arms, got up and walked round to ease the stiffness out of his limbs. Monica marvelled at his stamina, his encyclopaedic memory which forgot nothing.

The staff running the European sectors were based in a building further along the Crescent – together with the complex technical communications, including satellite reception from the weird seeing eyes orbiting in space. Tweed suddenly returned to his swivel chair.

'I've overlooked something vital. Imagine the position of that *Spetsnaz* group. They've lost their Exmoor base, they're blown. After they accomplish their mission – as they hope – they need an *escape route*. Contact Roberts at Lloyd's. Ask about any Iron Curtain vessel sailing off our shores.'

'Sorry. Roberts is taking a weekend holiday. Don't know where. I could try to ask someone else . . .'

'Don't. Roberts knows the need for secrecy. Monday will have to do.' He took off his tie, loosened his collar. 'I'm going to get some sleep.'

Monica was already folding back the blankets from the

camp bed in the corner for him. She plumped up the pillow. He was taking off his shoes when he stopped.

'I wonder what happened to that cleaning woman Paula saw at the bungalow estate . . .'

'Bed,' said Monica firmly. Then she swore. The phone was ringing. She listened for a moment, then looked at Tweed. 'It's Paula. Calling from Somerset. I can tell her you're asleep . . .'

'I'll take it.' Tweed grasped the receiver, standing in his socks. 'Something wrong? You should be in bed.'

'So should you, but I took a chance. I'm talking from the public box in Minehead. I got lost in the dark. Don't worry – I called The Anchor and the night porter will let me in. Lucky I've stayed there before. The main thing is I wasn't stopped by any police checkpoint. That worried me.'

'That was because you were *entering* Somerset. The checkpoints are concealed. They're checking everyone *leaving*. I'm glad you called. In the morning contact Inspector Farthing in Minehead. He's reliable – the chap who turned up when Partridge's body was brought down from Exmoor into Winsford. Tell him frankly about the three men you're watching. You'll need help.'

'OK. Will do. Now, get some rest . . .'

'Bed,' Monica repeated. 'Stop thinking. Sunday is going to be hell.'

He put his head on the pillow, his mind churning. Then he fell fast asleep.

Sunday, 6 December. Foster was up early at Cherry Farm despite his night duty. They ate a hurried breakfast while he outlined the plan. 'I will be going over the route with Seton-Charles and Saunders. We'll use Anton's Austin Metro. That's the safest vehicle. I want several places where the furniture vans can be hidden *east* of Brize Norton

545

– the direction Gorbachev will be flying in from. The hiding-places have to be well away from the airfield perimeter. Security there is already ferocious.'

'What will I do?' Anton asked truculently.

'You will help Sully clean up this place. Ready for instant departure tomorrow. As soon as we've grabbed that Post Office van and dealt with the driver. Stack all the Elsan closets except one by the back door. What's that?'

He stood up, ran to the back of the house. Round the table they could now all hear what Foster's acute ears had caught. A steady chug-chug of a helicopter's motor. They froze as Foster peered out of the back door he had opened a few inches.

'Only a Traffic Control chopper,' he said when he returned. 'We get moving in the Metro now.'

Inside the Wessex helicopter – roomy enough to take ten men – Tweed peered out of the window from his seat. Newman sat in front of him by the door where the swivel-mounted machine-gun was positioned. A member of an airborne division sat beside him, his beret slanted at a slight angle. He was satisfied Newman could handle the weapon. They'd had a practice shoot while the machine hovered above Fairoaks Airport. The target, a pile of wooden crates, had been shattered by Newman's first burst. The airfield had a notice at the entrance. *Closed for Repairs*.

Marler was travelling with Nield in the second machine which was not visible. The radio op was keeping in close touch with its twin helicopter. Tweed was impressed with the swift conversion job. Both machines carried the legend *Traffic Control* in large letters. Only Butler was somewhere on the ground, riding one of the two waiting BMW motor-cycles. Nield had said, 'Thanks, but no thanks. I'm not riding one of those death-traps.' Butler had made a rude

546

reply and wheeled his bike aboard the other Wessex.

The second machine had landed on a deserted main road, waited briefly while Butler disembarked with his BMW near Brize Norton, and had immediately taken off.

Tweed stared down at Cherry Farm from two hundred feet. Raising the glasses looped round his neck, he scanned the buildings carefully. No sign of life. He dropped the glasses and spoke into the microphone, part of the headset he had attached to himself.

'Nothing down there, Bob. That place has been derelict for a decade at least.'

They flew on as the airborne soldier, Harper, shifted to the seat on the starboard side and raised his own glasses. Very little traffic on the roads at this hour. The wind was strong and Tweed was thankful he'd had the foresight to take Dramamine as the chopper rocked like a boat in a storm.

At the last minute Howard had been forbidden to join them, much to his chagrin. The PM had phoned. 'Someone must be there to mind the shop . . .'

But every member of the search party had copies of the car outlines Howard had produced – together with Paula's photographs of the furniture van seen from different angles. Everyone – including Butler riding his motorcycle round the country lanes – was concentrating on detecting a furniture van. Except Tweed who kept studying the car silhouettes, with an Austin Metro added.

They had been cruising round the edge of the forbidden flying zone over Brize Norton for an hour without seeing anything. Marler came on the radio from his machine at regular intervals. 'Nothing to report.'

Then Tweed saw the Austin Metro.

Behind the wheel of the Metro Foster was driving along a winding country lane east of Brize Norton, close to the

547

village of Ducklington. He saw the chopper appear over a ridge straight ahead about half a mile away. Beside him Saunders leaned forward. In the rear seat Seton-Charles peered out of the window.

'Yes, it's that bloody Traffic Control machine,' Foster snapped. 'Something funny about it – there's no traffic round here.'

He slowed down as a large copse of trees masked them from the helicopter. The copse was beyond a bend in the road. Glancing to his left, Foster saw a crumbling barn, the roof still intact, open at both ends. He looked in his wing mirror. Road deserted, behind as well as ahead. He jammed on the brakes in an emergency stop. Saunders was thrown forward; only his safety belt saved him diving through the windscreen.

'What the hell,' he rasped.

Foster made no reply. He swung the Metro through ninety degrees, drove off the road straight at the ancient farm gate. As the car hit it the gate fainted, collapsed inwards. Foster drove over it and continued across the field, pulling up inside the barn.

'Let the bloody thing find us in here.' He switched off the engine. 'At least we've found four possible places to site the vans tomorrow.'

'The chopper's coming,' warned Seton-Charles.

'You must have imagined it,' Newman commented. 'I didn't see a car.'

'Please keep flying along the country road below us,' Tweed instructed the pilot. He raised his glasses again as he replied to Newman. 'I tell you, I saw an Austin Metro. It matched the outline. And it was darkish – could have been blue.'

'We'll find it . . .'

'Which is exactly what we're trying to do.'

548

They were flying at eight hundred feet – the minimum altitude permitted because they were close to the forbidden flying zone round Brize Norton. The pilot followed the winding course of the empty road below. Tweed had the glasses screwed tightly against his eyes. He scanned every likely hiding-place.

A dense copse of evergreens came up in his lenses, a copse which straddled the road where it turned a bend. He ordered the pilot to circle it so he could study it from every angle. Where the devil had the Metro gone to? The pilot completed one circuit, commenced another.

Tweed saw an isolated barn standing in the fields a short distance from the road. From that height he looked down on the sagging roof. Nothing. Anywhere.

'Fly a mile or two, behind that ridge we came over. Then turn and come back,' he ordered.

Inside the Metro the chopper sounded like a giant bee circling. Saunders was sweating. He mopped his forehead. Foster sat patiently, gloved hand tapping the wheel. Saunders stiffened, lowered his window. A blast of icy air came inside.

'We might as well keep warm,' Foster told him.

'That chopper's going away. I can hear the engine sound receding. We've done the job. We might as well get back.'

'Not yet. It could be a trick. Go away and then come back – find us in the open.'

'You're assuming it's looking for us.'

'I always assume the worst. We wait . . .'

Five minutes later they heard the helicopter returning. Foster stared ahead in silence. It wasn't his way to say, 'I told you.' He waited half an hour until the machine had flown off a second time, then started the motor, backed on to the road, drove back the way they had come.

The Wessex cruised round the approaches to the

perimeter of Brize Norton air base for another three hours. They frequently crossed the Vale of White Horse, maintaining the permitted altitude of eight hundred feet. Tweed's eyes were aching from staring through his field glasses. As they returned to Fairoaks, coming in to land, Newman made his comment.

'Well, you were wrong about the Metro. And we've found damn-all. Marler reports the same result from his machine.'

Tweed had a map of the Brize Norton area spread out on his lap. He had marked with a cross the place where he was sure he had spotted the Metro. Using a ruler, he measured three miles in each direction from the cross, then drew a circle with a diameter of six miles. He handed the map over the seat to Newman.

'That's the area we concentrate on tomorrow.'

'Why? We never found your Metro.'

'For that very reason. I could have been wrong – the car could have belonged to anyone. But it did a vanishing trick. And we scoured the ground without finding it. I think it went into hiding. That's highly suspicious. I scanned every road after it disappeared. No sign of it.'

'If you say so.'

'And,' Tweed added as they were landing, 'I'm changing the dispositions of Force Z tomorrow. We need more men on the ground.'

They drove back to London to spend the night at Park Crescent, to see if any further information had come through. Butler left his motorcycle at Fairoaks. 'Didn't see a thing,' he reported as they drove back. 'But I have a few more roads to check – to the east of the air base.'

'Which I'd guess is where Winterton's men would place their missile launchers,' Tweed remarked. '*East*. Because that's the direction Gorbachev's plane will fly in from. And

550

I have to call the PM when I get back. She was insistent on that for some reason I can't fathom . . .'

They had just arrived back at Park Crescent when Paula called from Somerset. 'I'm speaking from Minehead again,' she opened. 'I've had quite a day. The police brought back a woman's body found in the Somerset Levels – that sinister area we crossed on our first trip here.'

'I remember. Sounds a bit grisly.'

'A peat digger found a hand sticking out of the place where he was digging. When Inspector Farthing told me I had an idea. I asked to visit the mortuary. It was the cleaning woman from the bungalow estate. I showed Farthing the photo I'd taken. She'd been shot once in the back of the neck.'

'They were cleaning up before they left. No macabre pun intended.'

'And Farthing has been very helpful. He's put two men in plain clothes to help me watch the commando trio. They're all still here. That's it.'

'Take care. I have an important call to make.'

The four men sitting in his office and Monica watched him as he called the PM on scrambler. He listened, said he understood and put down the phone. He looked around at Newman, Marler, Butler and Nield.

'She's just heard from Moscow Gorbachev will be flying here in *four* Ilyushin 62s.'

'Four?' Newman enquired. 'I know he's unusual but how can he do that?'

'It's a clever Soviet precaution – security. No one will know which of the four machines Gorbachev and his wife will be aboard. Maybe the PM gave him a hint of possible trouble. I don't know. Now, we've eaten, so everyone get some sleep. Tomorrow is the day.'

53

Monday, 7 December. 7 a.m. Sully lay in the road covered with blood near the entrance to Cherry Farm. It was real blood: Foster, against Anton's protests, had used a knife to cut his forearm lightly. He had then smeared blood all over Sully's face and neck. Inside the farmhouse Seton-Charles was using sticking plaster to cover the flesh wound.

Nearby Sully the Austin Metro had its bonnet pushed against a tree trunk, positioned at an angle across the road. The driver's door was wide open. George Hobart, driving his Post Office van, slowed, then stopped as he saw the body sprawled in the road. He jumped out. Only twenty-two years old, he wore his Post Office cap, unlike the more veteran postmen who went bareheaded.

'Nasty accident,' said Foster, appearing from behind a tree. 'It just happened. Could you take him to hospital? We've no transport.'

'Of course I'll help.' Hobart approached the 'body' and swallowed. 'He looks in a bad way.'

'Something for your help . . .'

Foster reached into his breast pocket, hauled out his wallet, dropped it on the road at Hobart's feet. He was slow retrieving it and Hobart bent forward to pick up the wallet. Foster pressed the muzzle of his Luger against the back of Hobart's neck, pulled the trigger. The old method of execution used in the motherland when he'd been young. Hobart slumped to the ground.

Saunders appeared with a large wheelbarrow. Foster picked up the dead youngster and his cap, askew, dropped off. When he'd dumped the body inside the wheelbarrow and Saunders was taking it towards the farmhouse Foster picked up the cap. Climbing into the cab of the large van, he drove it off the road along a track into the woods opposite the farm entrance.

Then he checked his watch. They'd all better give Anton a hand to fill in the grave. He got behind the wheel of the Metro, closed the door, backed it on to the road and drove it back to the shed. They'd be on their way in fifteen minutes.

Tweed wore a thick woollen pullover, a heavy sports jacket, a woollen scarf round his neck, and corduroy trousers tucked inside knee-length boots with rubber-grip soles.

The Wessex chopper was again flying at eight hundred feet and Tweed sat in the same seat, map in his lap, binoculars looped round his neck. In front of him Newman sat holding the handle of the swivel-mounted machine-gun by the closed door. On the starboard side the airborne soldier, beret slanted at exactly the same angle, sat peering out of the window through his field glasses.

There had been very little conversation since the machine took off from Fairoaks. There was an atmosphere of rising tension inside the helicopter. Then the pilot passed on the message to Tweed through his earphones.

'Marler and Butler have landed. They are on the ground.'

'Thank you,' said Tweed.

Marler would now be driving the Land Rover waiting for him at the appointed rendezvous, a crossroads in the middle of nowhere near Ducklington village. Butler would be riding the BMW motorcycle which had been transported to the crossroads by truck during the night. All arranged by Tweed over the phone in the early hours. Nield was at Fairoaks, running the radio control room set up inside an administrative office.

Tweed studied the area he had circled on the map the

previous day. He was gambling everything that the attack would be launched from somewhere in that area. It was logical. And Winterton had shown himself to be logical in everything he organized.

The second chopper would return to Fairoaks. At the last moment Security Control at Brize Norton had sanctioned one machine, not two. Tweed gathered they did not take Force Z too seriously. He raised his glasses as they crossed the Vale of White Horse. They were moving into the danger zone.

The furniture van driven by Foster, with Saunders alongside him, turned off the road into the worked-out chalk quarry. It had been carved out in a semi-circle. A chalk cliff enclosed it on the west, south and north sides. To the east it looked out across open country and the sky. Foster backed the vehicle until it was facing due east with the rear of the van a few feet away from the cliff. Then he stopped the engine.

They jumped out, went to the back, lowered the tail-board and went inside. Foster led the way, squeezing past the piles of old furniture. He climbed the steps to the platform, sat in the chair and pressed the switch. The panel in the roof slid back. He settled himself in the chair, picked up the Stinger launcher, inserted a missile.

He picked up the walkie-talkie Anton had specially amplified to increase its range. Holding it close to his mouth with his left hand, he spoke.

'Coastguard Number One in position.'

There was a crackle. Then he clearly heard Sully's voice.

'Coastguard Number Two in position . . .'

Marler drove the Land Rover along the narrow country lane at speed. He was moving through open country so he couldn't miss anything. He was following routes which

Butler had not covered the previous day but which were inside Tweed's circle. Half a mile behind him Butler followed on his motorcycle.

He reached a crossroads and drove straight on. Round a bend he was confronted with a tarring machine taking up the whole road. A workman came up to him.

'Didn't you see the bloody diversion sign, mate?'

'No, because there wasn't one.'

'Must be blind as a bat. You can't pass.'

Marler swore, turned the Land Rover and went back to the crossroads. He turned right just as Butler appeared over a rise. He drove on, more slowly: there were clumps of trees on either side, clumps which became woodland. He turned a corner and saw a sign in the distance. *Diversion*. The sign pointed right at a point where the road forked. Marler frowned, then drove his vehicle straight at the sign, sending it into the ditch as he took the left fork.

On the floor lay his rifle, telescopic sight attached. They had installed a small transceiver, complete with microphone. He had tested it earlier and it was tuned to the waveband Nield was operating on at Fairoaks. He turned the wheel as the winding road curved round another bend. Then he slowed to a stop.

At the base of the chalk cliff Foster saw four Ilyushin 62s flying one behind another coming in from the east. He grabbed the microphone. 'Coastguard One reporting. Four blackbirds in view. Repeat, *four* blackbirds. I'll arrest three and four. You take one and two. Over.'

'Four blackbirds sighted,' Sully confirmed. 'Will take one and two. Over and out . . .'

Marler had stopped where the rear of a large furniture van was parked half inside a wood. Beyond, the trees had been felled by storms, leaving the sky open. On the tailboard sat Seton-Charles, eating a sandwich. A rug covered his lap. He threw back the rug and pointed an Uzi machine-pistol point blank at Marler. Somewhere beyond the pile of furniture Marler detected signs of further movement. Behind him he heard the sound of an approaching motorcycle.

'Stay very still. Hands in sight,' rasped Seton-Charles, dressed in overalls. 'Wait like that till the biker has gone.'

Marler raised both hands in the air. 'Drop them!' screamed the professor. 'In your lap.' Marler let his hands drop. The BMW was very close. He hoped Butler had seen his gesture. The BMW slowed down, turned out to pass Marler's stationary Land Rover.

As he cruised slowly past Butler tossed the grenade he'd extracted from his saddlebag into Seton-Charles' lap. Marler ducked, fell crouched on the floor. There was an ear-splitting *crack!* Marler's windscreen shattered.

He looked up, grabbing his rifle. Seton-Charles was plastered all over the furniture. Blood and flesh strips everywhere. Marler saw movement high up at the front of the van. The mass of ancient furniture had saved Sully. His head peered over the top. Marler shot him through the forehead.

He leapt out and ran to the right side as Butler ran to the left. They met on opposite sides of the cab. Empty. Somewhere beyond the trees a vehicle's engine started up, moved off. Marler ran to the rear, pushed his way inside, leapt up the steps. Sully, flopped over the back of the chair, was dying but not dead. He looked into Marler's eyes as the Englishman bent over him. His eyes were glazed. The bullet had missed the brain and his expression showed a glimmer of hatred.

'Anton,' he whispered. 'Bastard ran for it. In Post Office van. Ex . . .' Then he died.

* * *

556

Foster aimed his launcher to take out Ilyushin Number Three, the plane carrying Gorbachev. He waited for the first two machines to disintegrate. Then decided he could wait no longer. In his concentration he failed to hear the sound of the chopper.

Aboard the Wessex Tweed was scanning the countryside below. He swept over a chalk quarry, then swung his glasses back again. The van came up clearly in his high-powered glasses. So clearly he could see the open panel in the roof, the man seated inside holding something rammed into his shoulder.

'The chalk quarry!' he shouted into his mike. 'It's there . . .'

The airborne soldier swung open his door. Icy air blasted into the chopper. Newman aimed his gunsight, pressed the trigger, swept the opening in the roof with bullets. Inside Foster was training the Stinger's sophisticated gunsight on the third Ilyushin. The chopper pilot – at Tweed's urgent request – had earlier ignored regulations, descending to one hundred feet, and now he hovered. In response to Newman's shouted request. He held the trigger back in the firing position. A stream of bullets laced Foster's back and chest. Blood splotches burst out of his overalls. He sagged in the chair. His last reflex action was to fire the launcher's missile.

But as he'd slumped the barrel had dropped, was now aimed inside the vehicle. The heat-seeking missile *whooshed* from the launcher, sped the few feet towards the vehicle's engine, which was still warm.

'Climb!' Newman shouted.

The pilot reacted instantly, began to ascend vertically. Tweed was staring at the quarry. As the missile detonated there was a blinding flash, a low rumble like thunder. The climbing chopper rocked from side to side as the blast hit it, then steadied. Tweed and Newman gazed down.

The furniture van had disappeared, blown into a million fragments. A cloud of white chalk dust rose from the quarry. Tweed searched in vain for any debris which might be a relic of the van. His hands were sweating and he wiped them on his handkerchief as the airborne soldier hauled the door shut. The interior of the machine was like an ice box from the raw wind which had penetrated inside.

'Fairoaks reporting,' the pilot said, his tone calm. 'Marler has intercepted Vehicle One.'

'Thank God! Tell Fairoaks Vehicle Two also intercepted. Pass the message to Marler,' Tweed told him.

Overhead the four Ilyushin 62s were continuing their descent to Brize Norton. Tweed finished wiping his hands, put on a pair of gloves. He spoke again to the pilot.

'Please return to Fairoaks. We have unfinished business to attend to.'

54

Monday, 7 December. 'I will be driving down to interrogate Colonel Winterton,' Tweed told Monica, Newman, Butler and Nield in his Park Crescent office. 'Before he leaves the country.'

'On Exmoor?' Butler queried. 'You know who he is?'

'Yes. Monica has heard from Roberts at Lloyd's. The Shipping Index shows the only Iron Curtain vessel off our shores is an East German freighter, the *Stralsund*. At this moment it is unloading timber at Swansea. It sails for Rostock in the Baltic before the end of the day. That means it could heave to after dark at the mouth of the Bristol Channel. Ready to take aboard Winterton.'

'You really know who he is?' Monica asked. 'And he is one of the three ex-commandos?'

'Yes to both questions.' He turned to Butler. 'We left Fairoaks in a hurry. You talked with Marler. Why did he wait instead of coming with us?'

'Apparently just before Sully died he told Marler Anton had fled in a Post Office van. Heard the grenade I threw, then the shot Marler fired, I suppose. Ran for it. Headed for Exmoor, according to Marler. He's going after him. Trouble was the chopper we didn't use had a mechanical defect. And the pilot of our machine insisted on a thorough check-up before he'd fly Marler anywhere. That blast from the quarry really hit us.'

'Up to Marler, then. You heard me call Paula. She'll wait to meet us in the Mercedes by the call box in Minehead. Newman, you can come with me. Butler and Nield, you stay here. We're desperately understaffed if something else breaks.'

The phone rang. Monica said it was the call Tweed had booked to Arthur Beck at Federal Police headquarters in Berne. Tweed took the phone.

'Arthur. Check with Sarris, I suggest. But I think it's safe to send Christina back to Athens. Send me the bill.'

'No bill.' Beck chuckled. 'But now you owe me one. And don't think I won't call in the debt when it suits me. 'Bye.'

Newman stood up. 'I'm ready to leave when you are. As it is, we won't reach Exmoor before dark. Winterton could be aboard the *Stralsund* if we don't move. I'll drive the Cortina.'

'We need to be armed.' Tweed opened a drawer, took out from it a Smith & Wesson short-barrelled .38. Plus a shoulder holster. 'The armourer recommended this for me. You agree?'

'You never normally carry a gun. I'll give you some practice at a quiet spot on the way. Yes, that's OK. A hip holster would have been better. But it's short-barrelled, shouldn't snag if you have to snatch it out. I'm keeping the Magnum .45.'

'That blows a hole as big as a cave through your target.'

'Which means it does the job.'

Newman had become harder since he first knew him, Tweed reflected. His experience behind the lines in East Germany. Newman seemed to read his mind.

'Why is Winterton boarding an East German vessel?'

'Because the East Germans are not sympathetic to *glasnost*. And I doubt he'll report precisely what he was involved in. We'd better go.'

'Do give us a clue,' Monica begged. 'About the identity of this Winterton.'

'He must have needed to keep contact with the *Spetsnaz* group when it moved to a new base close to Brize Norton, wherever that was. So, he needed a phone he could use which wasn't his own – in case we'd put a phone tap on it. Which I wouldn't risk. A phone, Monica . . .'

It was early evening, just before dark, when the Wessex carrying Marler approached Dunkeswell Airfield south of Exmoor. On his lap Marler nursed his rifle with the telescopic sight as he peered out of the window. 'Can you land somewhere close to Dunkeswell, but not on the airfield?' he asked the pilot.

'Might manage it. You spoke in time. Not yet dark. How long a walk do you fancy?'

'No more than five minutes. It's an emergency.'

'When isn't it? There's Dunkeswell.'

Marler looked out of the window, frowned. Two main runways crossed each other almost at right angles. One had lights on at either side. Ready for a plane to take off?

The chopper was descending towards a deserted country road. Marler grabbed his rifle, headed for the door after one last word.

'Land me on that road. Then you'd better take off, head back for Fairoaks . . .'

He tore off his headset, splaying his feet as he made for the door. The machine was rocking gently. He felt it touch down, opened the door, dropped to the ground. Ducking to keep clear of the rotors, he ran towards the main airport building. He reached the open gate at the main entrance as an old Rover driven by a middle-aged man appeared from the opposite direction. The car stopped, half-turned to drive through the entrance. The driver lowered his window, leaned out.

'Who are you?' he enquired, staring at the rifle Marler held in his right hand.

'Don't go in there,' Marler warned. He used his left hand to extract his Special Branch card, shoved it in the driver's face. 'And who are you?'

'I'm the controller of this airfield. Those damned gates should be kept closed. I've told Abbott before . . .'

'Who is Abbott? Quick. There's probably an armed terrorist inside.'

'Maintenance mechanic. Odd-job man. Really runs the place . . .'

'Where do I find this Abbott?'

'Should be inside that office with the lights on . . .'

'Drive off. Up the road. Unless you want to risk getting shot.'

Marler darted inside the entrance, crouched low as he ran, rifle gripped in both hands. He avoided the office door, which was closed. Very carefully he raised his head, peered in through the window. Then he ran back to the door, turned the handle, threw it open. He had found Abbott.

The mechanic was sprawled forward over a desk. Blood

was congealing from a hole in the side of his skull. Marler felt the neck pulse. Nothing. In the distance he heard the sound of a light aircraft starting up. He ran outside, keeping close to the side of the building, peered round the corner.

A Cessna was taxiing slowly along a runway. As he watched, it turned. The engine revolutions increased in speed. He raised his rifle, peered through the sight. Inside the cockpit a face wearing a pilot's helmet jumped at him. Anton Gavalas. The machine began to move forward along a course parallel to the building. Moving target. Marler held the crosshairs fixed on the Greek's head. He took the first pressure on the trigger, waited until the small plane was opposite him, pulled the trigger rapidly three times.

He saw the perspex craze. The aircraft proceeded on down the runway. Marler thought he'd missed. The machine began leaving the ground. It was gaining height when the nose dipped and plunged swiftly down on to the runway. The tail was poised in mid-air. Then the fuel tanks exploded. Fire enveloped the Cessna, a fierce blaze which was smothered with a cloud of the blackest smoke. Silence suddenly descended on Dunkeswell.

'Lord, I'm glad to see you.'

Paula jumped out of the Mercedes parked by the call box in Minehead as the Cortina driven by Newman pulled up. It was dark as Tweed stepped out and she hugged him. 'They go to bed early here,' Tweed commented, glancing along the deserted street. He squeezed her, let her go as Newman approached.

'Look what Inspector Farthing gave me.' She took them both by the arm, guided them to the Mercedes and pointed at the dashboard. A mobile phone unit had been attached. Tweed got in behind the wheel, pressed the switch which operated the aerial and watched it slide down out of sight in the wing mirror.

562

'No, elevate that,' Paula protested as she got in beside him and dropped her shoulder bag in her lap. 'It helps contact. Farthing has a policeman with a walkie-talkie watching each of the houses. Barrymore, Robson and Kearns. They report back to a radio car and I hear their observations over that phone. In a kind of code I can understand. They're all at home. Farthing has been marvellous.'

'I have to get moving,' Tweed said as he elevated the aerial. 'Bob, take Paula with you. Drive to The Anchor and keep your eyes open.'

'For what?' Newman asked.

'In case he gets away from me. I'd say a four-wheel drive – heading past The Anchor and west over that pebble beach. And cover him with that Magnum. He's lethal. Out you get, Paula.'

'I'm coming with you.' She spoke calmly and produced from her bag the Browning. 'I can protect myself. I did with Norton and Morle.'

It was the controlled way she spoke which stopped Tweed arguing. He shrugged, glanced at the call box. 'Has Barrymore used that this evening?'

'Not so far.'

'Then we'd better move off.' He waved to Newman, drove through Minehead and climbed Porlock Hill. The Mercedes purred up the steep ascent. At the top he passed Culbone Inn, continued along the coast road, took the first turning to the left.

'It's the Doone Valley,' Paula said quietly as they descended the steep winding lane, crossed the ford at the bottom, turned right. Towards the Doone Valley.

'We located the two furniture vans they were using as mobile missile launcher platforms,' Tweed remarked. 'Just in time. One was blown to bits. Marler found a dead Middle Easterner in his. Maybe a Shi-ite. They were going to be left behind as the scapegoats. Monica read out a news

563

story about two Arabs being airlifted from Gartree Prison. Shi-ites.' He stopped and backed the car through a gap in the hedge into a field, switched off the lights. 'No one will see you here. Keep the Browning in your lap until I get back.'

'You've stopped midway between Quarme Manor and Endpoint.'

'Lock all the doors,' Tweed said, then he was gone.

He pressed the bell. The man who opened the door was dressed in a leather windcheater unzipped down the front, cavalry twill trousers tucked into riding boots, a woollen scarf round his neck. The hall beyond was as cold as the biting wind moaning across the moor.

'May I have a word with you, Dr Robson?' Tweed asked.

'Come in, my dear fellow. Can't give you long. I'm expecting a call from a patient. They phone me at all hours. Goes with the territory as the Americans say.'

All this as Robson closed the door, led the way into the sitting room. The curtains were almost drawn with a gap where they should have met. Tweed sat down at a polished wooden table as Robson gestured and then sat opposite him. His host moved an old-fashioned doctor's bag on to the floor by his side without bothering to close it.

'I've come to arrest you for murder,' Tweed said. 'Quite a few murders. You've probably heard on the news your plan failed. Gorbachev is now in Washington.'

Robson's face crinkled into a smile. His pale blue eyes watched Tweed as he pulled at his straggly moustache.

'I don't follow any of this. You look sane enough.'

'One thing which pinpointed you was your conversation at The Luttrell Arms over dinner. Barrymore referred to the Greek Key. You pooh-poohed the idea. Out of character. When you all had houses like fortresses. Especially this place. I asked my man Nield, who was recording secretly, who was *facing* him. Barrymore was. So were you. The tape sounded like someone had spotted the tie pin microphone Nield kept fiddling with to get the right angle. And you made the mistake of asking Barrymore if Nield was wearing an earpiece when he met him on the moor. Only a professional would spot that. You spotted it. Hence your strange remark – considering you were all supposed to be scared stiff someone was coming from Greece to avenge the murder of Ionides . . .'

'Gavalas . . .' Robson stopped. His expression changed. The eyes were blank and cold.

'I never told you Ionides was a Gavalas,' Tweed remarked.

Robson sat very still. The only illumination was a plastic-shaded bulb which hung low above the table. Robson reached down into his bag. He pointed the Luger as Tweed reached inside his jacket.

'Don't bring your hand out with anything in it but your fingers. I still find your reasoning feeble.'

'Winterton – as we codenamed the killer – needed access to a safe phone. You wouldn't like using the one here. Your sister, May, could have overheard you. Where is she?'

'I sent her off for a holiday to my brother's place in Norfolk . . .'

'You needed access to a safe phone,' Tweed continued, 'to keep in touch with the *Spetsnaz* group you'd set up on that bungalow estate, to give orders when they'd moved to their new base. You kept visiting the bedridden old lady down in Dulverton at night. She has an extension upstairs by her bedside. That means the main phone is downstairs – the one you used.'

'Pure guesswork. You're crazy . . .'

'The first thing which drew my attention to *you* was when I heard you'd found homes for Barrymore and Kearns on Exmoor. Two reasons would be my guess, as you call it. Camouflage, in case suspicion centred on this area. Three

565

suspects – and you made Barrymore look the most suspicious. I heard in Greece the voice changing the call sign in English over Florakis' transceiver. Very upper-crust. Very Barrymore. You mimicked him. The second reason for bringing your two commando friends here was a genuine fear of the vindictive Petros.'

'Why should I fear him?' Robson moved his left hand and then held it still: he had felt the need of his pipe, his prop.

'Because you murdered Andreas Gavalas on Siros. Another guess. You took a spare knife on the raid to do the job.'

'You'll be accusing me of stealing the diamonds next.'

'Of course you did. Which is why Andreas was killed. He was going to hand them to the right-wing EDES people. Probably you were told by your controller in Cairo to keep the diamonds for future use . . .'

'And I live in such luxury,' Robson sneered.

'Not for you. But it must have cost Colonel Winterton – again a pointer towards Barrymore – a packet to build that bungalow estate ready for the *Spetsnaz* group you'd been told to establish. Plus financing them in little businesses to give authentic backgrounds for them when they arrived from Russia. Plus buying the Stinger launchers and missiles from Gallagher, the Lisbon arms dealer. By then those diamonds were worth far more than the original hundred thousand pounds.'

'And what other murders am I supposed to have committed?' Robson enquired sarcastically.

'Stephen Ionides in the Antikhana Building for one. There was a lot of blood. My guess – again – is you wore an Army waterproof buttoned to the neck to save your uniform.'

'Oh, really? Entering the realms of fantasy now, are we? I suppose you worked out how I escaped when there wasn't even a convenient fire escape?'

'Poor Sam Partridge worked that out. There was a strong iron rail elevated above the wall on the roof. You took inside a briefcase – or something – a length of knotted rope. When you had cleaned up the blood from your hands in the bathroom you went back on the roof. You dropped the rope over the rail on the native quarter side – an equal length on either side. You shinned down the wall, holding both pieces of rope with the knots. Reaching the empty street, you simply hauled one length of rope down and coiled the lot in a loop. Very easy to lose that inside the available native quarter.'

'Any reason for all these acrobatics? And my killing Ionides?'

'Commandos *are* acrobatic. And Ionides – who was really Stephen Gavalas – had become suspicious of the killing of his brother, Andreas. You tied up a loose end.'

'Two murders so far. Any more?'

'It's not amusing. Mrs Larcombe's death was a fresh pointer – clue, if you like. She was a careful woman. Who would she let in to her house at night without fear? The local doctor. You said you needed to use her phone for an emergency?'

Robson ran his tongue briefly over his lips. In the dim light there was moisture on his brow, but the muzzle of the Luger aimed at Tweed's chest was steady.

'One thing which put me off the track,' Tweed went on. He had to keep Robson talking. 'Barrymore kept making clandestine phone calls from a public box in Minehead. What was wrong with using the phone at Quarme Manor?'

An unpleasant smile. 'A touch of romance, Tweed. Barrymore has fallen in love with a woman in London, hopes she will agree to marry him. But not sure of his chances. If it doesn't come off he'll still need Mrs Atyeo to run Quarme Manor. So he goes to extreme lengths to make sure she doesn't know anything. She might up and leave.'

567

'Extraordinary.' Tweed was momentarily non-plussed. 'A small domestic detail I never dreamed of.'

'Like your theories. All bits and pieces . . .'

'Which complete the jigsaw. And expose the face of Dr Robson. The killing of Sam Partridge on Exmoor was another pointer. The knife was driven in at exactly the right angle, the pathologist told me. A doctor would know how to do that. Much better than ex-commandos who had grown rusty with the passage of time. And Harry Masterson, who visited you, sent me a clue. *Endstation*. A clever clue. Pointing in two directions – here to your bungalow, Endpoint, and describing the atmosphere down at Porlock Weir, the end of the world. Harry was clever – I think he guessed it was you. He hoped to get confirmation by telling all three of you he was flying to Greece – to see which one of you turned up when he arrived.'

'I didn't.' Robson gripped the trigger of the Luger more firmly under the lampshade. 'I'm holding this gun on you because I appear to face a lunatic with a gun under his own arm.' He glanced at his watch.

'No. You sent a message to Doganis to do the job for you.' Tweed noted the glance at the time – which must be running out. But like a real professional, Robson was curious as to how he had tripped up. 'And,' Tweed went on, 'you fired at my Mercedes, aiming to miss – you couldn't afford the furore which would follow my murder at that stage. But you aimed – literally – to throw suspicion on Kearns. I'd just left his house.'

'You simply have no proof of these mad assertions.'

'Then take me up into the conning tower where you spend so much time at night. That curious structure which is supposed to be a watch-tower. Then I can satisfy myself there is no transceiver up there. Plus an aerial which automatically elevated while you were transmitting to Florakis in Greece, receiving messages from him. The retracting aerial on a Mercedes gave me that idea.'

The Luger wavered, then steadied. Robson's eyes became colder still. No smile. The bedside manner had vanished. His face became a frozen image, reminded Tweed of pictures of the statues on Easter Island.

'You're clever, I'll grant you that. But it was all in a great cause. Lenin's cause which I embraced when I was a young man. The cause Gorbachev is trying to pervert with his mad *glasnost*.'

'You killed Partridge because he was getting too close to the truth,' Tweed went on. 'You killed Mrs Larcombe because her window creaked and you heard it that first night you collected Anton Gavalas off the *Oporto*. You couldn't afford to risk her seeing you the second time when you brought the Stinger launchers ashore.'

'Dear me.' Robson's lips curled cruelly. 'You have worked it all out.'

'And you killed Jill Kearns in London. Why?'

'Simply to divert attention to London from Exmoor. She was a foolish sort of woman . . .'

Tweed saw movement by the gap in the curtains out of the corner of his eye. There was a tremendous smashing sound, glass breaking under a hammerblow. He thought he saw a rifle butt. Robson glanced at the window, swung the Luger round. Tweed reached up, grasped the plastic shade, pulled it down over the bulb. There was a brief flash, the room was plunged into darkness. Tweed threw himself sideways on to the floor as the Luger roared. Confusion. Bodies moving, feet running. A door shut. A vehicle's engine started up, moving at speed down the slope, skidded as though turning along the lane.

Tweed felt his way into the hall, along the wall, opened the front door. The sound of a second vehicle starting up, driving along the lane towards Quarme Manor. He ran down the slope, ran all the way back to where the Mercedes was parked, jumped in behind the wheel. Paula had released the locks as she saw him coming.

'Two vehicles driving at speed along the lane,' she said tersely. 'First a four-wheel-drive job, like we saw parked by the side of Robson's house. Then a car. Couldn't see the make.'

'We must hurry.' Tweed was driving through the gateway, turning along the lane, lights full on, driving away from the Doone Valley. In his wing mirror he saw a police patrol car coming up behind him. He passed Quarme Manor, reached the ford gushing with deep water, drove through it. Behind him the patrol car stopped half-way through the ford. He drove up the hill, kept going when he turned right on the coast road, heading back towards Minehead.

'The Toll Road!' Paula shouted.

He was almost past it, swung the wheel, began the descent and slowed as he nearly took them over the brink. They arrived in front of The Anchor and Newman was just climbing into the Cortina. He left it as Tweed approached, dived into the back.

'Two vehicles heading for the pebble beach,' he reported.

'I know. It was Robson . . .'

'Robson?' Paula gasped. 'I thought it was Kearns.'

They had driven along the track, began bouncing across the pebble-strewn beach. Something jumped up under the Mercedes, there was a loud clang. The car stopped. Tweed jumped out, began running over the pebbles, careful not to lose his footing. In the distance both vehicles had also been stopped by the terrain. He glimpsed two running figures, a hundred yards between them. Behind him Newman ran with Paula, ready to catch her arm if she slipped. Then the searchlight beam came on, aimed at the foot of the looming cliffs. The light shone from the edge of the sea.

570

It took Newman a moment to grasp the searchlight was mounted at the bow of a motorboat which had been driven up on to the edge of the beach. Tweed ran on past the sign reading, *Warning. Keep clear. Danger of cliff falls*. He passed an empty Renault, then the four-wheel drive vehicle.

Robson was caught in the searchlight beam as he kept to the lee of the cliffs. A shot rang out. The bullet sang past Newman's head. Paula was fumbling for her Browning when Newman saw inside the beached boat a bulky figure, clad like a seaman, aiming a gun. He swung up the Magnum, gripped in both hands, fired two shots. The seaman was hurled back, tried to recover his balance, toppled, fell over the stern of the boat. His body drifted with the outgoing tide.

Robson, hair awry, flung up a hand to shield his eyes against the glare of the light supposed to lead him to the boat. Tweed saw the tall figure a hundred yards from Robson reach inside a satchel slung from his shoulder. He hoisted his right arm like a cricket bowler, threw an object high up the cliff.

His hand delved again inside the satchel, came out and his arm hoisted a second time. There was a deafening crack on the cliff top above Robson. Tweed stopped, grabbed Paula by the forearm to halt her. She was gasping for breath as the second grenade detonated.

From high up on the cliff they heard a muttering rumble, prelude to a cataclysm. A vast slab of cliff broke free, slowly slid downwards, then faster. Robson looked up, opened his mouth. A cascade of rocks roared towards him. He turned to flee. The cascade engulfed him, like a rising tide, swallowing him up to the waist. In the searchlight beam he was a man half buried alive. He opened his mouth again and screamed and screamed, waving his arms. Then a Niagara of boulders stormed down, bounding against each other. One struck his head and seemed to telescope it deep into his body. Paula gulped.

571

A fresh fall of massive rocks poured down, tumbling over each other like some mad race. The head vanished. The boulders piled over the invisible corpse, building a grisly funeral pyre. Slowly the noise receded, the cliff settled, returned to stability as a great cloud of dust, a dense fog, spread over the whole ghastly scene.

Kearns, still carrying the satchel, walked back to Tweed, his wrists held out, as though waiting for handcuffs.

'He killed Jill,' he said in a choked voice. 'It had to be one of them. I've lived with the conviction Robson or Barrymore killed those Greeks during the war. But we were afraid of Petros, so we stuck together. I followed you the previous walk you took along here, saw the landslip. I kept several Mills hand grenades when I left the Army. I tested one up at Dunkery Beacon the other night – to make sure they were still working. I'm ready to go.'

'Two questions,' Tweed replied. He opened his hand, exposing the stick of French chalk he'd taken from his pocket. 'Paula picked that up in your house – you used it to simulate grief, to chalk your face. Why?'

Kearns walked a few slow paces until they were on their own. 'When Barrymore phoned, asked me to come and meet you at his house, I'd been sobbing like a child – because of Jill. So I had to clean up my face somehow. I used that stick of French chalk – the one Jill used when she occasionally did a bit of dressmaking.'

'I see.' Tweed changed the subject. 'During the raid on Siros, why land below a German lookout post?'

'Bravado. Barrymore's. And because of the lookout there were few German patrols at that point. Made tactical sense – we relied on a sea mist to cover us, which it did most of the way. Now, I'm ready to go.'

'Then go,' said Tweed. 'I don't recall ever seeing you here. Leave Exmoor. Petros is in prison. Go,' he repeated, 'build yourself a new life.'

'Thank you . . .'

572

'I said go!'

As Kearns walked slowly away Tweed stared towards Porlock Weir. No sign of activity: they were too far west for the thunder of the falling cliff to have been heard. 'Poor devil,' he commented. He glanced at the pile of rocks where the dust was settling. 'It will be months before they find out what is under that lot, if ever. Now, let's get rid of that boat.'

Standing on either side of the motorboat, Tweed and Newman exerted all their strength. They heaved it upside down, pushed it over the pebbles, which made a grinding noise. The craft slid over the edge, floated for some distance half-submerged, drifted out to sea.

Kearns had managed to start up his Renault while they were occupied and it disappeared into the distance. Between them they tackled the Land Rover which still had the key in the ignition. Within ten minutes Newman had driven it to the water's brink. One final shove propelled it off the pebbles and it sank from view.

'Back to The Anchor,' Tweed ordered. He put an arm round Paula who was shivering with reaction. 'You need a good stiff drink. It's all over. Détente is intact – for better or worse. And I'll report to the PM on the quiet about Lucharsky and his allies. It's up to her what she does after that.'

Epilogue

It is reported that Deputy Chief of General Staff, Andrei Lucharsky, General Budienny, and a third unnamed general, together with their aides, Colonels Rykovsky and Volkov, perished while flying in a helicopter over the Caspian Sea. The pilot saved himself by parachuting from the machine. No further details are available of this tragic accident.

Extract from December issue of PRAVDA.

'Odd that so much top brass should be committed to one chopper,' Tweed commented after reading the report. He handed it back to Monica. 'File it.'